TOLSTOY

was born on his noble family's estate, Yasnaya Polyana, in 1828. In 1844, he was sent to the University of Kazan, which he later left in dissatisfaction.

Tolstoy's military service in the war against Napoleon, and his life as a gentleman of wealth and fashion, in Moscow and St. Petersburg, provide part of the material for his greatest novel, WAR AND PEACE.

His prestige was so enormous in his own lifetime that even the Czar did not dare to challenge him. But his radical beliefs caused an estrangement between him and most of his family. He left home for the last time in 1910, with his daughter, Alexandra, and died suddenly on a railway platform at Astapovo.

War
AND
Peace

by Leo Tolstoy

Edited and abridged for today's readers
by Manuel Komroff

with an introduction and critical appreciation
by CLIFTON FADIMAN

profusely illustrated by John Groth

published by Bantam Books, Inc.

ACKNOWLEDGMENT—*For the many days and nights of work and for many important suggestions in preparing this new edition for the American reader the editor here acknowledges with gratitude the invaluable assistance of his wife Odette Komroff.*

WAR AND PEACE
A Bantam Book
Published August 1956
Second Printing
Third Printing
Fourth Printing
Fifth Printing
Sixth Printing
Seventh Printing
Eighth Printing
Ninth Printing
Tenth Printing

Library of Congress Catalog Card Number: 56-10503
Bantam Books, Inc., 25 West 45th Street, New York, N.Y.

War and Peace, Fifteen Years After

BY CLIFTON FADIMAN

Fifteen years ago I wrote an introduction to an edition of Tolstoy's *War and Peace.* I wrote it after six months of careful study of what is universally acknowledged, often by people who have actually read the whole book, as one of the greatest novels ever written. This introduction, now that I have re-read it, gives the impression of being almost as long as the novel. I must have been infected by Tolstoy's own mania for inclusiveness, for in it I tried to say everything—and of course failed. No final statements about a first-rate work of art are possible. The work itself is the final statement. That is one reason for its first-rateness.

Now, after fifteen years during which the whole world has experienced its own very real wars and even a certain reasonable facsimile of peace, I have re-read Tolstoy's masterpiece in about eight virtually uninterrupted hours. It is a good way to read it. Indeed it is the only natural way, for no novel was ever written to be studied. I do not say it *should* not be studied, merely that such was not the author's intention.

So I plunged into these wide waters and then began to swim as rapidly as I could. By so doing I avoided the mental lockjaw that often afflicts the man who sits down deliberately to read a "classic". Often the poor fellow is so rigid with pre-conceived reverence, so stuffed with the unyielding upholstery of other men's opinions, that (a) he does not know whether or not he is enjoying the book and (b) he does not know what to think of it when he has finished it. It is like being introduced to a very great man. You and he are not really shaking hands. You are shaking hands with History or some other paralyzing abstraction.

Re-reading a classic entails other dangers and difficulties. You are afraid that you may not find there what once you found. Or, on the other hand, your enjoyment may be clouded by nostalgia, by the sense of familiarity, pleasant but sometimes mentally blurring, that overcomes you when you revisit the scenes of your childhood.

We would probably all enjoy classics a good deal more if the publishers could be induced to issue them casually, with a changed title and an unfamiliar author's name. But this is too much to ask: literature, like commerce, is permanently cursed with the Brand Name complex.

At any rate I tried hard to re-read *War and Peace* as though it were a new book sent me for review. This is impossible, of course, but even the attempt brought with it certain rewards that were not mine fifteen years ago. Perhaps I can pass on to you a few of them. I am especially anxious to do this for it seems clear that this book, by virtue of the film version that will soon be seen by tens of millions of people, is in for a re-revival. What all the world's finest literary critics find difficulty in doing, Anita Ekberg and Audrey Hepburn will accomplish with ease.

In a way writing about *War and Peace* is a self-defeating activity. Criticism in our day has become largely the making of finer and finer discriminations. But *War and Peace* does not lend itself to such an exercise. If you say the book is about the effect of the Napoleonic wars on a certain group of Russians, most of them aristocrats, you are not telling an untruth. But you are not telling the truth either. Its subject has been variously described—even Tolstoy tried his hand at the job—but none of the descriptions leaves one satisfied.

You can't even call the book a historical novel. It describes events that are part of history, but to say that it is about the past is to utter a half-truth. *Ivanhoe, Gone With the Wind*—these are historical novels. Kipling has suddenly become for us a historical novelist: Gandhi made him one. But the only sections of *War and Peace* that seem historical are the battle-pieces. War is now apocalyptic; it was not so in Tolstoy's time. Austerlitz and Cannae are equally historical, equally antique, equally part of the springtime of war. Now our weapons think for us; that is the revolutionary change that has outmoded all previous narratives of conflict.

But, except for these battle-pieces, *War and Peace* is no more a historical novel than is the *Iliad*. Homer is not history, not Greek history, not Trojan history, he is—Homer. So with Tolstoy.

No, you say little when you say that *War and Peace* has to do with the Napoleonic Wars, Borodino, the burning of Moscow, the retreat of 1812. As a matter of fact the vaguer your critical vocabulary, the less precisely you describe the subject of *War and Peace*, the nearer you get to the truth. It really—yes, let us use un-twentieth century words—is about Life and People and Love; those abhorred capital-letter abstractions that irritate our modern novelists and against which they persistently warn us.

Another impression I got from my re-reading was an odd one indeed. That is to say, I did not seem to be reading a "work of art". In a sense, Tolstoy is not an artist at all, as, let us say, Virginia Woolf, Hemingway, Faulkner, Proust are artists. He does not appear, at least in translation, to have any "style". There is no such thing as a Tolstoyan sentence or a Tolstoyan vocabulary. The poor chap has no technique. He knows nothing of flashbacks, streams of consciousness, symbols, objective correlatives. He introduces his people flatly and blurts out at once their dominant characteristics. He has unending insight, but no subtlety. Compared to such a great master as Henry James, or such a little master as Kafka, he seems deficient in sheer brain power, the power to analyze, the power to discriminate.

He never surprises you. All his characters are recognizable, most of them are normal. Even his villain, Anatole Kuragin, seems merely an impetuous fool compared to the monsters of labyrinthine viciousness that our Southern novelists can create with a touch of the pen.

He isn't even a good story-teller, if by a good story-teller one means a master of suspense. You do not read *War and Peace* in order to see "how it comes out", any more than you live your life in order to see how it will end. His people grow, love, suffer, die, commit wise or foolish actions, beget more people who are clearly going to pass through the same universal experiences; and that's about all there is to the "story". There are plenty of events but they are not arranged or balanced or patterned. Tolstoy is not a neat writer, any more than your biography or mine is neat. He is as shapeless as the Russian land itself.

I found myself struck with the originality of *War and Peace*, but by a kind of reverse English. It is original because it is unoriginal. Kafka is original. Faulkner is original. Eudora Welty is original. In fact most of our most admired modern writing is original, full of strange people, strange feelings, strange ideas, strange confrontations. But Tolstoy portrays pleasant, lively, ordinary girls like Natasha. His book is crowded with people who are above the average in intelligence or wealth or insight—but not extraordinarily so. He balks at portraying genius: he makes of Napoleon a fatuity, and of the slow-thinking, almost vacant-minded Kutuzov the military hero of the war. And when he writes about war, he does not describe its horrors or its glories. He seizes upon the simplest of the truths about war, and sticks to that truth: that war is *foolish*.

Tolstoy has a genius for the ordinary, which does not mean the commonplace. It is this ordinariness that to us moderns, living on a literary diet of paprika, truffles and cantharides, makes him seem so unusual. When we read him we seem to be escaping into that almost forgotten country, the real world.

Another odd thing—Tolstoy does not seem to have any "personality". Many fine writers are full of personality, Hemingway for instance; but the *very* finest write books in which they are concealed, books like the *Iliad* or *Don Quixote* or *War and Peace*. I do not mean that Tolstoy writes like an impersonal god, but that he seems to intrude into his book only in the sense that he and the book are one and the same. I believe this effect of de-singularization springs from his instinctive refusal to load any scene or indeed any sentence with more meaning than it will bear. He has no "effects". He is unable to call attention to his own mastery. He knows what he is doing but he does not know how to make *you* know what he is doing. The consequence is that, despite the enormous cast of characters, everything (once you have waded through the rather difficult opening chapters) is simple, understandable, recognizable, like someone you have known a long time. In our own day the good novelists tend to be not very clear, and the clear novelists tend to be not very good. Tolstoy is clear and he is good.

To the professional literary critic *War and Peace* is an irritating book. It is irritating because it forces you to say simple things, such as those I have already said. Any sympathetic critic of Faulkner will inevitably find himself saying quite profound things. Indeed that is one reason for his popularity among the technicians of criticism. But *War and Peace* forces you into non-sophistication.

For example: *War and Peace,* I need hardly say, is not a transcript of life. Nothing could be more alien to it than the photograph or the tape-recording. But the one thing you find yourself saying as you read it is, "Yes, this is the way life is." Not "the way life was". Not "the way Russian life was". Not "the way these aristocrats, so different from plain, down-to-earth American me, must have been." But—the way life is. And, as you say it, you feel rise up in you a peculiar satisfaction, a pervasive, un-analysable sense of the richness, the palpability of human experience. This is not the only thing a good novel can give you, but it is a great thing nonetheless—and of how many novels of the last twenty years that you have read can you say the same? *The Man in the Gray Flannel Suit* is about life as it is, that is to say, a narrow sector of life as it is—but once you have recognized the simple identity, nothing else happens to you, no welling up of emotion, no throat-catching sense of richness. You *spot* the reality in such a book. But spotting is not an emotion, it is a parlor game. That is what most current best-sellers are: pleasant invitations to a parlor game.

On re-reading *War and Peace* after fifteen years, I came upon another equally obvious fact. Here it is: when you re-read a classic you do not see more in the book than you did before; you see more in *you* than there was before. A lesser book often on re-reading reveals new subtleties. A great one is more like an instrument of self-discovery. Thus, fifteen years ago, I did not see at all plainly that *War and Peace* is, among other things, about love—love between men and women, love of country, but more especially Christian apostolic love. Fifteen years ago Christian apostolic love did not, as it happens, occupy any great place in my mental world. Today, as it happens, it occupies a greater place. The Bomb is responsible for that, of course; it is the severe teacher who is making clear to all of us, one after another, that hatred is destroying our whole world, that, as Auden says, we must love one another or die. A platitude? Yes—but for many of us a relatively fresh and new platitude. And, curiously enough, the addition of that platitude to our emotional stock enables us to see in *War and Peace* what was there all along, the fact that this is a preachment in story form of the original, not the contemporary, Christian doctrine.

And this doctrine is not mere moralizing. It is the foundation of Tolstoy's esthetic theory, if we may use such un-Tolstoyan jargon. Somewhere in his notebooks Tolstoy writes: "The first condition of an author's popularity, the means of making himself beloved, is the love he bears to all his created characters." Ask yourself to how many modern novelists this statement applies.

In a letter to one of his friends Tolstoy sets down another deceptively simple statement: "I have read [Turgenev's] *On the Eve*. This is my opinion of it: writing novels is useless in general, and even more so if those writing them are dispirited or do not have a good idea of what they want to get out of life." If this last clause is admitted to be true, how much of the contemporary novel, in Tolstoy's view, at once becomes "useless"?

War and Peace is written by a man who knew what he wanted to get out of life, or at any rate spent his life in a relentless search for it; and his characters are all engaged in the same search, most of them, as with us, unsuccessfully. But it is precisely because Tolstoy will not settle for a subject-matter any less serious than this that he continues to engage us, even to engage Hollywood, after so much time has elapsed.

It is an unusual thing to read a novel by a grown-up who refuses the temptation to be merely interesting or entertaining; who does not use his novel to prove a private thesis; or to work off a resentment; or to recall his youthful sufferings; or to cure himself of his obsessions; or to educate himself by the mere exercise of writing. *War and Peace* is not Tolstoy's *mechanism* of self-comprehension; it is the *result* of this comprehension. He dares to write a long story—a story, not a philosophical essay—about the meaning and value of human life. This is the platitudinous subject that most modern novels are either afraid to touch, or touch with bitterness or frenzy or incoherence. How many of our best-selling novelists, many of whom are admirable in other respects, would be interested in setting down such a dialogue as that in which André and Pierre debate how men should live well?

It is because Tolstoy is *continually* reflecting on such questions that he is able, it would seem without calculation, to break our hearts and suddenly enlarge our minds with those moments of "crystallization" for which he is so renowned. The face of the little Princess Lise, dead in childbirth, says "What have you done to me, and why?" Prince André hears Natasha's happy voice at the window at one a.m.—and his life turns on its base. At the Peronsky ball Natasha disregards the entrance of the Tsar—she thinks only of whether she will be chosen as a dance-partner. Old Prince Nicholas Bolkonsky is dying; he does not speak of his beloved Russia, or of his family, or of his approaching death. But he says to his daughter Mary, to whom he has always been a tyrannical taskmaster: "Put on your white dress. I like it."

A half-dozen of such moments, such summatory sentences, would make the fortune of a dramatist. But Tolstoy offers hundreds of them; he knows and *loves* (and to love enough is to know enough) his characters so well that he cannot help seeing always, describing always, the shattering, beautiful, tragic moment of truth.

A word about the edition the reader holds in his hand. It is an abridgment of one of the longest novels ever written. It contains rather more than half of the entire original book. Such matter as Tolstoy's long essays on his philosophy of history has been deleted. So have the lengthy passages on the development and influence of freemasonry in Russia and in Europe. Beyond this major surgery, Mr. Komroff has simplified and quite properly abbreviated many of the leisurely late-victorian sentences of the Garnett version on which this edition is based. There are also—and I find this a most valuable feature—retranslated from the Russian a number of key scenes and passages, so that the present version has rather more vitality than the older nineteenth century translations, naturally couched in their own now somewhat faded idiom, could well possess.

What general defense can be offered of abridgment of a major masterpiece? I think none. What specific defense can be offered of the abridgment of this particular masterpiece? I think considerable, provided one admits at the outset that such an abridgment can never be a *substitute* for the original and that in it you will not get the full *range* of Tolstoy's mind. But you *will* get the *novelist* Tolstoy—or at least enough of him to lead you at a later time to attempt the whole book.

I can think of very few long novels of which it can truly be said that they contain relatively extraneous matter, matter put in by the author in a kind of defiance of his story, or because such digressions were fashionable in his time. One of these books is *Don Quixote*. Another is *War and Peace*. I would be hard put to it to name a third.

It is not because it is so long that *War and Peace* is abridgeable. *Remembrance of Things Past* is just as long; but it is not abridgeable, because each part is there for a calculated *novelistic* purpose. But Tolstoy is not Proust: he is both greater and less. Into *War and Peace* he threw everything he happened to be thinking about at the time, reflections on history, on free thought, on Napoleon's conquests, on the littleness of great men, on the philosophy of military strategy. All of this is interesting. But not all of it is *essential* to the enjoyment of his novel.

The serious reader will want to read the whole book and I hope he will. But in this particular case a supreme, even though incomplete, reading experience is now open to hundreds of thousands of readers who—let us tell the truth—would be discouraged by *War and Peace* in the full version.

To abridge *Pride and Prejudice* or *Wuthering Heights* or *The Red and the Black* (and this has been tried) is both irreverent and injudicious. To abridge *War and Peace,* as skillfully, as intelligently as Mr. Komroff has here done, is perhaps irreverent. But it is not injudicious. What remains is not a betrayal of *War and Peace*. It is an invitation to it.

WAR AND PEACE

1805

BOOK ONE

"WELL, PRINCE, Genoa and Lucca are now little more than private estates of the Bonaparte family. But I warn you, that if you do not admit we are at war, if you again defend all the infamies and atrocities of this Antichrist, upon my word, I believe he is, I will not know you in future, and you are no longer my friend, no longer my faithful slave, as you say. But how do you do? I see I have frightened you, sit down and talk to me."

These words were spoken in July 1805 by Anna Pavlovna Scherer, a distinguished lady of the court, and favorite of the Empress. It was her greeting to Prince Vassily, a man high in rank and office, who was the first to arrive at her *soirée*.

In the notes she had sent round in the morning by a footman in red livery, she had written: "If you have nothing better to do, Count (or Prince), and if the prospect of spending an evening with a poor invalid is not too frightening, I shall be charmed to see you between 7 and 10. Anna Scherer."

"Heavens! what a violent outburst!" the prince replied, not in the least disconcerted by this reception. He was wearing an embroidered court uniform, knee breeches and slippers, and had stars on his breast, and a bright smile on his flat face.

He spoke in that refined French, and with those slow, patronizing intonations peculiar to a man of importance who has grown old in court society. He went up to Anna Pavlovna, kissed her hand, presenting her with a view of his perfumed, shining bald head, and settled himself on the sofa.

"First of all, dear friend, tell me how you are. Relieve my anxiety," he said, with no change of his voice and tone, in which affected sympathy, and even irony, was perceptible.

"How can one be well when one is in moral suffering? How can one be calm in these times, if one has any feeling?" said Anna Pavlovna. "You'll spend the whole evening with me, I hope?"

"And the English ambassador's? I must put in an appearance there," said the prince. "My daughter is coming to take me there."

"I thought to-day's reception had been put off. I confess that all these festivities and fireworks are becoming tiresome."

"If they had known that it was your wish, the reception would have been put off," said the prince, from habit, like a wound-up clock, saying things he did not even wish to be believed.

"Don't tease me. Well, what has been decided? You know everything."

"What can one tell?" said the prince in a tired, listless tone. "What has been decided? It has been decided that Bonaparte has burnt his ships, and I think that we are ready to burn ours."

Prince Vassily always spoke languidly, like an actor repeating his part in an old play. Anna Pavlovna Scherer, in spite of her forty years, was on the contrary brimming over with animation and impulsiveness. To be enthusiastic had become her pose in society, and at times even when she had no inclination to be so, she was enthusiastic. Her affected smile was out of keeping with her faded looks.

In the midst of a conversation about politics, Anna Pavlovna became greatly excited.

"Oh, don't talk to me about Austria! I don't understand it. But Austria has never wanted, and doesn't want war. She is betraying us. Russia alone must save Europe. Our gracious sovereign knows his destiny, and will be true to it. That's the one thing I have faith in. Our good and sublime emperor has the greatest part in the world to play, and he is so virtuous and noble that God will not forsake him, and he will fulfil his mission and crush the hydra of revolution, which is more horrible than ever in the person of this murderer and villain! Whom can we reckon on, I ask you? . . . England with her commercial spirit will not and cannot understand all the loftiness of soul of Emperor Alexander. They're incapable of understanding the self-sacrifice of our emperor, who desires nothing for himself, and everything for the good of humanity. And what have they promised? Nothing. What they have promised won't come to anything! Prussia has declared that Bonaparte is invincible, and that all Europe can do nothing against him. . . . I have no faith but in God and the lofty destiny of our adored emperor. He will save Europe!"

"I imagine," said the prince, smiling, "that if you had been sent instead of our ambassador, you would have carried the Prussian king's consent by storm,—you are so eloquent. Will you give me a cup of tea?"

"In a moment. By the way," she added, "there are two very interesting men coming here to-night, the vicomte de Mortemart; he is connected with the Montmorencies, one of the best families in France. He is one of the good emigrants, the real ones. And also the Italian, Abbé Morio; you know that profound intellect? He has been received by the emperor. Had you heard?"

"I shall be delighted," said the prince. "Tell me," he added, as though he had just recollected something, speaking with studied carelessness, though the question was the chief motive of his visit: "is it true that the Dowager Empress desires the appointment of Baron Funke as first secretary to the Vienna legation? He is a poor creature, by all accounts." Prince Vassily would have liked to see his son appointed to the post.

Anna Pavlovna almost closed her eyes to signify that neither she nor any one else could pass judgment on what the empress might be pleased or see fit to do.

"Baron Funke has been recommended to the Dowager Empress by her sister," was all she said in a dry, mournful tone. When Anna Pavlovna spoke of the empress her countenance suddenly assumed a profound and genuine expression of devotion and respect, mingled with melancholy. She said that Her Majesty had been graciously pleased to show great esteem to Baron Funke, and again a shade of melancholy passed over her face.

The prince was silent. But Anna Pavlovna, with the adroitness and quick tact of a courtier and a woman, wanted to chastise the prince for daring to speak in such terms of a person recommended to the empress, and at the same time to console him.

"But about your own family," she said, "do you know that your daughter, since she has come out, charms everybody? People say she is most beautiful."

The prince bowed to signify respect and gratitude.

"I often think," continued Anna Pavlovna, drawing nearer to the prince and smiling cordially, to show that political and worldly conversation was over and now intimate talk was to begin: "I often think how unfairly the blessings of life are distributed. Why has fate given you two such splendid children—I don't speak of Anatole, your youngest. I don't like him—such charming children? And you really seem to appreciate them less than any one, and so you don't deserve them."

And she smiled her affected smile.

"Perhaps I do not have the bump of paternity," said the prince.

"Don't joke. I wanted to talk to you seriously. You know I'm not pleased with your youngest son. Between ourselves people have been talking about him to her majesty and every one feels sorry for you . . ."

She waited in silence for his answer. Prince Vassily frowned.

"What would you have me do?" he said at last. "You know I have done everything for their education a father could do, and they have both turned out fools. Hippolite is at least a quiet fool, while Anatole is a fool that won't keep quiet. That's the only difference between them," he said, with a smile, more natural and more animated than usual.

"Why are children born to men like you? If you weren't a father, I could find no fault with you," said Anna Pavlovna.

"I am your faithful slave and to you alone I can confess. My children are the bane of my life. It's the cross I have to bear, that's how I explain it to myself. It can't be helped!" He broke off with a gesture expressing his resignation to cruel fate. Anna Pavlovna thought for a moment.

"Have you never thought of marrying your prodigal son Anatole? People say," she said, "that old maids have a mania for matchmaking. I have never been conscious of this failing before, but I know a little person, who is very unhappy with her father. She is a relation of yours, young Princess Mary Bolkonsky."

Prince Vassily made no reply, but with the rapidity of memory characteristic of worldly people, signified by a motion of his head that he was considering what she said.

"No, do you know that that Anatole is costing me forty thousand roubles a year?" he said. "What will it be in five years if this goes on? These are the advantages of being a father. . . . Is she rich, your young princess?"

"Her father is very rich and miserly. He lives in the country. You know that notorious Prince Bolkonsky, retired from the army under the late emperor, and nicknamed the 'Prussian King.' He's a very clever man, but eccentric and tedious. The poor girl is very unhappy. Her brother who has recently been married is an adjutant of Kutuzov's. He'll be here this evening."

"Listen, dear Anna," said the prince, suddenly taking her hand, and for some reason bending it downwards. "Arrange this matter for me and I will be your devoted slave for ever and ever. She's of good family and well off. That's all I want."

"Wait," said Anna Pavlovna, "I'll talk to Liza, the wife of young Bolkonsky, this very evening, and perhaps it can be arranged."

Anna Pavlovna's drawing-room gradually began to fill. The people of the highest Petersburg society were there, people very different in ages and character, but all belonging to the same social strata. The daughter of Prince Vassily, the beautiful Helen, came to take her father to the ambassador's reception. She was wearing a ball-dress with an imperial badge on it. The young Princess Bolkonsky was there, celebrated as the most seductive woman in Petersburg. She had been married the previous winter, and being pregnant was not now going out into the great world, but only to small parties. Prince Hippolite, the son of Prince Vassily, arrived with Mortemart, whom he introduced. The Abbé Morio was there too, and many others.

"Have you not yet seen, or not been introduced to my aunt?" Anna Pavlovna said to her guests as they arrived, and very seriously she led them up to a little old lady wearing large bows in her cap. The guests performed the ceremony of greeting the aunt, who was unknown, uninteresting and unnecessary to every one. Each visitor moved away from the old lady with a sense of relief at a tiresome duty accomplished, and did not approach her again all the evening.

The young Princess Bolkonsky had come with her work in a gold-embroidered velvet bag. Her pretty little upper lip, faintly darkened with down, was very short over her teeth, but was all the more charming when it was lifted, and still more charming when it was at times drawn down to meet the lower lip. As is always the case with perfectly charming women, her defect—the shortness of the lip and the half-opened mouth—seemed her peculiar, her characteristic beauty. Every one took delight in watching the pretty creature full of life and gaiety, so soon to be a mother, and so lightly bearing her burden. Old men and bored, depressed young men gazing at her felt as though they were becoming like her, by being with her and talking a little while to her. Any man who spoke to her imagined that he was being particularly successful this evening.

The little princess, moving with a slight swing, walked with rapid little steps round the table with her work-bag in her hand, and gaily arranging the folds of her gown, sat down on a sofa near the silver samovar; it seemed as though everything she did was a pleasure for herself and all around her.

"I have brought my work," she said, displaying her bag, and addressing the company generally. "Mind, Anna, I hope you have not played me a nasty trick," she turned to the lady of the house. "You wrote that it was to be a small gathering. See how I am dressed."

And she flung her arms open to show her elegant grey dress, trimmed with lace and girdled below the bosom with a broad sash.

"Never mind, Liza, you will always be prettier than any one else," answered Anna Pavlovna.

"You know my husband is deserting me," she went on in just the same voice, addressing a general. "He is going to get himself killed. Tell me what this horrid war is for," she said to Prince Vassily, and without waiting for an answer she turned to Prince Vassily's daughter, the beautiful Helen.

"How delightful this little princess is!" said Prince Vassily to Anna Pavlovna.

Soon after the arrival of the little princess, there walked in a heavily built, stout young man in spectacles, with a cropped head, light breeches in the fashion of the day, with a high lace ruffle and a ginger-coloured coat. This stout young man was the illegitimate son of a celebrated dandy of the days of Catherine the Great, Count Bezuhov, who was now dying at Moscow. He had not yet entered any branch of the service; he had only just returned from abroad, where he had been educated, and this was his first appearance in society. Anna Pavlovna greeted him with a nod reserved for persons of the very lowest social class in her drawing-room. But, in spite of this greeting, Anna Pavlovna showed signs on seeing Pierre of uneasiness and alarm, such as is shown at the sight something too big and out of place.

"It is very kind of you, Monsieur Pierre, to have come to visit a poor invalid," Anna Pavlovna said to him, exchanging anxious glances with her aunt, to whom she was conducting him.

Pierre murmured something unintelligible, and continued to look around as though in search of something. He smiled, bowing to the little princess as though she were an intimate friend, and went up to the aunt. Anna Pavlovna's alarm was not without grounds, for Pierre walked away from the aunt without waiting to hear her remarks. Anna Pavlovna stopped him in dismay with the words: "You don't know Abbé Morio? He's a very interesting man," she said.

"Yes, I have heard of his scheme for perpetual peace, and it's very interesting, but hardly possible."

"You think so?" said Anna Pavlovna in order to say something and to get away again to her duties as hostess. With head bent and legs planted wide apart, he began explaining to Anna Pavlovna why he considered the abbé's scheme impossible.

"We will talk of it later," said Anna Pavlovna, smiling.

And getting rid of this unmannerly young man she returned to her duties, keeping her eyes and ears open, ready to fly to the assistance at any point where the conversation was bogging down. But in the midst of these cares a special anxiety on Pierre's account was evident. She kept an anxious watch on him as he went up to listen to what was being said near Mortemart, and walked away to another group where the abbé was talking.

Pierre had been educated abroad, and this reception at Anna Pavlovna's was the first which he had attended in Russia. He knew that all the intellectual lights of Petersburg gathered together here, and his eyes gazed about like a child's in a toy-shop. He was afraid at every moment of missing some intellectual conversation which he might hear. Seeing the self-confident and refined expression on the faces of the people assembled here, he was expecting something exceptionally clever. At last he came up to Abbé Morio. Here the conversation seemed interesting, and he stood still waiting for an opportunity to express his own ideas, as young people are fond of doing.

Anna Pavlovna's reception was in full swing. Beside the aunt, was sitting an elderly lady with a thin, careworn face, who seemed rather out of her element in this brilliant society. The company was broken up into three groups. In one of these, the more masculine, the centre was the abbé; in the other, the group of young people, the chief attractions were the beautiful Princess Helen, Prince Vassily's daughter, and the little Princess Bolkonsky, with her rosy prettiness, too plump for her years. In the third group were Mortemart and Anna Pavlovna.

The vicomte was a pretty young gentleman with soft features and manners, who obviously regarded himself as a celebrity, but with good breeding modestly allowed the company the benefit of his society. Anna Pavlovna regarded him as the chief entertainment, a treat for her guests. As a clever head waiter serves a piece of beef which no one would have cared to eat in the kitchen, Anna Pavlovna that evening served up to her guests, first the vicomte and then the abbé, as something extra fine. In Mortemart's group the talk turned at once on the execution of the duc d'Enghien. The vicomte said that the duc d'Enghien had perished by his own magnanimity and that there were special reasons for Bonaparte's bitterness against him.

"Ah, come! Tell us about that, Vicomte," said Anna Pavlovna.

The vicomte bowed and smiled courteously in token of

his readiness to obey. Anna Pavlovna made a circle round the vicomte and invited every one to hear his story.

"The vicomte was personally acquainted with the duc," Anna Pavlovna whispered to one. "The vicomte tells a story perfectly," she said to another. "How one sees the man of quality," she said to a third.

The vicomte was about to begin his narrative, and he smiled.

"Come over here, dear Helen," said Anna Pavlovna to the young beauty who was sitting a little way off.

Princess Helen smiled. She got up with the same unchanging smile of the acknowledged beauty with which she had entered the drawing-room. Her white dress trimmed with ivy and moss rustled lightly. With a gleam of white shoulders, glossy hair, and sparkling diamonds, she passed between the men who made way for her. Not looking directly at any one, but smiling at every one, graciously allowing all the right to admire the beauty of her figure, her full shoulders, her bosom and back, which were extremely exposed in the fashion of the day, she moved up to Anna Pavlovna, and doing so brought with her the glamour of the ballroom. Helen was so lovely that she was free from all traces of coquetry. She actually seemed to wish to soften the effect of her beauty.

As though struck by something extraordinary, the vicomte shrugged his shoulders and dropped his eyes, when she seated herself near him and dazzled him too with the same unchanging smile.

"Madame, I doubt my ability before such an audience," he said, bowing with a smile.

The princess rested her plump, bare arm on the table and did not find it necessary to say anything. She waited, smiling. During the vicomte's story she sat upright, looking from time to time at her beautiful, plump arm, which lay with its line changed by pressure on the table, then at her still lovelier bosom, on which she set straight her diamond necklace. Several times she settled the folds of her gown, and when the narrative made a sensation upon the audience, she glanced at Anna Pavlovna and at once assumed the expression she saw on the maid-of-honour's face, then she relapsed again into her set smile. After Helen the little princess also left the tea-table.

"Wait for me, I will take my work," she said. "Come, what are you thinking of?" she said to Prince Hippolite. "Bring me my work-bag."

The little princess, smiling and talking to every one, at once effected a change of position, and settling down again, gaily smoothed out her skirts.

"Now I'm comfortable," she said, and begging the vicomte

to continue, she took up her work. Prince Hippolite brought her bag, and sat close beside her.

The vicomte very charmingly related the anecdote then current, that the duc d'Enghien had secretly visited Paris for the sake of an interview with the actress, Mlle. Georges, and that there he met Bonaparte, who also enjoyed the favours of the celebrated actress, and that, meeting the duc, Napoleon had fallen into one of his fainting spells to which he was subject and had been completely in the duc's power, and how the duc had not taken advantage of it. Later Bonaparte repaid this magnanimity by ordering the duc's death.

The story was very interesting. At the point when the rivals recognise each other the ladies looked agitated. "Charming!" said Anna Pavlovna, looking inquiringly at the little princess. "Charming!" whispered the little princess, sticking her needle into her work as an indication that the interest of the story prevented her working. The vicomte appreciated this silent homage, and smiling gratefully, resumed his narrative.

But meanwhile Anna Pavlovna, still keeping a watch on the dreadful young man, Pierre, noticed that he was talking too loudly and too warmly with the abbé and hurried to the spot of danger. Pierre had in fact succeeded in getting into a political conversation with the abbé on the balance of power, and the abbé, evidently interested by the simple-hearted fervour of the young man, was unfolding to him his cherished idea. Both were listening and talking too eagerly and too naturally, and Anna Pavlovna did not like it.

"The balance of power in Europe and the rights of the people," said the abbé. "One powerful state like Russia—with the prestige of barbarism—need only take a disinterested stand at the head of the alliance that aims at securing the balance of power in Europe, and it would save the world!"

"How are you going to get such a balance of power?" Pierre was beginning; but at that moment Anna Pavlovna came up, and glancing severely at Pierre, asked the abbé how he stood the Russian climate. The abbé's face changed instantly and assumed the look of offensive, affected sweetness, which was evidently its habitual expression in conversation with women. "I am so enchanted by the wit and culture of the society—especially of the ladies—in which I have had the happiness to be received, that I have not yet had time to think of the climate," he said.

Not letting the abbé and Pierre slip out of her grasp, Anna Pavlovna, for greater convenience in watching them, made them join the bigger group.

At that moment another guest walked into the drawing-room: young Prince André Bolkonsky, the husband of the little princess. Prince Bolkonsky was a very handsome young man, of medium height, with clear, clean-cut features. Everything in his appearance, from his weary, bored expression to his slow, measured step, formed a most striking contrast to his lively little wife. It was evident that all the people in the drawing-room were familiar to him, and more than that, he was unmistakably so weary of them that even to look at them and to listen to them was tedious to him. Of all the wearisome faces the face of his pretty wife seemed to bore him most. With a grimace that distorted his handsome face he turned away from her. He kissed Anna Pavlovna's hand, and with half-closed eyelids examined the whole company.

"You are enlisting for the war, prince?" said Anna Pavlovna.

"General Kutuzov has been kind enough to take me as an aide-de-camp," said Prince André.

"And Liza, your wife?"

"She is going to the country."

"Are you not ashamed to deprive us of your charming wife?"

"André," said his wife, addressing her husband in exactly the same coquettish manner in which she spoke to other men, "the vicomte has just told us such a story about Mlle. Georges and Bonaparte!"

Prince André scowled and turned away. Pierre, who had watched him with a happy and affectionate glance ever since he came in, went up to him and took hold of his arm. Prince André, without looking round, seemed annoyed at any one touching him, but seeing Pierre's smiling face, he gave him a smile that was unexpectedly kind and pleasant.

"Why, you! . . . And in such high society too," he said to Pierre.

"I knew you would be here," replied Pierre. "I'm coming to supper with you," he added in an undertone, not to interrupt the vicomte who was still talking. "May I?"

"Oh no, impossible," said Prince André, laughing, and with a squeeze of his hand giving Pierre to understand that there was no need to ask. He would have said something more, but at that instant Prince Vassily and his daughter Helen got up and the two young men rose to make way for them.

"Pardon me, my dear vicomte," said Prince Vassily in French, gently pulling him down by his sleeve to prevent him from getting up from his seat. "This unfortunate reception at the ambassador's deprives me of a pleasure and interrupts you. I am very sorry to leave your enchanting party," he said to Anna Pavlovna.

His daughter, Princess Helen, lightly holding the folds of her gown, passed between the chairs, and the smile glowed more brightly than ever on her handsome face. Pierre looked with rapturous, almost frightened eyes at this beautiful creature as she passed.

"Very lovely!" said Prince André.

"Very," said Pierre.

In passing Prince Vassily took Pierre by the arm, and said to Anna Pavlovna: "Get this bear into shape for me." "Here he has been staying with me for a whole month, and this is the first time I have seen him in society. Nothing's so necessary for a young man as the society of clever women."

Anna Pavlovna smiled and promised to look after Pierre. She knew he was related to Prince Vassily on his father's side.

The elderly lady, who had all this time been sitting by the aunt, got up hurriedly, and overtook Prince Vassily in the hall. All the affectation of interest she had assumed now vanished. Her kindly, careworn face now expressed nothing but anxiety and alarm.

"What have you to tell me, Prince, of my Boris?" she said, detaining him in the hall. "I can't stay any longer in Petersburg. Tell me what news am I to take to my poor boy?"

Although Prince Vassily listened reluctantly and not too politely to the elderly lady and even showed signs of impatience, she gave him an ingratiating and appealing smile, and to prevent his going away she took him by the arm. "What would it cost you to say a word to the Emperor, and he would be transferred at once to the Guards?" she implored.

"Believe me, I will do all I can, Princess," answered Prince Vassily; "but it's not easy for me to ask the Emperor. I should advise you to apply to Rumyantsov, through Prince Galitsin; that would be the wisest course."

The elderly lady was a Princess Drubetskoy, one of the best families in Russia; but she was poor, and having been a long while out of society she had lost her influential connections. She had come now to try and obtain the appointment of her only son to the Guards. It was simply in order to see Prince Vassily that she had invited herself to Anna Pavlovna's party, simply for that she had listened to the vicomte's story. She was worried by Prince Vassily's words; her once handsome face showed exasperation, but that lasted only one moment. She smiled again and grasped Prince Vassily's arm more tightly.

"Hear what I have to say, Prince," she said. "I have never asked you a favour, and never will I ask again. I have never reminded you of my father's affection for you. But now, for God's sake, I beseech you, do this for my son, and I shall consider you my greatest benefactor," she added hurriedly. "No, don't be angry, but promise me. I have asked Galitsin;

he has refused. Be as kind as you used to be," she said, trying to smile, though there were tears in her eyes.

"Father, we are late," said Princess Helen, turning her lovely head on her statuesque shoulders as she waited impatiently at the door.

But influence in society is a kind of capital, which must be carefully protected if it is not to disappear. Prince Vassily knew this. He knew that if he were to beg for all who asked him to do so, he would soon be unable to beg for himself. In Princess Drubetskoy's case, however, he felt after her second appeal somewhat guilty. She had reminded him of the truth; for his first step upwards in the service he had been indebted to her father. Besides this, he saw from her manner that she was one of those women—mostly mothers—who having once taken an idea into their heads will not give it up till their wishes are fulfilled.

"My dear Anna," he said, with his usual familiarity and boredom in his voice, "it's almost impossible for me to do what you wish; but to show you my devotion to you, and my reverence for your dear father's memory, I will do the impossible—your son shall be transferred to the Guards; here is my hand on it. Are you satisfied?"

"My dear Prince, you are our benefactor. I expected nothing less indeed; I know how good you are." He tried to get away. "Wait a moment, one word. Once in the Guards . . ." She hesitated. "You are on friendly terms with Michael Kutuzov, recommend Boris as adjutant. Then my heart will be set at rest, then indeed . . ."

Prince Vassily smiled. "That I can't promise. You don't know how Kutuzov has been besieged ever since he has been appointed commander-in-chief. He told me himself that all the Moscow ladies were in league together to give him all their offspring as adjutants."

"No, promise me; I can't let you go! My dear benefactor . . ."

"Father," repeated the beauty in the same tone, "we are late."

"Come, *au revoir*, good-bye. You see how it is."

"To-morrow then you will speak to the Emperor?"

"Certainly; but about Kutuzov I can't promise."

"Yes; do promise, promise," Anna Drubetskoy said, pursuing him with the smile of a coquettish girl, once perhaps characteristic, but now quite out of keeping with her careworn face. She had forgotten her age and from habit was bringing out every feminine device. But as soon as he had gone her face assumed once more the frigid, artificial expression it had worn all the evening. She went back to the

preserving all that was good—the equality of all citizens, and freedom of speech and of the press, and only for that reason has he taken power."

"Yes, if on obtaining power he had surrendered it to the lawful king, instead of making use of it to commit murder," said the vicomte, "then I might have called him a great man."

"He could not have done that. The people gave him power to rid them of the Bourbons, and that was just why the people believed him to be a great man. The Revolution was a wonderful thing!" continued Pierre, betraying by this desperate statement his extreme youth and desire to give full expression to everything.

"What! Revolution and terror a wonderful thing! . . . What next? . . . But won't you come to this table?" repeated Anna Pavlovna.

"I'm not speaking of terror. I'm speaking of the idea."

"The idea of plunder, murder, and violence!" said one.

"Those are extremes, of course," said Pierre. "But the whole meaning of the Revolution does not lie in them, but in the rights of man, in emancipation from conventional ideas, in equality. And all these Napoleon has maintained in full force."

Prince André, who obviously wished to tone down Pierre's remarks, got up, and made a sign to his wife that it was time to go.

Having thanked Anna Pavlovna for her charming party, the guests began to take their leave.

Pierre was clumsy, stout and uncommonly tall. He had large red hands. He did not know how to enter a drawing-room and still less how to leave. He did not know how to say something agreeable on departure. Moreover, he was absent-minded. He stood up, and picking up a three-cornered hat with the plume of a general in it instead of his own, he kept hold of it, pulling the feathers till the general took it out of his hand. But all his forgetfulness and his inability to enter a drawing-room or talk properly in it were atoned for by his good-nature, simplicity and modesty.

Anna Pavlovna turned to him, and with Christian meekness expressed her forgiveness for his misbehaviour. She nodded to him and said: "I hope I shall see you again, but I hope also you will change your opinions, my dear Monsieur Pierre."

He made no answer, he simply bowed and displayed to every one once more his smile, which seemed to say: "Opinions or no opinions, you see what a nice, good-hearted fellow I am." And Anna Pavlovna and every one else instinctively felt this.

Prince André had gone out into the hall and turning his shoulders to the footman who was helping him with his coat, listened indifferently to his wife's chatter with Prince Hippolite, who had also come out into the hall. Prince Hippolite stood close to the pretty princess, so soon to be a mother, and stared persistently straight at her through his eyeglass.

"Go in, Anna, you'll catch cold," said the little princess, saying good-bye to Anna Pavlovna. "It is settled," she added in a low voice.

Anna Pavlovna had managed to have a few words with the Princess Liza about the match she was planning between Anatole and her sister-in-law.

"I rely on you, my dear," said Anna Pavlovna, "you write to her and tell me how her father will view the matter. *Au revoir!*" And she left the hall.

Pierre, reaching the house first, went to Prince André's study, like one of the family, and at once lay down on the sofa. "What a shock you gave Mlle. Scherer! She'll be quite ill now," Prince André said, as he came into the study rubbing his small white hands.

Pierre smiled and waved his hand.

"Oh, that abbé was very interesting, only he's got a wrong notion about it. . . . To my thinking, perpetual peace is possible, but I don't know how to express it. . . . Not by a balance of political power. . . ."

Prince André was obviously not interested.

"One can't always say all one thinks. Come tell me, have you decided on anything? Are you going into the cavalry or the diplomatic service?" asked Prince André.

Pierre sat up on the sofa with his legs crossed under him.

"Can you believe it, I still don't know. I don't like either."

"But you must decide on something; you know your father's expecting it."

Ten-year-old Pierre had been sent with an abbé as tutor to be educated abroad, and there he remained till he was twenty. When he returned to Moscow, his father had dismissed the tutor and said to the young man: "Now you go to Petersburg, look about you and make your choice. I agree to anything. Here is a letter to Prince Vassily and here is money. Write and tell me everything; I will help you in everything." Pierre had been already three months choosing a career and had not yet made his choice. It was of this problem that Prince André spoke to him. Pierre rubbed his forehead.

"But he must be a freemason," he said, referring to the abbé he had seen that evening.

"That's all nonsense," Prince André pulled him up again; "we'd better talk of serious things. Have you been to the Horse Guards?"

"No, I haven't; but this is what struck me and I wanted to talk to you about it. This war now is against Napoleon. If it were a war for freedom, I could understand it, I would have been the first to go into the army. But to help England and Austria against the greatest man in the world—that's not right."

Prince André simply shrugged his shoulders at Pierre's childish words. He looked as though one really could not answer such absurdities. But in reality it was hard to find an answer to this naïve question other than the answer Prince André made. "If every one would only fight for his own convictions, there'd be no war," he said.

"And a very good thing that would be too," said Pierre.

Prince André smiled ironically. "Very likely it would be a good thing, but it will never come to pass."

"Well, why are you going to the war?" asked Pierre.

"What for? I don't know. Because I have to. Besides, I'm going . . ." he stopped. "I'm going because the life I lead here, this life is—does not suit me!"

The rustle of a woman's dress was heard in the next room. Prince André started up, and pulled himself together. His face assumed the expression it had worn in Anna Pavlovna's drawing-room. Pierre removed his feet from the sofa. The princess came in. She had changed her gown, and was wearing a house dress as fresh and elegant as the other had been. Prince André got up and politely drew up a chair for her.

"Why is it, I wonder," she began in French as always, while she fussily settled herself in the chair, "why is it Anna Pavlovna never married? How stupid you men all are not to have married her. You must excuse me, but you really have no sense about women. What an argumentative fellow you are, Monsieur Pierre!"

"I'm still arguing with your husband. I can't understand why he wants to go to war," said Pierre, addressing the princess.

The princess started. Pierre's words touched a tender spot.

"Oh, that's what I say," she said. "I don't understand, I simply can't understand why men can't live without war. Why is it we women want nothing of the sort? We don't need it. Come, you shall be the judge. I keep saying to him: here he is Uncle's aide-de-camp, a most brilliant position. He's so well known, so appreciated by every one. The other day I heard a lady ask: 'So that is the famous Prince André?' I did really!" She laughed. "He's received everywhere. He could very easily become aide-de-camp to the Emperor. You know the Emperor has spoken very graciously to him. Anna and I were saying it would be quite easy to arrange it. What do you think?"

Pierre looked at Prince André, and, noticing that his friend did not like this subject, he did not answer.

"When are you starting?" he asked.

"Oh, don't talk about his going away; don't talk about it. I won't even hear it spoken of," said the princess in the playful tone in which she had talked to Hippolite at the *soirée*. "This evening when I thought all these associations so precious to me must be broken off. . . . And then, you know, André?" She looked at her husband. "I'm afraid! I'm afraid!" she whispered, and a shudder ran through her. Her husband looked at her, surprised to observe that there was some one in the room besides himself and Pierre.

"What are you afraid of, Liza? I don't understand," he said.

"See how selfish men are; they are all, all egoists! Of his own accord, for his own whim, for no reason whatever, he is deserting me, locking me up alone in the country."

"With my father and sister, remember," said Prince André quietly.

"It's just the same as alone, without my own friends. . . . And he doesn't expect me to be afraid." Her tone was quarrelsome. She paused as though feeling it embarrassing to speak of her condition before Pierre, though the whole gist of the matter lay in that.

"I still don't understand what you are afraid of," Prince André said, not taking his eyes off her. The princess blushed, and waved her hands despairingly.

"No, André, I must say you are so changed, so changed . . ."

"Your doctor's orders were that you were to go to bed earlier," said Prince André. "It's time you were asleep."

The princess said nothing, and suddenly her short, downy lip began to quiver. Prince André got up and walked about the room, shrugging his shoulders.

Pierre looked over his spectacles from him to the princess, and stirred uneasily as though he too meant to get up, but had changed his mind.

"What do I care if Monsieur Pierre is here?" the little princess said suddenly, her pretty face distorted into a tearful grimace; "I have long wanted to ask you, André, why are you so changed? What have I done? You want to go away to the war, you have no pity for me. Why is it?"

"Liza!" was all Prince André said, but in that one word

there was entreaty and menace, and, most of all, a conviction that she would herself regret her words.

But she went on hurriedly. "You treat me as though I were ill, or a child. I see it all! You did not behave like this six months ago."

"Liza, I beg you to be silent," said Prince André, still more emphatically.

Pierre, who had been growing more and more disturbed during this conversation, got up and went to the princess. He seemed unable to endure the sight of her tears, and was ready to cry himself.

"Calm yourself, princess. You only fancy these things because . . . I assure you, I've felt so myself . . . because . . . through . . . Oh, excuse me, an outsider has no business . . . Oh, don't distress yourself . . . Good-bye."

Prince André held his hand and stopped him.

"No, wait a little, Pierre. The princess is so good, she would not wish to deprive me of the pleasure of spending an evening with you."

"No, he thinks only of himself," the princess declared, not attempting to check her angry tears.

"Liza," said Prince André, raising his voice to a pitch that showed his patience was at an end.

All at once the angry expression of the princess's lovely little face changed to a look of fear.

"Mon Dieu! mon Dieu!" murmured the princess, and lifting her gown with one hand, she went to her husband and kissed him on the forehead.

"Good-night, Liza," said Prince André, rising and kissing her hand courteously, as though she were a stranger.

The friends were silent. Neither of them cared to talk. Pierre looked at Prince André; Prince André rubbed his forehead with his small hand.

"Let us go and have supper," he said with a sigh, going to the door.

They entered the elegantly, newly and richly furnished dining-room. Everything from the dinner-napkins to the silver, the china and the glass, wore that peculiar stamp of newness that is seen in the household of newly married couples. When they were half through supper Prince André leaned on his elbow, and like a man who long had something on his mind, he began to speak with a look of nervous irritation which Pierre had never before seen in his friend.

"Never, never marry, my dear fellow! That's my advice to you; don't marry till you have faced the fact that you have done all you're capable of doing, and till you cease to love the woman of your choice, till you see her plainly, or else you will make a cruel mistake that can never be set right. Marry when you're old and good for nothing . . . Or else everything good and lofty in you will be done for. It will all be wasted on trifles. Yes, yes, yes! Don't look at me with such surprise. If you expect anything of yourself in the future you will feel at every step that for you all is over, all is closed up except the drawing-room, where you will stand on the same level with a court lackey and an idiot . . . And why!" . . . He waved his arm.

Pierre took off his spectacles, which made his face seem even more good-natured, and looked wonderingly at his friend.

"My wife," pursued Prince André, "is an excellent woman. She is one of those rare women with whom one can feel quite secure of one's honour; but, O God! what wouldn't I give now not to be married! You are the first and the only person to whom I mention this, because I like you."

As Prince André spoke these words he was less than ever like the Bolkonsky who had sat lolling in Anna Pavlovna's drawing-room with half-closed eyelids, uttering French phrases. His face was quivering with nervous excitement in every muscle; his eyes, which had seemed lifeless, now flashed. It seemed that the more lifeless he was at ordinary times, the more impassioned he became at such moments of irritability.

"You don't understand why I say this," he went on. "Why it is the whole story of life. You talk of Bonaparte and his career," he said, "but Bonaparte when he was working his way up, going step by step straight toward his goal, was free; he had nothing except his aim and he attained it. But tie yourself up with a woman, and, like a chained convict, you lose all freedom! And all the hope and strength there is in you only weighs you down and torments you with regret. Drawing-rooms, gossip, balls, vanity, triviality—that's the enchanted circle I cannot escape from. I am setting off now to the war, the greatest war there has ever been, and I know nothing, and am fit for nothing. I am very amiable and sarcastic," pursued Prince André, "and at Anna Pavlovna's every one listens to me. And this stupid society without which my wife can't exist, and these women . . . If you only knew what these society women are! My father's right. Selfish, vain, stupid, trivial in everything—that's what women are. Looking at them in society, one fancies there's something in them, but there's nothing, nothing, nothing! No, don't marry, my dear fellow, don't marry!" Prince André concluded.

"It seems absurd to me," said Pierre, "that you, you con-

sider yourself a failure, your life wrecked. You have everything, everything before you. And you . . ."

His tone showed how highly he thought of his friend, and how much he expected of him in the future.

"How can he talk like that?" Pierre thought.

Pierre regarded Prince André as a model of all perfection, because Prince André possessed in the highest degree just that combination of qualities which Pierre lacked, and which might be described as strength of will. Pierre always marvelled at Prince André's faculty for dealing with people, his exceptional memory, his wide knowledge. He had read everything, knew everything, had an opinion about everything, and above all he had a great capacity for work and study. If Pierre were frequently struck by André's lack of capacity for dreaming and philosophising, to which Pierre was himself greatly given, he did not regard this as a defect but as a sign of strength.

"My day is done," said Prince André. "Why talk of me? Let's talk about you," he said after a brief pause.

"Why, what is there to say about me?" said Pierre. "What am I? I'm a bastard." And he suddenly flushed crimson. Apparently it was a great effort to him to say this. "With no name, no fortune. . . . And after all, really . . ." He did not finish. "For the present I am free and I'm content. Only I don't know in the least what I am to do. I meant to ask your advice in earnest."

Prince André looked at him kindly. But in his eyes, friendly as they were, there was yet a trace of his own superiority.

"You are dear to me just because you are the one vital person in all our society. You're lucky. Choose what you will, it's all the same. You'll be all right anywhere, but there's one thing: give up visiting the Kuragins and leading this sort of life. it's not the right thing for you. This riotous living and dissipation and all . . ."

"What would you have?" said Pierre, shrugging his shoulders. "Women, my dear fellow, women."

"I can't understand it," answered André. "Ladies, that's another matter, but Kuragin's women! I can't understand!"

Pierre was living at Prince Vassily Kuragin's, and sharing in the dissipated mode of life of his son Anatole, the son whom they were proposing to marry to Prince André's sister to reform him.

"Do you know what," said Pierre, as though a happy thought had suddenly occurred to him; "seriously, I have been thinking about it for a long while. Leading this sort of life I can't decide on anything, or think about anything properly.

My head aches and my money's all gone. He invited me tonight, but I won't go."

"Give me your word of honour that you will not go."

"On my honour!"

It was already past one o'clock when Pierre left. The clear Petersburg summer night was cloudless. He hailed a passing cab, intending to go home. But the closer to home he got, the more impossible it seemed to him to go to bed on such a night as this, that was more like evening or morning. One could see everything far along the empty streets. On the way Pierre remembered that the usual card-playing crowd was to have met at Anatole Kuragin's that evening, after which there usually followed a drinking bout. But immediately he remembered his promise to Prince André that he would not visit Kuragin again.

And then, as so often happens with people of weak character, he began to wish so desperately for one more taste of this familiar, purposeless existence, that he decided to go after all. And instantly it occurred to him that the promise he had given Prince André was not binding at all because before promising Prince André, he had already promised Prince Anatole that he would drop in. Finally he told himself that all these promises solemnly given were in reality only relative when one considered that tomorrow one might die, or that something might happen so extraordinary as to make all consideration of either honour or dishonour negligible. Reflections of this sort often came to Pierre, negating whatever decisions or resolutions he might have made. He went on to Kuragin's.

Having driven up to the entrance of the big house where Anatole Kuragin lived, he went up the well-lighted stairway, and through an open door. There was no one in the hall, which was littered with empty bottles, overshoes, and coats; it smelled strongly of liquor; voices and shouts could be heard from an inner room.

The card game and the supper were over, but the party had not broken up. Pierre threw off his coat and went into the first room, where he saw the remains of supper and where a footman, thinking himself alone, was finishing off the wine in the half-empty glasses. From the room beyond came laughter, familiar voices shouting and also the roar of a bear. Eight or nine young men were crowding around an open window. Three others were dragging a young bear around by a chain, trying to frighten the others.

"I bet a hundred on Stevens!" someone shouted.

"No holding on!" cried someone else.

"I bet on Dolohov!" cried a third man. "You hold the bets, Kuragin!"

"But all at once, or the bet is lost!" shouted a fourth.

"Jacob! Bring in a bottle, Jacob!" shouted Anatole, a tall handsome young man who stood in the center of the room, wearing a thin shirt open at the throat. "Hold everything, gentlemen! Here he is, here's Pierre." He turned to Pierre.

From the window came another shout. It came from a man of medium height whose eyes were a clear light blue and whose voice, in the midst of all these drunken voices, was especially striking for its soberness. "Come here—hold the bets!" This was Dolohov, an officer of the Semenov regiment, a notorious gambler and duellist who lived with Anatole. Pierre smiled, looking about in a good-natured way.

"I don't understand—what's this all about?" he asked.

"Wait, wait, he's sober! Let's have a bottle," said Anatole, and taking a glass from the table he went up to Pierre.

"First of all, drink this."

Pierre began drinking glass after glass, at the same time looking at the drunken group that was now once more crowding around the window. Anatole kept pouring him more wine and explaining how Dolohov had bet the Englishman, Stevens, a visiting seaman, that he, Dolohov, could drink a full bottle of rum while sitting on the outer ledge of the third-story window, his legs dangling outside.

"Here, finish the bottle!" said Anatole, pouring Pierre a last glass.

"No, I don't want any more," said Pierre, and pushing Anatole aside he went toward the window.

Dolohov was holding the Englishman by the hand and clearly, distinctly, was stating the terms of the bet, while addressing himself primarily to Anatole and Pierre.

Dolohov was about twenty-five years old. Like all infantry officers he wore no mustache and his mouth, his most striking feature, was completely exposed. The upper lip closed firmly over the strong lower one. He was a man of small means and no connections. And although Anatole spent tens of thousands yearly yet Dolohov, living with him, somehow managed the situation so that all their acquaintances respected Dolohov more than they did Anatole. Dolohov played every conceivable game and nearly always won. No matter how much he drank he never lost his head. And both Anatole Kuragin and Dolohov were notorious in Petersburg's fashionable fast set.

The bottle of rum was brought in. The window frame which prevented anyone from sitting on the outside ledge, was being broken away by two footmen, who were intimidated by the shouts of advice given to them.

Anatole strode over to the window. He had an urge to break something. He pushed the footmen aside and tugged at the window frame which refused to give. He broke the glass pane.

"This is something for you, strong man," he turned to Pierre.

Pierre got a firm hold on the crossbeam, pulled hard, and with a crash half broke, half twisted out the massive oak frame.

Dolohov, holding the bottle, jumped to the window sill.

"Attention!" he shouted, balancing himself and turning to face the room. Everyone was silent.

"I take the bet." He spoke French in order to be understood by the Englishman. "I am betting fifty imperials—or do you want to make it a hundred?" he asked, turning to the Englishman.

"No, fifty," said the Englishman.

"All right, fifty imperials that I can drink the whole bottle of rum without once taking it from my lips—drink it all while sitting outside the window, right there." He bent and pointed to a sloping projection in the wall beyond the window sill. "And I'll do it without holding on to anything. . . . that right?"

"Right," said the Englishman.

Anatole turned to the Englishman and, catching him by a button of his coat and looking down at him, for the Englishman was a short man, began to repeat the terms of the bet in English.

"Wait!" cried Dolohov, banging the bottle against the window in order to attract attention. "Wait a minute, Kuragin! Listen, all of you! If anyone else can do the same, I'll pay him a hundred imperials. Is that clear?"

The Englishman nodded without making it in the least clear whether or not he meant to take up this new wager.

Setting the rum bottle on the sill where he could easily reach it, Dolohov now carefully and slowly climbed outside. Lowering his legs over the ledge and spreading both arms wide he tested his position, made himself comfortable, shifted slightly to the right, then to the left, and picked up the bottle. Anatole brought two candles and set them down on the sill although it was by then quite light outside. Everyone crowded around the window. The Englishman stood out in front. Pierre smiled but said nothing. However one of the guests, somewhat older than the rest, suddenly came forward, his face frightened and angry, and tried to grab Dolohov by his shirt.

Anatole stopped him. "Don't touch him, or you'll startle him and he'll be killed! And then what, eh?"

Dolohov turned, balancing himself again with his hands.

"The next one who interferes with me," he said, letting the words fall slowly through tightly drawn lips, "I will throw him down there! . . . Now."

And with the "Now," he turned back, let go of any support, picked up the bottle, put it to his mouth, tilted his head and raised his other arm to balance himself. One of the footmen, who had begun to clear away the broken glass, stopped still, his eyes fixed on Dolohov's back. Anatole stood, his eyes wide open. The Englishman bit his lips. All were silent.

Dolohov, sitting in exactly the same position, now bent his head so far back that his curly hair touched his shirt collar and the hand with the bottle rose higher and higher, trembling with effort. The bottle was nearly empty, and so was tipped still higher, forcing his head back further.

"Why is it taking so long?" thought Pierre. It seemed to him that a half hour or more must have gone by. Suddenly Dolohov made a backward movement and his arm shuddered convulsively. He slipped downward. One arm shot out to catch hold of the window frame, then dropped again. Pierre closed his eyes. Suddenly he felt everything coming to life around him. He glanced up. Dolohov was standing on the window ledge, his face pale but happy.

"Empty!"

He pitched the bottle to the Englishman, who caught it neatly. Dolohov jumped down.

"Hurray! That's what I call a bet! The devil take you, my friend!" came shouts from all sides.

The Englishman, reaching for his purse, began to count out the money. Dolohov frowned and stood silent.

Pierre jumped up on the window. "Gentlemen! I'll do what he did," he began to shout. "Better still, don't let's bet at all. Just have them bring in another bottle. I'll do it for nothing—just give me a bottle!"

"Let him, let him," Dolohov said, smiling.

"Have you gone out your mind? Do you think we'd let you? Why, you even get dizzy going down the stairs." Several began to argue with him.

"I'll finish a bottle—give me a bottle of rum!" cried Pierre.

Someone caught his hand. But he was so strong that he shoved away everyone.

"No, that isn't the way to handle him," said Anatole. "Wait, I think I can manage him. Listen, I'll take you up on your bet, but not now, tomorrow. Right now we're all on our way to . . ."

"Good!" roared Pierre. "If we're on our way, let's go! And we'll take the bear with us." And catching hold of the bear, he embraced him, lifted him up and began to waltz with him around the room.

Prince Vassily kept the promise he had made at Anna Pavlovna's to Princess Drubetskoy, who had petitioned him on behalf of her only son Boris. His case had been laid before the Emperor, and he received a commission as sub-lieutenant in the Guards of the Semenovsky regiment. But the post in Kutuzov's service was not obtained for Boris despite all Anna Drubetskoy's endeavors.

Shortly after the gathering at Anna Pavlovna's, Anna Drubetskoy went back to Moscow, to her rich relatives the Rostovs, with whom she stayed. It was with these relations that her adored Boris had been educated from childhood and had lived for years. The Guards had already left Petersburg on the 10th of August, and her son, who was remaining in Moscow to get his equipment, was to overtake them on the march to Radzivilov.

The Rostovs were celebrating the name-day of the mother and the younger daughter, both called Natasha. Ever since the morning, coaches with six horses had been driving here and there bringing visitors to Countess Rostov's big house, which was known to all Moscow. The countess and her handsome elder daughter were sitting in the drawing-room with the visitors, who came in continual succession to present their congratulations.

The countess was a woman with a thin face of Oriental cast, forty-five years old, and worn out by child-bearing. She had had twelve children. The deliberate slowness of her movements and conversation, arising from weak health, gave her an air of dignity which inspired respect. Princess Anna Drubetskoy, as an intimate friend of the family, sat with them receiving and entertaining their guests. The younger members of the family were in the back rooms, indifferent to the visitors. The count met his guests and escorted them to the door, inviting all of them to dinner.

"I thank you for myself and my two dear ones whose name-day we are keeping. Mind you come to dinner. I shall be offended if you don't, my dear. I beg you most sincerely from all the family." These words, invariably accompanied by the same expression on his full, good-humoured, clean-shaven face, and the same warm pressure of the hand, and repeated short bows, he said to all without exception or variation.

When he had escorted one of the guests to the hall, the count returned to those guests who were still in the drawing-room. Moving up a chair, and with the air of a man fond of society and at home in it, he would sit down, his legs apart, and his hands on his knees and offer predictions upon the weather, or give advice about health, sometimes in Russian, sometimes in very bad French. Then again he would get up, and with the air of a man weary but resolute in the performance of his duty, he would escort guests out, stroking up his grey hair over his bald patch, and again he would urge them to come to dinner. Sometimes on his way back from the hall, he would pass through the conservatory and the butler's room into a big dining room with a marble floor, where they were setting a table for eighty guests; and looking at the waiters who were bringing in the silver and china, moving tables and unfolding damask tablecloths, he would call Dmitry Vassilyevitch, a young man of good family, who performed the duties of a steward in his household, and would say: "Now then, Dmitry, mind everything's right. That's it, that's it," he would say, looking round with pleasure at the immense table opened out to its full extent; "the great thing is the service." And then he would return again with satisfaction to the drawing-room.

"Marya Lvovna Karagin and her daughter," the countess's huge footman announced in a deep bass voice at the drawing-room door. The countess thought a moment, and took a pinch from a golden snuff-box with her husband's portrait on it.

"I'm worn out with these callers," she said. "This is the last one I'll see. She's so affected. Show her up," she said in a dejected tone.

A tall, stout, haughty-looking lady and her round-faced, smiling daughter walked with rustling skirts into the drawing-room.

"Dear countess, it is such a long time . . . she has been laid up, poor child . . . at the Razumovskys' ball, and the Countess Apraxin . . . I was so glad," feminine voices chattered briskly, interrupting one another and mingling with the sound of rustling skirts and the scraping of chairs.

The conversation touched on the chief items of news in the town, on the illness of the wealthy old Count Bezuhov, a man who had been known for his handsome appearance in the days of Catherine, and on his illegitimate son, Pierre, who had behaved so improperly at Anna Pavlovna's. "I am very sorry for the poor count," declared the visitor; "his health in such a poor state, and now this distress brought on by his son. It will be the death of him!"

"Why, what has happened?" asked the countess, pretending she did not know what was meant, though she had already heard about the cause of Count Bezuhov's distress fifteen times.

"This is what comes of modern education! When he was abroad," the visitor continued, "this young man was left to his own devices, and now in Petersburg, they say, he has been doing such vile things that he has been sent away under police escort."

"Really!" said the countess.

"He has made a bad choice of his companions," put in Princess Anna Drubetskoy. "Prince Vassily's son—he and a young man called Dolohov, they say—God only knows the dreadful things they've been doing. And both have suffered for it. Dolohov has been degraded to the rank of a common soldier, while Bezuhov's son has been banished to Moscow. As for Anatole Kuragin . . . his father managed to hush it up somehow. But he has been sent out of Petersburg too."

"Why, what did they do?" asked the countess.

"They're perfect ruffians, especially Dolohov," said the visitor. "The three of them got hold of a bear somewhere, put it in a carriage with them, and were taking it to some actress's. The police ran up to stop them. They took the policeman, tied him back to back to the bear, and dropped the bear into the river. The bear swam with the policeman tied on his back."

"What a sight that must have been, my dear," cried the count, rolling with laughter.

"Oh, such a horror! How can you laugh at it, count?"

But the ladies could not help laughing at it themselves.

"It was all they could do to rescue the unlucky man," the visitor went on. "And that's the intellectual sort of amusement the son of Count Cyril Bezuhov indulges in!" she added. "And people said he was so well educated and clever! That's what foreign education has done for him. I hope no one will receive him here, in spite of his great wealth. They tried to introduce him to me. I gave an absolute refusal; I have daughters!"

"What makes you say the young man is so wealthy?" asked the countess, turning away from the girls, who at once looked as though they did not hear. "The count has none but illegitimate children. I believe that . . . Pierre, too, is illegitimate."

The visitor waved her hand.

Princess Anna Drubetskoy interrupted, obviously wishing to show her connections and intimate knowledge with every detail in society.

"This is how the matter stands," she said, speaking in a half whisper. "Count Cyril's reputation we all know. . . . He has lost count of his own children, indeed, but this Pierre was his favourite."

"How handsome the old man was," said the countess, "only last year! A finer-looking man I have never seen."

"Now he's very much altered," said Anna Drubetskoy. "Well, I was just saying, the direct heir to all the property is Prince Vassily through his wife, but the father is very fond of Pierre, has taken trouble over his education, and he has written to the Emperor . . . so that no one can tell, if he dies, he's so ill that it's expected any moment, and Doctor Lorrain has come from Petersburg, who will inherit that immense property, Pierre or Prince Vassily. Forty thousand serfs and millions of money! He's the richest man in Russia. I know this for a fact, for Prince Vassily himself told me so. And indeed Count Cyril happens to be a third cousin of mine on my mother's side, and he's Boris' godfather too," she added, as if she attached no importance to this circumstance.

"Prince Vassily arrived in Moscow yesterday. He's coming on some inspection business, so I was told," said the visitor.

"Yes, between ourselves," said the princess, "that's a pretext; he has come simply to see Count Cyril, hearing he is in such a serious state."

During a brief silence, the countess looked at her guests and smiled. But she did not disguise the fact that she would be glad if the guests were to get up and go.

The daughter was fingering at the folds of her gown and looking at her mother when suddenly they heard in the next room several girls and boys running, and the noise of a chair knocked over. A girl of thirteen ran in, hiding something in her short muslin petticoat. She stopped short in the middle of the room. She had evidently not intended to come so far but was unable to stop. At the same instant there appeared in the doorway a student with a crimson band on his collar, a young officer in the Guards, a girl of fifteen, and a fat, rosy-cheeked boy in a short jacket.

The prince jumped up, and held his arms out wide round the little girl.

"Ah, here she is!" he cried, laughing. "Our little darling, whose name-day it is. My pet!"

"My dear, there is a time for everything," said the countess, affecting severity. "You're always spoiling her," she added to her husband.

The dark-eyed little girl, plain, but full of life, with her wide mouth, her childish bare shoulders, her black hair brushed back, her slender bare arms and little legs in lace-edged long drawers and open slippers, was at that charming stage when the girl is no longer a child, while the child is not yet a young girl. Escaping from her father, she ran up to her mother, and taking no notice whatever of her severe remarks, she hid her flushed face in her mother's lace kerchief and broke into laughter. As she laughed she tried to say something about a doll, Mimi, which was poking out from under her petticoat.

"Come, run along, go away with your monstrosity!" said her mother, pushing her off with a pretence of anger. "This is my younger girl," she said to the visitor.

Natasha, pulling her face away from her mother's lace kerchief for a moment, looked down at her through tears of laughter, and hid her face again.

The visitor thought it necessary to say something.

"Tell me, my dear," she said, addressing Natasha, "how did you come by your Mimi? Your daughter, I suppose?"

Natasha did not like the visitor's tone of condescension. She made no answer, but stared solemnly at her.

Meanwhile, Boris the officer, Anna Drubetskoy's son; Nicholas, the student, the count's elder son; Sonya, the count's niece; and little Peter, his younger son, had all seated themselves about the drawing-room, and were obviously trying to restrain the excitement and mirth which beamed in their faces. They looked at one another and could hardly suppress their laughter.

The two young men, the student and the officer, friends from childhood, were of the same age, and both good-looking, but not like each other. Boris was a tall, fair-haired lad with delicate, regular features, and a look of composure on his handsome face. Nicholas was curly-headed, not tall, and with an open expression; his whole face expressed impulsiveness and enthusiasm. Nicholas flushed red as he came into the drawing-room. He was trying to find something to say, but couldn't. Boris, on the contrary, was at home immediately and talked easily and playfully of the doll Mimi, saying that he had known her as a young girl before her nose was broken, and she had grown older during the five years he remembered her, and how her head was cracked right across the skull. As he said this he looked at Natasha. Natasha turned away from him and jumped up and flew out of the room as quickly as her legs could carry her.

"You were meaning to go out, mother, weren't you? Do you want the carriage?" Boris asked now turning to his mother with a smile.

"Yes, go and tell them to get it ready," she said. Boris walked slowly to the door and went in search of Natasha. The plump little Peter also left the room, as though resenting the interruption of his fun.

Of the young people, not counting the countess's elder daughter, Vera, who was four years older than her sister and behaved quite like a grown-up person, and the young lady visitor, there were now left in the drawing-room only Nicholas and Sonya, the niece. Sonya was a slender, small brunette, with soft eyes shaded by long lashes. The grace of her movements, and something of slyness and reserve in her manner, suggested a lovely half-grown kitten. Apparently she thought it only proper to show an interest in the general conversation and to smile. But against her own will, her eyes turned under their thick, long lashes to her cousin, Nicholas, who was going away into the army, with girlish, passionate adoration. It was clear that the kitten only perched there waiting to skip off with her cousin as soon as they could, like Boris and Natasha.

"Yes," said the old count, addressing the visitor and pointing to his Nicholas; "here his friend Boris has received his commission as an officer, and he's so fond of his friend he doesn't want to be left behind. And so he is giving up the university and his poor old father to go into the army. And there was a place all ready for him in the archives department!"

"But they say that war has been declared, you know," said the visitor.

"They've been saying so a long while," said the count. "They'll say so again and again, and so it will be." Then he added: "He's going into the hussars."

The visitor, not knowing what to say, shook her head.

"It's not from friendship at all," answered Nicholas in anger. "Not friendship at all, but simply I feel that it's my duty."

He looked round at his cousin and the young lady visitor; both looked at him with a smile of approval.

"Schubert's dining with us to-night, the colonel of the Pavologradsky regiment of hussars. He has been here on leave, and is taking Nicholas with him. There's no help for it," said the count, shrugging his shoulders and speaking lightly of something that distressed him very much.

"I've already told you father," said his son, "that if you're unwilling to let me go, I'll stay. But I know I'm no good for anything except in the army. I'm not a diplomat, or a government clerk. I'm not clever at disguising my feelings," he said, glancing repeatedly at Sonya and the young lady.

"Well, well, all right!" said the old count. "He always gets so excited. Bonaparte's turned all their heads; they're all thinking of how he rose from lieutenant to Emperor. Well, and so may it turn out again, please God," he added, not noticing the visitor's sarcastic smile.

While their elders began talking about Bonaparte, Julie, Madame Karagin's daughter, turned to young Rostov.

"What a pity you weren't at the Arharovs' on Thursday. I was so dull without you," she said, smiling. The young man, highly flattered, moved nearer her, unaware that he had dealt a jealous stab to the heart of Sonya, who was flushing crimson and assuming a forced smile. In the middle of his talk with Julie he glanced round at her. Sonya gave him an intensely angry look, and, hardly able to restrain her tears, she got up and left the room. All Nicholas' animation was gone. He waited for the first break in the conversation, and, with a worried face, walked out of the room to look for Sonya.

"How all young people wear their hearts on their sleeves!" said Anna Drubetskoy pointing to Nicholas' retreating figure. "Cousinhood is a dangerous neighbourhood," she added.

"What a charming little thing your younger girl is!" said the visitor. "Full of fun and mischief!"

"Yes, that she is," said the count. "She takes after me!"

"And she's in love with Boris already! What do you say to that?" said the countess, smiling softly and looking at Boris's mother. And apparently concerned with something that was ever in her mind, she went on: "Why, you know, if I were strict with her, if I were to forbid her . . . Goodness knows what they might not be doing in secret." The countess meant that they might kiss each other. "But as it is I know every word she utters. She'll come to me this evening and tell me everything. I spoil her, perhaps, but I really believe it's the best way. I brought my elder girl up more strictly."

"Yes, I was brought up quite differently," said the handsome young Countess Vera; and she smiled. What she said was true and appropriate. But, strange to say, every one—both the visitors and the countess—looked at her, as though wondering why she had said it, and they all felt awkward.

"People are always too clever with their elder children; they try to do something exceptional with them," said the visitor.

"We won't conceal our errors, my dear! My dear countess was too clever with Vera," said the count. "But what of it? she has turned out very well all the same," he added, with a wink to Vera.

The guests got up and took their leave, promising to come to dinner.

"What manners! I thought they would never go!" said the countess, when she had seen her guests out.

When Natasha ran out of the drawing-room she only ran as far as the conservatory. There she stopped, listening to the talk in the drawing-room, and waiting for Boris. She was beginning to get impatient, and stamping her foot, was almost ready to cry at his not coming, when she heard his footsteps. At this she darted away swiftly and hid among the tubs of shrubs.

Boris stood still in the middle of the room, looked round him, brushed off the sleeve of his uniform, and going up to the looking-glass examined his handsome face. Natasha, keeping quiet, peeped out of her hiding-place, waiting to see what he would do. He stood a little while before the glass, smiled at his reflection, and then walked towards the door. Natasha was on the point of calling to him, but she changed her mind. "Let him look for me," she said to herself.

Boris had only just gone out, when at the other door Sonya came in, flushed and muttering angrily through her tears. Natasha checked her first impulse to run out to her, and remained in her hiding-place to learn what was going on in the world. She was experiencing a new and peculiar pleasure. Sonya was murmuring something as she looked towards the drawing-room door. Then the door opened and Nicholas came in.

"Sonya! what is the matter? How can you?" said Nicholas, running up to her.

"Nothing, nothing, leave me alone!" Sonya was sobbing.

"Oh, I know what it is."

"Very well, you do, so much the better, and you can go back to her."

"So-o-onya! Look here! How can you torture me and yourself for a mere fancy?" said Nicholas, taking her hand. Sonya did not pull her hand back. She stopped crying.

Natasha, not stirring and hardly breathing, watched with sparkling eyes from her hiding-place. "What's coming now?" she wondered.

"Sonya! I care for nothing in the whole world! You're everything to me," said Nicholas. "I'll prove it to you."

"I don't like you to talk like that."

"Well, I won't then; come, forgive me, Sonya." He drew her to him and kissed her.

"Oh, how nice," thought Natasha, and when Sonya and Nicholas had gone out of the room she followed them and called Boris.

"Boris, come here," she said with a sly look. "I've something to tell you. Here, here," she said, and she led him into the conservatory, to the place where she had hidden between the tubs. Boris followed her, smiling.

"What is the *something?*" he asked. She was a little embarrassed; she looked round her, and seeing her doll flung down on a tub she picked it up.

"Kiss the doll," she said. Boris looked at her eager face and made no answer. "Don't you want to? Well, then come here," she said, and went further in among the plants and tossed away the doll. "Closer, closer!" she whispered. She caught hold of the young officer's arms, and her flushed face looked serious and frightened.

"Would you like to kiss me?" she whispered, smiling and almost crying with excitement.

Boris reddened. "How funny you are!" he said, bending

down to her, flushing redder still, but doing nothing. Suddenly she jumped onto a tub, so that she was taller than he, flung both arms round him, clasped him above his neck, and throwing back her hair with a toss of her head, she kissed him on his lips.

Then she slipped down among the flower-pots on the other side, and stood with hanging head.

"Natasha," he said, "you know I love you, but . . ."

"You're in love with me," Natasha broke in.

"Yes I am, but, please, don't let us do like that. . . . In another four years . . . Then I shall ask for your hand."

Natasha pondered a moment. "Thirteen, fourteen, fifteen, sixteen . . ." she said, counting on her thin little fingers. "Very well. Then it's settled?" And her excited face beamed with a smile of joy and satisfaction.

"Settled!" said Boris.

"Forever?" said the little girl. "Till death?" And taking his arm, with a happy face, she walked with him into the next room.

After receiving her visitors the countess was eager for a heart-to-heart talk with the friend of her childhood, Anna Drubetskoy, whom she had not seen properly since she had arrived from Petersburg. Anna Drubetskoy, with her tear-worn and amiable face, moved closer up to the countess' easy-chair.

"With you I will be perfectly open," said Anna Drubetskoy. "We haven't many old friends left. That's why I value your friendship so."

Anna Drubetskoy looked at Vera and stopped. The countess pressed her friend's hand.

"Vera," said the countess to her daughter, who was not her favourite, "how is it you have no notion about anything? Don't you feel that you're not wanted here? Go to your sister or . . ."

The handsome young countess smiled scornfully.

"If you had told me, mother, I would have gone away sooner," she said, and went off towards her own room. But passing through the sitting-room, she noticed two couples sitting in the two windows. She stopped and smiled contemptuously at them. Sonya was sitting close beside Nicholas, who was copying out some verses for her, the first he had ever written. Boris and Natasha were sitting in the other window, and were silent when Vera came in. Sonya and Natasha looked at Vera with guilty, happy faces.

"How often have I asked you," Vera said, "'not to take my things? You have a room of your own." She took the inkstand away from Nicholas.

"One minute, one minute," he said, dipping his pen.

"You always manage to do things just at the wrong time," said Vera. "First you burst into the drawing-room so that every one was ashamed of you."

Because what she said was perfectly true, no one answered; all four simply looked at one another. She lingered in the room with the inkstand in her hand. "And what sort of secrets can you have at your age, Natasha and Boris, and you two! It's all silly nonsense!"

"Well, what has it to do with you, Vera?" Natasha said very gently. She was good-humoured and affectionate that day with every one.

"It's very silly," said Vera; "I am ashamed of you. What sort of secret . . ."

"Every one has secrets. We don't interfere with you and Berg," said Natasha.

"I should think you wouldn't interfere," said Vera, "because there could be no harm in any conduct of mine. But I shall tell mother how you behave with Boris."

"Natasha behaves very well," said Boris. "I have nothing to complain of."

"Don't, Boris!" said Natasha, in a shaking voice.

Then she added, addressing Vera, "You'll never understand because you've never cared for any one; you've no heart. And your greatest delight is in getting other people into trouble. You can flirt with Berg, as much as you like!"

"Well, I'm not likely to run after a young man before visitors. . . ."

"Well, now you have done what you always do!" said Nicholas. "You've said something nasty to everyone, and upset everybody. Let's go into the other room."

All four rose, like a flock of scared birds, and left.

The handsome girl who produced such an irritating and unpleasant effect on every one smiled; and, obviously unaffected by what had been said to her, she went up to the looking-glass and fixed her scarf and her hair. Looking at her handsome face, she seemed to become colder and more composed than ever.

In the drawing-room the conversation was still going on.

"Ah, my dear," said the countess, "in my life, too, everything is not rose-coloured. Do you suppose I don't see that, in the way we are going on, our fortune can't last long? And it's all the club and his good-nature. When we're in the country we have no rest from it,—it's nothing but theatricals, hunting parties, and God knows what. But I won't talk of myself. Come, tell me how you managed it all. I often wonder at you, Anna, the way you go racing off alone, at your age, to Moscow, and to Petersburg, to all the ministers, and all the great people, and know how to get round them all too. I admire you, really! Well, how was it arranged? Why, I could never do it."

"Oh, my dear!" answered Princess Anna Drubetskoy. "God grant that you never know what it is to be left a widow, with no one to support you, and a son whom you love to distraction. One learns how to do anything," she said with some pride. "If I want to see one of these great people, I write a note: 'Princess so-and-so wishes to see so-and-so,' and I go myself in a hired cab two or three times—four, if need be—till I get what I want. I don't mind what they think of me."

"Well, tell me, then, whom did you interview for your dear Boris?" asked the countess. "Here's your boy an officer in the Guards, while my Nicholas is going as an ensign. There's no one to manage things for him. Whose help did you ask?"

"Prince Vassily's. He was so kind. Agreed to do everything immediately; put the case before the Emperor," said Princess Anna Drubetskoy enthusiastically, not mentioning all the humiliation she had been through to attain her object.

"And how is he? beginning to get old, Prince Vassily?" inquired the countess. "I have not seen him in many years and I dare say he has forgotten me. He once paid me attentions," the countess recalled with a smile.

"He's just the same," answered Anna Drubetskoy, "so affable, brimming over. Greatness has not turned his head. But you know my love for my son. I don't know what I would not do to make him happy. And my means are so scanty," added Anna Drubetskoy, dropping her voice mournfully, "that now I am in a most awful position. I have not, can you conceive it, literally, not a penny in the world, and I don't know how to get Boris' equipment." She took out her handkerchief and brushed away a tear. "I must have five hundred roubles, and I have only a twenty-five rouble note. I'm in such a position. . . . My one hope now is in Count Cyril Bezuhov. If he will not come to the help of his godson—you know he is Boris' godfather—and allow him something for his maintenance, all my efforts will have been in vain; I shall have nothing for his equipment.

The countess was silent.

"I often think—perhaps it's a sinful thought," said the princess, "but I often think: here is Count Cyril living all alone . . . that immense fortune . . . and what is he living for? Life is a burden to him, while Boris is only just beginning life."

"He will be sure to leave something to Boris," said the countess.

"God knows, dear friend! These wealthy people are such egoists. But still I'm going to see him at once with Boris, and I will tell him plainly the state of the case. People may think what they choose of me, I really don't care, when my son's future depends on it." The princess got up. "It's now two o'clock, and you dine at four. I shall just have time to drive there and back."

And with the air of a Petersburg lady, accustomed to business, and knowing how to make use of every moment, Anna Drubetskoy sent for her son, and with him went out into the hall.

"Good-bye, my dear," she said to the countess, who accompanied her to the door. "Wish me good-luck," she added in a whisper unheard by her son.

"You're going to Count Cyril's, my dear?" said the count, coming out of the dining-room into the hall. "If he's better, invite Pierre to dine with us. He has been here; used to dance with the children. Be sure you invite him."

"My dear Boris," said Anna Drubetskoy as the Countess Rostov's carriage drove along the street strewn with straw and into the wide courtyard of Count Cyril Bezuhov's house. "My dear Boris," repeated his mother, putting her hand out from under her old cape, and laying it on her son's hand with a timid, caressing movement, "be nice, be attentive. Count Cyril is after all your godfather, and your future depends on him. Remember that, my dear, be charming, as you so well know how to be. . . ."

"If I knew anything would come of it but humiliation," her son answered coldly. "But I have promised, and will do it for your sake."

At the entrance, the hall-porter scrutinized the mother and son and inquired whom they wanted, the princesses or the count. Hearing that they wanted to see the count the hall-porter said that his excellency was worse to-day and could see no one.

Boris looked inquiringly at his mother.

"My friend," Anna Drubetskoy said in a quiet voice, "I know that Count Cyril is very ill . . . that is why I am here. . . . I am a relation. . . . I shall not disturb him, my good man. . . . I need only see Prince Vassily, he's staying here, I know. Announce us, please."

The hall-porter pulled the bell-rope that rang upstairs and turned away.

"Princess Drubetskoy to see Prince Vassily," he called to a footman, who ran down from above, and looked down from the turn in the staircase.

The mother straightened the folds of her silk gown, looked

at herself in the looking-glass on the wall, and then walked up the carpeted stair in her shabby shoes. Boris, with his eyes down, followed after her.

They went into a large room, from which a door led to the apartments assigned to Prince Vassily.

Just as the mother and son reached the middle of the room and were about to ask their way of an old footman, who had appeared at their entrance, the bronze handle of one of the doors turned, and Prince Vassily, dressed in a house jacket of velvet, with one star, entered the room. The celebrated Petersburg doctor, Lorrain, was with him.

"It is positive, then?" said the Prince.

"Prince, to err is human, but . . ."

"Very well, very well . . ."

Noticing Anna Drubetskoy and her son, Prince Vassily dismissed the doctor with a bow, and in silence, with an air of inquiry, came toward them. The son noticed how an expression of intense grief suddenly came into his mother's eyes, and he smiled slightly.

"In what sad circumstances we were destined to meet again, prince! . . . Tell me how is our dear patient?" she said, apparently not observing the cold look that was fixed on her. Prince Vassily stared at her, then at Boris with a perplexed look. Boris bowed politely. Prince Vassily, without acknowledging his bow, turned away to Anna Drubetskoy and to her question he replied by a movement of the head and lips, indicating there was little hope

"Is it possible?" cried Anna Drubetskoy. "Oh, this is terrible! It is dreadful to think . . . This is my son," she added, indicating Boris. "He wanted to thank you in person."

Boris again made a polite bow.

"Believe me, prince, a mother's heart will never forget what you have done for us."

"I am glad I have been able to do you a service, my dear Anna Drubetskoy," said Prince Vassily, pulling his lace frill straight. "Try to do your duty in the service, and to be worthy of it," he added, turning severely to Boris. "I am glad . . . you are here on leave?" he asked.

"I am awaiting orders, your excellency, to join my new regiment," answered Boris, showing no sign either of resentment at the prince's abrupt manner, nor of desire to get into conversation, but speaking with such quiet composure that the prince gave him a searching glance.

"You are living with your mother?"

"I am living at Countess Rostov's," said Boris, again adding: "your excellency."

"The Ilya Rostov, who married Natasha Shinshin," said Anna Drubetskoy.

"I know, I know," said Prince Vassily. "I have never been able to understand how Natasha Shinshin could marry that crude bear! A completely stupid and ridiculous person. And a gambler too, I am told."

"But a very fine man, prince," observed Anna Drubetskoy, with a pathetic smile, as though she recognised that Count Rostov deserved this criticism, but asked him not to be too hard on the poor old fellow. "What do the doctors say?" asked the princess, after a brief pause, and again the expression of deep sorrow appeared on her face.

"There is little hope," said the prince.

"And I was hoping to thank Uncle once more for all his kindness to me and to Boris. He is his godson," she added in a tone that suggested that Prince Vassily would be highly delighted to hear this fact.

Prince Vassily frowned. Anna Drubetskoy saw he was afraid of finding in her a rival with claims on Count Bezuhov's will. She hastened to reassure him. "If it were not for my genuine love and devotion for Uncle," she said, "I know his character; generous, upright; but with only the princesses about him. . . . They are young. . . ." She bent her head and added in a whisper: "Has he performed his last duties, Prince? How priceless are these last moments! It is absolutely necessary to prepare him, if he is so ill. We women, prince," she smiled tenderly, "always know how to say these things. I absolutely must see him. Hard as it will be for me, I am accustomed to suffering."

The prince evidently understood, and understood, too, as he had at Anna Pavlovna's, that it was no easy task to get rid of Anna Drubetskoy.

"Would not such an interview be trying for him, dear Anna Drubetskoy?" he said. "Let us wait till the evening; the doctors have predicted a crisis."

"But waiting's out of the question, Prince. Think, it is a matter of saving his soul! The duties of a Christian. . . ."

A door from the inner rooms opened, and one of the count's nieces entered with a cold and stern face, and a long waist strikingly out of proportion with the shortness of her legs.

Prince Vassily turned to her. "Well, how is he?"

"Still the same. What can you expect with all this noise?" said the princess, staring at Anna Drubetskoy, as at a stranger.

"Ah, dear, I did not recognise you," said Anna Drubetskoy, with a delighted smile. "I have just come, and I am at your service to help nurse my uncle. I imagine what you have gone through," she added, sympathetically turning her eyes up.

The princess made no reply, she did not even smile, but walked out of the room. Anna Drubetskoy took off her gloves, and entrenched herself as it were in an armchair, inviting Prince Vassily to sit down beside her.

"Boris!" she said to her son, smiling, "I am going in to the count, to our poor uncle, and you can go to Pierre, my dear, and don't forget to give him the Rostovs' invitation. They ask him to dinner. I suppose he won't go?" she said to the prince.

"On the contrary," said the prince, visibly depressed, "I should be very glad if you would take that young man off my hands. . . . He remains here and the count has not once asked to see him."

He shrugged his shoulders. A footman escorted the youth downstairs and up another staircase to the apartment of Pierre Bezuhov.

Pierre had not succeeded in choosing a career in Petersburg, and really had been banished to Moscow for disorderly conduct. The story told about him at Count Rostov's was true. He had helped to tie the policeman to the bear.

Arriving at his father's house in Moscow, Pierre assumed that this story would already be known, and that his cousins, the three princesses who were always with his father, and who did not like him, would have used it to turn the count against him. Entering the drawing-room where the princesses usually sat, he greeted them, two of whom were sitting at their embroidery frames, while one read aloud. The eldest, a trim, long-waisted, severe maiden-lady, the one who had come to Anna Drubetskoy, was reading.

"Good morning, cousin," said Pierre. "You don't recognise me?"

"I know you only too well, only too well."

"How is the count? Can I see him?" Pierre asked, awkwardly as always.

"The count is suffering both physically and mentally, and you seem to do your best to cause him as much suffering as possible."

"Can I see the count?" repeated Pierre.

"Hm . . . if you want to kill him, to kill him outright, you can see him. Olga, go and see if uncle's broth is ready, it will soon be time for it," she added, to show Pierre they were busy looking after his father's comfort.

Olga left the room. Pierre waited a moment, looked at the sisters and said: "Then I will go to my room. When I can see him, you will tell me." He went away.

The next day Prince Vassily arrived and settled in the count's house. He sent for Pierre and said to him: "My dear fellow, if you behave here as you did at Petersburg, you will come to a very bad end; that's all I have to say to you. The count is very, very ill. You must not see him."

Since then Pierre had not been disturbed, and he spent the whole day alone in his room upstairs.

When Boris entered, Pierre was walking up and down his room, murmuring indistinct words, shrugging his shoulders and imagining himself Napoleon, who had just succeeded in the dangerous crossing of the Channel and in the conquest of London. When he saw the young officer come in, he suddenly stopped. Pierre had seen Boris last as a boy of fourteen, and did not remember him in the least. But in spite of that he took his hand in his impulsive and warm-hearted manner, and smiled at him.

"You remember me?" Boris said with a pleasant smile. "I have come with my mother to see the count, but it seems he is not quite well."

"Yes, he is ill. People are always bothering him," answered Pierre, trying to recall who this youth might be.

Boris saw that Pierre did not know him, but did not think it necessary to introduce himself, and without the slightest embarrasment looked him straight in the face.

"Count Rostov asks you to come to dinner to-day," he said, after a rather long silence.

"Oh, Count Rostov," began Pierre, delighted. "So you are his son, Ilya? Can you believe it, for a moment I did not recognise you. Do you remember how we used to slide on the Sparrow Hills . . . long ago?"

"You are mistaken," said Boris, deliberately, with a bold and rather sarcastic smile. "I am Boris, the son of Princess Anna Drubetskoy. It is the father of the Rostovs who is called Ilya, the son's name is Nicholas."

Pierre shook his head and arms as though flies or bees were swarming about him.

"I've mixed it all up! There are such a lot of relatives in Moscow! You are Boris . . . yes. Well, now, I have it clear. Tell me, what do you think of the Boulogne expedition? Things will go badly with the English, you know, if Napoleon ever gets across the Channel. I believe that the expedition is very possible."

Boris knew nothing at all about the Boulogne expedition.

"Here in Moscow we are more occupied with dinner parties and scandal than with politics," he said in his self-possessed, sarcastic tone. "I know nothing and think nothing about it. Moscow's busy with scandal," he went on. "Just now they are all talking about you and your father."

Pierre smiled his good-natured smile, as though afraid for his companion's sake that he might say something he would regret. But Boris spoke distinctly, clearly and drily, looking straight into Pierre's eyes.

"There's nothing else to do in Moscow but talk scandal," he went on. "Everyone is wondering to whom the count will leave his fortune. Perhaps he will outlive us all, as I sincerely hope he may."

"Yes, it's all very horrid," Pierre replied, "very horrid." Pierre was still afraid this young officer would inadvertently drop into some remark disconcerting for himself.

"And it must seem to you," said Boris, flushing slightly, but not changing his voice or attitude, "it must seem to you that everyone's thinking of nothing but getting something from the rich man."

"That's just it," thought Pierre.

"And that's just what I want to say to you to prevent misunderstandings. You are very much mistaken if you count me and my mother among those people. We are very poor, but I—at least I speak for myself—just because your father is rich, I don't consider myself a relation of his. Neither I nor my mother would ever ask for anything or take anything from him."

It was a long while before Pierre understood, but, when he did understand, he seized Boris' hand with his characteristic quickness and awkwardness, and blushing far more than Boris, began speaking with a mixed feeling of shame and annoyance.

"Well, it's strange! Do you suppose I . . . how you could think . . . I know very well . . ."

But Boris again interrupted him. "I am glad I have told you everything frankly. Perhaps you did not like it? You must excuse me," he said, trying to put Pierre at his ease instead of being put at his ease by him. "But I hope I have not offended you. I make it a rule to speak out quite plainly. . . . Then what message am I to take? You will come to dinner at the Rostovs'?"

And Boris, with a sense of having discharged a duty, having freed himself from an awkward position, and put somebody else into one, became quite pleasant again.

"No, let me tell you," said Pierre, calming himself, "you are a wonderful person. What you have just said was very fine, very fine. Of course you don't know me, it's so long since we've seen each other . . . we were children. . . . You might think . . . I understand, I quite understand. I couldn't have done it, I wouldn't have had the courage, but it's splendid. I'm very glad I have made your acquaintance. A queer idea," he added smiling, "you must have had of me." He laughed. "But what of it? Let us know each other better, please!" He pressed Boris' hand. "Do you know I've not once seen the count? Nor has he sent for me . . . I am sorry for him, as a man . . . But what can one do?"

"And so you think Napoleon will succeed in getting his army across the Channel?" asked Boris.

Pierre saw that Boris was trying to change the conversation, and so he began explaining the advantages and difficulties of the Boulogne expedition.

A footman came in to call Boris. His mother, the princess, was going. Pierre promised to come to dinner in order to see more of Boris, and pressed his hand warmly at parting, looking affectionately into his face over his spectacles.

When he had gone, Pierre walked for some time longer up and down his room, not murmuring and shrugging his shoulders, but smiling at the memory of the young man.

Prince Vassily accompanied the princess to the hall. The princess was holding her handkerchief to her eyes, and her face was wet with tears.

"It is terrible, terrible!" she said. "But whatever it costs me, I will do my duty. I will come and stay the night. He can't be left like this. Every minute is precious. I can't understand why his nieces put it off. Perhaps God will help me to find a way to prepare him! Adieu, Prince, may God support you . . ."

"Adieu, my good friend," answered Prince Vassily, turning away from her.

"Oh, he is in an awful state!" said the mother to her son, when they were sitting in the carriage again. "He scarcely knows any one."

"I don't understand, mamma, what his attitude is toward Pierre."

"The will should make all that plain, my dear. Our own fate, too, hangs upon it . . ."

"But what makes you expect he will leave us anything?"

"Oh, my dear! He is so rich, and we are so poor."

"Well, that's hardly a sufficient reason."

"Oh, my God. How ill he is, how ill he is!" cried his mother.

After Anna Drubetskoy had driven off with her son to Count Cyril's, Countess Rostov sat a long while alone, putting her handkerchief to her eyes.

The countess was upset by the troubles and degrading poverty of her friend. At last she rang the bell.

"Ask the count to come to me," she said to the maid.

The count came in to see his wife, looking, as usual, rather guilty. "Well, little countess! What a *sauté* of woodcocks and Madeira we're to have, my dear! I've tasted it. I did well to give a thousand roubles for Taras. He's worth it!"

He sat down by his wife, placing his elbow on his knee,

and ruffling up his grey hair. "What are your commands, little countess?"

"It's this, my dear—why, what is this mess on you here?" she said, pointing to his waistcoat. "It's the *sauté*, most likely," she added, smiling. "It's this, my dear, I want some money." Her face became sad.

"Ah, little countess! . . ." And the count fidgeted about, pulling out his wallet.

"I want a great deal. I want five hundred roubles." And taking out her cambric handkerchief she wiped her husband's waistcoat.

"Yes, immediately! Hey, who's there?" he shouted, certain that those called would run headlong at his summons. "Send Mitenka to me!"

Mitenka, a young man of noble family who had been brought up in the count's house, and now had charge of all his money affairs, walked softly into the room.

"Here, my dear boy," said the count to the young man. "Bring me," he thought a moment, "yes, seven hundred roubles, yes. And mind, don't bring me such torn and dirty notes as last time. I want nice ones, for the countess."

"Yes, Mitenka, clean ones, please," said the countess with a sigh.

"Your excellency, when do you want the money?" said Mitenka. "Your honour ought to know . . . But don't trouble," he added, noticing that the count was beginning to breathe rapidly and heavily, which was always the sign of approaching anger. "I was forgetting . . . Do you wish them at once?"

"Yes, yes, just so, bring them. Give them to the countess. What a treasure that Mitenka is," added the count, smiling, when the young man had gone out. "He doesn't know the meaning of impossible. That's a thing I can't bear. Everything's possible."

"Oh, money, money, what a lot of sorrow it causes in the world!" said the countess. "This money I really need."

"You are a famous spendthrift, little countess, we all know," said the count, and kissing his wife's hand he went back to his study.

When Anna Drubetskoy came back from the Bezuhovs', the money was already on the countess' little table, all in new notes, under her pocket-handkerchief. Anna Drubetskoy noticed that the countess was fluttered about something.

"Anna, for God's sake don't refuse me," the countess said suddenly with a blush, which was strangely incongruous with her elderly, thin, and dignified face. Taking the money from under her handkerchief, she added, "This is for Boris, from me, for his equipment . . ."

Anna Drubetskoy embraced her and began weeping. The countess wept too. They wept because they were friends, and because they were soft-hearted, and also because they, who had been friends in youth, should have to think of anything so base as money, and now their youth was over. . . . But the tears were pleasant to both of them.

Countess Rostov, with her daughters and a large number of guests, was sitting in the drawing-room. The count led the gentlemen of the party to his room. Now and then he went out and inquired: "Has she come yet?" They were waiting for Marya Ahrosimov, known in society as "the terrible dragon," a lady who owed her renown not to her wealth or her rank, but to her directness and her open, unconventional behaviour. Marya Ahrosimov was known to the imperial family; she was known to all Moscow and all Petersburg. And in both cities, while they marvelled at her, laughed secretly at her rudeness, and told good stories about her, nevertheless, all without exception respected and feared her.

In the count's room, full of smoke, they talked of the war, which had been declared in a manifesto, and of the recruiting. No one had read the manifesto, but every one knew it had been issued. The count was sitting on an ottoman with a man smoking and talking on each side of him.

One of these two was a civilian with a thin, wrinkled, bilious, close-shaven face, a man past middle age. He sat with one leg up on the ottoman, as though he were at home, and with the amber mouthpiece in the side of his mouth, he smoked spasmodically, screwing up his face. This was an old bachelor, Shinshin, a cousin of the countess, famed in Moscow drawing-rooms for his biting wit. He seemed condescending to his companion, a young officer of the Guards, irreproachably washed and brushed and buttoned. He held his pipe in the middle of his mouth, and drawing in a little smoke, sent puffs of rings out of his fine red lips. He was the Lieutenant Berg, an officer in the Semenovsky regiment with whom Boris was to travel to join the army, and about whom Natasha had taunted Vera, calling Berg her lover. The count sat between these two listening intently to them.

"Come," said Shinshin, laughing. "You think you'll get an income from the government, and you want to get a little something from your company too?"

"No, Peter, I only want to show that in the cavalry the advantages are few as compared with the infantry. Consider my position now, for instance." Berg talked very precisely, quietly, and politely. He always spoke about himself. When any subject was discussed that had no direct bearing on him, he remained silent. And he could be silent in that way for several hours at a time, neither experiencing nor causing others the slightest embarrassment. But whenever the conversation concerned him personally, he talked at length and with great satisfaction.

"Consider my position, Peter: if I were in the cavalry, I should get no more than two hundred roubles every four months, even at the rank of lieutenant, while as it is I get two hundred and thirty," he explained with a beaming smile, looking at Shinshin and the count as though he had no doubt that his success was always the desire of all who knew him. "Besides that, Peter, changing into the Guards, I'm so much nearer the front," continued Berg. "And vacancies occur so much more frequently in the infantry guards. Perhaps you wonder how I can manage on two hundred and thirty roubles. Why, I'm putting by and sending some off to my father too," he added, letting out a ring of smoke.

"There is a balance! A German will thrash wheat out of the head of an axe, as the Russian proverb has it," said Shinshin, winking to the count.

The count laughed. The other visitors seeing that Shinshin was talking came up to listen. Berg, without noticing either their sneers or their lack of interest, went on to explain how by changing into the guards he had already gained a step in advance of his old comrades in the Cadet Corps; how in wartime the commander of a company may easily be killed, and he as next in command might very easily succeed him. And he told how every one in the regiment liked him, and how pleased his father was with him. Berg was unmistakably enjoying himself as he related all this, and seemed never to suspect that other people too might have their own interests. But all he said was so nice, the naïveté of his youthful egoism was so apparent, that he disarmed his listeners.

"Well, my good fellow, whether you're in the infantry or in the cavalry, you'll always get along, that I venture to predict," said Shinshin, patting him on the shoulder. Berg smiled happily. The count, followed by the guests, went into the drawing-room.

It was that moment just before a big dinner when the guests, expecting to be summoned to the dining-room, feel it necessary to move about and not to be silent, so as to show that they are not impatient to sit down to table. The host and hostess look towards the door, and occasionally at one another. The guests try from these glances to guess whom or what they are waiting for; some important relation late in arriving, or some dish which is not ready.

Pierre arrived just at dinner-time, and sat down awkwardly

in the middle of the drawing-room, blocking everyone's way. The countess tried to get him to talk, but he looked naïvely round over his spectacles as though he were looking for some one, and replied in monosyllables to all the countess' questions. He was in the way, and was the only person unaware of it. A great number of the guests, knowing the story of the bear, looked curiously at this big, stout, inoffensive-looking person, puzzled to know how such a clumsy, modest young man could have played such a prank.

"You have only lately arrived?" the countess asked him.

"Yes, madam."

"You have not seen my husband?"

"No, madam." He smiled very inappropriately.

"You have recently been in Paris, I believe? I suppose it's all very interesting."

"Very interesting."

The countess exchanged glances with Anna Drubetskoy. And Anna Drubetskoy saw that she was asked to entertain the young man, and sitting down by him she began talking of his father. But to her, also, he replied only in monosyllables. The countess got up and went into the reception hall.

"Marya Ahrosimov?" she was heard saying.

"Herself," a rough voice came in reply. And Marya Ahrosimov walked into the room.

All the girls and even the ladies, except the very old ones, got up. Marya Ahrosimov, a stout woman of fifty, stopped in the doorway, and holding her head with its grey curls erect, she looked at the guests and leisurely arranged the wide sleeves of her gown as if rolling them up. Marya Ahrosimov, "the terrible dragon," always spoke Russian.

"Health and happiness to the lady whose name-day we are celebrating and to her children," she said in her loud, rich voice that drowned out all other sounds. "Well, you old sinner," she turned to the count who was kissing her hand, "I suppose you are tired of Moscow—nowhere to go out with the dogs? Well, my good man, what's to be done? These fledglings will grow up. . . ." She pointed to the girls. "Whether you like it or not, you must look out for young men for them."

"Well, how's my Cossack?" (Marya Ahrosimov liked to call Natasha a Cossack) she said, stroking the hand of Natasha, who came up to kiss her hand without shyness. "I know you're a wicked girl, but I like you."

She took out of her huge handbag some amber earrings with drops, and giving them to Natasha, whose beaming birthday face flushed red, she turned away immediately and addressed Pierre.

"Ay, ay! come here, sir!" she said in an intentionally quiet and gentle voice. "Come here, sir . . ." And she tucked her sleeve up higher.

Pierre went up, looking at her over his spectacles.

"Come nearer, my friend! I was the only person that told your father the truth when he was in high favour, and in your case it is my sacred duty." She paused. Every one was expectant of what was to follow, feeling that this was merely a prelude. "A pretty fellow, there's no denying! A pretty fellow! . . . His father is lying on his deathbed, and he's amusing himself, tying a policeman to a bear! For shame, sir, for shame! It would be better if you went to the war."

She turned away and gave her hand to the count, who could hardly keep from laughing.

"Well, I suppose dinner's ready, eh?" said Marya Ahrosimov. The count led the way with Marya Ahrosimov, then followed the countess, escorted by a colonel of hussars, a person of importance, as Nicholas was to travel in his company to join the regiment; then Anna Drubetskoy with Shinshin. Berg gave his arm to Vera, Julie Karagin walked in smiling with Nicholas. They were followed by a line of other couples, stretching right across the hall, and last of all, the children with their tutors and governesses filed in.

There was a bustle among the footmen and a creaking of chairs; the orchestra began playing, as the guests took their places. Then the strains of the music were drowned out by the clatter of knives and forks, the conversation of the guests, and the tread of the footmen.

The countess presided at one end of the table. On her right was Marya Ahrosimov; on her left Anna Drubetskoy and the other ladies of the party. At the other end sat the count, with the colonel of hussars on his left, and on his right Shinshin and the other male guests. On one side of the long table sat the more grown-up of the young people: Vera beside Berg, Pierre beside Boris. On the other side were the children with their tutors and governesses.

At the ladies' end there was a quiet chatter, but at the other end of the table the men's voices grew louder and louder, especially the voice of the colonel of hussars, who, getting more and more flushed, ate and drank so much that the count held him up as a pattern to the other guests. Berg with a smile was telling Vera that love was an emotion not of earth but of heaven. Boris was telling his new friend Pierre the names of the guests, while he exchanged glances with Natasha sitting opposite him. Pierre said little, but examined the new faces, and ate a great deal. Natasha, who sat opposite, looked at Boris as girls of thirteen gaze at the boy whom they have just kissed for the first time, and with whom they are in love. This gaze sometimes strayed to Pierre, and at the look on the funny, excited little girl's face, he felt an impulse to laugh without knowing why.

Nicholas was sitting a long way from Sonya, beside Julie Karagin. Sonya wore a company smile, but she was visibly jealous; at one moment she turned pale, then she crimsoned, and all her energies were concentrated on listening to what Nicholas and Julie were saying. The governess looked nervously about her, as though preparing to resent any slight that might be offered to the children. The German tutor was trying to learn by heart a list of all the kinds of dishes, desserts, and wines, in order to write a detailed description of them to his family at home in Germany, and was greatly mortified when the butler with a bottle in a napkin passed him by. He frowned and tried to look as though he would not have cared to take that wine, but he was offended.

At the men's end of the table the conversation was becoming more and more lively. The colonel was asserting that a proclamation of war had already been issued in Petersburg, and that a copy, which he had seen himself, had that day been brought by a courier to the commander-in-chief.

"And why the devil must we go to war with Bonaparte?" asked Shinshin. "He has already made Austria take a back seat. I am afraid it may be our turn this time."

The colonel was a stout, tall German, a devoted officer and good patriot. He resented Shinshin's words.

"The reason why, my good sir," he said, speaking with a German accent, "is just that the emperor knows that. In his proclamation he says that he cannot look calmly upon the danger threatening Russia, and the security of the empire, its dignity, and the sacredness of its alliances." He laid a special emphasis on the word alliances, as though the gist of the matter lay in that word. And with an unfailing memory for official matters that was peculiar to him, he repeated the introductory words of the proclamation. "That is the reason why, my dear sir," he concluded, tossing off a glass of wine, and looking towards the count for encouragement.

"Do you know the proverb, 'Jerome, Jerome, do not roam, but mind your spindle'?" asked Shinshin, frowning and smiling. "That suits us to a hair. Why, even Suvorov was defeated, and where are our Suvorovs nowadays? I just ask you that," he said.

"We ought to fight to the last drop of our blood," said the colonel, thumping the table, "and die for our emperor, and then all will be well. And discuss it as little as possible," he concluded, turning again to the count, and drawling out the word "possible." "That's how we old hussars look at it;

that's all we have to say. And how do you look at it, young man and young hussar?" he added, addressing Nicholas, who, when he heard that it was the war they were discussing, had dropped his conversation with Julie, and given his full attention to the colonel.

"I quite agree with you," answered Nicholas, growing hot all over, twisting his plate round, and changing the places of the glasses with a face as desperate and determined as though he were exposed to great danger at that moment. "I am convinced that the Russians must die or conquer!" he said. He was himself, like those who heard him, immediately conscious that he had spoken with an enthusiasm and fervour out of keeping with the occasion, and so he was embarrassed.

"You're a true hussar, young man," the colonel shouted, thumping on the table again.

"What are you making such a noise about over there?" Marya Ahrosimov's bass voice was suddenly heard asking across the table. "What are you banging the table for?" she addressed the colonel. "Whom are you so hot against? You imagine, I suppose, that the French are already here?"

"I speak the truth," said the hussar, smiling.

"It's all about the war," the count shouted across the table. "My son's going, Marya, my son's going."

"I've four sons in the army, but I don't complain. All's in God's hands; one may die in one's bed, and in battle God may spare you," Marya Ahrosimov's deep voice boomed, speaking without the slightest effort from the far end of the table.

"That's true."

And the conversation fell into two groups again, one at the ladies' end, and one at the men's.

"You don't dare to ask!" said her little brother to Natasha, "and you won't ask!"

"I will ask," answered Natasha. Her face suddenly glowed, expressing a desperate and mirthful resolution. She stood up, her eyes inviting Pierre to listen, and addressed her mother.

"Mother!" her childish voice rang out over the table.

"What is it?" the countess asked in dismay; but seeing from her daughter's face that it was mischief, she shook her finger at her sternly. All conversation was hushed.

"Mother! what dessert will there be?"

The countess tried to frown, but could not. Marya Ahrosimov shook her fat finger.

"Cossack!" she said threateningly.

Most of the guests looked at the parents, not knowing how they were to take this.

"Behave yourself, Natasha!" said the countess, sternly.

"Mother! what dessert will there be?" Natasha repeated, with bold and saucy gaiety, feeling sure that her prank would be taken in the right spirit. Sonya and fat little Peter were giggling. "You see I did ask," Natasha whispered to her little brother and Pierre, at whom she glanced again.

"Ice-pudding, only you are not going to get any," said Marya Ahrosimov.

Natasha saw there was nothing to be afraid of, and so she was not even frightened of Marya Ahrosimov.

"Marya Ahrosimov! what sort of ice-pudding? I don't like ice-cream."

"Carrot-ices."

"No, what sort, Marya Ahrosimov, what sort?" she almost shrieked. "I want to know." Marya Ahrosimov and the countess burst out laughing, and all the party followed their example. They all laughed, not at Marya Ahrosimov's answer, but at the irrepressible boldness and cleverness of the little girl, who had the pluck and the wit to tackle Marya Ahrosimov in this fashion.

Natasha only stopped when she had been told it was to be pineapple ice. Before the ices, champagne was passed round. Again the band struck up, the count kissed the countess, and the guests getting up from the table congratulated the countess, and clinked glasses across the table with the count, the children, and one another.

The card-tables were brought out, parties were made up for boston, and the count's guests settled themselves in the two drawing-rooms, the sitting room, and the library.

The count, holding his cards, and with some difficulty keeping himself from dropping into his customary after-dinner nap, laughed at everything. The young people, at the countess' suggestion, gathered about the clavichord and the harp. Julie was first asked to perform, and played a piece with variations on the harp. Then she joined the other young ladies in begging Natasha and Nicholas, who were noted for their musical talents, to sing something. Natasha, who was treated by every one as though she were grown-up, was visibly very proud of it, and at the same time felt shy.

"What shall we sing?" she asked.

"The 'Brook,'" answered Nicholas.

"Well, then, let's hurry. Boris, come here," said Natasha. "But where's Sonya?" She looked round, and seeing that she was not in the room, ran off to find her.

After running to Sonya's room, and not finding her there, Natasha ran to the nursery. Sonya was not there either. Natasha knew that she must be on the chest in the corridor. The chest in the corridor was the scene of the woes of the younger female generation of the house of Rostov. Yes, Sonya was on the chest, lying face downwards, crushing her gauzy pink frock on their old nurse's dirty striped feather-bed. Her face hidden in her hands, she was sobbing. Natasha's face that had been happy all day, changed at once; her eyes became fixed and the corners of her mouth drooped.

"Sonya! what is it? . . . What's the matter with you? Oo-oo-oo! . . ." and Natasha, letting her mouth drop open and becoming quite ugly, wailed like a baby, not knowing why, simply because Sonya was crying. Sonya tried to lift up her head, tried to answer, but could not, and again hid her face. Natasha cried, sitting on the edge of the blue feather-bed and hugging her friend. Making an effort, Sonya got up, began to dry her tears and to talk.

"Nicholas is going away in a week, his . . . paper . . . has come . . . he told me himself. . . . But still I shouldn't cry . . ." She opened a sheet of paper she was holding in her hand; on it were verses written by Nicholas. "I shouldn't have cried; but you can't . . . no one can understand . . . what a soul he has!"

And again she fell to weeping.

"It's all right for you . . . I'm not envious . . . I love you and Boris too," she said, controlling herself a little; "he's so nice . . . there are no difficulties in your way. But Nicholas is my cousin . . . the metropolitan chief priest himself . . . has to grant permission . . . or else it's impossible. And so, if mamma's told" (Sonya looked on the countess and addressed her as a mother), "she'll say that I'm spoiling his career, that I have no heart, that I'm ungrateful, though really . . . in God's name" (she made the sign of the cross) "I love her so, and all of you, only Vera . . . Why is it? What have I done to her? I am so grateful to you that I would be glad to sacrifice everything for you, but I have nothing. . . ."

Sonya could say no more, and again she buried her head in her hands and the feather-bed. Natasha tried to comfort her, and her face showed that she understood the seriousness of her friend's trouble.

"Sonya!" she said suddenly, as though she had guessed the real cause of her cousin's misery, "I'm sure Vera's been talking to you since dinner? Yes?"

"Yes, these verses Nicholas wrote himself, and I copied some others; and she found them on my table, and said she should show them to mamma, and she said that I was ungrateful, and that mamma would never allow him to marry me, but that he would marry Julie. You see how he has been with her all day . . . Natasha! why is it?"

And again she cried more bitterly than ever. Natasha lifted

her up, hugged her, and, smiling through her tears, began comforting her.

"Sonya, don't believe her, darling; don't believe her. Do you remember how we talked with Nicholas, all three of us together, in the sitting-room, do you remember, after supper? Why, we settled how it should all be. I don't quite remember now, but do you remember, it was all right and all possible. Why, uncle Shinshin's brother is married to his first cousin, and we're only second cousins, you know. And Boris said that it's quite easily arranged. You know I told him all about it. He's so clever and so good," said Natasha. . . . "Don't cry, Sonya, darling, sweet one, precious, Sonya," and she kissed her and laughed. "Vera's spiteful; never mind her! and it will all come right and she won't tell mamma. Nicholas will tell her himself, and he doesn't care at all for Julie." And she kissed her on the head.

Sonya got up. "Do you think so? Really? Truly?" she said quickly, smoothing her dress and hair.

"Really, truly," answered Natasha. They laughed. "Well, come along and sing the 'Brook.'"

"Let's go, then."

"And do you know that fat Pierre, who was sitting opposite me, he's so funny!" Natasha said suddenly, stopping. "I am enjoying myself so." Natasha ran along the corridor. And Sonya ran after her.

At the request of the guests the young people sang the quartette the "Brook," with which every one was delighted; then Nicholas sang a song he had lately learnt. And as soon as he finished the young people got ready to dance in the big hall, and the musicians in the gallery began stamping with their feet and coughing.

Pierre was sitting in the drawing-room, where Shinshin had started a conversation with him on the political situation. Several other persons joined them. When the orchestra struck up, Natasha walked into the drawing-room, and going straight up to Pierre, laughing and blushing, she said, "Mother told me to ask you to dance."

"I'm afraid of muddling the figures," said Pierre, "but if you will be my teacher . . ." and he gave his fat hand to the slim little girl, putting his arm low down to reach her level.

While the couples were taking their places and the musicians were tuning up, Pierre sat down with his little partner. Natasha was perfectly happy; she was going to dance with a grown-up person, with a man who had just come from abroad. She was sitting in view of every one and talking to him like a grown-up lady.

"What a girl! Just look at her, look at her!" said the old countess, crossing the big hall and pointing to Natasha. Natasha blushed and laughed.

"Why, what do you mean, mother? Why should you laugh? Is there anything strange about it?"

While in the Rostovs' hall they were dancing the sixth English dance, while the weary orchestra played wrong notes, and the tired footmen and cooks were getting the supper, Count Bezuhov had a sixth stroke. The doctors announced that there was no hope of recovery. The sick man received absolution and the sacrament while unconscious. Preparations were being made for administering extreme unction, and the house was full of the bustle and the kind of suspense usual at such moments. Outside the house undertakers were crowding beyond the gates, trying to escape the notice of the carriages that drove up, but eagerly anticipating a good order for an expensive funeral. The governor of Moscow, who had been constantly sending his adjutants to inquire after the count's condition, came himself that evening to say good-bye to the celebrated grandee of Catherine's court, Count Bezuhov.

The magnificent reception room was crowded. Every one stood up respectfully when the governor, after being half an hour alone with the dying man, came out of the sick-room. Acknowledging the bows with which he was received, he tried to escape as quickly as possible from the gaze of the doctors, churchmen, and relations. Prince Vassily, who had grown paler and thinner during the last few days, escorted the governor out, and softly repeated something to him several times over.

When the governor was gone, Prince Vassily sat down alone on a chair in the hall, leaning his elbows on his knees, and covering his eyes with his hand. After sitting in this position for some time he got up, and with steps more hurried than usual, he crossed the long corridor and went to the back part of the house to the apartments of the eldest princess.

Prince Vassily opened the door of the princess' room.

It was half dark in the room; there were only two small lamps burning before the holy pictures, and there was a sweet perfume of incense and flowers. A little dog barked.

"Oh, is that you, my cousin?"

She got up and smoothed her hair.

"Has anything happened?" she asked.

"Nothing, everything remains unchanged. I have only come to have a little talk with you, Catherine, about business," said the prince, sitting down wearily.

"I thought possibly something had happened," said the

princess, and with her severe expression unchanged, she sat down opposite the prince.

"Well, my dear?" said Prince Vassily, taking the princess' hand, and bending it downwards as was his habit. "I must have a little talk with you, Catherine, and a very serious one."

Prince Vassily paused, and his cheeks began twitching nervously, giving his face an unpleasant expression. His eyes, too, seemed changed, at one moment they stared with a sort of hard insolence and at the next they looked around in alarm.

The princess, holding her dog on her lap with her thin, dry hands, gazed intently at Prince Vassily, but resolved that she would not break the silence, if she had to wait till morning.

"You see, my dear princess and cousin, Catherine," continued Prince Vassily, "at such moments as the present, one has to think of everything. One must think of the future, of you . . . I care for all of you as if you were my own children; you know that."

The princess looked at him with the same dull expression.

"Finally, we have to think of my family too," added Prince Vassily, angrily pushing away a little table and not looking at her: "you know, Catherine, that you three Mamontov sisters and my wife,—we are the only direct heirs of the count. I know, I know how hard it is for you to speak and think of such things. And it's as hard for me; but, my dear, I am a man over fifty, I must be prepared for anything. Do you know that I have sent for Pierre, and that the count has asked for him?"

Prince Vassily looked at the princess, but he could not make out whether she was considering what he had just said, or was simply staring at him.

"I pray to God, continually, for one thing only, cousin," she replied, "that He may have mercy upon him, and allow his noble soul to leave this . . ."

"Yes, quite so," Prince Vassily interrupted, rubbing his bald head and again nervously moving the table, "but in fact . . . in fact the point is, as you are yourself aware, that last winter the count made a will by which, passing over his direct heirs and us, he left all his property to Pierre."

"He may have made many wills!" the princess said quietly, "but he can't leave it to Pierre. Pierre is illegitimate."

"But, my dear," said Prince Vassily suddenly speaking more rapidly: "but what if a letter has been written to the Emperor, and the count has petitioned him to legitimise Pierre? You understand, that due to the count's services his petition would be granted."

The princess smiled, as people smile who believe that they know much more about the subject than those with whom they are talking.

"I can say more," Prince Vassily went on, clasping her hand. "That letter has already been written, though it has not been sent off, and the Emperor has heard about it. The question only is whether it has been destroyed or not. If not, as soon as all is over, and the Count's papers are opened, the will with the letter will be given to the Emperor, and his petition will certainly be granted. Pierre, as the legitimate son, will receive everything."

"What about our share?" the princess inquired, smiling ironically as though anything but that might happen.

"Why, my poor Catherine, it is as clear as daylight. He will then be the only legal heir, and you won't receive anything. You ought to know, my dear, whether the will and the petition were written, and whether they have been destroyed, and if they have somehow been overlooked, then you ought to know where they are and to find them, because . . ."

"What next!" the princess interrupted him. "I am a woman, and you think we are all silly; but I do know this much, that an illegitimate son can't inherit . . . A bastard!" she added, supposing that this word would prove to the prince the falseness of his contention.

"How can you not understand, Catherine, really! You are so intelligent; how is it you don't understand that if the count has written a letter to the Emperor, begging him to recognise his son as legitimate, then Pierre will not be Pierre but Count Bezuhov, and he will inherit everything under the will? And if the will and the letter have not been destroyed, then you will have only the consolation of having been dutiful. That's the fact."

"I know that the will was made, but I know, too, that it is invalid, and you seem to take me for a perfect fool, dear cousin," said the princess, who imagined she was saying something witty and biting.

"My dear princess, Catherine!" Prince Vassily began impatiently, "I have come to you not to provoke you, but to talk to you, as a close relative, of your own interest. I tell you for the tenth time that if the letter to the Emperor and the will in Pierre's favour are among the count's papers, you, my dear girl, and your sisters are not heiresses. If you don't believe me . . ."

There was obviously some sudden change in the princess' ideas; her thin lips turned white. "That would be a pretty thing," she said. "I wanted nothing, and I want nothing." She pushed her dog off her lap and smoothed out the folds of her skirt. "That's the gratitude, that's the recognition people get who have sacrificed everything for him," she said. "Very nice! Splendid! I don't want anything, prince."

"Yes, but you are not alone, you have sisters," answered Prince Vassily. But the princess did not hear his words.

"Yes, I knew it long ago, but I'd forgotten that I could expect nothing in this house but baseness, deceit, envy, intrigue, nothing but ingratitude, the blackest ingratitude!"

"Do you, or do you not, know where that will is?" asked Prince Vassily.

"Yes, I was a fool. I still believed in people, and cared for them and sacrificed myself. But no one succeeds except those who are base and vile. I know who has been plotting."

The princess wanted to get up, but the prince held her by the arm. She had the air of a person who has suddenly lost faith in the whole human race. Her face was angry.

"There is still time, my dear. Remember, Catherine, that all this was done heedlessly, in a moment of rage, of illness, and then forgotten. Our duty, my dear girl, is to correct his mistake, to soften his last moments by not letting him commit this injustice, not letting him die with the thought that he has made miserable those . . ."

"Those who have sacrificed everything for him," the princess interrupted, "a sacrifice he has never known how to appreciate. No, cousin," she added. "I will remember that one can expect no reward in this world, that in this world there is no honour, no justice. Cunning and wickedness is what one wants in this world."

"Come, come, be reasonable. Calm yourself and let us talk sensibly while there is time—perhaps twenty-four hours, perhaps only one. Tell me all you know about the will, and where it is; you must know. We will take it now at once and show it to the count. He has no doubt forgotten about it and would wish to destroy it. You undertand that my desire is only to carry out his wishes. That is why I came here. I am only here to be of service to him and to you."

"Now I see it all. I know whose plotting this is. I know!" cried the princess.

"That's not the point, my dear."

"It's all your sweet Anna Drubetskoy, your *protégé* whom I wouldn't take as a housemaid, the nasty creature."

"Do not let us lose time."

"Oh, don't talk to me! Last winter she forced her way in here and told the count such a pack of vile, mean lies about all of us, especially Sophie. I can't repeat them. It made the count ill, and he wouldn't see us for over two weeks. It was at that time, I know, he wrote that hateful, infamous document, but I thought it was invalid."

"Why didn't you tell us about it before?"

"It's in the inlaid portfolio that he keeps under his pillow.

Now I know," said the princess, ignoring his question. "Yes, if I have a sin, a great sin, it's my hatred of that vile woman!" shrieked the princess. "And why does she force herself in here? But I'll have it out with her. The time will come!"

While these conversations were taking place in the reception-room and the princess' room, a carriage with Pierre, who had been sent for, and Anna Drubetskoy, who had thought fit to come with him, was driving into the court of Count Bezuhov's mansion. When the sound of the carriage wheels was muffled by the straw in the street, Anna Drubetskoy turned with words of comfort to her companion, discovered that he was asleep in his corner of the carriage, and woke him up.

Rousing himself, Pierre followed Anna Drubetskoy out of the carriage, and only then began to think of the interview with his dying father that awaited him. He noticed that they had driven not up to the visitors' approach, but to the back entrance. As he got down from the carriage step, two men who looked like tradesmen hurried away from the entrance into the shadow of the wall. Anna Drubetskoy hurried up the dimly lighted, narrow stone staircase, and urged Pierre on. Pierre had no notion why he had to go to the count at all, and still less why he had to come in by the back stairs. Half-way up the stairs they were almost knocked over by some men with pails, who ran down towards them, tramping loudly with their big boots. These men huddled up against the wall to let Pierre and Anna Drubetskoy pass, and showed no surprise at seeing them.

"Is this the princesses' wing of the house?" Anna Drubetskoy asked.

"Yes, it is," answered the footman. "The door on the left, ma'am."

"Perhaps the count has not asked for me," said Pierre, as he reached the landing. "I had better go to my own room." Anna Drubetskoy waited for him to come up.

"Ah, my friend," she said, touching his hand with the same gesture she had used in the morning with her son. "Believe me, I am suffering as much as you; but be a man."

"Really, had I not better go away?" Pierre asked, looking at her over his spectacles.

"Ah, my friend, forget the wrong that may have been done you, think that he is your father . . . and perhaps in his death agony," she sighed. "I have loved you like a son from the first. Trust me, Pierre. I shall look after your interests."

Pierre did not understand a word. Again he felt more strongly than before that all this had to be so, and he obediently followed Anna Drubetskoy who was already opening the door.

The door led into the vestibule of the back stairs. In the corner sat the princess' old man-servant knitting stockings. A maid-servant carrying a tray with a decanter overtook them, and Anna Drubetskoy, calling her "my dear," and "my good girl," asked her after the princesses' health, and drew Pierre further along the stone corridor. The first door to the left led into the princesses' living rooms. The maid with the decanter was in a hurry, and she did not close the door after her. Pierre and Anna Drubetskoy, as they passed by, glanced into the room where the eldest princess and Prince Vassily were sitting close together talking. On catching sight of their passing figures, Prince Vassily drew back, the princess jumped up, and with a despairing gesture closed the door, slamming it with all her might. Pierre stopped short and looked inquiringly over his spectacles. But Anna Drubetskoy showed no surprise; she simply smiled a little and sighed, as though she had expected it.

"Be a man, my friend, I am looking after your interests," she said in answer to his look of inquiry, and she walked more quickly along the corridor.

Pierre had no notion what was going on, and no inkling of what was meant by watching over his interests. But he felt that all this had to be so. From the corridor they went into the half-lighted hall adjoining the count's reception-room. This was one of the cold, sumptuously furnished rooms which Pierre knew, leading from the visitors' staircase. They were met here by a servant and a church attendant with a censer, who walked on tiptoe and took no notice of them. They went into the reception-room opening into the winter garden, a room Pierre knew well, with its two Italian windows, its big bust and full-length portrait of Catherine the Great. The same persons were all sitting almost in the same positions whispering to one another. All suddenly became silent and looked round at Anna Drubetskoy, and at the big, stout figure of Pierre.

Anna Drubetskoy's face showed that she believed that the crucial moment had arrived. She walked into the room boldly keeping Pierre at her side. She felt that as she was bringing the person the dying man wanted to see, she might feel secure as to her reception. With a rapid glance, scanning all the persons in the room, she noticed the count's spiritual adviser.

"Thank God that we are in time," she said to the priest. "All of us, his kinsfolk, have been in such anxiety. This young man is the count's son," she added more softly, "It is a terrible moment."

Having spoken these words she approached the doctor.

"Dear doctor," she said to him, "this young man is the count's son. Is there any hope?"

The doctor did not speak but rapidly shrugged his shoulders and turned up his eyes. With precisely the same gesture Anna

Drubetskoy moved her shoulders and eyes, sighed and came to Pierre. She spoke in a tender voice filled with melancholy.

"Have faith in His mercy," she said, and pointed to a sofa for him to sit down and wait for her. She went towards the door, and after noiselessly opening it, she vanished behind it.

Two minutes had not elapsed before Prince Vassily came majestically into the room, wearing his coat with three stars on his breast. He looked as though he had grown thinner since the morning. His eyes seemed larger than usual as he glanced round the room, and caught sight of Pierre. He went up to him, took his hand, a thing he had never done before, and drew it downwards.

"Courage, courage, my friend. He has asked to see you, that is well . . ." He would have continued, but Pierre interrupted him to ask: "How is . . . ?" He hesitated, not knowing whether it was proper for him to call the dying man "the count." He felt ashamed to call him "father."

"He has had another stroke half-an-hour ago. Courage, my friend."

Prince Vassily said a few words to the doctor as he passed and went to the door on tiptoe. He was followed by the eldest princess, then by the clergy and church attendants; some servants too went in at the door. Through that door a stir could be heard.

At last Anna Drubetskoy, with a face still pale but resolute in the performance of duty, ran out and, touching Pierre on the arm, said: "The goodness of heaven is inexhaustible! Unction is about to be administered. Come!"

Pierre went through the door, stepping on to the soft carpet.

Pierre well knew this large room, divided by columns and an arch, and carpeted with Persian rugs. The part of the room behind the columns, where on one side there stood a high mahogany bedstead with silken hangings, and on the other a huge case containing icons, was brightly lighted up, as churches are lighted for evening service. Under the gleaming icons stood a long invalid chair, and in the chair, on snow-white, uncrumpled pillows, Pierre recognised the majestic figure of his father, Count Bezuhov. A grey shock of hair like a lion's mane was over his broad forehead, and his aristocratic face. He was lying directly under the holy pictures. In his right hand a wax candle had been thrust between his thumb and forefinger, and an old servant bending down helped to hold it. About the chair stood the clergy in their shining ceremonial vestments, with their long hair. They held lighted candles in their hands, and were performing the service with great solemnity. A little behind them stood the two younger princesses holding handkerchiefs to their eyes, and in front of them the eldest, Princess Catherine, stood with a vindictive and determined air, never for an instant taking her eyes off the holy image.

Anna Drubetskoy with a face filled with meek sorrow and forgiveness stood at the door. Prince Vassily was standing close to the invalid chair. He had drawn a chair up to him, and was leaning on the back of it with his left hand, in which he held a candle, while with his right hand he crossed himself, turning his eyes upwards every time as he put his finger to his forehead. His face had in it a look of piety and submission to the will of God.

Behind him stood the adjutant, the doctors, and the men-servants; the men and the women had separated as though they were in church. All were silently crossing themselves, nothing was audible but the reading of the service, the deep bass singing, and in the intervals of silence sighs could be heard and the shuffling of feet.

With an air of importance, which showed she knew what she was about, Anna Drubetskoy walked boldly across the room to Pierre and gave him a candle. He lighted it. The youngest princess, Sophie, the rosy, laughing one with the mole, was looking at him. She smiled, hid her face in her handkerchief, and for a long while did not uncover it. She was apparently unable to look at him without laughing, but could not resist looking at him, and to be out of temptation, she moved behind a column.

Soon the sounds of the church singing ceased and the voice of the priest was heard, respectfully congratulating the sick man on his having received the sacrament. The dying man lay as lifeless and immovable as before. Every one began to stir and there was the sound of footsteps and of whispers, Anna Drubetskoy's whisper rising above the rest.

Pierre heard her say: "Surely he must be moved to the bed; here it's impossible . . ."

The sick man was so surrounded by the doctors, the princesses and the servants, that Pierre could no longer see his face and his grey mane. Pierre guessed from the cautious movements of the people about the chair that they were lifting the dying man up and moving him.

They were busy for several minutes round the high bed; then Anna Drubetskoy touched Pierre's arm and said, "Come along." Pierre approached the bed, on which the sick man had been laid in a ceremonial position. His head was propped high on the pillows. His hands were laid symmetrically on the green silk quilt with the palms turned downwards.

When Pierre came up, the count looked straight at him, but he looked at him with a gaze the intent and significance of which no man could fathom. Either these eyes said nothing, but simply looked because eyes must look at something, or they said too much. Pierre stopped, not knowing what he was to do. Anna Drubetskoy gave him a hurried glance, with a gesture indicating the sick man's hand and with her lips wafting towards it a phantom kiss. Pierre did as he was bid, and kissed the broad-boned, muscular hand. Pierre again looked inquiringly at Anna Drubetskoy and she glanced towards the armchair that stood beside the bed. Pierre sat down and Anna Drubetskoy nodded approvingly. The count's eyes gazed at the spot where Pierre's face had been, when he was standing up. Then suddenly a shudder passed over his thick muscles and across the furrows of his face. The shudder grew more intense. The eyes and face of the sick man showed impatience. He made an effort to glance at the servant, who remained close to the head of his bed.

"His excellency wants to be turned over on the other side," whispered the servant, and he got up to turn the heavy body of the count.

Pierre stood up to help the servant.

While the count was being turned over a weak, suffering smile came over his face. Suddenly, at the sight of that smile, Pierre felt a lump in his throat and tears dimmed his eyes. The sick man was turned towards the wall. He sighed.

"He is dozing," said Anna Drubetskoy. "Let us go."

Pierre went out.

There was no one left in the reception room except Prince Vassily and the eldest princess, and these two, seated side by side beneath the portrait of Catherine the Great, were deep in conversation with each other. As soon as they noticed Pierre and his companion, however, they fell silent. And Pierre thought he saw the princess hide something as she whispered, "I can't bear the sight of that woman."

"Catherine is having tea served in the small drawing room," Prince Vassily said to Anna Drubetskoy, "Go along, my poor Anna, have a little something, otherwise you won't last the night."

To Pierre he said nothing at all, just pressed his arm sympathetically. Pierre and Anna Drubetskoy went into the small drawing room.

"There's nothing like a cup of this fine Russian tea to revive one after a sleepless night," the doctor, Lorraine, was saying as he sipped tea from a fine Chinese porcelain cup. Around the table, fortifying themselves, had gathered all those who were spending the night in Count Bezuhov's house. Pierre well remembered this small circular drawing room with its mirrors and little tables. Whenever there had been a ball in the count's house Pierre, who seldom danced, had enjoyed sitting in this mirror-lined room watching the ladies in their ball dresses, with their bare shoulders adorned with pearls and diamonds, examining themselves as they passed the brilliantly lighted mirrors that caught their reflections from every side.

Pierre ate nothing, much as he would have liked to. He turned and saw that his companion was tiptoeing back to the reception room where Prince Vassily had remained with the eldest princess. Pierre assumed that that was as it should be, and after a moment he followed her. Anna Drubetskoy was standing next to the princess and both were talking at once in excited whispers.

"Please allow me, princess, to be the one to decide what need and what need not be done," the eldest princess was saying, and she seemed as upset as she had been when she'd slammed the door of her room.

"But, dear princess," Anna Drubetskoy was saying in a mild yet forceful voice, barring the way to the bedroom and not permitting the princess to get by her. "Won't it be just too taxing for poor uncle at a time like this when he needs his rest? At a time like this, when his soul has already been prepared for—to talk of worldly things—"

Prince Vassily sat deep in an arm chair. His cheeks were twitching violently. Yet he seemed to pay little attention to the conversation of the two ladies.

"Come now, my dear Anna Drubetskoy, let Catherine do what she thinks best. You know how fond the count is of her."

"Why, I don't even know what is in these papers," the eldest princess was saying, turning to Prince Vassily and indicating the inlaid portfolio she was holding. "I only know that the true will is in his desk, while this is just some forgotten document. . . ."

She tried to pass but Anna Drubetskoy, with a quick movement, again blocked her way.

"Yes, I know, my dear princess," Anna Drubetskoy said, taking hold of the portfolio so firmly that it became quite plain she had no intention of letting it get out of her hands again. "Dearest princess, I beg you, I implore you, have pity on him. I beseech you!"

Princess Catherine was silent. The only sounds were those of the scuffle over the portfolio. Anna Drubetskoy kept a tight grip on the leather case, yet her voice never lost its sweet drawling softness.

"Pierre, come here, dear boy. . . . Surely he'll not be in the way in this family council. Isn't that so, prince?"

"Why don't you speak, cousin!" the princess suddenly cried out so shrilly that the people in the drawing room beyond heard her and were startled. "Why do you remain silent while an outsider meddles in our affairs, making a scene on the very threshold of a dying man's room! Scheming creature!" And once more she tugged at the portfolio as hard as she could. But Anna Drubetskoy took a few steps forward so as not to lose her grip.

"Oh!" said Prince Vassily. He stood up. "Why this is ridiculous. Come, let go of it, I say!"

Princess Catherine let go.

"You too!"

Anna Drubetskoy ignored him.

"Let go, I say. I'm assuming all the responsibility. I'll go in and ask him myself . . . I . . . Enough, I say . . ."

"But Prince," said Anna Drubetskoy, "let him have a moment's rest after the holy sacrament. Here Pierre, tell us what you think?" She turned to Pierre.

"You evil woman!" shrieked the princess, suddenly turning on Anna Drubetskoy and tearing the portfolio out of her hands.

Prince Vassily lowered his head and threw up his hands.

At that very moment the door—that terrifying door which until now people had been opening and shutting so gently—was flung wide, so hard that it banged against the wall, and the second of the three sisters ran out, wringing her hands.

"What are you all thinking about?" she cried despairingly. "Here he is slipping away, and you're leaving me all alone with him!"

Princess Catherine dropped the portfolio. Anna Drubetskoy quickly picked it up and rushed into the bedroom. Princess Catherine and Prince Vassily went in after her. A few moments later Princess Catherine came out again, her face pale and dry, biting her lower lip. At sight of Pierre her expression turned to hatred.

"Well, you can be happy now," she said. "You've been waiting for this." And, sobbing, she covered her face with a handkerchief and rushed from the room.

The next to come out was Prince Vassily. Staggering, he made his way to the sofa where Pierre was sitting, and collapsed, covering his eyes with his hands. Pierre noticed how pale he was and that his lower jaw was working and trembling.

"Oh my friend," he said, taking Pierre by the elbow. There was in his voice a sincerity and a weakness Pierre had never noticed before. "How greatly we sin, what frauds we commit, and all for what? I'm almost sixty, my boy . . . Why I'm . . . And everything ends in death, everything . . . And death is terrible . . ." And he wept.

Anna Drubetskoy was the last to come out. She approached Pierre with slow, deliberate steps. "Pierre," she said. Pierre looked at her questioningly. She kissed his forehead, wetting it with her tears. She remained silent for a long moment. "He is no more!"

Pierre gazed at her over his glasses.

"Come, I'll go with you. Try to cry. Nothing relieves like tears."

She led him into the dim drawing room, and Pierre was glad that no one could see his face. Anna Drubetskoy left him there, and when she returned he was sleeping soundly, one arm under his head.

The next morning Anna Drubetskoy said to Pierre: "Yes, my dear, it is a great loss for us all. I do not speak of you. But God will uphold you; you are young, and now you are the head of an immense fortune, I hope. The will has not yet been opened. I know you well enough to know that this will not turn your head, but it will impose duties upon you and you must be a man."

Pierre did not reply.

"Perhaps, later, I may tell you, my dear boy, that if I had not been there God knows what would have happened. You know, your father promised me, only the day before yesterday, not to forget my son Boris. But he had no time. I hope, dear friend, that you will carry out your father's desire."

Pierre did not understand a word, and colouring shyly, looked blankly at Anna Drubetskoy. After talking to him, Anna Drubetskoy drove to the Rostovs', and went to bed. On waking in the morning, she told the Rostovs and all her acquaintances the details of Count Bezuhov's death. She said that the count had died, as she would wish to die herself, that his end was not only touching, but edifying; that the last interview of the father and son had been so moving that she could not recall it without tears. And that she did not know who had behaved more nobly in those terrible moments. The father had remembered everything and every one so well at the last, and had said such moving words to his son; and Pierre, whom it was heartbreaking to see, was so utterly crushed. "It was most painful, but it does one good; it uplifts the soul to see such men as the old count and his worthy son," she said. Then she told them about the behaviour of the princess and Prince Vassily, but in great secrecy, in whispers, and with much disapproval.

At Bleak Hills, the estate of Prince Nicholas Bolkonsky, the arrival of his son Prince André and his wife was expected daily. But this expectation did not upset the regular routine in which life moved in the old prince's household.

Prince Nicholas, once a commander-in-chief, known in the fashionable world by the nickname of "the King of Prussia," had been exiled to his estate in the reign of Paul. Here he remained at Bleak Hills with his daughter, Princess Mary, and her companion, Mademoiselle Bourienne. Even after Alexander became Czar, though he had received permission to return to the capital, he never left his home in the country, saying that if any one wanted to see him, he could travel the hundred and fifty miles from Moscow to Bleak Hills. For his part, he wanted nobody and nothing.

Prince Nicholas believed that human vices all sprang from only two sources: idleness and superstition. And that there were but two virtues: energy and intelligence. He had himself undertaken the education of his daughter; and to develop in her these important qualities, he continued giving her lessons in algebra and geometry up to her twentieth year, and mapped out her whole life so that every moment was occupied. He was himself writing his memoirs, working out problems in higher mathematics, turning snuff-boxes on his lathe, working in his garden, or looking after the construction of farm buildings on his estate.

Regularity in his household was carried to the highest point of exactitude. His meals were served in a fixed manner, and not only at a certain hour, but at a certain minute. With those about him, from his daughter to his servants, the count was strict and invariably exacting yet without being cruel. He inspired a degree of respect and awe. In spite of the fact that he was now on the retired list, and had no influence in political circles, every high official in the province felt obliged to call upon him, and had, just like his architect, the gardener, or Princess Mary, to wait till the regular hour at which the prince always made his appearance. And every one in the waiting-room felt the same respect, and even awe, when the immensely high door of the study opened and showed the small figure of the old man in a powdered wig, with his little withered hands and grey, bushy eyebrows, which when he frowned, hid the gleam in his shrewd, youthful-looking eyes.

On the day that the young people were to arrive, Princess Mary went as usual at the fixed hour in the morning to say good-morning to her father, and with dread in her heart crossed herself and repeated a prayer. Every morning she went to her father in the same way, and every day she prayed that their interview might pass off well. An old man-servant wearing powder, got up from his seat in the waiting-room and whispered: "Walk in."

Through the door came the regular hum of the lathe. The princess timidly opened the door, and stood still in the entrance. The prince was working at his lathe, and glancing round, he went on with what he was doing.

The immense study was filled with things obviously in constant use. The large table on which lay books and plans, the high bookcases with keys in the glass doors, the high table for the prince to write at, standing up, with an open manuscript-book upon it, the wood-turning lathe, with tools about it and shavings scattered around, all suggested continual, varied, and orderly activity. The movements of the prince's small foot in its Tartar, silver-embroidered boot, the firm pressure of his sinewy, lean hand, showed the strength of a vigorous old age.

After a few more turns, he took his foot from the pedal, wiped the chisel, dropped it into a leather pouch attached to the lathe, and going up to the table called his daughter. He never gave the usual blessing to his children; he simply offered her his scrubby, unshaven cheek, and said sternly and yet with intense tenderness, as he inspected her: "Quite well? . . . All right, then, sit down!" He took a geometry exercise-book written by himself, and drew his chair up with his foot.

"For to-morrow," he said quickly, turning to the page and marking it from one paragraph to the next with his rough nail. The princess bent over the exercise-book. "Stop, there's a letter for you," the old man said suddenly, handing her an envelope addressed in a feminine hand.

The princess' face coloured red in patches at the sight of the letter. She took it hurriedly and bent over it.

"From Julie?" asked the prince, showing his strong, yellow teeth in a cold smile.

"Yes, it's from Julie," replied the princess, looking timidly at him.

"Two more letters I'll let pass, but the third I shall read," said the prince. "I'm afraid you write a lot of nonsense. The third I shall read."

"Read this if you like, father," answered the princess, colouring still more and handing him the letter.

"The third, I said the third," the prince cried. Then pushing away the letter and leaning his elbow on the table, he drew up to him the geometry book.

"Now, madam," began the old man, bending over the book close to his daughter, and laying one arm on the back of the chair she was sitting on, so that the princess felt herself surrounded on all sides by the peculiar acrid smell of old age and tobacco, which she had known so long. "Come, madam, these triangles are equal; kindly note; the angle A B C. . . ."

The princess looked in a sacred way at her father's eyes glittering close beside her. The red patches spread over her whole face, and it was evident that she did not understand a word, that terror prevented her from understanding any of the explanations her father offered.

Whether it was the teacher's fault or the pupil's, every day the same scene was repeated. The princess' eyes grew dim; she could see and hear nothing; she could feel nothing but the withered face of her stern father, his breath and the smell of him, and could think of nothing but how to escape as soon as possible from the study and try to solve the problem alone in her own room. The old man lost his temper and with a loud, grating noise pushed back the chair he was sitting on. He made an effort to control himself, not to fly into a rage, but almost every day he did fly into a rage, and scold, and sometimes he flung the book away.

On this day, as on other days, the princess gave a wrong answer, and he cried out: "You are stupid!" Then he got up, walked up and down, laid his hand on the princess' hair, and sat down again. He drew himself up to the table and continued his explanations.

"This won't do; it won't do," he said, when Princess Mary, taking the exercise-book and shutting it, was about to leave the room: "mathematics is a great subject. And to have you like the common run of silly girls is what I don't want. Patience, and you'll get to like it." He patted her on the cheek. "It will drive all the nonsense out of your head."

She wanted to leave; he stopped her and took a new, uncut book from the high table.

"Here's a book, your friend Julie sends you. Some sort of Key to the Mystery. Religious. But I don't interfere with any one's belief. . . . I have looked at it. Take it. Come, run along, run along."

He patted her on the shoulder, and closed the door after her.

Princess Mary went back to her room with that dejected, scared expression that rarely left her, and made her plain, sickly face even plainer. She sat down at her writing-table, which was dotted with miniature portraits, and strewn with books and manuscripts. The princess was as untidy as her father was tidy. She put down the geometry book and opened the letter. The letter was from the princess' dearest childhood friend. This friend was none other than Julie Karagin, who had been at the Rostovs' name-day party.

Julie wrote in French:

"Dear Friend. What a terrible and frightful thing is absence! Why are we not together as we were this summer in your great study, on the blue sofa, the confidential sofa? Why can I not, as I did three months ago, draw strength from that gentle, calm, penetrating look of yours, a look that I loved so well and seem to see before me now as I write."

Princess Mary sighed and looked round into the mirror that stood on her right. The glass reflected a weak, ungraceful figure and a thin face. The eyes, always melancholy, were looking just now with a particularly hopeless expression. She flatters me, thought the princess, and she turned away and went on reading. But Julie did not flatter her; the princess' eyes, large, deep, and luminous, were really so fine, that very often in spite of the plainness of her face, her eyes made her appear beautiful. But the princess had never seen the beautiful expression of her eyes; the expression that came into them when she was not thinking of herself. As with every one, her face assumed a forced, unnatural expression as soon as she looked in the looking-glass. She went on reading.

"All Moscow talks of nothing but war. One of my two brothers is already abroad, the other is with the Guards, who are starting on the march to the frontier. Our dear Emperor has left Petersburg, and, people declare, intends to expose his precious person to the risks of war. God grant that the Corsican monster who is destroying the peace of Europe may be brought low by the angel whom the Almighty in His mercy has given us as sovereign! Without speaking of my brothers, this war has deprived me of one dear to my heart. I mean the young Nicholas Rostov. Dear Mary, I will confess to you that in spite of his extreme youth, his departure for the army has been a great grief to me. Some day I will tell you about our farewells and all that we said to each other as we parted. I know very well that Count Nicholas is too young ever to become more to me than a friend, but this friendship, this intimacy has fulfilled a need of my heart. But enough of this. The great news of the day, with which all Moscow gossips, is the death of old Count Bezuhov, and his inheritance. Fancy, the three princesses have hardly received anything, Prince Vassily nothing, and everything has been left to Monsieur Pierre, who has also been acknowledged as a legitimate son, so that he is now Count Bezuhov and has the finest fortune in all Russia. People say that Prince Vassily behaved very badly and that he has gone back to Petersburg quite depressed.

"I confess I understand very little about all these matters of legacies and wills; what I know is that since the young man whom we all used to know as plain Monsieur Pierre has become Count Bezuhov and possessor of one of the largest fortunes in Russia, I am much amused to observe the change in the tone and the manners of the mammas burdened with marriageable daughters and of those young ladies themselves, towards him. I may say, between ourselves, he has always seemed to me a poor creature. And talking about marriage, do you know that the universal aunt, Anna Drubetskoy, has confided to me, under the seal of the deepest secrecy, a marriage scheme for you. It is no one more or less than Prince

Vassily's son, Anatole, whom they want to settle by marrying him to some one rich and distinguished. And the choice has fallen on you. I don't know what you will think of it, but I thought it my duty to let you know. He is said to be very handsome and very wild; that is all I have been able to find out about him.

"But enough of gossip. Read the mystical book which I send you, and which is a great success here. Farewell. My respects to your father and my compliments to Mlle. Bourienne. I embrace you as I love you. JULIE.

Princess Mary thought a minute, smiling dreamily. Then she glanced at her watch, and seeing that it was already five minutes later than the hour fixed for her practice on the clavichord, she went quickly into the living room with a look of alarm. In accordance with the rules by which the day was mapped out, the prince rested from twelve to two, while the young princess practised on the clavichord.

The grey-haired valet was sitting in the waiting-room dozing and listening to the prince's snoring in the large study. From a far-off part of the house there came through closed doors the sound of difficult passages of a sonata repeated twenty times over.

Just then a carriage and a little cart drove up to the house, and Prince André got out, helped his little wife and let her pass into the house before him. Old Tihon in his wig came out of the door of the waiting-room, and reported in a whisper that the prince was taking a nap. Tihon knew that no extraordinary event, not even the arrival of his son, would be permitted to break through the routine of the day. Prince André was as well aware of the fact as Tihon. He looked at his watch and spoke to his wife.

"He will get up in twenty minutes. Let's go to Mary," he said.

The little princess had grown stouter during this time, but her short upper lip, with its smile, rose as gaily and charmingly as ever when she spoke.

"Why, it is a palace!" she said to her husband, looking round. And as she looked about, she smiled at Tihon and at her husband, and at the footman who was showing them in.

"It is Mary practising? Let us go quietly, we will surprise her." Prince André followed her with a courteous but sad expression.

"You're looking older, Tihon," he said as he passed to the old man, who kissed his hand.

Before they had reached the room, from which the sounds of the clavichord were coming, the pretty, fair-haired Frenchwoman came out from a side-door. Mademoiselle Bourienne seemed overwhelmed with delight.

"Ah, what a pleasure for the princess!" she exclaimed. "At last! I must tell her."

"No, no, please don't . . ." said the little princess, kissing her. "You are Mademoiselle Bourienne; I know you already through my sister-in-law's friendship for you. She does not expect us?"

They went up to the door of the room, from which came the sound of the same passage repeated over and over again. Prince André stood still and frowned as though he expected something unpleasant.

The little princess entered the room. The passage broke off in the middle; a cry was heard, then Princess Mary's heavy tread. And when Prince André went in, the two princesses, who had only seen each other once before at his wedding, were in each other's arms, kissing over and over. Mademoiselle Bourienne was standing near them, ready to weep or to laugh. Prince André shrugged his shoulders and scowled. The two princesses parted, then suddenly hugged and kissed each other again. Then they began to cry. Mademoiselle Bourienne cried too. Prince André was ill at ease. But to the two princesses it seemed a natural thing that they should weep; it seemed never to have occurred to them that their meeting could have taken place without tears.

"Oh my dear! . . . Oh Mary!" . . . Both began talking at once, and they laughed. "I had a dream last night. Then you did not expect us? Oh Mary, you have got thinner."

"And you have grown stouter."

"I recognized the princess at once," put in Mademoiselle Bourienne.

"And I had no idea!" cried Princess Mary. "Oh, André, I did not see you."

Prince André and his sister kissed each other, and he told her she was just as great a cry-baby as she always had been. Princess Mary turned to her brother, and through her tears, her luminous eyes, that were beautiful at that instant, rested with a loving, warm and gentle gaze on Prince André's face.

The little princess, in a happy mood, talked incessantly. She described an incident that had occurred to them on the road, and might have been serious for her in her condition. And immediately after that she informed them that she had left all her clothes in Petersburg, and God knew what she would have to wear. And that André was quite changed, and that a suitor had turned up for Princess Mary, "who was a suitor worth having," but that they would talk about that later.

Princess Mary was still looking at her brother, and her beautiful eyes were full of love and melancholy. It was clear that her thoughts were following a train of their own, apart from the chatter of her sister-in-law. In the middle of a description of the last fête-day at Petersburg, Princess Mary spoke to her brother.

"Is it quite settled that you are going to war, André?" she asked.

"Yes, I'm leaving tomorrow," he answered.

Liza, the little princess, looked up. "He is deserting me," she said. "And Heaven knows why, when he might have had a promotion . . ."

Princess Mary looked at her sister-in-law and asked again: "Is it really true?"

"Yes, it's true," answered Princess Liza. "Oh! It's so dreadful . . ." And she began to cry.

"She needs rest," said Prince André, frowning. "Don't you, Liza? Take her to your room, while I go to father. How is he —just the same?"

"The same, just the same; I don't know what you will think," Princess Mary answered pleasantly. There was almost a note of happiness in her voice.

"And the same hours, and the walks about the avenues, and the lathe?" asked Prince André with a smile, showing that, in spite of all his love and respect for his father, he understood his weaknesses.

"The same hours and the lathe, mathematics too, and my geometry lessons," Princess Mary answered gaily, as though those lessons were one of the most delightful events of her life.

When the twenty minutes had passed, and it was time for the old prince to get up. Tihon came to call the young man to his father. On this day the old man made a departure from his ordinary routine in honour of his son's arrival. He ordered that he should be admitted into his apartments during his time for dressing, before dinner.

The old prince used to wear an old-fashioned, long coat and powdered hair. And when Prince André went in to his father's room, he was sitting in a roomy leather chair, with his head in the hands of Tihon.

"Ah! the warrior! So you want to fight Bonaparte?" said the old man, shaking his powdered head. "Mind you look sharp after him, or he'll soon be putting us on the list of his subjects. How are you?" And he held out his cheek.

The old gentleman was in excellent humour after his nap before dinner. He took delighted, sidelong glances at his son from under his thick, overhanging brows. Prince André went up and kissed his father. He made no reply to his father's favourite topic—jesting banter at the military men of the day, and particularly at Bonaparte.

"Yes, I have come to you, father, bringing a wife with child," said Prince André, in a respectful voice. "How is your health?"

"None but fools and rakes are ever sick. You know me; busy from morning till night and abstemious, so of course I'm well."

"Thank God," said his son, smiling.

"God has nothing to do with it. Come, tell me," the old man went on, going back to his favourite subject, "how have the Germans taught you to fight with Bonaparte on their new scientific method—strategy as they call it?"

Prince André smiled.

"Give me time to recover, father," he said, with a smile that showed that his father's whims did not prevent his respecting and loving him. "Why, I have only just got here."

"Nonsense, nonsense," cried the old man, shaking his pigtail to see if it was tightly plaited, and taking his son by the hand. "The house is ready for your wife. Mary will look after her and show her everything, and they'll talk nineteen to the dozen. That's how women are. I'm glad to have her. Sit down, talk to me. Tell me about Mihelson's army, and Tolstoy's too . . . a simultaneous expedition . . . but what's the army of the South going to do? Prussia is neutral. . . . I know all that. What of Austria?" he said, getting up from his chair and walking about the room, with Tihon running after him, giving him various articles of clothing. "What about Sweden? How will they cross Pomerania?"

Prince André, seeing that his father insisted, began explaining the plan of the proposed campaign, speaking at first reluctantly, but becoming more interested as he went on. He told how an army of ninety thousand troops was to threaten Prussia so as to drive her out of her neutrality and draw her into the war, how part of these troops were to join the Swedish troops, how two hundred and twenty thousand Austrians were to combine with a hundred thousand Russians, and how fifty thousand Russians and fifty thousand English troops were to meet at Naples, and how the army, forming a total of half-a-million, was to attack the French on different sides at once. The old prince did not show the slightest interest in what André was saying. He went on dressing and walking about, and three times he interrupted him. Once he shouted: "The white one! the white one!"

This meant that Tihon had not given him the waistcoat he wanted. Another time, he asked: "And will she be confined soon?" and shook his head. "That's bad! Go on, go on."

A third time the old man hummed in French, in his cracked falsetto voice: "Malbrook goes off to battle, God knows when he'll come back."

His son only smiled.

"I don't say that this is a plan I would approve," he said. "I'm only telling you what it is. Napoleon has surely made a plan by now as good as this one."

"Well, you have told me nothing new." And thoughtfully the old man repeated, speaking quickly to himself: "God knows when he'll come back." Then he added, "Go into the dining-room."

At the exact hour, the prince, powdered and shaven, walked into the dining-room, where there were waiting for him Prince André, his daughter-in-law, Princess Mary, Mademoiselle Bourienne, and his architect, who, by a strange whim of the old gentleman's, dined at his table, though being an insignificant person of no social standing. The prince, who was very strict about social distinctions and rank, and rarely admitted to his table even important government officials, had chosen the architect Michael Ivanovitch, to illustrate the theory that all men are equal. And more than once he had impressed upon his daughter that Michael Ivanovitch was in every way as good as himself and her.

The prince walked in with a quick, lively step, as though intentionally contrasting the freedom of his movements with the rigid routine of the house. At that instant the big clock struck two. His keen, stern eyes gleaming under his bushy, overhanging brows scanned all the company and rested on the little princess. He went over to her and stroked her on the head, and then with an awkward movement patted her on her neck.

"I'm glad, glad to see you," he said, and after looking intently into her eyes he walked away and sat down in his place. "Sit down, sit down, Michael Ivanovitch, sit down."

He indicated a place for his daughter-in-law beside him. The footman moved the chair for her.

"Ho, ho!" said the old man, looking at her rounded figure. "You've not lost time. That's bad!" He laughed a dry, cold, unpleasant laugh. "You must have exercise, as much exercise as possible," he said.

The little princess did not hear, or did not care to hear his words. She sat silent and confused. But when the prince asked after her father, she began to talk and to smile. He asked her about common acquaintances; the princess became more and more animated, and began talking away, giving the prince greetings from various people and retailing the gossip of the town.

As she became livelier, the prince looked more and more sternly at her, and all at once, as though he had studied her sufficiently and had formed a clear idea of her, he turned away and addressed his architect, Michael Ivanovitch:

"Well, Michael Ivanovitch, our friend Bonaparte is going to have a bad time. Prince André," this was how he always spoke of his son, "has been telling me what forces are being massed against him! And all the time you and I have looked upon him as a very insignificant person!"

Michael Ivanovitch had never said anything of the sort about Bonaparte, but grasping that he was wanted as a peg on which to hang the prince's favourite subject, he looked questioningly at the young prince, not knowing what was to come next.

"He's a great tactician!" said the prince to his son, pointing to the architect. And the conversation turned again on the war, on Bonaparte, and the generals and political personages of the day. The old prince was, it seemed, convinced that all the public men of the period were mere fools who had no idea of the A B C of military and political matters. And Bonaparte, according to him, was an insignificant Frenchman, who had met with success simply because there were no Potemkins and Suvorovs to oppose him. He was firmly convinced that there were no political difficulties in Europe, that there was no real war, but only a sort of puppet show in which the men of the day took part, pretending to be doing something important. Prince André accepted his father's ridicule and even took pleasure in drawing him out.

"The past always seems good," he said; "but didn't Suvorov himself fall into the trap Moreau laid for him?"

"Who told you that? Who said so?" cried the prince. "Suvorov!" And he flung away his plate, which Tihon very neatly caught. "Suvorov! . . . Think again, Prince André. There were two men—Friedrich and Suvorov . . . Moreau! Moreau would have been a prisoner if Suvorov's hands had been free, but his hands were tied. The devil himself would have been in a tight place. Ah, you'll find out! Suvorov couldn't get the better of them, so how is Michael Kutuzov going to do it? No, my dear boy," he went on; "so you think you and your generals won't be able to get round Bonaparte! No, my boy, either you have all lost your wits, or I have outlived mine. God help you. Bonaparte's become a great military leader! H'm! . . ."

"I don't say that all our plans are good," said Prince André; "only I can't understand how you can have such a low opinion of Bonaparte. Laugh, if you like, but Bonaparte is any way a great general!"

"Michael Ivanovitch!" the old prince cried to the architect, who, busy with his roast meat, hoped they had forgotten him.

"Didn't I tell you that everyone thinks Bonaparte is a great tactician? Here he says so too!"

"To be sure, your excellency," replied the architect. The prince again laughed his frigid laugh.

"Bonaparte was born with a silver spoon in his mouth. He has splendid soldiers. And he began by attacking the Germans. And any fool can beat the Germans. From the very beginning of the world every one has beaten the Germans. And they've never beaten any one. They only conquer each other. He made his reputation fighting them." And the prince then analyzed all the blunders that in his opinion Bonaparte had committed in his wars and even in politics.

His son did not protest. But he could not help wondering how this old man, living so many years alone and never leaving his country estate, could know all the military and political events in Europe of the last few years in such detail and with such accuracy.

"You think I'm an old man and don't understand the actual position of affairs?" he concluded. "But I'll tell you I'm completely absorbed by it! I don't sleep at nights. Come, where has this great general of yours shown his skill?"

"That would be a long story," answered his son.

"Oh you go along to your Bonaparte! Mademoiselle Bourienne, here is another admirer of that self-appointed emperor of yours!" he cried in excellent French.

"You know that I am not a Bonapartist, prince."

"God knows when he'll come back . . ." the prince again hummed in his falsetto voice, and got up from the table.

The little princess had sat silent during the whole discussion looking frightened first at Princess Mary and then at her father-in-law. When they left the table, she took her sister-in-law's arm and drew her into another room.

"What a clever man your father is," she said. "Perhaps that is why I am afraid of him."

"Oh, he is so kind!" said Princess Mary.

The following evening Prince André was ready to leave. The old prince, not departing from his regular routine, went away to his own room after dinner. The little princess was with her sister-in-law.

Prince André, having changed his dress and put on a traveling coat without epaulettes, had been packing with his valet in the rooms set apart for him. After inspecting the coach and the packing of his trunks on it, he gave orders for the horses to be harnessed. Nothing was left in the room but the things that Prince André always carried with him: a traveling-case, a big silver wine flask, two Turkish pistols and a sabre, a present from his father. All Prince André's belongings for the journey were in good order; everything was new and clean, in cloth covers, carefully fastened with tape.

Prince André was alone in his room. Suddenly he heard footsteps in the hall outside. It was the heavy step of Princess Mary.

"They told me you had ordered the horses to be harnessed," she said, out of breath for she had evidently been running. "And I did so want to talk with you alone. God knows how long we shall be parted again. You're not angry with me for coming? You're very much changed, André," she added, as though to explain the question.

He smiled. "Where's Liza?" he asked.

"She was so tired that she fell asleep on the sofa in my room. Oh André, what a treasure of a wife you have," she said, sitting down on the sofa, facing her brother. "She is a perfect child; such a sweet, merry child. I like her so much." Prince André did not reply, but the princess noticed an ironical and contemptuous expression on his face.

"One must be indulgent to little weaknesses. Who is free from them, André? You mustn't forget that she has grown up and been educated in society. And now her position is not a very cheerful one. To understand is to forgive everything. Only think what it must be for her, after the life she has been used to, to part from her husband and be left alone in the country, and in her condition too. It's very hard."

Prince André smiled, looking at his sister as we smile at those we think we understand.

"You live in the country and think the life so awful?" he said.

"I—that's different. Why speak of me? I don't wish for any other life, and indeed I can't wish for anything different, for I know no other sort of life. But only think, André, what it is for a young woman used to fashionable society to be buried, for the best years of her life in the country, alone, because papa is always busy, and I . . . you know me . . . I am not a cheerful companion for women used to the best society. Mademoiselle Bourienne is the only person . . ."

"I don't like her at all, your Bourienne," said Prince André.

"Oh, no! She's very good and sweet, and what's more, she's very much to be pitied. She has nobody, nobody. To tell the truth, she is of little use to me; she's only in my way. I have always, you know, been a solitary creature, and now I'm getting more and more so. I like to be alone . . . Father likes her very much. She and Michael Ivanovitch are the two people he is always friendly and good-tempered with, because he has been a benefactor to both of them. As Sterne says: 'We don't love people so much for the good they have done us as for the good we have done them.' Father picked her up an orphan in the streets, and she's very good-natured. And he likes her way of reading. She reads aloud to him in the evenings. She reads very well."

"Come, tell me the truth, Mary, you suffer a good deal because of father's character, don't you?" Prince André asked suddenly. Princess Mary was at first surprised, then aghast at the question.

"Me? . . . Me? . . . Me suffer!" she said.

"He was always harsh, but now he's growing very trying," said Prince André, speaking slightingly of his father with the unmistakable intention of testing his sister.

"You are good in every way, André, but you have a sort of pride of intellect," said the princess, following her own train of thought, "and that's a great sin. Do you think it right to judge father? I am contented and happy with him. I could only wish you were as happy as I am."

Her brother shook his head.

"The only thing that troubles me, I'll tell you the truth, André, is our father's way of treating religious matters. I can't understand how a man of such intellect can fail to see what is as clear as day, and can fall into such error. That is the one thing that makes me unhappy. But even in this I have lately noticed a slight change for the better. His remarks are not so bitter, and there was a monk he received recently and talked to a long time."

"Well, Mary, I'm afraid you and your monk are wasting your powder." Prince André said ironically but affectionately.

"I can only pray to God and trust that He will hear me." Then after a moment's silence, she said timidly, "André, I have a great favour to ask you."

"What is it?"

"No; promise me you won't refuse. It will be no trouble to you, and there is nothing unworthy in it. Only it will be a great comfort to me. Promise, André," she said, putting her hand into her pocket and holding something. She looked timidly with imploring eyes at her brother.

"Even if it were a great trouble . . ." answered Prince André, seeming to guess what the favour was.

"You may think what you please about it. I know you are like father. Think what you please, but do this for my sake. Do, please. Father's father, our grandfather, always wore it in all his wars . . ." She still did not take out what she was holding in her hand. "You promise me, then?"

"Of course, what is it?"

"André, I am blessing you with this holy medal, and you must promise me you will never take it off. . . . You promise?"

"If it does not weigh a ton and won't drag my neck down . . . To please you," said Prince André. He noticed the pained expression that came over his sister's face at his words and felt sorry. "I am very glad, really very glad," he added.

"Against your own will He will save and will have mercy on you and bring you to Himself, because in Him alone is truth and peace," she said in a voice shaking with emotion. Then she held up in both hands before her brother a little, old-fashioned oval holy medal of the Saviour with a dark face in a silver setting, on a silver chain of delicate workmanship. She crossed herself and kissed the image.

"Please, André, for my sake."

Her large timid eyes shone. They lit up her thin, sickly face and made it beautiful. Her brother would have taken the image, but she stopped him. André understood, crossed himself, and kissed the image. He looked at her tenderly. He was touched.

"Thank you, André," she said handing it to him. She kissed him on the forehead. Both were silent.

"So as I was telling you, André, you must be kind and generous as you always used to be. Don't judge Liza harshly," she began; "she is so sweet, so good-natured, and her position is a very hard one just now."

"I fancy I have said nothing to you, Mary, of my blaming my wife for anything or being dissatisfied with her. What makes you say all this to me?"

Princess Mary blushed and was silent, as though she felt guilty.

"I have said nothing to you, but you have been talked to. And that makes me sad."

The red grew deeper on her forehead, neck and cheeks. She would have said something, but could not speak. Her brother had guessed right; his wife had shed tears after dinner, had said that she had a presentiment of a bad confinement, that she was afraid of it, and had complained of her hard lot, of her father-in-law and her husband. After crying she had fallen asleep.

Prince André felt sorry for his sister.

"Let me tell you one thing, Mary, I can't reproach my wife for anything, I never have and I never shall, nor can I reproach myself for anything in regard to her, and that shall always be so. But if you want to know the truth . . . if you want to know if I am happy . . . No. Is she happy? No. Why is it so? I don't know."

As he spoke these words, he went up to his sister, and kissed her on the forehead. His fine eyes lit up with an unaccustomed light. But he was not looking at his sister, but towards the darkness of the open doorway.

"Let us go to her; I must say good-bye. Or you go alone and wake her up, and I'll come in a moment. Peter!" he called to his valet, "come here and take these things. This is to go in the seat and this on the right side."

Princess Mary got up and moved toward the door. She stopped. "André, if you had faith, you would have asked God to give you the love that you do not feel, and your prayer would have been granted."

"Yes, perhaps so," said Prince André. "Go, Mary, I'll come immediately."

When he reached his sister's room, the little princess was awake and her gay little voice could be heard through the open door. She talked as though she wanted to make up for lost time, and, as always, she spoke in French.

"No, but imagine the old Countess Zubov, with false curls and her mouth full of false teeth as though she wanted to defy the years. Ha, ha, Mary!"

This was the same phrase about Countess Zubov and the same laugh Prince André had heard five times already. He walked softly into the room. The little princess, plump and rosy, was sitting in a low chair with her needle-work in her hands, trotting out her Petersburg reminiscences. Prince André stroked her head, and asked if she felt rested after the journey. She answered him and went on talking.

The coach with six horses stood at the steps. It was a dark autumn night. The coachman could not see the carriage shafts. Servants with lanterns were running back and forth. The big house was brilliant with its great windows lighted up. The serfs were crowding in the outer hall, anxious to say good-bye to their young prince. In the reception hall were gathered all the members of the household: Michael Ivanovitch, Mademoiselle Bourienne, Princess Mary, and the little princess.

Prince André had been summoned to the study of his father, who wanted to say good-bye to him alone. The old prince was in his white dressing-gown, in which he never received any one but his son. He was sitting at the table writing. He looked up.

"Going?" And he went on writing again.

"I have come to say good-bye."

"Kiss me here," he touched his cheek. "Thanks, thanks!"

"What are you thanking me for?"

"For not lingering, for not hanging on to a woman's petticoats. Duty before everything. Thanks, thanks!" And he went on writing, so that his quill spluttered and scratched.

"If you want to say anything, say it. I can do these two things at one time," he added.

"About my wife . . . I'm ashamed as it is to leave her on your hands. . . ."

"Don't talk nonsense. Say what you want."

"When my wife's confinement is due, please send to Moscow for a doctor . . . Let him be here."

The old man stopped and stared with stern eyes at his son, as though not understanding.

"I know that no one can be of use, if nature does not help," said Prince André, confused. "Out of a million cases only one goes wrong, but it's her fancy and mine. They've been telling her things; she's had a dream and she's frightened."

"H'm . . . h'm . . ." the old prince muttered to himself, going on with his writing. "I will do so." He scribbled his signature, and suddenly turned to his son and laughed.

"It's a bad business, eh?"

"What's a bad business, father?"

"Wife!" the old prince said significantly.

"I don't understand," said Prince André.

"But there's no help for it, my dear boy," said the old prince. "They're all like that, and there's no getting unmarried again. Don't be afraid, I won't say a word to any one, but you know it yourself."

He grasped André's hand with his thin, bony fingers, shook it, looked straight into his face with his keen eyes, that seemed to see right through him. And again he laughed his frigid laugh.

André nodded, acknowledging that his father understood him.

"It can't be helped. She's pretty. I'll do everything. Set your mind at rest," he said jerkily, as he sealed the letter.

André did not speak; it was both pleasant and painful to him that his father understood him. The old man got up and gave his son the letter.

"Listen," said he. "Don't worry about your wife; what can be done shall be done. Now, listen; give this letter to Michael Kutuzov. I write that he is to make use of you on good work, and not to keep you long an adjutant; a vile duty! Tell him I remember him and like him. And write to me how he receives you. If he's all right, serve him. The son of Nikolas Bolkonsky has no need to serve under any man as a favour. Now, come here."

He spoke so rapidly that he did not finish half of his words, but his son was used to understanding him. He led his son to the bureau, opened it, drew out a drawer, and took out of it a manuscript book filled with his bold, big compressed handwriting.

"I am sure to die before you. See, here are my notes, to be given to the Emperor after my death. Now here, see, is a bank note and a letter: this is a prize for any one who writes a history of Suvorov's wars. Send it to the academy. Here are my remarks, read them after I am gone for your own sake; you will find them profitable."

André did not tell his father that he probably had many years before him. He knew there was no need to say that.

"I will do all that, father," he said.

"Well, now, good-bye!" He gave his son his hand to kiss and embraced him. "Remember one thing, Prince André, if you are killed, it will be a grief to me in my old age . . ." He paused, and all at once in a shrill voice went on: "But if I learn that you have not behaved like the son of Nikolas Bolkonsky, I shall be . . . ashamed!"

"You needn't have said that to me, father," said his son, smiling.

The old man did not speak.

"There's another thing I wanted to ask you," went on Prince André. "If I'm killed, and if I have a son, don't let him slip out of your hands. Let him grow up with you . . . please."

"Not give him up to your wife?" said the old man, and he laughed.

They stood facing each other. The old man's sharp eyes were fixed on his son.

"We have said good-bye . . . Go along!" he said suddenly. "Go along!" he cried in a loud and angry voice, opening the study door.

"What is it, what's the matter?" asked the two princesses on seeing Prince André, and catching a glimpse of the old man in his white dressing-gown, wearing his spectacles and no wig.

Prince André did not answer.

"Now, then," he said, turning to his wife, and that "now then" sounded like a sneer, as though he had said, "Now, go through your performance."

"André? Already!" said the little princess, turning pale. He embraced her. She shrieked and fainted on his shoulder.

He cautiously withdrew the shoulder, on which she was lying, glanced into her face and carefully laid her in a low chair.

"Good-bye, Mary," he said gently to his sister, and they kissed one another's hands. Then he walked quickly out of the room.

The little princess lay in the arm-chair; Mademoiselle Bourienne rubbed her temples. Princess Mary, gazed with her eyes full of tears at the door by which Prince André had gone, and she made the sign of the cross. From the study came, like pistol shots, the repeated and angry sounds of the old prince blowing his nose. Then suddenly the door of the study was flung open, and the old man in his white dressing-gown peeped out.

"Gone? Well, and a good thing too!" he said, looking angrily at the little princess. He shook his head and slammed the door.

1805

BOOK TWO

In October of 1805 Russian troops were occupying the towns and villages of Austria, and fresh regiments kept arriving from Russia and encamping about the fortress of Braunau, burdening the inhabitants on whom they were billeted. Braunau was the chief headquarters of the commander-in-chief, Kutuzov.

On the 11th of October 1805, one of the infantry regiments that had just reached Braunau had halted a mile from the town, awaiting the inspection of Kutuzov. The soldiers after a twenty-five-mile march had not closed their eyes, but had spent the night mending and cleaning. And by the morning the regiment, instead of the straggling, disorderly crowd it had been on the march the previous evening, was an organised body of two thousand men, of whom every one knew his part and his duty, and had every button and every strap in its proper position, and shining with cleanliness. There was only one thing about which no one could feel comfortable. More than half the soldiers had holes in their boots. But this was not due to any fault on the part of their commanding officer, since in spite of his repeated demands boots had not yet been granted him by the Austrian authorities, and the regiment had marched nearly a thousand miles.

The commander of the regiment was a general past middle age, with grey whiskers and eyebrows, broad and thick-set. He wore a brand-new uniform with the creases still in it where it had been folded, and rich gold epaulettes, which seemed to stand up instead of lying down on his thick shoulders. He had the air of a man who has successfully performed one of the most solemn duties of his life and walked about in front of the line with a slight jerk of his back at each step. He was unmistakably admiring his regiment, and happy about it.

"Well, Mihail Mitritch, sir," he said, addressing a major.

The major came forward smiling; they were evidently in excellent spirits.

"We have had our hands full all night . . . But it'll do, I guess. The regiment's not so bad . . . eh?"

At that moment two figures on horseback came into sight on the road from the town. They were an adjutant, and a Cossack riding behind him.

The adjutant had been sent by the commander-in-chief, Kutuzov, to confirm what had not been clearly stated in the previous order, namely, that the commander-in-chief wished to inspect the regiment exactly as they had been on the march—wearing their overcoats, and carrying their packs, and without any sort of preparation.

A member of the high war council from Vienna had been with Kutuzov the previous day, demanding that he should move his Russian troops on as quickly as possible to effect a junction with the army of Archduke Ferdinand and Mack; and Kutuzov, not considering this advisable, had intended, among other arguments in support of his view, to point out to the Austrian general the dreadful condition of his troops. It was with this in mind that he planned to meet the regiment, so that the worse its condition, the better pleased he would be.

And although the adjutant did not know these details, he gave the general the message that Kutuzov absolutely insisted on the men being in their overcoats just as they had been on the march, otherwise Kutuzov would be displeased.

On hearing this the general shrugged his shoulders, and threw up his hands in anger.

"Oh, my God!" he said. Then stepping forward he shouted. "Captains! Sergeants! . . . Will his excellency be coming soon?" he said, turning to the adjutant.

"In an hour, I think."

"Have we time to change clothes?"

"I can't say, general. . . ."

Then the general, walking through the ranks, ordered the men to change back to their overcoats. The captains and the sergeants ran about among the companies. The soldiers ran in all directions, pulling their knapsacks off over their heads, taking out their overcoats and putting them on.

Half an hour later everything was in order again, only the squadrons were now grey instead of black. The general walked in front of the regiment again and looked at it from a distance.

"What next? What's this!" he shouted, stopping short. "Captain of the third company! You'll soon be dressing your men in petticoats! What's the meaning of it?" He pointed at a soldier, in the ranks of the third division, dressed in an overcoat of a colour different from the rest. "I'll teach you to rig your men out in dressing-gowns for inspection! . . . Well, why don't you speak? Who's that dressed up like a Hungarian?" he jested bitterly.

"Your excellency, that's Dolohov, the degraded officer," the captain said softly.

"Well, is he degraded to be a field-marshal, or a common soldier? If he's a soldier, then he must be dressed like all the rest, according to regulation."

"Your excellency, you gave him permission yourself."

"Gave him permission? There, you're always like that, you young men," said the general, softening a little. "Gave him permission? If one says a word to you, you go and . . ." The general paused. He then walked toward Dolohov.

"Why are you in a blue coat? Off with it! . . . Sergeant! Change his coat . . . the dirty . . ."

"General, I am bound to obey orders, but I am not bound to put up with . . ." Dolohov interrupted.

"No talking in the ranks! . . . No talking, no talking!"

"Not bound to put up with insults," Dolohov went on, loudly and clearly. The eyes of the general and the soldier met. The general paused, angrily pulling down his stiff scarf.

"Change your coat, if you please," he said as he walked away.

"Coming!" the sentinel shouted at that moment.

The general, turning red, ran to his horse, with trembling hands caught at the stirrup, swung himself up, settled himself in the saddle, drew out his sword, and shouted, "Silence!"

A high, blue Vienna coach with several horses was driving at a smart trot, rumbling on its springs, along the broad unpaved high-road. An escort of Croats galloped after the coach. Beside Kutuzov sat an Austrian general in a white uniform, that looked strange among the black Russian ones. The coach drew up on reaching the regiment. Kutuzov and the Austrian general stepped out of the carriage.

The word of command rang out. The regiment presented arms. Then it roared: "Good health to your Ex . . lency . . lency . . lency!" And all was still.

Then Kutuzov and the Austrian general, followed by their aides, began walking through the ranks. Closest to Kutuzov walked a handsome adjutant. It was Prince André Bolkonsky. Beside him was his friend Nesvitsky, a staff officer, tall stout but with a good-natured, handsome face. Kutuzov stopped now and then, saying a few friendly words to officers he had known in the Turkish war, and sometimes to the soldiers. Looking at their boots, he several times shook his head, and pointed them out to the Austrian general, as much as to say that he blamed no one for it, but that he could not help bringing this to his attention.

Kutuzov and his party walked slowly by the thousands of eyes which were almost rolling out of their sockets in the effort to watch him. On reaching the third company, he suddenly stopped. He seemed pondering, as though trying to recall something. Prince André stepped forward and said softly in French: "You asked me to remind you of the degraded officer, Dolohov, serving in the ranks in this regiment."

"Where is Dolohov?" asked Kutuzov.

Dolohov, now in the grey overcoat of a private soldier, did not wait to be called up. He stepped out of the line and went up to the commander-in-chief and presented arms.

"A complaint to make?" Kutuzov asked.

"This is Dolohov," said Prince André.

"Ah!" said Kutuzov. "I hope this will be a lesson to you, do your duty thoroughly. The Emperor is gracious. And I shall not forget you if you deserve it."

Dolohov looked boldly at the commander-in-chief tearing down the veil of convention that removed the commander-in-chief so far from the soldier.

"The only favour I beg of your most high excellency," he said in a deliberate voice, "is to give me a chance to atone for my offence, and to prove my devotion to his majesty the Emperor, and to Russia."

Kutuzov turned away and frowned, as though what Dolohov had said to him and all he could say, he had known long, long ago, that he was sick to death long ago of it, and that it was not at all what was wanted. He walked towards the coach.

The regiment broke into companies and started toward Braunau, where they hoped to find boots and clothes, and to rest after their hard marches.

"You won't bear me a grudge?" said the commanding general, overtaking the third company and riding up to the captain, whom he had shouted at because of Dolohov's blue overcoat. The general's face beamed after the successful inspection. "It's in the Tsar's service . . . can't be helped . . . sometimes one has to be a little sharp at inspection. I'm the first to apologise; you know me. . . . Kutuzov was very much pleased." And the general held out his hand to the captain. "Tell Dolohov that I won't forget him; he can be easy about that. And tell me, how's he behaving himself . . . I've been meaning to inquire . . ."

"He's very exact in the discharge of his duties, your excellency . . . but he's a character . . ." said the captain.

"Why, what sort of a character?" asked the general.

"It's different on different days, your excellency. At one time he's sensible and well-educated and good-natured. And then he'll be like a beast. In Poland, he nearly killed a Jew. . . "

"Well," said the general, "still one must help a young man in trouble. He has connections, you know. . . . So you . . ."

"Oh, yes, your excellency," said the captain, with a smile that showed he understood his general's wish in the matter.

The general sought out Dolohov in the ranks and pulled up his horse.

"In the first action you may win your epaulettes," he said to him.

Dolohov looked round and said nothing.

"Well, that's all right then," the general went on. "A glass of brandy to every man from me," he added, so that the soldiers could hear. "I thank you all. God be praised!" And riding round the company, he galloped off to another.

The cheerful mood of the officers after the inspection was shared by the soldiers. The companies went along happily, the soldiers talking freely among themselves.

"They say Kutuzov's blind in one eye."

"Yes, he is."

"He's more sharp-eyed than you are. See how he looked at our boots and things." . . .

"Did he say anything about when the battles are going to begin? You stood close. They say Bonaparte was in Brunovo."

"Bonaparte! What nonsense! What won't they say next!"

"Those devils of quartermasters! . . . The fifth company's turned into the village by now, and they're cooking their food, and we're not there yet."

"Singers to the front," the captain called. And from the different ranks about twenty men advanced. The drummer, who was their leader, turned round facing the chorus and waving his arms, struck up a soldier's song, beginning: "The sun was scarcely dawning," and ending with the words: "So, lads, we'll march to glory with Father Kutuzov."

Twenty voices caught up the refrain, and the castanet player, in spite of the weight of his gun and knapsack, bounded nimbly forward, and walked backwards facing the company, and clicking his castanets.

Behind the company came the sound of wheels, the rumble of springs, and the tramp of horses. Kutuzov and his party were returning to the town. He made a sign for the soldiers not to stop, and he and all his aides looked as though they took pleasure in the sound of the singing and the happy men. They could not help noticing Dolohov, who walked with a

a shoulder ornament on a military uniform

special jauntiness and grace in time to the singing, and seemed to pity every one who was not at that moment marching in the ranks.

Zherkov, an officer of Kutuzov's party, rode up to Dolohov. He had at one time belonged to the fast set in Petersburg, of which Dolohov had been the leader, and having met Dolohov as a common soldier, had not seen fit to recognise him. But now, after Kutuzov's conversation with Dolohov, he addressed him like an old friend.

"How are you?" he said.

"How am I?" Dolohov answered coldly. "As you see."

"Well, how do you get on with your officers?" asked Zherkov.

"All right; they're good fellows. How did you manage to squeeze yourself on to the staff?"

"I was appointed."

They were silent.

"Is it true, the Austrians have been beaten?" asked Dolohov.

"They say so."

"I'm glad," Dolohov replied.

"Come round to see me and my friends some evening. We'll have a game of faro," said Zherkov.

"Is money so plentiful among you?"

"Do come."

"I can't; I've sworn not to. I won't drink or gamble till I'm promoted."

Again they were silent.

"If you need anything come to me," said Zherkov. "One can always be of use on the staff. . . ."

Dolohov smiled. "Don't trouble yourself. What I want, I'm not going to ask for. I take it for myself."

On returning from the review, Kutuzov, accompanied by the Austrian general, went to his private room, and calling his aide, Prince André, asked him to bring him certain papers, relating to the condition of the newly arrived troops, and letters, received from Archduke Ferdinand, who was in command of the army at the front. Kutuvoz and the Austrian general were looking at a map that lay unfolded on the table.

"I have only one thing to say, general," said Kutuzov speaking in French. "If the matter depended on my personal wishes, the desire of the Emperor Francis should long ago have been accomplished; I should long ago have joined the archduke. And, upon my honour, believe me that for me personally to hand over the chief command of the army to more experienced and skilful generals—such as Austria is so rich in—and to throw off all this weighty responsibility would be a relief. But circumstances are too strong for us, general." And Kutuzov smiled with an expression that seemed to say: "You are perfectly at liberty not to believe me, and indeed it's a matter of perfect indifference to me whether you believe me or not."

The Austrian general looked dissatisfied, but he had no choice but to answer Kutuzov in the same tone.

"On the contrary," he said in an irritated voice, that contrasted with the flattering words he uttered; "on the contrary, the participation of your most high excellency in common action is highly appreciated by his majesty. But we imagine that the present delay robs the gallant Russian troops and you, their commander-in-chief, of the laurels you are accustomed to winning in action."

Kutuzov bowed, still with the same smile.

"But I am convinced of this, and relying on the last letter with which his Highness the Archduke Ferdinand has honoured me, I imagine that the Austrian troops under the command of so talented a leader as General Mack, have by now gained a decisive victory and have no longer need of our aid," said Kutuzov.

The Austrian general frowned. Though there was no positive news of the defeat of the Austrians, there were too many rumours. And so Kutuzov's remark about an Austrian victory sounded very much like a sneer. But Kutuzov smiled blandly, with an expression which seemed to say that he had a right to suppose so. And in fact the last letter he had received from the army of General Mack had given him news of victory, and of the most favourable strategical position of the army.

"But you know, your excellency, the wise saying that it is better to prepare for the worst," said the Austrian general, wishing to have done with jests and to come down to business. He could not help glancing round at Prince André.

"Excuse me, general," Kutuzov interrupted him, and he, too, turned to Prince André. "Here, my dear boy are two letters from Count Nostits, here is a letter from his Highness the Archduke Ferdinand, here is another," he said, giving him several papers. "Make out in French a memorandum showing all the information we have had of the movements of the Austrian Army. And show it to his excellency."

Prince André bowed. He gathered up the papers and went out into the reception-room.

Although only a short time had passed since Prince André had left Russia, he had changed greatly. In the expression of his face, in his gestures, in his walk, there was now scarcely a trace to be seen of his former affectation and indolence. He had the air of a man who has not time to think of the impression he is making on others, and is absorbed in work, both agreeable and interesting. His face showed more satisfaction with himself and those around him. His smile and his glance were more light-hearted and attractive.

Kutuzov, whom he had overtaken in Poland, had received him very cordially, had promised not to forget him, had marked him out among the other aides, had taken him with him to Vienna and given him the more serious commissions. From Vienna, Kutuzov had written to his old comrade, Prince André's father.

"Your son," he wrote, "gives promise of becoming an officer, who will make his name by his industry, firmness, and conscientiousness. I consider myself lucky to have such an assistant at hand."

On Kutuzov's staff, among his fellow-officers, and in the army generally, Prince André had, as he had had in Petersburg society, two quite opposite reputations. Some, the minority, regarded Prince André as a person different from themselves and from all other men, expected great things of him, listened to him, were enthusiastic in his praise, and imitated him, and with such people Prince André was frank and agreeable. Others, the majority, did not like Prince André, and regarded him as a sulky, cold, and disagreeable person. But with these people, Prince André knew how to behave so that he was respected and even feared by them.

Coming out of Kutuzov's room, Prince André went with the papers to the aide on duty, who was sitting in the window reading a book.

"What is it, prince?" asked the aide.

"I am ordered to make a report of the reason why our Russian troops are not advancing."

"And why aren't we?"

Prince André shrugged his shoulders.

"No news from Mack?" asked the aide.

"No."

"If it were true that he had been beaten, news would have come."

"Most likely," said Prince André, and he moved towards the door to go out. But at that moment a tall man walked into the reception-room, slamming the door. He was an Austrian general wearing a long coat and the order of Maria Theresa on his neck. His head was bandaged with a black cloth.

"Commander-in-chief Kutuzov?" the general asked quickly, speaking with a harsh German accent. He looked about him on both sides, and without a pause walked to the door of the private room.

"The commander-in-chief is engaged," said the aide barring his way to the door. "Whom am I to announce?"

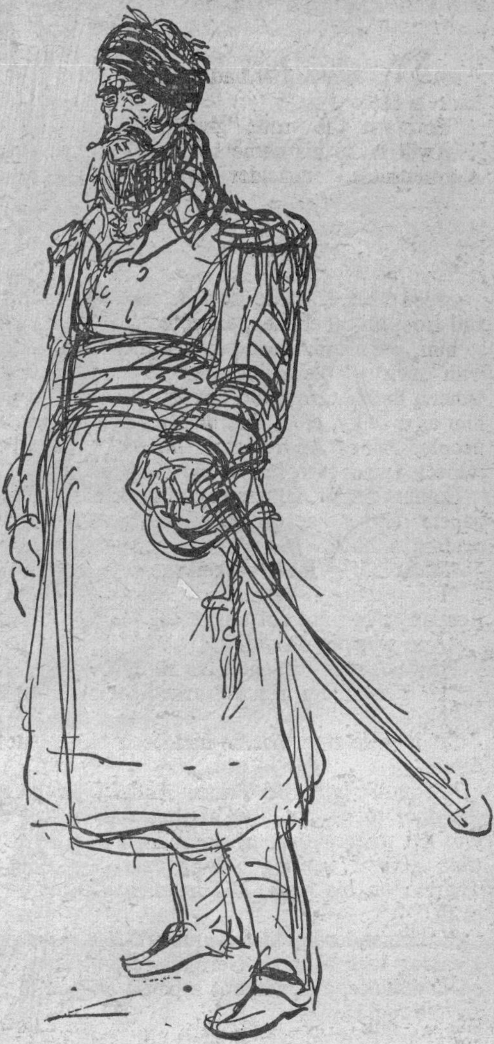

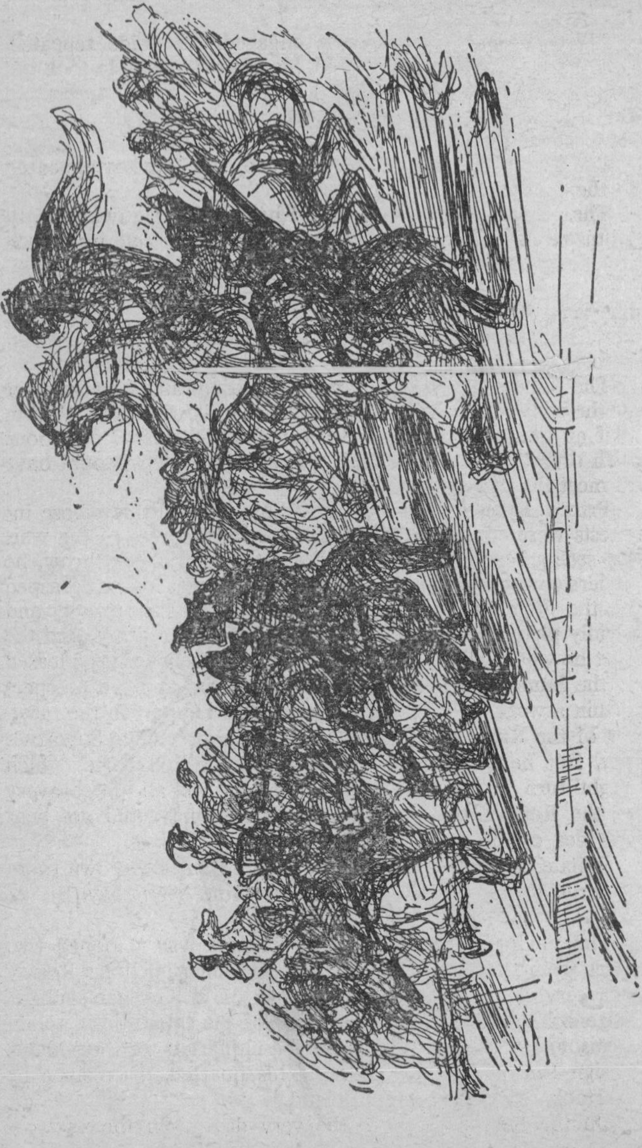

The unknown general looked disdainfully at the aide and then at Prince André as though surprised that they could be ignorant of his identity.

"The commander-in-chief is engaged," the aide repeated.

The general's face contracted, his lips twitched. He took out a notebook, hurriedly scribbled something in pencil, tore out the leaf, handed it to the aide and then walked to the window.

The door of the private room opened, and Kutuzov appeared in the doorway.

The general with the bandaged head walked quickly up to Kutuzov. "You see the unfortunate Mack," he said in French in a breaking voice.

Kutuzov stood in the doorway. A frown seemed to run over his face, like a wave, leaving his forehead smooth again; he bowed his head respectfully, closed his eyes, ushered Mack in before him without a word, and closed the door.

The rumour of the defeat of the Austrians and the surrender of the whole army at Ulm, turned out to be the truth. Within half an hour aides had been despatched in various directions with orders. It was now clear that Russian troops would have to meet the enemy.

Prince André was one of those rare staff-officers whose interests were concentrated on the general progress of the war. On seeing Mack and learning the details of his overthrow, he understood the fact that half the campaign was lost; he grasped all the difficulty of the position of the Russian troops, and vividly pictured to himself what lay before the army, and the part he would have to play. He could not help feeling pleased at the humiliation of self-confident Austria, and the prospect within a week, perhaps, of seeing and taking part in the meeting of the Russians with the French, the first since Suvorov's day. But he was afraid of the genius of Bonaparte, which might turn out to be more powerful than all the bravery of the Russian troops; at the same time he could not bear the idea of the disgrace of his favourite hero.

Irritated by these ideas, Prince André went to his own room to write to his father, to whom he wrote every day.

The Pavlogradsky regiment of hussars was stationed two miles from Braunau. The squadron in which Nicholas Rostov was serving as ensign was billeted on a German village, Salzeneck. The officer in command of the squadron, Captain Denisov, had been assigned the best quarters in the village. Ensign Rostov had been sharing his quarters, ever since he overtook the regiment in Poland.

On the 8th of October, the very day when the news of

Mack's defeat reached headquarters, the routine of life was going on as before among the officers of this squadron.

Denisov, who had been losing all night at cards, had not yet returned, when Rostov rode back early in the morning from a foraging expedition.

"Ah, Bondarenko, friend of my heart," he said to the hussar who rushed up to his horse. "Walk him up and down."

"Yes, your excellency."

Another hussar rushed up to the horse too, but Bondarenko already had hold of the reins. It was clear that Rostov was liberal with his tips.

Rostov stroked the horse on the neck and then on the haunch. "What a horse he will be!" he said to himself. And then smiling and holding his sword, he ran up the steps, clanking his spurs.

"Where's your master?" he asked of Lavrushka, Denisov's orderly, well known to all the regiment as a rogue.

"His honour's not been in since the evening. He's been losing, for sure," answered Lavrushka. "I know by now, if he wins, he'll come home early to boast of his luck; but if he's not back by morning, it means that he's lost. He'll come back in a rage. Shall I bring coffee?"

"Yes, bring it."

Ten minutes later, Lavrushka brought in the coffee.

"He's coming!" he said.

Rostov looked out of the window and saw Denisov returning.

"Oh! You're already up," said Denisov, coming into the room.

"Long ago," said Rostov; "I've already been out after hay."

"Really? And I've been losing, my boy, all night, like the son of a dog," cried Denisov. "Such bad luck! Such bad luck! . . . As soon as you left, my luck was gone."

Denisov began ruffling up his black hair with his short-fingered hands. Then rubbing his face he said: "The devil was in me to go to that rat. He didn't deal me one card, not one, not one card! . . . If there were only women. But here, except drinking, there's nothing to do. If only we could get to fighting soon. . . . Hey, who's there?" he called towards the door, hearing the sound of thick boots and clanking spurs.

"The sergeant!" said Lavrushka.

"What a nuisance!" Denisov said, flinging down a purse with several gold coins in it. "Rostov, count how much is left, and put the purse under my pillow," he said, and he went out to the sergeant. Rostov took the money and sorting the old and new gold, he began counting it over.

"Ah, Telyanin! Good-morning! I was cleaned out last night," he heard Denisov's voice saying from the other room.

"Where was that? At the rat's? . . . I knew it," said a thin voice, and there walked into the room Lieutenant Telyanin, a little officer in the same squadron.

Rostov put the purse under the pillow, and shook the damp little hand that was offered him. Telyanin had for some reason been transferred from the guards just before the regiment set out. He had behaved very well in the regiment, but he was not liked, and Rostov, in particular, could not endure him, and could not conceal his feelings.

"Well, how is my Rook doing for you?" Rook was a riding-horse Telyanin had sold to Rostov.

"Oh, he's all right; a good horse," answered Rostov, though the horse, for which he had paid seven hundred roubles, was not worth half that amount. "He's begun to go a little lame in the left foreleg . . ." he added.

"The hoof cracked! I'll show you what to do for it."

"Yes, please do," said Rostov.

"I'll show you, I'll show you; it's not a secret. But you'll be grateful to me for that horse."

"Then I'll have the horse brought round," said Rostov, anxious to be rid of Telyanin. He went out to order the horse to be brought round.

In the outer room Denisov was squatting on the floor facing the sergeant, who was giving him a report. On seeing Rostov, Denisov screwed up his eyes, and pointing over his shoulder with his thumb to the room where Telyanin was sitting, he frowned and shook his head.

Rostov shrugged his shoulders as though to say, "I don't like him either, but what can I do?" And having given his order, he went back to Telyanin, who was still sitting in the same place where Rostov had left him, rubbing his little white hands.

"Well, have you given orders for the horse to be brought out?" said Telyanin, getting up and looking carelessly about him.

"Yes."

"Well, then come along."

They went out down the steps and into the stable. Telyanin showed Rostov what to do and then went to his own quarters.

When Rostov came back Denisov was sitting at the table, and his pen was squeaking over the paper. He looked up gloomily.

"I am writing to her," he said. He leaned his elbow on the table with the pen in his hand, and began telling Rostov everything he was going to write. "You see," he said, "we are plunged in slumber, we are the children of dust and ashes, until we love . . . but the moment you love, you are a god, you are pure, as on the first day of creation. . . . Who's that now? Send him to the devil! I've no time!" he shouted to Lavrushka, who went up to him.

"Why, who should it be? You told him to come yourself. The sergeant has come for the money."

Denisov frowned. "It's a nuisance," he said to himself. "How much money was there left there in the purse?" he asked Rostov.

"Seven new and three old gold pieces."

Denisov went to the bed to take the purse from under the pillow.

"Where did you put it, Rostov?"

"Under the lower pillow."

"But it's not there." Denisov threw both pillows on the floor. There was no purse. "Well, that's a queer thing."

"Maybe you dropped it?" said Rostov, picking up the pillows one at a time and shaking them. He took off the quilt and shook it. The purse was not there.

"I laid the purse here," said Rostov. "Where is it?" He turned to Lavrushka.

"I never came into the room. It must be where you put it."

"But it isn't."

"You're always like that; you throw things down anywhere and forget them. Look in your pockets."

"I remember where I put it!"

Lavrushka ransacked the whole bed, looked under it and under the table. He ransacked the whole room. Denisov watched Lavrushka in silence, and when Lavrushka flung up his hands to signify that it was nowhere, he looked round at Rostov.

"Rostov, none of your jokes."

Rostov felt his blood rush to his face. He could hardly draw his breath.

"There's been no one in the room but the lieutenant and yourselves. It must be here somewhere," said Lavrushka.

"Now then, you devil's puppet, look for it!" Denisov shouted suddenly, turning purple and threatening his orderly. "I'll flog you! I'll flog you all!"

Rostov, his eyes avoiding Denisov, began buttoning up his jacket, fastening on his sword, and putting on his forage-cap.

"I tell you the purse is to be found," roared Denisov, shaking the orderly by the shoulders and pushing him against the wall.

"Denisov, let him be; I know who has taken it," said Rostov, going towards the door.

Denisov stopped, thought a moment, and understanding Rostov's hint, he clutched him by the arm.

"Nonsense!" he roared so that the veins stood out on his neck and forehead like cords. "I tell you, you've gone out of your mind; I won't allow it. The purse is here; I'll flay the skin off this rascal, and it will be here."

"I know who has taken it," repeated Rostov, in a shaking voice.

"And I tell you, you're not to dare to do it," shouted Denisov. Rostov pulled his arm away and looked directly at Denisov.

"Do you understand what you're saying?" he said in a trembling voice; "Except for me, there has been no one else in the room. So that, if it's not so, why then . . ."

He could not speak the rest, and ran out of the room.

Rostov went to Telyanin's quarters.

"The master's not at home, he's gone to the staff," Telyanin's orderly told him.

The staff quarters were two miles and a half from Salzeneck. Rostov took his horse and rode to the village, where the staff was quartered. There was a restaurant which the officers frequented. Rostov reached the restaurant and saw Telyanin's horse outside.

In the second room the lieutenant was sitting over a dish of sausages and a bottle of wine.

"Ah, you have come here too, young man," he said, smiling and lifting his eyebrows.

"Yes," said Rostov. And he sat down at the nearest table.

Both were silent; there were two Germans and a Russian officer in the room. Every one was quiet and the only sounds were the clatter of knives on the plates and the munching of the lieutenant.

When Telyanin had finished his lunch, he took out of his pocket a double purse; with his little white fingers, that were curved at the tips, he parted the rings, took out some gold, and raising his eyebrows, gave the money to the attendant.

The gold was new. Rostov got up and went to Telyanin.

"Let me look at the purse," he said in a low voice, scarcely audible.

With eyebrows still raised, Telyanin handed him the purse.

Rostov looked at the purse and at the money in it, and also at Telyanin. The lieutenant seemed suddenly to have grown very good-humoured.

"If we go to Vienna, I suspect I shall leave it all there, but now there's nowhere to spend our money in these wretched little places," he said. "Come, give it back to me, young man; I'm going."

He put out his hand and took hold of the purse. Rostov let go of it. Telyanin took the purse and began dropping it into the pocket of his riding trousers, as much as to say: "Yes, I'm putting my purse in my pocket and no one has anything to do with it."

"Come here," said Rostov, taking Telyanin by the arm. He almost dragged him to the window. "That's Denisov's money; you took it . . ." he whispered in his ear.

"What? . . . what? . . . How dare you? What?" . . . said Telyanin. But the words sounded like a plaintive, despairing cry. And as soon as Rostov heard them a great weight of suspense, like a stone, rolled off his heart.

"God knows what the people here may think," muttered Telyanin, snatching up his forage-cap and turning towards a small empty room. "You must explain . . ." His terrified white face began twitching in every muscle.

"Count! . . . don't ruin a young man . . . here is the wretched money, take it." Telyanin threw it on the table. "I've an old father and mother!" . . .

Rostov took the money and without saying a word, he went out of the room. But suddenly he stopped and turned back.

"My God!" he said. "How could you do it?"

"Count," said Telyanin, coming closer.

"Don't touch me," said Rostov, drawing back. "If you're in need, take the money."

He thrust a purse on him and ran out of the restaurant.

In the evening of the same day a discussion was taking place in Denisov's quarters between some officers of the squadron.

"But I tell you, Rostov, that you must apologise to the colonel, Bogdanitch," the tall staff-captain was saying, addressing Rostov, who was crimson with anger.

"I permit no one to tell me I'm lying!" cried Rostov. "He told me I was lying and I told him he was lying. And there it rests. He can put me on duty every day, he can place me under arrest, but no one can make me apologise."

"But you listen to me, young man," interrupted the staff-captain in his bass voice, calmly stroking his long whiskers. "You tell the colonel in the presence of other officers that an officer has stolen . . ."

"I'm not to blame for the conversation being in the presence of other officers. Maybe I shouldn't have spoken before them, but I'm not a diplomat. That's just why I joined the hussars; I thought that here . . . And he tells me I'm a liar . . . So let him give me satisfaction."

"That's all fine. No one imagines that you're a coward, but that's not the point. Ask Denisov if it's not out of the question for an ensign to demand satisfaction of his colonel?"

Denisov was listening to the conversation but he had no desire to take part in it. He replied by shaking his head.

"He said I was telling a lie," repeated Rostov.

"You must apologise."

"Never!" shouted Rostov.

"I didn't expect this of you," said the staff-captain. "You won't apologise, but young man, it's not only him, but all the regiment, all of us, that you're hurting. Look here, what is the colonel to do? Is he to bring the officer up for trial and disgrace the whole regiment? On account of one scoundrel is the whole regiment to be put to shame? Is that the thing for him to do? And now when they try to smooth the thing over, you won't apologise. What is it for you to apologise to an old and honourable officer! Bogdanitch is an honourable and gallant old colonel. You're offended, but disgracing the regiment's nothing to you." The staff-captain's voice began to quaver. "You, sir, have been next to no time in the regiment; you're here to-day, and to-morrow you'll be passed on somewhere as an aide; you don't care a straw for people saying: 'There are thieves among the Pavlograd officers!' But we do care! Don't we, Denisov?"

"That's the truth, damn it!" shouted Denisov, jumping up. "Come, Rostov, come!"

Rostov, turning crimson and white again, looked first at one officer and then at the other.

"No, gentlemen, no . . . you must think . . . I quite understand, you're wrong in thinking that of me . . . I . . . for me . . . for the honour of the regiment I'd . . . but why talk? I'll prove that in action and for me the honour of the flag . . . well, never mind, it's true, I'm to blame!" . . . There were tears in his eyes. "I'm wrong, wrong all round! Well, what more do you want?" . . .

"Come, that's right, count," cried the staff-captain, turning round and clapping him on the shoulder with his big hand. "That's better, count," he repeated beginning to address him by his title as though in acknowledgment of his confession. "Go and apologise, your excellency."

"Gentlemen, I'll do anything, no one shall hear a word from me," Rostov protested in an imploring voice, "but I can't apologise, by God, I can't, say what you will! How can I apologise, like a little boy begging pardon! I can't describe the feeling it gives me. I can't do it."

Denisov laughed.

"Well, as you like," said the staff-captain. "What has the scoundrel done with himself?" he asked Denisov.

"He has reported himself ill; to-morrow the order's given for him to be struck off," said Denisov.

"There's no other way of explaining it," said the staff-captain.

"Whether it's illness or whether it's not, he'd better not cross my path. I'll kill him," Denisov shouted.

They were suddenly interrupted. Zherkov walked into the room.

"To the front, gentlemen. Mack has surrendered with his whole army!"

"What!"

A regimental aide then came in and confirmed the news brought by Zherkov. They were under orders to advance next day.

"Well, thank God! We've been sticking here too long."

Kutuzov fell back to Vienna. On the 23rd of October the Russian troops crossed the river Enns. The day was warm, autumnal, and rainy. From the heights, where the Russian batteries stood guarding the bridge, the little town of Enns could be seen below with its white houses and its red roofs, its cathedral and its bridge, on both sides of which streamed masses of Russian troops. At the bend of the Danube could be seen ships and the island and a castle with a park, surrounded by the waters formed by the Enns falling into the Danube, and the precipitous left bank of the Danube, covered with pine forest. Beyond the pine forest, that looked wild and untouched, rose the turrets of a nunnery; and in the far distance in front, on the hill on the further side of the Enns, could be seen the scouts of the enemy.

Between the cannons on the height stood the general in command of the rear-guard and a staff officer scanning the country through a field-glass. A little behind them, there sat on the trunk of a cannon, Nesvitsky, who had been despatched by Kutuzov to the rear-guard. The Cossack who accompanied Nesvitsky had handed him a knapsack and a flask, and Nesvitsky was treating the officers to pies and real doppelkümmel. The officers surrounded him in a circle, some on their knees, some sitting cross-legged, like Turks, on the wet grass.

"Look, prince," said one, who would have liked to take another pie, but was ashamed to, and therefore pretended to be gazing at the countryside; "look, our infantry has just arrived. Over there, near the meadow behind the village, three of them are dragging something. They will ransack that palace nicely," he said, with evident approval.

"They certainly will," said Nesvitsky. "No; but what I should like," he added, munching a pie, "would be to slip in there." He pointed to the turreted nunnery that could be seen on the mountainside. He smiled, his eyes narrowing and gleaming. "There are Italian girls, they say, among them! I'd give five years of my life for it!"

The officers laughed.

Meanwhile the staff officer who was standing in front, pointed something out to the general. The general looked through the field-glass.

"Yes, so it is, so it is," said the general angrily, taking the field-glass away from his eye and shrugging his shoulders. "They are going to fire at them at the crossing of the river. And why do they delay so?"

With the naked eye, looking in that direction, one could see the enemy and their batteries, from which a milky-white smoke was rising. The smoke was followed by the sound of a shot in the distance, and Russian troops hurried to the place of crossing.

Nesvitsky got up puffing and went up to the general.

"Wouldn't your excellency like some lunch?" he said.

"It's a bad business," said the general, without answering him. "Our men have been too slow."

"Shouldn't I ride over, your excellency?" said Nesvitsky.

"Yes, ride over, please," said the general. "And tell the hussars that they are to cross last and to burn the bridge."

"Very good," answered Nesvitsky. He called the Cossack with his horse, told him to pick up the knapsack and flask, and swung himself into the saddle.

"I am going to pay a visit to the nuns," he called to the officers who were watching him, smiling. And he rode along the winding path down the mountain.

"Now then, captain, try how far it'll carry," said the general, turning to the artillery officer. "Let's have a little fun to pass the time."

"Men, to the guns!" commanded the officer, and in a moment the gunners ran from the camp fires and loaded the big guns.

"One!" they heard the word of command. Number one bounded back. The cannon boomed with a deafening metallic sound, and whistling over the heads of the Russian troops at the foot of the mountainside, the cannon ball flew across, falling a long way short of the enemy.

The faces of the soldiers and officers brightened up at the sound. Every one got up and watched the movements of the troops below, which could be seen as in the hollow of a hand, and the movements of the advancing enemy.

At the same instant, the sun came out from behind the clouds, and the clear sound of the solitary shot and the brilliance of the bright sunshine created a carefree mood.

There was a crush on the bridge and Nesvitsky, who had

dismounted, stood jammed against the railings. Every time he tried to move on, the advancing soldiers and waggons bore down upon him and shoved him back. There was nothing for him to do but to smile.

Looking down over the rails, Nesvitsky saw the noisy, rapid, but not high waves of the Enns, which, swirling in eddies round the piles of the bridge, chased one another down stream. Looking on the bridge he saw the living waves of soldiers, all alike as they streamed by: shakoes with covers on them, knapsacks, bayonets, long rifles, and under the shakoes broad-jawed faces, sunken cheeks, and looks of weariness. Sometimes among the monotonous streams of soldiers, like a crest of white foam on the waves of the Enns, an officer forced his way through, with a face of a different type from the soldiers. Sometimes, like a chip whirling on the river, there passed over the bridge among the waves of infantry a dismounted hussar, an orderly, or an inhabitant of the town. Sometimes, like a log floating down the river, there moved over the bridge, hemmed in on all sides, a baggage-waggon, piled up high and protected with leather covers.

"They're like a river bursting its banks," thought Nesvitsky. And standing there he heard fragments of passing voices.

"If the enemy starts popping at the bridge you'll forget to scratch yourself. . . . . Where the devil did you put the leg-wrappers? . . . . And didn't he up with the butt end of his gun and give him one right in the teeth. . . . It was a delicious ham." And they passed on, so that Nesvitsky never knew who had received the blow in the teeth, and what the ham had to do with it. Then came some soldiers who had been drinking. They too passed on.

And after them came a waggon, with two horses, unlike all that had passed over before. It was loaded with household goods. The horses were led by a German, and behind was fastened a handsome, brindled cow with an immense udder. On piled-up feather-beds sat a woman with a small baby, an old woman, and a good-looking, rosy-cheeked German girl.

The eyes of all the soldiers were turned upon the women, and, while the waggon moved by, a step at a time, all the soldiers' remarks related to them. Every face wore almost the same smile, reflecting indecent ideas.

"Sell us your women," called a soldier to the German, who trudged along with downcast eyes, looking angry and frightened.

"Look how she's dressed herself up!"

"Wouldn't you like to be billeted on them!"

"Where are you going?" asked an infantry officer, who was eating an apple. He too was half smiling and staring at the handsome girl. The German, shutting his eyes, signified that he did not understand.

"Take it, if you like," said the officer, handing the girl an apple. The girl smiled and took it.

Then when the waggon had passed by, there again moved on the same soldiers with the same talk.

With effort Nesvitsky finally succeeded in getting to his horse. Shouting, he moved forward. The soldiers pressed back to make way for him, but then jammed upon him again.

"Nesvitsky! Nesvitsky!" he heard a husky voice shouting from behind.

Nesvitsky looked round and saw, separated from him by the living mass of moving infantry, Denisov with a forage-cap on the back of his head, and a cape swung carelessly over his shoulder.

"Make way, damned devils!" roared Denisov. He waved a sheathed sword.

"Denisov!" Nesvitsky called. "What are you doing?"

"The squadron can't advance!" roared Denisov, spurring his raven thoroughbred "Bedouin," which, twitching its ears at the bayonets against which it pricked itself, snorting and foaming at its bit, tramped with metallic clang on the boards of the bridge, and seemed ready to leap over the railings.

"Sheep! You're all like sheep! Back . . . make way! . . . I'll cut you down with my sword!" He drew his sword out of the sheath and began to brandish it.

The soldiers, with terrified faces, squeezed together, and Denisov joined Nesvitsky.

Nesvitsky's imposing figure and Denisov, waving his sword and shouting, produced so much effect that they stopped the infantry and got to the other end of the bridge. Nesvitsky found the colonel, to whom he had to deliver the command, and having executed his commission he rode back.

The rest of the infantry quickly marched across the bridge. At last all the baggage-waggons had passed over; the crush was less. Only the hussars of Denisov's squadron were left on the further side of the river facing the enemy.

Suddenly on the road, where it ran up the rising ground opposite, troops came into sight wearing blue tunics and accompanied by artillery. They were the French.

The officers and the men of Denisov's squadron tried to talk of other things, and to look in other directions, but they all thought continually of nothing else but what was there on the hillside, and they kept constantly glancing towards the dark patches they saw coming into sight on the sky-line. The air was still, and from the hillside there came from time to time the sound of bugles and of the shouts of the enemy. An empty plain, about six hundred yards across, an unassailable borderland was the only dividing-line between the two armies.

One step across that line, that suggests the line dividing the living from the dead, and unknown sufferings and death. And what is there? And who is there? There, beyond that field and that tree and the roofs with the sunlight on them? No one knows, and one longs to know and dreads crossing that line, and still longs to cross it. And one knows that sooner or later one will have to cross it and find out what there is on the other side, just as one must inevitably find out what is on the other side of death. Yet one is strong and well and cheerful and nervously excited, and surrounded by men who are just as strong and excited. . . . That is how every man, even if he does not think, feels in the sight of the enemy, and that feeling gives a peculiar brilliance and keenness to one's impressions of all that takes place at such moments.

A cannon ball whizzed over their heads. The officers, who had been standing together, scattered. All the men looked first at the enemy and then at the commander of their squadron, expecting an order to be given. Another cannon ball flew over them, and a third. There was no doubt that the enemy was firing at them. The hussars did not look round, but at each sound of a flying ball, as though at the word of command, the whole squadron rose in the stirrups, holding their breath, as the ball whizzed by, then sank again. The soldiers did not turn their heads, but glanced out of the corners of their eyes at one another. Every face from Denisov down to the bugler showed about the lips and chin the same lines of conflict and nervous irritability and excitement. Only Rostov on his Rook—a handsome beast, in spite of his unsound legs—had the happy air of a schoolboy. He looked about as though calling upon all to see how unconcerned he was under fire.

Denisov, who could not keep still, galloped back and forth before the squadron.

The staff-captain rode at a walking pace to meet him.

"Well," he said to Denisov, "it won't come to a fight. You'll see, we'll retreat again."

"The devil only knows what they're about!" said Denisov. "Rostov!" he called, noticing his friend. "You've not had long to wait."

At that moment the colonel appeared at the bridge. Denisov galloped up to him.

"Your excellency, let us attack!"

"Attack, indeed!" said the colonel in a bored voice. "What

are you stopping here for? You see the flanks are retreating. Lead the squadron back."

The squadron crossed the bridge and passed out of range of the enemy's guns without losing a single man. It was followed by the second squadron, and the Cossacks last of all crossed, leaving the further side of the river clear.

The two squadrons of the Pavlograd regiment, after crossing the bridge, rode one after the other up the hill. Their colonel, Bogdanitch, was riding at a walking pace not far from Rostov, taking no notice of him, though this was the first time they had met since the incident in connection with Telyanin. Rostov, now feeling himself under the command of the man towards whom he admitted that he had been to blame, never took his eyes off him. It seemed to Rostov at one time that Bogdanitch was only pretending to ignore him and that his whole aim was to test him. Then he thought that Bogdanitch was riding close by him on purpose to show off his own valour. Then the thought struck him that Bogdanitch was now sending the squadron on a hopeless attack on purpose to punish him, Rostov. Then he dreamed of how after the attack he would go up to Bogdanitch as he lay wounded, and hold out his hand in reconciliation.

The high-shouldered figure of Zherkov, who was known to the Pavlograd hussars, as he had not long before left their regiment, rode up to Bogdanitch with an order from the commander of the rear guard.

"Colonel," he said, with gloomy seriousness, "there's an order to go back and burn the bridge."

"An order, *who to?*" asked the colonel grimly.

"Well, I don't know, colonel, *who to*." answered Zherkov, "only the prince commanded me: 'Ride and tell the colonel the hussars are to go back and burn the bridge.' "

Zherkov was followed by a staff officer who rode up to the colonel with the same command. Then Nesvitsky rode up.

"Colonel," he shouted, while still galloping towards him, "I told you to burn the bridge, and now some one's got it wrong. They're all frantic over there, there's no making out anything."

The colonel in a leisurely way stopped the regiment and turned to Nesvitsky. "You never told me to set fire to the bridge! I know my duty, and it's my habit to carry out my orders strictly. You said the bridge will be burnt, but who was going to burn it I couldn't tell. You said, . . ." continued the colonel in an offended tone.

"Colonel," interrupted the staff officer, "there is no time to waste or the enemy will move up their grape-shot guns."

The colonel looked dumbly at the staff officer, at Nesvitsky, at Zherkov, and scowled.

"I will burn the bridge," he said solemnly as though to express that in spite of everything they might do to annoy him, he would still do his duty.

Beating his long muscular legs against his horse, as though the beast were to blame for it all, the colonel moved forward and commanded the second squadron, the one under Denisov's command, in which Rostov was serving, to turn back to the bridge.

"Yes, it really is so," thought Rostov, "he wants to test me!" His heart throbbed and the blood rushed to his face. "Let him see whether I'm a coward!" he thought. Rostov looked steadily at his enemy, the colonel. But the colonel never once glanced at Rostov.

The word of command was given.

The hussars dismounted quickly, not knowing themselves what they were to do. The soldiers crossed themselves. Rostov did not look at the colonel now; he had no time. He dreaded, with a sinking heart he dreaded, being left behind.

"Stretchers!" shouted a voice behind him. Rostov did not think of the meaning of the need of stretchers. He ran along, trying only to be ahead of all. But just at the bridge, not watching where he was going, he slipped in the mud, and stumbling, fell on his hands. The others ran past him. Getting up and rubbing his muddy hands on his riding-breeches, he looked round at his enemy, the colonel. He wanted to run on further, thinking that the farther he went the better it would be.

Meanwhile Nesvitsky, Zherkov, and the staff officer were standing together out of range of the enemy, watching the little group of men in yellow shakoes, dark-green jackets, embroidered with frogs, and blue riding-breeches, swarming about the bridge, and on the other side of the river the blue tunics of the French approaching in the distance.

"Will they be able to burn the bridge or not? Who'll get there first? Will the French train their grape-shot on them and kill them?" These were the questions that, with sinking heart, each man was asking himself in the great mass of troops overlooking the bridge. In the brilliant evening sunshine they gazed at the bridge and the hussars and at the blue tunics of the French, with bayonets and guns, moving up on the other side.

"The hussars will be caught!" said Nesvitsky. "They're in range of grape-shot now."

"He was wrong to take so many men," said the staff officer.

"Yes, that's grape-shot," said Nesvitsky pointing to the French guns, which had just been taken out of the gun-carriages.

On the French side, smoke rose from the cannons. One puff, a second and a third almost at the same time; and at the very moment when they heard the sound of the first shot, there rose the smoke of a fourth; two booms came one after another, then a third.

"Oh!" cried Nesvitsky, clutching the arm of the staff officer. "Look, a man has fallen!"

"Two, I think."

"If I were Tsar, I'd never make war," said Nesvitsky, turning away.

The French cannons were quickly loaded again. The French infantry in their blue tunics ran towards the bridge. There were more puffs of smoke and grape-shot rattled and cracked on the bridge. A thick cloud of smoke had risen from it. The hussars had succeeded in setting fire to the bridge, and the French batteries were firing at them now, not to hinder them, but because their guns had been brought up and they had some one to fire at.

The French had time to fire three volleys of grape-shot before the hussars got back to their horses. The last volley fell in the middle of the group of hussars and knocked down three men.

Rostov stepped on the bridge, not knowing what he had to do. There was no one to slash at with his sword. That was how he always pictured a battle to himself. And he could be of no use in burning the bridge, because he had not brought with him any wisps of straw, like the other soldiers. He stood and looked about him, when suddenly there was a rattle on the bridge, like a lot of nuts being scattered, and one of the hussars, the one standing nearest him, fell with a groan on the railing. Rostov ran up to him with others. Again some one shouted. "Stretchers!" Four men took hold of the hussar and began lifting him up. "Oooo! . . . Let me be, for Christ's sake!" shrieked the wounded man. But still they lifted him up and laid him on the stretcher.

Rostov turned away, and began staring into the distance, at the waters of the Danube, at the sky, at the sun, as though he was searching for something. How fair that sky seemed, how blue and calm and deep! How brilliant seemed the setting sun. And the far-away mountains that showed blue beyond the Danube, the nunnery, the pine forests, filled with mist to the tree-tops . . . There all was peace and happiness. . . .

At that moment the sun went behind the clouds.

More stretchers were brought. And the terror of death and of the stretchers, and the loss of the sunshine and life, all blended into one sensation of sickening fear.

"Good God, Thou who art in Heaven, save and forgive, and protect me," Rostov whispered.

The hussars ran back to their horses; their voices grew

louder and more assured; the stretchers disappeared from sight.

"It's all over, and I'm a coward. Yes, I'm a coward," thought Rostov. And he mounted his Rook. "But no one seems to have noticed it," Rostov thought to himself.

And no one had noticed it at all.

"Inform the prince that I have burnt the bridge," said the colonel, in a triumphant tone.

"And if he inquires about the losses?"

"Not worth mentioning," boomed the colonel. "Two hussars wounded, and one stark dead on the spot."

Pursued by the French army of a hundred thousand men under the command of Bonaparte, received with hostility by the inhabitants, losing confidence in their allies, suffering from shortness of supplies, and forced to act under circumstances unlike anything that had been foreseen, the Russian army of thirty-five thousand men, under the command of Kutuzov, retreated to the lower ground about the Danube. The Austrian troops that had escaped capture at Ulm, and had joined Kutuzov's forces at Braunau, now parted from the Russian army, and Kutuzov was left unsupported with his weak and exhausted forces. The defence of Vienna could no longer be dreamed of. The sole aim—almost a hopeless one—that remained now for Kutuzov was to avoid losing his army, like Mack at Ulm, and to effect a junction with fresh troops marching from Russia.

On the 28th of October, Kutuzov took his army across to the left bank of the Danube, and then for the first time halted, leaving the Danube between his army and the greater part of the enemy's forces. On the 30th he attacked Mortier's division, which was on the left bank of the Danube, and defeated it. In this action for the first time trophies were taken —a flag, cannons, and two French generals. For the first time, after retreating for two whole weeks, the Russian troops had halted, and after fighting had not merely kept the field of battle, but had driven the French off it. Although the troops were without clothing and exhausted, and had lost a third of their strength in wounded, killed, and missing; although they had left their sick and wounded behind on the other side of the Danube, with a letter from Kutuzov commending them to the humanity of the enemy; although the hospitals and houses in Krems could not contain all the sick and wounded,—in spite of all that, the halt before Krems and the victory over Mortier had raised the spirits of the troops. Throughout the whole army, and also at headquarters, there were the most optimistic but groundless rumours of the near approach of the troops from Russia, of some victory gained by the Austrians, and of the retreat of Bonaparte panic-stricken.

During this time Prince André had been in attendance on the Austrian general Schmidt, who was killed in the battle. He himself had received a slight wound on his arm. And so as a mark of special favour on the part of Kutuzov, the commander-in-chief, he was sent with the news of this victory to the Austrian court, now at Brünn, as Vienna was threatened by the French.

It was quite dark when Prince André rode into Brünn. At the entrance of the palace an official ran out to meet him, and learning that he was a special messenger, led him to another entrance.

"Turn to the right at the end of the corridor. You will find the adjutant on duty," the official said to him. "He will conduct you to the minister of war."

The adjutant on duty asked Prince André to wait, and went in to the war minister. Five minutes later he returned, and with marked courtesy, bowing and ushering Prince André before him, he led him across the corridor to the private room of the war minister. The adjutant, by his elaborately formal courtesy, seemed to wish to guard himself from any attempt at familiarity on the part of the Russian adjutant. The joyous feeling of Prince André was considerably damped as he approached the door of the minister's room. He felt slighted, and the feeling of being slighted passed instantaneously—without his being aware of it himself—into a feeling of disdain, which was quite uncalled for. His subtle brain at the same instant supplied him with the point of view from which he had the right to feel disdain both of the adjutant and the minister of war. "No doubt it seems to them a very simple matter to win victories, never having smelt powder!" he thought. His eyelids drooped disdainfully; he walked with peculiar deliberateness into the war minister's room.

The minister of war was sitting at a big table, and for the first two minutes he took no notice of Prince André. His bald head, with grey curls on the temple, was held low between two wax candles. He was reading some papers, and marking them with a pencil. He went on reading to the end, without raising his eyes.

"Take this and give it to him," he said to his adjutant, handing him a few papers and still taking no notice of Prince André. Then he put the remaining papers together, making their edges level, and lifted his head. He had an intellectual face but the instant he turned to Prince André, his shrewd and determined expression changed in a manner evidently conscious and habitual. On his face was left the stupid smile—

hypocritical, and not disguising its hypocrisy—of a man who receives many petitioners, one after another.

"From General—Field Marshal Kutuzov?" he asked. "Good news, I hope? Has there been an engagement with Mortier? A victory? It was high time!"

He took the despatch, which was addressed to him, and began to read it.

"Oh! My God! My God! Schmidt!" he said in German. "What a tragedy! What a tragedy!" Skimming through the despatch, he laid it on the table and looked at Prince André, meditating on something.

"Oh, what a tragedy! So the action, you say, was a decisive one? Mortier was not taken, however," he added. "Very glad you have brought good news, though the death of Schmidt is a costly price for the victory. His majesty will certainly wish to see you, but not to-day. I thank you. . . . To-morrow, be at the levée after the review."

The stupid smile, which had disappeared while he was talking, reappeared on the war minister's face.

"*Au revoir,* I thank you indeed. His majesty the Emperor will most likely wish to see you," he repeated, and he bowed his head.

Prince André stayed at Brünn with Bilibin, a Russian of his acquaintance in the diplomatic service.

"Ah, my dear prince, there's no one I could have been more pleased to see," said Bilibin, coming to meet Prince André. "Franz, take the prince's things to my bedroom," he said to the servant, who was ushering Prince André in. "What, a messenger of victory? That's wonderful! I'm kept indoors ill, as you see."

After washing and dressing, Prince André came into Bilibin's luxurious study and sat down to the dinner prepared for him. Bilibin was sitting quietly at the fireplace.

Not his journey only, but all the time he had spent with the army on the march, deprived of all the conveniences of cleanliness and the elegancies of life, made Prince André feel now an agreeable sense of repose among the luxurious surroundings to which he had been accustomed from childhood. Moreover, after his Austrian reception, he was glad to speak—if not in Russian, for they talked French—at least to a Russian, who would, he imagined, share the general Russian dislike for the Austrians.

Bilibin was a man of five-and-thirty, a bachelor, of the same circle as Prince André. They had known each other in Petersburg, but had become more intimate during Prince André's last stay in Vienna with Kutuzov. Just as Prince André was a young man, who promised to rise high in military life, Bilibin promised to do even better in diplomacy. He was still a young man, but not a young diplomat, as he had been in the service since he was sixteen. He had been in Paris and in Copenhagen; and now in Vienna he filled a post of considerable importance. Both the foreign minister and the Russian ambassador at Vienna knew him and valued him. He was one of those diplomats who like work and understand it, and in spite of his natural indolence, he often spent nights at his writing-table. He worked equally well whatever the object of his work might be. Bilibin's merits were valued still more because of his ease in moving and talking in the higher spheres. His conversation was continually sprinkled with original, epigrammatic, polished phrases of general interest. He fashioned these phrases so that insignificant people could easily remember them and carry them from drawing-room to drawing-room. And Bilibin's good things were hawked about in Viennese drawing-rooms and afterwards had an influence on so-called great events.

"Come, now, tell us about your victories," he said.

Prince André in the most modest fashion, without once mentioning himself in connection with it, described the engagement, and afterwards his reception by the war minister. "They received me and my news like a dog," he concluded.

Bilibin grinned.

"All the same," he said, gazing from a distance at his finger-nails, "notwithstanding my high esteem for the holy Russian armament, I own that your victory is not so remarkably victorious."

He went on talking in French, only uttering in Russian those words to which he wished to give a contemptuous intonation.

"Why, with the whole mass of your army you fell upon the unlucky Mortier with one division, and Mortier slipped through your fingers? Where's the victory?"

Prince André answered, "We can at least say without boasting that it's rather better than Ulm . . ."

"Why didn't you capture, at least, one marshal?"

"Because everything isn't done as one expects it will be, and things are not as regular as on parade. We had expected, as I told you, to attack the enemy in the rear at seven o'clock in the morning, but we did not arrive until five o'clock in the evening."

"But why didn't you do it at seven in the morning? You ought to have done it at seven in the morning," said Bilibin, smiling. "You ought to have done it at seven in the morning. . . . I know you are thinking that it's very easy to capture marshals, sitting on the sofa by one's fireside. That's true, but still why didn't you capture him? And you needn't feel surprised if the most august Emperor and King Francis, like the war minister, is not very jubilant over your victory. Why, even I, a poor secretary of the Russian Embassy, feel no necessity to rejoice." He looked straight at Prince André.

"Now it's my turn to ask you 'why,'" said Prince André. "I must admit that I don't understand it. Mack loses a whole army. Archduke Ferdinand and Archduke Karl give no sign of life and make one blunder after another. Kutuzov alone gains a decisive victory, breaks the prestige of invincibility of the French, and the minister of war does not even care to learn the details!"

"What has the Austrian court to do with your victories? Archduke Karl does nothing, Archduke Ferdinand covers himself with disgrace, you abandon Vienna, give up its defence. One general, whom we all loved, Schmidt, you put in the way of a bullet, and then ask us to congratulate you on your victory! . . . You must admit that anything more exasperating than the news you have brought could not be conceived. It's as though it were done on purpose, done on purpose. But apart from that, if you were to gain a really brilliant victory, if Archduke Karl even were to win a victory, what effect could it have on the general course of events? It's too late now, when Vienna is occupied by the French forces."

"Occupied? Vienna occupied?"

"Not only is Vienna occupied, but Bonaparte is at Schönbrunn. Count Lichtenfels was here this morning," pursued Bilibin, "and he showed me a letter containing a full description of the parade of the French at Vienna. Prince Murat and all the rest of it."

"How was Vienna taken? And its bridge and its famous fortifications, and Prince Auersperg?" asked Prince André confused. "We heard rumours that Prince Auersperg was defending Vienna."

"Prince Auersperg is stationed on this side—our side—and is defending us; defending us very ineffectually, I imagine, but any way he is defending us. But Vienna's on the other side of the river. No, the bridge has not been taken, and I hope it won't be taken, because it is mined and orders have been given to blow it up. If it were not so, we should have long ago been in the mountains of Bohemia."

"But that doesn't mean that the campaign is over," said Prince André.

"I believe that it is over. And so does everyone here, though they don't dare to say so. And I'll tell you what else I think. Austria has been made a fool of! She is not used to that! And she'll avenge it. She has been made a fool of because in the first place her provinces have been pillaged by our Russian armies, her army has been destroyed, her capital has been taken . . . And so between ourselves my instinct tells me we are being deceived. My instinct tells me of negotiations with France and talks of peace, a secret peace, concluded separately."

"That's not possible!" said Prince André.

"Time will show," said Bilibin.

At the levée the Emperor Francis only looked intently into Prince André's face, and nodded his long head to him as he stood in the place assigned him among the Austrian officers. But after the levée the adjutant of the previous evening ceremoniously communicated to Prince André the Emperor's desire to grant him an audience. The Emperor Francis received him, standing in the middle of the room. Prince André was struck by the fact that before beginning the conversation, the Emperor seemed embarrassed, didn't know what to say, and reddened.

"Tell me when the battle began," he asked quickly. Prince André answered. This question was followed by others just as simple: "Was Kutuzov well?" "How long was it since he left Krems?" and so on. The Emperor spoke as though his sole aim was to ask a certain number of questions. The answers were of no interest to him.

"At what time did the battle begin?" asked the Emperor.

"I cannot inform your majesty at what time the battle began in the front lines, but at Dürenstein, where I was, the troops began the attack about six in the evening," said Prince André, growing more eager, and thinking that now there was a chance for him to give an accurate description, just as he had it ready in his head, of all he knew and had seen.

But the Emperor smiled and interrupted him: "How many miles?"

"From where to where, your majesty?"

"From Dürenstein to Krems?"

"Three and a half miles, your majesty."

"The French abandoned the left bank?"

"The last crossed the river on rafts in the night."

"Have you enough provisions at Krems?"

"Provisions have not been furnished to the amount . . ."

The Emperor interrupted him: "At what time was General Schmidt killed?"

"At seven o'clock, I think."

"At seven o'clock? Very sad! very sad!"

The Emperor thanked him, and bowed.

Prince André withdrew, and was at once surrounded by courtiers on all sides. Everywhere he saw friendly eyes gazing at him, and heard friendly voices speaking to him. The adjutant of the previous evening reproached him for not having stayed at the palace, and offered him the hospitality of his own house. The minister of war came up and congratulated him on the Order of Maria Theresa of the third grade, with which the Emperor was presenting him. The Empress's chamberlain invited him to her majesty. The archduchess, too, wished to see him. Prince André did not know whom to answer first.

The Russian ambassador took him by the shoulder, led him away to a window, and began to talk to him.

Contrary to Bilibin's warning, the news he brought was received with rejoicing. A thanksgiving service was arranged. Kutuzov was decorated with the great cross of Maria Theresa, and rewards were bestowed on the whole army. Prince André received many invitations and had to spend the whole morning paying visits to the principal officials of the Austrian Government.

After paying his visits, Prince André, at five o'clock in the evening, returned to Bilibin's, mentally composing a letter to his father about the battle and his reception at Brünn. At the steps of Bilibin's house stood a cart packed half full of things, and Franz, Bilibin's servant, came out of the doorway, with difficulty dragging a travelling-trunk.

"What are you doing?" asked Prince André.

"Ah, your excellency!" said Franz, pushing the trunk up on to the cart. "We are to move on still farther. The scoundrel is at our heels again!"

"What?" asked Prince André.

Bilibin came out. He was excited.

"Where do you come from that you don't know what every coachman in the town knows?" he asked Prince André.

"I come from the archduchess. I heard nothing there."

"And didn't you see that people are packing up everywhere?"

"I have seen nothing . . . But what's the matter?" Prince André asked impatiently.

"What's the matter? The matter is that the French have crossed the bridge that Auersperg was defending, and they haven't blown up the bridge, so that Murat is at this moment running along the road to Brünn, and to-day or to-morrow they'll be here."

"Here? But how is it the bridge wasn't blown up, since it was mined?"

"Why, that's what I ask you. No one—not Bonaparte himself—can tell why."

Prince André shrugged his shoulders. "If they have crossed the bridge, then it is all over with the army. It will be cut off," he said.

"That's the whole point," answered Bilibin. "Listen. The French enter Vienna, as I told you. Everything is satisfactory.

Next day, that is yesterday, the French marshals Murat, Lannes, and Beliard get on their horses and ride off to the bridge. 'Gentlemen,' says one, 'Our gracious Emperor Napoleon will be pleased if we take the bridge. Let us go us three and take it.' These three gentlemen advance to the bridge alone and wave white handkerchiefs; they declare that it's a truce, and that they, the marshals, are come for a parley with Prince Auersperg. They tell the officer on duty a thousand absurdities; say that the war is over, that Emperor Francis has arranged a meeting with Bonaparte, that they desire to see Prince Auersperg, and so on. The officer sends for Auersperg. These French gentlemen embrace the officers, make jokes, and sit about on the cannons, while a French battalion meantime advances unnoticed on the bridge. Finally the lieutenant-general himself appears, our dear Prince Auersperg von Mautern. 'My dear enemy! Flower of Austrian chivalry! Hero of the Turkish war! Hostility is at end, we can shake hands . . . the Emperor Napoleon burns with impatience to make the acquaintance of Prince Auersperg.' In a word, these French gentlemen so bewilder Auersperg with fair words, he is so flattered at this intimacy with French marshals, so dazzled by the spectacle of their cloaks, and of the ostrich feathers of Murat, that he forgets that he ought to be firing on the enemy. A French battalion comes upon the bridge, spikes the cannons, and the bridge is taken."

After a pause Bilibin continued. "And that's not the worst of it. The sergeant in charge of the cannon which was to give the signal for firing the mines and blowing up the bridge, this sergeant seeing the French troops running on to the bridge wanted to fire, but, the French marshal, Lannes, pulled his arm away. The sergeant, who was sharper than his general, goes up to Auersperg and says: 'Prince, they're deceiving you, here are the French!' Murat sees the game is up if he lets the sergeant have his say. With an affectation of surprise he addresses Auersperg: 'Is this the Austrian discipline so highly praised all over the world?' says he. 'Do you let a man of low rank speak to you like this?' It was a stroke of genius. The Prince of Auersperg, with his honour questioned, has the sergeant put under arrest!"

"It is treason!" said Prince André.

"No," said Bilibin. "It is not treason, nor cowardice, nor stupidity; it is just as it was at Ulm . . .

"Where are you off to?" he said, suddenly turning to Prince André who started into the house.

"I must go at once."

"Where to?"

"To the army."

"You meant to stay another two days?"

"But now I must go at once." And Prince André went to his room.

"Do you know," said Bilibin, coming into his room, "I have been thinking about you. What are you going for?"

Prince André looked at him and did not reply.

"Why are you going? I know you consider that it's your duty to gallop off to the army now that the army is in danger. I understand that, but look at things from the other side, and you will see that it is your duty, on the contrary, to take care of yourself. Leave that to others who are no good for anything else . . . You have received no orders to go back, and you are not dismissed from here, so that you can remain and go with us, where our ill-luck takes us. They say we are going to Olmütz. And Olmütz is a very charming town. And we can travel there comfortably together in my carriage."

Prince André did not answer.

"I am speaking to you sincerely as a friend," Bilibin continued. "Consider where are you going and with what object, when you can stay here. You have two alternatives before you. Either you won't reach the army before peace is concluded, or you will share the defeat and disgrace with Kutuzov's whole army."

The same night, Prince André set out to join the army, not knowing where he would find it, and at the risk of being caught by the French.

At Brünn all the court and every one connected with it was packing up, and the heavy baggage was already being sent on to Olmütz.

At one place Prince André came out on the road along which the Russian army was pushing ahead as fast as possible and in the greatest disorder. The road was so blocked by baggage-waggons that it was impossible to get by in a carriage. Prince André got a horse and a Cossack from the officer in command of the Cossacks, and hungry and weary he made his way in and out between the waggons and rode in search of Kutuzov and his own luggage.

On the road he heard the rumours about the position and condition of the Russian army. And seeing the disorder he believed the rumours. "If there's nothing left but to die?" he thought. "Well, if it must be! I will do it no worse than others."

Prince André looked at the endless, confused mass of companies, of baggage-waggons, artillery, store-waggons, carts, and waggons of every possible description, following one another and blocking the muddy road three and four abreast. On every side, behind and before, as far as the ear could hear in every direction there was the rumble of wheels, the rattle of carts, of waggons, and of gun-carriages, the tramp of horses, the crack of whips, the shouts of drivers, the swearing of soldiers, of orderlies, and officers. At the sides of the roads he saw fallen horses, and sometimes their skinned carcases, broken-down waggons, with solitary soldiers sitting on them waiting for something, groups of soldiers strayed from their companies, starting off to neighbouring villages, or dragging back from them chickens, sheep, hay, or other things. Where the road went uphill or downhill the crush became greater, and there was an uninterrupted roar of shouts. The soldiers floundering knee-deep in the mud clutched the guns and clung to the waggons in the midst of cracking whips, slipping hoofs, breaking traces and throat-splitting yells.

He rode up to a convoy, intending to ask where he could find the commander-in-chief. But just then a strange vehicle, with one horse, came along. A soldier was driving it, and under an improvised leathern hood sat a woman, muffled up in shawls. The officer, directing the traffic, aimed a blow at the soldier who drove the cart, for trying to push in ahead of others, and the lash fell on the leather hood. The woman shrieked. Then catching sight of Prince André, she held out her thin arms and screamed: "Adjutant! Sir! . . . For God's sake! . . . Protect me . . . I am the wife of the doctor of the Seventh Chasseurs . . . They won't let us pass, we have dropped behind, lost our own people. . . ."

"I'll thrash you into mincemeat! Turn back!" shouted the officer to the soldier. "Turn back with your hussy!"

"Sir, protect us!" screamed the doctor's wife.

"Kindly let this cart get through. Don't you see that it is a woman?" said Prince André, riding up to the officer.

The officer looked at him, and without answering turned again to the soldier. "I'll teach you how to push in. . . . Back! . . ."

"Let it pass, I tell you," repeated Prince André.

"And who are you?" cried the officer, turning upon him suddenly with fury. "Who are you? Are you in command? I'm commanding officer here, not you!" Then, again threatening the soldier, he repeated, "I'll lash you into mincemeat." The expression evidently pleased the officer.

The officer had hardly spoken the last words when Prince André rode up to him and, raising his riding-whip, cried: "Let—them—pass!"

The officer drew back. "It's all their doing, these staff-officers, all the disorder," he grumbled as he rode away.

Prince André then galloped on towards the village, where he was told that he would find Kutuzov.

On reaching the village, he got off his horse, and looked round. A familiar voice called his name. Out of a little window of the first house was thrust the handsome face of Nesvitsky.

Going into the house, Prince André found Nesvitsky and another adjutant eating. Had he any news? They looked alarmed and uneasy, especially Nesvitsky, whose face was usually so full of laughter.

"Where is the commander-in-chief?" asked Prince André.

"Here in this house," answered the adjutant.

"Well, is it true, about the peace and surrender?" asked Nesvitsky.

"I know nothing except that I have had great difficulty in getting through."

"I was wrong to laugh at Mack; there's worse in store for us," said Nesvitsky. "But sit down, have something to eat."

"You won't find your baggage or anything now, prince," said the adjutant.

"Well, I got everything I wanted packed up on two horses," said Nesvitsky. "I can go as far as the Bohemian mountains at least."

"What is Kutuzov doing here?" asked Prince André.

"I don't know," said Nesvitsky.

"I know one thing, it's all horrible, horrible!" said Prince André, and he went to find Kutuzov.

Kutuzov was in an inner room with Prince Bagration and Weierother, the Austrian general, who had taken Schmidt's place.

Prince André went towards the door from which the sound of voices came. But at the moment when he was going to open the door, the voices in the room paused, the door opened of itself, and Kutuzov with his eagle nose and podgy face appeared in the doorway. Prince André was standing exactly opposite Kutuzov; but from the expression of the commander-in-chief's one seeing eye it was evident that thought and anxiety so engrossed him as to veil, as it were, his vision. He looked straight into Prince André's face and did not recognise him.

Bagration, a short lean man, not yet elderly, with a resolute and impassive face of oriental type, came out after the commander-in-chief.

"I have the honour to report myself," Prince André said for the second time, rather loudly, as he handed Kutuzov an envelope.

"Ah, from Vienna? Very good! Later, later!" Kutuzov went out to the steps with Bagration.

"Well, prince, good-bye," he said to Bagration. "Christ be with you! May my blessing bring you a great victory!" Kutuzov's face suddenly softened, and there were tears on his cheeks. With his left arm he drew Bagration to him, while with his right hand, on which he wore a ring, he made the sign of the cross over him. Then he offered him his podgy cheek, but Bagration kissed him on the neck. "Christ be with you!" repeated Kutuzov, and he went towards his carriage. "Get in with me," he said to Prince André.

"Your Most High Excellency, I should have liked to be of use here. Allow me to remain in Prince Bagration's detachment."

"Get in," said Kutuzov, and seeing that Prince André still hesitated: "I have need of good officers myself, myself."

They took their seats in the carriage and drove for some minutes in silence.

"There is a great deal, a great deal of everything still before us," Kutuzov said, as though he knew everything that was in Prince André's heart.

Kutuzov had received from one of his spies information that showed the Russian army was in an almost hopeless position. The spy reported that the French, after crossing the bridge at Vienna, were moving in immense force on Kutuzov's line of communications with the reinforcements marching from Russia.

"If one-tenth part of Bagration's detachment comes in, I shall thank God," said Kutuzov, as though talking to himself.

Prince André looked at Kutuzov. And his eyes were caught by the carefully washed scar on his temple, where the bullet had gone through his head at Ismail, and the empty eyesocket. "Yes, he has the right to speak so calmly of the destruction of these men," thought Prince André. "That's why I ask you to send me to that detachment," he said aloud.

Kutuzov did not answer. He sat plunged in thought.

Five minutes later, swaying easily on the soft carriage springs, Kutuzov spoke to Prince André. There was no trace of emotion on his face now. With delicate irony he questioned Prince André about the details of his interview with the Emperor, about the comments he had heard at Court, and about ladies of their common acquaintance.

Before four o'clock in the afternoon Prince André, who had persuaded Kutuzov, reached Grunte, and joined Bagration.

In Bagration's detachment, they knew nothing of what had happened. They talked about peace, but did not believe it possible. They talked of a battle, but did not believe that a battle was close at hand either.

Knowing Prince André to be a favourite and trusted adjutant, Bagration received him with special graciousness and condescension. He told him that there would probably be an engagement that day or the next day, and gave him full liberty to remain in attendance on him during the battle, or to retire to the rear-guard to watch over the order of the retreat, also a matter of great importance.

"If this is one of the common run of little staff dandies, sent here to win a cross, he can do that in the rear-guard, but if he wants to be with me, let him . . . he'll be of use, if he's a brave officer," thought Bagration.

Prince André asked permission to ride round and look over the disposition of the forces. A staff officer was ordered to accompany him.

As they rode along, on all sides, they saw officers drenched through, with dejected faces, apparently looking for something, and soldiers dragging doors, benches, and fences from the village.

"We can't put a stop to this," said the staff-officer, pointing to them. "Their commanders let their companies get out of hand. And look here," he pointed to a canteen-keeper's booth, "they gather here, and sit. I drove them all out this morning, and look, it's full again. I must go and scare them, prince. One moment."

"Let us go together, and I'll get some bread and cheese there," said Prince André, who had not yet eaten.

They got off their horses and went into the canteen-keeper's booth. Several officers were sitting at the tables, eating and drinking.

"Now what does this mean, gentlemen?" said the staff-officer, in the reproachful tone of a man who has repeated the same thing several times. "The prince gave orders that no one was to leave his post. Come, really, captain," he said to a muddy, thin little artillery officer, who in his stockings stood up smiling not quite naturally.

"Now aren't you ashamed, Captain Tushin?" added the staff-officer. "I should have thought you as an artillery officer would set an example, and you have no boots on!"

"The soldiers say it's easier barefoot," said Captain Tushin, smiling shyly, trying to carry off his awkward position with a joke. But before he had finished speaking he could see that his joke had failed. He was confused.

"Go to your places," said the staff-officer.

Prince André glanced at the little artillery officer. There was something completely unsoldier-like about him, rather comic, but very attractive.

The staff-officer and Prince André got on their horses and rode on.

Riding out beyond the village, continually meeting or overtaking soldiers and officers of various ranks, they saw on the left earthworks being thrown up, still red with the freshly dug clay. Several battalions of soldiers, in their shirt-sleeves, in spite of the cold wind were working like ants at these entrenchments.

They rode up the opposite hill. From that hill they had a view of the French.

"You see there is where our battery stands," said the staff-officer pointing to the highest spot. "It is commanded by that queer fellow sitting without his boots; from there you can see everything; let us go there, prince."

"I am very grateful to you, I'll go on alone now," said Prince André. "Don't trouble yourself further, please."

The staff-officer left him, and Prince André rode on alone.

The further forward and the nearer to the French he went, the more orderly and cheerful he found the troops. At Grunte a certain alarm and vague dread could be felt. But the nearer Prince André got to the enemy line, the more self-confident were the men. They were dotted all over the plain, dragging logs and brushwood, building shanties, talking together, and laughing. They were sitting round the fires drying shirts and boots. They were gathered round the porridge-pots and caul-drons. In one company mess was ready, and the soldiers watched the steaming pots and waited. In another company, a lucky one, for not all had vodka, the soldiers stood in a group round a broad-shouldered, pock-marked sergeant, who was tilting a keg of vodka, and pouring it into the covers of the canteens held out to him.

As Prince André rode into the ranks of the Kiev Grenadiers, he came upon a platoon of grenadiers, before whom lay a man stripped naked. Two soldiers were holding him, while two others were beating him with switches. The man shrieked. A stout major was walking up and down in front of the platoon, and regardless of the screams, he kept saying: "It's a disgrace for a soldier to steal; a soldier must be honest, honourable, and brave, and to steal from a comrade, he must be without honour indeed, a monster. Again, again!"

Prince André, reaching the front line, rode along it until he came to the center. At this place the French and Russian lines came so close that the soldiers of the two armies could talk together. And although it was strictly forbidden the men were fraternizing and laughing together with such good humour that it seemed as though they must unload their guns, blow up their ammunition, and all hurry away back to their homes.

But the guns remained loaded, the port-holes in the earth-works looked out as menacingly as ever, and the cannons, taken off their platforms, confronted one another.

After making a circuit round the whole line of the army, from the right flank to the left, Prince André rode up to that battery from which the staff-officer had told him that the whole field could be seen. Here he dismounted and standing close to one of the four cannons looked out over the countryside where the French and Russian forces were encamped. He studied the scene for a long time and all the while he heard voices coming from a little shanty close by.

At first Prince André did not pay attention to what the men were saying, but then he recognised a voice which seemed familiar. He listened.

"No," said the familiar voice. "If one knew what would happen after death, then not one of us would be afraid of death."

Another voice answered: "But afraid or not afraid, there's no escaping it."

"Why, you're always afraid!" said a third voice laughing.

"Still one is afraid," repeated the first voice, the one Prince André knew. "One's afraid of the unknown, that's what it is. It's all very well to say the soul goes to heaven . . . But this we do know, that there is no heaven, but only atmosphere."

The third voice interrupted.

"Give us a drop of your herb-brandy, Tushin," it said.

"Oh, it's the captain, who had his boots off in the canteen booth," thought Prince André.

"Herb-brandy . . ." said Tushin. "But still to conceive of a future life . . ." He did not finish his sentence.

At that moment there was a whiz heard in the air. Nearer, nearer, faster and more distinctly, and faster it came. And the cannon-ball, as though not uttering all it had to say, pounded into the earth not far from the shanty, tearing up the soil. The earth seemed to moan. At the same moment there dashed out of the shanty, before any of the rest, little Tushin. His shrewd, good-humoured face was pale. After him came an infantry officer, who ran off to his company, buttoning his coat as he ran.

Prince André mounted his horse but he did not ride off. His eyes moved rapidly over the wide plain. He saw the great masses of the French troops suddenly come to life. Two Frenchmen on horseback, doubtless adjutants, were galloping on the hill. A small column of the enemy, distinctly visible, was moving downhill, to strengthen the front line. The smoke of the first shot had not cleared away, when there was a fresh puff of smoke and another shot.

Prince André turned his horse and galloped back toward Grunte to look for Prince Bagration. Behind him he heard the cannonade becoming louder and more frequent. Musket shots could also be heard below at the place where the lines were the closest.

"It has begun! Here it comes!" thought Prince André, feeling the blood rush to his heart.

Passing between the companies that had been eating porridge and drinking vodka a quarter of an hour before, he saw soldiers forming in ranks and getting their guns.

Before he reached the earthworks that were being thrown up, he saw in the evening light of the dull autumn day men on horseback crossing towards him. The first, wearing a cloak and an Astrakhan cap, was riding on a white horse. It was Prince Bagration. With him were three staff-officers and his private adjutant, Zherkov. Prince Bagration, recognising Prince André, nodded to him and stopped. He still looked ahead while Prince André told him what he had been seeing, and nodded in answer to Prince André's words, as though to say: "Very good." He did this with an expression that seemed to say that all that happened, and all that was told him, was exactly what he had foreseen.

A few minutes later, as they were all riding up toward Tushin's battery, a ball struck the ground before them. Then again there was a sudden whiz, which ended abruptly in a thud. A Cossack, riding a little behind dropped from his horse to the ground. Zherkov and one of the staff-officers bent forward over their saddles and turned their horses away. The Cossack was dead, the horse was still struggling.

Prince Bagration dropped his eyelids, looked round, and seeing the cause of the delay, turned away indifferently, seeming to ask, "Why notice these trivial details?"

They then rode up to the very battery from which Prince André had surveyed the field of battle.

"Whose company?" Prince Bagration asked of the artilleryman standing at the ammunition boxes.

"Captain Tushin's, your excellency."

"To be sure, to be sure," said Bagration. And he rode to the end cannon. Just as he reached it, a shot boomed from the cannon, deafening him and his aides. A big broad-shouldered soldier, gunner number one, with a mop, darted up to the wheel and planted himself, his legs wide apart; while number two, with a shaking hand, put the charge into the cannon's mouth; the officer Tushin dashed forward, not noticing the general, and looked out, shading his eyes with his little hand.

"Another two points higher, and it will be just right," he shouted in a shrill voice. "Two!" he piped. "Smash away!"

Bagration called and Tushin went up to him, putting three fingers to the peak of his cap with a timid and awkward gesture, more like a priest blessing some one than a soldier saluting. Though Tushin's guns were supposed to blast the valley, he was instead firing shells at the village of Schöngraben, where there were great masses of French soldiers.

No one had given Tushin instructions at what to fire, and after consulting his sergeant, for whom he had a great respect, he had decided that it would be a good thing to set fire to the village. "Very good!" Bagration said.

Just as he was leaving the battery, shots were heard in the woods on the left. And as it was too far for him to go himself, Prince Bagration despatched Zherkov to tell the senior general, the general whose regiment had been inspected by Kutuzov at Braunau, to retreat as rapidly as possible as the right flank would probably not long be able to hold the enemy. Tushin, and the battalion that was to have defended his battery, was forgotten. Prince André listened carefully to Bagration's conversations with the commanding officers, and to the orders he gave them. And he noticed, to his astonishment, that no orders were really given by Prince Bagration at all but that he confined himself to trying to appear as though everything that was being done of necessity, by chance, or at the will of individual officers, was all done, if not by his order, at least in accordance with his wishes.

After riding up to the highest point of the right flank, Prince Bagration and his party began to go downhill, where a continuous roll of musketry was heard and nothing could be seen for the smoke. The nearer they got to the hollow the less they could see, and the more distinctly could be felt the nearness of the actual battle. They began to meet wounded men. Two soldiers were dragging one along, supporting him on each side. His head was covered with blood. He had no cap, and was coughing and spitting. The bullet had apparently entered his mouth or throat. Another one came towards them, walking alone without his gun, groaning aloud.

Crossing the road, they began going down a steep slope where they saw several men lying on the ground. They were met by a crowd of soldiers, among them some who were not wounded. The soldiers were hurrying up the hill, gasping for breath, and talking loudly together. Their commanding officer, seeing Bagration, ran after them, calling them to come back.

Bagration rode up to the ranks, along which there was here and there a rapid snapping of shots drowning the talk of the soldiers and the shouts of the officers. The whole air was reeking with smoke. The soldiers' faces were smudged with powder. Some were plugging with their ramrods, others were putting powder on the touch-pans, and getting charges out of their pouches, others were firing their guns. But it was impossible to see at whom they were firing from the smoke, which the wind did not lift.

A thin, weak-looking colonel, with an amiable smile and eyelids that half-covered his old-looking eyes, rode up to Prince Bagration and received him as though he were welcoming an honoured guest into his house. He announced to

Prince Bagration that his regiment had had to face a cavalry attack of the French, that though the attack had been repulsed, the regiment had lost more than half of its men. The colonel said that the attack had been repulsed but he did not really know himself what had been taking place. All he knew was that at the beginning of the action balls and grenades were flying all about his regiment and killing men; that then some one had shouted "cavalry," and his men had begun firing. And they were firing still, though not now at the cavalry, who had disappeared, but at the French infantry, who had come into the hollow.

Turning to an adjutant, Bagration commanded him to bring down from the hill the two battalions of the Sixth Chasseurs. Prince André was struck by the change that came over Prince Bagration's face. The lustreless, sleepy look in the eyes, the affectation of profound thought was suddenly gone.

The colonel protested to Prince Bagration, urging him to go back, as it was too dangerous for him. "I beg of you, your excellency, for God's sake!" he kept saying.

But Bagration did not answer. He merely gave the order to cease firing, and to make room for the two battalions of reinforcements. Just as he was speaking the cloud of smoke covering the hollow was lifted as by an unseen hand and blown by the rising wind from right to left, and the opposite hill came into sight with the French moving across it. All eyes fastened on that French column moving down upon them and winding in and out over the ups and downs of the ground. The front part of the column was already dipping down into the hollow. The engagement would take place then on the nearer side of the slope . . .

The attack of the Sixth Chasseurs covered the retreat of the right flank. In the centre, Tushin's forgotten battery had succeeded in setting fire to Schöngraben and delaying the advance of the French. The French stayed to put out the fire, which was fanned by the wind, and this gave time for the Russians to retreat. But the left flank was attacked and surrounded by the French army under Lannes.

The command of the left flank belonged by right of seniority to the general of the regiment in which Dolohov was serving—the regiment which Kutuzov had inspected before Braunau. But the command of the extreme left flank had been entrusted to the colonel of the Pavlograd hussars, in which Nicholas Rostov was serving. Both commanding officers were jealous of each other, and at the moment when the French began their attack, they were arguing with one another. Their regiments—cavalry and infantry alike—were by no means in readiness for battle. No one from the common soldier to the general expected an attack, and they were all unprepared—feeding their horses in the cavalry, gathering wood in the infantry.

"He is my senior in rank," said the German colonel of the hussars, growing very red and addressing an adjutant, who had ridden up. "So let him do as he likes. I can't sacrifice my hussars. Bugler! Sound the retreat!"

Things were becoming urgent. The fire of cannon and musketry thundered in the centre.

The infantry general walked up to his horse, and mounting it and drawing himself up very erect and tall, he rode up to the Pavlograd colonel. The two officers met with bows and concealed fury in their hearts.

"Again, colonel," the general said, "I cannot leave half my men in the wood. I beg you, I beg you," he repeated, "to occupy the position, and prepare for an attack."

"And I beg you not to meddle in what's not your business," answered the colonel. "If you were a cavalry officer . . ."

"I am not a cavalry officer, colonel, but I am a Russian general, and if you are unaware of the fact . . ."

"I am fully aware of it, your excellency," the colonel screamed, suddenly turning purple in the face. "If you care to come to the front with me, you will see that this position cannot be held. I don't want to massacre my regiment for your satisfaction."

Taking the colonel's words as a challenge to his courage, the general squared his chest and rode beside him to the front line, as though their whole difference would inevitably be settled there under the enemy's fire. When they reached the line, several bullets flew by them, but they stood still without a word. To look at the front line was useless, since from the spot where they had been standing before, it was clear that the cavalry could not act, owing to the bushes and the steep and broken character of the ground, and also because the French were outflanking the left wing. The general and the colonel glared at one another, seeking in vain for a symptom of cowardice. Both stood the test without flinching. Since neither was willing to be the first to withdraw from under fire, they might have remained a long while standing there, if there had not at that moment been heard in the woods, almost behind them, the snap of musketry and the shout of voices. The French were attacking the soldiers gathering wood. The hussars could not now retreat, nor could the infantry. They were cut off from falling back. Now they must attack to fight their way through.

The hussars of the squadron in which Rostov was an ensign had hardly time to mount their horses when they were confronted by the French. Again, as on the Enns bridge, there lay between them that terrible border-line of uncertainty and dread, like the line dividing the living from the dead. All the soldiers were conscious of that line, and the question whether they would cross it or not, and how they would cross it, filled their minds.

The colonel rode up to the front, made some angry reply to the questions of the officers, and, like a man desperately insisting on his rights, gave some command. No one said anything distinctly, but through the whole squadron there ran a vague rumour of attack. The command to form in order rang out, then there was the clank of sabres being drawn out of their sheaths. But still no one moved. The troops of the left flank, both the infantry and the hussars, felt that their commanders themselves did not know what to do, and the uncertainty of the commanders infected the soldiers.

"Hurry, if only they'd hurry," thought Rostov.

"With God's help, lads! Forward!" rang out the command. And Rostov felt the drooping of Rook's hindquarters as he broke into a gallop.

He saw a solitary tree ahead of him. The tree was at first in front of him, in the middle of that border-land that had seemed so terrible. But now he and the other hussars had galloped past it and nothing terrible had happened. Grasping the hilt of his sabre, Rostov thought, "Now, let him come on, whoever he may be." And driving the spurs into Rook, he let him go at full gallop.

The enemy could now be seen in front.

Rostov lifted his sabre, ready to strike, but at that instant he felt as though he were in a dream being carried forward with supernatural swiftness and yet remaining at the same spot.

"What's the matter? I'm not moving? I've fallen, I'm killed . . ." He was alone in the middle of the field. Instead of the moving horses and the hussars, he saw around him the motionless earth and stubble. There was warm blood under him.

"No, I'm wounded, and my horse is killed!" Rook tried to get up on his forelegs, but he sank again, crushing Rostov's leg. Blood was flowing from the horse's head. The horse struggled, but could not get up. Rostov tried to get up, and fell down too. His sabre strap had caught in the saddle. Where were his comrades, where were the French, he did not know. All around him there was no one.

Freeing his leg, he stood up. "Which side? Where now was that line that had so sharply divided the two armies?" he asked himself, and could not answer. "Hasn't something gone wrong with me? Do such things happen?" he wondered. Then he felt that his left arm was numb. The wrist seemed not to belong to it. He looked at his hand, carefully searching for blood.

Then seeing some men running towards him, he thought, "They will help me!"

In front of the men ran a single figure in a strange shako and a blue coat, with a sunburnt face and a hooked nose. Then came two men, and many more were running up behind. One of them said some strange words, not Russian. Between some other men in the same kind of shakoes stood a Russian hussar. He was being held by the arms.

"It must be one of ours taken prisoner. . . . Yes. Surely they couldn't take me too? What sort of men are they?" Rostov was still wondering, unable to believe his own eyes. "Can they be the French?" He gazed at the approaching French. And although only a few seconds before he had been longing to get at these Frenchmen and to cut them down, their being so near to him now seemed so awful that he could not believe his eyes. "Who are they? What are they running for? Can it be to me? Can they be running to me? And what for? To kill me? *Me,* whom every one's so fond of?" He recalled his mother's love, the love of his family and his friends, and the enemy's intention of killing him seemed impossible. "But they may even kill me." For more than ten seconds he stood, not moving from the spot.

The Frenchman with the hook nose was running towards him with his bayonet lowered. Rostov was seized with terror. He snatched up his pistol, but instead of firing it, he flung it at the Frenchman and ran toward the bushes.

Fear for his young happy life took possession of him. Leaping over the hedges like he used to when he played games, he ran over the field, now and then turning his pale, good-natured, youthful face. "No, it's better not to look," he thought. But as he got near to the bushes he looked round once more. The French had given up, and just at the moment when he looked round the nearest man was dropping from a run into a walk, and shouting something loudly to a comrade behind. Rostov stopped. "There's some mistake," he thought. "It can't be that they meant to kill me." His left arm was as heavy as if a hundred pound weight were hanging on it. He could run no further.

The Frenchmen took aim. One bullet and then another flew hissing by him. He took his left hand in his right, and with a last effort ran as far as the bushes. In the bushes there were Russian sharpshooters.

The infantry, caught unawares in the woods, retreated in disorder.

"Outflanked! Cut off! Lost!" they shouted as they ran.

When their general heard the firing and the shouts in the rear he grasped that something was happening to his regiment. And the thought that he, who had served twenty-two years without a reprimand, might be held responsible by his superiors for negligence or lack of discipline, so affected him that he galloped off to the regiment under a hail of bullets that luckily missed him.

Galloping between the French forces, he reached the field across which his men were running. But in spite of his despairing yells, in spite of his infuriated purple face distorted out of all likeness to itself, in spite of his flashing sword, the soldiers still ran, shooting into the air and not listening to the word of command.

All seemed lost. But at that moment the French, suddenly, for no apparent reason, ran back from the edge of the woods. Russian sharpshooters appeared. It was Timohin's division.

Timohin had rushed with such a desperate yell upon the French, and with such desperate and drunken energy had he dashed at them with only a sword in his hand, that they flung down their weapons and fled.

Dolohov, running beside Timohin, killed one French soldier and was the first to seize by the collar an officer who surrendered. The fleeing Russians came back; the battalions were brought together; and the French, who had been on the point of splitting the forces of the left flank into two parts, were for the moment held in check. The reserves had time to join the main forces, and the rout was stopped. The general stood watching the companies go by, when a soldier ran up to him. He was wearing a blue coat. His head was bound up and across his shoulders was slung a French cartridge case. In his hand he held an officer's sword.

"Your excellency, here are two trophies," said Dolohov, pointing to the French sword and cartridge case. "I took an officer prisoner. I stopped the company." Dolohov breathed hard. He spoke in jerks. "The whole company can bear witness. I beg you to remember me, your excellency!"

"Very good, very good," said the general, and he turned away. But Dolohov did not leave him. He undid the bandage, and showed the blood on his head.

"A bayonet wound. I kept my place in the front. Remember me, your excellency."

Tushin's battery had been forgotten. The force which had been stationed near Tushin's cannons to protect them had by somebody's orders retreated in the middle of the battle. But the battery still kept up its fire and had succeeded in setting fire to Schöngraben.

"Look! It's in flames! What smoke!" cried the gunners.

All the guns were now aimed at the burning town. The soldiers, as though they were urging each other on, cheered at every volley. The fire, fanned by the wind, soon spread. In retaliation the French stationed ten cannons a little to the right of the village, and began firing on Tushin.

Tushin's men only noticed this battery when two cannon-balls and then four more fell among their cannons. One knocked over two horses and another tore off the foot of a gunner. The horses were replaced by others from the ammunition carriage; the wounded were removed, and the four cannons were turned facing the ten of the enemy's battery. After an hour's time, of the forty gunners of the battery, seventeen were disabled. But they went on firing. Twice they noticed the French appearing below and they sent volleys of grapeshot at them.

"Smash away, boys!" Tushin kept saying. And he clutched at the cannon wheels himself and unscrewed the screws. The incessant booming of the cannons made him shudder. He ran from one cannon to the other. At one moment he was taking aim, at another reckoning the charges, then arranging for the changing and unharnessing of the killed and wounded horses. And all the time he shouted in his weak, shrill voice.

Tushin was not the least bit afraid and the idea that he might be killed or badly wounded never entered his head. Although he thought of everything, considered everything, did everything the very best officer could have done in his position, he was in a state of mind like that of a drunken man.

The deafening sound of his own guns, the hiss and thud of the enemy's shells, the sight of the perspiring, flushed gunners hurrying about the cannons, the sight of the blood of men and horses, and of the puffs of smoke from the enemy on the opposite side—always followed by a cannon-ball that flew across and hit the earth, a man, a horse, or a cannon—all these images made up for him a fantastic world of his own, in which he found enjoyment at the moment. The French seemed to be ants swarming about their cannons. And he himself figured in his imagination as a mighty man of immense stature, who was flinging cannon-balls at the French with both hands.

Suddenly he heard a strange, unfamiliar voice calling him. "Captain Tushin! Captain!"

Tushin looked round. It was the same staff-officer who had turned him out of the booth at Grunte. He was shouting to him in a breathless voice: "Are you mad? You've been commanded twice to retreat, and you . . ."

Tushin looked at him wondering what he was talking about. He had received no command to retreat. "I . . . don't . . ." he began, putting two fingers to the peak of his cap. "I . . ."

But the staff-officer did not say all he had meant to. A cannon ball flying near him made him duck. He paused, and was just going to say something more, when another ball stopped him. He turned his horse's head and galloped away.

"Retreat! Retreat!" he shouted from a distance.

The soldiers laughed.

A minute later an adjutant arrived with the same message. He was Prince André.

The first thing he saw was an unharnessed horse with a broken leg, which was neighing beside the harnessed horses. The blood was flowing in a stream from its leg. Among the platforms lay several dead men.

One cannon-ball after another flew over him. But the very idea that he was afraid was enough to rouse him again. "I can't be frightened," he thought, and he deliberately dismounted from his horse between the cannons. He gave his message, but he did not leave the battery. He decided to stay and help move the cannons from the position and get them away. Stepping over the bodies of dead men, under the fire from the French, he helped Tushin and his gunners.

"The officer that came just now ran off quicker than he came," said a gunner to Prince André, "not like your honour."

When they had got the two out of the four cannons that were uninjured on to the platforms and were moving downhill (one cannon that had been smashed and a howitzer were left behind), Prince André went up to Tushin.

"Well, good-bye till we meet again," he said.

"Good-bye," said Tushin. "Good-bye," he said with tears, which for some unknown reason started suddenly into his eyes.

The wind had sunk, black storm-clouds hung low over the battlefield, melting on the horizon into the clouds of smoke. Darkness had come. The booming of the cannons had grown less, but the snapping of gun-fire in the rear and on the right was heard nearer and more often.

As Tushin with his cannons got out of fire and was descending the ravine, he was met by the staff, among whom were the staff-officer and Zherkov, who had twice been sent to Tushin's battery, but had not once reached it because he was too frightened. They all vied with one another in giving him orders, telling him how and where to go, finding fault and making criticisms.

Though orders were given to abandon the wounded, many of them dragged themselves after the troops and begged for a seat on the cannons. The jaunty infantry-officer—the one who had run out of Tushin's shanty just before the battle—was laid on a gun-carriage with a bullet in his stomach.

At the bottom of the hill a pale ensign of hussars, holding one arm, came up to Tushin and begged for a seat.

"Captain, for God's sake. I've hurt my arm," he said timidly. "For God's sake. I can't walk. For God's sake!" It was evident that this was not the first time the ensign had asked for a lift, and that he had been refused each time. He asked in a hesitating and piteous voice, "Tell them to let me get on, for God's sake!"

"Let him get on, let him get on," said Tushin. "Put a coat under him." He turned to his favourite gunner. "But where's the wounded officer?"

"We took him off; he was dead," answered some one.

"Help him on. Sit down. Sit down. Lay the coat there."

The ensign was Nicholas Rostov. He was pale and his lower jaw was trembling as though in a fever. They put him on the gun-carriage from which they had just removed the dead officer. There was blood on the coat that was laid under him, and Rostov's riding-breeches and arm were smeared with it.

"What, are you wounded?" said Tushin, going up to Rostov.

"No; it's a sprain."

"How is it there's blood on the frame?" asked Tushin.

"That was the officer, your honour, stained it," answered an artilleryman, wiping the blood off with the sleeve of his coat, as if to apologise for the dirty state of the cannon.

With difficulty, aided by the infantry, Tushin and his men dragged the cannon uphill, and halted on reaching the village of Guntersdorf. All of a sudden there came the sound of firing and shouts close by on the right. The flash of shots could be seen in the darkness. It was met by the Russian soldiers in ambush in the houses of the village. Tushin's cannons could not move, and the artillerymen, Tushin, and the ensign looked at one another. Then the firing on both sides suddenly stopped.

The French had been repulsed for the last time. And again, in the complete darkness, Tushin's cannons moved forward, surrounded by the infantry, who kept up a hum of talk.

In the darkness they flowed on like an unseen, gloomy river always in the same direction, with a buzz of talk and the thud of hoofs and rumble of wheels. But above all other sounds, rose the moans and cries of the wounded. Their moans seemed to fill all the darkness. Their moans and the darkness seemed to melt into one.

A little later some one followed by a suite rode by on a white horse. And a rumour passed through that the order had been given to halt. All halted in the muddy road, just where they were.

Fires were lighted. Captain Tushin, after giving instructions to his battery, sent some of his soldiers to look for an ambulance or a doctor for the ensign, and then sat down by the fire his soldiers had lighted by the roadside. Rostov dragged himself to the fire. His whole body was trembling with fever from the pain, the cold, and the damp. He was dreadfully sleepy, but he could not go to sleep for the agonising pain in his arm. He closed his eyes, then opened them to stare at the fire, which seemed to him dazzling red, and then at the stooping, feeble figure of Tushin, squatting in Turkish fashion near him. The big, kindly, and shrewd eyes of Tushin were fixed upon him with sympathy. He saw that Tushin wished with all his soul to help him, but could do nothing for him.

On all sides they heard the footsteps and the voices of the infantry going and coming and settling themselves round them. The sounds of voices, of steps, and of horses' hoofs tramping in the mud, the crackling firewood far and near, all melted into one.

An infantry soldier came up to the fire, squatted on his heels, held his hands to the fire, and turned his face.

"You don't mind, your honour?" he said, looking at Tushin. "I've lost my company. I don't know where I am!"

An infantry officer with a bandaged face then approached the fire. He asked Tushin to have the cannon moved a little so as to let a store waggon pass by. After the officer two soldiers ran up fighting, trying to pull a boot from one another.

Then a thin, pale soldier approached, his neck bandaged with a blood-stained rag. He asked for water.

Next a soldier ran up, to beg for some red-hot embers for the infantry.

"Some of your fire for the infantry! Thanks, we'll pay it back with interest," he said, carrying some glowing firebrands away into the darkness.

Next four soldiers passed by, carrying something heavy in an overcoat. One of them stumbled.

"Devils! They've left firewood in the road," grumbled one.

"He's dead; why carry him?" said another. And they vanished into the darkness with their burden.

"Does it ache, eh?" Tushin asked Rostov in a whisper.

"Yes, it does."

A gunner, coming up to Tushin said: "The general wants to see you. He's over there in the cottage."

Tushin got up and walked away from the fire, buttoning up his coat and setting himself straight.

In a cottage that had been prepared for him not far from the artillerymen's fire, Prince Bagration was sitting at dinner, talking with several commanding officers, who had gathered about him. The little old colonel with the half-shut eyes was there, greedily gnawing at a mutton-bone, and the general of twenty-two years' irreproachable service, flushed with a glass of vodka and his dinner, and the staff-officer, and Zherkov, stealing uneasy glances at every one, and Prince André, pale with set lips and feverishly glittering eyes. In the corner of the cottage stood a French flag, that had been captured.

Prince Bagration thanked the officers, and inquired into details of the battle and of the losses.

The general, whose regiment had been inspected at Braunau, told the prince that as soon as the engagement began, he had fallen back from the woods, mustered the men who were cutting wood, and letting them pass by him, had made a bayonet charge with two battalions and repulsed the French.

"As soon as I saw, your excellency, that the first battalion was thrown into confusion, I stood in the road and thought, 'I'll let them get through and then open fire on them'; and that's what I did."

The general had so longed to do this, he had so regretted not having succeeded in doing it, that it seemed to him now that this was just what had happened. Indeed might it not actually have been so? Who could make out in such confusion what did and what did not happen?

"And by the way I ought to note, your excellency," he continued, recalling Dolohov's conversation with Kutuzov and his own late interview with the degraded officer, "that the private Dolohov, degraded to the ranks, took a French officer prisoner before my eyes and particularly distinguished himself."

"I saw here, your excellency, the attack of the Pavlograd hussars," Zherkov put in, looking uneasily about him. He had not seen the hussars at all that day, but had only heard about them from an infantry officer. "They broke up two squares, your excellency."

When Zherkov began to speak, several officers smiled, as they always did, expecting a joke from him. But when they realised that what he was saying had to do with the glory of the day, they assumed a serious expression, although many were very well aware that what Zherkov was saying was a lie utterly without foundation.

Prince Bagration turned to the old colonel.

"I thank you all, gentlemen; all branches of the service behaved heroically—infantry, cavalry, and artillery. But how did two cannons come to be abandoned in the centre?" he inquired, looking about for some one. "I think it was you I sent," he added, addressing the staff-officer.

"One had been disabled," answered the staff-officer, "but the other, I can't explain; I was there all the while myself, giving instructions, and I had scarcely left. . . ."

Some one said that Captain Tushin was close by in the village, and that he had already been sent for.

"Oh, but you went there," said Prince Bagration, addressing Prince André.

"Yes, we rode there almost together," said the staff-officer, smiling at Prince André.

"I did not have the pleasure of seeing you," said Prince André abruptly. Every one was silent.

Tushin appeared in the doorway, timidly edging in behind the generals' backs, embarrassed as he always was in the presence of his superior officers.

"How was it a cannon was abandoned?" asked Bagration, frowning.

"I don't know . . . your excellency . . . I hadn't the men, your excellency."

"You could have got them from the battalions that were covering your position!"

Tushin did not say that there were no battalions there, although that was the fact. He was afraid of getting another officer into trouble by saying so. Without uttering a word he gazed straight into Bagration's face.

There was a silence.

Prince Bagration, though he had no wish to be severe, apparently found nothing to say; the others did not venture to intervene.

Prince André looked at Tushin.

"Your excellency," Prince André broke the silence. "You sent me to Captain Tushin's battery. I went there and found two-thirds of the men and horses killed, two cannons disabled and no forces near to defend them."

Prince Bagration and Tushin looked at Prince André, as he went on speaking with emotion.

"And if your excellency will permit me to express my opinion," he went on, "we owe the success of the day more to the action of that battery and the heroic steadiness of Captain Tushin and his men than to anything else," said Prince

André, and he got up at once and walked away from the table, without waiting for a reply.

Prince Bagration looked at Tushin and, apparently loath to express his disbelief in Prince André's off-handed judgment, and yet unable to put complete faith in it, he bent his head and said to Tushin that he could go. Prince André walked out after him.

"Thank you," Tushin said to him.

Prince André looked at Tushin, and walked away without saying a word. He felt bitter and sad. It was all so strange, so unlike what he had been hoping for.

"Who are they? Why are they here? What do they want? And when will it all end?" thought Rostov, looking at the shadowy figures that kept flitting before his eyes. The pain in his arm became even more agonising. He was heavy with sleep. Crimson circles danced before his eyes, and the impression of the voices and the faces and the sense of his loneliness all blended with the misery of the pain. It was they, these soldiers, wounded and unhurt alike, it was they crushing and weighing upon him, and twisting his veins and burning the flesh in his sprained arm and shoulder. To get rid of them he closed his eyes.

He dozed off for a minute. He saw his mother and her large, white hands; he saw Sonya's thin shoulders, Natasha's eyes and her laugh, and Denisov with his voice, and Telyanin, and all the affair with Telyanin and Bogdanitch. All that affair was mixed up with this soldier with the harsh voice, and that affair and this soldier here were so agonisingly, so ruthlessly pulling, crushing, and twisting his arm always in the same direction. He was trying to get away from them, but they would not let go of his shoulder for a second. It would not ache, it would be all right if they wouldn't drag at it; but there was no getting rid of them.

He opened his eyes. The black pall of darkness hung only a few feet above the light of the fire. In the light fluttered tiny flakes of falling snow. Tushin had not returned, the doctor had not come. He was alone, only a soldier was sitting naked on the other side of the fire, warming his thin, yellow body.

"Nobody cares for me!" thought Rostov. "No one to help me, no one to feel sorry for me," he moaned.

"In pain?" asked the soldier, shaking his shirt out before the fire, and without waiting for an answer, he added: "Oh, what a lot of men died today! It was awful!"

Rostov did not hear the soldier. He gazed at the snowflakes whirling over the fire and thought of the Russian winter with his warm, brightly lighted home, his cosy fur cloak, his swift sledge, his good health, and all the love and tenderness of his family. "What did I come here for!" he wondered.

On the next day, the French did not renew the attack and the remnant of Bagration's detachment joined Kutuzov's army.

1805

BOOK THREE

PRINCE VASSILY did not think of doing harm to others for the sake of his own interest. He was simply a man of the world. Various plans and calculations were continually forming in his mind. Of such plans and calculations he had not one or two, but dozens in train at once, some of them only beginning to occur to him, others being concluded, others again coming to nothing. He never said to himself, for instance: "That man is now in power, I must secure his friendship and confidence"; nor, "Now Pierre is a wealthy man, I must get him to marry my daughter and borrow the forty thousand I need."

Pierre was in Moscow, and Prince Vassily secured an appointment as gentleman of the bedchamber for him. And he insisted on the young man's travelling with him to Petersburg, and staying at his house. Without apparent design, but yet with unhesitating conviction that it was the right thing, Prince Vassily did everything to ensure Pierre's marrying his daughter.

Pierre, on suddenly becoming rich and inheriting the title of Count Bezuhov, after his lonely and careless manner of life, felt so surrounded, so occupied, that he never succeeded in being alone except in his bed. He had to sign papers, to present himself at legal institutions, to visit his estate near Moscow, and to receive a great number of persons, who previously had not cared to be aware of his existence, but now would have been hurt and offended if he had not chosen to see them. All these people, business men, relations, acquaintances, were equally friendly and well disposed towards the young heir. They were all convinced of Pierre's noble qualities. He was continually hearing phrases, such as, "With your exceptionally kind disposition"; or, "Considering your generous heart"; or, "You are so pure-minded yourself, count . . ." or, "If he were as clever as you," and so on, so that he was beginning genuinely to believe in his own exceptional goodness and his own exceptional intelligence.

Even people, who had before been spiteful and openly hostile, became tender and affectionate. The ill-tempered, eldest princess, with the long waist and the hair plastered down like a doll, had gone into Pierre's room after the funeral. Dropping her eyes and turning crimson, she said that she very much regretted the misunderstanding that had arisen between them, and that now she felt she had no right to ask him for anything except permission, after the shock she had suffered, to remain for a few weeks longer in the house which she was so fond of and in which she had made such sacrifices. She could not control herself and wept. Touched at seeing the princess so changed, Pierre took her by the hand and begged her pardon, though he could not have said what for. From that day the princess began knitting a striped scarf for Pierre, and was completely changed towards him.

"Do this for my sake, my dear boy; she had to put up with a great deal from the deceased, any way," Prince Vassily said to him, giving him some deed to sign for the princess's benefit. Prince Vassily felt that this note for thirty thousand was a sop worth throwing to the poor princess, so that it might not occur to her to gossip about his part in the scheme concerning the will. Pierre signed the note, and from that time the princess became even more amiable.

In these early days Prince Vassily, more than all the rest, took control of Pierre's affairs, and of Pierre himself. On the death of Count Bezuhov he did not let Pierre slip out of his hands. During the few days he had stayed on in Moscow after Count Bezuhov's death, he went to see Pierre, and had dictated to him what he was to do in a tone of weariness and certainty which seemed to say: "You know that I am overwhelmed with business and that it is out of pure charity that I concern myself with you, and moreover you know very well that what I propose to you is the only feasible thing."

"Well, my dear boy, to-morrow we are off at last," he said one day, speaking as though the matter had long ago been settled between them.

"To-morrow we set off. I'll give you a place in my coach. I'm very glad. All our important business is settled. And I ought to have been back long ago. Here, I have received this from the chancellor. I petitioned him in your favour, and you are put on the diplomatic corps, and created a gentleman of the bedchamber. Now a diplomatic career lies open to you."

Pierre tried to protest. But Prince Vassily broke in on his protest in droning, bass tones, that precluded all possibility of interrupting the flow of his words. This was the resource he fell back upon when extreme measures of persuasion were needed.

"But, my dear boy, I have done it for my own sake, for my conscience' sake, and there is no need to thank me. No one has ever complained yet of being too much loved; and then you are free, you can give it all up to-morrow. You'll see for yourself in Petersburg. And it is high time you were getting away from these terrible associations." Prince Vassily sighed. "So that's all settled, my dear fellow. And let my valet go in your coach. Oh, yes, I was almost forgetting," Prince Vassily added. "You know, my dear boy, I had a little account to settle with your father, so as I have received something from the Ryazan estate, I'll keep that; you don't want it. We'll go into accounts later."

What Prince Vassily called "something from the Ryazan estate" was several thousands of roubles. This sum he kept for himself.

In Petersburg, Pierre was surrounded by the same atmosphere of affection and tenderness as in Moscow. He could not decline the post, or rather the title, for he did nothing, that Prince Vassily had obtained for him. And acquaintances, invitations, and social duties were so numerous that he was continually conscious of a strange feeling of hurry and expectation of some future good which was always coming and was never realised.

Of his old bachelor friends there were not many left in Petersburg. The Guards were on active service; Dolohov had been degraded to the ranks; Anatole had gone into the army and was somewhere in the provinces; Prince André was abroad. And so Pierre could not spend his nights in the way he had so loved spending them before, nor could he open his heart in intimate talk with Prince André. All his time was spent at dinners and balls, or at Prince Vassily's in the society of his fat wife, Princess Kuragin, and the beauty, his daughter Helen.

Like every one else, Anna Pavlovna Scherer showed Pierre the change that had taken place in the attitude of society towards him.

In former days, Pierre had always felt in Anna Pavlovna's presence that what he was saying was unsuitable, tactless, not the right thing; that the phrases, which seemed to him clever as he formed them in his mind, became somehow stupid as soon as he uttered them aloud. Now everything he said was always "delightful." Even if Anna Pavlovna did not say so, he saw she was longing to say so, and only refraining from doing so from regard for his modesty.

At the beginning of the winter of 1805, Pierre received one of Anna Pavlovna's pink notes of invitation, in which the words occurred: "You will find the fair Helen at my house, whom one never gets tired of seeing."

On reading this, Pierre felt for the first time that there was being formed between himself and Helen some sort of tie, recognised by other people. And this idea at once alarmed him and pleased him.

Anna Pavlovna's evening party was like her first one, only the attraction which she had provided for her guest was not on this occasion Mortemart, but a diplomat, who had just arrived from Berlin, bringing the latest details of the Emperor Alexander's stay at Potsdam, and of the alliance the two exalted friends had sworn together, to maintain the true cause against Napoleon, the enemy of the human race.

Pierre was welcomed by Anna Pavlovna with a shade of melancholy, bearing unmistakable reference to the recent loss he had suffered in the death of Count Bezuhov. Her melancholy was of precisely the same kind as that more exalted melancholy she always displayed at any allusion to Her Most August Majesty the Empress.

Anna Pavlovna had arranged the groups in her drawing-room with her usual skill. The larger group, in which were Prince Vassily and some generals, had the benefit of the diplomat. Another group gathered about the tea-table. Pierre would have liked to join the first group, but Anna Pavlovna, who was in the nervous excitement of a general on the battlefield, detained him: "Wait, I have designs on you for this evening."

She looked around at Helen and smiled.

"My dear Helen, my poor aunt adores you. Go and keep her company for ten minutes. And that you may not find it too tiresome, here's our dear count, who certainly won't refuse to follow you."

The beauty joined the old aunt. But Anna Pavlovna still detained Pierre, with the air of having some last arrangement to make with him.

"She is exquisite, isn't she?" she said to Pierre. "How she carries herself! For such a young girl, what tact, what a finished perfection of manner. The most unworldly of men would take a brilliant place in society as her husband. That's true, isn't it? I only wanted to know your opinion." And Anna Pavlovna let Pierre go.

The old aunt received the two young people in her corner. But instead of showing her adoration of Helen she displayed her fear of Anna Pavlovna. She glanced at her nervously as though to inquire what she was to do with them.

Anna Pavlovna disregarded her aunt and spoke to Pierre: "I hope you will never say that people are bored at my house." She looked at Helen.

Helen smiled with an air, which seemed to say that she did not admit the possibility of any one's seeing her without being enchanted.

The old aunt coughed, swallowed the phlegm, and said in French that she was very glad to see Helen.

In the middle of a halting and tedious conversation, Helen looked round at Pierre and smiled at him with the bright, beautiful smile with which she smiled at every one. Pierre was so used to this smile, it meant so little to him, that he did not even notice it. The aunt was speaking at that moment of a collection of snuff-boxes belonging to Pierre's father, Count Bezuhov, and she showed them her snuff-box. Helen asked to look at the portrait of the aunt's husband, which was on the snuff-box.

"It's probably the work of Vines," said Pierre, mentioning a celebrated miniature painter. He bent over the table to take the snuff-box. But the aunt handed it to him passing it across Helen, behind her back. Helen bent forward to make room, and looked round smiling. She was, as always in the evening, wearing a dress cut in the fashion of the day, very low in the neck both in front and back. Her bust was so close to Pierre's short-sighted eyes that he could feel all the living charm of her neck and shoulders, and so near his lips that he need scarcely have stooped to kiss it. He felt the warmth of her body, the fragrance of scent, and heard the creaking of her corset as she moved. He saw, not her marble beauty, making up one whole with her gown; he saw and felt all the charm of her body, which was only veiled by her clothes.

"So you have never noticed till now that I am lovely?" Helen seemed to be saying. "You haven't noticed that I am a woman? Yes, I am a woman, who might belong to any one—to you, too," her eyes said. And at that moment Pierre felt that Helen not only could, but would become his wife, that it must be so.

He knew it at that moment as surely as he would have known it, standing under the wedding crown beside her. How would it be? And when? He knew not. Knew not even if it would be a good thing, he had a feeling, that for some reason it would not, but he knew it would be so.

Pierre dropped his eyes, raised them again, and tried once more to see her as a distant beauty, far removed from him, as he had seen her every day before. But he could not do this. She was terribly close to him. Already she had power over him. And between him and her there now existed no barriers of any kind, but the barrier of his own will.

"Very well, I will leave you in your little corner. I see you are comfortable there," said Anna Pavlovna's voice. And Pierre, trying panic-stricken to think whether he had done anything wrong, looked about, crimsoning. It seemed to him as though every one knew what was passing in him.

A little later, when he went up to the bigger group, Anna

Pavlovna said to him: "I am told you are making improvements in your Petersburg house." This was the fact. The architect had told him it was necessary, and Pierre, without knowing with what object, was having his immense house in Petersburg redecorated. "That is all very well, but do not move from Prince Vassily's. It is a good thing to have such a friend as the prince," she said, smiling to Prince Vassily. "I know something about that. Don't I? And you are so young. You need advice. You mustn't be angry with me for making use of an old woman's privileges." She paused, as women always do pause, in anticipation of something, after speaking of their age. "If you marry, it's a different matter."

Pierre did not look at Helen, nor she at him. But she was still terribly close to him.

He muttered something and blushed.

After Pierre had gone home, it was a long while before he could get to sleep. He kept wondering what was happening to him. What was happening? Nothing. Simply he had grasped the fact that a woman, whom he had known as a child, of whom he had said without giving her a thought, "Yes, she's nice-looking," when he had been told she was a beauty, he had grasped the fact that that woman might belong to him.

"But she's stupid. I used to say myself that she was stupid," he thought. "There is something nasty in the feeling she excites in me. . . . I have been told that her brother, Anatole, was in love with her, and she in love with him, that there was a regular scandal, and that's why Anatole was sent away. Her brother is Hippolite. . . . Her father is Prince Vassily. . . . That's bad." And at the very moment he caught himself smiling, and became conscious that other thoughts had risen to the surface across the first, that while he was thinking of her worthlessness, he was also dreaming of how she would be his wife, how she might love him, how she might become quite different, and how all he had thought and heard about her might be untrue. And again he saw her, not as the daughter of Prince Vassily, but saw her whole body, only veiled by her grey gown. "But, no, why didn't that idea ever occur to me before?" And again he told himself that it was impossible, that there would be something nasty, unnatural, and dishonourable in this marriage. He recalled her past words and looks, and the words and looks of people, who had seen them together. He remembered the words and looks of Anna Pavlovna, when she had spoken about his house. He recollected thousands of such hints from Prince Vassily and other people. And he was overwhelmed with terror that he might have bound himself in some way to do a thing obviously wrong, and not what he ought to do.

But at the very time that he was saying these things to himself, in another part of his mind, Helen's image floated to the surface in all its womanly beauty.

In November Prince Vassily had to go on an official tour of inspection through four provinces. He had secured this appointment for himself, in order to be able at the same time to visit his estates, which were in a neglected state. He intended to pick up his son, Anatole, on the way, where his regiment was stationed, and to pay a visit to Prince Nicholas Bolkonsky, with a view to marrying his son to the rich old man's daughter Princess Mary. But before going away and entering on these new affairs, Prince Vassily wanted to settle matters with Pierre. Pierre had, it was true, of late spent whole days at home, that is, at Prince Vassily's, where he was staying, and was as absurd, as agitated, and as stupid in Helen's presence, as a young man in love should be, but still made no offer.

"This is all very fine, but the thing must come to a conclusion," Prince Vassily said to himself one morning, thinking that Pierre, who was so greatly indebted to him, was not behaving quite nicely. "Youth . . . Frivolity . . . well, God be with him," thought Prince Vassily, enjoying the sense of his own goodness of heart. "But the thing must come to a conclusion. The day after to-morrow is Helen's name-day, I'll invite some people, and if he doesn't understand what he's to do, then it will be my affair to see to it. Yes, my affair. I'm her father."

Six weeks after Anna Pavlovna's party, and the sleepless night after it when Pierre had decided that he must avoid Helen and go away; six weeks after that night Pierre had still not left Prince Vassily's. Perhaps he might have mastered himself, but not a day passed without a party at Prince Vassily's, where receptions had not been frequent, and Pierre was bound to be present if he did not want to disturb the general satisfaction and disappoint every one. At the rare moments when Prince Vassily was at home, he took Pierre's hand and said, "till to-morrow," or "be in to dinner, or I shan't see you," or "I shall stay at home on your account," or some such remark. But although, when Prince Vassily did stay at home for Pierre, as he said, he never spoke two words to him, Pierre did not feel equal to disappointing him.

Every day Pierre said the same thing over and over to himself. "I must really make up my mind." But he was unable to do so.

Helen always spoke to him now with a smile—a smile having reference to him alone, and full of something more significant than the society smile that always adorned her face. Pierre knew that every one was only waiting for him to say one word, to cross a certain line, and he knew that sooner or later he would cross it. But a kind of horror seized upon him at the mere thought of this. A thousand times in the course of those six weeks, during which he felt himself being drawn on further and further toward the abyss that horrified him, Pierre had said to himself: "But what does it mean? I must act with decision! Can it be that I haven't any will?"

On Helen's name-day, Prince Vassily gave a little supper party of just their own people, as his wife said, that is, of friends and relations. All these friends and relations were made to feel that the day was to be a very important one in their daughter's life. The guests were seated at supper. Princess Kuragin, a massive woman of imposing presence, who had once been beautiful, sat in the hostess' place, with the most honoured guests on each side of her—an old general and his wife, and Anna Pavlovna Scherer. Towards the other end of the table sat the less elderly and less honoured guests, and there too sat as members of the family Pierre and Helen, side by side. Prince Vassily did not take supper. He moved about the table, in excellent spirits, sitting down beside one guest after another. To every one he dropped a few careless and agreeable words, except to Pierre and Helen, whose presence he seemed not to notice.

The wax candles burned brightly, there was a glitter of silver and crystal on the table, of ladies' ornaments and the gold and silver of epaulettes. The servants threaded their way in and out round the table in their red coats. There was the clatter of knives, glasses, and plates, and the sound of eager talk from several conversations round the table. The old chamberlain at one end could be heard asserting to an elderly baroness his ardent love for her, while she laughed. In the centre Prince Vassily was telling the ladies a very funny story about the ridiculous new military governor-general of Petersburg, named Sergey Kuzmitch.

Every one laughed.

"Don't be mean," said Anna Pavlovna, from the other end of the table, shaking her finger at Prince Vassily. "He is such a worthy, excellent man, our good Sergey Kuzmitch."

At the upper end of the table, the place of honour, every one seemed in good spirits. Only Pierre and Helen sat silently side by side. They smiled, the smile of bashfulness at their own feelings. Gaily as the others laughed and talked and joked, appetising as were the Rhine wine, the *sauté*, and the ices, carefully as they avoided glancing at the young couple, yet it was somehow obvious that the anecdote about Sergey Kuzmitch, and the laughter were all affectation, and that every one's attention was really concentrated simply on Pierre and Helen.

While Prince Vassily mimicked Sergey Kuzmitch, his expression seemed to say: "Yes, yes, it's all going well, it will all be settled to-day." While Anna Pavlovna shook her finger at him for laughing at "our good Sergey Kuzmitch," Prince Vassily read in her eyes congratulations on his future son-in-law. And while old Princess Kuragin offered wine to the lady next her with a pensive sigh, she looked angrily at her daughter, and her sigh seemed to say: "Yes, there's nothing left for you and me now, my dear, but to drink sweet wine, now that the time has come for the young people to be so indecently, provokingly happy!"

The jests fell flat, the news was not interesting, the liveliness was unmistakably forced. Not the guests only, but the footmen waiting at table seemed to feel the same and forget their duties, glancing at the lovely Helen with her radiant face and the broad, red, happy and uneasy face of Pierre.

Pierre felt that he was the centre of it all, and this both pleased him and embarrassed him. "So it's all over!" he thought. "How has it all been done? So quickly! They all expect it, they are all so convinced that it will be, that I cannot, I cannot, disappoint them. But how will it be?" thought Pierre, glancing at the dazzling shoulders that were so close to his eyes.

Then he suddenly felt a vague shame. He felt awkward at being the centre of attention, at being a happy man in the eyes of others, with his ugly face being a sort of Paris in possession of a Helen. "I came here from Moscow with Prince Vassily. What reason was there for not staying with him?" Pierre asked himself. "Then I played cards with her and picked up her purse, and went skating with her. When did it begin, when did it all come about?" And here he was sitting beside her as her betrothed, hearing, seeing, feeling her closeness, her breathing, her movements, her beauty.

All at once he heard a voice, a familiar voice, addressing him for the second time.

"I'm asking you, when you heard last from Prince André," Prince Vassily repeated a third time. "How absent-minded you are, my dear boy." Prince Vassily smiled, and Pierre saw that every one, every one was smiling at him and at Helen. And he smiled himself his gentle, childlike smile. And Helen smiled.

"When did you get a letter? From Olmütz?" repeated Prince Vassily, who wanted to know in order to settle an argument.

"Yes, from Olmütz," Pierre answered.

After supper Pierre escorted Helen to the drawing-room. The guests began to leave. Several went away without saying good-bye to Helen, as though unwilling to take her away from a serious occupation. Others went up to her for an instant and hurried off, refusing to let her accompany them out. The old general growled angrily at his wife when she inquired how his leg was. "The fool," he thought. "Look at Helen, she'll still be beautiful at fifty."

"I believe I may congratulate you," Anna Pavlovna whispered to Princess Kuragin, as she kissed her warmly. "If I hadn't a headache, I would stay on." The princess did not reply. She was tormented by envy of her daughter's happiness.

While the guests were leaving, Pierre and Helen were alone in the little drawing-room, where they were sitting. Often before, during the last six weeks, Pierre had been left alone with Helen, but he had never spoken of love to her. Now he felt that it was inevitable, but he could not make up his mind to this final step. He felt ashamed; it seemed to him that here at Helen's side he was filling some other man's place. "This is not for you," some inner voice said to him. But he had to say something, and he began to speak. He asked Helen whether she had enjoyed the evening. And with her usual directness she answered that this name-day had been one of the most pleasant she had ever had.

A few of the nearest relatives were still lingering on. They were sitting in the big drawing-room. Prince Vassily walked with languid steps towards Pierre. Pierre rose and observed that it was getting late. Prince Vassily looked sternly at him, as though what he had said was so strange that he could not believe his ears. Then taking Pierre's hand he drew him down into a seat and smiled affectionately.

"Well, Helen?" he said, addressing his daughter in that careless tone of tenderness which comes natural to parents who have petted their children from infancy, but in Prince Vassily's case was only arrived at by imitation of other parents. And he turned to Pierre. Then all at once he muttered something and went away. Pierre looked at Helen confused. And her glance seemed to say: "Well, it's your own fault."

"I must inevitably cross the barrier, but I can't, I can't," thought Pierre, and he began again speaking of extraneous subjects, of Sergey Kuzmitch, inquiring what was the point of the anecdote, as he had not caught it all. Helen, with a smile, replied that she did not know either.

When Prince Vassily went into the drawing-room, the princess was talking in subdued tones with an elderly lady about Pierre.

"Of course it is a very brilliant match, but happiness, my dear . . ."

"Marriages are made in heaven," answered the elderly lady.

Prince Vassily walked to the furthest corner and sat down on a sofa, as though he had not heard the ladies.

"Aline," he said to his wife, "go and see what they are doing."

The princess went up to the door, walked by it, and glanced into the little drawing-room. Pierre and Helen were sitting and talking as before.

"Just the same," she said, coming back to her husband.

Prince Vassily frowned. Twisting his mouth on one side, his cheeks twitched with an unpleasant, brutal expression peculiar to him at such moments. He got up and crossed over to the little drawing-room. He walked quickly. The prince's face was so extraordinarily solemn that Pierre got up in alarm on seeing him.

"Thank God!" he said. "My wife has told me all about it." He put one arm round Pierre, the other round his daughter. "My dear boy! Helen! I am very, very glad." His voice shook. "I loved your father . . . And she will make you a good wife . . . God's blessing on you both! . . ." He embraced his daughter, then Pierre. Tears were actually moist on his cheeks.

"Aline, come here," he called.

The princess went in and wept too. The elderly lady also put her handkerchief to her eye. They kissed Pierre, and he several times kissed the hand of the lovely Helen. A little later they were again left alone.

"All this had to be so and could not have been otherwise," thought Pierre. "It's no use to ask whether it was a good thing or not. It's a good thing because it's definite, and there's none of the agonising suspense there was before." Pierre held Helen's hand in silence and gazed at the heaving and falling of her lovely bosom.

"Helen!" he said aloud, and stopped. "Something special is said on these occasions," he thought; but he could not recollect what it was. He looked into her face. She bent forward closer to him. Her face flushed rosy red.

"Now it's too late, it's all over, and besides I love her," thought Pierre.

"I love you!" he said, remembering what had to be said on these occasions. But the words sounded so poor that he felt ashamed of himself.

Six weeks later he was married, and the lucky possessor of a lovely wife and millions of money, as people said. He took up his residence in the great, newly decorated Petersburg mansion of the Count Bezuhov.

In December, the old Prince Nicholas Bolkonsky received a letter from Prince Vassily, announcing that he intended to visit him with his son. "I am going on an inspection tour, and of course a hundred miles is only a step out of the way for me to visit you, my deeply-honoured benefactor," he wrote. "My Anatole is accompanying me, and I hope you will permit him to express to you in person the profound veneration that, following his father's example, he entertains for you."

"Well, there's no need to bring Mary out, it seems; suitors come to us of themselves," the little princess said heedlessly on hearing of this.

The old Prince Nicholas scowled and said nothing. He had always had a poor opinion of Prince Vassily, and this opinion had grown stronger of late since Prince Vassily had, under the new reigns of Paul and Alexander, advanced to high rank and honours. Now from the letter and the little princess's hints, he saw what the object of the visit was, and his poor opinion of Prince Vassily passed into a feeling of ill-will and contempt. He snorted indignantly whenever he spoke of him.

On the day of Prince Vassily's arrival, the old prince was particularly discontented and out of humour. At nine o'clock, he went out for a walk, as usual, wearing his short, velvet, fur-lined cloak with a sable collar and a sable cap. There had been a fall of snow on the previous evening. The path along which Prince Nicholas walked to the conservatory had been cleared.

"Could a sledge drive up?" he asked the respectful steward, who was escorting him to the house.

"The snow is deep, your excellency. I gave orders for the avenue to be cleared too. Otherwise it would be hard to drive up," said the steward. "I hear, your excellency, there's a minister coming to visit your excellency?" The prince turned to the steward and stared at him.

"Eh? A minister? What minister? Who gave you orders?" he began in his shrill, cruel voice. "For the princess my daughter, you do not clear the way, but for the minister you do! For me there are no ministers!"

"Your excellency, I supposed . . ."

"You supposed," shouted the prince. "You supposed . . . Brigands! Fools! . . . I'll teach you to suppose," and raising his stick he waved it at the steward, and would have hit him, had not the man shrunk back. "You supposed . . . Fools! . . ." he cried again. But although the steward, shocked at his own insolence in dodging the blow, went closer to the prince, with his bald head bent humbly before him, or perhaps just because of this, the prince did not lift his stick again. And shouting, "Fools! . . . Fill up the road . . ." he ran into the house.

Princess Mary and Mademoiselle Bourienne stood, waiting for the old prince before dinner, well aware that he was out of temper. Mademoiselle Bourienne's beaming face seemed to say, "I know nothing about it, I am just the same as usual," while Princess Mary stood pale and terrified with downcast eyes. What made it harder for Princess Mary was that she knew that she ought to act like Mademoiselle Bourienne at such times, but she could not do it. She felt, "If I behave as if I did not notice it, he'll think I have no sympathy for him. If I behave as if I were depressed and out of humour myself, he'll say that I'm sulky . . ."

The prince glanced at his daughter's scared face and snorted.

"Stuff!" or perhaps "stupid!" he muttered. "And the other is not here!" noticing that the little princess was not in the dining-room.

"Where's Princess Liza?" he asked. "In hiding?"

"She's not quite well," said Mademoiselle Bourienne with a bright smile. "She is not coming down. In her condition it is only to be expected."

"H'm! h'm!" growled the prince, and he sat down to the table. He thought his plate was not clean: he pointed to a mark on it and threw it away. Tihon caught it and handed it to a footman.

The little princess was quite well, but she had such an overwhelming terror of the prince, that on hearing he was in a bad temper, she had decided not to come in.

"I am afraid for my baby," she said to Mademoiselle Bourienne. "God knows what might not be the result of a fright."

The little princess, in fact, lived at Bleak Hills in a state of continual terror of the old prince. And she became particularly fond of Mademoiselle Bourienne; she spent her days with her, begged her to sleep in her room, and often talked of her father-in-law, and criticised him to her.

"We have company coming, prince," said Mademoiselle Bourienne, her rosy fingers unfolding her dinner-napkin. "His excellency Prince Vassily Kuragin with his son, as I have heard say?" she said in a tone of inquiry.

"H'm! . . . his *excellence* is an upstart. I got him his place in the college," the old prince said huffily. "And what his son's coming for, I can't make out. Princess Liza and Princess Mary can perhaps tell us. I don't know what he's bringing this son here for. I don't want him." And he looked at his daughter, who turned crimson.

Unsuccessful as Mademoiselle Bourienne had been in the subject she had started, she did not stop, but went on prattling away about the conservatories, the beauty of a flower that had just opened, and after the soup the prince subsided.

After dinner he went into the waiting-room. The steward was standing there with downcast head.

"Filled up the road again?"

"Yes, your excellency. For God's sake, forgive me, it was simply a blunder."

The prince cut him short with his unnatural laugh.

"Oh, very well, very well." He held out his hand, which the steward kissed, and then he went to his study.

In the evening Prince Vassily arrived. He was met on the way by the coachmen and footmen of the Bolkonskys, who with shouts dragged his carriages and sledge to the lodge over the road, which had been purposely filled up again with snow.

Prince Vassily and his son Anatole were conducted to separate apartments.

Anatole shaved and scented himself with the care and elegance that had become habitual with him, and with his usual expression of all-conquering good-humour, he walked into his father's room. Two valets were busy dressing Prince Vassily. He nodded to his son, as he entered with an air that said, "Yes, that's just how I wanted to see you looking."

"Come, joking apart, father, is she so plain?" Anatole asked in French, reverting to a subject more than once discussed on the journey.

"Nonsense! The thing for you is to try and be respectful and sensible with the old prince. Remember that for you everything depends on it."

Meanwhile, Princess Mary was sitting alone in her room.

"Why did they write? Why did Liza tell me about it? It cannot be!" she thought, looking at herself in the mirror. "How am I to go into the drawing-room? Even if I like him, I can never be myself with him now." The mere thought of her father's eyes reduced her to terror.

The little princess Liza and Mademoiselle Bourienne had already obtained all necessary information from the maid, Masha. They had learned what a handsome fellow the minister's son was, how his father had dragged his legs upstairs with difficulty, while he, like a young eagle, had flown up after him three steps at a time. On receiving these items of news, the little princess and Mademoiselle Bourienne went into Princess Mary's room.

"They have arrived, Mary. Did you know?" said the little princess, waddling in and sinking heavily into an armchair. She was not wearing the gown in which she had been sitting in the morning, but had put on one of her best dresses. Her hair had been carefully arranged, and her face was full of excitement, which did not, however, conceal its wasted and pallid look. Mademoiselle Bourienne, too, had put some finishing touches to her costume, which made her fresh, pretty face even more attractive.

"What, and you are not dressing, dear princess. They will come in a minute to tell us the gentlemen are in the drawing-room," said Princess Liza. And getting up from her chair she rang for the maid, and hurriedly and eagerly began to arrange what Princess Mary was to wear.

Princess Mary did not want to get dressed but she knew that to refuse would have been exposing herself to criticism and insistence. She flushed; her beautiful eyes grew dim; her face was covered with patches of crimson; and with the victimised expression which was the one most often seen on her face, she abandoned herself to Mademoiselle Bourienne and Liza.

"No, really, Mary, that dress isn't pretty," said Liza, looking sideways at Princess Mary from a distance. "Tell the maid to bring your maroon velvet dress. Yes, really! Why, you know, it may be the turning-point in your whole life. That one's too light, it's not right, no, it's not!"

Mademoiselle Bourienne and the little princess felt that if they were to put a blue ribbon in her hair, and do it up high, and put the blue sash lower on the maroon dress and so on, then all would be well. They forgot that the frightened face and figure of Princess Mary could not be changed.

After two or three changes, to which Princess Mary submitted passively, the little princess gazed at her with her head first on one side and then on the other.

"No, it won't do," she said, throwing up her hands. "No, Mary, decidedly that does not suit you. I like you better in your everyday grey dress. Bring the princess her grey dress, and look, Mademoiselle Bourienne, how I'll arrange it."

But when the maid brought the dress, Princess Mary with tears in her eyes was on the point of breaking into sobs.

"Come, dear princess," said Mademoiselle Bourienne.

The little princess, taking the dress from the hands of the maid, went up to Princess Mary.

"Now, we'll try something simple and charming," she said. Her voice and Mademoiselle Bourienne's and the giggle of the maid blended into a sort of gay babble like the twitter of birds.

"No, leave me alone," said Princess Mary. There was such seriousness and such suffering in her voice that the twitter of the birds ceased at once. They saw the great, beautiful eyes, full of tears looking at them imploringly and they knew that to insist was useless and even cruel.

"At least alter your hair," said the little princess. "I told you," she said reproachfully to Mademoiselle Bourienne, "there are faces which that way of doing the hair does not suit a bit. Not a bit, not a bit, please alter it."

"Leave me alone, leave me alone," answered a voice scarcely able to struggle with tears.

"You will change it, won't you?" said Liza, and when Princess Mary made no answer, Liza and Mademoiselle Bourienne went out of the room.

Princess Mary was left alone. She did not re-arrange her hair, she did not even glance into the looking-glass. She sat dreaming. She pictured her husband, a man, a strong, masterful, and attractive creature, who would bear her away into an utterly different, happy world. A child, her own, at her breast. Her husband standing, looking tenderly at her and the child. "But no, it can never be, I am too ugly," she thought.

"Kindly come to tea. The prince will be going in immediately," said the maid's voice at the door. She started and was horrified at what she had been thinking.

Before going downstairs she went into the oratory, and fixing her eyes on the black outline of the great image of the Saviour, she stood for several minutes before it with clasped hands.

When Princess Mary entered, Prince Vassily and his son were already in the drawing-room, talking to the little princess and Mademoiselle Bourienne. When she walked in with her heavy step, treading on her heels, the gentlemen and Mademoiselle Bourienne rose, and the little princess, with a gesture indicating her to the gentlemen, said: "Here is Mary!"

Princess Mary saw them all and saw them in detail. She saw the face of Prince Vassily, growing serious for an instant at the sight of her, and then quickly smiling, and the face of the little princess, scanning the faces of the guests to see the impression Mary was making on them. She saw Mademoiselle Bourienne, too, with her ribbon and her pretty face, turned towards *him* with a look of more eagerness than she had ever seen on it. But *him* she could not see, she could only see something large, bright-coloured, and handsome moving towards her, as she entered the room.

Prince Vassily approached her first; and she kissed his bald head, as he bent over to kiss her hand, and in reply to his words said, that on the contrary, she remembered him very well. Then Anatole went up to her. She still could not see him. She only felt a soft hand taking her hand firmly, and she touched with her lips a white forehead, over which there was beautiful fair hair, smelling of pomade. When finally she glanced at him, she was impressed by his looks.

Anatole was not quick-witted, he was not ready, not eloquent in conversation, but he had that faculty, so invaluable for social purposes, of assurance. It was clear that he could be silent with serenity for a very long while. "If anybody feels silence awkward, let him talk, but I don't care," he seemed to say. Moreover, in his manner to women, Anatole had that air, which does more than anything else to excite curiosity, awe, and even love in women, the air of supercillious consciousness of his own superiority. His manner seemed to say to them: "I know you, I know, but why trouble my head about you? You'd be pleased enough, of course!"

Princess Mary felt this, and as though to show him she did not even venture to think of inviting his attention, she turned to his father. The conversation was general and lively, thanks to the little princess. She met Prince Vassily in that playful tone so often adopted by chatty and lively persons. And he readily fell in with this tone. Anatole too was drawn into the conversation. Mademoiselle Bourienne also succeeded in taking a part. And even Princess Mary felt with pleasure that she was being made to share in their gaiety.

"Do you remember our dear Anna Pavlovna?" the little princess asked Prince Vassily.

"Ah yes, but then you mustn't talk to me about politics, like Anna!"

"And why is it you never used to be at Anna's?" the little princess asked of Anatole. "Ah, I know, I know," she said, winking. "Your brother, Hippolite, has told me tales of your doings. Oh!" She shook her finger at him. "I know about your days in Paris too!"

Mademoiselle Bourienne then ventured to inquire if it were long since Anatole was in Paris, and how he had liked that city. Anatole very readily answered the Frenchwoman, and smiling and staring at her, he talked to her about her native country. At first sight of the pretty Mademoiselle, Anatole had decided that even here at Bleak Hills he would not be bored. "Not half bad-looking," he thought. "She's not half bad-looking, that companion! I hope Mary will bring her along when we're married," he mused. "She's a nice little thing."

The old prince was dressing in his room, scowling and thinking of what he was to do. The arrival of these visitors angered him. "What's Prince Vassily to me, he and his son? Prince Vassily is a braggart, an empty-headed fool, and a nice fellow the son is, I expect," he growled to himself. What angered him was that this visit revived in his mind the unsettled question, continually thrust aside, the question in regard to which the old prince always deceived himself. That question was whether he would ever bring himself to part with his daughter and give her to a husband. The prince could never bring himself to put this question directly to himself, knowing beforehand that if he did he would have to answer it justly, but against justice in this case was ranged more than feeling, the very possibility of life. Life without Princess Mary was unthinkable to the old prince, little as in appearance he prized her. "And what is she to be married for?" he thought; "to be unhappy, beyond a doubt. Look at Liza with André, a better husband it would be difficult to find. And who would marry Mary for love? She's plain and ungraceful. She'd be married for her connections, her wealth. And don't old maids get on well enough? They are happier really!" So old Prince Nicholas mused, as he dressed, yet the question constantly deferred demanded an immediate decision. Prince Vassily had brought his son obviously with the intention of making an offer, and probably that day or the next he would ask for a direct answer. The name, the position in the world, was suitable. "Well, I'm not against it," the prince kept saying to himself. "Only let him be worthy of her. That's what we shall see. That's what we shall see," he said aloud. "That's what we shall see."

And with his usual alert step he walked into the drawing-room, taking in the whole company in a glance. He noticed the change in the dress of the little princess and Mademoiselle Bourienne's ribbon, and the way in which Princess Mary's hair was done, and the smiles of the Frenchwoman and Anatole, and the isolation of his daughter in the general talk. "She's decked herself out like a fool!" he thought, glancing vindictively at her. "No shame in her; while he doesn't even care to speak to her!"

He went up to Prince Vassily.

"Well, how d'ye do, how d'ye do, glad to see you."

"For a friend that one loves seven miles is close by," said Prince Vassily, quoting a Russian proverb, and speaking in his usual rapid, self-confident, and familiar tone. "This is my second, I beg you to love him and welcome him, as they say."

Old Prince Nicholas scrutinized Anatole.

"A fine fellow, a fine fellow!" he said. "Well, come and give me a kiss," and he offered him his cheek. Anatole kissed the old man, and looked at him with curiosity and perfect composure, waiting for some eccentricity his father had told him to expect.

The old prince sat down in his customary place in the corner of the sofa, moved up an armchair for Prince Vassily, pointed to it, and began questioning him about political affairs and news. He seemed to be listening with attention to what Prince Vassily was saying, but glanced continually at Princess Mary.

"So they're writing from Potsdam already?" He repeated Prince Vassily's last words, and suddenly getting up, he went to his daughter.

"So it was for visitors you dressed yourself up like this, eh?"

he said. "Nice of you, very nice. You do your hair up in some new fashion before visitors, and before visitors, I tell you, never dare in the future to change your dress without my leave."

"It was my fault . . ." stammered little Princess Liza, flushing.

"You are quite at liberty," said the old prince, bowing to his daughter-in-law. "But Mary has no need to disfigure herself—she's ugly enough without that." And he sat down again in his place, taking no further notice of his daughter, whom he had reduced to tears.

"On the contrary, that coiffure is extremely becoming to the princess," said Prince Vassily.

"Well, my young prince, what's your name?" said the old prince, turning to Anatole. "Come here, let us talk to you a little and make your acquaintance."

"Now the fun's beginning," thought Anatole, and with a smile he sat down by the old prince.

"That's it; they tell me, my dear boy, you have been educated abroad. Not taught to read and write by the deacon, like your father and me. Tell me, are you serving now in the Horse Guards?" asked the old man, looking closely and intently at Anatole.

"No, I have transferred into the line," answered Anatole smiling.

"Ah! a good thing. So you want to serve your Tsar and your country? These are times of war. Such a fine young fellow ought to be on service, he ought to be on service. Ordered to the front, eh?"

"No, prince, our regiment has gone to the front. But I'm attached. What is it I'm attached to, father?" Anatole turned to his father with a laugh.

"He is a credit to the service, a credit. What is it I'm attached to! Ha-ha-ha!" laughed the old Prince Nicholas, and Anatole laughed still louder. Suddenly the old prince frowned. "Well, you can go," he said to Anatole, and Anatole with a smile returned to the ladies.

"So you had him educated abroad, eh?" said the old prince to Prince Vassily.

"I did what I could, and I assure you the education there is far better than ours."

"Yes, nowadays everything's different, everything's new-fashioned. A fine fellow! A fine fellow! Well, come to my room." He took Prince Vassily's arm and led him away to his study.

Left alone with the old prince, Prince Vassily promptly made known to him his wishes and his hopes.

"Why, do you imagine," said the old prince, "that I keep

her, that I can't part with her? What an idea!" he protested angrily. "I am ready for it to-morrow! Only, I tell you, I want to know my future son-in-law better. You know my principles: everything open! To-morrow I will ask her in your presence; if she wishes it, let him stay on. Let him stay on, and I'll see." The prince snorted. "Let her marry, it's nothing to me," he screamed in the piercing voice in which he had screamed at saying good-bye to his son.

"I will be frank with you," said Prince Vassily in the tone of a crafty man, who is convinced of the uselessness of being crafty with so penetrating a companion. "You see right through people, I know. Anatole is not a genius, but a straightforward, good-hearted lad, good as a son or a kinsman."

"Well, well, very good, we shall see."

With the arrival of Anatole the three women in old Prince Nicholas' house felt that their lives had not been real till then.

Princess Mary did not remember her face and her hair-do. The handsome, open face of the man who might, perhaps, become her husband, absorbed her whole attention. She thought him kind, brave and manly. Thousands of dreams of her future married life floated across her mind. And she tried and knew not how to be cordial to him.

"The poor girl is devilish ugly," Anatole was thinking about her.

Mademoiselle Bourienne had long been looking forward to a "Russian prince" who would see her superiority to the ugly, badly dressed, ungainly Russian princesses—who would fall in love with her and carry her away. And now this "Russian prince" at last had come. And she tried to attract Anatole as much as possible.

The little princess, like an old warhorse hearing the blast of the trumpet, was prepared to gallop off into a flirtation as her habit was, unconsciously forgetting her position, with no ulterior motive, no struggle, nothing but frivolous gaiety in her heart.

That night they all went to their rooms. Anatole fell asleep instantly.

"Can he possibly be—my husband, that stranger, that handsome man," thought Princess Mary, and a feeling of terror, such as she had never known, came upon her. She was afraid to look round; it seemed to her that there was some one there—the devil. . . . She rang for her maid and asked her to sleep in her room.

Mademoiselle Bourienne walked up and down the winter garden for a long while in vain expectation of some one.

The little princess kept grumbling to her maid that her bed

had not been properly made. She could not lie on either side. She felt uncomfortable and ill at ease in every position. Her burden oppressed her, oppressed her more than ever that night, because Anatole's presence had carried her vividly back to another time when it was not so, and she had been light and gay. She sat in a low chair in her night-cap and dressing-jacket. The sleepy maid for the third time beat and turned the heavy feather bed. "I told you it was all in lumps and hollows," the little princess repeated. "I want to go to sleep, it's not my fault." And her voice quivered like a child's when it is going to cry.

The old Prince Nicholas could not sleep either. He paced up and down blowing his nose. He felt as though he had been insulted through his daughter. He said to himself that he would think the whole matter over thoroughly and decide what was right and what must be done, but instead of doing so, he only worked up his irritation more and more.

"The first stray comer that appears! and I'm forgotten, and she runs upstairs, and does up her hair, and rigs herself out, and doesn't know what she's doing! She's glad to abandon me! . . . And don't I see the fool of a boy has no eyes but for Bourienne! And how can she have so little pride, as not to see it? If not for her own sake, if she has no pride, at least for mine. I must show her that the blockhead doesn't give her a thought, and only looks at Bourienne. She has no pride, but I'll make her see it . . . "

By telling his daughter that she was making a mistake, that Anatole was flirting with Mademoiselle Bourienne, the old prince knew that he would wound Mary's self-respect, and so his object, not to be parted from his daughter, would be gained. And so with this in mind he grew calmer.

He called Tihon and began undressing. "The devil brought them here!" he thought, as Tihon slipped his nightshirt over his dried-up old body and his chest covered with grey hair. "I didn't invite them. They come and upset my life. And there's not much of it left. Damn them!"

"They had no reason, no reason . . ." the prince said aloud. And slipping his feet into his slippers and his arms into his dressing-gown, he went to the couch on which he always slept.

The next morning it was with even more than her usual fear that Princess Mary went to the door of her father's study.

The old Prince came to the point at once and began talking. "A proposal has been made to me on your behalf," he said, with an unnatural smile. "I dare say, you have guessed," he went on, "that Prince Vassily has not come here and brought his protégé for the sake of my charms. Yesterday, they made me a proposal on your behalf. And as you know my principles, I refer the matter to you."

"I don't understand you, father," said the princess, turning pale and red.

"Don't understand me!" cried her father angrily. "Prince Vassily finds you to his taste as a daughter-in-law, and makes you a proposal for his protégé. That's how to understand it. Don't understand it! . . . Why, I ask you."

"I don't know how you, father . . ." the princess began in a whisper.

"I? I? What have I to do with it? Leave me out of it. I'm not going to be married. What do you say? That's what I want to know."

The princess saw that her father looked with ill-will on the proposal, but she felt that now or never the fate of her life would be decided. She dropped her eyes so as to avoid the gaze under which she felt incapable of thought, and capable of nothing but her habitual obedience. "My only desire is to carry out your wishes," she said. "If I had to express my own desire . . ."

She had not time to finish. The prince cut her short. "Very good, then!" he shouted. "He shall take you with your dowry, and hook on Mademoiselle Bourienne into the bargain! She'll be his wife, while you . . ." The prince stopped. He watched the effect of these words on his daughter. She had bowed her head and began to cry.

"Come, come, I was joking, I was joking," he said. "Remember one thing, princess, *I* stick to my principles, that a girl has a full right to choose. And I give you complete freedom. Remember one thing; the happiness of your life depends on your decision. No need to talk about me."

"But I don't know . . . father."

"No need for talking! Anatole has been ordered, and he's ready to marry any one, but you are free to choose. . . . Go to your room, think it over, and come to me in an hour's time and tell me in his presence: yes or no. I know you will pray over it. Well, pray if you like. Only you'd do better to think. You can go."

"Yes or no, yes or no, yes or no!" he shouted again as the princess went out of the room.

Princess Mary was decided. She had decided to marry Anatole. But what her father had said about Mademoiselle Bourienne . . . It was not true, of course, but still she could not help thinking of it.

She walked through the winter garden, when all of a sudden, before her, she saw Anatole with his arms round Mademoiselle Bourienne, whispering something to her. Anatole suddenly looked round and saw Princess Mary, but he did not take his arm away from the waist of Mademoiselle Bourienne, who had not seen her. But at last Mademoiselle Bourienne shrieked and ran away. With a gay smile Anatole bowed to Princess Mary, as though inviting her to share his amusement, and with a shrug of his shoulders he went to the door that led to his apartment.

An hour later Tihon came to summon Princess Mary to her father, adding that Prince Vassily was with him. Princess Mary was sitting on the sofa holding the weeping Mademoiselle Bourienne. She was softly stroking her head. Her beautiful eyes had regained all their luminous peace.

"Oh, princess, I am ruined for ever in your heart," Mademoiselle Bourienne was saying.

"Why? I love you more than ever," said Princess Mary.

"But you despise me, you who are so pure, you will never understand . . ."

"I understand everything," said Princess Mary, smiling kindly. "Calm yourself, my dear. I am going to my father now," she said, and she went out.

When the princess went into her father's study, Prince Vassily was sitting with one leg crossed high over the other, and a snuff-box in his hand.

"Ah, my dear, my dear!" he said, getting up and taking her by both hands. He heaved a sigh, and went on: "My son's fate is in your hands. Decide, my good dear, sweet Marie, whom I have always loved like a daughter." He drew back. There were tears in his eyes.

The old prince snorted. "The prince in his protégé's . . . his son's name makes you a proposal. Are you willing or not to be the wife of Prince Anatole Kuragin? You say: yes or no," he shouted, "and then I reserve for myself the right to express my opinion. Yes, my opinion, and nothing but my opinion," added the old prince. "Yes or no!"

"My wish, father, is never to leave you; never to divide my life from yours. I do not wish to marry," she said looking steadily with her beautiful eyes at Prince Vassily and at her father.

"Nonsense, fiddlesticks! Nonsense, nonsense!" shouted the old prince, frowning. He took his daughter's hand, drew her towards him and did not kiss her, but bending over, touched her forehead with his, and wrung the hand he held so violently that she winced and uttered a cry.

Prince Vassily got up. "My dear, let me tell you that this is a moment I shall never forget, never. But my dear, will you not give us a little hope. Say, perhaps. . . . The future is so wide. . . . Say, perhaps."

"Prince, what I have said is from my heart. I thank you for the honour you do me, but I shall never be your son's wife."

"Well, then it's all over, my dear fellow. Very glad to have seen you, very glad to have seen you. Go to your room, princess; go along now," said old Prince Nicholas. "Very, very glad to have seen you," he repeated, embracing Prince Vassily.

It was a long time since the Rostovs had had news from their son Nicholas. But in the middle of the winter a letter was handed to Count Rostov, and in alarm and haste, he ran on to his room, trying to escape notice.

Anna Drubetskoy learned, as she always did learn all that passed in the house, that he had received a letter, and she went to the count and found him with the letter in his hand, sobbing and laughing. Anna Drubetskoy, though her fortunes had been looking up, was still living with the Rostovs.

"Our Nicholas has been wounded," sobbed the count. "My dear, my darling boy. Promoted, thank God . . . How are we to tell the little countess?"

Anna Drubetskoy sat down by his side, and tried to soothe him. Then she decided that before dinner and before tea she would prepare the countess; and after tea, wth God's help, tell her all.

During dinner Anna Drubetskoy talked of the war, of Nicholas, inquired when his last letter had been received, though she knew perfectly well, and observed that they might well be getting a letter from him to-day. Every time that the countess began to be uneasy, Anna Drubetskoy turned the conversation in the most unnoticeable way to other subjects.

Natasha was, however, certain that there was some secret between her father and Anna Drubetskoy, and that it had something to do with her brother. Natasha knew how easily upset her mother was by any references to news from Nicholas, and so she did not say anything at dinner. But she was too excited to eat and kept wriggling about on her chair, regardless of the protests of her governess.

After dinner she rushed to overtake Anna Drubetskoy, and in the living-room flung herself on her neck: "Auntie, darling, do tell me what it is."

"Nothing, my dear."

"No, darling, sweet, precious peach, I won't stop. I know you know something."

Anna Drubetskoy shook her head.

"A letter from Nicholas? I'm sure of it!" cried Natasha.

"But, for God's sake, be more careful. You know what a shock it may be to your mother."

"I will. I will, but tell me about it. You won't? Well, then, I'll run and tell her this minute."

Anna Drubetskoy told Natasha what was in the letter, on condition that she would not tell a soul.

"On my word of honour," said Natasha, crossing herself. "I won't tell any one," and she ran at once to Sonya. "Nicholas has been wounded. . . . A letter . . ." she proclaimed in triumph.

"Nicholas!" was all Sonya could say.

Natasha seeing the effect of the news on Sonya, for the first time realised the seriousness of it all.

She rushed to Sonya, hugged her, and began to cry. "He's only a little wounded and has been made an officer. He's all right now. He writes himself," she said through her tears.

"One can see all you women are regular cry-babies," said Peter. "I'm very glad, really very glad, that my brother has distinguished himself so. You all start blubbering! You don't understand anything about it."

"You haven't read the letter?" asked Sonya.

"No; but she told me it was all over, and that he's an officer now . . ."

"Thank God," said Sonya, crossing herself. "But perhaps she was deceiving you. Let us go to mother."

"If I were in Nicholas' place, I'd have killed a lot more of those Frenchmen," said Peter. "They're such beasts! I'd have killed them till there was a regular heap of them."

"Keep quiet Peter, you're so silly."

"I'm not silly. People are silly who cry for trifles," said Peter.

"Do you remember him?" Natasha asked suddenly, after a moment's silence.

Sonya smiled.

"Do I remember Nicholas?"

"No, Sonya, but do you remember him so as to remember him thoroughly, to remember him completely," said Natasha, as though she were trying to put into her words the most earnest meaning. "I don't remember Boris. I don't remember him a bit . . ."

"What? You don't remember Boris?" Sonya asked in surprise.

"I don't mean I don't remember him. I know what he's like, but when I shut my eyes I can't see him." She shut her eyes. "No, nothing!"

"Oh, Natasha!" said Sonya, looking earnestly at her, as though she considered her unworthy to hear what she meant to say, and was saying it to some one else with whom joking was out of the question. "I love Nicholas once and for all, and whatever happens to him and to me, I will love him all my life."

With wondering eyes, Natasha gazed at Sonya, and she did not speak. She felt that what Sonya was saying was the truth, that there was love such as Sonya was speaking of. But Natasha had never known anything like it. She believed that it might be so, but she did not understand it.

The countess had been prepared by Anna Drubetskoy's hints during dinner. On returning to her room she had sat down in a low chair with her eyes fixed on the miniature of her son, painted on the lid of her snuff-box, and the tears started into her eyes. Anna Drubetskoy, with the letter, approached the countess's room on tiptoe, and stood still at the door.

"Don't come in," she said to the count, who was following her. "Later," and she closed the door. The count put his ear to the keyhole, and listened.

At first he heard the sound of indifferent talk, then Anna Drubetskoy's voice alone, then a cry, then silence, then both voices talking at once. Then there were steps, and Anna Drubetskoy opened the door.

"It is done," she said to the count triumphantly. On seeing the count, the countess held out her arms to him and embraced him.

Vera, Natasha, Sonya, and Peter came into the room, and the reading of the letter began. The letter briefly described the march and the two battles in which Nicholas had taken part, and the receiving of his commission, and said that he kissed the hands of his mother and father, begging their blessing, and sent kisses to Vera, Natasha, and Peter. He sent greetings, too, to Monsieur Schelling and Madame Schoss, and his old nurse, and begged them to kiss for him his darling Sonya, whom he still loved and thought of the same as ever. On hearing this, Sonya blushed till the tears came into her eyes. And she ran into the big hall, ran about with a flushed and smiling face, whirled round and round and ducked down, making her skirts into a balloon.

The countess was crying. "What are you crying about?" said Vera. "From all he writes, we ought to rejoice instead of crying."

This was perfectly true, but the count and the countess and Natasha all looked at her reproachfully. "Who is it that she takes after!" thought the countess.

Nicholas' letter was read over hundreds of times, and those who were considered worthy of hearing it had to come in to the countess, who did not let it go out of her hands. The tutors went in, the nurses, and several acquaintances, and the countess read the letter every time with fresh enjoyment and every time she discovered new virtues in her Nicholas.

"How charmingly he describes everything!" she said, reading over the descriptions in the letter. "And of himself not a word . . . not a word! A great deal about a man called Denisov, though he was himself, I'm sure, braver than any one. He doesn't write a word about his sufferings. How like him it is! I always, always said, when he was no more than that high, I always used to say . . ."

For over a week the Rostovs were hard at work preparing letters to Nicholas from all the household, writing out rough copies, copying out fair copies. With the watchful care of the countess, and the fussy solicitude of the count, all sorts of necessary things were got together, and money, too, for the equipment and the uniform of the young officer. Anna Drubetskoy, practical woman, had succeeded in obtaining special patronage for herself and her son in the army, that even extended to their correspondence. She had opportunities of sending her letters to the Grand Duke, who was in command of the guards. And so the Rostovs sent their letters, and a sum of six thousand roubles, by the special messenger of the Grand Duke to Boris, and Boris was to forward them to Nicholas.

On the 12th of November, Kutuzov's army, encamped near Olmütz, was preparing to be reviewed on the following day by the two Emperors—the Russian and the Austrian.

That day Nicholas Rostov received a note from Boris saying that his regiment was quartered for the night fifteen miles from Olmütz, and that he wanted to see him to give him a letter and some money. Rostov needed the money just now because the troops after active service were stationed near Olmütz, and the camp swarmed with well-equipped canteen keepers, offering all kinds of attractions. Besides a certain Caroline the Hungarian had recently opened a restaurant in Olmütz with girls as waiters. Rostov had also been celebrating his commission as a cornet; he had bought Denisov's horse Bedouin, and was in debt all round to his comrades and the canteen keepers.

On receiving the note from Boris, Rostov rode to Olmütz and then on to the guards' camp to find Boris. He was wearing a shabby ensign's jacket with a private soldier's cross, equally shabby riding-trousers lined with worn leather, and an officer's sabre with a sword-knot. A crushed hussars' cap was stuck jauntily back on one side of his head. As he rode up to the camp of Boris' regiment, he was thinking of how he would impress Boris and all his comrades in the guards by looking so completely a veteran hussar who has been under fire.

The guards had made their march from Russia as though

it were a pleasure excursion, priding themselves on their smartness and discipline. They moved by short stages, their knapsacks were carried in the transport waggons, and at every halt the Austrian government provided the officers with excellent dinners. The regiments made their entry into towns and their exit from them with bands playing. Boris had throughout the march walked and stayed with Berg, who was by this time a captain. Berg had succeeded in gaining the confidence of his superior officers by his conscientiousness and accuracy, and had established his financial position on a very satisfactory basis. Boris had during the same period made the acquaintance of many persons likely to be of use to him, and by means of a letter of recommendation brought from Pierre, had made the acquaintance of Prince André Bolkonsky, through whom he had hopes of obtaining a post on the staff of the commander-in-chief, Kutuzov.

It was almost six months since Nicholas Rostov and Boris had seen each other. Both had changed greatly since they were last together, and both wanted to show as soon as possible what a change had taken place.

"Oh, you damned floor polishers! Smart and clean, as if you'd been enjoying yourselves; not like us poor devils at the front," said Rostov. He pointed to his mud-stained riding-breeches. The German woman of the house popped her head out of a door at Rostov's loud voice.

"A pretty woman, eh?" said he, winking.

"Why do you shout so?" said Boris. "I didn't expect you to-day," he added. "I only sent the note off to you yesterday—through an adjutant of Kutuzov's, who's a friend of mine—Prince André Bolkonsky. I didn't expect he would send it to you so quickly. Well, how are you? Been under fire already?" asked Boris.

Without answering, Rostov, shook the cross of St. George that hung on the cording of his uniform, and pointed to his arm in a sling.

"Yes, yes," said Boris, smiling. Then he added: "You know his Highness travelled with our regiment while we were on the march, so that we had every convenience and advantage. In Poland, the receptions, the dinners, the balls!—I can't tell you. And the Grand Duke was very gracious to all our officers." And both the friends began talking at once; one describing the life at the front; the other telling of the advantages of service under the command of royalty.

"Oh, you guards," said Rostov. "But let's send for some wine."

Boris went to the bedstead, took a purse from under the clean pillows, and ordered some wine. "Oh, Nicholas, I have letters and money to give you," he added.

With the letters and money from his family there had been inserted a letter of recommendation to Prince Bagration, on Anna Drubetskoy's advice, which Countess Rostov had obtained through acquaintances, and had sent to her son, begging him to take it to its address, and to make use of it.

"What nonsense!" said Rostov, throwing the letter under the table.

"What did you throw that away for?" asked Boris.

"It's a letter of recommendation of some sort. What the devil do I want with a letter like that!"

"What the devil do you want with it?" said Boris, picking it up and reading the address; "That letter would be of great use to you."

"I'm not in want of anything, and I'm not going to be an adjutant to anybody."

"Why not?" asked Boris.

"A lackey's job!"

Over the bottle of wine the conversation between the three officers became livelier. The guardsmen told Rostov about their march and how they had been fêted in Russia, in Poland, and abroad. They talked of the sayings and doings of their commander, the Grand Duke, and told anecdotes of his kind-heartedness and his irascibility. Berg was silent, as he always was, when the subject did not concern him personally, but *à propos* of the irascibility of the Grand Duke he related with gusto how he had had some words with the Grand Duke in Galicia, when his Highness had inspected the regiments and had flown into a rage over some irregularity. With a bland smile on his face he described how the Grand Duke had ridden up to him in a violent rage, shouting. "Would you believe me, count, I wasn't in the least alarmed, because I knew I was right. Without boasting, you know, count, I may say I know all the regimental drill-book by heart, and the standing orders, too, I know as I know 'Our Father that art in Heaven.' And so that's how it is, count, there's never the slightest detail neglected in my company. So my conscience was at ease. I came forward." Berg stood up and mimicked how he had come forward with his hand to the beak of his cap. It would certainly have been difficult to imagine more respectfulness and more self-complacency in a face. "Well, he raged at me, and shouted 'damn,' and 'to Siberia,' " said Berg, with a subtle smile. "I knew I was right, and so I didn't speak; how could I, count? 'Why are you dumb?' he shouted. Still I held my tongue, and what do you think, count? Next day there was nothing about it in the orders of the day. That's what comes of keeping one's head. Yes, indeed, count," said Berg, pulling at his pipe and letting off rings of smoke.

Boris then changed the conversation. He asked Rostov to

tell them how and where he had been wounded. That pleased Rostov, and he began telling them, getting more and more eager as he talked. He described to them his battle at Schöngraben exactly as men who have taken part in battles always do describe them, as they would have liked them to be. Rostov was a truthful young man; he would not have intentionally told a lie. He began with the intention of telling everything precisely as it had happened, but unconsciously, and inevitably he passed into falsehood. He could not tell them simply that they had all been charging full gallop, that he had fallen off his horse, sprained his arm, and run with all his might away from the French into the woods. Besides his listeners expected to hear how he had forgotten himself, had flown like a tempest on the enemy, hewing men down right and left, how a sabre had been thrust into his flesh and how he had fallen unconscious. And so he described all that.

In the middle of his tale, just as he was saying: "You can't imagine what a frenzy takes possession of you at the moment of the charge," there walked into the room Prince André Bolkonsky, whom Boris was expecting. Prince André liked to encourage and assist younger men. He was flattered at being applied to for his influence, and well disposed to Boris, who had succeeded in making a favourable impression on him the previous day. He was eager to do for the young man what he desired. Having been sent with papers from Kutuzov to the Grand Duke, he called upon Boris, hoping to find him alone. When he came into the room and saw the hussar, Rostov, with his soldierly swagger describing his warlike exploits, he frowned. He regretted having dropped into such undesirable society.

But turning to Boris, he smiled warmly and said: "As to your business, we will have to talk of it later." He glanced at Rostov. "You come to me after the review, and we'll do what we can." And looking round the room he added: "On Friday, after the review, I shall expect you, Drubetskoy. Goodbye till then." And he went out.

The day after Rostov's visit to Boris, both Emperors, the Russian Emperor with the Grand Duke, and the Austrian with the Archduke, reviewed the allied forces, making up an army of eighty thousand men.

The whole army was drawn out in three lines. In front was the cavalry; behind, the artillery; still further back, the infantry.

Like a wind passing over the leaves, an excited whisper fluttered over the plain: "They are coming! they are coming!"

A group came into sight. It was the Emperors' suite.

In the deathlike stillness, the only sound was the tramp of hoofs. The Emperors rode towards the flank, and the trumpets of the first cavalry regiment began playing a march. Through the music could be distinctly heard one voice, the genial, youthful voice of the Emperor Alexander. He uttered some words of greeting, and the first regiment boomed out: "Hurrah!" with a shout deafening, prolonged, and joyful.

"Hurrah! Hurrah! Hurrah!" thundered on all sides, and one regiment after another greeted the Tsar with the strains of the march, then hurrah! . . . Then the march, and again hurrah! And hurrah! Which growing stronger and fuller, blended into a deafening roar.

In the terrific uproar of those voices, between the square masses of troops, immobile as though turned to stone, moved carelessly and freely, some hundreds of men on horseback, the suite, and in front of them two figures—the Emperors.

Rostov, standing in the foremost ranks of Kutuzov's army, was possessed by the feeling, common to every man in that army—a feeling of self-oblivion, of proud consciousness of their might and passionate devotion to the man who was the centre of that solemn ceremony.

He felt that at one word from that man all that vast mass and he, an insignificant atom bound up with it, would rush through fire and water, to crime, to death, or to the grandest heroism.

The handsome, youthful Emperor Alexander, in the uniform of the Horse Guards, halted before the Pavlograd regiment. He said something in French to the Austrian Emperor and smiled.

Seeing that smile, Rostov unconsciously began to smile himself and felt an even stronger rush of love for his Emperor. He longed to express his love for the Tsar in some way. He knew it was impossible, and he wanted to cry. The Tsar called up the colonel of the regiment and said a few words to him which Rostov did not catch. And the soldiers, straining their lungs, roared "hurrah!"

Then the Tsar's foot, in the narrow-pointed boot of the day, touched the belly of the bay English thoroughbred he was riding. The Tsar's hand in its white glove gathered up the reins and he moved off, accompanied by the heaving sea of adjutants. Further and further he rode away, stopping at the other regiments, and at last the white plume of his hat was all that Rostov could see.

Among the gentlemen of the suite, Rostov recognised Prince André Bolkonsky.

When the Tsar had made the round of almost all the regiments, the troops began to file by him in a parade march. Thousands of legs and bayonets moved with flags waving. With the rhythmic tramp of hoofs, the smartly dressed cavalry in blue and red and green laced uniforms rode jingling by on black and chestnut and grey horses, the bandsmen in front covered with embroidery. Between the infantry and the cavalry the artillery, in a long line of polished, shining cannons rattling on their carriages, crawled slowly past. The generals in their full parade uniform, wearing scarves and all their decorations, with waists, portly and slim alike, pinched in to the uttermost, and red necks squeezed into stiff collars, rode proudly by. Every soldier, with his clean, washed, and shaven face, and weapons polished to the utmost glitter, marched in perfect order. Every horse was rubbed down till its coat shone like satin, and every hair in its moistened mane lay in place.

The day after the review Boris Drubetskoy put on his best uniform and rode to Olmütz to see Prince André Bolkonsky.

"It's all very well for Rostov, whose father sends him ten thousand at a time, to talk about not caring to cringe to any one, and not being a lackey. But I, with nothing of my own but my brains, have my career to make, and mustn't let opportunities slip by."

When the review was over, the officers, both of the reinforcements and of Kutuzov's army, began to gather together in groups. They spoke about the honours that had been conferred, about the Austrians and their uniforms, about Bonaparte and the bad time in store for him now. But the chief subject of conversation in every circle was the Emperor Alexander. Every word he had uttered, every gesture was described and commented upon with enthusiasm.

There was but one desire. Under the Emperor's leadership, all wanted to face the enemy as soon as possible. Under the command of the Emperor himself they could not fail.

After the review they all felt certain of victory.

Prince André took Boris to Prince Dolgorukov. It was late in the evening as they entered the palace at Olmütz, occupied by the Emperors and their retinues.

There had been on that same day a council of war, at which all the members of the Austrian high command and the two Emperors had been present. At this council it had been decided, contrary to the advice of the elder generals, Kutuzov and Prince Schwarzenberg, to advance at once and to fight a general engagement with Bonaparte.

The council of war was only just over when Prince André and Boris went into the palace in search of Prince Dolgorukov. Every one at headquarters was still under the spell of the success gained that day by the younger party at the council of war. The voices of those who urged delay, and counselled waiting had been so unanimously drowned out and their arguments had been over-ruled by such positive proof of the advantages of advancing, that the coming battle was already counted as a victory. All the advantages, it was agreed, were on Russia's and Austria's side. Their immense forces, undoubtedly superior to those of Napoleon, were concentrated in one place; the troops were encouraged by the presence of the two Emperors, and were eager for battle. The strategic position on which they were to act was to the minutest detail known to the Austrian general Weierother, who was at the head of the troops. And as luck would have it, the Austrian troops had chosen for their manœuvres the very fields in which they were now to fight the French. Every detail of the surrounding neighbourhood was known and put down on maps, while Bonaparte, apparently growing feebler, was taking no measures.

Dolgorukov, who had been one of the strongest supporters of attack, had just come back from the council, weary, exhausted, but eager and proud of the success he had gained. Prince André introduced Boris, but Prince Dolgorukov, though he shook hands politely and warmly, said nothing to Boris. Obviously unable to restrain his thoughts, he addressed Prince André in French.

"Well, we have won! God only grant that the battle will also be a victory. I must admit though," he said eagerly, "my shortcomings compared with the Austrians, and especially Weierother. What accuracy, what minuteness, what knowledge of the locality, what foresight of every possibility, every condition! The combination of Austrian organization with Russian valour—what more could you wish for?"

"So an attack has been decided upon?" asked Prince André.

"Yes, definitely. I tell you, Napoleon is in our hands. Victory is ours!"

"But, prince," said André, changing the subject, "I have come to see you on behalf of this young friend. You see . . ." But before Prince André could finish, an adjutant came into the room to summon Prince Dolgorukov to the Emperor.

"Oh, how annoying!" said Dolgorukov, getting up hurriedly and shaking hands with Prince André and Boris. "You know I shall be very glad to do everything possible for . . ." Once more he shook hands with Boris in a good-natured way. "But you see . . . another time!"

Next day the troops set off on the march, and up to the time of the battle of Austerlitz, Boris did not succeed in seeing Prince André or Dolgorukov again, and remained in his old regiment.

At dawn on the 16th, Denisov's squadron, in which Nicholas Rostov was serving, and which formed part of Prince Bagration's detachment, moved on from its halting place for the night to advance into action. After about a mile's march, in the rear of other columns, it was brought to a standstill on the high-road. Rostov saw the Cossacks, the first and second squadron of hussars, and the infantry battalions with the artillery pass and march on ahead. He also saw the Generals Bagration and Dolgorukov ride by with their adjutants. All the panic he had felt, as before, at the prospect of battle, all the inner conflict by means of which he had overcome that panic, all his dreams of distinguishing himeslf in true hussar style in this battle—all were for nothing. His squadron was held back in reserve, and he spent a tedious and wretched day. About nine o'clock in the morning he heard firing ahead, and shouts of hurrah, saw the wounded being brought back, and finally saw a whole detachment of French cavalry being brought back by a company of Cossacks. Obviously the action was over, and successful. The soldiers and officers as they came back were talking of a brilliant victory, of the taking of the town of Vishau, and a whole French squadron.

"Rostov, come here, have a drink," shouted Denisov, sitting at the roadside before a bottle and some food. The officers were gathered in a ring, eating and talking, round Denisov's wine-case.

"The Emperor! The Emperor!" was suddenly heard among the hussars. Everything was bustle and hurry, and Rostov saw behind them on the road several horsemen riding up with white plumes in their hats. In a single moment all were in their places.

The young Emperor could not resist being present at the battle, and in spite of the protests and warnings of his courtiers, at twelve o'clock, he galloped to the vanguard. Before he reached the hussars, several adjutants met him with news of the successful engagement.

The action, which had simply consisted in the capture of a squadron of the French, was magnified into a brilliant victory, and so the Tsar and the whole army believed, especially while the smoke still hung over the field of battle, that the French had already been defeated and had been forced to retreat.

A few minutes after the Tsar had galloped on, the division of the Pavlograd hussars received orders to move forward.

The advance forces were posted before Vishau in sight of the enemy's line, which had been all day retreating at the slightest exchange of shots. The Tsar's thanks were conveyed to the men, rewards were promised, and a double allowance of vodka was served out. The camp fires crackled, and the happy soldiers sang their songs. Denisov on that night celebrated his promotion to major, and, after a good deal of drinking, Rostov proposed a toast to the health of the Emperor, but "not our Sovereign the Emperor, as they say at official dinners," said he, "but to the health of the Emperor, the good great man, let us drink to his health, and to a decisive victory over the French!"

"If we fought before," he added, "and would not yield an inch to the French, as at Schöngraben, what will it be now when he is leading us? We will all die, we will gladly die for him. Eh, gentlemen? Perhaps I'm not saying it right. I've drunk a good deal, but that's how I feel. To the health of Alexander the First! Hurrah!"

"Hurrah!" rang out the voices of the officers. And the old captain shouted no less heartily and sincerely than Rostov, the boy of twenty.

The following day the Tsar stayed in Vishau. His medical attendant, Villier, was several times summoned to him. At headquarters and among the troops that were near, the news circulated that the Tsar was unwell. He was eating nothing and had slept badly that night. It was said that he was ill because of the shock of seeing the killed and wounded.

On the 18th and 19th the troops moved forward two days' march, and the enemy's outposts, after a brief interchange of shots, retired. In the higher departments of the army an intense, bustling excitement and activity prevailed from noon of the 19th till the morning of the following day, the 20th of November, on which was fought the memorable battle of Austerlitz. Up to midday of the 19th the activity, the eager talk, the bustle, and the despatching of adjutants was confined to the headquarters of the Emperors; after midday the activity had reached the headquarters of Kutuzov and the staff of the commanding officers of the columns. By evening this activity had been carried by the adjutants in all directions into every part of the army, and in the night of the 19th the multitude of the eighty thousands of the allied army rose from its halting-place, and moved on, a heaving mass nine miles long.

Prince André was on duty that day, and in close attendance on the commander-in-chief. At six o'clock in the evening Kutuzov visited the headquarters of the Emperors, and after a brief interview with the Tsar, went in to see the high marshal Count Tolstoy.

Prince André took advantage of this interval to visit Dolgorukov. He felt that Kutuzov was disturbed and displeased about something, and that they were displeased with him at headquarters, and that all the persons at the Emperor's headquarters took the tone with him of people who knew something other people are not aware of. And for that reason Prince André wanted to have some talk with Dolgorukov.

"The fun is for tomorrow," said Dolgorukov, who was sitting at tea with Bilibin. "How's your old fellow Kutuzov? Out of humour?"

"I won't say he's out of humour, but I think he would like to get a hearing."

"But he did get a hearing at the council of war, and he will get another hearing whenever he begins to talk sense. But to delay and wait, when Bonaparte fears a general engagement more than anything, is out of the question. In spite of my profound respect for old Kutuzov," he continued, "what fools we should be to wait about and let him have a chance to get away or cheat us. No, we mustn't forget Suvorov and his rule—always to attack. Believe me, the energy of young men is often a safer guide in warfare than all the experience of old generals."

"But where are you going to attack him? I have been at the outposts to-day, and there is no making out where his chief forces are concentrated," said Prince André.

"Oh, that's a matter of no consequence whatever," Dolgorukov said quickly, getting up and unfolding a map on the table. "Every contingency has been provided for. If he is concentrated at Brünn. . . ." And Prince Dolgorukov gave a rapid and vague account of Weierother's plan of a flank movement.

Prince André began to make objections and to offer suggestions. But Dolgorukov seemed bored.

"There is to be a council of war at Kutuzov's to-night. You can explain all that then," he said.

"That's what I am going to do," said Prince André, moving away from the map.

"And what are you worrying yourselves about, gentlemen?" said Bilibin, with sarcasm. "Whether there is victory or defeat to-morrow, the glory of Russian arms is secure. Except for Kutuzov, there's not a single Russian in command of a column. The commanders are: Herr General Wimpfen, le comte de Langeron, le prince de Lichtenstein, le prince de Hohenlohe and Prishprshiprsh, or some such Polish name."

"Keep quiet," said Dolgorukov. "It's not true, there are two Russians: Miloradovitch and Dohturov, and there would have been a third, but for his weak nerves."

On returning to his quarters Prince André could not resist asking Kutuzov, who sat near him in silence, what he thought about the coming battle.

Kutuzov looked sternly at him, and after a pause, answered quietly: "I think the battle will be lost, and I said so to Count Tolstoy and asked him to give that message to the Tsar. And what do you suppose was the answer he gave me? 'O, my dear general, can't you see I am busy eating rice and chops. . . .' Yes. . . . That's the answer I got!"

At ten o'clock in the evening, Weierother with his plans rode

over to Kutuzov's quarters, where the council of war was to take place. All the commanders of columns were summoned to the commander-in-chief's, and with the exception of Prince Bagration, who declined to come, all of them arrived at the appointed hour.

Weierother, who was entirely responsible for the strategy of the proposed battle, in his eagerness and hurry, was a striking contrast to the ill-humoured and sleepy Kutuzov, who presided as chairman. Weierother obviously felt himself at the head of the movement that had been set going and could not be stopped. Twice that evening he had made a personal inspection of the enemy's line, and twice he had been with the Emperors, Russian and Austrian.

He was evidently so much engrossed with his plans that he forgot to be respectful to Kutuzov. He interrupted him, talked rapidly and indistinctly, failed to answer questions that were put to him, and was exhausted, distracted, and at the same time self-confident and haughty.

Kutuzov, his uniform unbuttoned, and his fat neck as though set free from bondage, bulging over the collar, was sitting in a low chair with his podgy old hands laid symmetrically on the arms. He was almost asleep.

At the sound of Weierother's voice, he made an effort and opened his solitary eye.

"Yes, yes, please, it's late as it is," he assented, and nodding his head, he let it droop and closed his eye again.

Weierother glanced at Kutuzov and satisfying himself that he was asleep, he took up a paper and in a loud, monotonous tone began reading a report of the disposition of the troops in the coming battle. It was very complicated and intricate.

The generals listened reluctantly. The tall, fair-haired general, Buxhevden, stood leaning against the wall, and fixing his eyes on a burning candle, he seemed not to be listening, not even to wish to be thought to be listening. Exactly opposite to Weierother, was Miloradovitch, a ruddy man, with whiskers, sitting with his hands on his knees. He sat in obstinate silence, staring into Weierother's face, and only taking his eyes off him when the Austrian staff-commander ceased speaking. Next to Weierother sat Count Langeron. He gazed at his delicate fingers as he twisted round a golden snuff-box with a portrait on it. Przhebyshevsky, with respectful but dignified courtesy, put his hand up to his ear on the side nearest Weierother. Dohturov, a little man, sat opposite Weierother with a studious and modest look on his face. Bending over the map, he was conscientiously studying the arrangement of the troops and the unfamiliar locality. Several times he asked Weierother to repeat words and difficult names of villages that he had not caught. Weierother did so, and Dohturov made a note of them.

When the reading, which lasted more than an hour, was over, Langeron stopped twisting his snuff-box and began to speak without looking at Weierother or any one else in particular. He pointed out how difficult it was to carry out such manœuvres while the enemy was in movement. Langeron's objections were valid, yet it was evident that their principal object was to make Weierother, who had read his plans, as though to a lot of schoolboys, feel that he had to deal not with fools, but with men who could teach him something in military matters.

When the monotonous sound of Weierother's voice ceased, Kutuzov opened his eye, listened to Langeron, and as though saying to himself: "Oh, you're still at the same nonsense!" closed his eye again, and let his head sink still lower.

Weierother met all Langeron's objections with a confident and contemptuous smile.

"You suppose Napoleon, then, to be powerless?" said Langeron.

"I doubt if he has forty thousand troops," answered Weierother.

"In that case, he will meet defeat by awaiting our attack," said Langeron with an ironical smile, looking round for support from Miloradovitch. But Miloradovitch was obviously thinking at that instant of something completely removed from the dispute between the generals.

Weierother smiled again. "The enemy have extinguished their fires and a continual noise has been heard in their camp," he said. "What does that mean? Either they are retreating, the only thing we have to fear, or changing their position."

"How can that be? . . ." said Prince André, who had been looking out for an opportunity of expressing his doubts.

Kutuzov waked up, cleared his throat huskily, and looked round at the generals. "Gentlemen, the disposition for tomorrow, for to-day indeed, for it's going on to one o'clock, can't be altered now," he said. "You have heard it, and we will all do our duty. And before a battle nothing is of so much importance . . ." He paused. "Nothing is of so much importance as a good night's rest."

He rose from his chair. The generals bowed themselves out. It was past midnight. Prince André left.

The council of war had left Prince André with an impression of uncertainty and uneasiness. Which was right: Dolgorukov and Weierother, or Kutuzov and Langeron and the others, who did not approve of the plan of attack; he did not know. But could it not have been managed differently? Because of personal and court considerations were tens of thousands of lives to be risked, "And my life, mine?" he thought.

"I may be killed to-morrow."

And all at once, at the thought of death, a whole chain of memories, the most remote and closest to his heart, rose up in his imagination. He recalled his last farewell with his father and his wife; he recalled the early days of his love for her, thought of her approaching motherhood; and he felt sorry for her and for himself, and in a nervously overwrought and softened mood he went out of the cottage at which he and Nesvitsky were staying, and began to walk back and forth. The night was foggy, and the moonlight glimmered mysteriously through the mist. "Yes, to-morrow, to-morrow!" he thought. "To-morrow, maybe, all will be over for me, all these memories will be no more, all these memories will have no more meaning for me. To-morrow, perhaps . . ."

Nicholas Rostov had been sent that night with a platoon on picket duty to the foremost part of Bagration's detachment. His hussars were scattered about the outposts. And he himself rode about the line trying to struggle against the sleepiness which kept overcoming him. Behind him stretched miles of dimly burning Russian and Austrian camp fires. Before him was the misty darkness.

However intently Rostov gazed into this misty distance, he could see nothing. At one moment there seemed something greyish, at the next something blackish, then something like the glimmer of a fire over there where the enemy must be. Then he thought the glimmer had been only in his own eyes. His eyes kept closing, and there floated before his mind the image of the Emperor, then of Denisov, and Moscow memories, and again he opened his eyes and saw close before him the head and ears of the horse he was riding. But in the distance there was still the same misty darkness. "Where am I? Yes, in the picket line. How annoying that our squadron will be in reserve . . ." he thought. "I'll ask to go to the front. It won't be long before I'm off duty. I'll ride round once more, and when I come back, I'll go to the general and ask him." He sat up straight in the saddle and set off to ride once more round his hussars. ". . . Na . . . tasha, my sister, her black eyes. Na . . . tasha. Won't she be surprised when I tell her how I've seen the Emperor! Natasha . . . tasha . . ."

"Keep to the right, your honour, there are bushes here," said the voice of a hussar, by whom Rostov was riding as he fell asleep. Rostov lifted his head and pulled up beside the hussar. He could not shake off his childish drowsiness. "What was I thinking? I mustn't forget. Yes! Natasha . . . Ah, a fine fellow, Denisov! But that's all nonsense. The great thing is that the Emperor's here now at the head of our troops. Natasha . . ." And again his head dropped.

All at once it seemed to him that he was being fired at. "What? What? . . . Cut them down! What?" Rostov was saying, as he awakened. At the instant that he opened his eyes, Rostov heard over where the enemy were, the prolonged shouting of thousands of voices. His horse and the horse of the hussar near him pricked up their ears. Over where the shouts came from, a light was lighted and put out, then another, and all along the line of the French troops on the hillside fires were lighted and the shouts grew louder and louder.

"What is it? What do you think?" Rostov asked the hussar. "That's in the enemy's camp?"

The hussar did not answer.

"Why, don't you hear it?" Rostov asked again.

"Who can tell, your honour?"

"From the direction it must be the enemy," Rostov said again.

"May be 'tis, and may be not," said the hussar. "It's dark. Now steady!" he shouted to his horse. Rostov's horse too was restless, and pawed the frozen ground as it listened to the shouts and looked at the lights. The shouting grew louder and passed into a roar that could only be produced by an army of thousands. The lights stretched further and further.

"Vive l'Empereur! l'Empereur!" Rostov could hear distinctly now.

The shouts and lights in the French army were due to the fact that Napoleon himself was riding through the ranks. And the soldiers on seeing their Emperor were lighting wisps of straw and running after him.

There suddenly sprang up out of the night mist the figure of a sergeant of hussars on horseback.

"Your honour, the generals!" said the sergeant, riding up to Rostov. Rostov, still looking away towards the lights and shouts, rode with the sergeant to meet several men galloping along the line. One was on a white horse. Prince Bagration with Prince Dolgorukov and his adjutant had ridden out to look at the strange lights and shouts in the enemy's army. Rostov, going up to Bagration, reported what he had heard and seen, and joined the adjutants, listening to what the generals were saying.

"Take my word for it," Prince Dolgorukov was saying to Bagration, "it's nothing but a trick; they have retreated and ordered the rearguard to light fires and make a noise to deceive us." Dolgorukov was still insisting on his opinion that the French were retreating.

"It's very clear they have not all retired, at all, prince," said Bagration in anger.

"The picket's on the hill, your excellency, still where it was in the evening," Rostov announced, his hand to his cap.

"Very good, very good," said Bagration, "I thank you, officer."

"Your excellency," added Rostov, "may I ask a favour?"

"What is it?"

"To-morrow our squadron is ordered to the rear; would you assign me to the first squadron?"

"What's your name?"

"Count Rostov."

"Ah, very good! You may stay in attendance on me. I will give the order."

"To-morrow!" he thought. "Thank God!"

And once more they saw the strange lights and heard the roar of voices: *"Vive l'Empereur!"*

At five o'clock in the morning it was still quite dark. The troops of the centre, of the reserves, and of Bagration's right flank, were still at rest. But on the left flank the columns of the infantry, cavalry, and artillery, according to Weierother's plan, were to attack the French right flank who were already up and astir. The smoke from the camp fires made the eyes smart. It was cold and dark. The officers were hurriedly drinking tea and eating breakfast; the soldiers were munching biscuits and stamping their feet, while they gathered about the fires warming themselves, and throwing into the blaze the remains of shacks, chairs, tables, wheels, tubs, everything that they could not take away with them. Austrian officers were moving in and out among the Russian troops. At their orders the soldiers ran from the fires, threw bags into waggons, checked their muskets, and formed into ranks. The officers buttoned their coats, put on their sabres and pouches, and moved up and down the ranks shouting. The officers' servants harnessed the horses, packed and tied up the waggons. The adjutants and the officers in command of regiments and battalions got on their horses, crossed themselves, gave final orders, and the monotonous thud of thousands of feet began. The columns moved, not knowing where they were going, and unable from the crowds round them, the smoke, and the thickening fog, to see either the place which they were leaving, or that into which they were advancing.

The fog was so thick that though it was growing light, they could not see ten steps in front of them. Anywhere, on any side, they might stumble upon unseen enemies. But for a long while the columns marched on in the fog, going downhill and uphill, passing gardens and fences, in new and unknown country, without coming upon the enemy anywhere.

Though not one of the officers in command of the columns rode up to the ranks nor talked to the soldiers, yet the soldiers marched on in good spirits, as they always do when advancing into action, especially when on the offensive.

But after they had been marching on for about an hour in the thick fog, a great part of the troops had to halt, and an unpleasant impression of mismanagement and misunderstanding spread through the ranks.

"What are we stopping for?"

"After hurrying us . . . Here we are in the middle of a field."

"The cavalry is blocking the road," said an officer.

"Which division are you?" shouted an adjutant, riding up.

"Eighteenth."

"Then why are you here? You ought to have been in front long ago. You won't get there now before evening." He rode off.

Then a general galloped up, and shouted something in a foreign tongue.

Ahead of the troops an argument had arisen between an Austrian officer and a Russian general. The Russian general shouted that the cavalry should stop. The Austrian tried to explain that he was not responsible. The troops meanwhile stood, growing listless and dispirited. After an hour's delay the troops moved on at last, and began going downhill. The fog, that overspread the hill, lay even more densely on the low ground to which the troops were going. Ahead in the fog they heard a shot, and another; at first at random, at irregular intervals; then growing more regular and frequent. And a skirmish began.

Coming upon the French unexpectedly in the fog, not hearing a word of encouragement from their commanding officers, and with a general sense of being too late, the Russians fired slowly at the enemy. They never received a command in time from their officers and adjutants, who wandered about in the fog unable to find their own divisions. This was how the battle of Austerlitz began for the first, the second, and third columns, who had gone down into the low-lying ground.

The fourth column, with which Kutuzov was, was still on the plateau of Pratzen.

Nine o'clock came. The fog lay stretched in an unbroken sea over the valley where the skirmish had begun, but on the high ground where Napoleon was, surrounded by his marshals, it was now perfectly clear. There was bright blue sky overhead.

Napoleon was standing in front of his marshals, on a little grey Arab horse. He was looking intently and silently at the hills, which stood up out of the sea of mist, and at the Russian troops moving across them in the distance. And he listened to the sounds of firing in the valley. His face did not stir a single muscle; his gleaming eyes were fixed intently on one spot. His forecasts were turning out correct. Part of the Russian forces were going down into the valley towards the ponds and lakes, while part were evacuating the heights of Pratzen, which he regarded as the key position, and which he had intended to take. He saw through the fog, in the dip between two hills near the village of Pratzen, Russian columns with glittering bayonets moving always in one direction towards the valley, and vanishing one after another into the mist. From information he had received during the night, from the loose order of the march of the Russian columns, from all evidence, he saw clearly that the Russians and Austrians believed him to be a long way off. But still he delayed beginning the battle.

That day was for him a day of triumph, the anniversary of his coronation. He had slept for a few hours in the early morning, and felt fresh, and in good health and spirits, in that happy frame of mind in which everything seems possible and everything succeeds. He stood without stirring, looking at the heights that rose out of the fog. His marshals stood behind him, mounted on their horses.

Then when the sun had completely emerged from the fog, and was glittering with dazzling brilliance over the fields and the mist, he took his glove off his hand, made a signal with it to his marshals, giving the order for the battle to begin.

Kutuzov rode out to Pratzen greeting the men of the fourth column. He gave them the command to march, showing that he meant to lead them himself. Prince André was among the immense number of persons who made up the commander-in-chief's suite.

Kutuzov seemed exhausted and irritable that morning. The infantry marching by him halted without any command being given, apparently because something in front blocked up the way.

An Austrian officer wearing a white uniform and green plumes in his hat, galloped up to Kutuzov and asked him in the Emperor's name: Had the fourth column started?

Kutuzov turned away without answering, and his eye fell casually on Prince André, who was standing near him. Seeing him, Kutuzov let his vindictive and bitter expression soften, as though recognising that his adjutant was not to blame for what was being done. And still not answering the Austrian adjutant, he addressed Prince André.

"Go and see whether the third division has passed the village. Tell them to stop and wait for my orders."

Prince André had scarcely started when he stopped him.

"And ask whether the sharpshooters are posted," he added. "What they are doing, what they are doing!" he murmured to himself, still making no reply to the Austrian.

Prince André galloped off. Overtaking all the advancing battalions, he stopped the third division and found there actually was no line of sharpshooters. The officer in command of the advance regiment was greatly surprised on the order being brought him from the commander-in-chief to send a flying line of sharpshooters in advance. The officer had believed that there were other troops in front of him, and that the enemy could not be less than ten miles away. In reality there was nothing in front of him but an empty stretch of ground, sloping downhill and covered with fog.

Prince André galloped back. Kutuzov was still at the same place; his bulky frame drooped in the saddle with the lassitude of old age, and he was yawning. The troops had not yet moved on.

"Good, good," he said to Prince André, and he turned to the general who, watch in hand, was saying that it was time they started, as all the columns of the left flank had gone down already.

"We have plenty of time, your excellency," Kutuzov said between yawns. "Plenty of time!" he repeated.

At that moment in the distance behind Kutuzov there were sounds of regiments saluting; the shouts came rapidly nearer along the whole drawn-out line of the advancing Russian columns. When the soldiers of the regiment, in front of which Kutuzov was standing, began to shout, he rode off a little on one side, and wrinkling up his face, looked round. Along the road from Pratzen, galloped what looked like a whole squadron of horsemen of different colours. Two of them galloped side by side ahead of the rest. One was in a black uniform with a white plume, on a chestnut English thoroughbred, the other in a white uniform on a black horse. These were the two Emperors and their suites.

With a sort of affectation of the manner of an old soldier at the head of his regiment, Kutuzov gave the command, "Steady," to the standing troops and rode up to the Emperors, saluting. His whole figure and manner were suddenly transformed. He assumed the air of a subordinate, a man who accepts without criticism. With a show of respectfulness which unmistakably made an unpleasant impression on the Tsar Alexander, he rode up and saluted him.

The Tsar was flushed a little from the three-mile gallop,

and as he pulled up his horse, he looked round at those among the faces of his suite that were as young and eager as his own. They were all richly dressed, gay young men on splendid, well-groomed horses. The Emperor Francis, a long-faced young man, sat erect on his handsome horse, casting anxious looks around him. With the Emperors' suite were a certain number of fashionable young aristocrats—Russians and Austrians—selected from the regiments of the guards and the line. Among them were postillions leading extra horses, beautiful beasts from the Tsar's stables, covered with embroidered horsecloths.

Like a breath of fresh country air rushing into a stuffy room through an open window was the youth, energy, and confidence of success that this cavalcade of brilliant young people brought with them into Kutuzov's cheerless staff.

"Why aren't you beginning?" the Emperor Alexander said hurriedly, addressing Kutuzov, while he glanced courteously towards the Emperor Francis.

"I am waiting to see, your majesty," Kutuzov answered bowing.

The Emperor turned his ear towards him, with a slight frown and an air of not having caught his words.

"I'm waiting to see, your majesty," repeated Kutuzov. His upper lip quivered. "Not all the columns are massed yet, your majesty."

The Tsar heard him, but the answer apparently did not please him. He shrugged his sloping shoulders and his expression seemed to complain of Kutuzov.

"We are not on the Parade Ground you know, where the review is not begun till all the regiments are ready," said the Tsar, glancing again at the Emperor Francis as though inviting him, if not to take part, at least to listen to what he was saying. But the Emperor Francis still gazed away and did not listen.

"That's just why I'm not beginning, sire," said Kutuzov in a resounding voice, as though foreseeing a possibility his words might be ignored. And once more there was a quiver in his face. "That's why I am not beginning, sire; because we are not on review and not on the Parade Ground," he articulated clearly and distinctly.

Everyone in the Tsar's suite exchanged glances with one another. "However old Kutuzov may be, he ought not, he ought never to speak like that," the glances seemed to say.

The Tsar looked steadily and attentively into Kutuzov's face, waiting to see if he were not going to say more. But Kutuzov bending his head respectfully, also seemed to be waiting.

The silence lasted about a minute.

"However, if it's your majesty's command," said Kutuzov, lifting his head and relapsing into his former affectation of the uncritical general, who obeys orders. He moved away, and signaling the commanding officer of the column, gave him the order to advance.

The troops began to move again, and three battalions passed before the Tsar.

Kutuzov, accompanied by his adjutants, rode behind at a walking pace.

Having ridden for about half a mile at the end of the column, he stopped at a crossroads. Both roads led downhill, and both were crowded with marching troops.

The fog was beginning to lift, and in the distance, about two miles away, French troops could be vaguely seen on the opposite heights. Below, to the left, the firing became more distinct. Kutuzov stood talking with an Austrian general. Prince André, standing a little behind, watched them both intently; then he turned to another adjutant to ask for a pair of field glasses.

"Look, look!" the adjutant said, his eyes focused not on the distant troops but on the road directly below and ahead of them. "It's the French!"

They had supposed the French to be over two miles away, and here they suddenly appeared confronting them!

"The enemy . . . No! But look, it is the French!" could be heard from every side.

Prince André saw, to the right below, a solid column of French troops coming up. It was not over five hundred paces from the very spot where Kutuzov stood.

Suddenly everything disappeared in a cloud of smoke, shots sounded close by, and a soldier's voice in terror called out; "It's all up!" And this voice was like a command. There was a rush.

Panic-stricken crowds of troops, growing ever larger and larger, ran back toward the spot where, not five minutes before, they had paraded before the two Emperors. It was impossible not to be carried back with it. Prince André tried to escape it, and he looked about bewildered, unable to understand what was happening. Nesvitsky, his face red and furious, was shouting to Kutuzov that unless he left immediately he would be taken prisoner. Kutuzov did not move. Without answering he reached for his handkerchief. There was blood on his cheek. Prince André pushed his way through to him.

"Stop them!" Kutuzov shouted. And at the same moment, apparently understanding it would be impossible to stop them, he spurred his horse and rode off to the right. A fresh wave of panic-stricken troops caught up with him and carried him along.

Freeing himself, Kutuzov with his suite, which by now had shrunk to less than half, rode toward the sound of nearby cannon fire. Prince André, who was doing his best not to get separated from Kutuzov, suddenly saw, in the smoke on the downward slope, a Russian battery that was still keeping up its fire and some French soldiers running toward it. Above stood some Russian infantrymen neither moving forward to help the battery nor back with the fleeing troops. Of Kutuzov's suite there were only four men left. All were pale, and looked at one another dumbly.

"Stop those wretches!" Kutuzov shouted at the officer in command. He pointed to the running men. But at that very instant bullets rained over the regiment and over Kutuzov's suite. The French were attacking the battery and, having spotted Kutuzov, had aimed at him. A number of soldiers fell, and the second lieutenant standing with the flag let it drop from his hands. The flag toppled catching on the guns of the nearest soldiers. The soldiers began to fire without waiting for orders.

Kutuzov moaned with despair, looking around. "Prince André," he whispered in a voice that shook with the consciousness of his old age and helplessness. "Prince André," he whispered, pointing to the battalion in flight and the enemy, "what is happening!"

But before he could finish, Prince André was already off his horse and running toward the flag.

"Forward!" he shrieked with childish shrillness, seizing the staff of the flag. Several more soldiers fell.

"Forward!" shouted Prince André and, barely able to hold up the heavy staff, he ran forward in the unshaken conviction that the entire battalion would follow.

And as a matter of fact he ran alone not more than a few steps. First one soldier, then another followed him, and then the entire battalion, shouting "hurrah!" began to rush forward, overtaking him. A junior officer, hurrying over, took the flag that was too heavy for Prince André to carry, but he was instantly killed. Prince André again caught up the flag and, dragging it by the staff, ran forward with the battalion. Overhead he heard the ceaseless whizz of bullets, to the right and to the left of him soldiers were crying out and falling. But he hardly saw them at all; he saw only what was going on straight ahead of him, at the battery. He could now distinguish clearly the figure of an artilleryman, frantically pulling on a mop which a French soldier was doing his best to get away from him.

"What are they doing?" wondered Prince André. "Why

doesn't the artilleryman run away since he has no gun? And why doesn't the Frenchman bayonet him? He won't have time to run away. . . ."

But Prince André never saw how it all ended. "What is happening? Am I falling? My legs won't hold me up," he thought, and fell on his back.

He opened his eyes, hoping to see how the struggle of the French soldier with the artilleryman was going to end. And whether the cannons at the battery had been taken or saved. But he saw nothing of all that. Above him there was nothing but the sky—the lofty sky, not clear, but still immeasurably lofty, with grey clouds creeping quietly over it. "How quietly, peacefully, and triumphantly, and not like us running, shouting, not like the Frenchman and the artilleryman fighting over the mop with frightened and frantic faces, how differently are those clouds creeping over that lofty, limitless sky. How was it I did not see that lofty sky before? And how happy I am to have found it at last. Yes! all is vanity, all is fraud, except that infinite sky. There is nothing, nothing but that. But even that is not, there is nothing but peace and stillness. And . . ."

Prince Bagration, fearing to send his forces into action and anxious to pass on all responsibility, suggested to Dolgorukov that they send a messenger to the commander-in-chief asking his advice.

Bagration looked up and down his suite with his large, expressionless eyes, and the childish face of Rostov was the first that caught his eye. And he sent him.

"And if I meet his majesty before the commander-in-chief, your excellency?" said Rostov, with his hand to the peak of his cap.

"You can give the message to his majesty," said Dolgorukov, hurriedly interposing before Bagration.

All Rostov's hopes had been fulfilled that morning; there was a battle and he was taking part in it; more than that, he was in attendance on the bravest general; more than that, he was being sent on a commission to Kutuzov, perhaps even to the Tsar himself. It was a fine morning, he had a good horse under him, his heart was full of joy and happiness. On receiving his orders, he spurred his horse and galloped along the line.

Down the slopes of the hillsides before Pratzen, he could hear volleys of musketry, interspersed with such frequent shots of cannon that sometimes several booming shots could not be distinguished from one another, but melted into one roar of sound.

He could see puffs of musket smoke floating down the hillside as though chasing one another, while cannon smoke hung about in heavy clouds. He could see, from the gleam of bayonets in the smoke, that masses of infantry as well as artillery, with green caissons, were moving down into the valley.

He stopped his horse to try and make out what was going on. But he could not make out and understand what he saw; there were men of some sort moving about there in the smoke, lines of troops were moving both backwards and forwards; but what for? Who? Where were they going? It was impossible to make out.

Again he galloped along the line, penetrating further and further into the part where the troops were already in action.

He was now riding almost along the front line. A group of horsemen came galloping towards him. They were a troop of Russian cavalry returning in disorder from the attack. And as they passed he saw that one of them was covered with blood. He galloped on.

A foreboding of evil suddenly came upon Rostov. It grew stronger and stronger the further he advanced into the region behind the village of Pratzen, which was full of disorganized troops of all sorts.

"What does it mean? What is it? Whom are they firing at? Who is firing?" Rostov kept asking, as he met Austrian and Russian soldiers running in confusion across his path.

"The devil knows! Killed them all! Damn it all," he was answered in Russian, in German, and in Czech.

The idea of defeat could not force its way into Rostov's head. Though he saw the French cannons and troops on Pratzen hill, the very spot where he had been told to look for the commander-in-chief, he could not and would not believe in it.

"Where's the Emperor? Where's Kutuzov?" Rostov kept asking of every one he could stop. And from no one could he get an answer.

"Who is it you want?" asked a wounded officer who was passing by. "The commander-in-chief? Go that way, over there to that village," he pointed. Then he added, "All the commanding officers are there." And he walked on.

Rostov rode on at a walking pace, not knowing to whom and with what object he was going now. The battle was lost. There was no refusing to believe it now. Rostov rode in the direction which had been pointed out to him and saw in the distance turrets and a church. What had he to hurry for now? What was he now to say to the Tsar or to Kutuzov?

"Go along this road, your honour, that way you will be killed!" a soldier shouted to him. "You'll be killed that way!"

Rostov hesitated and then rode off in the very direction in which he had been told he would be killed.

He rode into the section where more men had been killed than anywhere, in fleeing from Pratzen. The French had not yet taken that region, though the Russians had long abandoned it. All over the field, like ridges of dung on plough-land, lay the heaps of dead and wounded. The wounded were crawling two or three together, and their shrieks and groans tore the air.

Rostov was suddenly filled with fear. He was afraid of losing not his life, but his courage.

In the village there were Russian troops who had just come from the field of battle. Here they were out of range of the French cannons, and the sounds of firing seemed far away. Here every one saw clearly that the battle was lost, and all were talking of it. But no one to whom Rostov spoke could tell him where was the Tsar, or where was Kutuzov.

One officer told Rostov that, behind the village to the left, he had seen some one from headquarters, and Rostov rode off in that direction. After going about two miles and passing the last of the Russian troops, Rostov saw, near a kitchen-garden enclosed by a ditch, two horsemen standing. One with a white plume in his hat seemed somehow familiar to Rostov, the other was a stranger.

"But it can't be he, alone, in the middle of this empty field!" thought Rostov. "It can't be he, the Tzar, all alone!"

At that moment the man with the white plume in his hat turned his head and Rostov saw the beloved features of the Tsar Alexander, those features so vividly imprinted on his memory. The Tsar was pale, his cheeks looked sunken, and his eyes hollow, but the charm, the mildness of his face was only the more striking.

Rostov knew that he ought to go straight to the Tsar and give him the message he had been commanded to give. But he did not knew how to approach, and thousands of reasons why it was unsuitable, unseemly, and impossible came into his mind.

"It may be disagreeable and painful to him, to see an unknown face at such a moment of sadness; besides, what can I say to him now? How can I ask the Emperor for his instructions when the battle is lost?" And Rostov rode away, continually looking back at the Tsar, who still stood alone with the stranger.

And as he looked back another horseman rode up to Alexander, and helped him dismount. The Tsar then sat down under an apple tree and, burying his face in his hands, he wept.

1806

BOOK FOUR

At the beginning of the year 1806, Nicholas Rostov was coming home on leave. Denisov, too, was going home and Rostov persuaded him to go with him to Moscow. In spite of the jolting of the road Denisov slept soundly lying at the bottom of the sledge beside Rostov, who grew more and more impatient, as they got nearer to Moscow.

"Will it come soon? Soon? Oh, these endless streets, shops, street lamps, and sledge drivers!" thought Rostov, when they had presented their papers at the city gates and were driving into Moscow.

"Hurry," he shouted to the driver. "Wake up!" he said to Denisov.

"Come, hurry! Three silver roubles for vodka!" shouted Rostov, when they were close to his home. It seemed to him that the horses were not moving. At last the sledge turned to the right into the approach. Rostov jumped out of the sledge while it was moving and ran onto the porch. Then he ran along the porch and up the familiar, crooked steps. Still the same door handle, the dirtiness of which so often angered the countess, turned in the same halting fashion. In the hall there was a single tallow candle burning.

The footman, a man so strong that he had lifted up a carriage, was sitting there nodding. He glanced towards the opening door.

"Merciful Heavens! The young count!" he cried, recognising his young master. "Can it be?" And he made a dash towards the drawing-room door to announce him; but he changed his mind and came back. "Let me have a look at you, your excellency!"

Rostov, completely forgetting Denisov, flung off his fur coat and, anxious that no one should prepare the way for him, he ran into the big, dark reception-hall. Everything was the same, the same card-tables, the same candelabra with a cover over it. But some one had already seen the young master, and he had not reached the drawing-room when from a side door something swooped headlong, like a storm upon him, and began hugging and kissing him. A second and a third figure dashed in at a second door and at a third; more huggings, more kisses, more outcries and tears of delight. He could not distinguish where and which was his father, which was Natasha, and which was Peter. All were screaming and talking and kissing him at the same moment. Sonya, Natasha, Peter, Anna Drubetskoy, Vera, and the old count were all hugging him; and the servants and the maids flocked into the room with talk and outcries. Only his mother was not among them.

Peter hung on his legs. "Me too!" he kept shouting.

Natasha, after pulling him down to her and kissing his face all over, skipped back from him and pranced like a goat up and down in the same place with shrieks of delight.

All round him were loving eyes shining with tears of joy, all round were lips seeking kisses.

Sonya too, as red as crimson, clung to his arm and beamed all over, gazing blissfully at his eyes for which she had so long been waiting. Sonya was just sixteen and she was very pretty. She gazed at him smiling, unable to take her eyes off him. He glanced gratefully at her. But he was looking for some one. His mother the countess had not come in yet.

Now steps were heard at the door. The steps were so rapid that they could hardly be his mother's footsteps. But it was the countess in a new dress that he did not know, made during his absence. He ran to her. She sank on his bosom, sobbing. She could not lift up her face, and only pressed it to the cold braiding of his hussar's jacket.

Denisov, who had come into the room unnoticed by any one, stood still looking at them.

"Vassily Denisov, your son's friend," he said, introducing himself to the count, who looked at him.

"Very welcome. I know you, I know you," said the count, kissing and embracing Denisov. "Nicholas wrote to us . . . Natasha, Vera, here he is, Denisov."

The same happy faces turned to the tousled figure of Denisov and surrounded him.

"Darling Denisov," squealed Natasha, and, beside herself with delight, she darted up to him, hugging and kissing him. Every one was disconcerted by Natasha's behaviour. Denisov too reddened, but he smiled, took Natasha's hand and kissed it.

Denisov was conducted to the room assigned him, while the Rostovs all gathered about Nicholas in the living-room.

The old countess sat beside him, holding his hand. The others thronged round them, gloating over every movement, every glance, every word he uttered, and never taking their loving eyes off him. His brother and sisters quarrelled and snatched from one another the place nearest him and disputed over which was to bring him tea, a handkerchief, a pipe.

Next morning he slept till ten o'clock.

The adjoining room was littered with swords, bags, open

trunks, and dirty boots. The servants brought in wash-basins, and hot water for shaving. The room was full of a masculine odour and reeked of tobacco.

"Hi, a pipe!" shouted the husky voice of Denisov. "Rostov, get up!"

Rostov, rubbing his eyes, lifted his head from the warm pillow.

"Why, is it late?"

"Nearly ten," answered Natasha's voice, and in the next room they heard the rustle of starched skirts and girlish laughter. The door was opened a crack, and there was a glimpse of something blue, of ribbons, black hair and merry faces. Natasha with Sonya and Peter had come to see if he were getting up.

"Nicholas, get up!" Natasha's voice was heard again at the door.

"At once!" Meanwhile in the outer room Peter had caught sight of the swords and seized them with the rapture small boys feel at the sight of a soldier brother. And regardless of its not being the proper thing for his sisters to see the young men undressed, he opened the bedroom door.

"Is this your sword?" he shouted.

The girls hurried away. Denisov hid his hairy legs under the bedclothes, looking with a scared face. Peter came in and closed the door after him. A giggle was heard from outside.

"Nicholas, come out in your dressing-gown," cried Natasha's voice.

Rostov put on his dressing-gown and went out. Natasha had put on one spurred boot and was just getting into the other. Sonya had just whirled her skirt into a balloon and was ducking down, when he came in. They were dressed alike in new blue frocks, both fresh, rosy, and good-humoured. Sonya ran away, but Natasha, taking her brother's arm, led him into the schoolroom, and they began talking. Natasha laughed at every word he said and at every word she said, not because what they said was amusing, but because she was in high spirits and unable to contain her joy.

"Oh, isn't it nice!" she kept saying. Under the influence of the warm sunshine of love, Rostov felt that for the first time for a year and a half his soul and his face were expanding in that childish smile, he had not once smiled since he left home.

"Oh," she said, "you're a man now. I'm awfully glad you're my brother." She touched his moustache.

"Why did Sonya run away?" asked Nicholas.

"I'll tell you why afterwards."

"Why?"

"Well, I'll tell you now. You know that Sonya's my friend, such a friend that I burnt my arm for her sake. Here, look."

She pulled up her muslin sleeve and showed him a red mark.

"I burnt that to show her my love. I simply heated a ruler in the fire and pressed it on."

Sitting in his old schoolroom on the sofa with little cushions on the arms, and looking into Natasha's eager eyes, Rostov was carried back into that world of home and childhood which had no meaning for any one else. And burning one's arm with a ruler as a proof of love did not strike him as pointless. He understood it, and was not surprised.

"Well, is that all?" he asked.

"Well, we are such friends, such great friends! That's nonsense—the ruler; but we are friends for ever. If she once loves any one, it's for ever; I don't understand that, I forget so quickly."

"Well, what then?"

"Yes, so she loves me and you." Natasha suddenly flushed. "Well, you remember before you went away . . . She says you are to forget it all . . . She said, I shall always love him, but let him be free. That really is noble! Yes, yes; very noble? Yes?" Natasha asked with such seriousness that it was clear that what she was saying now she had talked of before with tears.

Nicholas thought a little. "I never take back my word," he said. "And besides, Sonya's so charming that who would be such a fool as to renounce his own happiness?"

"No, no," cried Natasha. "She and I have talked about that already. We knew that you'd say that. But that won't do, because, don't you see, if you say that—if you consider yourself bound by your word, then it makes it as though she had said that on purpose. It makes it as though you were, after all, obliged to marry her, and it makes it all wrong."

Rostov saw that it had all been well thought over by them. On the previous day, Sonya had struck him by her beauty. In the glimpse he had caught of her to-day, she seemed even prettier. And he thought, why should he not love her now, even if he did not marry her. Yes, Natasha and Sonya were right. He must remain free.

"Well, that's all right, then," he said. "We'll talk about it later. Oh, how glad I am to be back with you!" he added. "Come, tell me, you've not been false to Boris?"

"That's nonsense!" cried Natasha, laughing. "I never think of him nor of any one else, and don't want to."

"Oh, you don't, don't you! Then what do you want?"

"I'm never going to marry any one. I'm going to be a dancer. Only, don't tell anybody."

Rostov laughed so loudly that Denisov in his room felt envious. And Natasha could not help laughing with him.

"Oh. So you don't want to marry Boris now?"

Natasha got angry.

"I don't want to marry any one. I'll tell him so myself when I see him."

"Oh, will you?" said Nicholas.

"That's all nonsense," Natasha prattled on. "Is Denisov nice?" she asked.

"Yes, he's nice. He's lots of fun."

"Well, good-bye, go and dress. Hurry and come to tea. We are all going to have it together."

And Natasha rose on to her toes and stepped out of the room, as dancers do, but smiling as only happy girls of fifteen can smile.

Nicholas reddened on meeting Sonya in the drawing-room. He felt that every one, his mother and his sisters, were looking at him, and wondering how he would behave with her. He kissed her hand, and called her *you* and *Sonya*. But their eyes when they met spoke more fondly and kissed tenderly. Her eyes asked his forgiveness for having dared, with Natasha's help, to remind him of his promise, and thanked him for his love. His eyes thanked her for offering him his freedom, and told her that whether so, or otherwise, he should never cease to love her, because it was impossible not to love her.

"How queer it is," said Vera, during a moment of silence, "that Sonya and Nicholas meet now and speak like strangers."

Vera's observation was true, as were all her observations. But like most of her observations it made every one uncomfortable. Not only Sonya, Nicholas, and Natasha crimsoned, but the countess, too. She was afraid that her son's love for Sonya might prevent him from making a brilliant marriage. She blushed like a girl.

On his return to Moscow from the army, Nicholas Rostov was received by his family as a hero, as the best of sons; by his relations, as a charming, agreeable, and polite young man; by his acquaintances as a handsome lieutenant of hussars, a good dancer, and one of the best matches in Moscow.

All Moscow was acquainted with the Rostovs; the old count had plenty of money that year, because all his estates had been mortgaged, and so Nicholas who kept his own racehorse, and wore the most fashionable riding-breeches of a special cut, unlike any yet seen in Moscow, and the most fashionable boots, with extremely pointed toes, and little silver spurs, was able to pass his time very agreeably. After the first brief interval of adapting himself to the old conditions of life, Nicholas felt very happy at being home again. He felt that he had grown up and become a man. Now he was a lieutenant of hussars with a silver-braided jacket, and a soldier's cross of St. George, and he kept company with well-known racing men, elderly and respected persons. He had struck up an acquaintance, too, with a lady living in a boulevard, whom he used to visit in the evening. He led the mazurka at the Arharovs' balls, talked to Field-Marshal Kamensky about the war, and used familiar forms of address to a colonel of forty, to whom he had been introduced by Denisov.

During this brief stay in Moscow, before his return to the army, Nicholas did not come nearer to Sonya, but on the contrary drifted further away from her. She was very pretty and charming, and it was obvious that she was passionately in love with him. But when he thought about her, he said to himself: "Oh! there are many, many more like her to come, and there are many of them somewhere now, though I don't know them yet. There's plenty of time before me to think about love when I want to." Moreover, it seemed to him that feminine society was somewhat beneath his manly dignity. He went to balls, and into ladies' society with an air of doing so against his will. Races, the English Club, parties with Denisov, and the midnight visits that followed—all that was different, all that was the correct thing for a dashing young hussar.

At the beginning of March Count Rostov was very busily engaged in arranging a dinner at the English Club, to be given in honour of Prince Bagration.

The count, in his dressing-gown, was continually walking up and down in the big hall of his home interviewing the club manager and the head cook, and giving them instructions about asparagus, fresh cucumbers, strawberries, veal, and fish. From the day of its foundation, the count had been a member of the club, and was its steward. He had been chosen to arrange the banquet, because it would have been hard to find any one so well able to organize a banquet on a large and hospitable scale, and still more hard to find any one so able and willing to advance his own money, if funds were needed.

The cook and the club manager listened to the count's orders with good-humoured faces, because they knew that with no one better than with him could one make a handsome profit out of a dinner costing several thousands.

"Well, then, there are scallops, scallops in pie-crust, you know."

"Cold *entrées,* I suppose—three? . . ." questioned the cook.

The count pondered.

"Couldn't do with less, three . . . *mayonnaise,* one," he said.

"Then it's your excellency's order to serve big sturgeons?" asked the manager.

"Yes; it can't be helped, we must buy them even if they won't knock the price down. Oh, I was forgetting. Of course we must have another *entrée* on the table. Ah, good heavens!"

he clutched at his head. "And who's going to get me the flowers? Mitenka! Hey, Mitenka! You gallop, Mitenka," he said to a servant who came in at his call, "you gallop off to my country estate and tell the gardener to set the serfs to work to get flowers from the greenhouses. Tell him everything from his conservatories is to be brought here, and is to be packed in felt. I'm to have two hundred pots here by Friday."

Young Nicholas entered the room. "Oh, my boy!" said the old count. "Come to my aid! We still need singers. The music is all settled, but should we have some gypsy singers? You military men like that sort of thing."

"Really father, Prince Bagration made less fuss over getting ready for the battle of Schöngraben than you are making now," said his son, smiling.

The old count pretended to be angry.

"Well, you talk, you try!" And the count turned to the cook, who with a shrewd and respectful face looked from father to son.

"What are young people coming to?" he said. "They laugh at us old fellows!"

"To be sure, your excellency, they enjoy eating a good dinner, but to arrange it and serve it up . . ."

"True, true!" cried the count. And turning again to his son he cried: "Take a sledge and pair this minute and drive off to Bezuhov, and say that Count Rostov has sent to ask him for strawberries and fresh pineapples. There's no getting them from any one else. And, I say, from there you drive to the Gaiety—the coachman knows the place—and look up the gypsy who danced at Count Orlov's, do you remember, in a white Cossack dress, and bring him here to me."

"And bring his gypsy girls here with him?" asked Nicholas laughing.

"Come, come! . . . "

At that moment Anna Drubetskoy came into the room with that air of Christian meekness, mingled with practical and anxious preoccupation, that never left her face.

"I am just going to see Bezuhov," she said. "He has arrived, and now we shall get all we want, count, from his greenhouses. I was going to see him on my own account. He has forwarded me a letter from Boris. Thank God, Boris is now on the staff."

The count was overjoyed at Anna Drubetskoy's undertaking one part of his commissions.

"Tell Pierre to come. I'll put his name down. Brought his wife with him?" he asked.

An expression of sadness came into Anna Drubetskoy's face.

"Oh, my dear, he's very unhappy," she said. "If it's true what we have been hearing, it's awful. How little did we think of this when we were rejoicing in his happiness! Yes, I pity him from my soul!"

"Why, what is the matter?" inquired both the Rostovs, young and old together.

"Dolohov," she said in a mysterious whisper, "has, they say, utterly compromised his wife, Helen. Bezuhov invited Dolohov to his house in Petersburg, and now this! . . . Helen has come here, and that scoundrel has come after her," said Anna Drubetskoy. She wished to express nothing but sympathy for Pierre, but through her intonations and half smile, she betrayed her sympathy for Dolohov. "Pierre himself, they say, is utterly crushed by his trouble."

"Well, any way, tell him to come to the club—it will divert his mind. It will be a banquet on a grand scale."

On receiving the news of the defeat of Austerlitz, all Moscow had at first been thrown into bewilderment. The Russians were so used to victories, that on receiving news of a defeat, some people were simply incredulous, while others sought an explanation of so strange an event in exceptional circumstances of some kind.

Causes were discovered to account for the fact—so incredible, unheard-of, and impossible—that the Russians had been beaten, and all became clear, and the same version was repeated from one end of Moscow to the other. These causes were: the treachery of the Austrians; the poor supply lines, the treachery of two officers, one a Pole and one a Frenchman; the incapacity of Kutuzov; and the youth and inexperience of the Emperor, who had put faith in men of no character and ability. This last reason was whispered in subdued tones. But the army, the Russian army, said every one, had been extraordinary, and had performed miracles of valour. The soldiers, the officers, the generals—all were heroes.

Anecdotes were to be heard on every side of individual feats of gallantry performed by officers and men at Austerlitz. Here a man had saved a flag, another had killed five Frenchmen, another had kept five cannons loaded single-handed. The story was told of Berg, by those who did not know him, that wounded in his right hand, he had taken his sword in his left and charged on the enemy. Nothing was said about Prince André, and only those who had known him intimately regretted that he had died so young, leaving a wife with child, and his queer old father. But the hero among heroes was Prince Bagration, who had distinguished himself in his Schöngraben engagement and in the retreat from Austerlitz, where he alone had withdrawn his column in good order, and had succeeded in repelling an enemy twice as strong.

What contributed to Bagration's being chosen for the popular hero at Moscow was the fact that he was an outsider, that he had no connections in Moscow. And besides, bestowing upon him such honours was the best possible way of showing their dislike and disapproval of Kutuzov.

Of Kutuzov people did not speak at all, or whispered abuse of him, calling him the court weathercock and the old satyr.

On the 3rd of March the rooms of the English Club were full of the hum of voices, and the members and guests in uniforms and frock-coats, some even in powder and Russian caftans, were running to and fro like bees swarming in spring. Powdered footmen in livery, wearing slippers and stockings, stood at every door, anxiously trying to follow every movement of the guests and club members, so as to offer their services. The majority of those present were elderly and respected persons, with broad, self-confident faces. A small number of those present were casual guests; young men, among them Denisov, Rostov, and Dolohov, who was now an officer again. Nesvitsky, an old member of the club, was there too. Pierre, who at his wife's command had let his hair grow, was walking about the rooms dressed in the height of the fashion, but looking melancholy and depressed. In years, he belonged to the younger generation, but by his wealth and connections he was a member of the older circles, and so he passed from one set to the other.

Count Rostov kept hurrying in his soft boots from the dining-room to the drawing-room, giving hasty greeting to important and unimportant persons, all of whom he knew, and all of whom he treated alike, on an equal footing. Now and then his eyes sought out the dashing figure of his young son and beamed on him. Young Rostov was standing at the window with Dolohov, whose acquaintance he had lately made, and greatly prized. The old count went up to them, and shook hands with Dolohov.

"I hope you will come and see us; so you're a friend of my son's . . . Been together, playing the hero together out there. . . . Ah! Vassily Ignatitch . . . A good day to you, old man," he turned to an old gentleman who had just come in. But before he had time to finish his greetings to him there was a general stir, and a footman running in announced: "He has arrived!"

Bells rang. The stewards rushed forward. The guests, scattered about the different rooms, gathered together and waited at the door of the great drawing-room.

At the door of the ante-room appeared the figure of Bagration, without his hat or sword, which, in accordance with the club custom, he had left with the hall porter. He was not wearing an Astrakhan cap, and had not a riding-whip over his shoulder, as Rostov had seen him on the night before the battle of Austerlitz, but wore a tight new uniform with Russian and foreign orders and the star of St. George. He walked shyly and awkwardly, not knowing what to do with his hands. He would have been more at home and at his ease walking over a ploughed field under fire.

The officers of the club met him at the first door, and expressed their pleasure at having such an honoured guest. They surrounded him without waiting for an answer, and, as it were, taking possession of him, led him off to the drawing-room. There was no possibility of getting in at the drawing-room door from the crowds of members and guests, who were crushing one another in their efforts to get a look over each other's shoulders at Bagration.

Count Rostov laughed more than any one, and continually repeating, "Make way for him, my dear boy, make way, make way," shoved the crowd aside, led the honoured guest into the drawing-room, and seated him on the sofa in the middle of it. The great men, and the more honoured members of the club, surrounded the newly arrived guest.

Count Rostov, shoving his way again through the crowd, went out of the drawing-room, and reappeared a minute later with another club official carrying a great silver dish, which he held out to Prince Bagration. On the dish lay a poem, composed and printed in the hero's honour.

The author of the verse took them, and began to read them aloud. Prince Bagration bowed his head and listened:

Be thou the pride of Alexander's reign!
And save for us our Titus on the throne!
Be thou our champion and our country's stay!
A noble heart, a Cæsar in the fray!
Napoleon in the zenith of his fame
Learns to his cost to fear Bagration's name,
Nor dares provoke a Russian foe again, . . .

But he had not finished the poem, when the butler boomed out "Dinner is ready!"

The door opened. From the dining-room thundered the strains of the Polonaise: *Raise the shout of victory, valiant Russian, festive sing,* and Count Rostov, looking angrily at the author, who went on reading his verses, bowed to Bagration as a signal to go in. All the company rose, feeling the dinner of more importance than the poem, and Bagration, preceding all the rest, went in to dinner. Three hundred persons were ranged about the tables according to their rank and importance, those of greater consequence, nearer to the distinguished guest—as naturally as water flows to find its own level.

Nicholas Rostov, with Denisov and his new friend Dolohov, sat together almost in the middle of a long table. Facing them sat Pierre with Prince Nesvitsky. Count Rostov was sitting with other officers of the club facing Bagration, and, the very impersonation of Moscow hospitality, did his best to regale the prince.

His efforts had not been in vain. The banquet was sumptuous, but he was not at ease till the end of dinner. He made signs to the carver, gave whispered directions to the footmen, and nervously awaited each new dish. Everything was perfect. At the second course, with the gigantic sturgeon, the footmen began popping corks and pouring out champagne. After the fish, which was a sensation, Count Rostov exchanged glances with the other club officers. "There will be a great many toasts, it's time to begin!" he whispered, and, glass in hand, he got up. All were silent, waiting for what he would say.

"To the health of our sovereign, the Emperor!" he shouted, and at the moment his kindly eyes grew moist with tears of pleasure and enthusiasm. At that instant they began playing: *Raise the shout of victory!* All rose from their seats and shouted "Hurrah!" And Bagration shouted "Hurrah!" in the same voice in which he had shouted it in the field at Schöngraben. Emptying their glasses at one gulp, they flung them on the floor. And the loud shouts lasted for a long while. When the uproar subsided, the footmen cleared away the broken glass, and all began settling themselves again; and smiling at the noise they had made, began talking.

Count Rostov rose once more, glanced at a note that lay beside his plate, and proposed a toast to the health of the hero of the last campaign, Prince Bagration. And again the count's blue eyes were dimmed with tears.

"Hurrah!" again shouted the three hundred guests. But instead of music this time a chorus of singers began to sing a cantata composed especially for the occasion.

As soon as the singers had finished, more and more toasts followed, at which Count Rostov became more and more moved, and more glasses were broken and even more uproar was made. They drank to the health of their war heroes, to the health of the club officers, to the health of the committee, to the health of all the club members, to the health of all the guests of the club, and finally to the health of the organiser of the banquet, Count Rostov. At this last toast the count took out his handkerchief and, hiding his face in it, wept.

Pierre ate greedily and drank heavily, as he always did. But those who knew him could see that some change had taken place in him. He was silent all through dinner, and blinking and screwing up his eyes, looked about him, with an air of complete absent-mindedness, and rubbed the bridge of his nose with his finger. He was depressed and gloomy.

He was worried about hints dropped by the princess, his cousin, in regard to Dolohov's close intimacy with his wife, and about an anonymous letter he had received that morning, which said that he didn't seem to see clearly through his spectacles, and that his wife's connection with Dolohov was a secret from no one but him. Pierre did not absolutely believe either the princess's hints nor the anonymous letter, but he was now afraid to look at Dolohov, who sat opposite him. Every time his glance met Dolohov's handsome, insolent eyes, Pierre felt as though something hideous was rising up in his soul, and he turned away. Recalling all his wife's past and her attitude to Dolohov, Pierre saw clearly that what was said in the letter might well be true. He could not help recalling how Dolohov, returning to Petersburg, had taken advantage of their acquaintance in their old rowdy days and had come straight to his house; how he had invited Dolohov to stay and lent him money. Pierre also recalled how Helen, smiling, had opposed Dolohov's staying in their house, and how cynically Dolohov had praised his wife's beauty to him, and how he had never since left them up to the time of their coming to Moscow.

"Yes, he is very handsome," thought Pierre, "but I know him. He would get a particular pleasure in disgracing my name just because I have befriended him and helped him. I know. I understand what pleasure that would be sure to give him." He recalled the expression on Dolohov's face in his moments of cruelty, such as when he was tying the police officer to the bear and dropping him into the water, or when he had without provocation challenged a man to a duel or killed a sledge-driver's horse with a shot from his pistol. That expression now came into Dolohov's face when he was looking at him. "Yes, he's a brute," thought Pierre. "To him it means nothing to kill a man, it must seem to him that every one's afraid of him. He must like it. He must think I am afraid of him. And, in fact, I really am afraid of him." And again at these thoughts Pierre felt as though something terrible and hideous were rising up in his soul.

Dolohov, Denisov, and Rostov were sitting facing Pierre and seemed to be greatly enjoying themselves. Rostov talked away to his two friends, and now and then cast ironical glances at Pierre. He looked with disfavour upon Pierre. In the first place, because Pierre, in the eyes of the smart hussar, was a rich civilian, and husband of a beauty, was altogether, in fact, an old woman. And secondly, because Pierre in his preoccupation and absent-mindedness had not recognised Rostov and had failed to return his bow.

"Why don't you renew the acquaintance?" said Dolohov to Rostov.

"Oh, he's a fool," said Rostov.

"One has to be polite to the husbands of pretty women," said Denisov.

Pierre did not hear what they were saying, but he knew they were talking of him. He flushed and turned away.

"Well, to the health of pretty women," said Dolohov, and with a serious expression, though a smile lurked in the corners of his mouth, he turned to Pierre.

"To the health of pretty women, Pierre, and their lovers too," he said.

Pierre sipped his glass, without looking at Dolohov or answering him. The footman, distributing copies of the cantata, laid a copy by Pierre, as one of the more honoured guests. He was about to take it, but Dolohov bent forward, snatched the paper out of his hands and began reading it. Pierre glared at Dolohov. He bent the whole of his ungainly person across the table. "Don't you dare take it!" he shouted.

Hearing this, Nesvitsky and Pierre's neighbour on the right looked at him in alarm.

"Hush, hush, what are you about?" whispered panic-stricken voices.

Dolohov looked at Pierre with his clear, cruel eyes, still with the same smile, as though he were saying: "Come now, this is what I like."

"I won't give it up," he said distinctly.

Pale and with quivering lips, Pierre snatched the copy.

"You . . . You . . . Scoundrel! . . . I challenge you," he said, and moving back his chair, he got up from the table.

The moment Pierre did this he felt that the question of his wife's guilt, that had been torturing him for the last twenty-four hours, was finally answered. He hated her and was severed from her for ever.

In spite of Denisov's entreaties that Rostov should have nothing to do with the affair, Rostov agreed to be Dolohov's second, and after dinner he discussed with Nesvitsky, Pierre's second, the arrangements for the duel.

Next day at eight o'clock in the morning, Pierre and Nesvitsky reached the place chosen for the duel and found Dolohov, Denisov, and Rostov already there. Pierre's face looked hollow and yellow. He had not slept all night. He looked about him absent-mindedly, and screwed up his eyes, as though in glaring sunshine. He was absorbed by two things: the guilt of his wife, of which after a sleepless night he had not a vestige of doubt, and the position of Dolohov. "Maybe I would have done the same in his place," thought Pierre. "Then why this duel, this murder? Either I shall kill him, or he will shoot me." To get away, to run, to bury himself somewhere, was the longing that came into his mind. But with a peculiarly calm and unconcerned face, he turned and asked: "Will it be soon? Aren't we ready?"

"Well, let us begin," said Dolohov.

"Yes," said Pierre.

A feeling of dread was in the air. Denisov was the first to come forward to the barrier and pronounce the words: "Since the antagonists refuse all reconciliation, would it not be as well to begin? Take your pistols, and at the word 'three' begin to advance together. O . . . one! Two! Three! . . ." Denisov shouted, and he walked away from the barrier.

The combatants had the right to fire when they chose as they approached the barrier. Dolohov walked slowly, not lifting his pistol, and looking intently with his clear, shining eyes into Pierre's face. His mouth wore, as always, the semblance of a smile.

"So when I like, I can fire," thought Pierre, as he walked forward with rapid steps. He held his pistol at full length in his right hand and fired.

Not expecting so loud a report, Pierre started at his own shot, then smiled and stood still. The smoke prevented him from seeing for the first moment; but the other shot that he was expecting did not follow. All that could be heard were Dolohov's rapid footsteps, and then his figure came into view through the smoke. With one hand he was clutching his left side, the other was clenched on the pistol. His face was pale. Rostov was running up and saying something to him.

"N . . . no," Dolohov muttered through his teeth. "No, it's not over." And struggling on a few staggering steps he sank into the snow. His left hand was covered with blood. He rubbed it on his coat. His face was pale.

"Co . . ." Dolohov began, but he could not speak the words: "Come up," he said, with effort. Pierre ran towards Dolohov, and would have crossed the space that separated the barriers, when Dolohov cried: "To the barrier!" And Pierre, grasping what was wanted, stood still. Now only ten paces divided them. Dolohov putting his head down, greedily bit at the snow, lifted his head again, sat up, tried to get on his legs and sat down. He took a mouthful of the cold snow, and sucked it. His lips quivered, but still he smiled. His eyes glittered with the strain of the struggle. He raised the pistol.

With his gentle smile of remorse, Pierre stood with his legs and arms straddling helplessly, and his broad chest directly

facing Dolohov, and looked at him. There came a shot and Dolohov's cry.

"Missed!" shouted Dolohov, and he dropped helplessly, face downwards, in the snow.

Pierre turned back, and walked into the woods, muttering incoherent words.

"Stupid . . . stupid! Death . . . lies . . ." he kept repeating. Nesvitsky stopped him and took him home.

Rostov and Denisov took the wounded Dolohov away.

Dolohov lay in the sledge with closed eyes, in silence. But as they were driving into Moscow, he suddenly came to himself, and lifting his head with an effort, he took Rostov's hand. Rostov was struck by the utterly tender expression on Dolohov's face.

"I have killed her, killed her. . . ." he said in a breaking voice. "She won't get over this. She can't bear . . ."

"Who?" asked Rostov.

"My mother. My mother, my angel, my adored angel, my mother," and squeezing Rostov's hand, Dolohov burst into tears. When he was a little calmer, he explained to Rostov that he was living with his mother, that if his mother were to see him dying, she would not get over the shock. He begged Rostov to go to her and prepare her.

Rostov drove on ahead to carry out his wish, and to his surprise he found that Dolohov, this daring duellist, lived with his old mother and a hunchback sister, and was the most tender son and brother.

Pierre had of late rarely seen his wife alone. Both at Petersburg and at Moscow their house had been constantly full of guests. On the night following the duel he did not go to his bedroom, but spent the night, as he often did, in his huge study, formerly his father's room, the very room indeed in which Count Bezuhov had died.

He lay down on the couch and tried to go to sleep, so as to forget all that had happened to him, but he could not do so. Such a tempest of feelings and thoughts arose in his mind, that, far from going to sleep, he could not even lie still and got up from the couch and paced about the room. At one moment he had a vision of his wife, as she was in the first days after their marriage, with her bare shoulders, and languid, passionate eyes; and then immediately by her side he saw the handsome, hard face of Dolohov, as he had seen it at the banquet, and again the same face of Dolohov, pale, quivering, in agony as it had been when he sank in the snow.

"What has happened?" he asked himself; "I have killed her lover. Yes, killed the lover of my wife. Yes, that is what has happened. Why? How have I come to this?"

"Because you married her," answered an inner voice.

"But how am I to blame?" he asked.

"For marrying without loving her, for deceiving yourself and her."

And vividly he recalled that moment after supper at Prince Vassily's when he had said those words he found so difficult to utter: "I love you."

"It has all come from that. Even then I felt it," he thought. "I felt at the time that it wasn't the right thing, that I had no right to do it. And so it has turned out."

He recalled the honeymoon, and blushed at the recollection of it. Particularly vivid, humiliating, and shameful was the memory of how one day soon after his marriage he had come in his silk dressing-gown out of his bedroom into his study at noon and had found his head steward, who looking at him had smiled, as though to express by that smile his respectful sympathy with his happiness. "And how often I have been proud of her, proud of her majestic beauty, her social tact," he thought; "proud of my house, in which she received all Petersburg, proud of her beauty. So this was what I prided myself on. I used to think then that I did not understand her. How often, reflecting on her character, I have told myself that I was to blame, that I did not understand her, did not understand that everlasting composure and complacency, and the absence of all preferences and desires. And all the time the answer lay in the fact that she is a dissolute woman. All is now clear.

"Her brother, Anatole, used to come to borrow money from her, and used to kiss her on her bare shoulders. She didn't give him money; but she let herself be kissed. Her father used to try, jokingly, to rouse her jealousy. With a smile she used to say she was not fool enough to be jealous. Let him do as he likes, she used to say about me. I asked her once if she felt no symptoms of pregnancy. She laughed contemptuously, and said she was not such a fool as to want children, and that she would never have a child by me."

Then he thought of the coarseness, the bluntness of her ideas, and the vulgarity of the expressions that were characteristic of her, although she had been brought up in the highest aristocratic circles. "Not quite such a fool . . . You just try . . . You clear out of this," she would say. Yet she made a favourable impression on young and old, on men and women. And Pierre could not understand why it was he did not love her. "Yes; I never loved her," Pierre said to himself. "I knew she was a dissolute woman," he repeated to himself. "But I did not dare admit it to myself."

"And now Dolohov . . . There he sits in the snow and forces

himself to smile and dies with maybe some swaggering affectation on his lips in answer to my remorse."

"She, she alone is to blame for everything," he said to himself. "But what of it? Why did I bind myself to her. Why did I say to her 'I love you,' which was a lie, and worse than a lie," he said to himself. "I am to blame, and ought to bear . . What? The disgrace to my name, the misery of my life? Oh that's all rubbish," he thought. "Disgrace to one's name and honour, all that's relative, all that's apart from myself. . . Who is right, who is wrong? No one. But live while you live, to-morrow you die, as I might have died an hour ago. And is it worth worrying oneself, when life is only one second in comparison with eternity?"

But at the moment when he believed himself soothed by reflections of that sort, he suddenly had a vision of *her,* and of her at those moments when he had most violently expressed his most insincere love to her, and he felt a rush of blood to his head. "Why did I say to her 'I love you'?" he kept repeating to himself.

And he resolved that next day he would go away, leaving her a letter, in which he would announce his intention of parting from her for ever.

In the morning when the valet came into the study with his coffee, Pierre was lying asleep with an open book in his hand.

He woke up and looked about him unable to grasp where he was.

"The countess sent to inquire if your excellency were at home," said the valet.

But before Pierre had time to make up his mind what answer he would send, Helen herself walked calmly into the room. She was wearing a white satin dressing-gown embroidered with silver, and had her hair in two immense coils wound like a coronet round her head. With her accustomed self-control and composure she did not begin to speak till the valet had left the room. She knew of the duel and had come to talk of it. Pierre looked timidly at her over his spectacles, and then tried to go on reading. But he felt that this was senseless and impossible, and again he glanced timidly at her. She did not sit down, but stood looking at him with a disdainful smile.

"What's this about now? What have you been up to? I'm asking you," she said sternly.

"I? I? What?" said Pierre.

"You going in for deeds of valour! Now, answer me, what does this duel mean? What did you want to prove by it? I ask you."

Pierre turned heavily on the sofa, opened his mouth but could not answer.

"If you won't answer, I'll tell you . . ." Helen went on. "You believe everything you're told. You were told . . ." Helen laughed, "that Dolohov was my lover," she said in French, with her coarse plainness of speech, uttering the word "lover" like any other word. "And you believed it! But what have you proved by this duel? That you're a fool! But every one knew that already. What does it lead to? Why, that I'm made the laughing-stock of all Moscow; that every one's saying that when you were drunk and didn't know what you were doing, you challenged a man of whom you were jealous without grounds." Helen raised her voice and grew more and more passionate. "He's a better man than you in every respect. . . . And how did you come to believe that he's my lover? . . . Because I like his society? If you were more clever and more agreeable, I should prefer yours."

"Don't speak to me . . . I beseech you," Pierre muttered huskily.

"Why shouldn't I speak? I can speak as I like, and I tell you boldly that it's not many a wife who with a husband like you wouldn't have taken a lover, but I haven't done it," she said.

Pierre tried to say something, glanced at her with strange eyes, whose meaning she did not comprehend, and lay down again. He was in physical agony at that moment. He felt a weight on his chest so that he could not breathe. He knew that he must do something to put an end to this agony but what he wanted to do was too horrible.

"We had better part," he said slowly.

"Part? By all means, only if you pay me," said Helen.

Pierre leaped up from the couch and rushed towards her.

"I'll kill you!" he shouted, and picking up a marble table-top with a strength he had not known in himself he went toward her.

She shrieked and backed away. He flung down the slab shattering it into fragments and screamed "Go!" in a voice so terrible that it was all over the house.

Helen ran from the room.

A week later Pierre signed over to Helen the revenue from all his estates in Great Russia, which made up the larger half of his property, and left for Petersburg.

Two months had passed since the news of the defeat of Austerlitz and the loss of Prince André had reached Bleak Hills.

In spite of all inquiries and letters through the Russian embassy, his body had not been found, nor was he among the prisoners. What made it worst for his father and sister was the fact that there was still hope that he might have been picked up on the battlefield by the people of the country, and

Mary went on hoping. She prayed for her brother, as living, and every moment she expected news of his return.

One morning a few weeks later the little princess complained of not feeling well.

"I am afraid this morning's breakfast has disagreed with me," she said to Princess Mary.

"What is the matter? You look pale. Oh, you are very pale," said Princess Mary in alarm.

"Shouldn't we send for Marie Bogdanovna, your excellency?" said one of the maids who was present. Marie Bogdanovna was a midwife from a district town, who had been for the last two weeks at Bleak Hills.

"Yes," said Princess Mary, "perhaps it is really that. I'll go and get her." She kissed Liza and was going out of the room.

"Oh, no, no!" And besides her pallor, the face of the little princess expressed a childish terror at the inevitable physical suffering before her.

"No, it is indigestion, say it is indigestion, say so, Mary, say so!" And the little princess began to cry, with childish misery. Princess Mary ran out of the room to call Marie Bogdanovna.

"Mon Dieu! Mon Dieu! Oh!" she heard behind her.

The midwife was already on her way rubbing her plump white hands with a face of significant composure.

"Marie Bogdanovna! I think it has begun," said Princess Mary, looking with wide-open, frightened eyes at the midwife.

"Well, I thank God for it," said Marie Bogdanovna, not quickening her step. "You young ladies have no need to know anything about it."

"But how is it the doctor has not come from Moscow yet?" said the princess. In accordance with the wishes of Liza and Prince André, they had sent to Moscow for a doctor, and were expecting him every minute.

"It's no matter, princess, don't be uneasy," said Marie Bogdanovna. "We shall do very well without the doctor."

Five minutes later the princess from her room heard something heavy being carried by. She looked out. The footmen were for some reason moving into the bedroom the leather sofa which stood in Prince André's study. There was a solemn and subdued look on the men's faces.

Princess Mary sat alone in her room, listening to the sounds of the house, now and then opening the door when someone passed by and looking at what was taking place in the hall. Several women passed back and forth treading softly. They glanced at the princess and turned away from her. She did not dare to ask questions, and going back to her room closed the door and sat in an armchair, or took up her prayer-book, or knelt down before the shrine. And to her distress and astonishment she felt that prayer did not soothe her.

All at once the door of her room was quietly opened, and she saw her old nurse, with a kerchief over her head. The old woman hardly ever, owing to the old prince's orders, came into her room.

"I've come to sit a bit with thee, Mary, my angel," said the nurse. "And here I've brought the Prince André's wedding candles to light before his saint," she said, sighing.

"Ah, how glad I am, nurse!"

"God is merciful, my darling." The nurse lighted the gilt candles before the shrine, and sat down with her knitting near the door. Princess Mary took a book and began reading. Only when they heard steps or voices, the princess and the nurse looked at one another, one with alarmed inquiry, the other with soothing reassurance in her face.

The feeling that Princess Mary was experiencing as she sat in her room had overpowered the whole house and taken possession of every one. Owing to the belief that the fewer people who know of the sufferings of a woman in labour, the less she suffers, every one pretended to know nothing of it. No one talked about it, but over and above the habitual staidness and respectfulness of good manners that always reigned in the prince's household, there was apparent in all a sort of anxiety, a softening of the heart, and a consciousness of some great, unfathomable mystery being accomplished at that moment. There was no sound of laughter in the big room where the maids sat. In the waiting-room the men all sat in silence, as it were on the alert. Torches and candles were burning in the serfs' quarters, and that night no one slept. The old prince walked about his study and sent Tihon to Marie Bogdanovna to ask what news.

"Inform the prince that the labour has commenced," said Marie Bogdanovna. Tihon went and gave the prince this message.

"Very good," said the prince, closing the door behind him, and after that Tihon heard not the slightest sound in the study.

After a short interval Tihon went into the study, as though to attend to the candles. Seeing the prince lying on the couch, Tihon looked at him, looked at his worried face, shook his head, and went up to him dumbly and kissed him on the shoulder. Then he went out without touching the candles or saying why he had come.

It was one of those March nights when winter seems to regain its sway, and flings its last snows and storms. A relay of horses had been sent to the high-road for the German doctor who was expected every minute, and men were despatched on horseback with lanterns to the turning at the cross-roads to guide him over the holes and treacherous places in the ice.

Princess Mary had long abandoned her book; she sat in silence, her luminous eyes fixed on the wrinkled face of her old nurse. The old nurse, with her knitting in her hand, talked away in a soft voice, not hearing herself nor following the meaning of her own words; telling, as she had told hundreds of times before, how the late princess had been brought to bed of Princess Mary and had only a Moldavian peasant woman instead of a midwife.

"God is merciful, doctors are never wanted," she said.

Suddenly a gust of wind blew open one of the windows and the chill, snowy draught blew out the candle. Princess Mary shuddered. The nurse, putting down her knitting went to the window to close it. The cold wind flapped the ends of her kerchief and the grey locks of her hair.

"Princess, my dear, there's some one driving up the avenue!" she said. "With lanterns. It must be the doctor. . . ."

"Oh, my God! Thank God!" said the Princess Mary. "I must go and meet him. He does not speak Russian."

Princess Mary hurried out. As she passed through the anteroom, she saw through the window a carriage and lanterns standing at the entrance. She went out on to the stairs. At the post of the balustrade stood a tallow-candle guttering in the draught. The footman, looking scared, stood below on the first landing of the staircase, with another candle in his hand. Still lower down, at the turn of the winding stairs, footsteps in thick overshoes could be heard coming up. And a voice was saying something.

"Thank God!" said the voice. "And father?"

"He has gone to bed," answered the voice of the butler, who was below.

Then the voice said something more, and the footsteps in thick overshoes began approaching up the unseen part of the staircase.

"It is André!" thought Princess Mary. "No, it cannot be!"

And at the very instant she was thinking so, on the landing where the footman stood with a candle, there came into sight the face and figure of Prince André, in a fur coat, with a deep collar covered with snow. He had been picked up by peasants on the battlefield and nursed back to health. Yes, it was he, but pale and thin, and with a strangely softened expression on his face. He went up the stairs and embraced his sister.

Then turning back, and with the doctor who was behind him—they had met at the last station—he ran again rapidly upstairs and again embraced his sister.

"What a strange fate!" he said, "Mary, darling!" And throwing off his fur coat and boots, he went towards the little princess's room.

The little princess was lying on the pillows in her white nightcap. The agony had only left her for a moment. Her black hair lay in curls about her swollen and perspiring cheeks. Her rosy, charming little mouth was open.

Prince André went into the room, and stood facing her at the foot of the bed. The glittering eyes, staring in childish terror and excitement, rested on him with no change in their expression. "I love you all, I have done no one any harm; why am I suffering? Help me," her face seemed to say. She saw her husband, but she did not understand the meaning of his presence.

Prince André went round the bed and kissed her on the forehead.

"My precious," he said, a word he had never used speaking to her before. "God is merciful. . . ." She stared at him with a look of childish reproach.

"I hoped for help from you, and nothing, nothing, you too!" her eyes said. She was not surprised at his having come; she did not understand that he had come. His coming had nothing to do with her agony and its alleviation. The pains began again. And Marie Bogdanovna advised Prince André to leave.

The doctor went into the room. Prince André came out, and, meeting Princess Mary, went to her. They talked in whispers. They were waiting and listening.

"Go to her," said Princess Mary.

Prince André went again to his wife and sat down in the adjoining room, waiting. A woman ran out of the bedroom with a frightened face, and was startled on seeing Prince André. He hid his face in his hands and sat so for some minutes. Piteous, helpless, animal groans came from the next room. Prince André got up, went to the door, and wanted to open it but some one was holding the door.

"Can't come in, can't!" a frightened voice said from within.

He began walking about the room. The screams ceased. Several seconds passed. Suddenly a fearful scream came from the room. Prince André ran to the door. The scream ceased. He heard the cry of a baby.

Tears choked him, and leaning both elbows on the window-sill he cried, sobbing as children cry. The door opened. The doctor with his shirt sleeves tucked up, and no coat on, came out of the room, pale, and his lower jaw twitching. Prince André spoke to him, but the doctor passed by without saying a word. A woman ran out, and, seeing Prince André, stopped, hesitating at the door.

Prince André went into his wife's room. She was lying dead in the same position in which he had seen her five minutes before. And in spite of the fixed gaze and white cheeks, there was the same expression still on the charming childish face. "I love you all, and have done no harm to any one. And what have you done to me?" said her piteous, dead face.

In a corner of the room was something red and tiny, squealing and grunting in the trembling white hands of Marie Bogdanovna.

Two hours later Prince André went into his father's room. The old prince knew everything already. He was standing near the door, and, as soon as it opened, his rough old arms closed like a vice round his son's neck, and without a word he burst into sobs like a child.

Three days later the little princess was buried, and Prince André went to the steps of the tomb to take his last farewell of her. Even in the coffin the face was the same, though the eyes were closed. "What have you done to me?" it still seemed to say. And Prince André felt that something was being torn out of his soul, that he was guilty of a crime that he could never set right nor forget. He could not weep. The old prince, too, went in and kissed the little waxen hand that lay so peacefully crossed over the other, and to him, too, her face said: "What have you done to me, and why?" And the old man turned angrily away.

In another five days there followed the christening of the young prince, Nicholas André. The nurse held the swaddling clothes up to her chin, while the priest with a goose feather anointed the baby's red, wrinkled hands and feet.

His grandfather, who was his godfather, trembling and afraid of dropping the baby, carried him round the battered tin font, and handed him over to his godmother, Princess Mary.

Faint with terror that they would let the baby drown in the font, Prince André sat in an adjoining room, waiting for the end of the ceremony. He looked happily at the baby when the nurse brought him out, and nodded approvingly when the nurse told him that a bit of wax with the baby's hairs in it, thrown into the font, had not sunk in the water but floated on the surface.

Rostov's share in the duel between Dolohov and Pierre had been hushed up by the efforts of the old count, and instead of being degraded to the ranks, as Nicholas had expected, he was appointed an adjutant to the governor of Moscow. Because of this, he could not go to the country with the rest of the family, but had to stay all summer in Moscow. Dolohov recovered, and Rostov became particularly friendly with him during this time.

In the autumn the Rostov family returned to Moscow. At the beginning of the winter Denisov too came back and stayed again with the Rostovs. The early part of the winter of 1806 spent by Nicholas Rostov in Moscow, was one of the happiest and liveliest periods for him and all the family. Nicholas brought a lot of young men home with him. Vera was a handsome girl of twenty; Sonya, a girl of sixteen, with all the charm of an opening flower; Natasha, half grown up, half a child, at one time childishly absurd, and at another completely fascinating.

Among the young men Rostov brought to the house was Dolohov, who was liked by every one except Natasha. She almost had a quarrel with her brother over Dolohov. She insisted that he was a spiteful man; that in the duel with Pierre, Pierre was right and Dolohov wrong, and that he was horrid and not natural.

"He's spiteful and heartless," Natasha cried. "Your Denisov now, you see, I like; he's a rake, and all that, but still I like him, so I do understand. I don't know how to tell you; with Dolohov everything is done on a plan, and I don't like that. Denisov, now . . ."

"Oh, Denisov's another matter," answered Nicholas, in a tone that implied that in comparison with Dolohov even Denisov was not of much account.

"I know nothing about that, but I don't feel at home with him. And do you know he's falling in love with Sonya!"

Natasha's prediction was fulfilled. Dolohov, who did not as a rule care for ladies, began to come often to the house; and the question, for whose sake he came, was soon decided—it was on Sonya's account. And though Sonya would never have ventured to say so, she knew it.

Dolohov showed marked attention to Sonya, and looked at her with such an expression in his eyes that Sonya could not bear his eyes on her without turning crimson, and even the old countess and Natasha blushed when they saw that look.

In the autumn of 1806 every one was beginning to talk again of war with Napoleon, and with even greater fervour than in the previous year.

A levy was decreed, not only of ten recruits for active service, but of nine militiamen for the reserve as well, from every thousand of the population. Everywhere Bonaparte was cursed and the only thing talked of in Moscow was the impending war. To the Rostov family the war rumours centered entirely in the fact that Nicholas refused to remain longer in Moscow, and was only waiting for the end of Denisov's leave to rejoin his regiment with him after the holidays. His approaching departure, far from keeping him from enjoying himself, gave an added zest to his pleasures. The greater part of his time he spent away from home, at dinners, parties, and balls.

On the third day after Christmas Nicholas dined at home, which he had rarely done of late. This was a farewell dinner in his honour, as he was soon to set off with Denisov to rejoin his regiment. Twenty persons were dining, among them Dolohov and Denisov.

After exhausting two pairs of horses, as he did every day without having been everywhere he ought to have been, and everywhere he had been invited, Nicholas reached home just at dinner-time. As soon as he went in he became conscious of a strange embarrassment. Sonya seemed particularly disturbed. So did Dolohov and the old countess, and in a lesser degree Natasha. Nicholas saw that something must have passed before dinner between Sonya and Dolohov, and he was wary with both of them during dinner.

On that evening there was to be one of the dances given by Iogel, the dancing-master, during the holidays for his pupils.

"Nicholas, are you going to Iogel's? Please, do come," said Natasha. "He particularly begged you to, and Denisov is going."

"Where would I not go at Natasha's commands!" said Denisov, who had jestingly taken up the rôle of Natasha's knight in the Rostov household.

"If I have time! I promised the Arharovs. They are having a party," said Nicholas.

"And you? . . ." he turned to Dolohov. And as soon as he had asked the question, he saw that he should not have asked it.

"Yes, possibly . . ." Dolohov answered coldly. And he looked at Nicholas with exactly the same expression with which he had looked at Pierre at the club dinner.

"There's something wrong," thought Nicholas. And he was still more sure of this when immediately after dinner Dolohov went away. He called Natasha, and asked her what had happened.

"I was looking for you," said Natasha, running out to him. "I told you so, and still you wouldn't believe me," she said triumphantly. "He has made Sonya an offer."

Little as Nicholas had been thinking of Sonya of late, he felt as if something were being torn from him when he heard this. Dolohov was a good, and in some respects a brilliant, match for the penniless orphan Sonya. From the point of view of the countess and of society it was out of the question for her to refuse him. And so Nicholas' first feeling when he heard of it was one of exasperation against Sonya. He braced himself to say, "Of course she must forget her childish promises and accept the offer."

But he had not succeeded in saying this when Natasha said: "Just think! she has refused him, absolutely refused him! She says she loves some one else," she added after a brief pause.

"Mother begged her ever so many times to marry him, but she refused. And I know she won't change, if she has said a thing. . . ."

"Mother begged her to marry him!" Nicholas said reproachfully.

"Yes," said Natasha. "Do you know, Nicholas—don't be angry—but I know you won't marry her. I know—I don't know why—but I know for certain that you won't marry her."

"Natasha, you can't know a thing like that," said Nicholas. Then he added smiling: "I want to talk to her."

"I'll send her in to you." And Natasha kissed her brother and ran away.

A minute later Sonya came in, looking frightened and guilty. Nicholas went up to her and kissed her hand. It was the first time since his return that they had talked alone and of their love.

"Sonya," he said to her, at first timidly, but more and more boldly as he went on, "if you were simply refusing a brilliant, an advantageous match—but he's a wonderful fellow . . . He's my friend . . . If you are refusing him for my sake, I am afraid that I . . ."

With frightened, imploring eyes Sonya looked at him.

"Nicholas, don't say that to me," she said.

"No, I must. It's better to say it. If you are refusing him on my account, I ought to tell you the whole truth. I love you, I believe, more than any one . . . But I have been in love a thousand times, and I shall fall in love again . . . Then I am young and mother does not wish it. Well—in fact—I can make no promise. And I beg you to consider the offer of Dolohov," he said, with an effort.

"Don't speak to me of such things. I shall always love you, and I want nothing more," Sonya answered.

Nicholas kissed her hand again.

For the next two days Nicholas did not see Dolohov. On the third day he received a note from him.

"As I do not intend to be at your house again and am going to rejoin the regiment, I am giving a farewell supper—come to the English Hotel."

On the day fixed Rostov went. He was at once conducted to the best room in the hotel, which Dolohov had taken for the occasion.

Some twenty men were gathered about a table before which Dolohov was sitting. On the table lay money and notes, and Dolohov was keeping the bank. Nicholas had not seen him since Sonya's refusal, and he felt uneasy at the thought of meeting him.

Dolohov's clear, cold glance met Rostov in the doorway as though he had been expecting him a long while.

"It's a long while since we've met," he said. "Thanks for coming. I'll just finish dealing here, and then I'll call the gypsies."

"I went to your home looking for you," said Rostov, flushing.

Dolohov did not answer him.

"You might put down a stake," he said. "Or are you afraid to play with me?" Dolohov said as though guessing Rostov's thoughts. And he smiled. Behind his smile Rostov saw in him that mood which he had seen in him at the club dinner and at other times, when Dolohov seemed, as it were, weary of the monotony of daily life, and felt a craving to escape from it by some strange cruel act.

Rostov felt ill at ease. He racked his brain but could not find a joke to reply to Dolohov's words.

Throwing down a pack he had just opened, Dolohov said, "Bank, gentlemen!" And moving the money forward, he began dealing.

Rostov sat near him, and at first he did not play. Dolohov glanced at him.

"Why don't you play?" said Dolohov. And strange to say, Nicholas felt that he could not help taking up a card and staking a trifling sum on it.

"I have no money with me," said Rostov.

"I'll trust you!"

Rostov staked five roubles on a card and lost it, staked again and again lost. Dolohov "killed," that is, beat ten cards in succession from Rostov.

"Gentlemen," he said, after dealing again for a little while. "I beg you to put the money on the cards or else I shall get muddled over the reckoning."

One of the players said that he hoped he could trust him.

"I can trust you, but I'm afraid of making mistakes. I beg you to lay the money on the cards," answered Dolohov. "You needn't worry, we'll settle our accounts," he added to Rostov.

The play went on. A footman kept bringing round champagne.

All Rostov's cards were beaten, and the sum of eight hundred roubles was scored against him. He wrote on a card eight hundred roubles, but while champagne was being poured out for him, he changed his mind and again wrote down the usual stake, twenty roubles.

"Leave it," said Dolohov, though he did not seem to be looking at Rostov. "You'll win it back. I lose to the rest, while I win from you. Or perhaps you are afraid of me," he repeated.

Rostov excused himself, left the stake of eight hundred and laid down the seven of hearts, a card with a corner torn, which he had picked up from the ground. He wrote on it with a broken piece of chalk 800 in bold round figures. And then with a sinking heart he waited. He watched Dolohov's hands that held the pack. The loss or gain of that card meant a great deal for Rostov. On the previous Sunday his father the Count had given him two thousand roubles, and though he never liked speaking of money difficulties, he told him that this money was the last they would get till May, and so he begged him to be a little more careful. Nicholas said that that was too much really for him, and he gave his word of honour not to come for more before May. Now there was only twelve hundred out of that two thousand left. So that on the seven of hearts there hung not merely the loss of sixteen hundred roubles, but the betrayal of his word. With a sinking heart he watched Dolohov's hand and thought: "Well, hurry and deal me that card, and I'll drive home to supper with Denisov, Natasha, and Sonya, and I'm sure I'll never take a card in my hand again." He could not conceive that a stupid chance, leading the seven to the right rather than to the left, could deprive him of all his happiness.

"So you're not afraid to play with me?" repeated Dolohov. And as though he were about to tell a good story, he laid down the cards, leaned back in his chair, and began deliberately with a smile: "Yes, gentlemen, I have been told there's a story going about Moscow that I'm too sharp with cards, so I advise you to be a little on your guard with me."

"Come, deal away!" said Rostov.

"These Moscow gossips!" said Dolohov, and he took up the cards with a smile.

"Oh!" Rostov almost screamed. The seven he needed was lying uppermost, the first card in the pack. He had lost more than he could pay.

"Don't swim beyond your depth," said Dolohov, with a passing glance at Rostov, and he went on.

Within an hour and a half the players were no longer interested in their own play. Their attention was concentrated on Rostov. Instead of a mere loss of sixteen hundred roubles he had by now scored against him more than twenty thousand roubles.

Dolohov was not now listening to stories, nor telling them. He followed every movement of Rostov's hands, and from time to time took a look at his score. He had resolved to keep playing until Rostov's losses reached forty-three thousand. He had fixed on that number because it represented the sum of his and Sonya's ages.

Rostov sat with his head propped in both hands, before the wine-stained table scrawled over with scorings and littered with cards. One torturing sensation never left him; those broad-boned, reddish hands, with the hairs visible under the shirt-cuffs, those hands which he loved and hated, held him in their power.

"Six hundred roubles, ace, nine . . . Winning it back's out of the question! . . . How happy I would be at home. . . . The jack double or quits, it can't be! . . . And why is he doing this to me? . . ." Rostov pondered. Sometimes he put a higher stake on a card but Dolohov refused it and fixed the stake himself. Nicholas submitted to him. And at one moment he was praying to God, as he had prayed under fire on the bridge at the Enns. At the next moment he tried his fortune on the chance that the card that he would first pick up among the heap of crumpled ones under the table would save him. Then he counted up the rows of braidings on his coat, and tried staking the whole amount of his losses on a card of that number. Then he looked round for help to the others playing, or stared into Dolohov's face, which looked quite cold now, and tried to penetrate into what was passing within him.

The score reached the fateful number of forty-three thousand roubles. Rostov had the card ready which he meant to stake for double or quits on the three thousand, that had just been put down to his score, when Dolohov slapped the pack of cards down on the table, pushed it away, and taking the chalk began rapidly in his clear, strong hand, writing down the total of Rostov's losses, breaking the chalk as he did so.

"Supper, supper-time. And here are the gypsies." And some swarthy men and women came in. Nicholas understood that it was all over.

"When am I to receive the money, count?" Dolohov asked.

"To-morrow," said Rostov. And he went out of the room.

To say "to-morrow," and maintain the right tone was not difficult. But to arrive home alone, to see his sisters and brother, his mother and father, to confess and beg for money to which he had no right after giving his word of honour, was terrible.

At home they had not yet gone to bed. Sonya and Natasha, wearing the light blue dresses they had put on for the theatre, stood at the clavichord, pretty and conscious of being so, happy and smiling. Vera was playing draughts with Shinshin in the drawing-room. The old countess, waiting for her son and her husband to come in, was playing patience with an old gentlewoman, who was one of their household. Denisov, with shining eyes and ruffled hair, was sittting with one leg behind him at the clavichord. He was singing in his small, husky, but true voice a poem of his own composition, "The Enchantress," to which he was trying to fit music. He sang, his black eyes gleaming at the frightened and delighted Natasha.

"Oh, and here's Nicholas." Natasha ran up to him.

"Is father at home?" he asked.

"How glad I am that you have come," said Natasha, not answering his question. "We are having such fun. Denisov is staying a day longer for me, do you know?"

"No, father has not come in yet," answered Sonya.

"Nicholas, is that you? Come to me, darling," said the voice of the countess from the drawing-room. Nicholas went to his mother, kissed her hand, and sitting down began silently watching her hands as she dealt the cards. From the hall he kept hearing the sound of laughter and merry voices, persuading Natasha to do something.

"It's your turn to sing the barcarolle," Denisov cried.

The countess looked round at her son. "What's the matter?" she asked.

"Oh, nothing," he said. And he went back to the hall, where the clavichord was.

Sonya was sitting at the clavichord, playing the prelude of the barcarolle that Denisov particularly liked. Natasha was preparing to sing. Denisov was watching her.

"Are you ready, Sonya?" Natasha asked walking into the middle of the room, where to her mind the resonance was best. She held her head up and let her arms hang lifelessly as dancers do. "Behold me, here I am!" she seemed to say, in response to the gaze with which Denisov followed her.

Natasha had for the first time begun that winter to take singing seriously, especially since Denisov had been so enthusiastic about her singing. She no longer sang like a child. There was not now in her singing that comical childish effort which used to be perceptible in it. Her voice now had a virginal purity, a velvety softness.

As soon as Natasha had finished her barcarolle, Nicholas,

saying nothing, went down stairs to his own room. A quarter of an hour later, the old prince came in, good-humoured and satisfied. Nicholas heard him come in, and went to him.

"Well, had a good time?" said the old count smiling proudly at his son. Nicholas tried to say "Yes," but could not. He was on the point of sobbing. The count was lighting his pipe, and did not notice.

Then all at once, as though he were asking for the carriage to drive into town, he said to his father in the most casual tone, that made him feel vile to himself: "Father I have come to you on a matter of business. I want some money."

"You don't say so?" said his father, who happened to be in particularly good spirits. "I told you that we were short. Do you want a large sum?"

"Very large," said Nicholas smiling a stupid, careless smile, for which long after he could not forgive himself. "I have lost a little at cards, that is, a good deal, really, a great deal, forty-three thousand."

"What! To whom? . . . You're joking!" cried the count, flushing, as old people flush, an apoplectic red over his neck and the back of his head.

"I have promised to pay it to-morrow," said Nicholas. "It can't be helped! It happens to every one." He continued in a free and easy tone, while in his heart he was feeling himself a cad whose whole life could not atone for his crime. He would have liked to kiss his father's hands, to beg his forgiveness on his knees, while carelessly, rudely even, he was telling him that it happened to every one.

Count Rostov dropped his eyes when he heard those words from his son, and began moving hurriedly, as though looking for something.

"Yes, yes," he said. "It will be difficult, I fear, difficult to raise . . . happens to every one! Yes, it happens to every one . . ." And glancing at Nicholas he walked out of the room.

Nicholas had been prepared to face resistance, but he had not expected this.

"Father! Father!" he cried, running after him. "Forgive me!" And clutching at his father's hand, he pressed it to his lips and burst into tears.

While Count Rostov and Nicholas were together, Natasha, in great excitement, had run in to her mother.

"Mother! . . . Mother! . . . He has made me . . ."

"Made you what?"

"He's made, made an offer. Mother! Mother!" she kept crying.

The countess could not believe her ears. Denisov had made

an offer . . . to whom? . . . To this child Natasha, who had only just given up playing with dolls, and was still having lessons.

"Natasha, enough of this silliness!" she said, hoping it was a joke.

"Silliness! I am telling you the truth," said Natasha angrily. "I have come to ask you what to do, and you talk to me of 'silliness' . . ."

The countess shrugged her shoulders.

"If it is true that Monsieur Denisov has made you an offer, then tell him he is a fool, that's all."

"No, he's not a fool," said Natasha, resentfully and seriously.

"Well, what would you have, then? You are all in love, it seems, nowadays. Oh, well, if you're in love with him, better marry him," said the countess, laughing angrily. "And God bless you."

"No, mother, I'm not in love with him. I suppose I'm not in love with him."

"Well, then, tell him so."

"Mother, are you cross? Don't be cross, darling; it's not my fault, is it?"

"No. . . . If you like, I will go and tell him so," said the countess, smiling.

"No, I'll do it myself; only tell me how to say it. Everything comes easy to you," she added, responding to her smile. "And if you could have seen how he said it to me! I know he did not mean to say it, but said it by accident."

"Well, any way you must refuse him."

"No, I mustn't. I feel so sorry for him! He's so nice."

"Oh, well, accept his proposal, then. High time you were married, I suppose," said her mother angrily and ironically.

"No, mother, but I'm so sorry for him. I don't know how to say it."

"Well, there's no need for you to say anything. I'll speak to him myself," said the countess, indignant that any one should have dared to treat her little Natasha as grown up.

"No, I'll go myself, and you listen at the door." And Natasha ran across the drawing-room to the hall, where Denisov, his face in his hands, was still sitting in the same chair at the clavichord. He jumped up at the sound of her footsteps.

"Natasha!" he said, going towards her.

"I'm so sorry for you! . . . No, but you are so nice . . . But it won't do . . . that . . . But I shall always love you as I do now."

Denisov bent over her, and she heard strange sounds that she did not understand. She kissed his tangled curly black head. At that moment they heard the hurried rustle of the countess's skirts. She came up to them.

"Monsieur Denisov, I thank you for the honour you do us," said the countess, in an embarrassed voice, which sounded severe to Denisov. "But my daughter is so young, and I should have thought that as my son's friend you would have come first to me. In that case you would not have forced me to make this refusal."

"Countess! . . ." said Denisov, with a guilty face. He tried to say more, and stammered.

Natasha could not see him in such a piteous plight. She began to whimper.

"Countess, I have acted wrongly," Denisov went on in a breaking voice. "But I so adore your daughter and all your family that I'd give my life twice over . . ." He looked at the countess and noticed her stern face. . . . "Well, good-bye, countess," he said, kissing her hand, and without glancing at Natasha he walked out of the room.

Next day Nicholas saw Denisov off, as he was unwilling to remain another day in Moscow. All his Moscow friends gave him a farewell party at the Gypsies', and he had no recollection of how they got him into his sledge, or of the first three stations he passed.

After Denisov's departure Rostov spent another two weeks in Moscow, waiting for the money to pay his debt, which the count was unable to raise all at once. He hardly left the house, and spent most of his time in the young girls' room.

He copied music for them, and wrote verses in their albums. And after at last sending off all the forty-three thousand roubles, and receiving Dolohov's receipt for it, he left Moscow towards the end of November and joined his regiment, which was already in Poland.

1806—1807

BOOK FIVE

AFTER HIS interview with his wife, Pierre set off for Petersburg. At the post station of Torzhok there were no horses and he had to wait. Without removing his overcoat he lay down on a leather sofa in front of a round table, put up his big feet in their thick overboots on the table and sank into thought.

"Shall I bring in the trunks? Make up a cot? Will you take tea?" the valet kept asking.

Pierre did not answer for he heard nothing and said nothing. He had been deep in thought since he left the last post station, and still went on thinking of the same thing—of something so important that he did not notice what was passing around him. "I shot Dolohov because I considered myself injured. Louis XVI was executed because they considered him a criminal, and a year later his judges were also executed for something. What is wrong? What is right? What must one love? What must one hate? What is life for, and what am I? What is life? What is death? What force controls it all?" he asked himself. And there was no answer to these questions, except one illogical reply that was in no way an answer to any of them. That reply was: "One dies and it's all over. One dies and ceases asking."

A Torzhok pedlar woman in a whining voice proffered her wares, especially some goatskin slippers. "I have hundreds of roubles I don't know what to do with, and she's standing in her torn cloak looking timidly at me," thought Pierre. "And what does she want the money for? As though the money could give her one hairsbreadth of happiness, of peace of soul. Is there anything in the world that can make her and me less enslaved to evil and to death? Death, which ends all, and must come to-day or to-morrow—which beside eternity is the same as an instant's time."

Everything within himself and around him struck him as confused, meaningless, and loathsome. But in this very loathing Pierre found a tantalising satisfaction.

"I make bold to beg your excellency to make room for this gentleman here," said the station master, coming into the room and ushering in after him another traveller, brought to a standstill from lack of horses. The traveller was a thickset, wrinkled old man, with gleaming eyes of an indefinite grey colour.

Pierre took his feet off the table, stood up and went to lie down on the cot that had been made ready for him, glancing now and then at the newcomer, who, without looking at Pierre, was taking off his overcoat with the aid of his servant. The traveller then sat down on the sofa and leaning back his close-cropped head, which was very large and broad across the temples, he glanced at Bezuhov. The stern, shrewd, and penetrating expression in that glance impressed Pierre. The gleaming old eyes drew him irresistibly to them.

"I have the pleasure of speaking to Count Bezuhov, if I am not mistaken," said the stranger, in a loud deliberate voice.

Pierre looked in silence over his spectacles at the speaker.

"I have heard of you," continued the stranger, "and I have heard, sir, of what has happened to you, of your misfortune." He underlined, as it were, the last word, as though to say: "Yes, misfortune, whatever you call it, I know what happened to you in Moscow was a misfortune."

"I am very sorry for it, sir." Pierre reddened. He smiled timidly and unnaturally.

"I have not mentioned this to you, sir, from curiosity, but from graver reasons." He paused, not letting Pierre escape from his gaze, and moved aside on the sofa, inviting him to sit beside him. Pierre disliked entering into conversation with this old man, but involuntarily submitting to him, he came and sat down beside him.

"You are unhappy, sir," he went on. "You are young, and I am old. I should like, as far as it is in my power, to help you."

"Oh, yes," said Pierre, with an unnatural smile. "Very much obliged to you . . . Where have you been travelling from?"

The stranger's face was not cordial, it was even cold and severe, but in spite of that, he was irresistibly attractive to Pierre. And glancing at the stranger's hands Pierre noticed he was wearing a large iron ring with the head of Adam, the token of masonry. "Allow me to ask," he said. "Are you a mason?"

"Yes, I belong to the brotherhood of freemasons," said the stranger, looking now more searchingly into Pierre's eyes. "And in their name I hold out to you a brotherly hand."

"I am afraid," said Pierre, smiling and hesitating between the confidence inspired in him by the personality of the freemason and the habit of ridiculing the articles of the masons' creed; "I am afraid that I am very far from a comprehension—how shall I say—I am afraid that my way of thinking in regard to the whole theory of the universe is so opposed to yours that we shall not understand one another."

"I am aware of your way of thinking," said the freemason. "And that way of thinking is the way of thinking of the majority of men, and is the invariable fruit of pride, indolence, and ignorance. Excuse my saying, sir, that if I had not been aware of it, I should not have addressed you. Your way of thinking is a melancholy error."

"Just as I may take for granted that you are in error," said Pierre, faintly smiling.

"I would never be so bold as to say I know the truth," said the mason, the definiteness and decision of whose manner of speaking impressed Pierre more and more. "No one alone can attain truth; only stone upon stone, with the co-operation of all, by the millions of generations from our first father Adam down to our day is that temple being reared that should be a fitting dwelling-place of the Great God," said the freemason, and he shut his eyes.

"I ought to tell you that I don't believe, don't . . . believe in God," said Pierre, feeling it essential to speak the whole truth.

The freemason looked intently at Pierre and smiled as a rich man, holding millions in his hands, might smile at a poor wretch, who should say to him that he, the poor man, has not five roubles that would secure his happiness.

"Yes, you do not know Him, sir," said the freemason. "You cannot know Him. That is why you are unhappy."

"Yes, yes, I am unhappy," Pierre agreed. "But what am I to do?"

"You know not Him, sir, and that's why you are very unhappy. You know not Him, but He is here, He is within me, He is in my words, He is in thee, and even in these scoffing words that thou hast just uttered," said the mason in a stern, vibrating voice.

He paused, evidently trying to be calm.

"If He were not," he said softly, "we should not be speaking of Him, sir. Of what, of whom were we speaking? Whom dost thou deny?" he said all at once, with authority in his voice. "Who invented Him, if He be not? How came there within thee the conception that there is such an incomprehensible Being? How comes it that thou and all the world have assumed the existence of such an inconceivable Being, a Being all powerful, eternal and infinite in all His qualities? . . ." He stopped. There was a long pause.

Pierre could not and would not break this silence.

"He exists, but to comprehend Him is hard," the mason began again, not looking into Pierre's face, but straight before him, while his old hands, which could not keep still for inward emotion, turned the leaves of a book. "If it had been a man of whose existence thou hadst doubts, I could have brought thee the man, taken him by the hand, and shown him thee. But how am I, an insignificant mortal, to show all the power, all the eternity, all the blessedness of Him to one who is blind, or to one who shuts his eyes that he may not see, may not understand Him, and may not see, and not understand all his own vileness and viciousness." He paused. "Who art thou? What art thou? Thou dreamest that thou art wise because thou couldst utter those scoffing words," he said, with a gloomy and scornful irony, "while thou art more foolish and artless than a little babe, who, playing with the parts of a cunningly fashioned watch, should rashly say that because he understands not the use of that watch, he does not believe in the maker who fashioned it. To know Him is a hard matter. For ages, from our first father Adam to our day, have we been striving for this knowledge, and are infinitely far from the attainment of our aim; but in our lack of understanding we see only our own weakness and His greatness . . ."

Pierre gazed into the freemason's face, listening to his words. He did not interrupt him, nor ask questions. But with all his soul he believed what this strange man was telling him. With his whole soul he longed to believe, and believed and felt a joyful sense of soothing, of renewal, and of return to life.

The freemason smiled a mild, fatherly smile.

"The highest wisdom is founded not on reason only, not on those worldly sciences, of physics, history and chemistry, into which knowledge of the intellect is divided. The highest wisdom is one. The highest wisdom knows but one science—the science of the whole, the science that explains the whole creation and the place of man in it. To instil this science into one's soul, it is needful to purify and renew one's inner man, and so, before one can know, one must believe and be made perfect. And for the attainment of these aims there has been put into our souls the light of God, called the conscience."

"Yes, yes," Pierre agreed.

"Look with the spiritual eye into thy inner man, and ask of thyself whether thou art content with thyself. What hast thou attained with the guidance of the intellect alone? What art thou? You are young, you are wealthy, you are cultured, sir. What have you made of all the blessings given you? Are you satisfied with yourself and your life?"

"No, I hate my life," said Pierre, frowning.

"Then change it. Look at your life, sir. How have you been spending it? In riotous orgies and debauchery, taking everything from society and giving nothing in return. You have received wealth. How have you used it? What have you done for your neighbour? Have you given a thought to the tens of thousands of your serfs, have you helped them physically and morally? No. You have profited by their toil to lead a dissipated life. That's what you have done. Have you chosen a post in the service where you might be of use to your neighbour? No. You have spent your life in idleness. Then you married, sir, took upon yourself the responsibility of guiding a young woman in life, and what have you done? You have not helped her, sir, to find the path of truth, but have cast her into an abyss of deception and misery. A man injured you, and you have killed him, and you say you do not know God, and that you hate your life. There is no wisdom in all that, sir."

After these words the freemason leaned on the back of the sofa and closed his eyes, as though weary of talking. Pierre gazed at that stern, immovable, almost death-like face, and moved his lips without uttering a sound. He wanted to speak but he dared not break the silence. Then suddenly the freemason cleared his throat huskily, as old men do, and called his servant.

"How about horses?" he asked, without looking at Pierre.

"They have brought round some that were given up," answered the old man. "You won't rest?"

"No, tell them to harness them."

"Can he really be going away and leaving me all alone, without telling me everything and promising me help?" thought Pierre, getting up and walking up and down the room, casting a glance from time to time at the freemason. "Yes, I had not thought of it, but I have led a dissolute life, but I did not like it, and I didn't want to," thought Pierre. "And this man knows the truth, and if he liked he could reveal it to me." Pierre wanted to say this to the freemason and dared not.

After packing his things the old traveller buttoned up his overcoat. Then he turned to Pierre, and in a polite, indifferent tone, said to him: "Where are you going now, sir?"

"I? . . . I'm going to Petersburg," answered Pierre in a tone of childish indecision. "I thank you. But do not suppose that I have been so bad. With all my soul I have desired to be what you would wish me to be. But I have never met with help from any one. . . . Though I was myself most to blame for everything. Help me, and perhaps I shall be able . . ."

Pierre could not say more. His voice broke and he turned away.

The freemason was silent, obviously pondering something.

"Help comes only from God," he said. "But such measure of aid as it is in the power of our order to give you, it will give you, sir. You go to Petersburg, and give this to Count Villarsky." He took out his notebook and wrote a few words on a large sheet of paper folded into four. "One piece of advice let me give you. When you reach the capital, devote your time at first there to solitude and to self-examination, and do not return to your old manner of life. . . . I wish you a good journey, sir," he added, noticing that his servant had entered the room. "And all success . . ."

The stranger was Osip Alexyevitch Bazdyev, as Pierre found out from the station master's book, a well-known freemason. For a long while after he had gone, Pierre walked about the station, neither lying down to sleep nor asking for horses. He reviewed his past, and with a sense of beginning anew, pictured to himself an irreproachable future, which seemed to him easy of attainment. There was left in his soul not a trace of his former doubts. He firmly believed in the possibility of the brotherhood of man, united in the aim of supporting one another in the path of virtue. And freemasonry he pictured to himself as such a brotherhood.

On reaching Petersburg, Pierre let no one know of his arrival, went out to see nobody, and spent whole days in reading

Thomas à Kempis, a book which had been sent him, he did not know by whom.

A week after his arrival, the young Polish count, Villarsky, whom Pierre knew very slightly in Petersburg society, came one evening into his room.

"I have come to you with a message and a suggestion, count," he said to him, not sitting down. "A person of very high standing in our brotherhood has been interceding for you to be admitted into our society before the usual term, and has asked me to be your sponsor. I regard it as a sacred duty to carry out that person's wishes. Would you like under my sponsorship to enter the brotherhood of freemasons?"

"Yes, I do wish it," said Pierre.

Villarsky bent his head.

"One more question, count," he said, "to which I beg you, not as a future mason, but as an honest man to answer me in all sincerity. Have you renounced your former convictions? Do you believe in God?"

Pierre thought a moment.

"Yes . . . yes, I do believe in God," he said.

"In that case . . ." Villarsky was beginning, but Pierre interrupted him.

"Yes, I believe in God," he said once more.

"In that case, we can go," said Villarsky. "My carriage is waiting."

During the drive Villarsky was silent. In answer to Pierre's questions of what he would have to do, and how he would have to answer, Villarsky simply said that brothers, more worthy than he, would prove him, and that Pierre need do nothing but tell the truth.

They drove in at the gates of a large house, where the lodge had its quarters, and, passing up a dark staircase, entered a small, lighted ante-room, where they took off their overcoats. From the ante-room they walked into another room. A man in strange attire appeared at the door. Villarsky said something to him in French in a low voice, and went up to a small cupboard, where Pierre noticed garments unlike any he had seen before. Taking a handkerchief from the cupboard, Villarsky put it over Pierre's eyes and tied it in a knot behind, catching his hair painfully in the knot. Then taking him by the hand led him away somewhere. Pierre walked with timid and uncertain steps.

Villarsky stopped. "When you hear a knock at the door, you may uncover your eyes," he said. "I wish you good courage and success." And, pressing Pierre's hand, Villarsky went away.

When he was left alone, Pierre raised his hand to the

handkerchief, as though to take it off, but he let it drop again.

At last there came loud knocks at the door. Pierre took off the bandage and looked about him. It was dark in the room; only in one spot was there a little lamp burning before something white. Pierre went nearer and saw that the lamp stood on a black table, on which there lay an open book. The book was the gospel. The white thing in which the lamp was burning was a human skull. After reading the first words of the gospel, "In the beginning was the Word and the Word was with God," Pierre went round the table and caught sight of a large open box filled with something. It was a coffin full of bones. He was not in the least surprised by what he saw. Hoping to enter upon a completely new life, utterly unlike the old life, he was ready for anything extraordinary, more extraordinary indeed than what he was seeing. The skull, the coffin, the gospel—it seemed to him that he had been expecting all that; had been expecting more, indeed. "God, death, love, the brotherhood of man," he kept saying to himself, associating with those words vague but joyful conceptions of some sort.

The door opened and a short man entered. He went towards the table, and laid on it both his small hands covered with leather gloves.

He was wearing a white leather apron, that covered his chest and part of his legs. Around his neck could be seen something like a necklace, and a high white ruffle stood up from under the necklace, framing his long face, on which the light fell from below.

"For what are you come hither?" asked the newcomer, turning towards Pierre. "For what are you, an unbeliever in the truth of the light, who have not seen the light, for what are you come here? What do you seek from us? Wisdom, virtue, enlightenment?"

For a long while Pierre could not utter a word, so that the man was obliged to repeat his question.

"Yes; I . . . I . . . wish to begin anew," Pierre said with difficulty.

"Very good," said the man and he went on calmly and rapidly.

"Have you any idea of the means by which our holy order will assist you in attaining your aim? . . ."

"I . . . hope for . . . guidance . . . for help . . . in renewing . . ." said Pierre, with a tremble in his voice.

"What idea have you of freemasonry?"

"I assume that freemasonry is the fraternity and equality of men with virtuous aims," said Pierre, feeling ashamed as he spoke of the incongruity of his words with the solemnity of the moment. "I assume . . ."

"Have you sought the means of attaining your aim in religion?"

"No; I regarded it as untrue and have not followed it," said Pierre, so softly that the man did not catch it, and asked him what he was saying. "I was an atheist," answered Pierre.

"You seek the truth in order to follow its laws in life; consequently, you seek wisdom and virtue, do you not?"

"Yes, yes," said Pierre.

The man cleared his throat, folded his gloved hands across his chest, and continued.

"Now I must reveal to you the chief aim of our order," he said, "and if that aim coincides with yours, you may with profit enter our brotherhood. The first and greatest aim and united basis of our order, on which it is established and which no human force can destroy, is the preservation and handing down to posterity of a certain important mystery . . . that has come down to us from the most ancient times, even from the first man—a mystery upon which, perhaps, the fate of the human race depends. But since this mystery is of such a kind that no one can know it and profit by it if he has not been prepared by a prolonged and diligent self-purification, not every one can hope to attain it quickly. Hence we have a second aim, which consists in preparing our members, as far as possible reforming their hearts, purifying and enlightening their intelligence by those means which have been revealed to us by tradition from men who have striven to attain this mystery, and thereby to render them fit for the reception of it. Purifying and regenerating our members, we endeavour, thirdly, to improve the whole human race, offering it in our members an example of piety and virtue, and thereby we strive with all our strength to combat the evil that is paramount in the world. Ponder on these things, and I will come again to you," he said, and went out of the room.

"To combat the evil that is paramount in the world . . ." Pierre repeated, and alone in the room he dwelt on what the man had said to him.

Half an hour later the man returned to enumerate to him seven virtues corresponding to the seven steps of the temple of Solomon, in which every freemason must train himself. Those virtues were: discretion, obedience, morality, love for mankind, courage, liberality, and love of death.

"If you are resolved, I must proceed to your initiation," continued the man, coming closer to Pierre. "In token of obedience I beg you to undress."

Pierre took off his coat and waistcoat and left boot at the man's instructions. The mason opened his shirt over the left side of his chest and pulled up his breeches on the left leg above the knee. Then he gave him a slipper to put on his left foot. With a childish smile of embarrassment, of doubt, and of self-mockery, which would come into his face in spite of himself, Pierre stood with his legs wide apart and his hands hanging at his sides, facing the man and awaiting his next commands. The freemason did not speak nor stir for a long while. At last he moved up to Pierre, took the handkerchief that lay on the table, and again tied it over his eyes.

"For the last time I say to you: turn all your attention upon yourself, put a bridle on your feelings, and seek blessedness not in your passions, but in your own heart. The secret of blessing is not without but within us. . . ."

Shortly after this, there walked into the dark temple to fetch Pierre, his sponsor Villarsky, whom he recognised by his voice.

In reply to fresh inquiries as to the firmness of his resolve, Pierre answered: "Yes, yes, I agree," and with a beaming, childlike smile he walked forward, stepping timidly and unevenly with one booted and one slippered foot, while Villarsky held a sword pointed at his fat, uncovered chest. He was led out of the room along corridors, turning backwards and forwards, till at last he was brought to the doors of the lodge. Villarsky coughed; he was answered by masonic taps with hammers; the door opened before them. A bass voice put questions to Pierre, who he was, where and when he was born, and so on. Then he was again led away somewhere with his eyes still bandaged, and as he walked they spoke to him in allegories of the toils of his pilgrimage, and of holy love, of the Eternal Creator of the world, of the courage with which he was to endure toils and dangers.

During this time Pierre noticed that he was called sometimes the *seeker*, sometimes the *sufferer*, and sometimes the *postulant*, and that they made various tapping sounds with hammers and with swords. While he was being led up to some object, he noticed that there was hesitation and uncertainty among his conductors. He heard a whispered dispute among the people round him, and one of them insisting that he should be made to cross a certain carpet. After this they took his right hand, laid it on something, while they bade him with the left hold a compass to his left breast, while they made him repeat after some one who read the words aloud, the oath of fidelity to the laws of the order. Then the candles were extinguished and a spirit lamp was lighted, as Pierre knew from the smell of it, and he was told that he would see the lesser light. The bandage was taken off his eyes, and in the faint light of the burning spirit lamp Pierre saw as though it were in a dream, several persons who stood facing him in aprons and held swords pointed at his breast.

Among them stood a man in a white shirt stained with blood. On seeing this, Pierre moved with his chest forward towards the swords, meaning them to stab him. But the swords were drawn back, and the bandage was at once replaced on his eyes.

"Now you have seen the lesser light," said a voice. Then again they lighted the candles, told him that he had now to see the full light, and again removed the bandage, and more than ten voices said all at once: *"Sic transit gloria mundi."*

Pierre looked about at the room and the people in it. Round a long table covered with black were sitting some dozen men, all in the same strange garment that he had seen before. Several of them Pierre knew in Petersburg society. In the president's chair sat a young man, with a peculiar cross on his neck, whom he did not know. On his right hand sat the Italian abbé whom Pierre had seen two years before at Anna Pavlovna's. There were among them a dignitary of very high standing and a Swiss tutor, who had once been in the Kuragin family. All preserved a solemn silence, listening to the president, who held a hammer in his hand. In the wall was carved a blazing star; on one side of the table was a small rug with various figures worked upon it; on the other was something like an altar with the gospel and a skull on it. Round the table stood seven big candesticks. Two of the brothers led Pierre up to the altar, set his feet at right angles and bade him lie down, saying that he would be casting himself down at the gates of the temple.

"He ought first to receive the spade," said one of the brothers in a whisper.

"Oh! hush, please," said another.

Pierre did not obey, but with uneasy short-sighted eyes looked about him, and suddenly doubt came over him. "Where am I? What am I doing? Aren't they laughing at me? Shan't I be ashamed to remember this?" But this doubt only lasted a moment. Pierre looked round at the serious faces of the people round him, thought of all he had just been through, and felt that there was no stopping half-way. He was terrified at his own hesitation, and he cast himself down at the gates of the temple.

When he had lain there some time, he was told to get up, and a white leather apron such as the others wore was put round him, and a spade and three pairs of gloves were put in his hands; then the grand master addressed him. He told him that he must try never to stain the whiteness of that apron, which symbolised strength and purity. Then of the unexplained spade he told him to toil with it at clearing his heart from vice, and with forbearing patience smoothing the way in the heart of his neighbour. Then of the first pair of gloves he said that he could not know yet their significance, but must treasure them; of the second pair he said that he must put them on at meetings; and finally of the third pair—they were women's gloves—he said: "Dear brother, and these woman's gloves are destined for you too. Give them to the woman whom you shall honour beyond all others. That gift will be a pledge of your purity of heart to her whom you select as a worthy helpmeet in masonry." After a brief pause, he added: "But beware, dear brother, that these gloves never deck hands that are impure."

While the grand master uttered the last words Pierre blushed, looking about him uneasily. An awkward silence followed.

This silence was broken by one of the brothers who, leading Pierre to the rug, began reading out of a manuscript book the interpretation of all the figures delineated upon it: the sun, the moon, the hammer, the balance, the spade, the rough stone and the shaped stone, the post, the three windows, etc. Then Pierre was shown his appointed place, he was shown the signs of the lodge, told the password, and at last permitted to sit down.

The grand master began reading the exhortation concluding with: "In our temples we know of no distinctions but those between virtue and vice. Beware of making any difference that may transgress against equality. Fly to the aid of a brother whoever he may be, exhort him that goeth astray, lift up him that falleth, and cherish not malice nor hatred against a brother. Be thou friendly and courteous. Kindle in all hearts the fire of virtue. Share thy happiness with thy neighbour, and never will envy trouble that pure bliss. Forgive thy enemy, revenge not thyself on him but rather do him good. Fulfilling in this wise the highest law, thou wilt regain traces of the ancient grandeur thou hadst lost." The grand master then got up, embraced Pierre and kissed him.

The ceremony was over. And it seemed to Pierre on returning home that he had come back from a long journey on which he had spent dozens of years, and had become utterly changed, and had renounced his old habits and manner of life.

The day after his initiation at the Lodge, Pierre heard that the rumour of the duel had reached the Emperor's ears, and that it would be wise for him to leave Petersburg. He therefore thought of going to his estates in the south, and occupying himself with the care of his peasants. A week later he left, after saying good-bye to his new friends, the freemasons, and leaving large sums in their hands for charity. His new brethren gave him letters for Kiev and Odessa, to

masons living there, and promised to write to him and guide him in his new life.

Pierre's duel with Dolohov was, in time, smoothed over, and in spite of the Tsar's severity in regard to duels, neither the principals nor the seconds suffered for it. But the scandal of the duel, confirmed by Pierre's rupture with his wife, made a great noise in society. Pierre had been looked upon with patronising condescension when he was an illegitimate son; he had been made much of and extolled for his virtues while he was the wealthiest match in the Russian empire. But after his marriage, when young ladies and their mothers had nothing to hope from him, he had fallen greatly in the opinion of society, especially as he had neither the wit nor the wish to ingratiate himself in public favour. Now the blame of the whole affair was thrown on him. It was said that he was insanely jealous, and subject to fits of fury. And when, after Pierre's departure, Helen returned to Petersburg, she was received by all not only cordially, but with a shade of deference that was a tribute to her distress.

When the conversation touched upon her husband, Helen assumed an expression of dignity, which her characteristic tact prompted her to adopt, though she had no conception of its significance. That expression suggested that she had resolved to bear her affliction without complaint, and that her husband was a cross God had laid upon her.

Prince Vassily expressed his opinion more openly. He shrugged his shoulders when the conversation turned upon Pierre, and pointing to his forehead, said: "Crackbrained, I always said so."

"I used to say so even before," Anna Pavlovna would say of Pierre. "At the time I said that he was an insane young man, corrupted by the dissolute ideas of the age. I used to say so at the time when every one was in such ecstasies over him; and he had only just come home from abroad. And how has it ended? Even then I was against this marriage, and foretold all that has come to pass."

Towards the end of the year 1806, when Russia's second war with Napoleon was beginning, Anna Pavlovna was giving one of her *soirées*. On this evening "the cream of really good society, the flower of the intellectual essence of Petersburg society," as Anna Pavlovna called her guests, consisted of the fascinating and unhappy Helen, abandoned by her husband, of two diplomats, of a newly appointed maid of honour and her mother, and several other less noteworthy persons.

The novelty Anna Pavlovna was offering her guests that evening was Boris Drubetskoy, who had just arrived as a special messenger from the Prussian army, and was in the suite of a personage of very high rank.

Thanks to the efforts of his mother, Anna Drubetskoy, his own tastes and the peculiarities of his reserved character, Boris had succeeded by that time in getting into a very advantageous position in the service. He was an adjutant in the suite of a personage of very high rank, he had received a very important commission in Prussia, and had only just returned thence as a special messenger. He had completely mastered the art of getting on with those who have the bestowal of promotion, and he often himself marvelled at the rapidity of his own progress, and that others failed to grasp the secret of it. He was not well off, but he spent his last penny to be better dressed than others. He would have deprived himself of many pleasures rather than have allowed himself to drive in an inferior carriage, or to be seen in the streets of Petersburg in an old uniform. He sought the acquaintance and cultivated the friendship only of persons who were in a higher position, and could consequently be of use to him. He loved Petersburg and despised Moscow. His memories of the Rostov household and his childish passion for Natasha were distasteful to him, and he had not once been at the Rostovs' since he had entered the army. In Anna Pavlovna's drawing-room, his entry into which he looked upon as an important step upward in the service, he at once took his cue, and let Anna Pavlovna make the most of what interest he had to offer, while himself attentively watching every face and appraising the advantages and possibilities of intimacy with every one of the persons present. He sat on the seat indicated to him beside the fair Helen and listened to the general conversation.

After a while Anna Pavlovna turned the conversation upon the courage and firmness of the Prussian king, with the object of bringing Boris into action.

Boris listened attentively to the person who was speaking, and waited for his turn, but meanwhile he had leisure to look round several times at the fair Helen, who met the handsome young adjutant's eyes with a smile.

Very naturally, speaking of the position of Prussia, Anna Pavlovna asked Boris to describe his journey to Glogau, and the position in which he had found the Prussian army. Boris in his pure, correct French, told them very deliberately a great many interesting details about the armies, and the court, studiously abstaining from any expression of his own opinion in regard to the facts he was relating. For some time Boris engrossed the whole attention of the company, and Anna Pavlovna felt that the novelty she was serving her guests was being accepted by them with pleasure. Of all the party, the person who showed most interest in Boris's description was Helen. She asked him several questions about his journey, and seemed to be extremely interested in the position of the Prussian army.

As soon as he had finished, she turned to him with her usual smile. "You absolutely must come and see me," she said in a tone that suggested that for certain considerations, of which he could have no knowledge, it was absolutely essential. "On Tuesday between eight and nine. It will give me a great pleasure."

Boris promised to do so.

And later that evening when every one got up to leave, Helen turned to Boris again with a request, and a caressing, impressive command that he would come to her on Tuesday.

"It is of great importance to me," she said with a smile, looking round at Anna Pavlovna. And Anna Pavlovna, with the same mournful smile with which she accompanied any reference to the Empress, gave her support to Helen's wishes. It appeared that from some words Boris had uttered that evening about the Prussian army Helen had suddenly discovered the absolute necessity of seeing him. She seemed to promise him that when he came on Tuesday she would disclose to him that necessity.

But when Boris entered Helen's magnificent reception-room on Tuesday evening he received no clear explanation of the urgent reasons for his visit. Other guests were present, the countess talked little to him, and only as he kissed her hand at taking leave, with a strangely unsmiling face, she whispered to him unexpectedly: "Come to dinner to-morrow . . . in the evening . . . you must come . . . come."

During that stay in Petersburg Boris was constantly at the house of the Countess Bezuhov on a footing of the closest intimacy.

War had broken out close to the borders of Russia. On all sides could be heard curses upon the enemy of the human race, Bonaparte. In the villages there were levies of recruits and reserve men, and from the theatre of war came news of the most conflicting kind, false as usual.

The life of the old Prince Bolkonsky, of Prince André, and of Princess Mary was greatly changed since the year 1805.

In 1806 the old prince had been appointed by the Tsar as one of the eight commanders-in-chief, created at that time for the equipment of the militia throughout all Russia. In spite of his weakness and age, which had been particularly noticeable during the time when he believed his son to have been killed, the old prince did not think it right to refuse a duty to which he had been appointed by the Emperor himself. This new field for his activity gave him fresh energy and strength. He was continually away on tours about the three provinces that were put under his command; he was punctilious in the performance of his duties, severe to cruelty with his subordinates, and entered into the minutest details of the work himself. Princess Mary no longer took lessons in mathematics from her father, and only went into her father's room on the mornings when he was at home, accompanied by the wet nurse and little Prince Nicholas. The baby, with his wet nurse, occupied the rooms that had been his mother's, and Princess Mary spent most of her time in the nursery taking a mother's place. Mademoiselle Bourienne, too, appeared to be passionately fond of the child.

Soon after Prince André's return, the old prince made over a part of the property to him, giving him Bogutcharovo, a large estate about thirty miles from Bleak Hills. Partly to escape the painful memories associated with Bleak Hills, partly because Prince André did not always feel equal to bearing with his father's peculiarities, and partly from a craving for solitude, Prince André made use of Bogutcharovo. He spent the greater part of his time there.

After the Austerlitz campaign, Prince André had resolved never to serve again in the army. And when war broke out and all were bound to serve, he took service under his father in the levying of the militia, so as to escape active service. Since the campaign of 1805 the old prince and his son had as it were exchanged parts. The old prince, stimulated by activity, expected the best results from the present campaign. Prince André, on the contrary, taking no part in the war, and secretly regretting his inaction, saw in it nothing but what was bad.

On the 26th of February, 1807, the old prince set off on a tour of inspection. Prince André was staying at Bleak Hills, as he usually did in his father's absence. The coachman, who had driven the old prince away, returned some days later bringing papers and letters. One of the letters was from the old prince. Another was from Prince André's friend, Bilibin.

The old prince in his big, sprawling hand, making use of occasional abbreviations, wrote on blue paper as follows: "I have this moment received, through a special messenger, very joyful news, if it's not a falsehood. Bennigsen has gained it seems a complete victory over Bonaparte near Eylau. In Petersburg every one's jubilant and rewards have been sent to the army without stint. Though he's a German—I congratulate him. I have a letter too about the Prussian battle at

Preussisch-Eylau from Petenka, he took part in it,—it's true. If people don't meddle who've no business to meddle, even a German beats Bonaparte. They say he's running away in great disorder."

Prince André broke open Bilibin's letter. The letter was dated some time back, before the battle of Eylau, and Bilibin in his usual way wrote with sarcasm.

"Since our great success at Austerlitz, I have not left headquarters. Decidedly I have acquired a taste for warfare, and it is just as well for me. What I have seen in these three months is incredible. . . . I will begin *ab ovo*. 'The enemy of the human race,' as you know, is attacking the Prussians. The Prussians are our faithful allies, who have only deceived us three times in three years. We stand up for them. But it occurs that the enemy of the human race pays no attention to our fine speeches, and in his uncivil and savage way flings himself upon the Prussians without giving them time to finish the parade that they had begun, and by a couple of conjuring tricks thrashes them completely, and goes to take up his quarters in the palace of Potsdam.

" 'I most earnestly desire,' writes the King of Prussia to Bonaparte, 'that your majesty may be received and treated in my palace in a manner agreeable to you, and I have hastened to take all the measures to that end which circumstances allowed. I hope I have succeeded!' The Prussian generals pride themselves on their politeness towards the French, and lay down their arms at the first summons.

"The head of the garrison at Glogau, who has ten thousand men, asks the King of Prussia what he is to do if he is summoned to surrender. . . . All these are actual facts.

"In short, hoping only to produce an effect by our military attitude, we find ourselves at war in earnest, and, what is more, at war on our own frontiers *with and for the King of Prussia*. Everything is fully ready, we only want one little thing, that is a commander-in-chief. As it is thought that the successes at Austerlitz might have been more decisive if the commander-in-chief had not been so young, the men of eighty have been passed in review, and of Prosorovsky and Kamensky the latter is preferred. The general comes to us and is greeted with acclamations of joy and triumph.

"On the 4th comes the first post from Petersburg. The mails are taken to Kutuzov's room, for he likes to do everything himself. I am called to sort the letters and take those meant for us. Kutuzov looks on while we do it, and waits for the packets addressed to him. We seek—there are none. Kutuzov gets impatient, sets to work himself, and finds letters from the Emperor for Count T., Prince V., and others. Then he throws himself into one of his furies. He rages against everybody, snatches hold of the letters, opens them, and reads those from the Emperor to other people.

" 'Oh, so that's how I'm being treated! No confidence in me! Oh, ordered to keep an eye on me, very well!'

"And then he writes a letter to the Tsar. 'All my expeditions on horseback, have given me a saddle sore, which, after my former journeys, quite prevents my sitting a horse, and commanding an army so widely scattered. And therefore I have handed over my command to the general next in seniority to me, Count Buxhevden, having despatched to him all my suite and appurtenances of the same, advising him, if bread should run short, to retreat further into the interior of Prussia, seeing that bread for one day's rations only is left, and some regiments have none and the peasantry of the country have had everything eaten up. I shall myself remain in the hospital at Ostrolenka till I am cured. In regard to which I must humbly submit the report that if the army remains another fortnight in its present bivouac, by spring not a man will be left in health.

" 'Graciously discharge from his duty an old man who is sufficiently disgraced by his inability to perform the great and glorious task for which he was chosen. I shall await here in the hospital your most gracious acceptance of my retirement, that I may not have to act the part of a secretary rather than a commander. My removal is not producing the slightest sensation—a blind man is leaving the army, that is all. More like me can be found in Russia by thousands!'

"Kutuzov is angry with the Emperor and punishes all of us; isn't it logical!"

On reaching Kiev, Pierre sent for all his stewards to his head counting-house, and explained to them his intentions and his desires. He told them that steps would very shortly be taken for the complete liberation of his peasants from serfdom, that till that time his peasants were not to be overburdened with labour, that the women with children were not to be sent out to work, that assistance was to be given to the peasants, that wrong-doing was not to be met with corporal punishment; and that on every estate there must be established hospitals, almshouses, and schools. Several of the stewards, among them were some bailiffs barely able to read and write, listened in dismay, supposing the upshot of the young count's remarks to be that he was dissatisfied with their management and embezzlement of his money. Others, after the first shock of alarm, derived amusement from Pierre's lisp and the new words he used that they had not heard before. Others again found a simple satisfaction in hearing the sound of their master's voice. But some, among them the head steward, gathered from this speech how to deal with their master for their own ends.

The head steward expressed great sympathy with Pierre's projects; but observed that, apart from these innovations, matters were in a bad way and needed thoroughly going into.

In spite of the late Count Bezuhov's enormous wealth, Pierre ever since he had inherited it, and had been, as people said, in receipt of an annual income of five hundred thousand, had felt much less rich than when he had been receiving an allowance of ten thousand from his father. His large income was spent—he hardly knew how—and almost every year he was forced to borrow. Moreover every year the head steward wrote to him of fires, or failures of crops, or of the necessity of rebuilding factories or workshops. And so the first duty with which Pierre was confronted was the one for which he had the least capacity and inclination—attention to practical business.

He did not like discussing business and only tried to keep up a pretence of going into practical matters with the head steward.

In Kiev Pierre had acquaintances. And those not acquaintances made haste to become so, and gave a warm welcome to the young man of fortune, the largest landowner of the province, who had come into their midst. Again whole days, weeks, and months of his life were busily filled up with parties, dinners, breakfasts, and balls, giving him as little time to think as at Petersburg. Instead of the new life Pierre had hoped to lead, he was living just the same old life only in different surroundings.

Of the three precepts of freemasonry, Pierre had to admit that he had not fulfilled that one which prescribes for every mason the duty of being a model of moral life; and of the seven virtues he was entirely without two—morality and love of death. He comforted himself by reflecting that, on the other hand, he was fulfilling the other precept—the improvement of the human race; and had other virtues, love for his neighbour and liberality.

In the spring of 1807, Pierre made up his mind to go back again to Petersburg. On the way back he intended to make the tour of all his estates to see what had been done and in what position the people now were who had been entrusted to him by God.

The head steward, who regarded all the young count's freaks as almost insanity—disastrous to him and to his peasants—made concessions to his weaknesses. While continuing to represent the liberation of Pierre's serfs as impracticable, he made arrangements on all his estates for the building of schools, hospitals, and asylums on a large scale to be begun for the master's visit. He prepared everywhere for Pierre to be met, not with ceremonious processions, which he knew would not be to Pierre's taste, but with just the devotionally grateful welcomes, with holy images and bread and salt, such as would, according to his understanding of the count, impress him and delude him.

The southern spring, the easy, rapid journey in his Vienna carriage, and the solitude of the road, had a good influence on Pierre. The estates, which he had not before visited, were one more picturesque than the other; the peasantry seemed everywhere thriving, and touchingly grateful for the benefits conferred on them. Everywhere he was met by welcomes, which though they embarrassed Pierre, yet at the bottom of his heart, rejoiced him. At one place the peasants had brought him bread and salt and begged permission in honour of his patron saints, Peter and Paul, to erect at their own expense a new chapel in the church. At another place he was welcomed by women with babies in their arms, who came to thank him for being released from the obligation of heavy labour. In a third place he was met by a priest with a cross, surrounded by children, whom he was instructing in reading and writing and religion. On all his estates Pierre saw with his own eyes stone buildings erected, or in course of erection, all on one plan, hospitals, schools, and almshouses, which were in short time to be opened. Everywhere Pierre heard touching thanks from peasants in blue, full-skirted coats.

But Pierre did not know that where they brought him bread and salt the chapel of Peter and Paul had been built long ago by wealthy peasants and that nine-tenths of the peasants of that village were in the utmost destitution. He did not know that since by his orders nursing mothers were not sent to work on their master's land, those same mothers did even harder work on their own bit of land. He did not know that the priest who met him with the cross oppressed the peasants with his exactions, and that the pupils gathered around him were yielded up to him with tears and redeemed for large sums by their parents. He did not know that the stone buildings being built by his labourers increased the forced labour of his peasants. He did not know that where the steward pointed out to him in the account book the reduction of rent to one-third in accordance with his will, the labour exacted had been raised by one-half. And so Pierre was pleased by his journey over his estates, and came back completely to the philanthropic frame of mind in which he had left Petersburg. And he wrote enthusiastic letters to the grand master of his lodge.

"How easy it is, how little effort is needed to do so much

good," thought Pierre. "And how little we trouble ourselves to do it!"

Returning from his southern tour in the happiest frame of mind, Pierre carried out an intention he had long had, of visiting his friend Prince André, whom he had not seen for two years.

Bogutcharovo lay in a flat, ugly part of the country, covered with fields and woods of fir and birch-trees, in parts cut down. The manor house was at the end of the straight village that ran along each side of the high road, behind an overflowing pond newly dug, and still bare of grass on its banks.

The homestead consisted of a threshing floor, serfs' quarters, stables, bath-houses, lodges, and a large stone house with a semicircular façade, still in course of erection. Round the house a garden had been newly laid out. The fences and gates were solid and new; under a shed stood two fire-engines and a tub painted green. The paths were straight, the bridges were strong and furnished with stone parapets. Everything had an air of being cared for and looked after.

The house serfs, in reply to inquiries where the prince was living, pointed to a small new lodge at the very edge of the pond. Prince André's old body-servant, Anton, after assisting Pierre out of his carriage, said that the prince was at home, and conducted him into a clean little lobby.

Pierre was struck by the modesty of this little, clean house, after the splendid surroundings in which he had last seen his friend in Petersburg.

He went hurriedly into the little parlour, still unplastered and smelling of pine wood, and would have gone further, but Anton ran ahead on tip-toe and knocked at the door.

"What is it?" A harsh, unpleasant voice called.

"A visitor," answered Anton.

Pierre went to the door, and came face to face with Prince André, who came out frowning and looking older. Pierre embraced him, and taking off his spectacles, looked close at him.

"Well, I didn't expect you. But I am glad," said Prince André.

Pierre said nothing; he was looking in wonder at his friend, and could not take his eyes off him. He was struck by the change in Prince André. His words were warm, there was a smile on his lips but there was a lustreless, dead look in his eyes.

On meeting after such a long separation, their conversation did not rest on one subject. They asked questions and gave brief replies about things of which they knew themselves they must talk at length. At last the conversation began to revolve about their life in the past, their plans for the future, Pierre's journeys, and what he had been doing, the war, and so on.

The look which Pierre had noticed in Prince André's eyes was more striking now, especially when he was telling him with earnestness and delight of his past or his future. It was as though Prince André would have liked to take interest in what Pierre was telling him, but could not. Pierre began to feel that to express enthusiasm, ideals, and hopes of happiness and goodness was unseemly before Prince André. He felt ashamed of giving expression to all the new ideas he had gained from the masons. He restrained himself, afraid of seeming naïve. At the same time he felt an irresistible desire to show his friend at once that he was now a quite different Pierre, better than the one he had known in Petersburg.

"I can't tell you how much I have passed through during this time. I don't know my old self."

"Yes, you are very, very much changed," said Prince André.

"Well, and what of you?" asked Pierre. "What are your plans?"

"Plans?" repeated Prince André ironically. "My plans?" he repeated, as though wondering what was the meaning of such a word. "Why, you see, I am building. I hope next year to settle in here altogether . . ."

Pierre looked intently at Prince André.

"I tell you what, my dear fellow," said Prince André, who was unmistakably dreary and ill at ease with his visitor. "I'm simply camping here. I only came over to have a look at things. I'm going back again to my sister to-day. I will introduce you to her. But I think you know her, though," he added. "We will set off after dinner. And now would you care to see my place?"

They went out and walked about till dinner time, talking of political news and common acquaintances, like people not very intimate. The only thing of which Prince André now spoke with some eagerness and interest was the new buildings and homestead he was building; but even in the middle of a conversation on this subject, he suddenly stopped. "There's nothing interesting in that, though, let us go in to dinner."

At dinner the conversation turned to Pierre's marriage.

"I was very much surprised when I heard of it," said Prince André.

Pierre blushed as he always did at any reference to his marriage, and said hurriedly: "I'll tell you one day how it all happened. But you know that it's all over and forever."

"For ever?" said Prince André. "Nothing's for ever."

"But do you know how it all ended? Did you hear of the duel?"

"Yes."

"The one thing for which I thank God is that I didn't kill that man," said Pierre.

"Why?" asked Prince André. "To kill a vicious dog is a very good thing to do."

"No, to kill a man is bad, wrong . . ."

"Why is it wrong?" repeated Prince André. "What's right and wrong is a question it has not been given to men to decide. Men are forever in error, and always will be in error."

"What does harm to another man is wrong," said Pierre, feeling with pleasure that for the first time since his arrival Prince André was beginning to speak eagerly.

"And who has told you what is harm to another man?" he asked.

"Harm? Harm?" said Pierre. "We all know what harms us."

"Yes, we know that, but it's not the same harm we do to another man," said Prince André, growing more and more eager, and evidently anxious to express to Pierre his new view of things. He spoke in French. "I only know two very real ills in life, remorse and sickness. To live for myself so as to avoid these two evils: that's the sum of my wisdom now."

"And love for your neighbour, and self-sacrifice?" began Pierre. "No I can't agree with you! To live with the sole object of avoiding doing evil, so as not to be remorseful, that's very little. I used to live so, I used to live for myself, and I spoilt my life. And only now, when I'm living, at least trying to live for others, only now I have learnt to know all the happiness of life. No, I don't agree with you, and indeed, you don't believe what you're saying yourself."

Prince André looked at Pierre without speaking, and smiled ironically. "Well, you'll see my sister Mary. You will get on with her," he said. "Perhaps you are right for yourself," he added, after a brief pause, "but every one lives in his own way. You used to live for yourself, and you say that by doing so you almost spoilt your life, and have only known happiness since you began to live for others. And my experience has been the reverse. I lived for others and almost spoilt my life. And I have become more peaceful since I live only for myself."

"But how are you living only for yourself?" Pierre asked, getting angry. "What of your son, your sister, your father?"

"Yes, but that's all the same as myself, they are not others," said Prince André. "But others, one's neighbours, as you and Mary call them, they are the great source of error and evil. One's neighbours are those—your Kiev peasants—whom one wants to do good to."

And he looked at Pierre with a glance of challenge. He unmistakably meant to draw him on.

"You are joking," said Pierre, getting more and more earnest. "What error and evil can there be in my wishing to do good? Where can be the harm if unhappy people, our peasants, people just like ourselves, growing up and dying with . . . What harm and error can there be in my giving them doctors, and a hospital, and a refuge for the aged, when men are dying of disease without help, and it is so easy to give them material aid? And isn't there good, when the peasants and the women with young children have no rest day or night, and I give them leisure and rest? . . ." said Pierre, talking hurriedly and lisping. "And I have done that; badly it's true, and too little of it, but I have done something towards it, and you'll not only fail to shake my conviction that I have done well, you'll not even shake my conviction that you don't believe that yourself. And the great thing," Pierre continued, "is that I know that the enjoyment of doing good is the only real happiness in life."

"Oh, if you put the question like that, it's a different matter," said Prince André. "I'm building a house and laying out a garden, while you are building hospitals. Either occupation may serve to pass the time. But as to what's right and what's good, it's not for us to decide."

They left the table and went outside on to the balcony. "You talk of schools," Prince André went on, "instruction, and so forth. That is, you want to raise the peasant out of his animal condition and to give him spiritual needs. But it seems to me that the only possible happiness is animal happiness, and you want to deprive him of it. I envy him, while you are trying to make him into me, without giving him my circumstances. Another thing you speak of is lightening his toil. But to my notions, physical labour is as much a necessity for him, as much a condition of his existence, as intellectual work is for me and for you. You can't help thinking. I go to bed at three o'clock, thoughts come into my mind, and I can't go to sleep; I turn over, and can't sleep till morning, because I'm thinking, and I can't help thinking, just as he can't help ploughing and mowing. If he didn't, he would go to the tavern, or become ill. Just as I could not stand his terrible physical labour, but should die of it in a week, so he could not stand my physical inactivity. He would grow fat and die. The third thing—what was it you talked about? Oh, yes, hospitals, medicine. He has a fit and dies, but you have him bled and cure him. He will drag about an invalid for ten years, a burden to every one. It would be ever so much simpler and more comfortable for him to die. Others are born, and there are always plenty. But you want to cure him from love for him. But he has no need of that."

Prince André gave such clear and precise utterance to his ideas that it was evident he had thought more than once of this already, and he talked rapidly and eagerly, as a man does who has long been silent. His eyes grew keener, the more pessimistic were the views he expressed.

"Oh," said Pierre, "I don't understand how one can live with such ideas. I have had moments of thinking like that; it was not long ago at Moscow, but then I become so depressed that I don't live at all, everything's hateful to me . . . myself, most of all. Then I don't eat, I don't wash . . . how can you go on? . . ."

"On the contrary, one has to try and make one's life more agreeable as far as one can," said Prince André. "I'm alive, and it's not my fault that I am, and so I have to try without hurting others to get on as well as I can till death."

"But how can you live with such ideas? You would sit still without stirring, taking no part in anything. . . ."

"Life won't leave you in peace even so. I should be glad to do nothing, but here you see on one side, the local nobility have done me the honour of electing me a marshal; it was all I could do to get out of it. They could not understand that I haven't what's needed, haven't that good-natured, fussy vulgarity we all know so well, that's needed for it. Then there's this house here, which had to be built that I might have a nook of my own where I could be quiet. Now there's the militia."

"Why aren't you serving in the army?"

"After Austerlitz!" said Prince André. "No, thank you; I swore to myself that I would never serve in the Russian army again. And I will not, if Bonaparte were stationed here at Smolensk, threatening Bleak Hills! Even then I wouldn't serve in the Russian army. Well, so I was saying," Prince André went on, regaining his composure. "Now, there's the militia; my father's commander-in-chief of the third circuit, and the only means for me to escape from active service is to serve under him."

"So you are in the service, then?"

"Yes." He was silent for a while.

"Then why do you serve?"

"I'll tell you why. My father is one of the most remarkable men of his time. But he's grown old, and he's not cruel exactly, but he's of too energetic a character. He's terrible from his habit of unlimited power, and now with this authority given him by the Emperor as a commander-in-chief in the militia. If I had not arrived in time he would have hanged the register-clerk at Yuhnovo," said Prince André with a smile.

"So I serve under him now because no one except me has any influence over my father, and I sometimes save him from an act which would be a source of misery to him afterwards."

"Ah, there you see!"

"Yes, it is not as you think," Prince André continued. "I didn't, and I don't wish well in the slightest to that scoundrelly register-clerk who had stolen boots or something from the militiamen. Indeed, I would have been very glad to see him hanged, but I feel for my father, that is again myself."

Prince André grew more and more eager. His eyes glittered feverishly, as he tried to prove to Pierre that there was never the slightest desire to do good to his neighbour in his actions.

"Well, you want to liberate your serfs, too," he continued. "That's a very good thing, but not for you—I expect you have never flogged a man nor sent one to Siberia—and still less for your peasants. If a peasant is beaten, flogged, sent to Siberia, I dare say he's not a bit the worse for it. In Siberia he can lead the same brute existence. The stripes on the body heal, and he's as happy as before. But it's needed for the people who are ruined morally, who are devoured by remorse, who stifle that remorse and grow callous from being able to inflict punishment all round them. Perhaps you have not seen it, but I have seen good men, brought up in the traditions of unlimited power with years, as they grew more irritable, become cruel and brutal, conscious of it, and unable to control themselves, and growing more and more miserable."

Prince André spoke with such earnestness that Pierre could not help thinking those ideas were suggested to him by his father. He did not answer him.

"So that's what I grieve for—for human dignity, for peace of conscience, for purity, and not for their backs or their heads, which always remain just the same backs and heads, however you thrash or shave them."

"No, no, a thousand times no! I shall never agree with you," said Pierre. "It can't be so. I used to think like that, and I have been saved, do you know by what? Freemasonry. No, you must not smile. Freemasonry is not a religious sect, nor mere ceremonial rites, as I used to suppose. Freemasonry is the expression of the highest, eternal aspects of humanity." And Pierre began expounding to Prince André freemasonry, as he understood it.

He said that freemasonry is the teaching of Christianity, freed from its political and religious fetters; the teaching of equality, fraternity, and love.

"Our brotherhood is the only thing that has real meaning in life; all the rest is a dream," said Pierre. "You understand that outside this brotherhood all is filled with lying and falsehood, and I agree with you that there's nothing left for an intelligent and good-hearted man but, like you, to get through his life, only trying not to hurt others. But make our fundamental convictions your own, and you will at once feel yourself, as I felt, a part of a vast, unseen chain, the origin of which is lost in the skies," said Pierre, looking straight before him.

Prince André listened to Pierre's words in silence.

". . . there is truth and there is goodness; and the highest happiness of man consists in striving for their attainment. We must live, we must love, we must believe," said Pierre, "that we are not only living to-day on this clod of earth, but have lived and will live for ever there in everything." He pointed to the sky. Pierre stopped speaking. There was perfect stillness.

Prince André with a childlike, tender look in his eyes glanced at Pierre.

"Yes, if only it were so!" he said. And then he looked up at the sky, to which Pierre had pointed. And he saw the lofty, eternal sky, as he had seen it lying on the field of Austerlitz, and something that had long been slumbering, something better that had been in him, suddenly awoke.

Pierre's visit was for Prince André an epoch, from which there began a new life.

That same evening Prince André and Pierre got into a coach and drove to Bleak Hills. It was dark by the time they drove up to the main entrance. While they were driving in, Prince André with a smile drew Pierre's attention to a commotion that was taking place at the back entrance. A bent little old woman with a bag on her back, and a short man with long hair, in a black garment, ran back to the gate on seeing the carriage driving up. Two women ran out after them, and all the four, looking round at the carriage with scared faces, ran in at the back entrance.

"Those are Mary's God's folk," said Prince André. "They took us for my father. It's the one matter in which she does not obey him. He orders them driven off, but she receives them."

"What are God's folk?" asked Pierre.

"You shall see. Let us go to my sister," said Prince André. "She is in hiding now, sitting with them. Serve her right; she will be put to shame, and you will see God's folk. It's curious, upon my word."

Princess Mary was disconcerted, and reddened in patches when they went in. In her snug room, with lamps before the holy picture, there was sitting, on the sofa beside her, a young man with a long nose and long hair, wearing a monk's cassock. In a low chair near sat a wrinkled, thin, old woman, with a meek expression on her childlike face.

"André, why did you not let me know?" Princess Mary said with mild reproach, standing before her pilgrims like a hen before her chickens.

"I am very glad to see you," she said to Pierre, as he kissed her hand. She had known him as a child, and now his friendship with André, his unhappy marriage, and above all, his kindly, simple face, won her favour. She looked at him with her beautiful, luminous eyes, and seemed to say: "I like you very much, but, please, don't laugh at my friends."

They sat down.

Princess Mary had not the slightest need to feel embarrassment on her friends' account. They were quite at their ease. The old woman cast down her eyes, but stole sidelong glances at the new-comers, and turning her cup upside down in the saucer, and laying a nibbled lump of sugar beside it, sat calmly without stirring in her chair, waiting to be offered another cup. The young man, sipping out of the saucer, peeped from under his brows with his sly eyes at the young men.

"Where have you been, in Kiev?" Prince André asked the old woman.

"I have, good sir," answered the old woman, who was conversationally disposed. "Just at the Holy Birth I was deemed worthy to be a partaker in holy, heavenly mysteries from the saints. And now, good sir, a great blessing has been revealed."

"What, new relics?" asked Prince André with a smile.

"Hush, André," said Princess Mary. "Don't tell us about it, Pelageyushka."

"Not . . . nay, ma'am, why not tell him? I like him. He's a good gentleman, chosen of God, he's my benefactor; he gave me ten roubles, I remember. When I was in Kiev, Kiryusha, a pilgrim, tells me—verily a man of God, winter and summer he goes barefoot—why are you not going to your right place, says he; go to the wonder-working ikon, a holy Mother of God has been revealed. On these words I said good-bye and off I went . . ."

All were silent, only the pilgrim woman talked on in her measured voice. "I came, good sir, and folks say to me: a great blessing has been vouchsafed, drops of myrrh trickle from the cheeks of the Holy Mother of God . . ."

"Come, that will do, that will do; you shall tell me later," said Princess Mary, flushing.

"Let me ask her a question," said Pierre. "Did you see it yourself?" he asked.

"To be sure, good sir, I myself was found worthy. Such a brightness overspread the face, like the light of heaven, and from the Holy Mother's cheeks drops like this and like this . . ."

"Why, but it must be a trick," said Pierre, after listening attentively to the old woman.

"Oh, sir, what a thing to say!" said Pelageyushka with horror, turning to Princess Mary for support.

"They impose upon the people," he repeated.

"Lord Jesus Christ!" said the pilgrim woman, crossing herself. "Oh, don't speak so, sir. There was a general did not believe like that, said 'the monks cheat,' and as he said it, he was struck blind. And he dreamed a dream, the Holy Mother comes to him and says: 'Believe in me and I will heal thee.' And so he kept beseeching them: 'Take me to her, take me to her.' It's the holy truth I'm telling you, I've seen it myself. They carried him, blind as he was, to her; he went up, fell down, and said: 'Heal me! I will give thee,' says he, 'what the Tsar bestowed on me.' I saw it myself. Well—he regained his sight! It's a sin to speak so. God will punish you," she said admonishingly to Pierre.

"How?" asked Pierre.

"And didn't they make the Holy Mother a general?" said Prince André, smiling.

Pelageyushka turned suddenly pale and flung up her hands.

"Sir, sir, it's a sin of you, you've a son!" she said, suddenly turning from white to dark red. "Sir, for what you have said, God forgive you." She crossed herself. "Lord, forgive him. Lady, what's this? . . ." she turned to Princess Mary. She got up, and almost crying began gathering up her belongings. Plainly she was both frightened and ashamed at having accepted bounty in a house where they could say such things, and sorry that she must henceforth deprive herself of the bounty of that house.

"What did you want to do this for?" said Princess Mary. "Why did you come to me? . . ."

"No, I was joking really," said Pierre. "I said it, meaning nothing. Don't think of it, I was joking," he said, smiling timidly and trying to smooth over his mistake. "It was all my fault."

The old woman was still mistrustful, but Pierre's face wore a look of such genuine penitence, and Prince André looked so mildly from Pelageyushka to Pierre, that she was gradually reassured and being drawn into conversation again, told them a long story of Father Amfilohey, who was so holy that his hands smelt of incense, and how some monks of her acquaintance had, on her last pilgrimage to Kiev, given her the keys of the catacombs, and how taking with her some dry bread she had spent two days and nights in the catacombs with the saints. "I pray a bit in one, chant a hymn, and go into another. I fall asleep, again I go and kiss the holy relics; and such peace, ma'am, such blessedness, that one has no wish to come out into God's world again."

Prince André went out of the room. And leaving God's folk to finish their tea, Princess Mary followed him with Pierre.

On returning from his leave, Nicholas Rostov for the first time felt how strong was the tie that bound him to Denisov and his regiment.

He experienced a sensation the same as he had felt on reaching his home at Moscow. When he caught sight of the first hussar in the unbuttoned uniform of his regiment, when he saw the chestnut horses, when Lavrushka shouted, "The count has come!" and Denisov, who had been asleep on his bed, ran all dishevelled out of the mud-hut, and embraced him, and the officers gathered around to welcome him—Rostov felt the same as when his mother had embraced him, and his father and sisters. The regiment was a home, too.

After reporting to his colonel, being assigned to his own squadron, and serving on orderly duty and going for forage, after entering into all the little interests of the regiment, and feeling himself deprived of liberty and nailed down within one narrow, unchangeable framework, Rostov had the same feeling of peace and of moral support and the same sense of being at home here, and in his proper place, as he had felt as a child under his father's roof. Here was none of all that confusion of the free world, where he did not know his proper place, and made mistakes in exercising free choice. There was no Sonya, with whom one ought or ought not to have a clear understanding. There were none of those vague and undefined money relations with his father; no memories of his awful loss to Dolohov. Here in the regiment everything was clear and simple. The whole world was divided into two unequal parts: one, the Pavlograd regiment, and the other—all the remainder. And with all that great remainder one had no concern. In the regiment everything was well known: this man was a lieutenant, that one a captain; this was a good fellow and that one was not; but most of all, every one was a comrade.

Regimental life was the greater relief to Rostov, because after his loss to Dolohov, for which, in spite of his family's efforts to console him he could not forgive himself, he had resolved not to serve as before, but to atone for his fault by good conduct. He had decided to be a thoroughly good soldier and officer, that is a good man, a task so difficult in the world, but so possible in the regiment.

Rostov had determined to repay his gambling debt to his parents in the course of five years. He had been sent ten thousand a year; now he had made up his mind to take only two thousand, and to leave the remainder to repay the debt.

In April the Pavlograd hussars were encamped near an utterly ruined, empty German village.

It was thawing, muddy, and cold, the ice had broken upon the river, the roads had become impassable. For several days there had been neither provender for the horses nor provisions for the men. Seeing that the transport of provisions was impossible, the soldiers wandered about the abandoned and deserted villages to try and find potatoes, but very few were to be found.

Everything had been eaten up, and most of the inhabitants of the district had fled; those that remained were worse than beggars, and there was nothing to be taken from them; indeed, the soldiers, although little given to compassion, often gave their last ration to them.

The Pavlograd regiment had only lost two men wounded in action, but had lost almost half its men from hunger and disease.

The horses, too, had for the last two weeks been fed on the thatched roofs of the houses; they were hideously thin, and still covered with their shaggy, winter coats, which were coming off in tufts.

But in spite of their destitute condition, the soldiers and officers went on living exactly as they always did. Just as always, though now with pale and swollen faces and torn uniforms, the hussars were drawn up for inspection, went out to collect forage, cleaned down their horses, and rubbed up their arms, dragged in straw from the thatched roofs in place of fodder, and assembled for dinner round the cauldrons, from which they rose up hungry, making jokes over their vile food and their hunger. Just as ever, in their spare time off duty the soldiers lighted camp fires, and warmed themselves naked before them, smoked, picked out, and baked the sprouting, rotten potatoes, and told stories.

The officers lived as usual in twos and threes in the roofless, broken-down houses and huts. Rostov lived as before with Denisov, and the bond of friendship between them had become still closer since their furlough. Denisov never spoke of any of Rostov's family, but from the affection the senior officer showed his junior, Rostov felt that the older hussar's luckless passion for Natasha had something to do with the strengthening of their friendship. There was no doubt that Denisov tried to take care of Rostov, and to expose him as rarely as possible to danger. And after action it was with unmistakable joy that he saw him return safe and sound.

One night Rostov had been on duty. At eight o'clock in the

morning, on coming home, he sent for hot embers, changed his rain-soaked underclothes, said his prayers, drank some tea, warmed himself, put things tidy in his corner and on the table, and with a wind-beaten, heated face, and with only his shirt on, lay down to rest. He was expecting Denisov to come in. He wanted to talk to him.

Suddenly through the wall he heard Lavrushka, Denisov's rogue of a valet, telling Denisov something about transports, biscuits and oxen he had seen, while on the look-out for provisions.

Then he heard Denisov shout: "Saddle! Second platoon!"

Five minutes later Denisov came into the hut and put on his riding-whip and sword. In reply to Rostov's question, where was he going? he answered angrily and vaguely that he had business to attend to.

"God and our gracious Emperor be my judges!" said Denisov, as he went out.

Outside the hut Rostov heard the hoofs of several horses splashing through the mud. Rostov did not even trouble himself to find out where Denisov was going. He fell asleep, and it was only towards evening that he came out of the hut. Denisov had not yet come back. The weather had cleared; near the next hut two officers were playing quoits, with a laugh sticking big radishes for pegs in the soft muddy earth. Rostov joined them. In the middle of a game the officers saw transport waggons driving up. Some fifteen hussars on lean horses rode behind them.

A little further back rode Denisov, accompanied by two infantry officers, with whom he was in conversation. Rostov went to meet them.

"I warn you, captain," one of the officers was saying, a thin, little man, visibly angry.

"Well, I have told you, I won't give them up," answered Denisov.

"You will have to answer for it, captain. It's mutiny—carrying off transports from your own army! Our men have had no food for two days."

"Mine have had nothing for two weeks," answered Denisov.

"It's looting. You will answer for it, sir!" repeated the infantry officer, raising his voice.

"Why do you keep pestering me?" roared Denisov, suddenly getting furious. "I will have to answer for it, and not you!" he shouted at the officers.

"All right!" the little officer answered, not the least intimidated, and not moving away. "It's robbery, so I tell you. . . ."

"Go to the devil!" And Denisov moved towards the officer.

"All right, all right," said the officer and he turned his horse and trotted away, swaying in the saddle.

The stores carried off by Denisov and his hussars had been intended for an infantry regiment, but learning from Lavrushka that the transport was unescorted, the hussars had carried off the stores by force. Biscuits were dealt out freely to the soldiers; they even shared them with the other squadrons.

Next day the colonel sent for Denisov. He said to him: "I look at the matter like this; see, I know nothing, and will take no steps; but I advise you to ride over to the staff, and smooth the thing over, and if possible give a receipt for so much stores. If not, and a claim is entered for the infantry regiments, there will be trouble and it may end unpleasantly."

Denisov went straight from the colonel to the staff with a sincere desire to follow his advice. And in the evening he came back to his hut in a condition such as Rostov had never seen him in before.

"Me to be court-martialled for looting! Let them court-martial me. I will, I always will, beat scoundrels and I'll tell the Emperor," he kept saying.

"I got there," Denisov continued. " 'Well, where are your chief's quarters?' I asked. They showed me. 'Will you please wait?' 'I have come on business, and I have come over thirty miles, I haven't time to wait; announce me.' Very good; but the over-thief appears; he, too, thought fit to lecture me. 'This is robbery!' says he. 'The robber,' said I, 'is not the man who takes the stores to feed his soldiers, but the man who takes them to fill his pockets.' 'Will you please be silent?' Very good. 'Give a receipt,' says he, 'to the commissioner, but the affair will be reported at headquarters.' I go before the commissioner. I go in. Sitting at the table . . . Who? No, think of it! . . . Who is it that's starving us to death?" roared Denisov, bringing his fist down so violently on the table that the glasses jumped. "Telyanin! . . . 'What, it's you that's starving us to death?' And I socked him. 'You so-and-so . . .' and I beat him up. I should have killed him. But they pulled me off."

The next day the adjutant of the regiment came with a formal communication to Major Denisov from the colonel, in which inquiries were made about the incidents of the previous day. The adjutant informed them that a court-martial was to be held; and that, with the strictness now prevailing as regards pillaging and breach of discipline, Denisov would be lucky if he got off with only being degraded to the ranks.

The case, as presented, was that Major Denisov, after carrying off the transports, had without any provocation come in a drunken condition to the chief commissioner of the commissariat, had called him a thief, threatened to beat him; and, when he was led out, had rushed into the office, attacked two officials, and sprained the arm of one of them.

Denisov tried to laugh about the whole thing. But Rostov knew him too well not to detect that he was worrying. Documents began to come every day, and notices from the court, and Denisov received a summons to put his squadron under the command of the officer next in seniority, and on the first of May to appear before the staff of the division for an investigation.

That same day the hussars undertook a reconnaissance of the enemy. Denisov, with his usual swaggering gallantry, rode in the front of the line. One of the bullets fired by the French sharpshooters struck him in the fleshy upper part of the leg. At any other time Denisov would not have left the regiment for so slight a wound, but now he took advantage of it to excuse himself from appearing before the staff, and went into the hospital.

In the month of June Rostov got a leave to visit Denisov in the hospital.

The hospital was in a little Prussian town, which had twice been sacked by Russian and French troops. It was a stone house with remnants of a fence torn up in the yard, and window frames and panes partly broken. Several soldiers bandaged up, and with pale and swollen faces, were walking or sitting in the sunshine in the yard.

As soon as Rostov went in the stench of hospital and putrefying flesh was all about him. On the stairs he met a Russian army doctor with a cigar in his mouth. He was followed by an assistant.

"I can't be everywhere at once," the doctor was saying. "Do as you think best! What difference will it make?"

The doctor caught sight of Rostov.

"What are you here for, your honour?" said the doctor. "This is a pest-house. Typhus. It's death to go in. It's only we two," he pointed to the assistant, "who are still alive. Five of us, doctors, have died here already. As soon as a new one comes, he's done for in a week."

Rostov explained that he wanted to see Major Denisov of the hussars, who was lying wounded here.

"I don't know, can't tell you, sir. I have three hospitals to look after alone—over four hundred patients. It's a good thing the Prussian charitable ladies send us coffee and lint—two pounds a month—or we should be lost." He laughed. "Four hundred, sir; and they keep sending fresh cases. It is four hundred, isn't it?" He turned to the assistant.

"Major Denisov," repeated Rostov. "He was wounded at Moliten."

Rostov described Denisov's appearance.

"He was here, was he?" the doctor asked. "He must be dead. But go to the officers' ward, there you'll see for yourself," he added.

Rostov and the assistant went into the corridor. The stench was so strong in that dark corridor that Rostov could barely breathe. A door was opened on the right, and there limped out on crutches a thin yellow man with bare feet. Leaning against the doorpost, he gazed with glittering, anxious eyes at the persons approaching. Rostov glanced in at the door and saw that the sick and wounded were lying there on the floor, on straw and on overcoats.

Rostov went in. It was a soldiers' ward. The stench was more intense. In the long room, brightly lighted by the sun in the big window, lay the sick and wounded in two rows with their heads to the wall, leaving a passage down the middle. The greater number of them were unconscious, and took no notice of Rostov and the assistant. Those who were conscious got up or raised their thin, yellow faces, and all gazed intently at Rostov, with the same expression of hope of help, of reproach, and envy of another man's health. Rostov went into the middle of the room, glanced in at the open doors of adjoining rooms, and on both sides saw the same thing. He stood still, looking round him. He had never expected to see anything like this. Just before him lay right across the empty space down the middle, on the bare floor, a sick man, probably a Cossack, for his hair was cut round in basin shape. His face was of a purple red, his eyes were sunk in his head so that only the whites could be seen. He was knocking his head against the floor, and repeating something over and over.

Rostov wanted to get away, but he felt that someone was staring at him and he looked round. In the corner there was an old soldier with a stern yellow face, thin as a skeleton's, and an unshaved grey beard. He was looking at Rostov. The man next to the old soldier was whispering something to him, pointing to Rostov. Rostov saw the old man wanted to ask him something. He went closer and saw that the old man had only one leg bent under him, the other had been cut off above the knee. On the other side of the old man, there lay with head thrown back the motionless body of a young soldier with a waxen pallor on his snub-nosed and still freckled face, and eyes sunken under the lids.

"We've begged and begged, your honour," said the old soldier with a quiver in his lower jaw. "He died early in the morning. We're men, too, not dogs. . . ."

"I'll see to it directly; they shall take him, they shall take him away," said the assistant hurriedly. "Come, your honour."

"Let us go, let us go," said Rostov quickly. And trying to pass unnoticed through the lines of reproachful and envious eyes he went out of the room.

The assistant walked along the corridor and led Rostov to the officers' wards, three rooms with doors opening between them. In these rooms there were bedsteads; the officers were sitting and lying upon them. Some were walking about the room in hospital dressing-gowns. The first person who met Rostov in the officers' ward was a thin little man who had lost one arm. He was walking about with a short pipe between his teeth. Rostov, looking intently at him, tried to recall where he had seen him.

"See where it was God's will for us to meet again," said the little man. "Tushin, Tushin, do you remember I brought you along after Schöngraben? They have sliced a bit off me, see, . . . " he said smiling and showing the empty sleeve of his dressing-gown. "Is it Denisov you are looking for?" he said. "Here, here," and he led him into the next room.

Denisov, covered up to his head with a quilt, was still in bed, though it was twelve o'clock. His wound, trifling as it was, had still not healed, though six weeks had passed since he was wounded. His face had the same swollen pallor as all the faces in the hospital. But that was not what struck Rostov. What struck him was that Denisov did not seem pleased to see him, and his smile was forced. Denisov asked him nothing either of the regiment or of the general progress of the war. When Rostov talked of it, Denisov did not listen.

The only thing which seemed to interest him was his pending court-martial. He drew from under his pillow a letter he had received from the commissioner, and a rough copy of his answer. He grew more eager as he began to read his answer, and specially called Rostov's attention to the biting sarcasm with which he addressed his foes. Denisov's companions in the hospital, who had gathered round Rostov, as a person newly come from the world of freedom outside, began to move away as soon as Denisov began reading his answer. From their faces Rostov surmised that all these men had more than once heard the whole story, and were now bored with it. Only his nearest neighbor, a stout Uhlan, sat on his pallet-bed, scowling gloomily and smoking a pipe, and little one-armed Tushin still listened, shaking his head disapprovingly. In the middle of the reading the Uhlan interrupted Denisov.

"What I say is," he said, turning to Rostov, "he ought simply

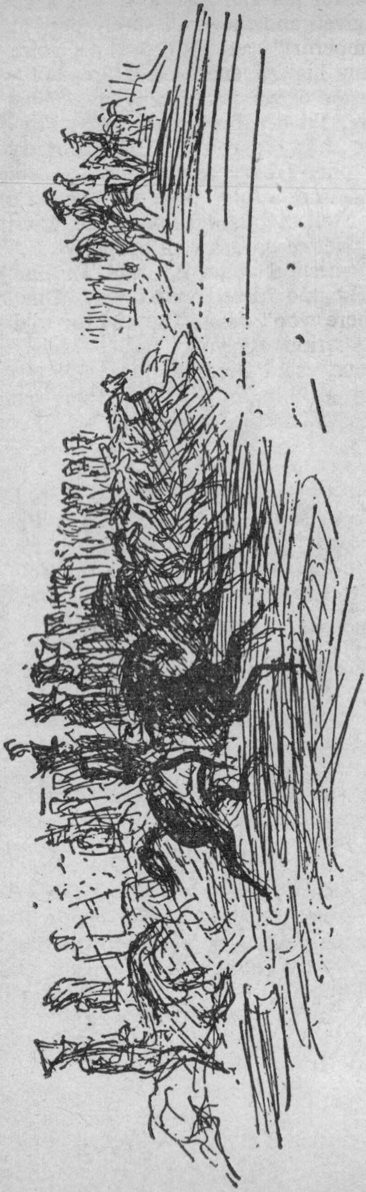

to petition the Emperor for pardon. Just now, they say, there will be great rewards given and they will surely pardon."

"Me petition the Emperor!" said Denisov in a voice into which he tried to throw his old energy and fire, but which sounded like the expression of impotent irritability. "What for? If I had been a robber, I'd beg for mercy; why, I'm being called up for trying to show up robbers. Let them try me, I'm not afraid of any one; I have served my Tsar and my country honestly, and I'm not a thief! And degrade me to the ranks and . . . Listen, I tell them straight out, see, I write to them, 'If I had been a thief of government property . . .' "

"It's neatly put, no question about it," said Tushin. "But that's not the point," he too turned to Rostov. "One must submit, and Denisov here won't do it. The auditor told you, you know, that it looks serious for you."

"Well, let it be serious," said Denisov.

"The auditor wrote a petition for you," Tushin went on. "And you ought to sign it and send it by your friend. No doubt he has influence on the staff. You won't have a better opportunity."

"I won't go cringing and fawning," Denisov interrupted, and he went on reading his answer.

Rostov did not dare to try and persuade Denisov. Though he felt instinctively that the course proposed by Tushin and the other officers was the safest, he knew Denisov's stubbornness and temper.

So Rostov said nothing, and in the most dejected frame of mind spent the rest of the day with Denisov, and his companions who had again gathered about him. He told them what he knew, and listened to the stories told by others.

Late in the evening, when Rostov was about to leave, he asked Denisov if there were something he could do.

"Yes, wait a minute," said Denisov. He looked round at the officers, and taking his papers from under his pillow, he went to the window where there was an inkstand, and sat down to write.

"It seems it's no good knocking one's head against a stone wall," he said coming from the window and giving Rostov a large envelope. It was the petition addressed to the Emperor that had been drawn up by the auditor. In it Denisov, making no reference to the shortcoming of the commissariat department, simply begged for mercy. "Give it, it seems . . ." He did not finish, and smiled a forced and sickly smile.

The battle of Friedland, which was fought at the beginning of June was followed by a truce. And on the 13th the French and Russian Emperors met at Tilsit.

Boris Drubetskoy had asked to be included in the suite destined to be staying at Tilsit. And so he was among the few present at Niemen on the day of the meeting of the Emperors. He saw the raft with the royal monograms, saw Napoleon's progress through the French guards along the further bank, saw the pensive face of the Emperor Alexander as he sat silent in the inn on the bank of the Niemen waiting for Napoleon's arrival. He saw both the Emperors get into boats, and Napoleon reaching the raft first, walked rapidly forward, and meeting Alexander, gave him his hand. Then both the Emperors disappeared into a pavilion.

As the Emperors' suite were few in number, to be present at Tilsit at the meeting of the Emperors was a matter of great consequence for a man who valued success in the service, and Boris, when he succeeded in obtaining this privilege, felt that his position was henceforth perfectly secure. He was not simply known, he had become an observed and familiar figure. On two occasions he had been sent with commissions to the Emperor himself, so that the Emperor knew him personally, and the court no longer held aloof from him.

Boris was staying with another adjutant, a Polish count, Zhilinsky. Zhilinsky, educated in Paris, was a wealthy man, devotedly attached to the French, and almost every day of their stay in Tilsit, French officers of the Guards and of the French head staff were dining and breakfasting with Zhilinsky and Boris.

On the 24th of June Zhilinsky was giving a supper for his French friends. There were present one of Napoleon's adjutants, several officers of the French Guards, and a young man of an aristocratic old French family, a page of Napoleon's. On the same evening Nicholas Rostov, taking advantage of the darkness to pass through unrecognised, came to Tilsit in civilian dress, with Denisov's petition to the Emperor. He went straight to the quarters of Zhilinsky and Boris.

Rostov, like the whole army indeed, was far from having passed through that revolution of feeling in regard to Napoleon and the French—transforming them from foes into friends—that had taken place at headquarters. In the army every one still felt mingled hatred, fear, and contempt for Bonaparte and the French. Consequently it struck Rostov as strange to see French officers everywhere. That feeling of war, of hostility, which he always experienced at the sight of the enemy, came upon him at once. He stood on the threshold and asked in Russian whether Drubetskoy lived there. Boris, hearing a strange voice in the passage, went out to meet him. For the first moment when recognised Rostov, his face betrayed his annoyance.

"Oh, it's you. Very glad, very glad to see you," he said, however, smiling and moving towards him.

"I have come at a bad time, it seems," said Nicholas. "I shouldn't have come, but it's on a matter of importance," he said coldly.

"No, I was only surprised at your getting away from the regiment. . . . I will be with you in a moment," Boris said in reply to a voice calling him.

"I see I have come at a bad time," repeated Rostov.

The expression of annoyance had by now completely vanished from Boris's face. Having reflected and made up his mind how to act, he led Nicholas into the next room and introduced him to his guests, explaining that he was not a civilian, but an officer in the hussars, and his old friend. Rostov looked at the Frenchmen, bowed reluctantly, and was silent.

Zhilinsky was obviously not pleased to receive this Russian outsider into his circle, and said nothing to Rostov. Boris appeared not to notice the constraint produced by the newcomer, and with composure he tried to enliven the conversation. With characteristic French courtesy one of the French officers turned to Rostov, as he sat in stubborn silence, and said to him that he had probably come to Tilsit to see the Emperor.

"No, I came on business," was Rostov's short reply.

Rostov had been out of humour from the moment when he had seen the dissatisfaction on the face of Boris, and as is always the case with persons who are ill-humoured, it seemed to him that every one looked at him with hostile eyes, and that he was in every one's way. And in fact he was in every one's way, and he was the only person left out of the general conversation, as it sprang up again. And what is he sitting on here for? was the question asked by the eyes of the guests turned upon him. He got up and went up to Boris.

"I'm in your way," he said to him in an undertone. "Let us talk about my business, and I'll go away."

"Oh, no, not the least," said Boris. "But if you are tired, come to my room and lie down and rest."

"Well, really . . ."

They went into the little room where Boris slept. Rostov, without sitting down, began speaking at once with irritation, as though Boris were in some way to blame in the matter. He told him of Denisov's scrape, asking whether he would and could through his general intercede with the Emperor in Denisov's favour, and present the petition.

Boris, crossing one leg over the other and stroking the slender fingers of his right hand, listened to Rostov, as a general listens to a report presented by a subordinate, at one time looking away, at the next looking Rostov straight in the face.

Every time he did so, Rostov felt ill at ease, and dropped his eyes.

"I have heard of affairs of the sort, and I know that the Emperor is very severe in such cases. I think it had better not be taken before his majesty. To my mind, it would be better to apply directly to the commander of the corps. . . . But generally speaking, I believe . . ."

"Then you don't care to do anything!" Rostov almost shouted. Boris smiled. "On the contrary, I will do what I can, only I imagine . . ."

Rostov had arrived at Tilsit on the day least suitable for interceding in Denisov's behalf. It was out of the question for him to go himself to the general in attendance, since he was wearing civilian dress, and had come to Tilsit without permission. On that day, the 27th of June, the preliminaries of peace were signed. The Emperors exchanged orders: Alexander received the Legion of Honour, and Napoleon the Order of St. André of the first degree, and that day had been fixed for the dinner to be given by a battalion of French guards to the Preobrazhensky battalion. The Emperors were to be present at this banquet.

Rostov strolled about the town, staring at the French and their uniforms, examining the streets and the houses where the Russian and the French Emperors were staying. In the market-place he saw tables set out and preparations for the banquet; in the streets he saw draperies hung across with flags of the Russian and French colours, and huge monograms of A and N. In the windows of the houses, too, there were flags and monograms.

"Boris doesn't care to help me. That question's closed," thought Nicholas. "Everything's over between us, but I'm not going away from here without having done all I can for Denisov, and, above all, getting the letter given to the Emperor. To the Emperor? . . . He is here!" thought Rostov, who had unconsciously gone back to the house occupied by Alexander.

Saddle horses were standing at the entrance, and the suite were riding up, evidently getting ready for the Emperor to come out.

"Any minute I may see him," thought Rostov. "If only I could give him the letter directly, and tell him all . . . He would understand on which side the truth lay. Who can be more just and more magnanimous than he?" Then seeing an officer go into the house he thought, "why people go in!" And fingering the letter in his pocket, he went straight into the house where the Emperor was staying.

"Whom are you looking for?" some one asked him.

"To give a letter, a petition, to his majesty," said Nicholas with a quiver in his voice.

"A petition? To the officer on duty. This way; please."

An attendant opened the door to the officer's room for him, and Rostov went in.

A short, stout man of about thirty in white breeches and high boots was talking with some one in the adjoining room.

"A good figure and in her first bloom," he was saying. But seeing Rostov he broke off and frowned.

"What do you want? A petition?"

"What is it?" asked the person in the next room.

"Another petition," answered the stout man.

"Tell him to come later. The Emperor will be coming out directly. We must go."

"Later, later, to-morrow. It's too late. . . ."

Rostov turned away and would have gone out, but the stout man stopped him.

"From whom is it? Who are you?"

"From Major Denisov," answered Rostov.

"Who are you—an officer?"

"A lieutenant, Count Rostov."

"What audacity! Send it through the proper channel. And go along with you, go. . . ." And he began putting on his jacket.

Rostov went out into the hall again, and noticed that by this time there were a great many officers and generals in full dress, and he had to pass through their midst.

Cursing his temerity, Rostov made his way out of the house, and through the crowd of the gorgeously dressed suite. Suddenly a familiar voice called to him, and a hand detained him.

"Well, sir, what are you doing here in a frock coat?"

It was a cavalry general who had won the Emperor's special favour, and had formerly been in command of the division in which Rostov was serving.

Rostov began in dismay to try and excuse himself, but seeing the good-natured face of the general, he moved to one side, and in an excited voice told him of the whole affair, begging him to intercede for Denisov, whom the general knew.

The general on hearing Rostov's story shook his head. "I'm sorry, very sorry for Denisov. Give me the letter."

Rostov had scarcely time to give him the letter when the clank of rapid footsteps with spurs was heard on the stairs, and the general left his side and moved up to the steps. The gentlemen of the Emperor's suite ran downstairs and went to their horses. The postillion, the same one who had been at Austerlitz, led forward the Emperor's horse, and on the stairs was heard a light footstep, which Rostov knew at once.

Rostov moved right up to the steps together with some curious people from the town; and again after two years he saw the features, the same face, the same glance, the same walk, the same combination of majesty and mildness. . . . The Emperor wore the uniform of the Preobrazhensky regiment, white elkskin breeches and high boots, and a star which Rostov did not recognise (it was the star of the Legion of Honour). He was holding his hat under his arm, and putting on his glove. He stopped, looking round. He said a few words to some of the generals and he recognised the former commander of Rostov's division, smiled to him and summoned him.

All the suite stood back, and Rostov saw the general talking at some length to the Emperor.

The Emperor said a few words to him, and took a step towards his horse. Again the crowd of the suite and the street gazers, pushing Rostov along, moved up closer to the Emperor. Standing still with his hand on the saddle, the Emperor turned to the cavalry general and said aloud with the obvious intention of being heard by all: "I cannot, general. I cannot because the law is mightier than I am," and he put his foot in the stirrup. The general bent his head respectfully. The Emperor took his seat and galloped up the street.

In the public square towards which the Tsar rode there stood, facing each other, the battalion of the Preobrazhensky regiment on the right and the battalion of the French guards in bearskin caps on the left.

While the Emperor was riding up to one flank of the battalions, who presented arms, another crowd of horsemen was galloping up to the opposite flank, and at the head of them Rostov recognised Napoleon. He galloped up, wearing a little hat, the ribbons of St. André across his shoulder, and a blue uniform open over a white vest. He was riding a grey Arab horse of extremely fine breed, with a crimson, gold-embroidered saddle-cloth.

Riding up to Alexander, he raised his hat. The battalions shouted hurrah, and *vive l'Empereur!* Napoleon said something to Alexander. Both Emperors dismounted from their horses and took each other by the hands. Napoleon's face wore an unpleasantly hypocritical smile. Alexander was saying something to him with a cordial expression.

In spite of the kicking of the horses of the French gendarmes, who were keeping back the crowd, Rostov watched every movement of the Emperor Alexander and of Bonaparte, and never took his eyes off them. What struck him as something unexpected and strange was that Alexander behaved as though Bonaparte were his equal, and that Bonaparte in his manner to the Russian Tsar seemed perfectly at ease, as though this equal and intimate relation with a monarch were something natural and customary with him.

Alexander and Napoleon, moved towards the right flank of the Preobrazhensky battalion, close up to the crowd which was standing there. The crowd found itself unexpectedly so close to the Emperors, that Rostov, who stood in the front of it could hear what was said.

"Sire, I ask your permission to give the Legion of Honour to the bravest of your soldiers," said a harsh, precise voice, fully articulating every letter.

It was Bonaparte speaking. Alexander listened and bending his head smiled amiably.

"To him who bore himself most valiantly in this last war," added Napoleon, emphasising each syllable, and with an assurance and composure, revolting to Rostov, scanning the rows of Russian soldiers drawn up before him.

"Will your majesty allow me to ask the opinion of the colonel?" said Alexander, and he took a few hurried steps towards the commander of the battalion.

"Lazarev!" the colonel called with a scowling face. And Lazarev, the soldier who was the best shot in firing at the range, stepped smartly forward.

Napoleon gave a slight backward turn of his head, and a slight motion of his little fat hand, as though seeking something with it. The members of his suite, who guessed what was wanted, whispered together, passing something from one to another, and a page ran forward, with an order on a red ribbon. Napoleon approached Lazarev. Napoleon looked round at the Emperor Alexander, as though to show that what he was doing now he was doing for the sake of his ally. Napoleon laid the cross on Lazarev's breast, and, dropping his hand, turned to Alexander.

Then the Emperors mounted their horses and rode away. The Preobrazhensky battalion broke up, and, mingling with the French guards, sat down to the tables prepared for them.

Lazarev was put in the place of honour. French and Russian officers embraced him, congratulated him, and shook hands with him. Crowds of officers and townspeople flocked up to look at him. There was a continual hum of laughter and French and Russian chatter round the tables in the square. Two officers with flushed faces passed by Rostov, looking cheerful and happy.

"They say the Russians are to give the French a dinner tomorrow."

"What luck for Lazarev! Twelve hundred francs pension for life."

"One day our Emperor gives it, and next day Napoleon.

To-morrow the Emperor is to present the St. George to the bravest of the French guards!"

Rostov stood a long while looking at the celebration. His brain was seething in an agonising confusion, which he could not work out to any conclusion. Horrible doubts were stirring in his soul. He thought of Denisov with his changed expression, his submission, and all the hospital with torn-off legs and arms, with the filth and disease. So vividly he recalled that hospital smell of corpse that he looked round to see where the stench came from. Then he thought of that self-satisfied Bonaparte, with his white hands—treated now with cordiality and respect by the Emperor Alexander. For what, then, had those legs and arms been torn off, those men been killed? Then he thought of Lazarev rewarded, and Denisov punished and unpardoned. He caught himself in such strange reflections that he was terrified at them.

1808—1810

BOOK SIX

IN THE year 1808 the Emperor Alexander visited Erfurt for another interview with the Emperor Napoleon; and in the highest Petersburg society a great deal was said of the significance of this meeting.

In 1809 the friendship between the two sovereigns of the world, as Napoleon and Alexander were called, had become so close that when Napoleon declared war that year with Austria, a Russian corps crossed the frontier to help him against their old ally, the Austrian Emperor; so close that in the highest society there was talk of a possible marriage between Napoleon and one of the sisters of the Emperor Alexander.

Life meanwhile, the actual life of men with their real interests of health and sickness, labour and rest, with their interests of thought, science, poetry, music, love, affection, hatred, passion, went its way, as always, independently, apart from the political friendship or enmity of Napoleon Bonaparte.

Prince André had spent two years in the country. All those projects which Pierre had attempted on his estates, and had never carried out successfully, all those projects had been carried out by Prince André without display. He possessed in the highest degree the quality Pierre lacked, that practical tenacity which, without fuss or any great effort on his part, set things in working order.

On one of his estates three hundred serfs were transformed into free workers. It was one of the first examples in Russia. On other estates forced labour was replaced by payment of rent. On Bogutcharovo a trained midwife had been engaged at his expense to assist the peasant-women in childbirth, and a priest, at a fixed salary, was teaching the children of the peasants and house servants to read and write.

Half his time Prince André spent at Bleak Hills with his father and his son, who was still in the nursery. The other half he passed at his Bogutcharovo retreat, as his father called his estate. In spite of the indifference to all the external events of the world that he had shown to Pierre, he studiously followed them, received many books, and, to his own surprise, when people coming fresh from Petersburg, the very vortex of life, visited him or his father, he noticed that those people, in knowledge of all that was passing in home and foreign politics, were far behind him, though he had never left the country.

Besides looking after his estates, and much general reading of the most varied kind, Prince André was busily engaged at this time upon a critical survey of Russia's two late disastrous campaigns and the composition of a proposal for reforms in army rules and regulations.

In the spring of 1809 Prince André set off to visit the Ryazan estates, the heritage of his son, whose trustee he was. His duties necessitated an interview with the marshal of the district. This marshal was Count Rostov, and in the middle of May Prince André went to see him.

It was by now late spring. The forests were already in full leaf. It was dusty, and hot.

Prince André drove along the avenue leading to the Rostovs' house at Otradnoe, thinking of what questions he must ask the marshal about his business. Behind some trees on the right he heard merry girlish cries, and caught sight of a party of girls running across the avenue along which his coach was driving. In front of all the rest there ran towards the coach a black-haired, very slender, strangely slender, black-eyed girl in a yellow cotton gown. She was shouting something, but seeing a stranger, she ran back laughing.

Prince André for some reason felt a sudden pang. The day was so lovely, the sun so bright, everything around him so gay, and that slim and pretty girl was content and happy in her own life—foolish doubtless—but gay and happy and remote from him. What was she so glad about? What was she thinking of? Not of army regulations; not of the organisation of the Ryazan rent-paying peasants. "What is she thinking about, and why is she so happy?" Prince André could not help wondering.

Count Rostov was in this year living at Otradnoe, exactly as he had always done in previous years; that is to say, entertaining almost the whole province with hunts, theatricals, dinner parties and concerts. He was delighted to see Prince André, as he always was to see any new guest, and insisted that he stay the night.

Prince André spent a tedious day, entertained by his elderly host and hostess and the more honoured among the guests, of whom the count's house was full in honour of an approaching name-day. Several times in the course of it, Prince André glanced at Natasha, continually laughing and full of gaiety among the younger members of the company. And he asked himself each time, "What is she thinking of? What is she so glad about?"

In the evening, alone in a new place, he was for a long while unable to sleep. He read for a time, then put out his candle, and afterwards lighted it again. It was hot in the bedroom with the shutters closed on the inside. He felt irritated that this foolish old gentleman, as he called Count Rostov, had detained him. And he was vexed with himself for staying.

Prince André got up and went to the window to open it. As soon as he opened the shutter, the moonlight broke into the room as though it had been waiting a long while outside on the watch for this chance. He opened the window. The night was fresh and bright and still. And above he saw the moon nearly full, in a clear, almost starless sky. Prince André leaned on the window.

His room was on the second story; there were people in the room over his head, and awake too. He heard girls' chatter.

"Only this once more," said a girlish voice, which Prince André recognised at once.

"But when are you coming to bed?" answered another voice.

"I'm not coming! I can't sleep; what's the use? Come, for the last time. . . ."

Two feminine voices sang a musical phrase, the finale of some song.

"Oh, it's lovely! Well, now go to sleep."

"You go to sleep, but I can't," answered the first voice.

She was evidently leaning right out of the window, for he could hear the rustle of her garments and even her breathing. All was hushed and stonily still, like the moon and its lights and shadows. Prince André dared not stir for fear of betraying his presence.

"Sonya! Sonya!" he heard the first voice again. "Oh, how

can you sleep! Do look how lovely! Oh, how lovely! Do wake up, Sonya!" she said, almost with tears in her voice. "Do you know such a beautiful night has never, never been before."

Sonya made some reluctant reply.

"No, do look what a moon! . . . Oh, how lovely it is! Do come here. Darling, precious, do come here. There, do you see? One has only to squat on one's heels like this—see—and to hold one's knees—as tight, as tight as one can—give a great spring and one would fly away. . . . Like this—see!"

"You'll fall."

Prince André heard sounds of a scuffle and Sonya's voice in a tone of vexation: "Why, it's past one o'clock."

"Oh, you only spoil it all for me. Well, go to bed then, go along."

All was hushed again. But Prince André knew she was still sitting there. He heard at times a soft rustle.

And suddenly there stirred within him a medley of youthful hopes and ideas, running counter to the whole tenor of his life.

Next day Prince André took leave of the count alone and set off on his way home, without waiting for the ladies to appear.

On getting home after his journey, Prince André made up his mind to go to Petersburg in the autumn. Just as a month before he could not have understood how the idea of leaving the country could ever occur to him, it now seemed clear to him that all his experience of life would be wasted and come to naught, if he did not take an active part in life again. His former pursuits no longer interested him, and often sitting alone in his study, he got up, went to the looking-glass and gazed a long while at his face. Then he turned to the portrait of Liza, who, with her curls tied up *à la grecque,* looked gaily out of the gold frame at him. She did not say those terrible words to him; she looked curiously and merrily at him. And, clasping his hands behind him, Prince André would walk a long while up and down his room, frowning and smiling by turns, as he brooded over those irrational thoughts, that could not be put into words, and were secret as a crime—the thoughts connected with Pierre, with glory, with the girl at the window, with woman's beauty, and love, which had changed the whole current of his life. And if any one came into his room at such moments, he would be particularly short, severely decided and disagreeably logical.

Prince André arrived in Petersburg in August of 1809. It was the period when the young Speransky was at the height of his fame and his reforms were being carried out with the utmost vigour. In that very month the Tsar was thrown out of his carriage, hurt his foot, and was laid up for three weeks at Peterhof, seeing Speransky every day and no one else. At that period a whole new political constitution was under discussion, destined to transform the legal, administrative and financial system of government from the Privy Council to the district tribunals. At this time the vague, liberal ideals with which the Emperor Alexander had ascended the throne were taking shape and being carried into practice.

Soon after his arrival, Prince André, as a gentleman-in-waiting, presented himself at court at a levée. The Tsar, meeting him on two occasions, did not deign to bestow a single word upon him. Prince André had felt even before then that he was disliked by the Tsar; that the Tsar disliked his face and his whole personality. Courtiers explained the Tsar's slight to Prince André by saying that his majesty was displeased at his having retired from active service in 1805.

"I know myself that one has no control over one's likes and dislikes," thought Prince André. "And so it is of no use to think of presenting my plan on army reform in person to the Tsar, but the thing will speak for itself." He sent word about his plan to an old field-marshal, a friend of his father's. The field-marshal fixed an hour to see him, received him cordially, and promised to lay it before the Tsar. A few days later, Prince André received notice that he was to call upon the minister of war, Count Araktcheev.

At nine o'clock in the morning on the day appointed, Prince André entered Count Araktcheev's reception-room. Prince André did not know Araktcheev personally and had never seen him, but all that he knew about him had inspired him with little respect for the man.

"He is the minister of war, a person the Tsar trusts, and no one need have any concern with his personal qualities; he has been commissioned to look at my plan, consequently he is the only person who can get it adopted," thought Prince André, as he waited among many persons of importance and unimportance in Count Araktcheev's anteroom.

After several people had been let in and let out of the minister's room by the adjutant, an officer was admitted whose panic-stricken face had struck Prince André. The officer's audience lasted a long while. Suddenly the roar of a harsh voice was heard through the door, and the officer, with a white face and trembling lips, came out and crossed the anteroom. After that, Prince André was conducted to the door, and the adjutant in a whisper said: "To the right, at the window."

Prince André went into a plain, neat study, and saw at the table a man of forty with a long waist, with a long, closely-cropped head, deep wrinkles, scowling brows over brown-green, dull eyes, and a red, overhanging nose. Araktcheev turned his head towards him, without looking at him.

"What is it you are petitioning for?" asked Araktcheev.

"There is nothing that I am . . . petitioning for, your excellency," Prince André said softly. Araktcheev's eyes turned to him.

"Sit down," said Araktcheev. "Prince Bolkonsky?"

"I have no petition to make, but his majesty the Tsar has graciously sent to your excellency a plan submitted by me——"

"I have read your plan," Araktcheev interrupted, uttering only the first words civilly, again looking away from him, and relapsing more and more into a tone of grumbling contempt. "Is it new army regulations you propose? There are regulations in plenty; no one will carry out the old ones. Nowadays every one's drawing up regulations; it's easier writing than doing."

"I have come by the desire of his majesty the Tsar to learn from your excellency how you propose to deal with my project," said Prince André courteously.

"I have proposed a resolution in regard to your plan, and have sent it to the committee. I do *not* approve," said Araktcheev, getting up and taking a paper out of the writing-table. "Here." He gave it to Prince André. Right across the plan had been scrawled, without punctuation or capital letters and with words misspelt: "Superficially compiled seeing that it's drawn up in imitation of the French army regulations and needlessly departing from the standing orders."

"To what committee has it been referred?" asked Prince André.

"To the Committee on Army Regulations, and I have proposed your honour being enrolled among its members. Only without salary."

Prince André smiled.

"I am not seeking a salary."

"A member without salary," repeated Araktcheev. "I wish you good day. Hey! call! Who's the next?" he shouted, as he bowed to Prince André.

While awaiting the announcement of his name having been put on the committee, Prince André looked up old acquaintances, especially those whom he knew could be of use to him. He was always well received in the highest and most various circles of Petersburg society. The party of reform welcomed him warmly, and sought him out, in the first place, because he had the reputation of being clever and very well read, and secondly because he had already gained the reputation of being a liberal by the emancipation of his serfs. The conservative party of the dissatisfied older generation welcomed him simply as the son of his father, and counted upon his sympathy in their disapproval of the reforms. The feminine world received him cordially because he was a wealthy match of high rank, and a person almost new, encircled by a halo of romance from his narrow escape from death and the tragic loss of his young wife. Moreover the general verdict of all who had known him previously was that he had greatly changed for the better during the last five years, had grown softer and more manly; that he had lost his old affectation, pride, and sarcastic irony. People talked of him, were interested in him, and eager to see him.

The day after his interview with Count Araktcheev, Prince André was at a *soirée*. The host, wishing to help him and knowing of his unpleasant interview with the minister of war, took Prince André by the arm and introduced him to a tall, bald, fair-haired man of forty, who had just come in. He had a large, open forehead, and his long face was of a strange, exceptional whiteness; he wore a blue frock coat and had a cross at his neck and a star on the left side of his breast. It was Speransky, the secretary of state, the Tsar's confidential adviser, who had accompanied him to Erfurt, and there had more than once seen and talked with Napoleon. Prince André recognised him at once.

Speransky's whole figure had a peculiar character by which he could be distinguished immediately. Never in any one of the circles in which Prince André had moved had he seen such calm and self-confidence as in this man's heavy and ungainly movements. Never in any one had he seen a glance so resolute, and yet so soft, as in those half-closed and moist-looking eyes; never had he seen such firmness as in that smile that meant nothing. Never had he heard a voice so delicate, smooth, and soft. But what struck him most of all was the tender whiteness of the face, and still more the hands, which were rather broad, but extremely plump, soft, and white.

He spoke slowly, with conviction that he would be listened to, and looked only at the person to whom he was speaking. Prince André watched every word and gesture.

"I am very glad to make your acquaintance. I have heard of you, as every one has," he said when Prince André was introduced to him.

The host said a few words about the reception Araktcheev had given Prince André. Speransky's smile broadened.

"The chairman of the Committee of Army Regulations is a friend of mine—M. Magnitsky," he said, articulating fully every word and every syllable. "And, if you wish it, I can introduce you to him. I think that he will be sympathetic and glad to help. If you will call on Wednesday, then I shall have seen Magnitsky . . . And besides I shall have the pleasure of more conversation with you." Closing his eyes, he bowed.

Speransky had a long and confidential talk with Prince André on Wednesday at his own home, where he received him alone.

Prince André regarded the mass of men as worthless creatures, and he had such a longing to find in some other man the living pattern of that perfection after which he strove himself, that he was ready to believe that in Speransky he had found this ideal of a perfectly rational and virtuous man. Had Speransky belonged to the same world as Prince André, had he been of the same breeding and moral traditions, Prince André would soon have detected the weak, human, unheroic sides of his character. But this logical turn of mind was strange to him and inspired him with the more respect from his not fully understanding it. Besides this, Speransky, either because he appreciated Prince André's abilities or because he thought it as well to win his friendship, flattered him with that delicate flattery that goes hand in hand with conceit, and consists in a tacit assumption that one's companion and oneself are the only people capable of understanding all the folly of the rest of the world and the wisdom and profundity of their own ideas.

In the course of their long conversation Speransky said more than once: "Among *us* everything that is out of the common rut of tradition is looked at," . . . or with a smile: "But *we* want the wolves to be well fed and the sheep to be unhurt." . . . or: "*They* can't grasp that" . . . And always with an expression that said: "We, you and I, we understand what *they* are and who *we* are."

Prince André saw in Speransky a man of vast intellect and sober, accurate judgment, who had attained power by energy and persistence, and was using it for the good of Russia only. In Prince André's eyes Speransky was precisely the man that he would have liked to be himself.

Everything was right, everything was as it should be, yet one thing disconcerted Prince André. That was the cold, mirror-like eye of Speransky, which seemed to refuse all admittance to his soul, and his flabby, white hand, at which Prince André instinctively looked, as one usually does look at the hands of men who have power. That mirror-like eye and that flabby hand vaguely irritated Prince André.

During the first period of his acquaintance with Speransky, Prince André had a passionate admiration for him, akin to what he had once felt for Bonaparte. The very fact that Speransky was the son of a priest, which enabled many foolish people to regard him with vulgar contempt, as a member of a despised class, made Prince André peculiarly delicate in dealing with his own feeling for Speransky, and unconsciously strengthened it in him.

On that first evening that Prince André spent with him, they talked of the commission for the revision of the legal code; and Speransky described ironically to Prince André how the commission had been sitting for one hundred and fifty years, had cost millions, and had done nothing.

"And that's all the state has got for the millions it has spent!" said he. "We want to give new judicial powers to the Senate, and we have no laws. That's why it is a sin for men like you, prince, not to be in the government."

Prince André observed that some education in law was necessary for such work, and that he had none.

"But no one has! It's a vicious circle which must be broken."

Within a week Prince André was a member of the committee for the reconstruction of the army regulations, and—a thing he would never have expected—he was also chairman of a section of the commission for the revision of the legal code. At Speransky's request he took the first part of the civil code under revision. And with the help of the Napoleonic Code and the Code of Justinian he worked at the revision of the section on Personal Rights.

Two years before, at the beginning of 1808, Pierre had returned to Petersburg from his visits to his estates, and by no design of his own had taken a leading position among the freemasons in Petersburg. He organised dining and funeral lodges, enrolled new members, took an active part in the formation of different lodges, and the acquisition of authentic acts. He spent his money on the construction of temples, and, to the best of his powers, made up the arrears, a matter in which the majority of members were niggardly and irregular. At his own expense, almost unaided, he maintained the poorhouse built by the order in Petersburg.

Meanwhile his life ran on in the old way. He liked a good dinner and he liked strong drink; and, though he thought it immoral and degrading to yield to them, he was unable to resist the temptations of the bachelor society in which he moved.

Yet even in the midst of his work and his dissipations, Pierre began, after the lapse of a year, to feel more and more as though the ground of freemasonry on which he had taken his stand was slipping away under his feet.

Osip Alexyevitch was not in Petersburg. He had withdrawn from all participation in the affairs of the Petersburg lodge, and now never left Moscow. All the brothers who were members of the lodge were people Pierre knew in daily life, and it was difficult for him to see in them simply brothers in freemasonry, and not Prince B., nor Ivan Vasilyevitch D., whom he knew in private life mostly as persons of weak and worthless character. Under their masonic aprons and emblems he could not help seeing the uniforms and the decorations they were striving after in mundane life. Often after collecting the alms and reckoning up twenty to thirty roubles promised—and for the most part left owing—from some ten members, Pierre thought of the masonic vow by which every brother promised to give up all his belongings for his neighbour; and doubts stirred in his soul from which he tried to escape.

His masonic brothers were men who, as far as Pierre could observe, had no belief in anything, nor desire of anything, but had entered the brotherhood simply for the sake of getting into touch with wealthy young men, powerful through their connections or their rank, who were numerous in the lodge.

Because of all this Pierre began to feel dissatisfied. And again he was overtaken by that despondency he so dreaded.

At this time he received a letter from his wife who begged him to see her, wrote of her unhappiness on his account, and her desire to devote her whole life to him.

At the end of the letter she told him that in a day or two she would arrive in Petersburg from abroad.

The letter was followed up by one of the freemasons, whom Pierre respected least, bursting in upon his solitude. Turning the conversation to Pierre's matrimonial affairs, he gave him, by way of brotherly counsel, his opinion that his severity to his wife was wrong, and that Pierre was departing from the first principles of freemasonry in not forgiving the guilty. At the same time his mother-in-law, Prince Vassily's wife, wrote to him, beseeching him to visit her, if only for a few minutes, to discuss a matter of great importance. Pierre saw there was a conspiracy against him, that they meant to reconcile him with his wife, and he did not even dislike this in the mood in which he then was. Nothing mattered to him. And because of his despondency he attached no significance either to his own freedom or to having his own way by punishing his wife.

"No one is right, no one is to blame, and so she, too, is not to blame," he thought.

If Pierre did not at once give his consent to being reunited to his wife, it was simply because in the despondent state into which he had lapsed, he was incapable of taking any line of action. Had his wife come to him, he could not now have driven her away. Could it matter, beside the questions that were absorbing Pierre, whether he now lived with his wife or not?

Without answering either his wife or his mother-in-law,

Pierre at once set off late in the evening, and drove to Moscow to see Osip Alexyevitch.

This is what Pierre wrote in his diary.

"Moscow, November 17.—I have only just come from seeing my benefactor, and I hasten to write down all I have been feeling. Osip Alexyevitch lives in poverty, and has been for three years past suffering from a painful disease of the bladder. No one has ever heard from him a groan or a word of complaint. From morning till late at night, except at the times when he eats the very plainest food, he is working at science. He received me graciously, and made me sit down on the bed on which he was lying. I made him the sign of the Knights of the East and of Jerusalem; he responded with the same. . . . He surprised me by asking whether I remembered the threefold aim of the order: the preservation and study of the holy mystery; the purification and reformation of self for its reception; and the improvement of the human race. Which, he asked, was the first and greatest of those three aims? Undoubtedly self-reformation and self-purification. It is only towards that aim that we can always strive. Talking of my private affairs, he said to me: 'The first duty of a mason, as I have told you, is the perfection of himself. But often we imagine that by removing all the difficulties of our life, we may better attain this aim. It is quite the contrary. It is only in the midst of the cares of the world that we can reach the great aims of self-knowledge, for a man can know himself only by comparison, and of greater perfection, which can only be obtained by conflict. Only the corruptions of life can show us all its vanity.' These words were the more remarkable as Osip Alexyevitch, in spite of his sufferings, is never weary of life. He advised me not to withdraw from my Petersburg brothers, and while undertaking duties only of the second order in the lodge, to try to draw the brothers away from the seductions of pride, and to turn them into the true path of self-knowledge and self-perfection. Moreover, for myself personally, he advised me first of all to keep a watch over myself, and with that aim he gave me a manuscript-book, the one in which I am writing now, and am to note down all my actions in the future."

"Petersburg, November 23.—I am reconciled with my wife. My mother-in-law came to me in tears, and said that Helen was here, and that she begged me to hear her; that she was innocent, that she was miserable at my desertion of her. I knew that if I once let myself see her, I should not be able to refuse her wishes. In my uncertainty, I did not know whose help and advice to get. If my benefactor had been here, he would have told me what to do. I retired to my own room, read over the letters of Osip Alexyevitch, recalled my conversations with him, and from all that I reached the conclusion that I

ought not to refuse Helen, and ought to hold out a helping hand to every one, and, above all, to a person so closely connected with me, and that I must bear my cross. But if I forgive her for the sake of doing right, at least let my reunion with her have a spiritual end only. So I decided, and so I wrote to Osip Alexyevitch. I said to my wife that I begged her to forget all the past, that I begged her to forgive whatever wrong I might have done her, and that I had nothing to forgive her. It was a joy to me to tell her that. May she never know how painful it was to me to see her again! I have installed myself in the upper rooms in this great house, and I am conscious of a happy feeling of beginning anew."

At that time, as always indeed, the exalted society that met at court and at the great balls was split up into several circles, each of which had its special tone. The largest among them was the French circle supporting the Napoleonic alliance. In this circle Helen took a leading position, as soon as she had established herself in her husband's house in Petersburg. She received the members of the French embassy, and a great number of people, noted for their wit and their politeness, and belonging to that political section.

Helen had been at Erfurt at the time of the famous meeting of the Emperors; and had there formed close ties with all the notable figures in Europe belonging to the Napoleonic circle. In Erfurt she had been brilliantly successful. Napoleon himself, seeing her at the theatre, had asked who she was, and admired her beauty.

Her triumphs in the character of a beautiful and elegant woman did not surprise Pierre, for with years she had become even more beautiful than before. But what did surprise him was that during the last two years his wife had succeeded in gaining a reputation as "a charming woman, as witty as she is beautiful." The distinguished Prince de Ligne wrote her letters of eight pages. Bilibin treasured up his clever remarks to utter them for the first time before her. To be received in Countess Bezuhov's salon was looked upon as a certificate of intellect. Young men read up subjects before one of Helen's *soirées,* so as to be able to talk of something in her salon, and secretaries of the embassy, and even ambassadors, confided diplomatic secrets to her, so that Helen was in a way a power.

It was with a strange feeling of perplexity and alarm that Pierre, who knew she was very stupid, sometimes at her dinners and *soirées,* listened to conversation about politics, poetry, and philosophy. At these *soirées* he experienced a sensation such as a conjuror must feel who expects every moment that his trick will be discovered. But either because stupidity was just what was needed for the successful management of such a salon, or because those who were deceived took pleasure in the deception, the cheat was not discovered, and the reputation of "a charming woman" clung so persistently to Helen Bezuhov, that she could utter the most vulgar and stupid speeches.

Pierre was exactly the husband needed by this brilliant society woman. He was that absent-minded, eccentric, grand seigneur of a husband, who got in nobody's way and far from spoiling the general lofty atmosphere of her drawing-room, formed by his contrast an advantageous foil to her. Pierre's continual concentration on immaterial interests during the last two years, and his genuine contempt for everything else, gave him in his wife's circle, which did not interest him, that tone of unconcern, indifference, and benevolence towards all alike, which cannot be acquired artificially, and for that reason commands involuntary respect. He entered his wife's drawing-room as though it were a theatre, was acquainted with every one, equally affable to all, and to all equally indifferent. Sometimes he took part in conversation on some subject that interested him, and then, without any consideration whether the "gentlemen of the embassy" were present or not, he mumbled out his opinions which were by no means always in harmony with the catch-words of the time. But the public estimate of the eccentric husband of "the most distinguished woman in Petersburg" was now so well established that no one took him seriously.

Among the many young men, who were daily to be seen in Helen's house, Boris Drubetskoy, who had by now achieved marked success in the service, was the most intimate friend of the Bezuhov household. Helen used to call him "my page," and treated him like a child. Her smile for him was the same smile she bestowed on all, but it was sometimes distasteful to Pierre to see that smile. Boris behaved to Pierre with a marked and dignified respectfulness. This too disturbed Pierre. He had suffered so much three years before from the mortification caused him by his wife, that now he secured himself from all possibility of similar mortification; in the first place, by being his wife's husband only in name, and secondly, by not allowing himself to suspect anything.

"No, now she has renounced for ever her former errors," he said to himself. But, strange to say, the presence of Boris had a physical effect on Pierre; it seemed to make all his limbs contract, and destroyed the freedom of his movement.

"Such a strange hate," thought Pierre. "And at one time I really liked him very much."

In the eyes of the world, Pierre was a great lord, the rather blind and absurd husband of a distinguished wife; a clever eccentric, who did nothing but who was no trouble to any one, a good-natured fellow. And in Pierre's soul all this while a complex and difficult process of inner development was going on that revealed much to him and led him to many spiritual doubts and joys.

The Rostovs' financial position had not improved during the two years they had spent in the country. Although Nicholas had kept firmly to his promise, and was spending comparatively little, the manner of life at Otradnoe, and still more Mitenka's management of affairs, were such that debts went on unchecked, growing bigger every year. The only way out for the old count was to enter the government service, and he had come to Petersburg to seek a post, and at the same time, as he said, to let his poor wenches enjoy themselves for the last time.

Although in Moscow the Rostovs belonged to the best society—themselves unaware of the fact, and never troubling themselves to consider what society they belonged to—yet in Petersburg their position was uncertain and indefinite. In Petersburg they were provincials and were not visited by the very people who in Moscow had dined at their home without their inquiring to what society they belonged.

Anna Drubetskoy was seeing less of the Rostovs. There was a marked dignity, too, in her manner with them, and she spoke on every occasion with thankfulness and enthusiasm of her son's great abilities and brilliant career. Her son Boris seldom visited them. He had a brilliant position in society, thanks to his intimacy with Countess Bezuhov; a brilliant position in the service, thanks to the protection of a great person whose confidence he had completely won; and he was beginning to make plans for marrying one of the richest heiresses in Petersburg, plans which might very easily be realised.

The Rostovs kept open house in Petersburg, just as they used to do in Moscow; and at their suppers people of every kind could be seen together: country neighbours, old and not well-to-do country gentlemen with their daughters, and the old-maid-of-honour, Madame Peronsky, Pierre Bezuhov, and the son of their district postmaster, who was in an office in Petersburg. Of the men who were constantly at the Rostovs' house in Petersburg, the most intimate friends of the family were very soon Pierre, who had been met in the street by the old count and dragged home by him, and Berg, who spent whole days with the Rostovs, and paid the elder of the young countesses, Vera, every attention a young man can pay who intends to make a proposal.

Not in vain had Berg shown everybody his right hand that had been wounded at Austerlitz, and the sword quite unnecessarily held in his left. He had related this episode to everybody so persistently and with such an air of importance, that every one had come to believe in the heroism of the feat, and Berg had received two decorations for Austerlitz.

In the war in Finland, too, he had succeeded in distinguishing himself. He had picked up a fragment of a grenade, by which an adjutant had been killed close to the commander-in-chief, and had carried this fragment to his commander. Again, as after Austerlitz, he talked to every one at such length and with such persistency about this incident that people ended by believing that this, too, was something that ought to have been done, and Berg also received two decorations for the Finnish war. In 1809 he was a captain in the guards with decorations on his breast, and was filling some particularly profitable posts in Petersburg.

Though there were some skeptics who smiled when Berg's merits were mentioned before them, it could not be denied that Berg was a gallant officer, punctual in the discharge of his duties, in excellent repute with the authorities, and a conscientious young man with a brilliant career before him and a secure position in society.

Four years before, on meeting a German comrade in the lobby of a Moscow theatre, Berg had pointed out to him Vera Rostov, and said to him in German, "That girl will be my wife." From that moment he had made up his mind to marry her. Now in Petersburg, after duly considering the Rostovs' position and his own, he decided that the time had come and made his offer.

Berg's proposal was received at first with a hesitation by no means flattering for him. It seemed a strange idea at first that the son of an obscure Livonian gentleman should propose for the hand of a Countess Rostov. But Berg's leading characteristic was an egoism so naïve and good-natured that the Rostovs unconsciously began to think that it must be a good thing since he was himself so firmly convinced that it would be a good thing, and indeed a very good thing. The Rostovs were, moreover, seriously embarrassed in their financial affairs, a fact of which the suitor could not but be aware; and what was more important Vera was now twenty-four, and had been brought out everywhere. And, in spite of the fact that she was undeniably good-looking and sensible, no one had proposed to her. The offer was accepted.

"You see," Berg said to a comrade, whom he called his friend—only because he knew all people do have friends—"you see, I have taken everything into consideration, and I should not consider marriage if I had not thought it over, or if it were unsuitable in any way. But at present my father and mother are well provided for, and I can live in Petersburg with my pay and her fortune and my careful habits. We can get along nicely. I'm not marrying for money, I consider that ungentlemanly, but the wife ought to bring her share and the husband his. I have my position in the service; she has connections and some small means. That's worth something nowadays, isn't it? And what's most important she's a handsome, estimable girl, and she loves me. . . ."

Berg blushed and smiled.

"And I love her because she has a character that is reasonable and very nice. Her sister, Natasha, now—though they are of the same family—is utterly different, and her character is disagreeable, and she has none of that intelligence, but something you know . . . I don't like. . . . But my fiancée . . . You must come and see us; come to . . ." Berg went on; he was going to say "to dinner," but on second thought he said "to tea," and putting out his tongue he blew a little ring of tobacco smoke that encircled for him all his dreams of happiness.

The first feeling of hesitation prompted by Berg's proposal had been followed by the festivity and rejoicing in the Rostov family usual on such occasions. But the rejoicing was not genuine.

A certain embarrassment could be sensed in regard to this marriage. It was as though their conscience smote them for not having been very fond of Vera and of being so ready now to get her off their hands. The old count was more disconcerted over it than any one. He would most likely have been unable to say what made him feel so, but his financial difficulties were at the root of the matter. He absolutely did not know what he had, how much his debts amounted to, and what he would be able to give for Vera's dowry. Each of his daughters had at their birth been assigned a portion, consisting of an estate with three hundred serfs on it. But one of those estates had by now been sold, and the other had been mortgaged, and the interest was so much in arrears that it would have to be sold, so that to give this estate was impossible. There was no money either.

Berg had been engaged more than a month, and it was only a week before the date fixed for the wedding, but the count was still unable to come to a decision on the subject of the dowry, and had not spoken of it to his wife. At one time the count thought of making over the Ryazan estate to Vera, then he thought of selling his forest, then of borrowing money.

A few days before the wedding, Berg went early in the morning into the count's study, and with an agreeable smile, respectfully invited his father-in-law to let him know what dowry would be given with the Countess Vera. The count was so much disconcerted by this long-foreseen inquiry that, without thinking, he said the first thing that came into his head.

"I like your being businesslike about it, I like it. You will be quite satisfied . . ."

And clapping Berg on the shoulder, he got up, intending to cut short the conversation. But Berg, smiling blandly, announced that if he were not to know for certain what would be given with Vera, and to receive at least part of the dowry in advance, he would be obliged to break off the marriage. "Because, you must consider, count, if I were to allow myself to marry now without having a definite security for the maintenance of my wife I should be acting like a scoundrel . . ."

The conversation ended by the count, in his anxiety to be generous and to avoid further requests, saying that he would give him a note for eighty thousand. Berg smiled gently and said that he was very grateful, but could not make his arrangements in his new life without receiving thirty thousand in ready money. "Twenty thousand at least, count," he added, "and then a note for sixty thousand."

"Yes, yes, very good," said the count hurriedly. "Only excuse me, my dear boy, I'll give you twenty thousand and the note for eighty thousand as well. That's all right, kiss me."

On the 31st of December, on the eve of the new year 1810, a ball was given by a grand personage who had been a favourite at the court of Catherine. The Tsar and the diplomatic corps were to be present at this ball.

The well-known mansion of this grandee in the English Embankment was ablaze with lights. The police were standing at the entry, laid with red carpet; and not merely policemen, but a police commander was on duty, and dozens of officers of the police. Carriages kept driving away, and fresh ones kept driving up, with grooms in red livery and grooms in plumed hats. From the carriages emerged men wearing uniforms, stars, and ribbons; while ladies in satin and ermine stepped carefully out on the carriage steps, that were let down with a bang, and then walked hurriedly and noiselessly over the red carpet.

A third of the guests had already arrived, while the Rostovs, who were to be present, were still busy in hurried preparations.

The Rostovs were to be accompanied by Marya Peronsky, a friend and relation of the countess, a thin and yellow maid-of-honour of the old court, who was acting as a guide to the provincial Rostovs in the higher circles of Petersburg society.

At ten o'clock the Rostovs were to drive to Tavritchesky Garden to call for the maid-of-honour. Meantime it was five minutes to ten, and the young ladies were not yet dressed.

Natasha was sixteeen and was going to her first great ball. She had got up at eight o'clock that morning, and had spent the whole day hurrying about. All her energies had since morning been directed to the one aim of getting herself, her mother, and Sonya as well dressed as possible. Sonya and her mother put themselves entirely in her hands. The countess was to wear a dark red velvet dress; the two girls white tulle dresses over pink silk slips, and roses on their bodices. They were to wear their hair *à la grecque*.

All the essentials were ready. Feet, arms, necks, and ears had been washed, scented, and powdered with particular care. Openwork silk stockings and white satin shoes with ribbons had been put on. The hairdressing was almost done. Sonya was finishing dressing, so was the countess; but Natasha, who had been busily looking after every one, was late. She was still sitting before the looking-glass. Sonya, already dressed, stood in the middle of the room, and was trying to fasten in a last ribbon, hurting her little finger as she pressed the pin with a scrooping sound into the silk.

"Will you soon be ready?" they heard the countess's voice. "It will be ten in a minute."

"Immediately, immediately. . . . And are you ready, mother?"

"Only my cap to fasten on."

"Don't do it without me," shouted Natasha. "You don't know how!"

"But it's ten o'clock already."

When her hair was finished, Natasha, in her mother's dressing-jacket and a short petticoat under which her dancing-shoes could be seen, ran up to Sonya, looked her over, and then ran to her mother. Turning her head round, she pinned on her cap, and hurriedly kissing her grey hair, ran back to the maids who were shortening her skirt.

All attention was now centred on Natasha's skirt, which was too long. Two maids were running it up round the edge, hurriedly biting off the threads. A third one, with pins in her teeth and lips, was running from the countess to Sonya.

"Mavrushka, quicker, darling!"

"Give me that thimble, miss."

"Will you be quick?" said the count standing at the door. "Here are your smelling-salts. Madame Peronsky must be tired of waiting."

"Ready, miss," said the maid, lifting up the shortened tulle skirt on two fingers, blowing something off it, and giving it a shake.

Natasha began putting on the dress.

"In a minute, in a minute, don't come in, father," she shouted from under the tulle of the dress that concealed all her face. Sonya slammed the door. A minute later the count was admitted. He was wearing a blue frock coat, stockings, and dancing-shoes, and was perfumed and pomaded.

"Oh, father, how nice you look!" said Natasha, standing in the middle of the room, stroking out the folds of her tulle.

At that moment the countess in her cap and velvet gown walked shyly into the room.

"Oo-oo! My beauty!" cried the count. "She looks nicer than any of you!" . . . He would have embraced her, but, flushing, she drew back to avoid being crumpled.

"Mother, the cap should be more on one side," said Natasha. "I'll pin it again," and she darted forward.

At a quarter past ten they were at last seated in their carriage and driving off. But they still had to go to Tavritchesky Garden.

Madame Peronsky was ready and waiting. In spite of her age and ugliness, just the same process had been going on with her as with the Rostovs, not with flurry, for with her it was a matter of routine. Her elderly and unprepossessing person had been also washed and scented and powdered; she had washed as carefully behind her ears, and like the Rostovs' nurse, her old maid had enthusiastically admired her mistress's attire, when she came into the drawing-room in her yellow gown adorned with her badge of a maid-of-honour.

Then, careful of their coiffures and their dresses, at eleven o'clock they settled themselves in the carriages and drove off.

Natasha had not had a free moment all that day, and had not once had time to think of what lay before her.

In the damp, chill air, in the closeness and half dark of the swaying carriage, she pictured to herself for the first time what was in store for her there, at the ball, in the brightly lighted halls—music, flowers, dancing, the Tsar, all the brilliant young people of Petersburg. The prospect before her was so splendid that she could not even believe that it would come to pass; so incongruous it seemed with the chilliness, darkness, and closeness of the carriage.

She could only grasp all that awaited her when, walking over the red carpet, she went into the vestibule, took off her cloak, and walked beside Sonya up the lighted staircase banked with flowers. Only then she remembered how she must behave at a ball, and moved on, filled with excitement, and trying with all her might to conceal it. And it was just in this mood that she looked her best. In front and behind them walked guests dressed in similar ball-dresses and conversing in similarly subdued tones. The looking-glasses on the staircases reflected ladies in white, blue, and pink dresses, with diamonds and pearls on their bare arms and necks.

Natasha looked into the looking-glasses and could not distinguish herself from the rest. All was mingled into one brilliant procession. At the entrance into the first room, the regular hum of voices, footsteps, greetings, deafened Natasha. The light and brilliance dazzled her still more. The host and hostess who had already been standing at the door for half an hour, saying exactly the same words to every guest on arrival, "Charmed to see you," gave the same greeting to the Rostovs and Madame Peronsky. The two young girls in their white dresses, made curtsies just alike, but unconsciously the hostess's eyes rested longer on the slender figure of Natasha. She looked at her, and smiled at her a smile that was something more than the smile of welcome she had for all. The host too followed Natasha with his eyes, and asked the count which of the girls was his daughter.

"Charming!" he said, kissing his finger-tips.

In the ballroom, guests stood crowding about the entry awaiting the Tsar. The countess and her party were in the front row of this crowd.

Madame Peronsky was pointing out the most distinguished persons at the ball.

"That is the Dutch ambassador, do you see, the grey-haired man," Madame Peronsky was saying, indicating an old man with a profusion of silver-grey curls, who was surrounded by ladies laughing at some story he was telling. "And here she comes, the queen of Petersburg society, Countess Bezuhov," she said, pointing to Helen who had just come in.

"How lovely! Look how attentive all the men are to her, young and old alike. She's both lovely and clever. . . . They say Prince So-and-So is wild about her. And you see these two, though they are not good-looking, they are even more run after."

She pointed out a lady who was crossing the room accompanied by a very ugly daughter.

"That's the heiress of a million," said Madame Peronsky. "And, look, here come her suitors. . . . That's Countess Bezuhov's brother, Anatole Kuragin," she said, pointing to a handsome officer in the Horse Guards, who passed by them looking from the height of his lifted head over the ladies to something beyond them. "He is handsome, isn't he? They say he is to be married to that heiress. And Boris Drubetskoy is very attentive to her too. They say she has millions. Oh, that's the French ambassador himself," she said in answer to the countess's inquiry as to the identity of Caulaincourt. "Just look, he's like some monarch. But yet they're nice. The French are very nice. No people more charming in society!"

"And that stout fellow in spectacles is a universal freemason," said Madame Peronsky, indicating Pierre. "Set him beside his wife: he's a motley fool!"

Swinging his stout frame, Pierre slouched through the crowd, nodding to right and to left, as casually and good-naturedly as though he were walking through a crowd in a market. He made his way through the crowd unmistakably looking for some one.

Natasha looked with joy at the familiar face of Pierre, 'the motley fool,' as Madame Peronsky called him, and knew that it was they, and she in particular, for whom Pierre was searching. Pierre had promised her to be at the ball and to find her partners. But before reaching them, Pierre came to a standstill beside a very handsome, dark man of medium height in the white uniform of a cavalry colonel, who was standing in a window talking to a tall man wearing stars and a ribbon.

Natasha at once recognised the handsome young man in the white uniform. It was Prince André, who seemed to her to have grown much younger, happier, and better looking.

"There's some one else we know, Bolkonsky, do you see, mother?" said Natasha, pointing out Prince André. "Do you remember he stayed a night at home, at Otradnoe?"

"Oh, do you know him?" said Madame Peronsky. "I can't bear him. Every one is crazy over him. And his conceit! It's beyond all bounds! He takes after his father! And he's hand in glove now with Speransky, making out some sort of plans for reform. Just look how he behaves with ladies! She's speaking to him, and he has turned his back on her," she said, pointing to him. "I would soon send him about his business if he were to treat me like that."

There was a sudden stir. The crowd rushed forward, then moved apart, and down the space, the Tsar walked to the strains of the band, which struck up at once. Behind him walked the host and hostess. The Tsar walked in rapidly, bowing to right and to left, as though trying to hurry over the first moments of greeting.

The Tsar went into the drawing-room, the crowd made a dash for the door. The crowd made another rush back, away from the drawing-room door at which the Tsar appeared in conversation with the hostess. A young man, looking distraught, pounced down on the ladies and begged them to move aside. Several, with faces that betrayed a total oblivion of all the rules of decorum, squeezed forward, crushing their dresses. The men began approaching the ladies, and couples were formed for the polonaise.

Then the Tsar, smiling, came out of the drawing-room door, leading the hostess. He was followed by the host. Then came ambassadors, ministers, and various generals, whose names Madame Peronsky never tired of reciting. More than half the ladies had partners, and were taking part, or preparing to take part, in the polonaise.

Natasha felt that she would be left with her mother and Sonya in that minority of the ladies who were crowded back against the wall, and not invited to dance the polonaise. She stood, her thin arms hanging at her sides. She gazed before her with shining, frightened eyes. She took no interest in the Tsar, nor in all the great people Madame Peronsky was pointing out; her mind was filled by one thought: "Is it possible no one will come up to me? Is it possible that I shall not be among the first to dance? Is it possible I shall not be noticed by all these men? No, it cannot be!" she thought.

The strains of the polonaise, which had already lasted some time, were beginning to sound like a melancholy reminiscence to Natasha. She wanted to cry. Madame Peronsky had left them. The count was at the other end of the ballroom, the countess, Sonya, and she stood in that crowd of strangers as lonely as in a forest.

Prince André with a lady passed close by, not recognising them. The handsome Anatole said something smiling to the lady on his arm, and he glanced at Natasha's face as one looks at a wall. Boris passed by them, twice, and each time turned away. Berg and his wife, who were not dancing, came towards them.

This family meeting here, in a ballroom, seemed a humiliating thing to Natasha, as though there were nowhere else for family talk. She did not listen, and did not look at Vera, who said something to her about her own green dress.

At last the Tsar stood still beside the last of his partners. He had danced with three. The music stopped. An anxious-looking adjutant ran up to the Rostovs, begging them to move a little further back, though they were already close to the wall, and from the orchestra came the circumspect, precise, seductively stately rhythm of a waltz. The Tsar glanced with a smile down the ballroom. A moment passed; no one had yet begun. An adjutant, who was a steward, went up to Countess Bezuhov and asked her to dance. Smiling, she raised her hand and laid it on the adjutant's shoulder without looking at him. With confident deliberation and smoothness they broke into the first gallop round the edge of the circle. And through the quickening strains of the music nothing could be heard but the regular jingle of the spurs on the adjutant's rapid, practised feet, and at every third beat the swish of Helen's flying velvet skirt as she whirled round.

Natasha looked at them, and was ready to cry that it was not she dancing that first round of the waltz.

Prince André stood not far from the Rostovs. A baron was talking to him of the proposed first sitting of the State Council. From his intimacy with Speransky, Prince André was in a position to give authoritative information in regard to that sitting, about which the most diverse rumours were current. But he did not hear what the baron was saying to him, and looked from the Tsar to the partners preparing to dance.

Pierre went up to Prince André and took him by the arm.

"You always dance. Here is Natasha, the younger Rostov girl, ask her," he said.

"Where?" asked Prince André. "I beg your pardon," he said, turning to the baron, "we will finish this conversation in another place, but at a ball one must dance." He went in the direction indicated by Pierre. Natasha's despairing, tremulous face broke upon Prince André. He recognised her, guessed her feelings, saw that it was her début, remembered what she had said at the window, and with an expression of pleasure on his face he approached Countess Rostov.

"Permit me to introduce you to my daughter," said the countess, reddening.

"I have the pleasure of her acquaintance already, if the countess remembers me," said Prince André, with a low and courteous bow, which seemed a direct contradiction to Madame Peronsky's remarks about his rudeness. He went up to Natasha, and raised his hand to put it round her waist before he had fully uttered the invitation to dance. Natasha's face brightened at once into a grateful, childlike smile.

"I have been a long while waiting for you," that alarmed and happy young girl's smile seemed to say to him as she raised her hand to his shoulder. They were the second couple that walked forward onto the floor.

And Prince André had no sooner put his arm round that slender, supple waist, and felt Natasha stirring close to him, and smiling close to him, than he felt full of life and youth again.

After Prince André, Boris came up to ask Natasha to dance, and he was followed by the dancing adjutant who had opened the ball, and many other young men. Natasha, flushed and happy, passed on her extra partners to Sonya, and never ceased dancing all the evening. She noticed nothing and saw nothing of what was absorbing every one else at the ball. She did not notice that the Tsar talked a long time with the French ambassador, that his manner was particularly gracious to a certain lady, that Prince So-and-So and Mr. So-and-So had said and done this and that, that Helen's success had been brilliant, and that So-and-So had paid her marked attention. She did not even see the Tsar, and was only aware that he was gone from noticing that the ball became livelier after his departure.

In one of the most enjoyable cotillions before supper, Prince André danced again with Natasha. He reminded her of how he had first seen her in the avenue at Otradnoe, and how she could not sleep on that moonlight night, and told her how he had accidently listened to her. Natasha blushed at these recollections, and tried to excuse herself, as though there were something to be ashamed of.

Like all men who have grown up in society, Prince André liked meeting anything not of the conventional society stamp. And such was Natasha with her wonder, her delight, her shyness. His manner was particularly tender and circumspect as he talked to her. Sitting beside her, and talking of the simplest and most trifling subjects, Prince André admired the radiant brilliance of her eyes and her smile, that had no concern with what was said but was due simply to her own happiness. When Natasha was chosen again, and she got up with a smile and was dancing, Prince André particularly admired her shy grace. In the middle of the cotillion, Natasha went back to her place, breathless at the end of a figure. Another partner again chose her. She was tired and panting, and evidently she thought for an instant of refusing, but immediately she put her hand on her partner's shoulder and was off again gaily, smiling to Prince André.

"I should have been glad to rest and sit by you. I'm tired; but you see how they keep asking me, and I'm glad of it, and I'm happy, and I love every one, and you and I understand all about it," and more, much more was said in that smile. When her partner left her side, Natasha flew across the room to choose two ladies for the figure.

'If she goes first to her cousin and then to another lady, she will be my wife," Prince André—greatly to his own surprise—caught himself saying, as he watched her. She did go first to her cousin.

At that ball Pierre felt humiliated by the position his wife took in the highest court circle. He was sullen and absent-minded. There was a broad furrow right across his forehead, as he stood in a window, staring over his spectacles and seeing no one. Natasha passed close by him on her way in to supper. Pierre's gloomy, unhappy face struck her. She stopped, facing him. She longed to come to his aid, to bestow on him some of her own overflowing happiness. "How delightful it is," she said. "Isn't it?"

Pierre smiled an absent-minded smile, obviously not grasping what was said to him. "Yes, I'm very glad," he said.

"How can people be discontented at anything!" thought Natasha. "Especially any one as nice as Pierre.

She was at that highest pitch of happiness, when one becomes completely good and kind, and disbelieves in the very possibility of evil, unhappiness, and sorrow.

A few days later Prince André paid calls on various people whom he had not visited before, and among them the Rostovs. Apart from politeness, which necessitated a call on the Rostovs, Prince André wanted to see at home that original, eager girl, who had left such a pleasant recollection with him.

Natasha was one of the first to meet him. She was in a blue everyday dress, in which she struck Prince André as looking prettier than in her ball-dress. She and all the family received Prince André like an old friend, simply and cordially. All the family, which Prince André had once criticised so severely, now seemed to him to consist of excellent, simple, kindly people. The hospitality and good-nature of the old count, particularly striking and attractive in Petersburg, was such that Prince André could not refuse to stay to dinner. "Yes, these are good-natured people," he thought. "Of course they have no conception what a treasure they possess in Natasha; but they are good people, who make the best possible background for that charming girl, so full of life!"

Prince André was conscious in Natasha of a special world, utterly remote from him, brimful of joys unknown to him, that strange world which even in the avenue at Otradnoe, and on that moonlight night at the window had tantalised him. Now that no longer tantalised him, it seemed no longer an alien world; but he himself was stepping into it, and finding new pleasures in it.

After dinner Natasha went to the clavichord, at Prince André's request, and began singing. Prince André stood at the window talking to the ladies, and listened to her. In the middle of a phrase, Prince André stopped speaking, and felt suddenly a lump in his throat. He looked at Natasha singing, and something new stirred within him. He was happy, and at the same time he was sad. He certainly had nothing to be sad about, but he was sad. For what? For his past love? For the little princess? For his lost illusions? . . . For his hopes for the future? . . .

It was late in the evening when Prince André left the Rostovs'. He went to bed from the habit of going to bed, but soon saw that he could not sleep. He lighted a candle and sat up in bed; then got up, then lay down again, not in the least wearied by his sleeplessness. He felt a new joy, as though he had come out of a stuffy room into the open daylight. It never occurred to him that he was in love with Natasha. He only pictured her to himself, and the whole of life rose before him in a new light as he did so. "Why do I struggle? Why am I troubled in this narrow, cramped routine, when life, all life, with all its joys, lies open before me?" he said to himself. And for the first time for a very long while, he began making happy plans for the future. He made up his mind that he ought to look after his son's education, to find a tutor, and entrust the child to him. Then he ought to go abroad, see England, Switzerland, Italy. "Pierre was right in saying that one must believe in the possibility of happiness, in order to be happy. Let us leave the dead to bury the dead. But while one is living, one must live and be happy," he thought.

One morning Colonel Adolphe Berg, whom Pierre knew just as he knew every one in Moscow and Petersburg, called upon him. He was wearing a brand-new uniform, and had his powdered locks standing up over his forehead, as worn by the Tsar Alexander.

"I have just been calling on the countess, your wife, and to my misfortune, my request could not be granted. I hope I shall be more fortunate with you, count," he said, smiling.

"What is it you desire, colonel? I am at your disposal."

"I am by now quite settled in my new quarters," Berg informed him, with perfect conviction that to hear this fact could not but be agreeable; "and so I am desirous of giving a little *soirée* for my friends and my wife." He smiled blandly. "I meant to ask the countess and you to do me the honour to come to us for a cup of tea, and . . . to supper."

Only the Countess Bezuhov, who considered it beneath her to associate with nobodies like the Bergs, could have had the cruelty to refuse such an invitation. Berg explained so clearly why he wanted to gather together a small and select company at his new rooms; and why it would be agreeable to him to do so; and why he would grudge spending money on cards, or anything else harmful; but was ready for the sake of good society to incur expense, that Pierre could not refuse, and promised to come.

"Only not late, count, if I may venture to beg. Ten minutes to eight, I venture to beg. We will make up a party for boston. Our general is coming; he is very kind to me. We will have a little supper, count, so I shall esteem it an honour."

Contrary to his usual habit—he was almost always late—Pierre arrived at the Bergs' not at ten minutes to eight, but at a quarter to eight.

The Bergs had made all necessary preparations for their little party, and were quite ready to receive their guests.

Berg and his wife were sitting in a new, clean, light study, furnished with little busts and pictures and new furniture. Berg, with his new uniform closely buttoned up, sat beside his wife, and was explaining to her that one always could and ought to cultivate the acquaintance of people above one, for only then is there anything agreeable in acquaintances. "You pick up something, you can put in a word for something. Look at me now, how I used to manage in the lower grades." Berg reckoned his life not by years but by promotions. "My comrades are nothing still, while I'm a lieutenant-colonel. I have the happiness of being your husband." He got up and kissed Vera's hand, but on the way turned back the corner of the rug, which was out of place. "And how did I obtain all this? Chiefly by knowing how to select my acquaintances. It goes without saying, of course, that one has to be conscientious and punctual in the discharge of one's duties."

Berg smiled with a sense of his own superiority over a mere weak woman, and paused, reflecting that this charming wife of his could never attain all that constituted a man's dignity,— Vera smiled, too, at the same time with a sense of her superiority over her conscientious, excellent husband, who yet, like all men, according to Vera's ideas of them, took such a mistaken view of life.

Berg got up, and cautiously embracing his wife so as not to crush the lace bertha, for which he had paid a large sum, he kissed her on the lips.

"There's only one thing: we mustn't have children too soon," he said, by a connection of ideas of which he was himself unconscious.

"Yes," answered Vera, "I don't at all desire that. We must live for society."

"Princess Yusupov was wearing one just like that," said Berg, pointing with a happy and good-humoured smile to the bertha.

At that moment they were informed that Count Bezuhov had arrived. Both exchanged glances of self-satisfaction, each mentally claiming the credit of this visit.

"See what comes of knowing how to make acquaintances," thought Berg. "See what comes of behaving properly!"

"But, please, when I am entertaining guests," said Vera, "don't interrupt me, because I know what to say in the company of different people."

Pierre was shown into the little drawing-room, in which it was impossible to sit down without disturbing the symmetry, tidiness, and order. But Pierre immediately moved out a chair for himself, and Berg and Vera promptly began their *soirée*, interrupting each other in their efforts to entertain their guest.

Vera, deciding in her own mind that Pierre ought to be entertained with conversation about the French Embassy, promptly embarked upon that subject. Berg, deciding that masculine conversation was what was required, interrupted his wife's remarks by reference to the question of war with

Austria, and made an unconscious jump from that general subject to personal considerations upon the proposal made him to take part in the Austrian campaign, and the reasons which had led him to decline it.

The next to arrive was Boris, an old comrade of Berg's. There was a certain shade of patronage and condescension in his manner. After Boris came a colonel and his lady, then the general himself, then the Rostovs, and the *soirée* now began to be exactly, incontestably, like all other *soirées*. Berg and Vera could hardly repress their smiles of pleasure at the sight, at the sound of the disconnected chatter, and the rustle of skirts and of curtsies. Everything was precisely as everybody always has it; especially so was the general, who admired their rooms, clapped Berg on the shoulder, and with paternal authority insisted on arranging the table for boston. The elderly guests were together, the younger people together, the hostess at the tea-table, on which there were cakes in a silver cake-basket.

Yes, their *soirée* was as like every other *soirée* as two drops of water—with the same conversation and tea and lighted candles.

Pierre, as one of the most honoured guests, was obliged to sit down to boston with the old count, the general, and the colonel. As he sat at the boston-table he happened to be directly facing Natasha and he was struck by the curious change that had come over her since the day of the ball. Natasha was silent, and not only was she not so pretty as she had been at the ball, she would have been positively plain but for the look of gentle indifference to everything in her face.

"What is wrong with her?" Pierre wondered, glancing at her. She was sitting by her sister at the tea-table; she gave reluctant answers to Boris at her side and did not look at him. After playing all of one suit and taking five tricks to his partner's satisfaction, Pierre, having caught the sound of greetings and the steps of some one entering glanced in her direction again.

Prince André was standing before her saying something to her with an expression of tenderness on his face. She was looking at him, flushing crimson. And the vivid glow of some inner fire that had been quenched before was alight in her again. She was utterly transformed. From a plain girl she was once more the beautiful creature she had been at the ball.

Several times Pierre changed his seat during the game, sitting sometimes with his back to Natasha, sometimes facing her. And during all the six rubbers he watched her and Prince André.

"Something is happening between them," thought Pierre, and a feeling at once of gladness and of bitterness made him forgetful of the game.

The general got up irritated, saying it was of no use playing like that, and Pierre was at liberty. Berg quickly drew them all into conversation. And the *soirée* continued just as successfully as before.

The next day Prince André went to dine at the Rostovs' and spent the whole day with them.

Every one in the house knew on whose account Prince André came, and he openly tried to be all day long with Natasha.

Not only in the soul of Natasha—scared, but happy—in the whole household, too, there was a feeling of awe, of something of great gravity being bound to happen. With sorrowful and sternly serious eyes the countess looked at Prince André as he talked to Natasha, and shyly and self-consciously tried to begin some insignificant talk with him as soon as he looked round at her. Sonya was afraid to leave Natasha, and afraid of being in their way if she stayed with them. Natasha turned pale in a panic of expectation every time she was left for a moment alone with him. Prince André's timidity impressed her. She felt that he wanted to tell her something, but could not bring himself up to the point.

When Prince André had gone away in the evening, the countess went up to Natasha and whispered: "Well?"

"Mother, for God's sake, don't ask me anything just now," said Natasha.

But in spite of this answer, Natasha lay a long while in her mother's bed that night, her eyes fixed before her, excited and scared. She told her mother how Prince André had praised her, how he had said he was going abroad and how he had asked where they were going to spend the summer.

"Nothing like this, like this . . . I have never felt before!" she said. "Only I'm afraid with him, I'm always afraid with him. What does that mean? Does it mean that it's the real thing? Mother, are you asleep?"

"No, my darling. I'm afraid of him myself," answered her mother. "Go to bed."

"I can't go to sleep! Mother! Nothing like this have I ever felt before," she said, with wonder and terror at the feeling she recognised in herself. "And could we ever have dreamed! . . ."

It seemed to Natasha that she had fallen in love with Prince André the first time she saw him at Otradnoe. She was terrified at the strange, unexpected happiness that the man she had chosen even then (she was firmly convinced that she had done so)—that that very man should meet them again now.

"And it seems as though it all happened on purpose—his coming to Petersburg just while we are here. And our meeting at that ball. It was all fate. It's clear that it is fate, that it has all led up to this. Even then, as soon as I saw him, I felt something quite different."

"What has he said to you?" said the mother thoughtfully.

"Mother, does it matter his being a widower?"

"Hush, Natasha. Pray to God. Marriages are made in heaven," she said, quoting the French proverb.

"Mother, darling, how I love you! How happy I am!" cried Natasha, hugging her mother.

At that very time Prince André was telling Pierre of his love for Natasha and of his determination to marry her.

That evening the Countess Helen Bezuhov gave a reception. The French ambassador was there, and a royal prince who had become a very frequent visitor at the countess's of late and many brilliant ladies and gentlemen. Pierre came down, wandered through the rooms and impressed all the guests by his look of gloom.

Pierre had been feeling one of his attacks of depression coming upon him ever since the day of the ball and had been making desperate efforts to struggle against it. Since his wife's intrigue with the royal prince, Pierre had been to his surprise appointed a gentleman-in-waiting, and ever since he had felt a sense of weariness and shame in court society, and his old ideas of the vanity of all things human began to come back often. The feeling he had lately noticed between Natasha and Prince André had aggravated his gloom by the contrast between his own position and his friend's. He tried equally to avoid thinking of his wife and also of Natasha and Prince André. Again everything seemed to him insignificant in comparison with eternity; again the question rose before him: "What for?" And for days and nights together he forced himself to work at masonic labours, hoping to force his gloom away.

Pierre had come out of the countess's apartments at midnight, and was sitting in a shabby dressing-gown at the table in his own low-pitched, smoke-blackened room upstairs, copying out long transactions of the Scottish freemasons, when some one came into his room. It was Prince André.

"Oh, it's you," said Pierre, with a preoccupied and dissatisfied air. "I'm at work, you see," he added, pointing to the manuscript book with that look of escaping from the ills of life with which unhappy people look at their work.

Prince André stood before Pierre, and with the egoism of happiness smiled at him without noticing his gloomy face.

"Well, Pierre," he said, "I wanted to tell you yesterday, and I have come to do so to-day. I am in love."

"With Natasha?" Pierre asked.

"Yes, yes, who else could it be? I would never have believed it, but the feeling is too strong for me. Yesterday I was in torment, in agony, but I would not exchange that agony for anything in the world. I have never lived till now, but I cannot live without her. But can she love me? . . . I'm too old for her. . . . Why don't you speak? . . ."

"I? I? What did I tell you?" said Pierre, suddenly getting up and walking about the room. "I always thought so. . . . That girl is a treasure. . . . She's a very rare sort of girl. . . . My dear André, don't, I entreat you, be too wise, don't doubt, marry, marry, marry! . . . And I am sure no man was ever happier than you will be."

"But she?"

"She loves you."

"Don't talk nonsense . . ." said Prince André, smiling and looking into Pierre's face.

"She loves you, I know it," Pierre cried angrily.

"No. Do listen," said Prince André, taking hold of him by the arm and stopping him. "I must talk about it to some one."

"Well, well, talk away. I'm very glad," said Pierre, and his face did really change. The line of care in his brow was smoothed away, and he listened gladly to Prince André. His friend seemed an utterly different man. What had become of his boredom, his contempt of life, his disillusionment? Pierre was the only person to whom he could have brought himself to speak quite openly; but to him he did reveal all that was in his heart. Readily and boldly he made plans reaching far into the future; said he could not sacrifice his own happiness to the caprices of his father; declared that he would force his father to agree to the marriage and like her, or dispense with his consent altogether. Then he marvelled at the feeling which had taken possession of him, as something strange and apart, independent of himself.

"I should never have believed it, if any one had told me I could love like this," said Prince André. "It is utterly different from the feeling I once had. The whole world is split into two halves for me: one—she, and there all is happiness, hope, and light; the other half—all where she is not, there all is dejection and darkness. . . ."

To get married the old prince's consent was needed. And to obtain this Prince André set off at once for Bleak Hills.

The old prince received his son's news with external composure, but with inward wrath. He could not comprehend how any one could want to alter his life, to introduce any new element into it, when life was for him so near its end. "If they would only let me live my life out as I want to, and then do as they like," the old man said to himself. With his son, however, he made use of that diplomacy to which he always had resort in cases of gravity. Assuming a calm tone, he went into the whole question judicially.

In the first place, the marriage was not a brilliant one from the point of view of birth, fortune, or distinction. Secondly, Prince André was not in his first youth, and was delicate in health. The old man laid special stress on this. And besides the girl was very young. Thirdly, there was his son, whom it would be a pity to entrust to a mere girl. "Fourthly, and finally," said the father, looking ironically at his son, "I beg you to defer the matter for a year. Go abroad, and get well. Find a German, as you want to do so, for little Prince Nicholas, and then, if your love, your passion, your obstinacy—what you choose—are so great, then get married. And that's my last word on the subject. You know, the last . . ." the old prince concluded, in a tone that showed that nothing would compel him to alter his decision.

Prince André saw clearly that the old man hoped that either his love or that of Natasha would not stand the test of a year or that he, the old prince, would die himself in the course of it. And he decided to act in accordance with his father's wish; to propose to Natasha and to defer the marriage for a year.

Three weeks after his last visit to the Rostovs, Prince André returned to Petersburg.

The day following her conversation with her mother, Natasha expected Prince André but he did not come. The next day, and the third, it was just the same. Pierre too stayed away, and Natasha, not knowing Prince André had gone away to see his father, did not know how to interpret his absence.

So passed the three weeks. Natasha would not go out anywhere, and wandered like a shadow about the house, idle and listless, wept at night in secret, and did not go in to her mother in the evenings. She was continually flushing and very irritable. It seemed to her that every one knew of her disappointment, was laughing at her, and pitying her. The wound to her vanity aggravated her misery.

She came in to the countess one day, tried to say something, and all at once burst into tears. Her tears were the tears of an offended child, who does not know why it is being punished. The countess tried to comfort Natasha. At first she listened to her mother's words, but suddenly she interrupted her:

"Stop, mother, I don't think of him or want to think of him! Why, he kept coming . . . And he has left off. And he has left off . . ." Her voice quivered, she almost began to cry, but recovered herself, and went on calmly: "And I don't want to be married at all. And I'm afraid of him. I have got over it now . . ."

The day after this conversation, Natasha put on the old dress she specially associated with the fun she had often had when wearing it in the mornings, and began from early morning to take up her old manner of life, which she had given up ever since the ball. After morning tea, she went into the big hall, which she particularly liked on account of the loud resonance in it, and began singing her vocal exercises. When she had finished the first exercise she stood still in the middle of the room and repeated a single musical phrase which particularly pleased her. She listened with delight, as though it were new to her, to the charm of these notes ringing out, filling the empty space of the great room and dying slowly away. And she felt all at once cheerful. "Why think so much about it. Things are nice even as they are," she said to herself. And she began walking up and down the room. Passing by the looking-glass, she glanced into it. "Yes, that's me!" the expression of her face seemed to say at the sight of herself. "Well, and very nice too. And I need nobody."

A footman wanted to come in to clear away something in the room, but she would not let him. She shut the door, and continued her promenade about the room. She had come back that morning to her favourite mood of loving herself. "What a charming creature that Natasha is!" she said again of herself, speaking as some third person, a generic, masculine person. "Pretty. A voice. Young. And she's in nobody's way, only leave her in peace." But, however much she might be left in peace, she could not now be at peace, and she felt that immediately.

In the vestibule the hall-door opened. Someone was asking, "At home?" and steps were audible. It was *he*. Natasha knew it for certain.

Pale and panic-stricken, she flew into the drawing-room. "Mother! Prince André has come," she said. "Mother! I don't want . . . to be tortured! What am I to do?"

The countess had not time to answer her before Prince André walked into the drawing-room. As soon as he saw Natasha his face beamed with delight. He kissed the countess's hand and Natasha's, and sat down beside the sofa.

"It's a long while since we have had the pleasure . . ." the countess was beginning, but Prince André cut her short, answering her implied question, and obviously in haste to say what he had to say.

"I have not been to see you all this time because I have been to see my father. I had to talk over a very important matter with him. I only returned last night," he said, glancing at Natasha. "I want to have a talk with you, countess," he added after a moment's silence.

The countess dropped her eyes.

"Run away, Natasha; I will call you," the countess whispered.

With frightened and imploring eyes Natasha glanced at Prince André and at her mother, and went out.

"I have come, countess, to ask for your daughter's hand," said Prince André.

The countess's face flushed hotly, but she said nothing.

"Your offer . . ." the countess began at last, sedately. He sat silent, looking into her face. "Your offer . . ." She hesitated in confusion. "Your offer is agreeable to us, and . . . I accept. I am glad of it. And my husband . . . I hope . . . but it must rest with Natasha . . ."

And she held out her hand to Prince André, and with mingled feelings of aversion and tenderness she pressed her lips to his forehead as he bent to kiss her hand. Her wish was to love him as a son. But she felt that he was a man alien to her. And she was afraid of him.

"I will send her to you," said the countess, and she went out of the room.

Natasha was in her bedroom. She was sitting on her bed, with a pale face and dry eyes. She was gazing at the holy picture, and murmuring something to herself as she rapidly crossed herself. Seeing her mother she leaped up and flew towards her.

"Well, mother . . . Well?"

"Go, go to him. He asks for your hand," said the countess, coldly. . . . "Yes . . . go . . ." the mother murmured as her daughter ran off.

Natasha could not have said how she reached the drawing-room. As she entered the door and caught sight of Prince André, she stopped: "Is it possible that this stranger has now become *everything* to me?" she asked herself, and instantly answered: "Yes, everything. He alone is dearer to me now than everything in the world."

Prince André walked towards her. "I have loved you from the first minute I saw . . ."

She came nearer to him and stopped. He took her hand and kissed it.

"Do you love me?"

"Yes, yes," said Natasha, almost angrily. And she burst into sobs.

"What is it? What's the matter?"

"Oh, I am so happy," she answered, smiling through her tears. She came closer to him, thought a second, as though wondering whether it were possible, and then kissed him on the lips.

Prince André held her hands, looked into her eyes and suddenly he could find no trace of his former love for her in his heart. Some strange reaction seemed to have taken place in his soul. There was none of the poetic and mysterious charm of desire left in it. Instead of that there was pity for her feminine and childish weakness, terror at her devotion and trustfulness, an irksome, yet sweet, sense of duty, binding him to her for ever.

"Forgive me," said Prince André after a silence. "But you are so young, and I have had so much experience with life. I am afraid for you. You don't know yourself. . . . My father has made it an express condition that our marriage cannot take place for a year. I shall go abroad . . ."

Natasha listened, trying to take in the meaning of his words. But she did not understand them.

"Hard as that year will be to me, delaying my happiness," continued Prince André, "in that time you will be sure of yourself. I beg you to make me happy in a year. But you are free. Our engagement shall be kept a secret, and if you should find out that you do not love me, or if you should come to love . . ." said Prince André with a forced smile.

"Why do you say that?" Natasha interrupted. "You know that from the very day when you first came to Otradnoe, I have loved you," she said, firmly persuaded that she was speaking the truth.

"In a year you will learn to know yourself. . . ."

"A whole year!" cried Natasha suddenly, only now grasping that their marriage was to be deferred for a year. "But why a year? . . . Why a year? . . ."

Prince André began to explain to her the reasons for this delay. Natasha did not hear him.

"And can't it be helped?" she asked. Prince André did not answer but his face expressed the impossibility of altering this decision.

"It's awful! It's awful!" Natasha cried, and she broke into sobs again. "I shall die if I have to wait a year. It's impossible. It's awful." She glanced at Prince André's face and saw a look of perplexity on it.

"No, no, I'll do anything," she said, suddenly checking her tears. "I'm so happy!"

There was no formal announcement made of the engagement. Prince André insisted upon that. He said that since he was responsible for the delay of their marriage, he ought to bear the whole burden of it. He said that he was bound for ever by his word, but he did not want to bind Natasha and would leave her perfect freedom. If in another six months she were to feel that she did not love him, she would have a perfect right to refuse him.

It need hardly be said that neither Natasha nor her parents would hear of this possibility. But Prince André insisted on having his own way. Prince André came every day to the Rostovs', but he did not behave with Natasha as though he were engaged to her; he addressed her formally and kissed only her hand.

Still from that day on the house was full of that atmosphere of dullness and silence, which always accompanies the presence of an engaged couple. Often as they all sat together every one was silent. Sometimes the others got up and went away, and the engaged pair were still as mute when they were left alone. Rarely they spoke of their future life together. Prince André felt frightened and ashamed to speak of it. Natasha shared the feeling, as she did all his feelings, which she never failed to guess.

The old count sometimes came up to Prince André, kissed him and asked his advice about some question relating to Peter's education or Nicholas' position. The old countess sighed as she looked at them. Sonya was afraid every instant of being in their way, and was always trying to find excuses for leaving them alone, even when they had no wish to be alone. When Prince André talked—he described things very well—Natasha listened to him with pride. When she talked, she noticed with joy and dread that he watched her with an intent and scrutinising look. She asked herself in perplexity: "What is it he seeks in me? What is it he is probing for with that look? What if I haven't in me what he is searching for?" Sometimes she fell into the mood of wild gaiety characteristic of her, and then she particularly loved to see and hear how Prince André laughed. He rarely laughed, but when he did laugh she always felt herself drawn closer to him.

On the day before Prince André was to leave Petersburg, he brought with him Pierre, who had not been at the Rostovs' since the day of the ball. Pierre seemed absent-minded and embarrassed. He talked chiefly to the countess. Natasha was sitting at the chess-board with Sonya, and invited Prince André to join them.

"You have known Pierre a long while, haven't you?" he asked. "Do you like him?"

"Yes; he's very nice, but very absurd."

And Natasha began, as people always did when speaking

of Pierre, to tell anecdotes of his absent-mindedness, anecdotes which were made up about him.

"You know, I have confided our secret to him," said Prince André. "I have known him from childhood. He has a heart of gold. I beg you, Natasha," he said, with sudden seriousness, "I am going away; God knows what may happen. You may change . . . Oh, I know I ought not to speak of that. Only one thing—if anything were to happen to you, while I am away . . .

"What could happen?"

"If any trouble were to come," continued Prince André. "I beg you, Sonya, if anything were to happen, to go to him and no one else for advice and help. He has the truest heart."

Neither her father nor her mother, neither Sonya nor Prince André could have foreseen the effect of the parting on Natasha. She wandered about the house all that day, flushed, excited, and tearless, busying herself about the most trivial matters as though she had no notion of what was before her. She did not weep even at the moment when Prince André kissed her hand for the last time.

"Don't go away!" was all she said, in a voice that made him wonder whether he ought not really to remain, and that he remembered long after. When he had gone, she still did not weep. But for several days she sat in her room, taking no interest in anything, and only saying from time to time: "Oh, why did he go?"

But a few days later she became herself again, only with a change in her spirit, such as one finds in the faces of children after a long illness.

After Prince André had gone abroad his old father's health declined. He became more irritable than ever, and it was Princess Mary who bore the brunt of his outbursts. He seemed to seek out tender spots so as to inflict on her the cruellest wounds possible. Princess Mary had two passions and consequently two joys: her nephew, little Nicholas, and religion. And both were favourite subjects for the old prince's attacks and jeers. Whatever was being spoken of, he would bring the conversation round to the superstitiousness of old maids, or the petting and spoiling of children. "You want to make little Nicholas into an old maid like you are. Prince André wants a son and not an old maid," he would say. Or addressing Mademoiselle Bourienne he would ask her, before Princess Mary, how she liked the village priests and holy pictures, and make jokes about them. . . .

He was constantly wounding Princess Mary's feelings, but his daughter needed no effort to forgive him. Could he be to blame in anything he did to her. Could her father, who as she knew in spite of it all, loved her, be unjust? And indeed what is justice? Princess Mary never gave a thought to that proud word, "justice." All the complex laws of humanity were summed up for her in one clear and simple law—the law of love and self-sacrifice, laid down by Him who had in His love suffered for humanity, though He was God Himself. What had she to do with the justice or injustice of other people? All she had to do was to suffer and to love. And that she did.

In the winter before going abroad Prince André had come to Bleak Hills, had been gay, gentle, and affectionate, as Princess Mary had not seen him for years. She felt that something had happened to him, but he said nothing to his sister of his love. Before his departure, Prince André had a long conversation with his father, and Princess Mary noticed that they were ill pleased with each other at parting.

Soon after Prince André had gone, Princess Mary wrote from Bleak Hills to her friend in Petersburg, Julie Karagin, whom Princess Mary had dreamed—as girls always do dream—of marrying to her brother. Julie was at this time in mourning for the death of a brother, who had been killed in Turkey.

"Sorrow, it seems, is our common lot, my sweet and tender friend Julie," wrote Princess Mary.

"Religion, and religion alone can—I don't say comfort us—but save us from despair. Religion alone can interpret to us what man cannot comprehend; why the good are called away to God, while the wicked, the useless, a burden to themselves and others, are left living. The first death which I have seen, and which I shall never forget—the death of my sister-in-law—made on me just the same impression. Just as you question destiny, and ask why your brother had to die, so did I wonder what reason there was for Liza to die, she who had never done the slightest harm to any one, never even had a thought in her heart that was not kind. And yet—do you know, five years have passed since then, and even I begin to understand clearly why she should die, and in what way that death was but an expression of the boundless grace of the Creator, all of whose acts are but manifestations of His infinite love for His creatures. That early and terrible death has had the most blessed influence on me and on my brother, in spite of all our grief. At the time, at the moment of our loss, I could not have entertained such thoughts; at that time I should have dismissed them in horror, but now it seems clear and incontestable. I write all this to you, dear friend, simply to convince you of the Gospel truth, which has become a principle of life for me. Not one hair of our head falls without His will. And the guiding principle of His will is only His infinite love for us, and so whatever may befall us, all is for our good.

"My father's health is noticeably weaker; he cannot endure contradiction and is easily irritated. This irritability is, as you are aware, most readily aroused on political subjects. He cannot endure the idea that Bonaparte is treating on equal terms with all the sovereigns of Europe, especially our own, the grandson of the great Catherine! As you know, I take absolutely no interest in politics, but from my father and his conversations with Mihail Ivanovitch, I know all that goes on in the world, and have heard of all the honours conferred on Bonaparte. It seems that Bleak Hills is now the only spot on the globe where he is not recognised as a great man—still less as Emperor of France.

"Our home life goes on in its old way, except for the absence of my brother André. As I wrote to you before, he has greatly changed of late. It is only of late, during this year that he seems to have quite recovered from the shock of his loss. He has become again just as I knew him as a child, good-natured, affectionate. He feels now, it seems to me, that life is not over for him. But he is thinner than ever and more nervous. I feel anxious about him and glad that he is taking this tour abroad, which the doctors prescribed long ago. I hope that it will help him.

"I wonder at the way reports fly from Petersburg to Moscow, and especially such groundless ones as the rumour you wrote to me about, of my brother's supposed engagement to the little Rostov girl. I don't imagine that André will ever marry any one at all, and certainly not her. And I will tell you why. In the first place, I know that though he rarely speaks of his late wife, the grief of his loss has penetrated too deeply into his heart. Secondly, because, as far as I can ascertain, that girl is not one of the kind of women who could attract my brother André. I do not believe that André has chosen her for his wife. And I will frankly confess, I should not wish for such a thing.

"But how I have been running on; I am finishing my second sheet! Farewell, my sweet friend; and may God keep you in His holy and mighty care. My dear companion, Mademoiselle Bourienne, sends you kisses.

MARY."

In the middle of the summer Princess Mary received a letter from Prince André, who was in Switzerland. In it he told her strange and surprising news. He informed his sister of his engagement to Natasha. His whole letter was full of loving enthusiasm for his fiancée.

He wrote that he had never loved as he loved now, and that it was only now that he saw all the value and meaning of life. He begged his sister to forgive him for having said nothing of his plans to her on his last visit to Bleak Hills, though he had spoken of them to his father. He had said nothing to her for fear she would beg her father to give his immediate consent, and, without attaining her object, would irritate her father and draw all the weight of his displeasure upon herself. The matter was not, however, then, he wrote to her, so completely settled as now. "At that time father insisted on a delay of a year, and now *six months,* half of the period is over. If it were not for the doctors keeping me here at the waters I should be back in Russia myself; but, as it is, I must put off my return for another three months. You know me and my relations with father. I want nothing from him. I have been, and always shall be, independent. But to act in opposition to his will, to incur his anger when he has perhaps not long left to be with us, would destroy half my happiness. I am enclosing a letter to him, and I beg you to choose a favourable moment to give it to him. Let me know how he looks at the whole matter, and if there is any hope of his agreeing to shorten the year by three months."

After long hesitations, doubts, and prayers, Princess Mary gave the letter to her father.

The next day the old prince said to her calmly: "Write to your brother to wait till I'm dead. . . . He won't have long to wait. I shall soon set him free."

The princess tried to answer, but her father would not let her speak, and went on, getting louder and louder. "Let him marry, let him marry! . . . A nice connection! . . . Clever people, eh? Rich, eh? Oh yes, a fine stepmother for little Nicholas she'll make! You write to him he can marry her to-morrow. Little Nicholas shall have her for a stepmother, and I'll marry little Bourienne! . . . Ha, ha, ha, and so he shall have a stepmother too! Only there's one thing, I won't have any more women-folk about my house; he may marry and go and live by himself. Perhaps you'll go and live with him too?" He turned to Princess Mary: "You're welcome to, and good luck to you!"

After this outburst the prince did not once refer to the subject again. But his repressed anger at his son's behaviour found vent in his treatment of his daughter. He now added to his former subjects for jeering and annoying her a new one—allusions to a stepmother and gallantries to Mademoiselle Bourienne.

"Why shouldn't I marry her?" he would say to his daughter. "A fine princess she will make!" And later, to her amazement, Princess Mary began to notice that her father was really beginning to attach himself more and more closely to the Frenchwoman.

Little Nicholas, her brother André and religion were Princess Mary's joys and consolations. But apart from those, Princess Mary cherished, in the deepest secrecy of her heart, a hidden dream and hope that was the source of the chief comfort in her life. This comforting dream and hope was given her by "God's folk"—the crazy prophets and the pilgrims, who visited her without her father's knowledge.

The longer Princess Mary lived, the more she wondered at the shortsightedness of men, who seek here on earth for enjoyment, toil, suffer, strive and do each other harm to attain that impossible, visionary, and sinful happiness. Prince André had loved a wife; she died. That was not enough for him, he wanted to bind his happiness to another woman. Her father did not want that, because he coveted a more distinguished or a wealthier match for André. And they were all striving, and suffering, and in torment, and sullying their souls, their eternal souls, to attain a bliss the duration of which was but a moment. Not only do we know that for ourselves. Christ, the Son of God, came down upon earth and told us that this life is but for a moment, is but a probation; yet we still cling to it and think to find happiness in it. "How is it no one has realised that?" Princess Mary wondered. "No one but these despised people of God who come to me by the back stairs, afraid of my father catching sight of them, and not from fear of ill-usage, but from fear of tempting him to sin. To leave home and country, give up all thoughts of worldly blessings, and clinging to nothing, to wander from place to place in a home-spun smock under a different name, doing people no harm, but praying for them, praying equally for those who drive them away and those who help them; higher than that truth and that life there is no truth and no life!"

There was one Pilgrim-woman, Fedosyushka, a quiet, little woman of about fifty, marked by smallpox, who had been wandering for over thirty years barefooted and wearing chains. Princess Mary was particularly fond of her. One day when sitting in a dark room, lighted only by the lamp before the holy picture, Fedosyushka told her about her life. Princess Mary felt all at once so strongly that Fedosyushka was the one person who had found the right way of life, that she resolved to go on a pilgrimage herself. When Fedosyushka had gone to bed Princess Mary pondered a long while over it, and at last made up her mind that—however strange it might be—she must go on a pilgrimage. She confided her intention to no one but a monk, Father Akinfy, and this priest approved. On the pretence of getting presents for pilgrim women, Princess Mary prepared for herself the complete outfit of a pilgrim: a smock, plaited shoes, a full-skirted coat, and a black kerchief. Often she went to her secret wardrobe, where she kept them, and stood in uncertainty whether the time to carry out her plan had come or not.

Often as she listened to the pilgrims' tales, their simple phrases—that had become mechanical to them, but were to her ears full of the deepest significance—worked upon her till she was several times ready to throw up everything and run away from home. In imagination she already saw herself with Fedosyushka in a coarse smock, trudging along the dusty road with her bundle and her staff, going on her pilgrimage, free from envy, free from earthly love, free from all desires, from one saint to another; and at last thither where there is neither sorrow nor sighing, but everlasting joy and blessedness.

"I shall come to one place. I shall pray there, and before I have time to grow used to it, to love it, I shall go on further. And I shall go on till my legs give way under me and I lie down somewhere, and reach at last that quiet, eternal haven, where is neither sorrow nor sighing! . . ." thought Princess Mary.

But then at the sight of her father, and of little Nicholas, she wavered in her resolution, wept in secret, and felt that she was a sinner, that she loved her father and her nephew more than God.

1810—1811

BOOK SEVEN

NICHOLAS ROSTOV remained in the Pavlograd regiment, in command of the squadron that had been Denisov's.

Rostov had become a bluff, good-natured fellow, who would have been thought rather rough by his old acquaintances in Moscow, though he was loved and respected by his comrades, his subordinates, and his superior officers, and was well content with his life. Of late—in the year 1809—he had found more and more frequently in letters from home complaints on the part of his mother that their financial position was going from bad to worse, and that it was high time for him to come home.

Nicholas dreaded their wanting to drag him out of the surroundings in which, by fencing himself off from all the complexities of existence, he was living so quietly and peacefully.

He felt that sooner or later he would have to plunge again into that whirlpool of life, with many difficulties and business to attend to, with the steward's accounts, with quarrels and intrigues, and ties, with society, with Sonya's love and his promise to her. All that was terribly difficult and complicated; and he answered his mother with cold letters in French, saying nothing of coming home.

In 1810 he received letters from home in which he was told of Natasha's engagement to Prince André, and of the marriage being deferred for a year, because the old prince would not consent to it. This letter mortified Nicholas. In the first place, he was sorry to be losing Natasha, whom he cared more for than all the rest of the family. Secondly, from his hussar point of view, he regretted not having been at home at the time, as he would have shown this Prince André that it was by no means such an honour to be connected with him, and that if he cared for Natasha he could get on just as well without his crazy old father's consent. For a moment Nicholas hesitated whether to ask for leave, so as to see Natasha engaged, but then the manœuvres were just coming on, and thoughts of Sonya, of complications, recurred to him, and again he put it off. But in the spring of the same year he got a letter from his mother, written without his father's knowledge. She wrote that if Nicholas did not come and look after things, their whole estate would have to be sold at auction, and they would all be beggars. The count was so weak, put such entire confidence in Mitenka, and was so good-natured, that things were going from bad to worse. "I beseech you, for God's sake, to come at once, if you don't want to make me and all your family miserable," wrote the countess.

Nicholas told Lavrushka—he had kept on Denisov's old valet—and the comrades who dropped in that evening, that he had applied for leave and was going home. It was strange and difficult for him to believe that he was going away without hearing from the staff whether he had been promoted to be a captain or had received the St. Anne for the last manœuvres. It was strange to him to think of going away like this without having sold Count Goluhovsky his three roan horses, over which the Polish count was haggling with him. Rostov had taken a bet that he would get two thousand for them. It seemed inconceivable that without him the ball could take place which the hussars were to give in honour of their favourite Polish belle, Madame Pshazdetsky, to outdo the Uhlans, who had given a ball to their favourite belle, Madame Borzhozovsky. Yet he knew he must leave this world, where all was well and all was clear, to go where all was nonsensical and complicated.

A week later permission for his leave came. His comrades—not only in the regiment, but throughout the whole brigade—gave Nicholas a dinner that cost fifteen roubles a head. Two bands of musicians played, two choruses sang; Nicholas danced the *trepak* with Major Bazov; the drunken officers tossed him in the air, hugged him, dropped him; the soldiers of the third squadron tossed him once more and shouted hurrah! Then they put Nicholas in a sledge and escorted him as far as the first posting-station on his way.

For the first half of the journey all Rostov's thoughts turned to what he had left behind—to his squadron. But after being jolted over the first half of the journey, he began to forget his three roans and his quartermaster, and he wondered uneasily what he should find on reaching Otradnoe. The nearer he got, the more intense were his thoughts of home.

After the excitement of the first meeting, and the strange feeling of disappointment after his expectations—the feeling that "it's just the same; why was I in such a hurry?"—Nicholas began to settle down in his old world of home. His father and mother were just the same, only a little older. All that was new in them was a certain uneasiness and at times a difference of opinion, which he had never seen between them before, and soon learned to be due to the difficulties of their position.

Sonya was nearly twenty. She would grow no prettier now; there was no promise in her of more to come; but what she had was enough. She was brimming over with love and happiness. And her faithful, steadfast love for him gladdened his heart. Peter and Natasha surprised Nicholas more than all the rest. Peter was a big, handsome lad of thirteen, whose voice was already cracking. Nicholas did not get over his wonder at Natasha for a long while, and laughed as he looked at her.

"You're utterly different," he told her.

"How? Uglier?"

"No, quite the contrary. But what dignity! A real princess!" he whispered to her.

"Yes, yes, yes," cried Natasha gleefully.

Natasha told him all the story of Prince André, of his visit to Otradnoe, and showed him his last letter.

"Well, are you glad?" asked Natasha. "I'm so happy."

"Very glad," answered Nicholas. "He's a fine fellow. Are you very much in love?"

"How shall I say?" answered Natasha. "I was in love with Boris, with Denisov; but this is utterly different. I know there is no one better than he in the world, and so I am calm now and content. It's utterly different from anything before . . ."

Nicholas complained about the marriage being put off for

a year. But Natasha fell on him with exasperation, proving to him that no other course was possible, that it would be a horrid thing to enter a family against the father's will, and that she would not consent to it herself.

"You don't understand at all, at all," she kept saying.

Nicholas paused a moment, and then said he agreed with her.

In the early part of his visit at home Nicholas was serious and even dull. He was worried by the necessity of meddling in the stupid business matters which his mother wanted him to look after. To be rid of this burden as soon as possible, on the third day after his return, he marched angrily off to Mitenka's lodge, and demanded from him an account in full. What he meant by an account in full, Nicholas knew even less than the panic-stricken and bewildered Mitenka. The conversation and Mitenka's accounts did not last long. The village elder, the deputy, and the village clerk, waiting in the entry of the lodge, heard with awe and delight at first the booming and snapping of the young count's voice, then terrible words of abuse, flung one after another.

"Robber! Ungrateful brute! . . . I'll thrash the dog! . . . Not father to deal with . . . Plundering us . . ." and so on.

Then, with no less awe and delight, they saw the young count dragging Mitenka out by the collar, kicking him at every appropriate moment between his words, and shouting: "Away with you! Never let me set eyes on you, thief!"

Mitenka flew head first down six steps and ran to the shrubbery. This shrubbery was well known as a haven of refuge for delinquents at Otradnoe. Mitenka had, on coming home drunk from the town, himself hidden in the shrubbery, and many of the residents of Otradnoe had been indebted to the saving power of this shrubbery when anxious to conceal themselves from Mitenka.

Mitenka's wife and sister-in-law, with frightened faces, peeped into the passage from the door of their room, where a bright samovar was boiling.

The young count walked by, taking no notice of them, and went into the house.

The countess heard at once through her maids of what had been happening in the lodge, and on one side was comforted by the reflection that now their position would be sure to improve, though on the other hand she was uneasy as to the effect of the scene on her son. She went several times on tiptoe to his door, and listened as he lighted one pipe after another.

The next day the old count drew his son to one side, and, with a timid smile, said to him, "But you know, my dear boy, you had no reason to be so angry. Mitenka has told me all about it."

"I knew," thought Nicholas, "that I should never make head or tail of anything in this crazy world."

"You were angry at his not having put down these seven hundred and eight roubles. But you see they were carried forward by double entry and you didn't look at the next page."

"Father, he's a thief, I am certain. And what I have done, I have done. But if you don't wish it, I will say nothing to him."

"No, my dear boy!" The old count was confused. He was conscious that he had mismanaged his wife's estate and had wronged his children. "No, I beg you to go into things. I am old. I . . ."

"No, father, forgive me if I have done what you dislike. I know less about it than you do."

"Damn them all, these peasants, and money matters and double entries," he thought. "I used once to understand scoring at cards, but bookkeeping by the double entry is quite beyond me," he said to himself. And from that time he did not meddle further with the management of the family affairs. But one day the countess called her son into her room, told him that she had a promisory note from Anna Drubetskoy for two thousand roubles, and asked Nicholas what he thought best to do about it.

"Well," answered Nicholas, "you say that it rests with me. I don't like Anna Drubetskoy, and I don't like her son Boris. But they were our friends, and they were poor. So that's what I would do!" and he tore up the note and by so doing made the countess sob with tears of joy.

After this young Rostov took no further part in business of any sort, but devoted himself with passionate interest to hunting which was kept up on a lavish scale on the old count's estate.

Count Rostov had given up being a marshal of nobility, because that position involved too heavy an expenditure. But his difficulties were not removed by that. And he often spoke of selling the sumptuous ancestral house of the Rostovs and the estate near Moscow.

When the count was no longer marshal it was not necessary to entertain on such a large scale, and the Rostovs led a quieter life at Otradnoe than in former years. But the immense house and the lodges were still full of people; more than twenty still sat down to table with them. These were all their own people almost members of the family, or persons who must, it seemed, live in the count's house. Such were

Dimmler, the music-master, and his wife; Vogel, the dancing-master, with his family; an old Madame Byelov, and many others besides; Peter's tutors, the girls' old governess, and persons who simply found it better or more profitable to live at the count's than in a house of their own.

The Rostovs did not entertain so many guests as before, but they still lived in that manner, apart from which the count and countess could not have conceived of life at all. There was still the same hunting establishment, increased indeed by Nicholas. There were still the same fifty horses and fifteen grooms in the stables; the same costly presents on name-days, and ceremonial dinners to the whole neighbourhood. There were still the count's games of whist and boston, at which, letting every one see his cards, he allowed himself to be plundered of hundreds by his neighbours, who looked upon the privilege of making up a rubber with the count as a profitable investment.

The count went into his affairs as though walking into a huge net, trying not to believe that he was entangled, and at every step getting more and more entangled. The countess with her loving heart felt that her children were being ruined, that the count was not to blame, that he could not help being what he was, that he was distressed himself at the consciousness of his own and his children's ruin, and was seeking means to improve their position. To her feminine mind only one way of doing so occurred—that was, to marry Nicholas to a wealthy heiress. She felt that this was their last hope, and that if Nicholas were to refuse the match she had found for him she must bid farewell for ever to all chance of improving their position. This match was Julie Karagin, the daughter of excellent and virtuous parents, known to the Rostovs from childhood, and now left a wealthy heiress by the death of her last surviving brother.

The countess wrote directly to Madame Karagin in Moscow and received a favourable reply from her. Madame Karagin replied that she was quite ready for her part to consent to the match, but everything must depend on her daughter's inclinations. Madame Karagin invited Nicholas to come to Moscow. Several times the countess, with tears in her eyes, had told her son that now that both her daughters were settled, her only wish was to see him married. She said that she could rest quietly in her grave if this were settled. Then she would say that she had an excellent girl in mind, and would try and get from him his views on marriage.

On other occasions she praised Julie and advised Nicholas to go to Moscow for the holidays to amuse himself a little. Nicholas guessed what his mother's hints were aiming at, and on one such occasion he forced her to complete frankness.

She told him plainly that all hope of improving their position rested now on his marrying Julie Karagin.

"What if I loved a girl with no fortune? Would you really want me, mother, to sacrifice my honour for the sake of money?" he asked his mother, with no notion of the cruelty of his question, but simply wishing to show his sentiments.

"No; you misunderstand me," said his mother, not knowing how to retrieve her mistake. "You misunderstand me, Nicholas. It is your happiness I wish for," she added, and she felt she was speaking falsely, that she was blundering. She burst into tears.

"Mother, don't cry. Only tell me that you wish it, and you know that I would give my whole life, everything for your peace of mind," said Nicholas. "I will sacrifice everything for you."

But the countess did not want the question put like that. She did not want to receive sacrifices from her son. She would have liked to sacrifice herself to him.

"No; you don't understand me. Don't let us talk of it," she said, wiping away her tears.

"I wonder how mother could say such a thing. Because Sonya is poor I must not love her," he thought. "And I should be happier with her than with any doll of a Julie! I love Sonya and that means more than anything to me."

Nicholas did not go to Moscow. The countess did not renew her conversations with him about marriage, and with grief, and sometimes with exasperation, saw symptoms of a growing attachment between her son and the portionless Sonya. She blamed herself for it, yet could not refrain from scolding and upbraiding Sonya, often reproving her without cause and addressing her as "my good girl." What irritated the kind-hearted countess more than anything was that this poor, dark-eyed niece was so meek, so good, so devoutly grateful to her benefactors, and so truly, so constantly, and so unselfishly in love with Nicholas that it was impossible to find any fault with her.

Life was not gay at the Rostovs'.

Christmas came and except for the High Mass, the solemn and wearisome congratulations to neighbours and house-serfs, and the new dresses worn by every one, nothing special happened to mark the holidays, though the still weather with twenty degrees of frost, the dazzling sunshine by day and the bright, starlit sky at night seemed to call for some special celebration.

On the third day of Christmas week, after dinner, all the members of the household had separated and gone to their respective rooms. It was the dullest time of the day. Nicholas, who had been calling on neighbours in the morning, was asleep in the study. The old count was resting in his own room. In the drawing-room Sonya was sitting at a round table copying a design for embroidery. The countess was playing patience. Natasha came into the room, went up to Sonya, looked at what she was doing, then went up to her mother and stood there silently.

"Why are you wandering about like an unquiet spirit?" said her mother. "What do you want?"

"I want *him* . . . I want *him* at once, this minute," said Natasha, with a gleam in her eyes and no smile on her lips. The countess raised her head and looked intently at her daughter.

"Don't look at me, mother. Don't look at me like that. I shall cry in a minute."

"Sit down. Come and sit by me," said the countess.

"Mother, I want *him*. Why should I be wasting time like this, mother?" . . . Her voice broke, tears filled her eyes, and to hide them, she turned quickly and went out of the room.

She went into the big hall, took up the guitar, and sat down with it in a dark corner behind a bookcase. She began fingering the strings in the bass, picking out a phrase she recalled from an opera she had heard in Petersburg with Prince André. For other listeners the sounds that came from her guitar would have had no sort of meaning, but these sounds called up in her imagination a whole series of reminiscences. She sat behind the bookcase with her eyes fixed on a streak of light that fell from the crack in the pantry door, and listened to herself and recalled the past. She was in the mood for brooding over memories.

"Oh, if he would come quickly! I'm so afraid it will never happen! Perhaps he is coming to-day, will be here immediately. Perhaps he has come, and is sitting there in the drawing-room. Perhaps he came yesterday, and I have forgotten." She got up, put down her guitar, and went into the living-room. All tutors, governesses, and guests were sitting at the tea-table. The servants were standing round the table. But Prince André was not there, and the same old life was still going on.

"Here she is," said the count, seeing Natasha coming in. "Come, sit by me." But Natasha stayed by her mother, looking about her as though seeking for something.

"Mother" she said. "Give me *him,* give me him, mother, quickly, quickly," and again she could hardly suppress her tears. She sat down at the table and listened to the talk of the elders and Nicholas, who had come in to tea. "My God, my God, the same people, the same talk. Father holding his cup, and blowing it just the same as always," thought Natasha, feeling with horror an aversion rising up in her for all her family, because they were always the same.

After tea Nicholas, Sonya, and Natasha went into the study to their favourite corner, where their most intimate talks always began.

"Does it happen to you," said Natasha to her brother, when they were settled, "to feel that nothing will ever happen—nothing; that all that is good is past?"

They went through their reminiscences; not the melancholy memories of old age, but the romantic memories of youth, those impressions of the past in which dreamland melts into reality. They laughed with quiet pleasure.

Sonya was, as always, left behind by them, though their past had been spent together. She did not remember much of what they recalled, and what she did remember, did not arouse the same romantic feeling in her. She was simply enjoying their pleasure, and trying to share it.

She could only enter into it fully when they recalled her arrival. Sonya described how she had been afraid of Nicholas, because he had cording on his jacket, and the nurse had told her that they would tie her up in cording.

"And I remember, I was told you were found under a cabbage," said Natasha. "And I remember I didn't dare to disbelieve it then, though I knew it was untrue, and I felt so uncomfortable."

In the middle of their talk they heard the countess calling from the next room.

"Natasha! Sing me something. Why are you sitting there so quietly, like conspirators?"

"Mother, I don't want to!" said Natasha. But she got up as she said it.

None of them wanted to break off the conversation, and come out of the corner of the study. But Natasha stood up, and Nicholas sat down to the clavichord. Standing, as she always did, in the middle of the room, and choosing the place where the resonance was greatest, Natasha began singing her mother's favourite song.

She had said she did not want to sing, but it was long since she had sung, and long before she sang again as she sang that evening. The old count listened to her singing from his study, where he was talking to Mitenka. And like a schoolboy in haste to finish his lesson and run out to play, he blundered in his orders to the steward, and at last paused, and Mitenka stood silent and smiling before him, listening too. Nicholas never took his eyes off his sister, and drew his breath when she did. Sonya, as she listened, thought of the vast difference between her and Natasha, and how impossible it was for her to be in ever so slight a degree fascinating like her cousin. The old countess sat with a blissful, but mournful smile, and tears in her eyes, and now and then she shook her head. She, too, was thinking of Natasha and of her own youth, and of how there was something terrible and unnatural in Natasha's marrying Prince André.

Dimmler, the music master, sitting by the countess, listened with closed eyes. "No, countess," he said, at last, "that's a European talent. She has no need of teaching: that softness, tenderness, strength . . ."

"Ah, I'm afraid for her, I'm afraid," said the countess, not remembering with whom she was speaking. Her instinct told her that there was too much of something in Natasha, and that it would prevent her from being happy.

Natasha had not finished singing when fourteen-year-old Peter ran into the room to announce the arrival of mummers.

Natasha stopped abruptly.

"Idiot!" she screamed at her brother. She ran to a chair, sank into it, and broke into such violent crying that it was a long while before she could stop.

"It's nothing, mother, it's nothing really, it's all right. Peter startled me," she said, trying to smile. But the tears still flowed, and the sobs still choked her.

The mummers—house-serfs dressed up as bears, Turks, tavern-keepers, and ladies—awe-inspiring or comic figures, at first huddled shyly together in the vestibule, bringing in with them the freshness of the cold outside, and a feeling of gaiety. Then, hiding behind one another, they crowded together in the big hall. And at first with constraint, but afterwards with more liveliness, they started singing songs, dancing, and playing Christmas games. The countess after identifying them, and laughing at their costumes, went away to the drawing-room. Count Rostov sat with a beaming smile in the big hall, praising them. The young people had disappeared.

Half an hour later there appeared in the hall among the other mummers an old lady in a crinoline—this was Nicholas. Peter was a Turkish lady, Dimmler was a clown, Natasha a hussar, and Sonya a Circassian with eyebrows and moustaches smudged with burnt cork.

After those of the household who were not dressed up had expressed wonder and approval, and had failed to recognise them, the young people began to think their costumes so good that they must display them to some one else.

Nicholas suggested driving to a so-called uncle's, taking about a dozen of the house-serfs in their mummer-dress with them.

"No; why should you disturb the old fellow?" said the countess. "Besides you wouldn't have room to turn round there. If you must go, let it be to the Melyukovs'."

Madame Melyukov was a widow with a family of children of various ages, and a number of tutors and governesses living in her house, four miles from the Rostovs'.

"That's a good idea, my love," the old count agreed.

And it was decided that Madame Schoss, the governess, would go with them. Half an hour later four sledges with bells drove up to the steps, their runners crunching the frozen snow.

Sonya, Natasha, Madame Schoss, and two maids got into Nicholas' sledge. In the second sledge were Dimmler with his wife and Peter. The other mummers were seated in the other two sledges.

"You go ahead, Zahar!" shouted Nicholas to the coachman of the second sledge.

The sledge with Dimmler and the others of his party started forward, its runners creaking as though they were frozen to the snow, and the deep-toned bell clanging. The trace-horses pressed close to the shafts and sticking in the snow kicked it up, hard and glittering as sugar.

Nicholas followed the first sledge. Behind him he heard the noise and crunch of the other two. At first they drove at a slow trot along the narrow road. As they drove by the garden, the shadows of the leafless trees often lay right across the road and hid the bright moonlight. But as soon as they were out of their grounds, the snowy plain, glittering like a diamond with bluish lights in it, lay stretched out on all sides, all motionless and bathed in moonlight. Now and again a hole gave the first sledge a jolt; the next was jolted in just the same way, and the next, and the sledges followed one another, rudely breaking the iron-bound stillness.

"A hare's tracks, a lot of tracks!" Natasha's voice rang out in the frostbound air.

"How light it is, Nicholas," said Sonya.

Nicholas looked round at Sonya, and bent down to look at her face closer. It was a quite new, charming face with black moustaches, and eyebrows that peeped up at him from the sable fur—so close yet so distant—in the moonlight.

"That used to be Sonya," thought Nicholas. He looked closer at her and smiled.

"What is it, Nicholas?"

"Nothing," he said, and turned to his horses again.

Madame Melyukov, a broad-shouldered, energetic woman in spectacles and a loose house dress, was sitting in her drawing-room, surrounded by her daughters, doing her utmost to keep them amused. They were dropping melted wax into water and watching the shadows of the shapes it assumed, when they heard the noise of steps in the vestibule, and the voices of people arriving.

The hussars, fine ladies, witches, clowns, and bears, coughing and rubbing the hoar-frost off their faces, came into the hall. The clown—Dimmler—and the old lady Nicholas—opened the dance. Surrounded by the shrieking children, the mummers hid their faces, and disguising their voices, bowed to their hostess and scattered about the room.

"Oh, there's no recognising them. And Natasha! See what she looks like! Really, she reminds me of some one. How good Dimmler is! I didn't know him. And how he dances! Oh, my goodness, and here's a Circassian too, upon my word; how it suits Sonya! And who's this? Well, you have brought us some fun! And we were sitting so quiet and dull!"

"Ha—ha—he! . . . The hussar, the hussar! Just like a boy; and the legs! . . . I can't look at him, . . ." voices cried.

Natasha, the favourite of the young Melyukovs, disappeared with them into rooms at the back of the house, and burnt cork and various dressing-gowns and men's clothes were sent for and taken from the footman by bare, girlish arms through the crack of the half-open door. In ten minutes all the younger members of the Melyukov family reappeared in fancy dresses too.

Madame Melyukov, busily giving orders for clearing the room for the guests and preparing for their entertainment, walked about among the mummers in her spectacles, looking close at them and not recognising any one. She not only failed to recognise the Rostovs and Dimmler, but did not even know her own daughters.

"And who is this?" she kept saying, addressing her governess and gazing into the face of her own daughter disguised as a Tatar of Kazan. "One of the Rostovs, I believe. And you, my hussar, what regiment are you in?" she asked Natasha. "Give the Turk a candied fruit," she said to the footman carrying round refreshments. "That's not forbidden by his law."

Sometimes, looking at the capers cut by the dancers, who, having made up their minds once for all that no one recognised them, were quite free from shyness, Madame Melyukov hid her face in her handkerchief, and all her portly person shook with good-natured, elderly laughter.

After Russian dances and songs in chorus, Madame Melyukov made all the party, servants and gentry alike, join in one large circle. They brought in a string, a ring, and a silver rouble, and began playing games. Then the guests were invited into the drawing-room for supper, while the servants were regaled in the hall.

"Oh, trying one's fate in a bath-house is awful!" was said at the supper-table by an old maiden lady who lived with the Melyukovs.

"Why?" asked the eldest daughter.

"Well, you won't go and try. It needs courage . . ."

"I'll go," said Sonya.

"Tell us what happened to the young lady," said the second girl.

"Well, it was like this," said the old maid. "The young lady went out; she took a cock, two knives and forks, and everything proper, and sat down. She sat a little while, and all of a sudden she heard some one coming—a sledge with bells driving up. She hears him coming. He walks in, precisely in the shape of a man, like an officer, and sits down beside her at the place laid for him."

"Oh! . . ." screamed Natasha with horror.

"But what did he do? Did he talk like a man?"

"Yes, like a man. And he began to try and win her over, and she should have kept him in talk till the cock crew; but she got frightened, and hid her face in her hands. And he picked her up. Luckily the maids ran in that minute . . ."

"Come, why are you scaring them?" said Madame Melyukov.

"And how do they try fate in a granary?" asked Sonya.

"Why, at a time like this you go to the granary and listen. And according to what you hear—if there's a knocking and a tapping, it's bad; but if there's a sound of sifting corn, it is good. But sometimes it happens . . ."

"Mamma, tell us what happened to you in the granary?"

"Why, I have forgotten . . ." said Madame Melyukov smiling. "I know none of you will go."

"I'll go," said Sonya.

"Oh, well, if you're not afraid."

"I'm not afraid of anything," said Sonya. "May I go at once?"

She got up. They told Sonya where the granary was; how she was to stand quite silent and listen, and they gave her a cloak. She threw it over her head and glanced at Nicholas. Then she went out into the corridor to go to the granary.

Nicholas quickly went out to the front porch, saying he was too hot.

Outside there was the same still frost, the same moonlight, only even brighter than before. The light was so bright, and there were so many stars sparkling in the snow, that the sky did not attract the eye, and the real stars were hardly noticeable. The sky was all blackness and dreariness, the earth all brightness.

"I'm a fool. A fool! What have I been waiting for all this time?" thought Nicholas. And he ran round the corner of the house along the path leading to the back door. He knew Sonya would come that way.

From the maid-servants' entrance came the sound of feet on the steps; there was a ringing crunch on the last step where the snow was heaped, and the voice of the old maid said: "Straight on, along this path, miss. Only don't look round!"

"I'm not afraid," answered Sonya's voice. And Sonya's little feet in their dancing-shoes came with a ringing, crunching sound along the path towards Nicholas.

Sonya was muffled up in the cloak. She was only a few steps away when she saw him.

He slipped his hands under the cloak that covered her head, embraced her, drew her to him, and kissed her lips. Sonya kissed him full on the lips, and putting out her little hands held them against his cheeks on both sides.

"Sonya! . . . Nicholas! . . ." was all they said. They ran to the granary and went back to the house, each at their separate door.

Soon after the Christmas holidays were over, Nicholas spoke to his mother of his love for Sonya, and his desire to marry her. The countess was expecting this. She listened to his words without comment, and then told him that he could marry whom he chose, but that neither she nor his father would give their blessing to such a marriage.

For the first time in his life Nicholas felt that his mother was displeased with him, that in spite of all her love for him she would not give way to him.

Coldly, without looking at her son, she sent for her husband. And when he came in, the countess would have briefly and coldly, in Nicholas' presence, told him her son's intention, but she could not control herself, burst into tears of anger, and went out of the room. The old count began irresolutely persuading and entreating Nicholas to give up his intention. Nicholas replied he could not be false to his word, and his father, visibly embarrassed, quickly cut short the conversation and went in to the countess. In all difficulties with his son, the old count could never lose his sense of guilt to him for having wasted their fortunes, and so he could not feel angry with his son for refusing to marry an heiress and choosing the portionless Sonya. He only felt more keenly that if their fortune had not been squandered, no better wife could have been desired for Nicholas than Sonya; and that he, with his Mitenka and his bad habits, was alone to blame for their fortune having been squandered.

The father and mother did not speak of the subject again with their son. But a few days later the countess sent for Sonya, and with cruelty she upbraided her niece for ensnaring her son and for ingratitude.

Sonya, with downcast eyes, listened in silence to the countess's cruel words, and did not understand what was expected of her. She could not help loving the countess and all the Rostov family, but neither could she help loving Nicholas. She was silent. She made no reply.

Nicholas could not endure this position any longer, and he went to his mother. He first begged her to forgive him and Sonya and to agree to their marriage. Then he threatened his mother that if Sonya were persecuted he would at once marry her in secret. The countess, with a coldness her son had never seen before, replied that he was of full age, that Prince André was marrying without his father's consent, and that he could do the same, but that she would never receive that "intriguing creature" as her daughter.

Stung to fury by the words "intriguing creature," Nicholas, raising his voice, told his mother that he had never expected her to try and force him to tell his feelings, and that since it was so, then for the last time he . . . But he had not time to utter the fatal word, which his mother seemed, from her expression, to be awaiting in terror, and which would, perhaps, have remained a cruel memory between them for ever. He had not time to finish, because Natasha, who had been listening at the door, ran into the room with a pale and set face.

"Nicholas, you are talking nonsense. Keep quiet! I tell you keep quiet!" . . . she almost screamed.

"Mother, darling, it's not at all so . . . my sweet, poor darling," she said, turning to her mother, who gazed in terror at her son, feeling herself on the edge of an abyss.

"Nicholas, you go away—listen, mother, darling," she said to her mother.

Her words were incoherent, but they attained the effect at which she was aiming.

The countess, with a deep sob, hid her face on her daughter's bosom, while Nicholas got up and went out of the room.

Natasha set to work to bring about a reconciliation, and succeeded so far that Nicholas received a promise from his mother that Sonya should not be worried. And he promised that he would take no step without his parents' knowledge.

Firmly resolved to settle things in his regiment, to retire, come home, and marry Sonya, Nicholas at the beginning of January went back to his regiment, sad and serious at being on bad terms with his parents, but, as it seemed to him, passionately in love.

After Nicholas' departure, it was more depressing than ever in the Rostovs' house. The countess fell ill from the emotional strains she had passed through.

Sonya was depressed at parting from Nicholas, and still more at the hostile tone the countess could not help adopting towards her. The count was more worried than ever by the difficulties of his position, which called for some decisive action. It was necessary to sell the Moscow house and the estate near Moscow, and to do so it was necessary to go to Moscow. But the countess's illness forced them to put off going from day to day.

Natasha, who had at first borne the separation from Prince André so easily and cheerfully, now grew more impatient and highstrung every day. The thought that time that might have been spent in loving him, was being wasted continually fretted her. Prince André's letters generally angered her. It mortified her to think that while she was simply living in the thought of him, he was living a real life, seeing new places and new people who were interesting to him. The more interesting his letters were, the more they vexed her. Her letters to him, far from giving her comfort, were looked upon by her as a wearisome and artificial duty. She could not write, because she could not express truly in a letter a thousandth part of what she expressed in voice and smile and eyes. She wrote him formal letters, all on one pattern. She did not attach the smallest importance to them herself, and the countess corrected the mistakes in spelling in the rough copy.

The countess's health still did not mend, but the visit to Moscow could be deferred no longer. The trousseau had to be ordered, the house had to be sold, and Prince André was soon to arrive in Moscow, where his father was spending the winter. The countess was left in the country, and towards the end of January the count took Sonya and Natasha with him to Moscow.

1811—1812

BOOK EIGHT

After Prince André's engagement to Natasha, Pierre suddenly, for no apparent reason, felt it impossible to go on living in the same way as before. Firm as his belief was in the truths revealed to him by his benefactor, the old freemason, and happy as he had been at first in the task of perfecting his inner spiritual self, yet after Prince André's engagement to Natasha, and the death of Osip Alexyevitch, the news of which reached him almost at the same time, the whole meaning of his religious life seemed to have suddenly vanished. Nothing but the skeleton of life remained: his house with his brilliant wife, now basking in the favours of a very grand personage indeed, the society of all Petersburg, and his service at court with its tedious formalities. And that life suddenly filled Pierre with loathing. He gave up keeping his diary, avoided the society of brother-masons, took to visiting the club again and to drinking a great deal; associated once more with gay bachelor companions, and began to lead a life so dissipated that Helen thought it necessary to speak to him about it. Pierre felt that she was right; and to avoid compromising her, he went to Moscow.

In Moscow, as soon as he entered his huge house with his cousins, the faded and fading princesses, and the immense retinue of servants, as soon as, driving through the town, he saw the Iversky chapel with the lights of innumerable candles before the golden setting of the Madonna, the square of the Kremlin with its untrodden snow, the sledge-drivers, and the hovels of Sivtsev and Vrazok; saw the old Moscow gentlemen quietly going on with their daily round, without hurry or desire of change; saw the old Moscow ladies, the Moscow balls, and the English Club—he felt himself at home, in a quiet haven of rest. In Moscow he felt comfortable, warm, at home, and snugly dirty, as in an old dressing-gown.

All Moscow society, from the old ladies to the children, welcomed Pierre back like a long-expected guest, whose place was always ready for him. For the Moscow world, Pierre was the most delightful, kind-hearted, intellectual, good-humoured, and generous eccentric, and a heedless and genial

Russian gentleman of the good old school. His purse was always empty, because it was always open to every one.

Benefit-entertainments, poor pictures and statues, benevolent societies, gypsy choruses, schools, subscription dinners, drinking parties, the masons, churches, and books—no one and nothing ever met with a refusal.

Not a dinner, not a *soirée* took place at the club without him. And as soon as he was lolling in his place on the sofa, after a couple of bottles of margot, he was surrounded by a circle of friends, and arguments, disputes, and jokes sprang up round him. Where there were quarrels, his kindly smile and casually uttered jokes were enough to reconcile the antagonists. The masonic dining lodges were dull and dreary when he was absent.

When after a bachelor supper, with a weak and good-natured smile, he yielded to the entreaties of the festive party that he would drive off with them to share their revels, there were shouts of delight and triumph. At balls he danced if there were a lack of partners. Girls and young married ladies liked him, because he paid no special attention to any one, but was equally amiable to all, especially after supper. "He is charming; he is of no sex," they used to say of him.

Pierre was just a gentleman-in-waiting, retired to end his days in Moscow, like hundreds of others. How horrified he would have been if, seven years before, when he had just come home from abroad, any one had told him that there was no need for him to look about him and rack his brains, that the track had long ago been trodden, marked out from all eternity for him, and that, struggle as he would, he would be just such another as all men in his position. He could not have believed it then! Had he not longed with his whole heart to establish a republic in Russia; then to be himself a Napoleon; then to be a philosopher; and then a great strategist and the conqueror of Napoleon? Had he not passionately desired and believed in the regeneration of the sinful race of man and the schooling of himself to the highest point of perfect virtue? Had he not founded schools and hospitals and liberated his serfs?

But instead of all that, here he was the wealthy husband of a faithless wife, fond of dining and drinking. Fond, too, as he unbuttoned his waistcoat after dinner, of indulging in a little abuse of the government, a member of the Moscow English Club, and a universal favourite in Moscow society. For a long while he could not reconcile himself to the idea that he was precisely the retired Moscow gentleman, the very type he had so profoundly scorned seven years before.

Sometimes he consoled himself by the reflection that it did not matter, that he was only temporarily leading this life. But later on he was horrified by another reflection, that numbers of other men, with the same idea of its being temporary, had entered that life and that club with all their teeth and a thick head of hair, only to leave it when they were toothless and bald.

Pierre no longer suffered from moments of despair, melancholy, and loathing for life as he had done. But the same sickness that had manifested itself in acute attacks in former days was driven inwards and never now left him for an instant. "What for? What's the use? What is going on in the world?" he asked himself in perplexity several times a day.

"Helen, who has never cared for anything but her own body, and is one of the most stupid women in the world," Pierre thought, "is regarded by people as the acme of wit and refinement. Napoleon Bonaparte was despised by every one while he was really great, and since he became a pitiful buffoon the Emperor Francis seeks to offer him his daughter in an illegal marriage. The Spaniards, through their Catholic Church, return thanks to God for their victory over the French on the 14th of June, and the French, through the same Catholic Church, return thanks to God for their victory over the Spaniards on the same 14th of June. My masonic brothers swear in blood that they are ready to sacrifice all for their neighbour, but they don't give as much as one rouble to the collections for the poor. We all profess the Christian law of forgiveness of sins and love for one's neighbour—the law, in honour of which we have raised forty times forty churches in Moscow—but yesterday we flogged to death a deserter; and the minister of that same law of love and forgiveness, the priest, gave the soldier the cross to kiss before his punishment."

Such were Pierre's reflections, and all this universal deception recognised by all, was always astounding him, as though it were something new. "I understand this deceit and tangle of cross-purposes," he thought, "but how am I to tell them all I understand? I have tried and always found that they understood it as I did, at the bottom of their hearts, but were only trying not to see it. So I suppose it must be so! But me—what refuge is there for me?" thought Pierre.

Meanwhile he had to live, he had to be occupied. It was too awful to lie under the burden of those insoluble problems of life, and he abandoned himself to the first distraction that offered, simply to forget them.

He read and re-read everything he came across. And although the doctors told him that because of his weight wine was bad for him, he drank a great deal. It was only after drinking a bottle or two of wine that he felt that the terrible tangled skein of life which had terrified him so before was not so terrible as he had imagined. With a buzzing in his head, chatting, listening to talk or reading after dinner and supper, he invariably saw that tangled skein on some one of its sides. It was only under the influence of wine that he said to himself: "Never mind. I'll disentangle it all; here I have a solution all ready. But now's not the time. I'll go into all that later on!" But that *later on* never came.

At the beginning of the winter old Prince Bolkonsky and his daughter moved to Moscow.

The prince had greatly aged during that year. He had sudden attacks of drowsiness, and forgetfulness of events nearest in time, and exact memory of remote incidents. But in spite of that, when the old man came into the drawing-room in the evenings to tea, in his wig and fur coat, and on being incited to do so by some one, began uttering abrupt observations on the past, or still more abrupt and harsh criticisms on the present—he aroused the same feeling of esteem and reverence in all his guests. For visitors, that old-fashioned house, with its huge mirrors, pre-revolutionary furniture, and powdered lackeys, and the stern and shrewd old man, himself a relic of a past age, with the gentle daughter and the pretty Frenchwoman, both so reverently devoted to him, made a stately and agreeable spectacle. But those visitors did not reflect that, apart from the couple of hours during which they saw the household, there were twenty-two hours of the day and night during which the secret, private life of the house went on its accustomed way.

That inner life had become very hard for Princess Mary. She was deprived in Moscow of her two greatest pleasures—talks with God's folk and the solitude which had refreshed her spirit at Bleak Hills, and she had none of the advantages and pleasures of town life. She did not go out into society. Every one knew that her father would not allow her to go anywhere without him, and owing to his failing health he could go nowhere himself. She was not even invited now to dinner-parties or balls.

Princess Mary had laid aside all hopes of marriage. She saw the coldness and hostility with which the old prince received and dismissed the young men, possible suitors, who sometimes appeared at the house. Friends, Princess Mary now had none; during this stay in Moscow she had lost all faith in the two friends who had been nearest to her. Mademoiselle Bourienne, with whom she had never been able to be perfectly open, she now regarded with dislike, and Julie, with whom she had kept up an unbroken correspondence for five years, seemed utterly alien to her.

Julie, who had become one of the wealthiest heiresses in Moscow, was surrounded by young men. She was at that age when a young lady is somewhat past her first youth and feels that her last chance of marrying has come, and that now or never her fate must be decided.

In Moscow Princess Mary had no one to speak to, no one to confide her sorrows to, and many fresh sorrows fell to her lot about this time. The time for Prince André's return and marriage was approaching, and any reference to the young Countess Rostov infuriated the old prince. Another trouble that weighed on Princess Mary of late was due to the lessons she gave to her six-year-old nephew. In her relations with little Nicholas she recognised to her horror symptoms of her father's irritable character in herself. However often she told herself that she must not let herself lose her temper when teaching her nephew, almost every time she sat down with him she would become angry. At the slightest thing she raised her voice and sometimes she pulled him by his little hand and stood him in the corner. When she had stood him in the corner she would begin to cry over her evil, wicked nature, and little Nicholas, also sobbing, would come out of the corner and pull her wet hands from her face and try to comfort her. But the greatest, far the greatest of the princess's burdens was her father's irascibility, which was invariably directed against her.

Of late he had taken a new departure, which caused Princess Mary more misery than anything—that was his closer and closer intimacy with Mademoiselle Bourienne. The idea that had occurred to him in jest—that if André got married he, too, would marry Mademoiselle Bourienne—obviously pleased him, and he had of late persisted in being particularly gracious to Mademoiselle Bourienne.

One day in Princess Mary's presence, the old prince kissed Mademoiselle Bourienne's hand, and drawing her to him embraced her affectionately. Princess Mary flushed and ran out of the room. A few minutes later, Mademoiselle Bourienne went into Princess Mary's room, smiling and making some cheerful remarks in her agreeable voice. Princess Mary wiped away her tears, went up to the Frenchwoman, and began screaming at her.

"It's loathsome, vile, inhuman to take advantage of feebleness . . ." She could not go on. "Get out of my room," she cried, and broke into sobs.

The next day the old prince did not say a word to his daughter, but she noticed that at dinner he gave orders for the dishes to be handed to Mademoiselle Bourienne first. When towards the end of dinner, the footman from habit handed the coffee, beginning with the princess, the old prince flew into a sudden frenzy of rage and immediately gave orders for the footman to be drafted into the army.

"He won't obey . . . twice I told him! . . . And he didn't obey. She's the first person in this house, she's my best friend," screamed the old prince. "And if you allow yourself," he shouted in a fury, for the first time addressing Princess Mary, "ever again, as you dared yesterday . . . to forget yourself in her presence, I'll show you who is master in this house. Away! Don't let me set eyes on you! Beg her pardon!"

Princess Mary begged Mademoiselle Bourienne's pardon and also her father's, both for herself and the footman, who implored her intervention.

At such moments the feeling in Princess Mary's soul was akin to the pride of sacrifice. But all of a sudden her father whom she was judging would look for his spectacles, fumbling by them and not seeing them, or would take a tottering step with his weak legs, and look round to see whether any one had noticed his feebleness, or what was worst of all, he would suddenly fall asleep, letting his napkin drop and his shaking head sink over his plate. "He is old and feeble, and I dare to judge him!" she thought, revolted at herself.

On St. Nicholas' day, the name-day of the old prince, all Moscow was driving up to the approach of his house, but he gave orders for no one to be admitted to see him. Only a few guests of whom he gave a list to Princess Mary, were to be invited to dinner.

At two o'clock the six people he had selected arrived to dinner. Those guests—the celebrated Count Rastoptchin, Prince Lopuhin and his nephew, General Tchatrov, an old comrade of the prince's in the field, and of the younger generation Pierre and Boris Drubetskoy—were awaiting him in the drawing-room. Boris, who had come on leave to Moscow shortly before, had been anxious to be presented to the old Prince Bolkonsky, and had succeeded in so far ingratiating himself in his favour, that the old prince made in his case an exception from his usual rule of excluding all young unmarried men from his house.

The prince did not receive what is called "society," but his house was the centre of a little circle into which—though it was not talked of much in the town—it was more flattering to be admitted than anywhere else. Boris had grasped that fact a week previously, when he heard Rastoptchin tell the commander-in-chief of Moscow, who had invited him to dine on St. Nicholas' day, that he could not accept his invitation.

"On that day I always go to pay my devotions to the relics of Prince Bolkonsky."

"Oh yes, yes . . ." agreed the commander-in-chief. "How is he? . . ."

The little party gathered before dinner in the old-fashioned, lofty drawing-room was like the solemn meeting of some legal council.

All sat silent, or if they spoke, spoke in subdued tones. The old prince came in, serious and taciturn. Princess Mary seemed meeker and more timid than usual. The guests showed no inclination to address their conversation to her, for they saw that she had no thought for what they were saying. Count Rastoptchin maintained the conversation alone, relating the latest news of the town and the political world. Lopuhin and the old general took part in the conversation at rare intervals. The old prince listened like a presiding judge.

At dinner the conversation turned to the latest political news.

"Bonaparte treats all Europe as a pirate does a captured vessel," said Rastoptchin, repeating a phrase he had uttered several times before. "One only marvels at the long-suffering or the blindness of the ruling sovereigns. Now it's the Pope's turn, and Bonaparte doesn't scruple to try and depose the head of the Catholic Church, and no one says a word. Our Emperor alone has protested against the seizure of the possessions of the Duke of Oldenburg. And even . . ." Count Rastoptchin broke off, feeling that he was on the very border line beyond which criticism was impossible.

"Other domains have been offered him instead of the duchy of Oldenburg," said the old prince. "He shifts the dukes about, as I might move my serfs from Bleak Hills to Bogutcharovo and the Ryazan estates."

"The Duke of Oldenburg supports his misfortune with admirable force of character and resignation," said Boris putting in his word respectfully. He said this because on his journey from Petersburg he had had the honour of being presented to the duke. The old prince looked at the young man as though he would have liked to say something in reply, but changed his mind, considering him too young.

After the meat, champagne was served. The guests rose to congratulate the old prince. Princess Mary too went up to him. He glanced at her with a cold, spiteful glance, and offered her his shaven, wrinkled cheek.

When they went into the drawing-room to coffee, the old prince grew more lively, and began to express his views on the impending war. He said that Russia's wars with Bonaparte would be unsuccessful so long as Russia sought alliances with the Germans and went meddling in European affairs, into which she had been drawn by the Peace of Tilsit. Russia had no business to fight for Austria or against Austria. Her political interests all lay in the East, and as regards Bonaparte, the one thing was an armed force on the frontier, and a firm policy, and he would never again dare to cross the Russian frontier, as he had done in 1807.

"And how should we, prince, fight against the French!" said Count Rastoptchin. "Can we arm ourselves against our teachers and divinities? Look at our young men, look at our ladies. Our gods are the French, and Paris—our Paradise."

He began talking more loudly, obviously with the intention of being heard by every one.

"Our fashions are French, our ideas are French, our feelings are French! Look at that French doctor, Metivier, who has recently come to Moscow. A real scoundrel! But our ladies are crawling on their hands and knees after him. Yesterday I was at an evening party, and out of five ladies three were Roman Catholics and had a papal indulgence for embroidering on Sundays. And they sitting all but naked, like the signboards of some public bath-house, if you'll excuse my saying so. Ah, when one looks at our young people, prince, one would like to take Peter the Great's old cudgel out of the museum and break a few ribs in good old Russian style, to knock the nonsense out of them!"

All were silent. The old prince looked at Rastoptchin with a smile on his face and shook his head approvingly.

Princess Mary, sitting in the drawing-room, and hearing the men's talk and criticisms, did not understand a word of what she was hearing. She thought of nothing but whether all their guests were noticing her father's hostile attitude to her. She did not even notice the marked attention and amiability shown her during the whole of dinner by Boris Drubetskoy, who was that day paying them his third visit.

Princess Mary turned with an absent-minded, questioning glance to Pierre, who, with a smile on his face, came up to her, hat in hand, the last of the guests, after the prince had gone out, and they were left alone together in the drawing-room.

"Can I stay a little longer?" he said, dropping his bulky person into a low chair beside Princess Mary.

"Oh, yes," she said. "You noticed nothing?" her eyes asked.

Pierre was in an agreeable, after-dinner mood. He looked straight before him and smiled softly. "Have you known that young man long, princess?" he said.

"Which one?"

"Drubetskoy."

"No, not long. . . ."

"Well, do you like him?"

"Yes; he's a very agreeable young man. Why do you ask me?" said Princess Mary, still thinking of her father.

"Because when a young man comes from Petersburg to Moscow on leave, it is invariably with the object of marrying an heiress. And that young man now manages matters so that wherever there are wealthy heiresses—there he is to be found. I can read him like a book. He is hesitating now between you and Julie Karagin. He is very attentive to her."

"Really!" said Princess Mary, looking at Pierre, and thinking all the time of her own trouble. "It would ease my heart," she was thinking, "if I could make up my mind to confide all I am feeling to some one. And it is just Pierre I should like to tell it all to. He is so kind and generous. He would give me advice."

"Would you marry him?" asked Pierre.

"Oh, there are moments when I would marry any one!" to her own surprise Princess Mary said, with tears in her voice. "Oh! how bitter it is to love some one near to one and to feel," she went on in a shaking voice, "that you can do nothing for him, but cause him sorrow. And when you know you cannot alter it. . . . There's only one thing—to go away. But where am I to go?"

"What is wrong? What is the matter with you, princess?"

Princess Mary burst into tears.

"I don't know what is the matter with me to-day. Don't take any notice of me. Forget what I said to you."

All Pierre's gaiety had vanished. He questioned the princess anxiously, begged her to speak out, to confide her trouble to him. But she would only repeat that she begged him to forget what she had said, that she did not remember what she had said, and that she had no trouble except the one he knew—her anxiety lest Prince André's marriage should cause a breach between him and his father.

"Have you heard anything of the Rostovs?" she asked to change the subject. "I was told they would soon be here. I expect André, too, every day. I should have liked them to see each other here."

"And how does he look at the matter now?" said Pierre, meaning by *he* the old prince. Princess Mary shook her head.

"But it can't be helped. There are only a few months left now before the year is over. And it can't go on like this. I should only have liked to spare my brother the first minutes. I could have wished the Rostovs were coming sooner. I hope to get to know Natasha well. . . . You have known them a long while," said Princess Mary. "Tell me the whole truth, speaking quite seriously. What sort of a girl is she, and how do you like her? But the whole truth, because, you see, André is risking so much in doing this against our father's will, that I should like to know . . ."

A vague instinct told Pierre that these pleas and repeated requests for the *whole truth* betrayed Princess Mary's ill-will towards her future sister-in-law, that she wanted Pierre not to approve of Prince André's choice. But Pierre said what he felt rather than what he thought. "I don't know how to answer your question," said he, blushing though he could not have said why himself. "I really don't know what kind of girl she is. I can't analyse her. She's fascinating. But why, I don't know. That's all that one can say about her."

Princess Mary smiled, and her face expressed: "Yes; that's what I expected and feared."

Boris had not succeeded in marrying a wealthy heiress in Petersburg, and it was with that object that he had come to Moscow. In Moscow Boris found himself hesitating between two of the wealthiest heiresses—Julie Karagin and Princess Mary. Though Princess Mary, in spite of her plainness, seemed to him more attractive than Julie, he felt vaguely awkward with her. On the old prince's name-day, she had met all his attempts to talk with irrelevant replies, and had obviously not heard what he was saying.

Julie, on the contrary, received his attentions eagerly.

Julie was twenty-seven. She had by now become decidedly plain. But she believed herself to be not merely as pretty as ever, but actually far more attractive than she had ever been. She was confirmed in this delusion by having become a very wealthy heiress, and also by the fact that as she grew older her society involved less risk for men, and they could behave with more freedom with her, and could profit by her suppers, her *soirées,* and the lively society that gathered about her, without incurring any obligations to her. A man who would have been afraid of going ten years before to a house where there was a young girl of seventeen, for fear of binding himself, would now boldly visit her every day, and treat her not as a marriageable girl, but as an acquaintance of no sex.

The Karagins' house was that winter one of the most agreeable and hospitable houses in Moscow. In addition to the dinner-parties and *soirées,* to which guests came by invitation, there were every day large informal gatherings, principally of men, who had supper there at midnight and stayed on till three o'clock in the morning. Julie did not miss a single ball, entertainment, or theatre. And her dresses were always the most fashionable.

Julie was particularly gracious to Boris. And Anna Drubetskoy, who often visited the Karagins, took a hand at cards with the mother, and meanwhile collected information as to the portion that Julie would receive on her marriage. Her dowry was to consist of two estates in the Penza province and forests in the Nizhnigorod province.

"Ah, my dear, how attached I have grown to Julie lately," she would say to her son, "I can't tell you. But, indeed, who could help loving her! A creature not of this earth! Ah, Boris! Boris!" She paused for a moment. "And how I feel for her mother," she would go on. "She showed me to-day the letters and accounts from Penza. They have an immense estate there. And she, poor thing, with no one to help her. They do take such advantage of her!"

Boris heard his mother with a faintly perceptible smile. He laughed blandly at her simple-hearted wiles, but he listened to her and sometimes questioned her carefully about the Penza and Nizhnigorod estates.

Julie had long been expecting an offer from Boris, and was fully prepared to accept it. But a sort of secret feeling of repulsion for her, for her passionate desire to be married, for her affectation, and a feeling of horror at renouncing all possibility of real love made Boris still delay. His leave was drawing to a close. Whole days at a time, and every day he spent at the Karagins'; and each day Boris resolved, as he thought things over, that he would make an offer the next day. But in Julie's presence, as he watched her red face and her chin, almost always sprinkled with powder and her moist eyes, Boris could not utter the decisive word, although in imagination he had long regarded himself as the owner of the Penza and Nizhnigorod estates, and had disposed of the expenditure of their several revenues. Julie saw the hesitation of Boris, and the idea sometimes occurred to her that she was distasteful to him. But feminine self-flattery promptly afforded her comfort, and she assured herself that it was love that made him retiring.

Not long before the end of Boris's leave she adopted a decisive plan of action. Just at this time there appeared in Moscow, and also in the drawing-room of the Karagins', no less a person than Prince Vassily's son Anatole, and Julie became exceedingly cordial to him.

"My dear," said Anna Drubetskoy to her son, "I know from a trustworthy source that Prince Vassily has sent his son to Moscow to marry Julie. I am so fond of Julie that I should be most sorry for her. What do you think about it, my dear?"

Boris was mortified at the idea of being unsuccessful, of having wasted all that month of courtship of Julie, and of seeing all the revenues of those Penza estates pass into other hands, especially into the hands of that fool Anatole. He drove off to the Karagins' with the firm determination to make an offer. Julie met him with a gay and careless face, casually mentioned how much she had enjoyed the ball of the evening, and asked him when he was leaving. Although Boris had come with the intention of speaking of his love, and was therefore resolved to take a tender tone, he began to speak irritably of the fickleness of woman. Julie was offended, and said that that was quite true, indeed, that a woman wanted variety, and that always the same thing would bore any one.

"Then I would advise you . . ." Boris was beginning, meaning to say something cutting; but he stopped short in the middle of the sentence, dropped his eyes, to avoid seeing her disagreeably exasperated face, and said, "But it was not to quarrel with you that I have come here. On the contrary . . ." He glanced at her to make sure whether he should go on.

"I can always manage so as to see very little of her," thought Boris. "And the thing's been begun and must be finished!" He flushed crimson, raised his eyes to her face, and said to her, "You know my feeling for you!"

There was no need to say more. Julie beamed with triumph and self-satisfaction. But she forced Boris to say everything that is usually said on such occasions, to say that he loved her, and had never loved any woman more than her. She knew that for her Penza estates and her Nizhnigorod forests she could demand that, and she got all she demanded.

The young engaged couple at once made plans for a brilliant home in Petersburg, paid visits, and made every preparation for a splendid wedding.

Count Rostov arrived in Moscow towards the end of January with Natasha and Sonya. The countess was still unwell, and unable to travel, but they could not put off coming till she recovered, for Prince André was expected in Moscow every day. They had, besides, to order the trousseau, to sell the estate in the suburbs of Moscow, and to take advantage of old Prince Bolkonsky's presence in Moscow to present his future daughter-in-law to him. The Rostovs' house in Moscow had not been heated all winter; and as they were coming only for a short time, and the countess was not with them, Count Rostov decided to stay with Marya Ahrosimov, "the terrible dragon," who had long been pressing her hospitality upon the count.

Late in the evening the four loaded sledges of the Rostovs drove into the courtyard of Marya Ahrosimov in Old Equerrys' Place. She lived alone. She had by now married off her daughter. Her sons were all in the service.

She still held herself as erect; still gave every one her opinions in the same loud, outspoken, decided fashion; and her whole bearing seemed a reproof to other people for every sort of weakness, passion, and temptation, of which she would not admit the bare possibility. In the early morning, in a house-jacket, she looked after the management of her household. Then she drove on saints' days to Mass, and from Mass to the prisons. And what she did there, she never told any one.

On ordinary days she dressed and received petitioners seeking her aid. Then she had dinner, an abundant and appetising meal, at which some three or four guests were always present. After dinner she played a game of boston; and at night had the newspapers and new books read aloud to her while she knitted. It was only as a rare exception that she went out in the evening. If she did so, it was only to visit the most important people in the town.

She had not gone to bed when the Rostovs arrived. She stood in the doorway of the hall, with her spectacles slipping down on her nose, and her head flung back, looking with a stern and irate face at the new-comers. It might have been supposed that she was irritated at their arrival, and would pack them off again at once, had she not at the very time been giving careful instructions to her servants where to install her guests and their belongings.

"The count's things? Bring them here," she said, pointing to the trunks, and not bestowing a greeting on any one. "The young ladies', this way to the left. Well, what are we puttering about for?" she called to her maids. "Warm the samovar! She's plumper, prettier," she pronounced of Natasha, flushed from the frosty air, as she drew her closer by her hood. "Foo! She's cold! Hurry and get your wraps off," she shouted to the count, who would have kissed her hand. "You're frozen. Rum for the tea! Sonya dear, *bonjour,*" she said to Sonya, indicating by this French phrase a slightly contemptuous attitude.

When they had all taken off their outdoor things, set themselves straight after the journey, and come in to tea, Marya Ahrosimov kissed them all in due course.

"Terribly glad you have come, and are staying with me," she said. "It's time you were here," she said, with a significant glance at Natasha. . . . "The old fellow's here, and his son's expected from day to day. You must, you must make their acquaintance. Oh, well, we shall talk of that later on," she added, with a glance at Sonya, showing that she did not care to talk of it before her. "Now, listen," she turned to the count. "What do you want to do to-morrow? Whom will you send for? Shinshin?" She paused. "The tearful Anna Drubetskoy? She's here with her son. The son's to be married too! Then Pierre. He's here, too, with his wife. He ran away from her, and she has come trotting after him. He dined with me last Wednesday. Well, and I'll take them"—she indicated the young ladies—"to-morrow to Iversky chapel, and then we shall go to Aubert-Chalmey. You'll be getting everything now, I expect! Don't judge by me—the sleeves nowadays are like this! The other day the young princess, Irina Vassilyevna, came to see me, just as though she had put two barrels on her arms, a dreadful fright. Every day there's a new fashion. And what sort of business is it you have come for yourself?" she said severely, addressing the count.

"Everything has come together," answered the count. "There's the girl's dresses to buy; and now there's a purchaser turned up for the Moscow estate and the house. If you'll graciously permit it, I'll choose an opportunity and drive over to Maryinskoe for a day, leaving my girls on your hands."

"Very good, very good, they'll be safe enough with me. I'm as safe as the Mortgage Bank. I'll take them where they must go, and scold them and pet them too," said Marya Ahrosimov, putting her big hand on the cheek of her favourite and god-daughter Natasha.

Next morning Marya Ahrosimov took the young ladies off to Iversky chapel and to Madame Aubert-Chalmey, who was so frightened of her that she always sold her dresses at a loss simply to get rid of her as soon as possible. Marya Ahrosimov ordered almost the whole trousseau. On their return, she sent every one out of the room but Natasha, whom she told to sit beside her.

"Well, now we can have a chat. I congratulate you on your betrothed. A fine fellow you have hooked! I'm glad of it for your sake, and I have known him since he was that high." She held her hand a yard from the floor. Natasha blushed. "I like him and all his family. Now, listen! You know, of course, that the old prince is very much against his son's marrying. He's a whimsical old fellow! Of course, Prince André is not a child, he can get on without him, but to enter a family against the father's will is not a nice thing to do. One wants peace and love in a family. You're a clever girl, you'll know how to manage things. You use your wits and your heart. And every thing will turn out all right."

Natasha was silent, not as Marya Ahrosimov supposed from shyness. She disliked any one's interfering in what touched her love for Prince André, which seemed to her something so apart from all human affairs, that no one, as she imagined, could understand it. She loved Prince André, and only him, and knew only him; he loved her, and was to arrive in a few days and carry her off. She did not care about anything else.

"I have known him a long while, do you see; and Mary, your sister-in-law, I love. Sisters-in-law are said to be mischief-makers, but she—well, she wouldn't hurt a fly. She has begged me to bring you two together. You must go to see her to-morrow with your father, and be as nice as possible. You are younger than she is. By the time your young man comes back, you'll be friends with his sister and his father, and they will have learned to love you. Yes or no? It will be better so, eh?"

"Oh yes!" Natasha responded reluctantly.

Next day, on the advice of Marya Ahrosimov, Count Rostov went with Natasha to call on the old Prince Bolkonsky. The count was by no means in a cheerful mood. He was afraid. He had vivid recollections of his last interview with the old prince at the time of the levying of the militia, when, in reply to his invitation to dinner, he had had to listen to a heated reprimand for furnishing less than the required number of men. Natasha in her best dress was, on the contrary, in the most cheerful frame of mind. "They can't help liking me," she thought. "Every one always does like me. And I'm so ready to do anything to please them, so ready to love them—him for being his father, and her for being his sister—they can have no reason for not loving me!"

They drove to the gloomy old house in Vosdvizhenka, and went into the vestibule.

"Well now, with God's blessing," said the count laughing. But Natasha noticed that her father was nervous as he went into the entry, and asked timidly and softly whether the prince and the princess were at home. After their arrival had been announced, there was some uneasiness among the prince's servants. The footman, who was running to announce them, was stopped by another footman in the big hall, and they whispered together. A maid-servant ran into the hall, and hurriedly said something, mentioning the princess. At last one old footman came out, and announced to the Rostovs that the prince was not receiving, but that the princess begged them to walk up.

The first person to meet the visitors was Mademoiselle Bourienne. She greeted the father and daughter with courtesy, and conducted them to the princess's apartment. The princess, with a frightened face, flushed in patches, ran in, treading heavily, to meet her visitors, doing her best to seem cordial and at ease.

From the first glance Prince Mary disliked Natasha. She thought her too fashionably dressed, too frivolously gay and vain. Princess Mary had no idea that before she had seen her future sister-in-law she had been unfavourably disposed to her, through unconscious envy of her beauty, her youth, and her happiness, and through jealousy of her brother's love for her. Apart from this feeling of hostility to her, Princess Mary was at that moment upset by the fact that on the Rostovs having been announced the old prince had shouted that he didn't want to see them, that Princess Mary could see them if she chose, but they were not to be allowed in to see him.

Princess Mary decided to see the Rostovs, but she was every instant in dread of her father.

"Well, here I have brought you my songstress, princess," said the count, bowing and scraping, while he looked round uneasily as though he were afraid the old prince might come in. "How glad I am that you should make friends. . . . Sorry, very sorry, the prince is unwell." And uttering a few more stock phrases, he got up. "If you'll allow me, princess, to leave you my Natasha for a quarter of an hour, I will drive round—only a few steps from here—to Dogs' Square to see an old friend, and then come back for her."

Count Rostov had plotted this diplomatic stratagem to give the future sisters-in-law greater freedom to express their feelings to one another. This is what he told Natasha afterward, but the truth was that he wanted to avoid meeting the prince, of whom he was afraid. But Natasha sensed this dread and uneasiness in her father, and felt mortified by it. She blushed for him, felt still angrier at having blushed, and glanced at the princess with a bold, challenging air, meant to express that she was not afraid of any one. The princess told the count that she would be delighted, and begged him to stay away as long as he liked.

In spite of the glances flung at her by Princess Mary, who wanted to talk to Natasha by herself, Mademoiselle Bourienne would not leave the room, and persisted in keeping up a conversation about Moscow entertainments and theatres. Natasha felt offended by the poor welcome, by her father's nervousness, and by the constrained manner of the princess, who seemed to be making a favour of receiving her. And then everything displeased her. She did not like Princess Mary. She seemed to her very ugly, affected, and frigid. Natasha suddenly, as it were, shrank into herself, and unconsciously assumed a nonchalant air, which repelled Princess Mary more and more.

After five minutes of irksome and constrained conversation, they heard the sound of slippered feet. Princess Mary's face expressed terror: the door of the room opened, and the old prince came in, in a white night-cap and dressing-gown.

"Ah, madam," he began. "Madam, countess. . . . Countess Rostov . . . If I'm not mistaken . . . I beg you to excuse me, to excuse me . . . I didn't know, madam. As God's above, I didn't know that you were deigning to visit us, and came in to my daughter in this costume. I beg you to excuse me . . . As God's above, I didn't know," he repeated so unnaturally, with emphasis on the word "God," and so unpleasantly, that Princess Mary rose to her feet with her eyes on the ground, not daring to look either at her father or at Natasha. Natasha, getting up and curtseying, did not know either what she was to do. Only Mademoiselle Bourienne smiled agreeably.

"I beg you to excuse me. I beg you to excuse me! As God's above, I didn't know," muttered the old man, and looking Natasha over from head to foot, he went out.

Mademoiselle Bourienne was the first to recover herself after this apparition, and began talking about the prince's ill-health. Natasha and Princess Mary gazed dumbly at one another, and the longer they gazed without saying what they wanted to say, the more unfavourably each felt toward the other.

When the count returned, Natasha hurried to get away. At that moment she almost hated that stiff, oldish princess, who could put her in such an awkward position, and spend half an hour with her without saying a word about Prince André. "I couldn't be the first to speak of him before that Frenchwoman," thought Natasha. Princess Mary meanwhile was tortured by the very same feeling. She knew what she had to say to Natasha, but she could not do it, both because Mademoiselle Bourienne prevented her, and because—she did not know herself why—it was difficult for her to begin to speak of the marriage.

The count was already going out of the room when Princess Mary came up to Natasha, took her hand, and, said: "Wait a moment, I want . . . Dear Natasha, I am so glad that my brother has found such happiness . . ." She paused, feeling that she was telling a lie. Natasha noticed the pause, and guessed the reason of it.

"I imagine, princess, that it is not now suitable to speak of that," said Natasha, with external dignity and coldness, though she felt the tears rising in her throat.

"What have I said, what have I done?" she thought as soon as she had gone out of the room.

They had to wait a long while for Natasha to come to dinner that day. She was sitting in her room, crying like a child, choking, and sobbing. Sonya stood over her, and kept kissing her on the head.

"Natasha, what is it?" she kept saying. "Don't bother about them? It will pass, Natasha."

"No, if only you knew how insulting it was . . . As though I . . ."

"Don't talk of it, Natasha. It's not your fault, you see, so what does it matter to you! Kiss me," said Sonya.

Natasha raised her head, and pressed her wet face against hers.

"I can't say; I don't know. It's no one's fault," said Natasha. "But why doesn't he come? . . ."

That evening the Rostovs went to the opera, for which Marya Ahrosimov had obtained a box.

Natasha did not want to go, but it was impossible to refuse after Marya Ahrosimov's kindness, especially as it had been arranged expressly for her. When she was dressed and waiting for her father in the hall, she looked at herself in the big looking-glass, and saw that she was looking pretty, very pretty.

The Rostovs' carriage fell into the line of carriages, and drove up to the theatre, its wheels crunching slowly over the snow. Natasha and Sonya skipped hurriedly out holding up their dresses; the count stepped out supported by the footmen, and all three walked to the corridor for the boxes in the stream of ladies and gentlemen going in and people selling programs. They could hear the music already through the closed doors.

"Natasha, your hair . . ." whispered Sonya. The box-opener hurriedly slipped before the ladies and opened the door of the box. The music became more distinctly audible at the door, and they saw the brightly lighted rows of boxes, with the bare arms and shoulders of the ladies, and the stalls below, noisy, and gay with uniforms. The curtain had not yet risen and they were playing the overture. Natasha went in with Sonya, and sat down looking round at the brightly lighted tiers of boxes facing them. The sensation she had not experienced for a long while—that hundreds of eyes were looking at her bare arms and neck—suddenly came upon her both pleasantly and unpleasantly, calling up a whole swarm of memories, desires, and emotions.

The two strikingly pretty girls, Natasha and Sonya, with Count Rostov, who had not been seen for a long while in Moscow, attracted general attention. Moreover, every one had heard vaguely of Natasha's engagement to Prince André, knew that the Rostovs had been living in the country ever since, and looked with curiosity at the girl who was to make one of the best matches in Russia.

Natasha had, so every one told her, grown prettier in the country; and that evening, owing to her excitement, she was particularly attractive. Her black eyes gazed at the crowd, seeking out no one, while her slender arm, bare to above the elbow, leaned on the velvet edge of the box, and her hand, holding the program, clasped and unclasped in time to the music with obvious unconsciousness.

"Look, there's Alenina," said Sonya, "with her mother, isn't it?"

"Heavens, Mihail Kirillitch is really stouter than ever," said the old count.

"Look! our Anna Drubetskoy in such a cap!"

"The Karagins, Julie, and Boris with them. One can see at once they are engaged."

Natasha looked in the direction her father was looking in and saw Julie with diamonds on her thick, red neck, sitting with a blissful face beside her mother.

Behind them could be seen the handsome, well-brushed head of Boris, with a smile inclining his ear towards Julie's mouth. He looked from under his brows at the Rostovs, and said something, smiling, to his betrothed. Their box was full of that atmosphere of an engaged couple which Natasha knew so well. She turned away. And suddenly all that had been humiliating in her morning visit came back to her mind.

"What right has he not to want to receive me into his family? Oh, better not think about it, not think till he comes back!" she said to herself, and began to look about at the faces, known and unknown, in the stalls.

In the front of the stalls, in the very centre, leaning back against the rail stood Dolohov, in a Persian dress, with his huge shock of curly hair combed upwards. He stood in the most conspicuous place in the theatre, well aware that he was attracting attention and as much at his ease as though he had been alone in his room. The most brilliant young men in Moscow were all thronging about him.

Count Rostov, laughing, nudged the blushing Sonya, pointing out her former admirer.

"Did you recognise him?" he asked. "And where has he dropped from?" said he, turning to Shinshin who had just come into their box. "I thought he had disappeared somewhere?"

"He did disappear," answered Shinshin. "He was in the Caucasus, and he ran away from there, and they say he has been acting as minister to some reigning prince in Persia, and there killed the Shah's brother. Well, all the Moscow ladies are wild about him! 'Dolohov the Persian,' that's what does it! Nowadays there's nothing can be done without Dolohov. They do homage to him, invite you to meet him, and offer him to you as though he were a dish of the finest sturgeon," said Shinshin. "Dolohov and Prince Vassily's son, Anatole Kuragin, have taken all the ladies' hearts by storm."

A tall, handsome woman with a mass of hair and very naked, plump, white arms and shoulders, and a double row of big pearls round her throat, walked into the next box, and was a long while settling into her place and rustling her thick silk gown. It was the Countess Bezuhov, Pierre's wife.

The count, who knew every one, bent over. "Have you

been here long?" he began. "I'm coming, I'm coming to kiss your hand. I have come to town on business and brought my girls with me. They say Semyonovna's acting is superb," the count went on.

At that moment they heard the last chords of the overture, and the tapping of the conductor's baton. Late comers hurried to their seats in the stalls, and the curtain rose.

After the country, and in her serious mood, Natasha felt it all grotesque and extraordinary. She could not follow the opera. She could not even listen to the music. She saw nothing but painted cardboard and strangely dressed-up men and women, talking, singing, and moving about in the bright light. She looked about her at the faces of the audience, seeking in them signs of the same bewilderment that she was feeling herself. But all the faces were watching what was going on. She looked alternately at the rows of pomaded masculine heads in the stalls, and at the naked women in the boxes, especially at Helen, who, sat gazing intently, with a quiet and serene smile, at the stage, and basking in the bright light that flooded the theatre, and the warm air, heated by the crowd.

Natasha began gradually to pass into a state of intoxication she had not experienced for a long while. She lost all sense of what she was and where she was and what was going on before her eyes. She gazed and dreamed, and the strangest ideas flashed unexpectedly and disconnectedly into her mind. At one moment the idea occurred to her to leap over the footlights and sing that air the actress was singing; then she felt inclined to hook her fan into an old gentleman sitting near her, or to bend over to Helen and tickle her.

At a moment when there was a lull on the stage before the beginning of a song, the door opening to the stalls creaked on the side nearest the Rostovs' box, and there was the sound of a man's footsteps. Countess Bezuhov turned smiling to the new-comer. Natasha saw an exceedingly handsome adjutant coming towards their box with a confident, but yet courteous, bearing. It was Anatole Kuragin, whom she had seen long before, and noticed at the Petersburg ball. He was now wearing an adjutant's uniform, with one epaulette and a shoulder knot. He walked with a jaunty strut, which would have been ridiculous if he had not been so handsome, and if his good-looking face had not expressed such simple-hearted satisfaction and good spirits. Although the performance was going on he walked without haste, along the carpeted corridor, holding his scented, handsome head high, and accompanied by a slight clank of spurs and sword. Glancing at Natasha, he went up to his sister, laid his hand in a close-fitting glove

on the edge of her box, nodded his head at her, and, bending down, asked her a question, with a motion towards Natasha.

"Very, very charming!" he said, obviously speaking of Natasha. She did not exactly hear the words, but guessed them from the movement of his lips. Then he went on to the front row and sat down beside Dolohov, giving a friendly and careless nudge. He smiled at him, and leaned his foot against the footlights.

"How like the brother is to his sister!" said the count. "And how handsome they both are!"

Shinshin began telling the count in an undertone some story of an intrigue of Kuragin's in Moscow, to which Natasha listened, simply because he had said of her "very charming."

The first act was over. Every one stood up in the stalls, changed places, and began going out and coming in.

Boris came to the Rostovs' box, received their congratulations very simply, and lifting his eyebrows with an absent-minded smile, gave Natasha and Sonya his fiancée's message, begging them to come to her wedding, and went away.

Helen's box was filled and surrounded on the side of the stalls by the most distinguished and intellectual men, who rivaled one another in their desire to show every one that they knew her.

Throughout the intermission Anatole Kuragin stood with Dolohov in front of the footlights staring at the Rostovs' box. Natasha knew he was talking about her, and that gave her satisfaction. She even turned so that he could see her profile from what she believed to be the most becoming angle. Before the beginning of the second act she saw in the stalls the figure of Pierre, whom the Rostovs had not seen since their arrival. His face looked sad, and he had grown stouter since Natasha had seen him last. He walked up to the front rows, not noticing any one. Anatole went up to him, and began saying something to him, with a look and a gesture towards the Rostovs' box. Pierre looked pleased at seeing Natasha, and walked hurriedly along the rows of stalls towards their box. Leaning on his elbow, he talked smiling to Natasha for a long while. While she was talking to Pierre, Natasha heard a man's voice speaking in Countess Bezuhov's box, and something told her it was Anatole. She looked round. He looked her straight in the eyes, almost smiling, with a look of such warmth and admiration that it seemed strange to be so near him, to look at him like that, to be so certain that he admired her, and not to be acquainted with him.

During the second act, every time Natasha glanced towards the stalls, she saw Anatole Kuragin, with one arm flung across the back of his chair, staring at her. It pleased her to see that he was so captivated by her, and it never entered her head that there could be anything wrong about it.

When the second act was over, Countess Bezuhov got up, turned towards the Rostovs' box, with her gloved little finger beckoned the old count to her, and taking no notice of the men who were thronging about her box, began with an amiable smile talking to him.

"Oh, do make me acquainted with your charming daughters," she said. "All the town is singing their praises, and I don't know them."

Natasha got up and curtseyed to the magnificent countess. Natasha was so delighted at the praise from this brilliant beauty that she blushed with pleasure.

"I quite want to become a Moscow resident myself," said Helen. "What a shame of you to bury such pearls in the country!"

Countess Bezuhov had some right to her reputation of being a fascinating woman. She could say what she did not think, especially what was flattering, with perfect simplicity and naturalness.

"No, dear count, you must let me help to entertain your daughters, though I'm not here now for very long, nor you either. But I'll do my best to amuse them. I have heard a great deal about you in Petersburg, and wanted to know you," she said to Natasha, with her unvarying beautiful smile. "I have heard of you, too, from my page, Boris Drubetskoy—you have heard he is to be married—and from my husband's friend, Bolkonsky, Prince André Bolkonsky," she said, with peculiar emphasis, by which she meant to signify that she knew in what relation he stood to Natasha. Then she asked that one of the young ladies might be allowed to sit through the rest of the performance in her box that they might become better acquainted, and Natasha moved into it.

During the intermission following the second act, the door to Helen's box was opened, and Anatole walked in, bending and trying not to brush against any one.

"Allow me to introduce my brother," said Helen, her eyes shifting uneasily from Natasha to Anatole. Natasha turned her pretty little head towards the handsome adjutant and smiled over her bare shoulder. Anatole, who was as handsome on closer view as he was from a distance, sat down beside her, and said he had long wished to have this pleasure, ever since the ball, at which he had had the pleasure he had not forgotten of seeing her. Anatole was far more sensible and straightforward with women than he was in men's society. He talked boldly and simply, and Natasha was strangely and agreeably impressed by finding nothing so formidable in this man, of whom such stories were told, but, on the contrary, seeing on his face the most innocent and simple-hearted smile.

Anatole asked her what she thought of the performance, and told her that at the last performance Semyonovna had fallen down while she was acting.

"And do you know, countess," said he, suddenly addressing her as though she were an old friend, "we are getting up a costume ball. You ought to take part in it. It will be great fun. They are all gathering at Julie Karagins'. Please, do come," he said. As he said this he never took his smiling eyes off the face, the neck, the bare arms of Natasha. Natasha knew beyond all doubt that he was fascinated by her. That pleased her, yet she felt for some reason constrained and oppressed in his presence. When she was not looking at him she felt that he was looking at her shoulders, and she could not help trying to catch his eyes that he might rather look in her face. But as she looked into his eyes, she felt with horror that, between him and her, there was not that barrier of modest reserve she had always been conscious of between herself and other men. In five minutes she felt—she did not know how—that she had come fearfully close to this man. When she turned away, she felt afraid he might take her by her bare arm and kiss her on the neck. They talked of the simplest things, and she felt that they were close as she had never been with any man. Natasha looked round at Helen and at her father, as though to ask them what was the meaning of it. But Helen was absorbed in talking to a general and did not respond to her glance, and her father's eyes said nothing to her but what they always said: "Enjoying yourself? Well, I'm glad then."

In one of the moments of awkward silence, during which Anatole gazed calmly and persistently at her, Natasha, to break the silence, asked him how he liked Moscow. Natasha asked this question and blushed as she did so. She felt all the while that there she was doing something improper in talking to him. Anatole smiled as though to encourage her.

"At first I didn't like it much, for what is it makes one like a town? It's the pretty women, isn't it? Well, but now I like it awfully," he said, with a meaning look at her. "You'll come to the fancy dress ball, countess? Do come," he said, and putting his hand out to her bouquet he said, dropping his voice, "You will be the prettiest. Come, dear countess, and as a pledge give me this flower."

Natasha did not understand what he was saying, nor did he himself, but she felt that there was some improper intention. She did not know what to say, and turned away as though she had not heard what he said. But as soon as she turned away she felt that he was there behind her, so close to her.

"What is he feeling now? Is he confused? Is he angry? Must I set it right?" she wondered. She could not refrain from looking round. She glanced straight into his eyes, and his nearness and confidence, and the simple-hearted warmth of his smile vanquished her. She smiled exactly as he did, looking straight into his eyes. And again, she felt with horror that no barrier lay between him and her.

The curtain rose again. Anatole walked out of the box. Natasha went back to her father's box, completely under the spell of the world in which she found herself. And all thoughts of Prince André, of Princess Mary, of her life in the country, seemed to belong to the distant past.

As the Rostovs came out of the theatre Anatole came up to them, called their carriage and helped them into it. As he assisted Natasha he pressed her arm above the elbow. Natasha flushed and looked round at him. He gazed at her with flashing eyes and a tender smile.

It was only on getting home that Natasha could form a clear idea of what had happened. And thinking of Prince André, she was horrified. "What does it mean? What is that terror I felt with him? What is the meaning of those gnawings of conscience I am feeling now?" she thought. "What has happened to me? Nothing. I have done nothing; I did nothing to lead him on. No one will ever know, and I shall never see him again," she told herself. Yet something told her that all the old purity of her love for Prince André was lost. And again, in her imagination, she went over all her conversation with Anatole, and saw again the face, the gestures, and the tender smile of that handsome, daring man at the moment when he had pressed her arm.

Anatole Kuragin was staying in Moscow because his father, Prince Vassily, had sent him away from Petersburg, where he had been spending twenty thousand a year in hard cash and running up bills for as much more, and his creditors had been dunning his father. The father informed his son that for the last time he would pay half his debts; but only on condition that he would go away to Moscow, where he had secured a post for him as adjutant to the commander-in-chief. He also told Anatole that it would be a good idea for him to marry while he was in Moscow. He suggested either Princess Mary or Julie Karagin.

Anatole consented, and went away to Moscow, where he stayed with Pierre. Pierre at first was not pleased to receive

Anatole, but after a while he got used to him; sometimes accompanied him on his wild parties, and gave him money.

As Shinshin had with truth said of him, Anatole had won the hearts of all the Moscow ladies, especially by the nonchalance with which he treated them and the preference he openly showed for gypsy girls and actresses. He never missed a single drinking party or other Moscow festivity, and was at every *soirée* and ball in the best society. There were rumours of several intrigues of his with Moscow ladies, and at balls he flirted with a few of them. But he fought shy of unmarried ladies, especially the wealthy heiresses, who were most of them plain. He had good reason for this, of which no one knew but his most intimate friends: he had been married for the last two years. Two years before, while his regiment had been stationed in Poland, a Polish landowner, by no means well-to-do, had forced Anatole to marry his daughter.

Anatole had very shortly afterwards abandoned his wife, and in consideration of a sum of money, which he agreed to send his father-in-law, he was allowed by the latter to pass as a bachelor unmolested.

Anatole was very well satisfied with his position, with himself, and with other people. He was instinctively and thoroughly convinced that he could not possibly live except just in the way he did live, and that he had never in his life done anything base. He had such perfect faith in this that, looking at him, others too were persuaded of it, and refused him neither the exalted position in society nor the money, which he borrowed right and left, obviously with no notion of repaying it.

Dolohov had that year reappeared in Moscow after his exile and his Persian adventures. He spent his time in luxury, gambling, and dissipation; renewed his friendship with his old Petersburg comrade Anatole, and made use of him for his own ends.

Anatole sincerely liked Dolohov for his cleverness and daring. Dolohov, for whom Anatole's name and rank and connections were of use in ensnaring wealthy young men for gambling, made use of Anatole without letting him feel it, and was amused by him too. Apart from needing Anatole, the process of controlling another man's will was a pleasure, a habit, and a necessity for Dolohov.

Natasha had made a great impression on Anatole. At supper, after the theatre, he described to Dolohov, with the manner of a connoisseur, the points of her arms, her shoulders, her foot, and her hair, and announced his intention of getting up a flirtation with her. What might come of such a flirtation —Anatole was incapable of considering, and had no notion, as he never had a notion of what would come of any of his actions.

"She's pretty, but she's not for us," Dolohov said to him.

"I'll tell my sister to ask her to dinner," said Anatole.

"You'd better wait till she's married. . . ."

"You know I adore little girls," said Anatole. "They're all confusion in a minute."

"You've come to grief once already over a 'little girl,'" said Dolohov, who knew of Anatole's marriage. "Beware!"

"Well, one can't do it twice! Eh?" said Anatole, laughing good-humouredly.

The next day the Rostovs did not go anywhere, and no one came to see them. Natasha twice that day sent a man to inquire whether Prince André had arrived. He had not. To her impatience there was now added the vague dread that he would never come.

As soon as she began to think of Prince André, her memory of him was mingled with the recollection of the old prince and Princess Mary, and of the theatre and of Anatole. Again the question presented itself whether she had not been to blame, whether she had not broken her faith to Prince André, and again she found herself going over in the minutest detail every word, every gesture, every shade in the play of expression on the face of Anatole.

On Sunday morning Marya Ahrosimov went alone to Mass to her parish church of Uspenya on Mogiltse.

"I don't like those fashionable churches," she said, obviously priding herself on her independence of thought. "God is the same everywhere. Our parish priest is an excellent man, and conducts the service in a suitable way, so that is all as it should be, and his deacon too. Is there something holier about it when there are concerts in the choir? I don't like it. It's simply self-indulgence!"

After Marya Ahrosimov had gone, a dressmaker arrived from Madame Aubert-Chalmey, and Natasha, very glad of a change, went into a room adjoining the drawing-room, and shutting the door between, began trying on her new dresses. Just as she had put on a bodice basted together, with the sleeves not yet tacked in, and was turning her head to look at the fit of the back in the looking-glass, she heard the sound of her father's voice in the drawing-room in conversation with another voice, a woman's voice, which made her flush red. It was the voice of Helen. Before Natasha had time to take off the bodice she was trying on, the door opened, and Countess Bezuhov walked into the room, wearing a dark heliotrope velvet gown with a high collar, and smiling graciously.

"O my enchantress!" she said to the blushing Natasha. "Charming! No, this is really beyond anything, count," she said to Count Rostov, who had followed her in, "How can you be in Moscow, and go nowhere? No, I won't let you off! This evening we have the famous French actress Mademoiselle George giving a recitation. She's a favourite of Bonaparte's, you know. A few people are coming. And if you don't bring your lovely girls, who are much prettier than Mademoiselle George, I give up knowing you! My husband's not here, he has gone away to Tver, or I should have sent him for you. You must come, you positively must, before nine o'clock."

She nodded to the dressmaker, who knew her, and was curtseying respectfully, and seated herself in a low chair beside the looking-glass, draping the folds of her velvet gown about her. She kept up a flow of light-hearted chatter, and repeatedly expressed her admiration of Natasha's beauty. She looked through her dresses and admired them.

The smile of pleasure never left Natasha's face. She felt happy, and as it were blossoming out under the praises of this charming Countess Bezuhov, who had seemed to her before a lady so unapproachable and dignified, and was now being so kind to her. Anatole had begged his sister to bring him together with Natasha, and it was with that object she had come to the Rostovs'. The idea of throwing her brother and Natasha together amused her.

As she was leaving the Rostovs', Helen drew Natasha aside.

"My brother was dining with me yesterday. We nearly died laughing at him. He won't eat, and does nothing but sigh for you, my charmer! He is madly, madly in love with you, my dear."

Natasha flushed crimson on hearing those words.

"How she blushes, how she blushes, my pretty!" Helen went on. "You must be sure to come. I am sure your fiancé would prefer you to go into society rather than to languish in boredom. There is no reason for you to cloister yourself."

"So then she knows I am engaged. Pierre must have told her," thought Natasha.

And under Helen's influence what had struck her before as terrible seemed to her simple and natural. "Why not enjoy myself," thought Natasha, gazing at Helen with wide-open, wondering eyes.

Count Rostov took his two girls to the Countess Bezuhov's and he observed with dissatisfaction that almost all the company consisted of men and ladies notorious for the freedom of their behaviour. Mademoiselle George was standing in one corner of the room, surrounded by young men. There were several Frenchmen present, among them the doctor Metivier, who had been a constant visitor at Countess Bezuhov's ever since her arrival in Moscow. And Count Rostov made up his mind not to take a hand at cards, not to leave his daughter's side, and to get away as soon as Mademoiselle George's performance was over.

Anatole was at the door, unmistakably on the look-out for the Rostovs. At once greeting the count, he went up to Natasha and followed her in. As soon as Natasha saw him, the same feeling came upon her as at the theatre—the feeling of gratified vanity at his admiration of her, and terror at the absence of any barrier between them.

Helen gave Natasha a delighted welcome, and was loud in her admiration of her loveliness and her dress. Soon after their arrival, Mademoiselle George went out of the room to change her dress. In the drawing-room chairs were set in rows and people began to sit down. Anatole moved a chair for Natasha, and would have sat down by her, but the count, who was keeping his eye on Natasha, took the seat beside her. Anatole sat down behind.

Mademoiselle George, with bare, fat, dimpled arms, and a red scarf flung over one shoulder, came into the empty space left for her between the chairs and threw herself into a pose. An enthusiastic whisper was audible.

She scanned her audience with stern and gloomy eyes, and began reciting French verses, describing her guilty love for her son.

"Exquisite, divine, marvellous!" was heard on all sides. Natasha gazed at the fat actress; but she heard nothing, saw nothing and understood nothing of what was passing before her. She felt nothing, but that she was borne away again irrevocably into that strange and senseless world so remote from her old world, a world in which there was no knowing what was good and what was bad, what was sensible and what was senseless. Behind her was sitting Anatole. And conscious of his nearness, she was in frightened expectation of something.

After the first monologue all the company rose and surrounded Mademoiselle George, expressing their admiration.

"How handsome she is!" said Natasha to her father, as he got up with the rest and moved through the crowd to the actress.

"I don't think so, looking at you," said Anatole, following Natasha. He said this at a moment when no one but she could hear him. "You are charming . . . From the moment I first saw you, I have not ceased . . ."

"Come along, come along, Natasha!" said the count, turning back for his daughter. "How pretty she is!"

Natasha, saying nothing, went up to her father, and gazed at him with eyes of inquiring wonder.

After several recitations, Mademoiselle George went away, and the Countess Bezuhov invited all the company to the great hall.

The count wanted to leave, but Helen begged him not to spoil her improvised ball. The Rostovs stayed on. Anatole asked Natasha for a waltz, and during the waltz, squeezing her waist and her hand, he told her she was bewitching and that he loved her. During the écossaise, which she danced again with Anatole, he simply looked at her. Natasha was in doubt whether she had not dreamed what he said to her during the waltz. At the end of the first figure he pressed her hand again. Natasha lifted her frightened eyes to his face, but there was an expression of such assurance and warmth in his fond look and smile that she could not as she looked at him say what she had to say to him. She dropped her eyes.

"Don't say such things to me. I am engaged, and I love another man . . ." she said quickly. She glanced at him. Anatole was neither disconcerted nor mortified.

"What is that to me," he said. "I tell you I am mad, mad with love for you. Is it my fault that you are so fascinating? . . . It's for us to begin."

Natasha looked about her with wide-open, frightened eyes, and seemed to be enjoying herself more than usual. She scarcely grasped anything that happened that evening. They danced the écossaise and "Grandfather." Her father suggested their going, and she begged to stay longer. Wherever she was, and with whomsoever she was speaking, she felt his eyes upon her. Then she asked her father's permission to go into a dressing-room to rearrange her dress. Helen followed her in, talked to her, laughing, of her brother's passion, and in the dressing-room she again met Anatole. Helen somehow vanished. They were left alone, and Anatole taking her by the hand, said in a tender voice:

"I can't come to see you, but is it possible that I shall never see you? I love you madly. Can I never . . . ?" and barring her way he brought his face close to hers.

His large, shining, masculine eyes were so close to her that she could see nothing but those eyes.

"Natasha?" his voice whispered, and her hands were squeezed till it hurt. "Natasha?"

Burning lips were pressed to her lips. And then she caught the sound of Helen's steps and rustling gown in the room again. She looked round towards Helen. Then, red and trembling, she glanced at Anatole with alarm and went towards the door.

"One word, just one word, for God's sake," Anatole was saying. She stopped. She so wanted him to say that word, that would have explained to her what had happened.

"Natasha, one word . . . one . . ." he kept repeating, plainly not knowing what to say. And he repeated it till Helen reached them.

Helen went back with Natasha to the drawing-room. The Rostovs went away without staying to supper.

The morning came with daily cares and bustle. Every one got up and began to move about and to talk. Dressmakers came again. Again Marya Ahrosimov went out and they were summoned to tea. And Natasha did her utmost to seem exactly as usual.

After luncheon when Natasha was alone a maid came to her with a letter.

"Madame," whispered the maid, coming into the room with a mysterious air. "A man told me to give you this. Only for Christ's sake . . ." said the girl, as Natasha, without thinking, mechanically broke the seal and began reading a love-letter from Anatole, of which she did not understand a word, but understood only that it was a letter from him, from the man whom she loved. "Yes, she loved him; otherwise, how could what had happened have happened? How could a love-letter from him be in her hand?"

With trembling hands Natasha held that passionate love-letter, composed for Anatole by Dolohov, and as she read it, she found in it echoes of all that it seemed to her she was feeling herself.

"Since yesterday evening my fate is sealed. To be loved by you or to die. There is nothing else left for me," the letter began. Then he wrote that he knew her family would never give her to him, that there were secret reasons for that which he could only reveal to her alone. But that if she loved him, she had but to utter the word *Yes,* and no human force could hinder their happiness. Love would conquer all. He could capture her and bear her away to the ends of the earth.

"Yes, yes, I love him!" thought Natasha, reading the letter over for the twentieth time, and finding some special meaning in every word.

That evening Marya Ahrosimov was going to the Arharovs', and wanted to take the young ladies with her. Natasha said she had a headache and stayed at home.

On returning late in the evening, Sonya went into Natasha's room, and to her surprise found her asleep on the sofa. On the table near her Anatole's letter lay open. Sonya picked up the letter and began to read it.

She read it, and looked at Natasha asleep, seeking in her face some explanation of what she had read and not finding it. Her face was quiet, gentle, and happy. Sonya, pale and shaking with horror and emotion, sat down in a low chair and burst into silent tears.

"How was it I saw nothing? How can it have gone so far? Can she have ceased loving Prince André? What will Nicholas —dear, noble Nicholas—do when he hears of it?" thought Sonya. "But it's impossible that she can care for him!"

She dried her tears and went up to Natasha, carefully studying her face again.

She was about to wake her but then she decided: "No. She can't possibly love Anatole. It's all a mistake. I won't say anything. But why doesn't Prince André come back. Why doesn't he return!"

On Wednesday the count went with an intending purchaser to his estate near Moscow.

That day Sonya and Natasha were invited to a big dinner-party at Julie Karagin's and Marya Ahrosimov took them. At that dinner Natasha met Anatole again, and Sonya noticed that Natasha said something to him, trying not to be overheard, and was all through the dinner more excited than before.

Hard as it was for Sonya, after that she kept watch over Natasha and never let her out of her sight.

On the day before that fixed for the count's return, Sonya noticed that Natasha sat all the morning at the drawing-room window, as though expecting something, and that she made a sign to an officer who passed by, whom Sonya took to be Anatole.

Sonya began watching Natasha even more closely, and she noticed that all through dinner and in the evening Natasha was in a strange and unnatural mood unlike herself. She made irrelevant replies to questions asked her, began sentences and did not finish them, and laughed at everything.

After tea Sonya saw the maid going into Natasha's room. And listening at the door, found out that another letter had arrived. And all at once it was clear to Sonya that Natasha had some dreadful plan for that evening. Sonya knocked at her door. Natasha would not let her in.

"She is going to run away with him!" thought Sonya. "She cried as she said good-bye to uncle," Sonya remembered. "Yes, it's certain, she's going to run away with him. But what am I to do?" wondered Sonya. "Her father is not here.

What am I to do? Write to Pierre, as Prince André asked me to do? . . ."

To tell Marya Ahrosimov, who had such faith in Natasha, seemed to Sonya a fearful step to take.

"No," thought Sonya, standing in the dark corridor. If I have to go three nights together without sleep, I won't tell any-one; I won't leave this corridor. And I will prevent her passing by force."

Anatole had recently moved into Dolohov's quarters. The plan for the abduction of Natasha had been worked out several days before by Dolohov.

Natasha had promised to come out to Anatole at the back entrance at ten o'clock in the evening. Anatole was to get her into a sledge that was to be all ready with three horses in it, and to drive her off sixty miles from Moscow to the village of Kamenka, where an unfrocked priest was to marry them. At Kamenka a relay of horses was to be ready to take them as far as the Warsaw road, and from there they were to hasten abroad by means of post-horses.

Anatole had a passport and an order for post-horses and ten thousand roubles borrowed from his sister, and ten thousand more raised by the assistance of Dolohov.

The two witnesses of the mock marriage ceremony—Hvostikov, once a petty official, a man of whom Dolohov made use at cards, and Makarin, a retired hussar, a weak and good-natured man, whose devotion to Kuragin was unbounded—were sitting over their tea in the outer room.

In Dolohov's big study, decorated from the walls to the ceiling with Persian rugs, bearskins, and weapons, Dolohov was sitting in a travelling tunic and high boots in front of an open bureau on which lay accounts and bundles of bank notes. Anatole, in an unbuttoned uniform, was walking to and fro from the room where the witnesses were sitting through the study into a room behind, where his French valet with some other servants was packing up the last of his belongings. Dolohov was counting up money and writing down sums.

"Well," he said, "you will have to give Hvostikov two thousand."

"Well, give it to him then," said Anatole.

"Makarin now, he would go through fire and water for you with nothing to gain by it. Well, here then, our accounts are finished," said Dolohov, showing him the paper. "That's all right?"

"Yes, of course, it's all right," said Anatole, evidently not listening to Dolohov, and looking straight before him with a smile that never left his face.

Dolohov shut the bureau with a slam, and put the money away. And calling a servant to give him orders about getting something to eat and drink before the journey, he went into the room where Hvostikov and Makarin were sitting. Anatole lay down on the sofa in the study.

"Come and have something to eat. Here, have a drink!" Dolohov shouted to him from the other room.

"I don't want to," answered Anatole.

"Come, Balaga is here."

Anatole got up, and went into the dining-room. Balaga was a well-known driver, who had known Dolohov and Anatole for the last six years, and driven them in his three-horse sledges. More than once, when Anatole's regiment had been stationed at Tver, he had driven him out of Tver in the evening, reached Moscow by dawn, and driven him back the next night. More than once he had driven Dolohov safe away when he was being pursued. Many a time he had driven them about the town with gypsies and "gay ladies," as he called them. More than one horse had he ruined in driving them. More than once he had driven over people and upset vehicles in Moscow, and always his "gentlemen," as he called them, had got him out of trouble. Many a time had they beaten him, many a time made him drunk with champagne and madeira, a wine he loved, and more than one exploit he knew of each of them, which would long ago have sent any ordinary man to Siberia. They often called Balaga in to their wild parties, made him drink and dance with the gypsies, and many a thousand roubles of their money had passed through his hands. In their service, twenty times a year, he risked his life and his skin, and wore out more horses than they repaid him for in money. But he liked them, liked their furious driving, eighteen miles an hour, liked upsetting coachmen, and running over people in Moscow, and always flew full gallop along the Moscow streets. He liked to hear behind him the wild shout of their drunken voices, "Get on; get on!" when it was impossible to drive faster; liked to give a lash on the neck to a passing peasant who was already hurrying out of his way more dead than alive. "Real gentlemen!" he thought.

Anatole and Dolohov liked Balaga because he liked the same things that they liked. With other people Balaga drove hard bargains; he would take as much as twenty-five roubles for a two hours' drive, and rarely drove himself, generally sending one of his young men. But with his own "gentlemen" he always drove himself, and never asked for anything for the job.

Only after learning through their valets when money was plentiful, he would turn up once every few months in the morning; and sober, and bowing low, would ask them to help him out of his difficulties. The "gentlemen" always made him sit down.

"Please, help me out of a scrape, your excellency," he would say. "I'm quite run out of horses. Lend me what you can."

And whenever they were flush Anatole and Dolohov would give him a thousand or two.

Balaga was a flaxen-headed, squat, snub-nosed peasant of twenty-seven, with a red face and a red thick neck, little sparkling eyes, and a little beard. He wore a fine blue silk-lined full coat, put on over a fur pelisse.

"Sit down. Have a drink," said Anatole, and he poured Balaga out a big glass of madeira. The driver's eyes sparkled at the sight of the wine. Refusing it at first for manners' sake, he tossed it off, and wiped his mouth with a red silk handkerchief that lay in his cap.

"Well, and when are we to start, your excellency?"

"Oh . . ." Anatole looked at his watch. "We must set off at once."

Anatole went out of the room, and a few minutes later he came back wearing a fur-lined coat, a silver belt, and a sable cap. Looking at himself in the mirror, and then standing before Dolohov in the same attitude, he took a glass of wine.

"Well, now, let's start," he said.

They all went out into the vestibule.

"But where's a fur cloak?" said Dolohov. "Hey, Ignatka! Run in to Matryona, and ask her for the sable cloak. I've heard what elopements are like," said Dolohov. "She'll come skipping out more dead than alive just in the things she had on indoors. The slightest delay and then there are tears, and dear father and dear mother, and she's frozen in a minute and all for going back again. Wrap her up in a cloak at once and carry her to the sledge."

The valet brought a woman's fox-lined pelisse.

"Fool, I told you the sable. Hey, Matryona, the sable," he shouted, so that his voice rang out through the rooms.

A handsome, pale gypsy woman, with shining black eyes and curly black hair, ran out, wearing a red shawl and holding a sable cloak on her arm.

"Here, I don't grudge it. Take it," she said, in visible fear of Dolohov, and regretful at losing the cloak.

Dolohov took the cloak, flung it about her, and wrapped her up in it.

"This is the way," said Dolohov. "And then this is the way," he said, and he turned the collar up round her head, leaving it open around the face. "And then this is the way, do you see?" and he moved Anatole's head forward to meet the open space left by the collar, from which Matryona's flashing smile could be seen.

"Well, good-bye, Matryona," said Anatole, kissing her. "Give my love to Styoshka. There, good-bye! Good-bye, Matryona; wish me happiness."

"God grant you great happiness, prince," she said with her gypsy accent.

At the steps stood two three-horse sledges. Two strong young drivers were holding them. Balaga took his seat in the first, and holding his elbows high, began arranging the reins. Anatole and Dolohov got in with him. Makarin, Hvostikov, and the valet got into the other sledge.

"Ready?" asked Balaga. "Off!" he shouted, twisting the reins round his hands, and the sledge flew at break-neck speed through the city streets.

At length Balaga pulled up, and stopped the horses at the Old Equerrys' crossing.

One of the young drivers jumped down to hold the horses. Anatole and Dolohov walked along the pavement. On reaching the gates, Dolohov whistled. The whistle was answered, and a maid-servant ran out.

"Come into the courtyard, or you'll be seen. She is coming in a minute," she said.

Dolohov stayed at the gate. Anatole followed the maid into the courtyard, turned a corner, and ran up the steps.

He was met by Gavrilo, Marya Ahrosimov's huge groom.

"Walk this way to the mistress," said the groom, blocking up the doorway.

"What mistress? And who are you?" Anatole asked.

"Walk in. My orders are to show you in."

"Anatole! Back!" shouted Dolohov. "Come back!"

Dolohov, at the gate where he had stopped, was struggling with the porter, who was trying to shut the gate and lock Anatole in. With a desperate effort Dolohov shoved away the porter, and clutching at Anatole, pulled him through the gate, and ran back with him to the sledge.

Marya Ahrosimov, coming upon Sonya late at night in the corridor, had forced her to confess everything. She went in to Natasha.

"Vile girl, shameless hussy!" she said to her. "I won't hear a word!" Pushing aside Natasha, who gazed at her with amazed but tearless eyes, she locked her into the room, and giving orders to her gate porter to admit the men who would be coming that evening, but not to allow them to pass out again, and giving her grooms orders to show those men up to her, she seated herself in the drawing-room to wait.

When Gavrilo came to announce to Marya Ahrosimov

that the persons who had come had run away, she got up frowning, and clasping her hands behind her, walked a long while up and down through her rooms, pondering what she was to do. At midnight she walked towards Natasha's room, feeling the key in her pocket. Sonya was sitting sobbing in the corridor, "Marya Ahrosimov, do, for God's sake, let me go in to her!" she said.

Marya Ahrosimov opened the door and went in. "Hateful. Disgusting. In my house, the nasty hussy. I'm sorry for her father!" Marya Ahrosimov was thinking. "Hard as it may be, I will forbid any one to speak of it, and will conceal it from the count." She walked with resolute steps into the room.

Natasha was lying on the sofa. She had her head hidden in her hands and did not stir. She was lying in exactly the same position in which Marya Ahrosimov had left her.

"You're a nice girl, a very nice girl!" said Marya Ahrosimov. "Encouraging meetings with lovers in my house! There's no use denying it. You listen when I speak to you." Marya Ahrosimov touched her on the arm. "You listen when I speak. You've disgraced yourself like the lowest wench. I don't know what I couldn't do to you, but I feel for your father. I will hide it from him."

Natasha did not change her position, only her whole body began to shake with noiseless, convulsive sobs. Marya Ahrosimov looked round at Sonya, and sat down on the edge of the sofa beside Natasha.

"It's lucky for him that he escaped. But I'll get hold of him," she said in her coarse voice. "Do you hear what I say, eh?" She put her big hand under Natasha's face, and turned it towards her. Both Marya Ahrosimov and Sonya were surprised when they saw Natasha's face. Her eyes were glittering and dry. Her lips tightly shut; her cheeks sunken.

"Let me be . . . What do I . . . I shall die. . . ." she said with effort, and tore herself away from Marya Ahrosimov, and fell back into the same position again.

"Natasha! . . ." said Marya Ahrosimov. "Lie still. Come lie still like that then. I won't touch you, listen. . . . I'm not going to tell you how stupidly you have acted. You know that yourself. But now your father's coming back to-morrow. What am I to tell him?"

Again Natasha's body heaved with sobs.

"Well, he will hear of it, so will your brother, and Prince André!"

"He means nothing to me now!" cried Natasha.

"When they hear of it, do you suppose they will let the matter rest? Suppose he—your father, I know him—if he challenges him to a duel, will that be all right? Eh?"

"Oh, let me be. Why did you interfere! Why? Why? Who asked you to?" cried Natasha, getting up from the sofa, and looking vindictively at Marya Ahrosimov.

"But what was it you wanted?" screamed Marya Ahrosimov, getting angry. "Why, you weren't shut up, were you? Who stopped his coming to the house? Why carry you off, like some gypsy wench? . . . If he had carried you off, do you suppose they wouldn't have caught him? Your father, your brother, Prince André? He's a wretch, a scoundrel, that's what he is!"

"He's better than any of you," cried Natasha. "If you hadn't interfered . . . O my God, what does it mean? Sonya, why did you? Go away! . . ." And she cried with a despair with which people only bewail a trouble they feel they have brought on themselves. And she flung herself again on the sofa.

Marya Ahrosimov went on for some time longer lecturing Natasha, and urging her that it must be kept from the count, that no one would know anything of it if Natasha would only forget it all, and not show that anything happened. Natasha did not answer. She did not cry any more. But she began to shiver and tremble. Marya Ahrosimov put a pillow under her head, laid two quilts over her, and brought her some lime-flower water. But Natasha did not answer when she spoke to her.

"Well, let her sleep," said Marya Ahrosimov, as she went out of the room, supposing her to be asleep. But Natasha was not asleep, her wide-open eyes gazed straight before her out of her pale face. All that night Natasha did not sleep, and did not weep, and said not a word to Sonya, who got up several times and went in to her.

Next day, at lunch time, as he had promised, Count Rostov returned from his estate in the suburbs. He was in very good spirits. He had come to terms with the purchaser, and since Prince André had not yet arrived, there was nothing now to detain him in Moscow away from his countess, for whom he was pining.

Marya Ahrosimov told him that Natasha had been very sick on the previous day, that they had sent for a doctor, and that now she was better. Natasha did not leave her room that morning. With tightly shut, parched lips, and dry, staring eyes, she sat at the window, watching the passers-by along the street, and hurriedly looking round at any one who entered her room. She was obviously expecting news of Anatole, expecting that he would come himself or would write to her.

When the count went in to her, she turned uneasily at the sound of his manly tread, and her face resumed its previous cold and even vindictive expression. She did not even get up to meet him.

"What is it, my angel. Are you ill?" asked the count.

Natasha was silent a moment.

"Yes, I am ill," she answered.

From his daughter's illness and the troubled faces of Sonya and Marya Ahrosimov, the count saw that something had happened in his absence. But it was so terrible for him to think that anything disgraceful had happened to his beloved daughter, and he so prized his own cheerful serenity, that he avoided inquiries and tried to assure himself that it was nothing very out of the way. He only grieved that Natasha's illness would delay their return to the country.

From the day of his wife's arrival in Moscow, Pierre had planned to go away somewhere else, simply not to be with her. He went to Tver to see the widow of Osip Alexyevitch, who had long before promised to give him papers of her dead husband's.

When Pierre came back to Moscow, he was handed a letter from Marya Ahrosimov, who asked him to come to her on a matter of great importance, concerning André Bolkonsky and Natasha. Pierre had been avoiding Natasha. It seemed to him that he had for her a feeling stronger than a married man should have for a girl engaged to his friend. And some fate was continually throwing him into her company.

"If only Prince André would hurry home and marry her," thought Pierre on the way to the house.

Driving along the boulevard some one shouted his name.

"Pierre! Been back long?" a familiar voice called to him. Pierre raised his head. Anatole, with his everlasting companion Makarin, dashed by in a sledge with a pair of grey trotting-horses, who were kicking up the snow on to the forepart of the sledge.

In Marya Ahrosimov's entrance-hall the footman, as he took off Pierre's fur coat, told him that his mistress begged him to come to her in her bedroom.

As he opened the door into the reception-room, Pierre caught sight of Natasha, sitting at the window with a thin, pale, and ill-tempered face. She looked round at him, frowned, and with an expression of frigid dignity walked out of the room.

"What has happened?" asked Pierre, going in to Marya Ahrosimov.

"Fine doings," she answered. "Fifty-eight years I have lived in the world—never have I seen anything so disgraceful."

And exacting from Pierre his word of honour not to say a word about all he was to hear, Marya Ahrosimov told him everything that had taken place between Natasha and Anatole, with whom Pierre's wife had thrown her.

Pierre, with hunched shoulders, listened to what Marya Ahrosimov was saying, hardly able to believe his ears. That Natasha should give up Prince André and elope with that fool Anatole, who was married already (Pierre knew the secret of his marriage), Pierre could not comprehend. He could not reconcile the lovely impression he had of Natasha, whom he had known from childhood, with this baseness, folly, and cruelty. He thought of his wife. "They are all alike," he said to himself, reflecting he was not the only man whose unhappy fate it was to be bound to a low woman. But still he felt ready to weep with sorrow for Prince André, with sorrow for his pride. And the more he felt for his friend, the greater was the contempt and even aversion with which he thought of Natasha, who had just passed him with such an expression of rigid dignity.

"What! get married?" cried Pierre at Marya Ahrosimov's words. "He can't get married. He is married."

"What, married!" said Marya Ahrosimov. "He's a rake. A perfect scoundrel. And she's expecting him. She's been expecting him these last two days. We must tell her. At least she will leave off expecting him."

After learning from Pierre the details of Anatole's marriage, and pouring out her wrath against him, Marya Ahrosimov told Pierre why she had sent for him. She was afraid that the count or Prince André, who might arrive any moment, might hear of the affair, though she intended to conceal it from them, and might challenge Anatole. And she begged Pierre to get his brother-in-law to leave Moscow. Pierre promised to do as she desired. Then she let him go to the drawing-room.

"Mind, the count knows nothing of it. We've told him that Natasha wants to break off her engagement but nothing more. You behave as though you know nothing," she said to him. "And I'll go and tell her it's no use for her to expect him! And stay to dinner, if you care to," Marya Ahrosimov called after Pierre.

Pierre met the old count. He was upset and anxious.

"I'm in trouble, in trouble, my dear fellow," he said to Pierre. "With those girls without the mother. I do regret now that I came. I will be open with you. Have you heard she wants to break off her engagement? I never did, I'll admit, feel very much pleased at the marriage. He's an excellent man, of course, but still there could be no happiness against a father's will, and Natasha will never want for suitors. Still it had been going on so long! And now she's ill, and God knows what it is. It's a bad thing, count, a bad thing to have a daughter away from her mother. . . ." Pierre saw the count was greatly troubled, and tried to change the conversation to some other subject, but the count went back again to his troubles.

Sonya came into the drawing-room.

"Natasha would like to see you. Marya Ahrosimov is with her and she asks you to come."

"Why, yes, you're such a great friend of Bolkonsky's; no doubt she wants to send him some message," said the count. "Ah, my God, my God! How happy it all was!" And the count went out of the room.

Marya Ahrosimov had told Natasha that Anatole was married. Natasha would not believe her, and insisted on the statement being confirmed by Pierre himself. Sonya told Pierre this as she led him across the corridor to Natasha's room.

Natasha, pale and stern, was sitting beside Marya Ahrosimov, and she met Pierre at the door with eyes of feverish brilliance and inquiry. She did not smile nor nod to him. She simply looked hard at him.

"He knows everything," said Marya Ahrosimov. "Let him tell you whether I have spoken the truth."

Natasha looked from one to the other.

"Natasha," Pierre began, dropping his eyes and conscious of a feeling of pity for her and loathing for what he had to say. "Whether it is true or not cannot affect you since . . ."

"Then it is not true that he is married?"

"Yes, it is true."

"Is he still here?" she asked.

"Yes, I have just seen him."

She was obviously incapable of speaking. She made a sign with her hands for them to leave her alone.

Pierre did not stay to dinner but went away at once on leaving Natasha's room. He drove about the town looking for Anatole. On the ice-hills, at the gypsies', at Somoneno he was not to be found. Pierre drove to the club. In the club everything was going on just as usual: the members who had come in to dinner were sitting in groups; they greeted Pierre, and talked of the news of the town. Someone asked him whether he had heard of Kuragin's elopement with Natasha Rostov, of which every one was talking. Was it true? Pierre said, laughing, that it was all nonsense, for he had just come from the Rostovs'. He asked everyone about Anatole. One man told him he had not come in yet; another said he was to dine there that day. It was strange to Pierre to look at that calm, indifferent crowd of people, who knew nothing of what was passing in his soul. He walked about the hall, waited till everyone had come in, and still seeing nothing of Anatole, he did not dine, but drove home.

Anatole dined that day with Dolohov, and discussed with him new plans for eloping with Natasha. In the evening he went to his sister's, to discuss with her means for arranging their meeting. When Pierre, after vainly driving about all Moscow, returned home, his valet told him that Anatole was with the countess. The drawing-room of the countess was full of guests.

Pierre did not greet his wife, whom he had not seen since his return. She was more hateful to him than ever at that moment. He walked into the drawing-room, and seeing Anatole, went straight up to him.

"Ah, Pierre," said the countess, going up to her husband. "You don't know what a plight our poor Anatole is in . . ." She stopped short, seeing in her husband's bowed head, in his eyes, in his tread, that terrible look of rage and power, which she knew and had experienced after the duel with Dolohov.

"Wherever you are, there is vice and wickedness," said Pierre to his wife. "Anatole, come along, I want a word with you," he said in French. Anatole looked round at his sister, and got up obediently, prepared to follow Pierre.

Pierre took him by the arm and walked out of the room.

"If you allow yourself in my drawing-room . . ." Helen whispered. But Pierre walked out of the room, without answering her.

Anatole followed him, with his usual jaunty swagger. But his face betrayed uneasiness. Going into his own room, Pierre shut the door, and addressed Anatole without looking at him. "Did you promise Countess Rostov to marry her? Did you try to elope with her?"

"My dear fellow," answered Anatole, in French. "I don't consider myself bound to answer questions put to me in that tone."

Pierre's face, which had been pale before, was distorted by fury. With his big hand he clutched Anatole by the collar of his uniform.

"You're a scoundrel and a cad. And I don't know what prevents me from braining you with this, see," said Pierre, taking up a heavy paper-weight. But he quickly put it down again. "Did you promise to marry her?"

"I, I . . . I . . . didn't think . . . I never promised, though, because . . ."

Pierre interrupted him.

"Have you any of her letters? Have you any letters?" Pierre repeated. Anatole glanced at him, and at once thrust his hand in his pocket, and took out a pocket-book.

Pierre took the letter he gave him, and pushing away a table that stood in the way, he plumped down on the sofa.

"Letters—one," said Pierre, as though repeating a lesson to himself. "Two"—after a moment's silence he went on, getting up again and beginning to walk about—"to-morrow you are to leave Moscow."

"But how can I . . . ?"

"Three"—Pierre went on, not heeding him—"you are never to say a word of what has passed between you and the young countess. That I know I can't prevent your doing, but if you have a spark of conscience . . ." Pierre walked several times up and down the room. Anatole sat at the table, scowling and biting his lips.

"You surely must understand that, apart from your own pleasure, there's the happiness, the peace of other people; that you are ruining a whole life, simply because you want to amuse yourself. Amuse yourself with women like my wife—with them you're within your rights, they know what it is you want of them. They are armed against you by experience. But to promise a girl to marry her . . . to deceive, to steal . . . Surely you must see that it's as base as attacking an old man or a child! . . ."

Pierre paused and glanced at Anatole, more with inquiry now than with anger.

"And here's money too, if you need some for your trip."

Anatole smiled.

The expression of that cringing smile, that Pierre knew so well in his wife, infuriated him. "What a heartless tribe!" he cried and walked out of the room.

Next day Anatole left for Petersburg.

Pierre drove to Marya Ahrosimov's to tell her that Anatole was gone. The whole house was in excitement and alarm. Natasha was very ill. After she had been told Anatole was married, she had taken arsenic. After swallowing a little, she had been so frightened that she waked Sonya, and told her what she had done. Antidotes had been given in time, and now she was out of danger. But she was still so weak, that they could not dream of moving her to the country, and the countess had been sent for. Pierre saw the count in great trouble, and Sonya in tears, but he could not see Natasha.

That day Pierre dined at the club, and heard on every side gossip about the attempted elopement of the young Countess Rostov, and persistently denied the story, assuring every one that the only foundation for it was that his brother-

in-law had made the young lady an offer and had been refused. It seemed to Pierre that it was part of his duty to conceal the whole affair, and to save Natasha's reputation.

He was looking forward with terror to Prince André's return, and drove round every day to ask for news of him.

The old prince heard all the rumours current in the town through Mademoiselle Bourienne. He seemed in better spirits than usual, and looked forward with impatience to seeing his son.

A few days after Anatole's departure, Pierre received a note from Prince André telling him that he had arrived, and begging him to come and see him.

The first minute after Prince André's arrival in Moscow, he heard from his father's lips the story of Natasha's elopement, with additions.

Prince André had arrived in the evening. Pierre came to see him the following morning. Pierre had expected to find Prince André almost in the same state as Natasha, and he was surprised when as he entered the drawing-room he heard the sound of Prince André's voice in the study, loudly and eagerly discussing some Petersburg intrigue. The old prince and some other voice interrupted him from time to time. Princess Mary came out to meet Pierre. She turned her eyes towards the door of the room, where Prince André was, plainly intending to express her sympathy with his sorrow. But Pierre saw by Princess Mary's face that she was glad both at what had happened and at the way her brother had taken the news.

"He said he expected it," she said. "I know his pride will not allow him to express his feelings. But anyway, he has borne it better, far better, than I had expected. It seems it was to be so . . ."

"But is it all really at an end?" said Pierre.

Princess Mary looked at him with surprise. She could not understand how one could ask such a question. Pierre went into the study. Prince André was very much changed, and visibly much more robust, but there was a new horizontal line between his brows. He was in civilian dress, and standing facing his father and another old man, he was arguing with them.

The subject was Speransky, of whose sudden dismissal and supposed treason news had just reached Moscow.

"Now Speransky will be criticised and condemned by all who supported him a month ago," Prince André was saying, "and were incapable of understanding his aims. It's very easy to condemn a man when he's out of favour, and to throw upon him the blame of all the mistakes of other people. But I maintain that if anything of value has been done in the present reign, it has been done by him—by him alone . . ."

He stopped, seeing Pierre. His face quivered, and at once assumed a vindictive expression. "And posterity will do him justice," he finished, and at once turned to Pierre. "Well, how are you, still getting stouter?" he said. And the new line was still more deeply furrowed on his forehead. "Yes, I'm very well," he answered to Pierre's question, and he smiled.

After saying a few words to Pierre of the awful road from the frontiers of Poland, of people he had met in Switzerland who knew Pierre, and of M. Dessalle, whom he had brought back from Switzerland as a tutor for his son, Prince André warmly took part again in the conversation about Speransky, which had been kept up between the two old gentlemen.

"If there had been treason, and there were proofs of his secret relations with Napoleon, they would have made them public," he said with heat. "I don't and I didn't like Speransky personally, but I do like justice."

Pierre recognized now in his friend that desire he knew only too well, for excitement and discussion of something apart from himself, simply in order to stifle thoughts that were too painful and too near his heart.

When the elderly guest had gone, Prince André took Pierre's arm, and asked him to come to his room. In that room there was a folding bedstead and open trunks and boxes. Prince André went up to one of them and took out a case. Out of the case he took a package of letters. He did all this in silence, and very rapidly. He stood up again and cleared his throat. He was frowning.

"Forgive me, if I'm troubling you . . ." Pierre saw that Prince André was going to speak of Natasha, and his broad face showed sympathy and pity. That expression in Pierre's face exasperated Prince André. He went on clearly, and disagreeably: "Rumours have reached me of your brother-in-law's seeking Countess Rostov's hand, or something of the kind. Is that true?"

"Both true and untrue," began Pierre. But Prince André cut him short.

"Here are her letters and her portrait," he said. He took the package from the table and gave it to Pierre.

"Give this to the countess . . . if you see her."

"She is very ill," said Pierre.

"So she's still here?" said Prince André. "And Prince Kuragin?" he asked quickly.

"He has been gone a long while. She has been at death's door."

"I am very sorry to hear of her illness," said Prince André. He laughed a cold, malignant laugh like his father's.

"But Kuragin, then, did not deign to bestow his hand on

Countess Rostov?" said Prince André. He snorted several times.

"He could not have married her, because he is married," said Pierre.

Prince André laughed unpleasantly, again recalling his father.

"And where is he now, your brother-in-law, may I ask?" he said.

"He went to Peter . . . but, really, I don't know," said Pierre.

"Well, it doesn't matter," said Prince André. "Tell Countess Rostov from me that she was and is perfectly free, and that I wish her well."

Pierre took the package. Prince André, as though reflecting whether he had not something more to say, or waiting for Pierre to say something, looked at him with a fixed gaze.

"Listen. Do you remember our discussion in Petersburg?" said Pierre. "Do you remember about . . . ?"

"I remember," Prince André answered quickly. "I said that a fallen woman should be forgiven, but I did not say I could forgive one. I can't."

"How can you compare it?" said Pierre.

Prince André cut him short. He cried harshly: "Yes, ask her hand again, be magnanimous, and all that sort of thing? . . . Oh, that's all very noble, but I'm not equal to following in that gentleman's tracks. If you care to remain my friend, never speak to me of that . . . Of all this business. Well, good-bye."

Pierre left him, and went in to the old prince and Princess Mary.

Looking at them, Pierre felt what a contempt and dislike they had for the Rostovs; felt that it would be impossible in their presence even to mention the name of the girl who could give up Prince André for any one in the world.

That evening Pierre went to the Rostovs' to fulfil Prince André's commission. Natasha was in bed, the count was at the club, and Pierre, after giving the letters to Sonya, went in to see Marya Ahrosimov, who wanted to know how Prince André had taken the news. Ten minutes later, Sonya came into the room.

"Natasha insists on seeing Pierre," she said. "She has dressed and gone into the drawing-room."

Marya Ahrosimov could only shrug her shoulders. "When will the Countess Rostov come? Natasha has worn me out! You mind now, don't tell her everything," she said to Pierre. "One hasn't the heart to scold her, she's so piteous, poor thing."

Natasha was standing in the middle of the drawing-room, looking thinner, and with a pale, set face. When Pierre appeared in the doorway, she made a hurried movement, uncertain whether to go to meet him, or to wait for him to come to her.

Pierre went towards her. He thought she would give him her hand as usual. But she stood still, breathing hard, and letting her hands hang lifelessly, exactly in the same pose in which she used to stand in the middle of the room to sing, but with an utterly different expression.

"Pierre," she began, speaking quickly. "Prince André was your friend—he is your friend," she corrected herself. It seemed to her that everything was in the past, and now all was changed. "He told me to go to you . . ."

Pierre choked dumbly as he looked at her. Till then he had in his heart blamed her, and tried to despise her, but now he felt so sorry for her, that there was no room in his heart for blame.

"He is here now, tell him . . . to for . . . to forgive me." She stopped short and breathed even more quickly, but she did not weep.

"Yes . . . I will tell him," said Pierre. "But . . ." He did not know what to say.

Natasha was dismayed at the idea that might have occurred to Pierre.

"No, I know that everything is over," she said hurriedly. "No, that can never be. I'm only wretched at the wrong I have done him. Only tell him that I beg him to forgive, to forgive, forgive me for everything . . ." She was trembling. She sat down on a chair.

A feeling of pity he had never known before flooded Pierre's heart.

"I will tell him, I will tell him everything once more," said Pierre. "But . . . I should like to know one thing . . ."

"To know what?" Natasha's eyes asked.

"I should like to know, did you love . . ." Pierre did not know what to call Anatole, and flushed at the thought of him. "Did you love Anatole?"

"I don't . . . know. I don't know . . ." She began crying, and Pierre was more than ever overwhelmed with pity, tenderness, and love. He felt the tears trickling under his spectacles.

"We won't talk any more of it, my dear," he said. It seemed suddenly so strange to Natasha to hear the gentle, tender, sympathetic voice in which he spoke. "We won't talk of it, my dear, I'll tell him everything. But one thing I beg you, look on me as your friend. And if you want help, advice, or simply want to open your heart to some one—not now, but when things are clearer in your heart—think of me." He took her hand and kissed it. "I shall be happy, if I am able . . ." Pierre was confused.

Natasha was crying and she wanted to leave the room, but Pierre held her hand. There was something more he wanted to say to her. But when he said it, he was surprised at his own words.

"Your whole life lies before you," he said to her. "If I were not myself, but the most handsome, the most clever, the best man in the world, and if I were free I would this minute beg for your hand and your love."

Natasha looked at Pierre tenderly through her tears, and ran out of the room.

Pierre followed her, almost running into the vestibule. And restraining the tears of happiness that made a lump in his throat, he flung on his fur coat, unable to find the armholes, and got into his sledge.

"Where to, your excellency?" asked the coachman.

"Where?" Pierre asked himself. "Where can I go now? Not to the club or to pay calls." All men seemed to him so pitiful, so poor in comparison with the feeling of tenderness and love in his heart, in comparison with that softened, grateful glance she had turned upon him that last minute through her tears.

"Home," said Pierre, throwing open the bearskin coat, in spite of ten degrees of frost.

It was clear and frosty. Over the dirty, half-dark streets, over the black roofs was a starlit sky.

1812

BOOK NINE

THE OUTBREAK of the war, which everyone had been expecting, at last took place.

On the 29th of May Napoleon left Dresden, where he had been spending three weeks surrounded by a court that included princes, dukes, kings, and one emperor.

He rode in a travelling carriage, drawn by six horses and surrounded by pages, adjutants, and an armed escort, along the route by Posen, Thorn, Danzig, and Königsberg. In each of these towns he was welcomed with enthusiasm and fear by thousands of people.

His army was moving from west to east, and he was driven

after it by continual relays of six horses. On the 10th of June he overtook the army and spent the night in the Vilkovik forest, in quarters prepared for him on the property of a Polish count.

The following day Napoleon drove on ahead of the army, reached the River Niemen, put on a Polish uniform in order to inspect the crossing of the river, and rode out on the river bank.

When he saw the Cossacks posted on the further bank, the Russian side of the river, and the expanse of the steppes—in the midst of which, far away, was the holy city, Moscow, capital of an empire—he ordered an immediate advance.

The troops knew of the Emperor's presence, and were on the lookout for him. When they caught sight of his figure in his greatcoat and hat standing apart from his suite on a hill, they threw up their caps and shouted, *"Vive l'Empereur!"* And one regiment after another, in a continuous stream, flowed out of the immense Vilkovik forest that had concealed them, and split up to cross the river. And every soldier's face wore an expression of pleasure at the beginning of the long-expected campaign, and enthusiasm and devotion to the man in the grey coat standing on the nearby hill.

The Russian Emperor had meanwhile been spending more than a month in Vilna, holding reviews and inspecting manœuvres. Nothing was in readiness for the war, though it was to prepare for it that the Tsar had come from Petersburg. There was no general plan of action. The vacillation between all the plans that were proposed and the inability to fix on any one of them, was more marked than ever after the Tsar had been for a month at headquarters. There was a separate commander at the head of each of the three armies; but there was no commander with authority over all of them, and the Tsar did not undertake the duties of such a commander-in-chief himself.

The longer the Tsar stayed at Vilna, the less ready was the Russian army for the war, which it had grown weary of expecting. Every effort of the men who surrounded the Tsar seemed to be devoted to making their sovereign spend his time pleasantly and forget the impending war.

Many balls and fêtes were given by the Polish aristocracy, by members of the court, and by the Tsar himself. And in the month of June it occurred to one of the Polish generals attached to the Tsar that all the generals on the staff should give a dinner and a ball to the Tsar. The suggestion was eagerly taken up. The Tsar gave his consent. The generals on the staff subscribed the necessary funds. The lady who was most likely to please the Tsar's taste was selected as hostess for the ball. Count Bennigsen, who had land in the Vilna province, offered his house in the outskirts for this fête, and the 13th of June was the day fixed for a ball, a dinner, with a regatta and fireworks.

On the very day on which Napoleon gave the order to cross the Niemen, and the vanguard of his army crossed the Russian frontier, driving back the Cossacks, Alexander was at the ball given by the generals on his staff at Count Bennigsen's house.

It was a brilliant and festive entertainment. Connoisseurs declared that rarely had so many beauties been gathered together at one place. Countess Bezuhov, who had been among the Russian ladies who had followed the Tsar from Petersburg to Vilna, was at that ball, her heavy, Russian style of beauty overshadowing the more refined Polish ladies. She was much noticed, and the Tsar had deigned to bestow a dance upon her.

Boris Drubetskoy, who had left his wife Julie at Moscow, and was living *"en garçon,"* as he said, at Vilna, was also at that ball; and although he was not a general on the staff, he had subscribed a large sum. Boris was now a wealthy man who had risen to high honours. He no longer sought patronage, but was on an equal footing with the most distinguished men of his age. At Vilna he met Helen, whom he had not seen for a long while. As Helen was enjoying the good graces of a very important personage indeed, and Boris had so recently been married, they made no allusion to the past, but met as good-natured, old friends.

At midnight dancing was still going on. Helen happening to have no suitable partner had herself proposed a mazurka to Boris. They were the third couple. Boris was looking coldly at Helen's splendid bare shoulders, which rose out of her dress of dark gauze and gold, and was talking to her of old acquaintances, and yet he never for a second ceased watching the Tsar who was in the same room. The Tsar was not dancing; he was standing in the doorway, stopping one person after the other with the gracious words he alone knew how to utter.

At the beginning of the mazurka, Boris saw that a general of the staff went up to him, regardless of court etiquette, while he spoke with a Polish lady. The Tsar glanced inquiringly and apparently seeing that the general had weighty reasons for doing so, he gave the lady a slight nod and turned to him. The Tsar betrayed amazement, as soon as the general had begun to speak. He took the general's arm and walked across the room with him and out into the lighted garden.

Boris went on performing the figures of the mazurka, but he was now wondering what the news could be that the general had brought, and in what way he could find it out before other people. In the figure in which he had to choose a lady, he whispered to Helen that he wanted to choose Countess Pototsky, who had, he thought, gone out on to the balcony, and hurrying away he rushed to the door that opened into the garden.

The Tsar in the tone of a man resenting a personal insult was saying: "To enter Russia with no declaration of war! I will consent to conciliation only when not a single enemy under arms is left in my country." Then seeing Boris and frowning, he added: "Let nobody know of it!"

Boris saw that this was aimed at him, and closing his eyes, bowed his head a little. The Tsar went back to the ballroom, and remained there another half hour.

In this way Boris was the first person to learn the news that French troops had crossed the Niemen. And because of this he was later able to prove to various persons of great consequence, that much that was hidden from others was commonly known to him, and he was thereby enabled to rise even higher than before in the opinion of those persons.

After his interview with Pierre in Moscow, Prince André went away to Petersburg, telling his family that he had business there. However, his true object was to meet Anatole Kuragin. But when he reached Petersburg, he found he was no longer there. Pierre had let his brother-in-law know that Prince André was on his track. And Anatole had promptly obtained a commission from the minister of war, and had gone to join the army near the Turkish border.

While in Petersburg Prince André met Kutuzov, his old general, and Kutuzov proposed that he should accompany him to the Turkish front, where the old general was being sent to take command of the army. Prince André received an appointment on his staff.

Prince André was seeking to encounter Anatole. But on the Turkish front too Prince André failed to come across him. Anatole had returned to Russia shortly after Prince André reached the Turkish lines.

In a new country, amid new surroundings, Prince André found life easier to bear. After Natasha's betrayal, which he felt more keenly, the more he strove to conceal its effect on him from others, he found it hard to bear the conditions of life in which he had been happy, and felt still more irksome the freedom and independence he had once prized so highly. He could not now think the thoughts that had come to him for the first time on the field of Austerlitz, that he had loved to develop with Pierre, and that had enriched his solitude at Bogutcharovo, and later on in Switzerland and in Rome. Now he dreaded those ideas that had then opened to him boundless vistas of light. Now he was occupied only with the most practical interests lying close at hand, and in no way associated with those old ideals. He clutched at these new interests the more eagerly, the more the old ideals were hidden from him. It was as though the infinite, fathomless arch of heaven that had once stood over him had been suddenly transformed into a low, limited vault weighing upon him, with everything in it clear, but nothing eternal and mysterious.

He performed the duties of a general on Kutuzov's staff with perseverance, surprising Kutuzov by his eagerness for work and his conscientiousness. When he missed Anatole in Turkey, Prince André did not feel it necessary to gallop back to Russia in search of him. Yet in spite of all his contempt for Anatole, in spite of all the arguments by which he sought to persuade himself that Anatole was not worth his stooping to quarrel with him, he knew that whatever length of time might elapse, when he did meet him, he would be unable to help challenging him. And the consciousness that the insult was not yet avenged, that his anger had not been expended, but was stored up in his heart, poisoned the artificial composure, which Prince André succeeded in obtaining in Turkey in the form of ambition and vain energy.

In 1812, when the news of the war with Napoleon reached Bucharest, where Kutuzov had been fourteen months, spending days and nights together with his mistress, Prince André asked to be transferred to the western army. Kutuzov, who was by now sick of Prince André's energy, and felt it a standing reproach to his laziness, was very ready to let him go, and gave him a commission for Barclay de Tolly.

Before joining the army of the west, which in May was encamped at Drissa, Prince André went to Bleak Hills, which was on the way, only three miles from the Smolensk high-road.

During the last three years Prince André had passed through such changes of thought and feeling, that it struck him as strange and amazing to find at Bleak Hills life going on in precisely the same routine as ever. He rode up the avenue to the stone gates of the house, feeling as though it were an enchanted, sleeping castle. The same sedateness, the same cleanliness, the same silence reigned in the house; there was the same furniture, the same walls, the same sounds, the same smell, and the same timid faces, only a little older.

Princess Mary was just the same timid, plain girl, no longer in her first youth, wasting the best years of her life in continual dread and suffering. Mademoiselle Bourienne was just the same self-satisfied, coquettish girl, enjoying every moment of her life, and filled with the most joyous hopes for the future. She seemed only to have gained boldness, so Prince

André thought. The tutor he had brought back from Switzerland, Dessalle, was wearing a coat of Russian cut, and talked broken Russian to the servants, but he was just the same narrow-minded, cultivated, conscientious, pedantic teacher. The only physical change apparent in the old prince was the loss of a tooth, that left a gap at the side of his mouth. In character he was the same as ever, only showing even more irritability and skepticism as to everything that happened in the world. Little Nicholas was the only one who had changed. He had grown taller, and had curly dark hair. He was the only one not in bondage to the law of sameness that reigned in that spellbound sleeping castle.

But though externally all was exactly as of old, the inner relations of all the persons concerned had changed since Prince André had seen them last. The household was split up into two hostile camps, which held aloof from one another, and only now came together in his presence, abandoning their ordinary habits on his account. To one camp belonged the old prince, Mademoiselle Bourienne, and the architect; to the other, Princess Mary, Dessalle, little Nicholas, and all the nurses.

During Prince André's stay at Bleak Hills all the family dined together, but every one was ill at ease, and Prince André felt that he was being treated as a guest for whom an exception was being made. The first day he could not help being aware of this at dinner, and sat in silence. The old prince noticed this, and he, too, preserved a sullen silence, and immediately after dinner withdrew to his own room. Later in the evening when Prince André went in to him, and began telling him about the campaign in Turkey to try and rouse him, the old prince, to his surprise, began talking about Princess Mary, grumbling at her superstitiousness, and her dislike of Mademoiselle Bourienne, who was, he said, the only person really attached to him.

The old prince declared that it was all Princess Mary's doing if he were ill; that she plagued and worried him on purpose, and that she was spoiling little Prince Nicholas by the way she petted him, and the silly tales she told him. "Why is it André, who sees it, says nothing about his sister?" the old prince wondered. "Why, does he suppose I'm a scoundrel or an old fool to be alienated from my daughter and friendly with this Frenchwoman for no good reason? He doesn't understand, and so I must explain it to him; he must hear what I have to say about it," thought the old prince. And so he began to explain the reason why he could not put up with his daughter's unreasonable character.

"If you ask me," said Prince André, not looking at his father (it was the first time in his life that he had blamed his father), "I did not wish to speak of it—but, if you ask me, I'll tell you my opinion frankly in regard to the whole matter. If there is any misunderstanding and estrangement between you and Mary, I can't blame her for it—I know how she loves and respects you. If you ask me," Prince André continued, losing his temper, as he very readily did in these days, "I can only say one thing; if there are misunderstandings, the cause of them is that worthless Frenchwoman, who is not fit to be my sister's companion."

The old man stared for a moment at his son, and a forced smile revealed the loss of the tooth, to which Prince André could not become accustomed.

"What companion? Eh! So you've talked it over already! Eh?"

"Father, I had no wish to judge you," said Prince André, in a hard tone. "But you have provoked me, and I have said, and shall always say, that Mary is not to blame, but the people to blame—the person to blame—is that Frenchwoman . . ."

"Ah, he has passed judgment! . . . he has passed judgment!" said the old man, in a low voice, and Prince André felt, with embarrassment. But immediately after he leapt up and screamed: "Go away, go away! Let me never set eyes on you again! . . ."

Prince André reached the headquarters of the army at the end of June. The first army, with which the Tsar was, was stationed in a fortified camp at Drissa. The second army was retreating, striving to effect a junction with the first army, from which—so it was said—it had been cut off by immense French forces. Every one was dissatisfied with the general course of events in the Russian army. But no one even dreamed of any danger of the Russian provinces being invaded, no one imagined the war could extend beyond the frontiers of the western Polish provinces.

Prince André found Barclay de Tolly, to whom he was sent, on the banks of the Drissa. Since there was not one large village nor dwelling-place in the neighbourhood of the camp, the numberless generals and courtiers accompanying the army were distributed about the neighbourhood for ten miles round in the best houses of the villages on both sides of the river. Barclay de Tolly was staying four miles away from the Tsar. He gave Prince André a dry and frigid reception, and said in his German accent that he would mention him to the Tsar so that a definite appointment might be given him, and that meanwhile he begged him to remain on his staff.

During the days that followed, Prince André had much

leisure time. He was not called upon to do anything and so he spent his time riding around all the fortifications, inspecting the army and talking to many officers. And he was shocked to discover that all seemed in a state of chaos. There were eight distinct and conflicting groups all rivaling each other and all trying to win the Tsar's approval for their special plans for the coming campaign. Prince André was further disturbed by the fact that many of the generals, those who spoke loudest, were foreigners. Some were Swedish, some French; but it was the Germans who were most insistent and most positive that their plans were the only plans that could be successful.

However at this time yet another, a ninth party, was being formed out of all the rest, and was just making its voice heard. It consisted of sensible men of age and political experience, sharing none of the conflicting opinions, and able to take a general view of all that was being done at headquarters, and to consider means for escaping from the vagueness, uncertainty, confusion, and feebleness.

The members of this party thought and said that the whole evil was primarily due to the presence of the Tsar with his military court in the army; that it brought into the army that indefinite, conditional, and fluctuating uncertainty of relations which is in place in a court, but harmful in an army; that it was for the Tsar to govern and not to lead his troops; that the only escape from the position was the departure of the Tsar and his court from the army; that the simple presence of the Tsar paralysed fifty thousand troops, which must be retained to secure his personal safety; that the worst commander-in-chief, acting independently, would be better than the best commander-in-chief with his hands tied by the presence and authority of the Tsar.

Sishkov, the secretary of state, one of the leading representatives of this last group, wrote to the Tsar a letter to which Balashov, a general in close attendance on the Tsar, and Araktcheev, the late Minister of War, agreed to add their signatures. In this letter he took advantage of the Tsar's permitting him to offer his opinion on the general question, and respectfully suggested the sovereign's leaving the army, urging as a pretext for his doing so the absolute necessity of his presence to rouse public feeling in the capital.

To appeal to the people, and to rouse them in defence of their country, was represented as urgently necessary to the Tsar, and was accepted by him as a sufficient reason for leaving.

Prince André pondered on all these things, on the clashes of personalities and on the idea which had long ago and often occurred to him during the period of his active service, that there was and could be no sort of military science, and that therefore there could not be such a thing as military genius. This seemed to him now to be an absolutely obvious truth. "What theory and science can there be of a subject of which the conditions and circumstances are uncertain and can never be definitely known, in which the strength of the active forces engaged can be even less definitely measured? No one can, or possibly could, know the relative positions of our army and the enemy's in another twenty-four hours. And no one can gauge the force of this or the other detachment. Victory or defeat depends in reality on the soldier in the ranks who first shouts 'Hurrah!' or 'We are lost!' And it is only in the ranks that one can serve with perfect conviction, that one is of use!"

Such were Prince André's reflections. And the next day at the review when the Tsar asked Prince André where he desired to serve, he ruined his chances for ever in the court world by asking to be sent to the front, instead of begging for a post in attendance on the Tsar's person.

Before the beginning of the campaign Nicholas Rostov had received a letter from his parents, in which they told him briefly of Natasha's illness and the breaking off of her engagement, and again begged him to retire from the army and come home to them. On receiving this letter Nicholas wrote to his parents that he would do everything in his power to follow their wishes.

It was, in fact, only the outbreak of the war that detained Nicholas and prevented him from returning home, as he had promised, and marrying Sonya. The autumn at Otradnoe with the hunting, and the winter with the Christmas festivities and Sonya's love had opened before him a vista of peace and quiet country delights unknown to him before, and this prospect now lured him back. "A charming wife, children, a good pack of hounds, the estate to look after, the neighbours, election to offices, perhaps, by the provincial nobility," he mused. But now war was breaking out, and he had to remain with his regiment. And since this had to be, Nicholas was characteristically able to be content with the life he led in the regiment, and to make that life a pleasant one.

On his return from his leave, Nicholas had been joyfully welcomed by his comrades. In his absence he had been promoted to captain, and when the regiment was being made ready with reinforcements for active service, he was again put in command of his old squadron.

The campaign was beginning, pay was doubled, the regiment was reinforced with new officers, new men, and fresh horses, and had moved into Poland. The army had been compelled to retreat from Vilna owing to various complex considerations of state, of policy, and tactics. Every step of that retreat had been accompanied by a complicated play of interests, arguments, and passions at headquarters. For the hussars of the Pavlograd regiment, however, this whole march in the finest part of the summer, with ample supplies, was a most simple and agreeable business. Intrigue was possible only at headquarters; the rank and file of the army never even wondered where and why they were going. If the retreat was a subject of regret, it was simply owing to the necessity of leaving quarters one had grown used to or a pretty Polish hostess.

On the 13th of July the Pavlograd hussars took part in their first serious action.

On the previous evening there had been a violent storm of rain and hail. The two Pavlograd squadrons were bivouacking in the middle of a field of rye, which was already ripe, but had been completely trodden down by cattle and horses. The rain was falling in torrents, and Rostov was sitting with a young officer, Ilyin, under a shanty, that had been rigged up for them.

Rostov smoked his pipe, and wriggled his neck, down which the water was trickling. He looked from time to time at Ilyin, who was squatting beside him. Ilyin, a boy of sixteen, who had lately joined the regiment, took the place Nicholas had taken seven years before with Denisov. He tried to imitate Rostov in everything and worshipped him.

"I can't stand this," said Ilyin. "I'm wet through. I'm going to look for shelter. I think the rain's not so heavy." He ran out.

Five minutes later he came back splashing through the mud.

"Hurrah! Rostov, hurry. I have found an inn. A lot of our fellows are there already. We can get dry."

Rostov flung on a cape, shouted to Lavrushka to follow them with their things, and went off with Ilyin, slipping in the mud, and splashing through the pools in the drizzling rain and the darkness, which was rent at intervals by distant lightning.

It was past two o'clock. No one at the inn was yet asleep, when the quartermaster appeared, bringing a command to advance upon a little place called Ostrovna. The officers began hurriedly getting ready; the samovar was filled up with dirty water. But Rostov, without waiting for tea, went off to his squadron. It was already light; the rain had stopped, and the clouds were parting. It was chill and damp.

Half an hour later the squadron stood drawn up on the road. The word of command was heard, "Mount!" and the soldiers crossed themselves and got on their horses. Rostov, riding ahead of them, gave the word: "Forward!" and drawing out four abreast, the hussars started with a sound of subdued talk, splashing hoofs, and jingling sabres. They trotted along the broad highway, with birch-trees on each side of it, following the infantry and artillery, who had gone on before.

As soon as the sun appeared in a clear strip of sky under the storm-clouds, the wind sank, as though not daring to spoil the beauty of the summer morning after the storm. The trees still dripped, but the drops fell vertically now, and all was hushed. Everything grew bright and shining. And with the bright light, as though in response to it, rang out shots in front of them.

Rostov had not time to collect his thoughts and decide how far off these shots were, when an adjutant of Count Osterman-Tolstoy galloped up from Vitebsk, bringing the order to advance at full speed along the road.

The squadron overtook and passed the infantry and the battery. Then the hussars raced downhill, passed through an empty and deserted village, and trotted uphill again and halted behind the Uhlans, who formed the front line. On the right was a dense column of infantry—they formed the reserves; on the hill above them, in the pure, clear air, in the brilliant, slanting, morning sunshine, could be seen cannons on the very horizon line. In front, beyond a hollow dale, could be seen the enemy's columns and cannons. In the dale could be heard advance pickets, already keeping up a lively interchange of shots with the enemy.

Rostov felt his spirits rise at those sounds, so long unheard, as though they had been the liveliest music. Trap-ta-ta-tap! rang out several shots, first together, then in rapid succession. All sank into silence again.

Then the command rang out among the Uhlans, "Form in column; make ready to charge!" The infantry in front parted in two to let the cavalry pass through. The Uhlans galloped off, the streamers on their lances waving, and trotted downhill towards the French cavalry, who came into sight below on the left.

As soon as the Uhlans had started downhill, the hussars received the order to ride off uphill to cover the battery. Just as the hussars were moving into the place of the Uhlans, there came flying from the outposts some cannon-balls, hissing and whistling out of the distance, and hitting nothing.

Five minutes later the Uhlans were dashing back, not towards the spot where they had been posted, but more to the left. Between the ranks of Uhlans on the chestnut horses, and in a great mass behind them, could be seen blue French dragoons on grey horses.

Rostov, was one of the first to spot these blue dragoons pursuing Uhlans. Nearer and nearer flew the disordered crowds of Uhlans and the French dragoons in pursuit of them. He could see now separate figures, looking small at the bottom of the hill, fighting, overtaking one another, and waving their arms and their swords.

Rostov gazed at what was passing before him as at a hunt. He felt instinctively that if he were to charge with his hussars on the French dragoons now, they could not stand their ground; but if he were to charge it must be that very minute or it would be too late. He looked round. The captain standing beside him had his eyes too fixed on the cavalry below.

"We could close them in, if . . ." said Rostov.

"Yes," said the captain, "and . . ."

Rostov, without waiting for his answer, set spurs to his horse and galloped off in front of his squadron. Before he had time to give the command, the whole squadron, sharing his feeling, flew after him. Rostov himself could not have said how or why he did it. He did it all without thinking or considering.

Letting his horse go at full speed, he galloped to cut off the broken ranks of the dragoons. One Uhlan halted; another, on foot, flung himself to the ground to avoid being knocked down; a riderless horse was carried along with the hussars. Almost all the dragoons were galloping back. Rostov picked out one of them on a grey horse and flew after him. On the way he rode straight at a bush; his gallant horse cleared it; and Nicholas was hardly straight in the saddle again when he saw in a few seconds he would overtake the enemy he had pitched upon as his aim. The Frenchman, an officer, sat crouched upon his grey horse, urging it on with his sword. In another instant Rostov's horse dashed up against the grey horse's hindquarters, almost knocking it over, and at the same second Rostov, not knowing why he did so, raised his sword, and aimed a blow at the Frenchman.

The instant he did this all Rostov's eagerness suddenly vanished. The officer fell to the ground, not so much from the sword cut, for it had only just grazed his arm above the elbow, as from fright and the shock to his horse. As Rostov pulled his horse in, his eyes sought his foe to see what sort of man he had attacked. The French officer was hopping along on the ground, with one foot caught in the stirrup. Screwing up his eyes, as though expecting another blow every instant, he looked at Rostov with terror. His pale, mud-stained face—fair and young, with clear blue eyes—was the most unwarlike, most good-natured face, more in place by a quiet fireside than on the field of battle. Before Rostov could make up his mind what to do with him, the officer shouted, "I surrender." He tried hurriedly and failed to free his foot from the stirrup, and still gazed with his frightened blue eyes

at Rostov. The hussars, galloping up, freed his foot, and got him into his saddle. The hussars were busily engaged on all sides with the dragoons; one was wounded, but though his face was streaming with blood he would not let go of his horse; another put his arm round an hussar as he sat perched up behind on his horse; a third was clambering on to his horse, supported by an hussar.

The French infantry were in front, firing as they ran. The hussars galloped quickly back with their prisoners. Rostov galloped back with the rest, conscious of some disagreeable sensation, a kind of ache at his heart. A glimpse of something vague and confused, of which he could not get a clear view, seemed to have come to him with the capture of that French officer and the blow he had dealt him.

Count Osterman-Tolstoy met the hussars on their return, summoned Rostov, thanked him and told him he would report his gallant action to the Tsar and would recommend him for the cross of St. George. Osterman's flattering words and promise of a reward should have been pleasant to Rostov; but he still suffered from that unpleasant vague feeling of moral nausea. "Why, what on earth is it that's worrying me?" he wondered, as he rode away from the general. "Ilyin? No, he's all right. Did I do anything disgraceful? No, that's not it either!" Something else fretted him like a remorse. "Yes, yes, that officer. And I remember clearly how my hand paused when I had lifted it."

Rostov saw the prisoners being led away, and galloped after them to look at his Frenchman. He was sitting in his strange uniform on one of the spare horses, looking uneasily about him. The sword-cut on his arm could hardly be called a wound. He looked at Rostov with a constrained smile, and waved his hand by way of a greeting. Rostov still felt the same discomfort and vague remorse.

There was something he could not fathom. "So they are even more frightened than we are," he thought. "Why, is this all that's meant by heroism? And did I do it for the sake of my country? And was he to blame with his blue eyes? How frightened he was! He thought I was going to kill him. Why should I kill him? My hand trembled. And they have given me the St. George's Cross. I can't make it out, I can't make it out!"

But while Nicholas was worrying over these questions in his heart and unable to find any clear solution of the doubts that troubled him, the wheel of fortune was turning in his favour, as so often happens in the service. He was brought forward after the affair at Ostrovna, received the command of a battalion of hussars, and when an officer of dauntless courage was wanted he was picked out.

Countess Rostov had not recovered her strength when she received the news of Natasha's illness. Weak as she still was, she set out at once for Moscow with Peter and the whole household. And the Rostovs moved from Marya Ahrosimov's into their own house.

Natasha's illness was so serious that, luckily for herself and her parents, all thought of what had caused it, of her conduct and of the breaking off of her engagement, fell into the background. She was so ill that no one could consider how far she was to blame for all that had happened, while she could not eat nor sleep, was growing visibly thinner, coughed, and was, as the doctors gave them to understand, in actual danger. Nothing could be thought of but how to make her well again.

The doctor came every day, felt her pulse, looked at her tongue, and made jokes, regardless of her dejected face. But then when he had gone into the next room, and the countess had hastily followed him, he assumed a serious face, and shaking his head gravely, said that though there was indeed danger, he had hopes from the effect of the most recent medicine, and that they could only wait and see; that the illness was more due to moral than physical causes, but . . . The countess slipped some gold into his hand, trying to conceal the action from herself and from him, and always went back to the sick-room with a lighter heart.

All the summer of 1812 the Rostovs did not visit the country. But in spite of the loss of the country life to which she was accustomed, youth gained the upper hand; Natasha's grief began to be covered up by the impressions of daily life; it ceased to lie like an aching load on her heart; it began to fade into the past; and Natasha began to return to health again.

Natasha was calmer, but no happier. She did not merely shun every amusement—balls, skating, concerts, and theatres—but she never even laughed without the sound of tears behind her laughter. She could not sing. As soon as she began to laugh or attempted to sing, tears choked her: tears of remorse; tears of regret for that time of pure happiness that could never return; tears of vexation that she should so wantonly have ruined her young life, that might have been so happy. Laughter and singing especially seemed to her like scoffing at her grief. She never even thought of desiring admiration; she had no impulse of vanity to restrain. She said and felt at that time that all men were no more to her than buffoons. An inner sentinel seemed to guard against every sort of pleasure. And, indeed, she seemed to have lost all the old interests of her girlish, careless life, that had been so full of hope. Most often, and with most pining, she brooded over the memory of those autumn months, and the Christmas holidays spent with Nicholas at Otradnoe. What would she not have given to bring back one single day of that time! But it was all over for her. Yet she had to live.

There was no gladness in life. She held aloof from all the household. It was only with her brother, Peter, that she felt at ease. She liked being with him better than being with the rest, and sometimes even laughed when she was alone with him. She hardly left the house to go anywhere; and of the guests who came to the house she was only glad to see one person—Pierre. No one could have been more tender, circumspect, and at the same time serious, than Pierre in his manner to her.

Natasha was unconsciously aware of this tenderness, and it was owing to it that she found more pleasure in his society. But she was not even grateful to him for it. Nothing good in him seemed to her due to an effort on Pierre's part. It seemed so natural to Pierre to be kind that there was no merit in his kindness. Sometimes Natasha noticed some confusion or awkwardness in Pierre in her presence, especially when he was trying to do something for her pleasure or afraid something in the conversation might suggest to her painful memories. She saw this, and put it down to his general kindliness and shyness, which she supposed would be the same with every one else. Ever since those unforeseen words—that if he had been free, he would have asked for her hand and her love—Pierre had said nothing of his feelings to Natasha. And it seemed to her clear that those words, which had so comforted her, had been uttered, just as one says any meaningless nonsense to console a weeping child. It was not because Pierre was a married man, but because Natasha felt between herself and him the force of that moral barrier—of the absence of which she had been so conscious with Anatole—that the idea never occurred to her that her relations with Pierre might develop into love on her side, and still less on his, or even into that tender, self-conscious, romantic friendship between a man and a woman, of which she had known several instances.

At the beginning of July the rumours of the war became more and more alarming. And there was talk of the Tsar's appeal to the people, and the Tsar himself was said to be coming from the army to Moscow. But since, up to the 11th of July, the manifesto and appeal to the people had not been received, the most exaggerated reports about them and the position of Russia were heard. It was said that the Tsar was coming away because the army was in danger. It was said that Smolensk had surrendered; that Napoleon had millions of troops, and that nothing short of a miracle could save Russia.

On Saturday, the 11th of July, the manifesto was received,

but was not yet in print; and Pierre, who happened to be at the Rostovs', promised to come next day, Sunday, to dinner, and to bring a copy of the manifesto, which he could obtain from Count Rastoptchin, the governor general of Moscow.

That Sunday the Rostovs attended service in the private chapel of the Razumovskys. It was a hot July day. Even by ten o'clock, when the Rostovs got out of their carriage before the chapel, the sultry air, the shouts of the street hawkers, the gay, light summer dresses of the crowd, the dusty leaves of the trees on the boulevard, the martial music and white trousers of the battalion marching by to parade, and the brilliant, hot sunshine, were all full of that summer languor, that content and discontent with the present, which is felt particularly vividly on a bright, hot day in town. All the fashionable world of Moscow, all the Rostovs' acquaintances were in the chapel. A great number of wealthy families, who usually spent the summer in the country, were staying on in Moscow, as though in vague anticipation of something.

A handsome, clean-looking old priest read the service with the mild solemnity that has such an elevating and soothing effect on the souls of those who pray. The sanctuary doors were closed, the curtain was slowly drawn, and a voice, mysteriously subdued, uttered some word from it. Tears, that she could not herself have explained, rose to Natasha's eyes.

"Teach me what to do, how to live my life, how to conquer my sins for ever, for ever!" . . . she prayed. The deacon came out to the steps before the altar screen; with his thumb held out apart from the rest, he pulled his long hair out from under his surplice, and laying the cross on his breast, he began in a loud voice solemnly reading the prayer:

"As one community let us pray to the Lord."

"As one community, all together without distinction of class, free from enmity, all united in brotherly love, let us pray," thought Natasha.

"For the world above and the salvation of our souls!"

"For the world of angels and the souls of all spiritual beings who live above us," prayed Natasha.

When they prayed for the army, she thought of her brother and Denisov. When they prayed for all travelling by sea and by land, she thought of Prince André, and prayed for him, and prayed that God would forgive her the wrong she had done him. When they prayed for all who love us, she prayed for all her family, her father and mother, and Sonya—for the first time feeling all the shortcomings in her behaviour to them, and all the strength of her own love for them. When they prayed for those who hate us, she tried to think of enemies, to pray for them. She counted as enemies all her father's creditors, and every one who had business relations with him; and always at the thought of enemies who hated her she thought of Anatole, who had done her so cruel an injury; she prayed for him, as an enemy. It was only at her prayers that she felt able to think calmly and clearly either of Prince André or of Anatole, with a sense that her feelings for them were as nothing compared with her feeling of worship and awe of God. When they prayed for the Imperial family and the Synod, she bowed and crossed herself more devoutly than ever, telling herself that if she did not comprehend, she could not doubt, and anyway loved the Holy Synod and prayed for it.

When the litany was over, the deacon crossed his stole over his breast and pronounced:

"Ourselves and our life we offer up to Christ the Lord!"

"Ourselves we offer up to God," Natasha repeated in her heart. "My God, I give myself unto Thy keeping!" she thought. "I ask for nothing, I desire nothing; teach me how to act, how to do Thy will! Yes, take me; take me to Thee!" Natasha said, with devout impatience in her heart. She did not cross herself, but stood with her thin arms hanging down, as though in expectation every moment that an unseen force would come and carry her off and rescue her from herself, from her regrets and desires and remorse and hopes and sins.

Several times during the service the countess looked round at her daughter and prayed to God to help her.

To the general surprise, in the middle of the service, which Natasha knew so well, the deacon brought forward the little bench, from which they repeated the prayers, kneeling, on Trinity Day, and set it before the sanctuary doors. The priest advanced in his lilac velvet calotte, threw back his hair, and, with an effort, dropped on his knees. All the congregation did the same, looking at one another in surprise. There followed the prayer, which had just been received from the Synod, the prayer for the delivery of Russia out of the hands of the enemy.

"Lord God of our might, God of our salvation," began the priest in a clear, mild, unemphatic voice.

"Lord God of might, God of our salvation! Look in grace and blessing on Thy humble people, and hear with loving-kindness, and spare and have mercy on us. The foe is confounding Thy land, and is fain to rise up against all the earth and lay it waste. These lawless men are gathered together to overwhelm Thy kingdom, to destroy Thy holy Jerusalem, Thy beloved Russia: to defile Thy temples, to overturn the altars and violate our holy shrines.

"Almighty God! Hear us when we pray to Thee, strengthen with Thy might our most gracious and supreme sovereign, Emperor Alexander. Be mindful of his truth and mercy, recompense him according to his good deeds, and let them preserve Thy chosen Israel. Bless his counsels, his undertakings, and his deeds; fortify his kingdom with Thy Almighty hand, and vouchsafe him victory over the enemy, even as Thou gavest Moses victory over Amalek, and Gideon over Midian, and David over Goliath. Preserve his army; put weapons of brass in the hands that wage war in Thy name, and gird them about with strength for the battle. Take Thou the lance and shield, and rise up to succour us, and put to shame and to confusion them that devise evil against us, and let them be scattered before the face of Thy faithful armament like dust before the wind; and may Thy mighty angel put them to flight and to confusion. And let the net ensnare them when they wot not of it, and their plots that they have hatched in secret be turned against them. And let them be laid low before the feet of Thy servants and vanquished by our hosts. Lord! it is nought for Thee to save both great and small. Thou art God, and man can do nought against Thee!

"God of our Fathers! Turn not Thy face away from us; be gracious to our unworthiness; overlook our transgressions and our iniquities. Fortify us with hope; let not the sceptre of the unrighteous be exalted above the destinies of Thy holy people.

"O Lord our God, in Whom we believe, and in Whom we put our trust, strike down our enemies and trample them swiftly under the feet of Thy faithful. Thou art the defence, the succour, and the victory of them that put their trust in Thee; and to Thee be the glory, to Father, and to Son, and to Holy Ghost, now and ever has been, for ever and ever. Amen!"

In Natasha's impressionable state, this prayer affected her strongly. She heard every word about Moses' victory over Amalek, and Gideon's over Midian, and David's over Goliath, and about the destruction of Thy Jerusalem; and she prayed to God with all the tenderness and fervour with which her heart was overflowing, but she had no distinct idea what she was asking for in this prayer. Yet she could have no doubts of the righteousness of this prayer that had been read by the priest on his knees. She felt in her heart a thrill of awe and horror at the punishment in store for men's sins, and especially for her sins, and prayed to God to forgive them all, and her too, and give them all and her peace and happiness. And it seemed to her that God heard her prayer.

Ever since that day when Pierre had seen the gentle grateful look in Natasha's tear-laden eyes, the haunting problem of the vanity and senselessness of all things earthly had ceased to torment him. That terrible question: Why? What for? which had till then haunted him in the midst of every occupation, was not now replaced by any other question, nor by an answer to the old question; its place was filled by the image of *her*. If he heard or talked of trivialities, or read or was told of some instance of human baseness or folly, he was not cast down as of old; he did not ask himself why people troubled, when all was so brief and uncertain. But he thought of her as he had seen her last, and all his doubts vanished; not because she had answered the questions that haunted him, but because her image lifted him instantly into a region of beauty and love, which was worth living for. Whatever infamy he thought of, he said to himself, "Well, let so-and-so rob the state and the Tsar, while the state and the Tsar heap honours on him; but she smiled at me yesterday, and begged me to come, and I love her, and nobody will ever know it."

Pierre still went into society, drank as much, and led the same idle and aimless life, because, apart from the hours he spent at the Rostovs', he had to get through the rest of his time somehow, and the habits and the acquaintances he had made in Moscow drew him irresistably into the same life. But of late, since the reports from the war had become more and more disturbing, and Natasha's health had improved, and she had ceased to call for the same tender pity, he had begun to be more and more possessed by a restlessness that he could not explain. He felt that the position he was in could not go on for long, that a catastrophe was coming that would change the whole course of his life, and he sought impatiently for signs of it.

The day before that Sunday on which the national prayer had been read in the churches, Pierre had promised the Rostovs to call on Count Rastoptchin, whom he knew well, and to get from him the Tsar's appeal to the country, and the last news from the army. On going to Count Rastoptchin's in the morning, Pierre found there a special courier, who had only just arrived from the army. The courier was a man whom Pierre knew, and often saw at Moscow balls.

"For mercy's sake, couldn't you relieve me of some of my burden," said the courier; "I have a sack full of letters to parents."

Among these letters was a letter from Nicholas Rostov to his father. Pierre took it and Count Rastoptchin gave him a copy of the Tsar's appeal to Moscow, which had just been printed, and the last announcements in the army. Looking through the army announcements, Pierre found in one of them, among lists of wounded, killed and promoted, the name of Nicholas Rostov, rewarded with the order of St. George, of the fourth degree, for distinguished bravery in the Ostrovna affair, and in the same announcement the appointment of

Prince André Bolkonsky to the command of a regiment of light cavalry. Though he did not want to remind the Rostovs of Bolkonsky's existence, Pierre could not resist bringing them the news of their son's decoration. Keeping the Tsar's appeal, to bring with him at dinner-time, Pierre sent the printed announcement and Nicholas' letter to the Rostovs.

The conversation with Rastoptchin, and his tone of anxiety and hurry, the meeting with the courier, who had casually alluded to the disastrous state of affairs in the army, the rumours of spies being caught in Moscow, of a sheet circulating in the town stating that Napoleon had sworn to be in both Moscow and Petersburg before autumn, of the Tsar's expected arrival next day—all combined to revive in Pierre with fresh intensity that feeling of excitement and expectation, that he had been conscious of since the beginning of the war.

The idea of joining the army had long before occurred to Pierre, and he would have acted upon it, but that, in the first place, he was pledged by his vow to the Masonic brotherhood, which preached universal peace and the abolition of war; and secondly, when he looked at the great mass of Moscow gentlemen, who put on uniforms, and professed themselves patriots, he felt somehow ashamed to take the same step.

A few intimate friends were, as usual on Sundays, dining with the Rostovs.

Pierre came early, hoping to find them alone.

Pierre had that year grown so stout, that he would have been grotesque, had not he been so tall, so broad-shouldered, and so powerfully built that he carried off his bulk with ease.

Puffing, and muttering something to himself, he went up the stairs. His coachman did not even ask whether he should wait. He knew that when the count was at the Rostovs', it was till midnight.

The first person he saw at the Rostovs' was Natasha. Before he saw her, while taking off his cloak, he heard her. She was practising her singing exercises in the hall. He knew she had given up singing since her illness, and so he was surprised and delighted at the sound of her voice. He opened the door softly, and saw Natasha, in her lilac dress. She had her back turned to him as he opened the door; but when she turned sharply round and saw his broad, surprised face, she flushed and ran quickly up to him.

"I want to try and sing again. How glad I am you have come! I'm so happy to-day," she said with the old eagerness that Pierre had not seen for so long. "You know, Nicholas has won the St. George's Cross. I'm so proud of him."

"Of course, I sent you the announcement. Well, I won't

interrupt you," he added, and would have gone on to the drawing-room.

Natasha stopped him.

"Pierre, is it wrong of me to sing?" she said, blushing, but still keeping her eyes fixed inquiringly on him.

"No. . . . Why should it be? On the contrary. . . . But why do you ask me?"

"I don't know myself," Natasha answered quickly. "But I don't want to do anything you wouldn't like. I trust you in everything. You don't know how much you are to me, and what a great deal you have done for me!" . . . She spoke quickly, and did not notice how Pierre flushed at these words. "I saw in that announcement, *he,* Prince André," she whispered quickly, "he is in Russia, and in the army again. What do you think," she said hurriedly, evidently in haste to speak because she was afraid her strength would fail her. "Will he ever forgive me? Will he not always have an evil feeling for me? What do you think? What do you think?"

"I think . . ." said Pierre. "He has nothing to forgive . . . If I were in his place . . ." From association of ideas, Pierre was instantly carried back in imagination to the time when he had comforted her by saying that if he were not himself, but the best man in the world and free, he would beg for her hand, and the same feeling of pity, tenderness, and love took possession of him, and the same words rose to his lips. But she did not give him time to utter them.

"Yes, you—you," she said, uttering that word *you* with enthusiasm, "that's a different matter. Any one kinder, more generous than you, I have never known—no one could be. If it had not been for you then, and now too . . . I don't know what would have become of me, because . . ." Tears suddenly came into her eyes. She turned away, held her music before her eyes, and began again singing and walking up and down the room.

At that moment Peter ran in from the drawing-room.

Peter was by now a handsome boy of fifteen, very like Natasha. He was being prepared for the university, but had lately resolved in secret with his comrade, Obolensky, to go into the hussars.

Peter rushed up to Pierre, to talk to him of this scheme. He had begged him to find out whether he would be accepted in the hussars.

Pierre walked about the drawing-room, not paying any attention to Peter.

The boy pulled him by the arm.

"Come, tell me about my plan, Pierre, for goodness' sake! You're my only hope."

"Oh yes, your plan. To be an hussar? I'll speak about it; to-day I'll tell them all about it."

"Well, my dear fellow, have you got the manifesto?" asked the old Count Rostov, entering the room. "My little countess was at the service in the Razumovsky's chapel; she heard the new prayer there. Very fine it was, she tells me."

"Yes, I have got it," answered Pierre. "The Tsar will be here to-morrow. . . . There's to be an extraordinary meeting of the nobility and a levy they say of ten per thousand. Oh, I congratulate you."

"Yes, yes, thank God. Well, and what news from the army?"

"Our soldiers have retreated again. They are before Smolensk, they say," answered Pierre.

"Mercy on us, mercy on us!" said the count. "Where's the manifesto?"

"The Tsar's appeal? Ah, yes!" Pierre began looking for the papers in his pockets, and could not find them. Still slapping his pockets, he kissed the countess's hand as she came in, and looked round uneasily, evidently expecting Natasha, who had left off singing now, but had not come into the drawing-room. "Good Heavens, I don't know where I have put it," he said.

"To be sure, he always mislays everything," said the countess.

Natasha came in and sat down, looking at Pierre. As soon as she came into the room, Pierre's face, which had been overcast, brightened, and while still searching for the paper, he looked several times at her.

"By God, I'll drive round, I must have forgotten them at home. Of course . . ."

"Why, you will be late for dinner."

"Oh! And the coachman has not waited."

But Sonya had gone into the vestibule to look for the papers, and there found them in Pierre's hat, where he had carefully put them under the lining. Pierre wanted to read them.

"No, after dinner," said the old count, who was obviously looking forward to the reading of them as a great treat.

At dinner they drank champagne to the health of the new cavalier of St. George, and Shinshin told them of the news of the town, of the illness of the old Georgian princess, and of the disappearance of the French doctor Metivier from Moscow.

"And did you hear," continued Shinshin, "Prince Galitzin has engaged a Russian teacher—he's learning Russian. It begins to be dangerous to speak French in the streets."

"Well, Pierre, now if they raise a general militia, you will have to mount a horse too, ah?" said the old count.

Pierre looked at the count as though not understanding.

"Yes, yes, for the war," he said. "No! A fine soldier I should make! And yet everything's so strange; so strange! Why, I don't understand it myself. I don't know, I am far from being military in my taste, but in these days no one can answer for himself."

After dinner the count settled himself comfortably in a low chair, and with a serious face asked Sonya to read the Tsar's appeal.

"To our metropolitan capital Moscow. The enemy has entered our border with an immense host and comes to lay waste our beloved country," Sonya read conscientiously in her thin voice. The count listened with closed eyes, heaving abrupt sighs at certain passages.

Natasha sat erect, looking inquisitively and directly from her father to Pierre.

Pierre felt her eyes on him and tried not to look round. The countess shook her head disapprovingly at every solemn expression in the manifesto. In all these words she saw nothing but that the danger menacing her son would not soon be over. Shinshin, pursing his lips up into a sarcastic smile, was clearly preparing to make a joke at the first subject that presented itself: at Sonya's reading, the count's next remark, or even the manifesto itself, if no better pretext should be found.

After reading of the dangers threatening Russia, the hopes the Tsar rested upon Moscow, and particularly on its illustrious nobility, Sonya, with a quiver in her voice, due principally to the attention with which they were listening to her, read the last words: "We shall without delay be in the midst of our people in the capital, and in other parts of our empire, for deliberation, and for the guidance of all our militia levies, both those which are already barring the progress of the foe, and those to be formed for conflict with him, wherever he may appear. And may the ruin with which he threatens us recoil on his own head, and may Europe, delivered from bondage, glorify the name of Russia!"

"That's right!" cried the count, opening his wet eyes. He went on, "Only let our sovereign say the word, we will sacrifice everything without grudging."

Before Shinshin had time to utter the joke he was ready to make on the count's patriotism, Natasha had jumped up from her seat and run to her father.

"What a darling father is!" she cried, kissing him, and she glanced again at Pierre with the unconscious coquetry that had come back with her fresh interest in life.

"Oh, what a patriot she is!" said Shinshin.

"Not a patriot at all, but simply . . ." Natasha began, irritated. "You think everything funny, but this isn't a joke . . ."

"A joke," repeated the count. "Only let him say the word, we will all go . . . We're not a set of Germans!"

"Did you notice," said Pierre, "the words, 'for deliberation . . .' "

"Yes, to be sure, for whatever might come . . ."

Meanwhile Peter, to whom no one was paying attention, went up to his father, and very red, said in a voice that passed abruptly from gruffness to shrillness, "Well, now, father, I tell you positively—and mother too, say what you will—I tell you, you must let me go into the army, because I cannot . . ."

The countess in dismay said angrily to her husband: "See, what your talk has brought us to!"

But the count recovered the same instant.

"Come, come," he said. "A fine warrior you'd make! Don't talk nonsense; you have your studies to attend to."

"It's not nonsense, father. Obolensky's younger than I am, and he's going. And what's more, I can't anyhow study now, when . . ." Peter stopped, flushed till his face was perspiring, yet stoutly went on . . . "when the country's in danger."

"Hush, hush, nonsense! . . ."

"Why, but you said yourself you would sacrifice everything."

"Peter! I tell you be quiet," cried the count, looking at his wife, who was gazing with a white face and fixed eyes at her younger son.

"Let me say . . . Pierre here will tell you . . ."

"I tell you, it's nonsense; the milk's hardly dry on his lips, and he wants to go into the army! Come, come, I tell you," and the count, taking the papers with him, was going out of the room, probably to read them once more in his study before his nap.

"Pierre, let us have a smoke. . . ."

Pierre felt embarrassed and hesitated. Natasha's unusually brilliant and eager eyes, continually turned upon him with more than cordiality in them, had reduced him to this condition.

"No; I think I'll go home. . . ."

"Go home? But you meant to spend the evening with us. . . . You come rarely enough, as it is. And this girl of mine," said the count good-humouredly, looking towards Natasha, "is never in good spirits but when you are here. . . ."

"But I have forgotten something. I really must go home. . . . Business. . . ." Pierre said hurriedly.

"Well, good-bye then," said the count as he went out of the room.

"Why are you going away? Why are you so upset? What for?" Natasha asked Pierre, looking into his face.

"Because I love you!" he wanted to say, but he did not

say it. But instead he said, "Because it is better for me not to be so often with you. . . . Because . . . no, simply I have business. . . ."

"What for? No, do tell me," Natasha was beginning to insist, and she suddenly stopped. Both, in dismay and embarrassment, looked at one another. He tried to laugh, but could not. And he kissed her hand and went out without a word.

Pierre made up his mind not to visit the Rostovs again.

Next day, the Tsar arrived in Moscow. Several of the Rostovs' servants asked permission to go out to see the Tsar. And Peter without saying anything to any one, put on his cap and went out of the house by the back door.

He moved along with the growing crowd. And when he got close to the Kremlin he was pushed against a wall where he was forced to wait while carriages drove by with a rumbling sound.

When all the carriages had driven by, the crowd made a rush, and swept Peter along with it into the square, which was already full of people. Not only in the square, but on the slopes, and the roofs, and everywhere there were crowds of people.

As soon as Peter got into the square, he heard the ringing of bells and the joyous hum of the crowd filling the whole Kremlin.

For a while the crush was less in the square, but all at once all heads were bared, and there was another rush forward. And there was continual shouting: "Hurrah! Hurrah! Hurrah!"

A shopkeeper's wife standing near Peter sobbed, and tears flowed down her cheeks.

"Father, angel!" she kept saying, wiping her tears with her fingers.

"Hurrah!" shouted the crowd on all sides.

Then there was another rush forward.

Peter, beside himself with excitement, clenched his teeth, rushed forward, elbowing his way and shouting "Hurrah!" as though he were prepared to kill himself and every one else at that moment. But faces just as savage pushed on each side of him with the same shouts of "hurrah!"

In spite of that, he still forced his way forward as desperately, and over the backs of those in front of him caught a glimpse of open space with a passage covered with red cloth. But at that moment the crowd began heaving back; the police in front were forcing back those who had pressed too close to the procession. The Tsar was passing from the palace to the Uspensky Sobor.

When the Tsar had entered the Uspensky Sobor the crowd spread out again, and Peter, pale and breathless, climbed on to a big cannon, from which he hoped to see the Tsar, who was to walk back.

During the service in the Uspensky Sobor, in celebration of the Tsar's arrival, and also in thanksgiving for the peace with the Turks, the crowd dispersed about the square, and hawkers appeared crying kvass, gingerbread, and poppyseed sweets—of which Peter was particularly fond—and he could hear the usual talk among the people. One shopkeeper's wife was showing her torn shawl, and saying how much she had paid for it, while another observed that all silk things were very dear nowadays. A deacon was talking to a clerk of the different priests who were taking part in the service that day with the most reverend bishop. Two young workmen were joking with some servant-girls.

Suddenly cannon shots were heard from the embankment—the firing was in celebration of the peace with the Turks—and the crowd made a dash for the embankment to see the firing. Peter, too, would have liked to run there, but he did not want to lose his place. The firing still continued, when officers, generals, and gentlemen-in-waiting came running out of the Uspensky Sobor. Then others came out with less haste, and again caps were lifted, and those who had run to look at the cannons ran back. At last four men in uniforms covered with decorations came out from the doors of the Sobor. "Hurrah! hurrah!" the crowd shouted again.

"Which? Which one?" Peter asked of those around him, but no one answered him. Every one was too much excited, and Peter, picking out one of the four, concentrated all his enthusiasm on him, though it happened not to be the Tsar. He shouted "Hurrah!" in a voice of frenzy, and resolved that the next day, come what might, he would join the army.

The crowd ran after the Tsar, accompanied him to the palace, and began to disperse. It was late. But Peter did not go home. He remained with a smaller crowd before the palace during the Tsar's dinner-time. He gazed up at the palace windows, expecting something to happen, and envying equally the grand personages who drove up to the entrance to dine with the Tsar, and the footmen waiting at table, of whom he caught glimpses at the window.

At the Tsar's dinner, someone said, looking out of the window: "The people are still hoping to get a sight of your majesty."

The Tsar got up, and still munching a biscuit, came out on the balcony. The crowd, with Peter in the midst, rushed towards the balcony.

"Angel, father! Hurrah!" . . . shouted the crowd, and with it Peter. And again women, and some men, shed tears of happiness.

A good-sized piece of the biscuit in the Tsar's hand broke off, fell on the balcony railing, and from the railing to the ground. A coachman, who stood nearest, pounced on the piece of biscuit and snatched it up. Several persons rushed at the coachman. Noticing this the Tsar asked for a plate of biscuits, and began dropping them from the balcony. Peter's eyes almost started out of his head and he rushed at the biscuits. He did not know why, but he felt he must have a biscuit from the Tsar's hands, and he must not give in. He made a dash and upset an old woman, who was just about to seize a biscuit. But the old woman refused to consider herself beaten. Though she was on the ground she snatched at the biscuits on her hands and knees. Peter pushed her hand away with his knee, snatched up a biscuit, and as though afraid of being late, quickly shouted again, "Hurrah!" in a hoarse voice.

The Tsar went in, and after that the greater part of the crowd dispersed.

On getting home, Peter announced that if they would not let him join the army he would run away. And next day, though Count Rostov had not quite yielded, he went to inquire if a commission could be obtained for Peter somewhere where there would be little danger.

The next day, a great number of carriages stood outside the Slobodsky palace.

The great halls were full. In the first were the noblemen in their uniforms; in the second there were merchants with medals and long beards, wearing blue, full-skirted coats.

The noblemen, whom Pierre saw every day either at the club or at their houses, were all in uniforms; some in those of Catherine's court, some in those of the Emperor Pavel, and some in the new uniforms of Alexander's reign, others in the common uniforms of the nobility.

Pierre, who had been since early morning in an uncomfortable uniform, that had become too tight for him, was in the room. He was in a state of excitement; this extraordinary assembly, not only of the nobility, but of the merchant class too, called up in him a whole series of ideas of the *Contrat Social* and the French Revolution, ideas imprinted deeply on his soul, though they had long been laid aside. The words he had noticed in the manifesto, that the Tsar was coming to the capital *for deliberation* with his people, confirmed him in this chain of thought. And supposing that something of importance in that direction was near at hand, that what he had long been looking for was coming, he looked and listened attentively, but he saw nowhere any expression of these ideas.

The Tsar's manifesto was read, and evoked enthusiasm; and then all moved about, talking. Apart from their everyday interests, Pierre heard discussion as to where the marshals were to stand when the Tsar should come in, when the ball was to be given for the Tsar, whether they were to be divided according to districts or the whole province together . . . and so on. But as soon as the war and the whole object of their meeting together was touched upon, the talk was uncertain and hesitating.

A handsome, middle-aged man, wearing the uniform of a retired naval officer, was speaking, and a little crowd was gathered about him in one of the rooms. The officer was speaking very boldly.

"What if the Smolensk people have offered the Emperor a levy of militia. Are the Smolensk people any rule for us? If the nobility of the Moscow province thinks fit, it can show its devotion to our sovereign the Emperor by other means. Have we forgotten the militia in the year 1807? It was only the beggarly priests' sons and thieves made a good thing of it. . . ."

Count Rostov, in his uniform of Catherine's court, smiling blandly, nodded his head in approval.

"And were our militiamen of any service to the state? Not the slightest! They only ruined our agriculture. Even conscription is better. . . . As it is, a man comes back to you neither soldier nor peasant, nothing, but only demoralised. The nobility don't grudge their lives. We will go ourselves to a man; take recruits, too; and the Tsar has but to say the word, and we will all die for him," added the orator, warming up.

Pierre wanted to speak too. He was just opening his mouth to speak when he was interrupted by a toothless senator with a shrewd face.

"I imagine, my dear sir," said the senator, mumbling with his toothless mouth, "that we are summoned here not to discuss which is more suitable for the country at the present moment—conscription or the militia. We are summoned to reply to the appeal which our sovereign the Emperor graciously deigns to make to us. And to judge which is the fitter means—recruiting or a levy for militia—we leave to a higher power. . . ."

Pierre felt exasperated with the senator, who introduced this conventional and narrow view of the duties that lay before the nobility. He stepped forward and cut him short.

"Excuse me, your excellency," he began. . . . "But I imagine the estate of the nobility, apart from the expression of its sympathy and enthusiasm, has been convoked also to deliberate upon the measures by which we can assist our country. I imagine," said Pierre, growing warmer, "that the Tsar would himself be displeased if he should find in us only the owners of peasants, whom we give up to him, not find in us co . . co . . . counsel. . . ."

Many persons moved a little away from the circle, noticing the disdainful smile of the senator and the freedom of Pierre's words. Count Rostov was the only person pleased at what Pierre said, just as he had been pleased with the naval officer's speech and the senator's, as he always was with the last speech he had heard.

"I consider that before discussing these questions," Pierre continued, "we ought to ask the Emperor most respectfully to communicate to us what forces we have, what is the position of our men and our army, and then . . ."

Pierre had hardly uttered these words when he was promptly attacked on three sides at once. The most violent onslaught was made upon him by an old acquaintance and partner at boston, who had always been on the friendliest terms with him. This man was, of course, in uniform, and whether it was due to the uniform or to other causes, Pierre saw before him quite a changed person. With an old man's anger he screamed at Pierre:

"In the first place, let me tell you that we have no right to ask such questions of the Emperor; and secondly, if the nobility had any such right, the Emperor could not answer such questions. The movements of the troops depend on the movements of the enemy; the troops are augmented and decreased . . ."

Another voice interrupted. The speaker was a man of forty, of medium height, whom Pierre had seen in former days at the gypsies' entertainments, and knew as a bad card-player. But now he, too, was quite transformed by his uniform.

"Yes, and it's not the time for deliberation," said this nobleman. "What's needed is action; there is war in Russia. Our foe comes to ruin Russia, to desecrate the tombs of our fathers, to carry away our wives and children." The gentleman struck himself a blow on the chest. "We will all rise up; we will all go to a man, we will follow our father the Tsar!" he cried. Several approving voices could be heard in the crowd. "We are Russians and we do not grudge our blood for the defence of our faith, our throne, and our country. But we must put a stop to idle talk, if we are true sons of our fatherland. We will show Europe how Russia can defend Russia!" shouted this gentleman.

Pierre tried to reply but he could not get in a word. He wanted to say that he was by no means averse to the sacrifice of his money, or his peasants, or himself, but that one ought to know the true position of affairs, in order to be able to assist, but he could not speak.

The editor of the *Russian Messenger*, Glinka, who was

recognised and greeted with shouts of "the author, the author!" said that hell must be driven back by hell.

The crowd approached a great table, where grey or bald old noblemen of seventy were sitting, wearing uniforms and decorations. Almost all of them Pierre had seen in their own homes or playing boston at the club. The crowd drew near the table, still with the same buzz of talk. The old grandees at the table sat looking from one to another, and their expression for the most part betrayed nothing but that they were very hot. Pierre did not disavow his ideas, but felt somehow in fault and tried to defend himself.

"I only said that we could make sacrifices to better purpose when we know what is needed," he cried, trying to shout down the other voices.

One old man close by him looked round, but his attention was immediately called off by a shout at the other end of the table.

"Yes, Moscow will be surrendered! She will be sacrificed!" one man was shouting.

"He is the enemy of mankind!" another shouted.

"Allow me to say . . ."

"Gentlemen, you are crushing me! . . ."

At that moment the governor general of Moscow, Count Rastoptchin, with his prominent chin and alert eyes, strode in wearing the uniform of a general and a ribbon over his shoulder.

"Our sovereign the Emperor will be here immediately," said Rastoptchin. "I have just come from him. I presume that in the position in which we are placed, there is no need of much discussion. The Emperor has graciously seen fit to summon us and the merchants," said Count Rastoptchin. "They will pour out their millions," he pointed to the merchants' hall, "it is our duty to raise men and not to spare ourselves. . . . It is the least we can do."

A consultation took place between the great noblemen at the table. The whole consultation was more than subdued, it seemed even mournful, when, after all the hubbub that had gone before, the old voices could be heard, one at a time, saying "agreed," or for the sake of variety, "I am of the same opinion."

The secretary was told to write down the resolution of the Moscow nobility: that the nobles of Moscow, like those of Smolensk, would furnish a levy of ten men in every thousand, with their complete equipment.

The gentlemen, who had been sitting, got up with an air of relief; there was a scraping of chairs and they walked about to stretch their legs.

"The Tsar! The Tsar!" was suddenly heard all through the rooms, and the whole crowd rushed towards the entrance.

The Tsar walked in along the wide, free space left for him, between walls of noblemen close packed on each side. Every face expressed reverent and awe-stricken curiosity. The Tsar spoke of the danger in which the empire was placed, and the hopes he rested on the Moscow nobility. He was answered by a voice informing him of the resolution just passed by the nobility.

"Gentlemen!" said the trembling voice of the Tsar. A stir passed through the crowd, and then a hush fell on it again. "I have never doubted of the devotion of the Russian nobility. But this day it has surpassed my expectations. I thank you in the name of our beloved Russia. Gentlemen, let us act—time is more precious than anything. . . ."

The crowd began pressing round the Tsar, and cries of enthusiasm were heard on all sides.

Pierre felt nothing at that moment but the desire to show that nothing was too much for him and that he was ready to sacrifice everything. His speech weighed on him like a sin; he sought an opportunity of glossing it over. On hearing that Count Mamonov was furnishing a regiment, Pierre at once told Count Rastoptchin that he would furnish one thousand men and their equipment.

Later Count Rostov could not tell his wife what had passed without tears. And he agreed at once to Peter's wishes, and went himself to enter his name.

Next day the Tsar went away. All the assembled noblemen went back to their homes and their clubs, took off their uniforms, and with some groans gave orders to their stewards to raise the levy, wondering themselves at what they had done.

1812

BOOK TEN

THE DAY after Prince André's departure, his old father sent for Princess Mary.

"Well, now are you satisfied?" he said to her. "You have made me quarrel with my son! Are you satisfied? That was what you wanted! Satisfied? . . . It's a grief to me, a grief. I'm old and weak, and it was your wish. Well, now, rejoice over it. . . ." And after that, Princess Mary did not see her father again for a week. He was ill and did not leave his study.

Princess Mary noticed to her surprise that during this illness the old prince excluded Mademoiselle Bourienne from his room. Tihon was the only person who looked after him.

A week later the prince reappeared, and began to lead the same life as before, showing marked energy in the laying out of farm buildings and gardens, and completely breaking off all relations with Mademoiselle Bourienne. His frigid tone and air with Princess Mary seemed to say: "You see, you plotted against me, told lies to Prince André of my relations with that Frenchwoman, and made me quarrel with him, but you see I can do without you, and without the Frenchwoman too."

One half of the day Princess Mary spent with little Nicholas, giving him his Russian lessons, and talking to Dessalle. The rest of the day she spent in reading, or with her old nurse and "God's folk."

Princess Mary looked upon the war as women look on war. She was afraid for her brother who was at the front, and was horrified at the cruelty of men, that led them to kill one another. But she had no notion of the meaning of this war, although Dessalle tried to explain his views on the subject to her, and although "God's folk," with terror, told her in their own way of the rumours among the peasantry of the coming of Antichrist, and although Julie, now Princess Drubetskoy, was continually writing her patriotic letters from Moscow.

"I write to you in Russian, my sweet friend," Julie wrote, "because I feel a hatred for the French and for their language too. I can't bear to hear it spoken. . . . In Moscow we are all wild with enthusiasm for our adored Emperor.

"My poor husband is enduring hardships and hunger, but the news I get from him only increases my ardour.

"We kill time here as best we can. Princess Alina and Sophie spend whole days with me, and we, unhappy widows of living husbands, have delightful talks over scraping lint."

The main reason why Princess Mary failed to grasp the significance of the war was that the old prince never spoke of it, refused to recognise its existence, and laughed at Dessalle when he mentioned the war at dinner-time. The prince's tone was so calm and confident that Princess Mary put implicit faith in him.

During the whole of July the old prince was excessively active and even lively. He laid out another new garden and a new wing for the servants. The only thing that made Princess Mary anxious about him was that he slept badly, and gave up his old habit of sleeping in his study, and had a bed made up for him in a new place every day. One night he would have his travelling bedstead set up in the gallery, the next night he would spend dozing dressed on the sofa or in the lounge-chair in the drawing-room, while some one read aloud to him; then he would try spending a night in the dining-room.

On the first of August a second letter came from Prince André. In his first letter, which had been received shortly after he left home, Prince André had humbly asked his father's forgiveness. To this letter, the old prince had sent an affectionate answer, and from that time he had kept the Frenchwoman at a distance. Prince André's second letter consisted of a brief account of the whole campaign, with a plan sketched to illustrate it, and of reflections on the probable course it would take in the future. In this letter Prince André pointed out to his father the danger of his staying on at Bleak Hills which was in the direct line of the enemy's advance. He advised him to move to Moscow.

At dinner that day, on Dessalle's observing that he had heard that the French had already entered the city of Vitebsk, the old prince remembered Prince André's letter.

"I have heard from Prince André to-day," he said to Princess Mary, with a contemptuous smile. "He writes about the war."

"It must be very interesting," said Dessalle. "Prince André is in a position to know. . . ."

"Ah, very interesting!" said Mademoiselle Bourienne.

"Go and get it for me," said the old prince to Mademoiselle Bourienne. "You know, on the little table under the paper-weight."

Mademoiselle Bourienne jumped up eagerly.

"Ah, no," he shouted, frowning. "You run, Mihail Ivanitch!" Mihail Ivanitch got up and went to the study. But he had hardly left the room when the old prince, looking about him nervously, threw down his dinner napkin and went himself.

"They never can do anything, always make a muddle."

As he went out, Princess Mary, Dessalle, Mademoiselle Bourienne, and even little Nicholas, looked at one another without speaking. The old prince accompanied by Mihail Ivanitch came back, bringing the letter and a plan, which he laid beside him.

When they went into the drawing-room, he handed the letter to Princess Mary, and spreading out before him the plan of his new buildings, he fixed his eyes upon it, and told her to read the letter aloud.

After reading the letter, Princess Mary looked inquiringly at her father. He was gazing at the plan, evidently engrossed in his own ideas.

"What do you think about it, prince?" Dessalle ventured to inquire.

"I? Eh? . . ." said the old prince, seeming to rouse himself with a painful effort, and not taking his eyes from the plan of the building.

"It is very possible that the field of operations may be brought so close to us . . ."

"Ha-ha-ha! The field of operations indeed!" said the old prince. "I have always said, and I say still, that the field of operations is bound to be Poland, and the enemy will never advance beyond the Niemen." Dessalle looked in amazement at the prince, who was talking of the Niemen, when the enemy was already at the Dnieper. But Princess Mary, forgetting the geographical position of the Niemen, supposed that what her father said was true.

"When the snows thaw they'll drown in the marshes of Poland. It's only that they can't see it," said the old prince, obviously thinking of the campaign of 1807, which seemed to him so recent. "Bennigsen ought to have entered Prussia earlier, and things would have taken quite another turn. . . ."

"But, prince!" said Dessalle timidly, "the letter speaks of Vitebsk. . . ."

"Ah, the letter? Yes, . . ." said the prince, with displeasure. "Yes . . . yes . . ." His face suddenly assumed a gloomy expression. He paused. "Yes, he writes, the French have been beaten. On what river was it?"

Dessalle dropped his eyes. "The prince says nothing about that," he said gently.

"Doesn't he? Why, you don't suppose I imagined it."

Every one was for a long time silent.

"Yes . . . yes . . . Well, Mihail Ivanitch," he said suddenly, raising his head and pointing to the plan of the building. "Tell me how you propose to make that alteration. . . ."

Mihail Ivanitch went up to the plan, and the old prince, talking to him about it, went off to his own room, casting an angry glance at Princess Mary and Dessalle.

Princess Mary was struck by the fact that her father had left Prince André's letter forgotten on the drawing-room table. But she was afraid to speak of it.

In the evening Mihail Ivanitch was sent by the prince to Princess Mary to ask for the letter. Princess Mary gave him the letter, and much as she disliked doing so, she ventured to ask what her father was doing.

"Still very busy," said Mihail Ivanitch, in a tone of deferential irony, that made her turn pale. "Worrying very much over the new wing. Been reading a little: but now"—Mihail Ivanitch dropped his voice—"he's at his desk looking after his will." One of the old prince's favourite occupations of late had been going over the papers which he meant to leave at his death, and called his "will."

"And is Alpatitch being sent to Smolensk?" asked Princess Mary.

"To be sure; he's been waiting a long while for his orders."

When Mihail Ivanitch went back to the study with the letter, the old prince was sitting in his spectacles, with shades on the candles, at his open desk. He was in a rather solemn mood, reading the papers (the "remarks," as he called them) which were to be given to the Tsar after his death.

When Mihail Ivanitch went in, there were tears in his eyes, called up by the memory of the time when he had written what he was now reading. He took the letter out of Mihail Ivanitch's hand, put it in his pocket, folded up his papers and called in Alpatitch, the manager of his estates, who had been waiting a long while to see him.

The old prince had noted down on a sheet of paper what he wanted in Smolensk, and he began walking up and down the room, as he gave his instructions to Alpatitch, standing at the door.

"First, letter paper, do you hear, eight quires, like this pattern, you see; gilt edged . . . take the pattern, so as to be sure to match it; varnish, sealing-wax—according to Mihail Ivanitch's list."

He walked up and down the room and glanced at the memorandum.

"Then deliver the letter about the enrolment to the governor in person."

Then bolts for the doors of the new building were wanted, and must be of a new pattern, which the old prince had himself designed. Then an iron-bound box was to be ordered for keeping his will in.

Giving Alpatitch his instructions occupied over two hours. The prince still would not let him go. He sat down, sank into thought, and closing his eyes, dropped into a doze. Alpatitch made a slight movement.

"Well, go along, go along," said the old prince.

Alpatitch went away. The prince went back to his desk, and sat down to the table to write to the governor.

It was late when he sealed the letter and got up. He was sleepy.

He called Tihon, and went through the rooms with him, to tell him where to make up his bed for that night. He walked about, measuring every corner.

There was no place that pleased him, but worst of all was the couch in the study that he had been used to. That couch had become an object of dread to him. No place was quite right, but best of them all was the corner behind the piano; he had never slept there yet.

Tihon brought the bedstead in with the footmen, and began putting it up.

"That's not right, that's not right!" cried the old prince. With his own hands he moved the bed an inch further from the corner, and then closer to it again.

Frowning at the effort he had to make to take off his coat and trousers, the prince undressed, dropped heavily down on his bed, and seemed to sink into thought, staring contemptuously at his yellow, withered legs. He was not really thinking, but simply pausing before the effort to lift his legs up and lay them in the bed. Pinching his lips tightly, he made that effort for the twenty thousandth time, and lay down. But he had hardly lain down, when all at once the bed seemed to rock under him, as though it were heaving and jolting. He had this sensation almost every night. He opened his eyes.

"No peace, damn them!" he grumbled, with inward rage. "Yes, yes, there was something else of importance—something of great importance I was saving up to think of in bed. The bolts? No, I did speak about them. No, there was something, something in the drawing-room. Princess Mary talked some nonsense. Dessalle—he's a fool—said something, something in my pocket—I don't remember."

"Tihon! What were we talking about at dinner?"

"About Prince André . . ."

The prince slapped his hand down on the table. "Yes, I know, Prince André's letter. Princess Mary read it. Dessalle said something about Vitebsk. I'll read it now."

He told Tihon to get the letter out of his pocket, and to move up the little table with the spiral wax candle on it, and putting on his spectacles he began reading. Only then in the stillness of the night did he grasp its meaning. "The French are at Vitebsk, in four days' march they may be at Smolensk; perhaps they are there by now. Tihon!" Tihon jumped up. "No, nothing, nothing!" he cried.

He put the letter under the candlestick and closed his eyes. And there rose before his mind the Danube, bright midday, the reeds, the Russian camp, and he, a young general, without one wrinkle on his brow, bold, gay, ruddy, entering Potyomkin's gay-coloured tent, and the burning sensation of envy of the favourite stirs within him as keenly as at the time. And he recalls every word uttered at that first interview with Potyomkin. And then he sees a plump, short woman with a sallow, fat face, the mother empress, her smiles and words at her first gracious reception for him; and then her face as she lay on the bier, and the quarrel with Zubov over her coffin for the right to kiss her hand. . . .

Bleak Hills was sixty miles from Smolensk and three miles from the main road to Moscow.

When Alpatitch had received all his orders, he put on his white beaver hat—a gift from the prince—and carrying a stick in his hand, like the prince, went out, accompanied by all his household, to get into the leather gig harnessed to three sleek, roan horses.

"If there's anything . . . you turn back. For Christ's sake, think of us," his wife called to him, alluding to the rumours of war and of the enemy near.

"Ah, these women and their fuss!" Alpatitch muttered to himself as he drove off, looking about him at the fields. He saw rye turning yellow, thick oats still green, and here and there black patches, where they were only just beginning the second ploughing.

On reaching Smolensk, three days later, Alpatitch put up at an inn where he had been in the habit of putting up for the last thirty years.

The inn-keeper was standing in his print shirt and his waistcoat in front of his place. He saw Alpatitch, and went up to him.

"You're kindly welcome, Alpatitch. Folk are going out of the town, while you come into it," said he.

"How's that? Out of town?" said Alpatitch.

"To be sure, I say folks are fools. Frightened of the French."

"Women's nonsense, women's nonsense!" replied Alpatitch.

"That's just what I think, Alpatitch. There's a notice put up that they won't let them come in, so to be sure that's right. But the peasants are asking as much as three roubles for a cart and horse . . . !"

Alpatitch heard without heeding. He asked for a samovar, and for hay for his horses; and after drinking tea lay down to sleep.

Next day Alpatitch put on a tunic, which he kept for wearing in town, and went out to execute his commissions. It was a sunny morning, and by eight o'clock it was hot. "A day for the harvest," Alpatitch thought.

From early morning firing could be heard from beyond the town. At eight o'clock the boom of cannon mingled with the rattle of musketry. The streets were thronged with people, hurrying about, and also with soldiers, but drivers plied for hire, the shopkeepers stood at their shops, and services were being held in the churches just as usual. Alpatitch went to the shops, to the government offices, to the post and to the governor's. Everywhere that he went every one was talking of the war, and of the enemy who was attacking the town. All were asking one another what was to be done, and trying to calm each other's fears.

At the governor's house, Alpatitch found a great number of people, and a travelling carriage belonging to the governor at the entrance. On the steps Alpatitch met two gentlemen, one of whom he knew. This gentleman, a former police-captain, was speaking with great heat.

"Well, this is no joking matter," he said. "Good luck for him who has only himself to think of. It's bad enough for one alone, but when one has a family of thirteen and a whole property. . . . Things have come to such a pass that we shall all be ruined; what's one to say of the government after this? . . . Ugh, I'd hang the fools. . . ."

"Come, come, hush!" said the other.

"What do I care! Let him hear! We're not dogs!" said the former police-captain, and looking round, he caught sight of Alpatitch.

"Ah, Alpatitch, how do you come here?"

"By command of his excellency to his honour the governor," answered Alpatitch, lifting his head proudly and putting his hand into his bosom, as he always did when he mentioned the old prince. . . . "His honour was pleased to bid me inquire into the position of affairs," he said.

"Well, you may as well know then," cried the gentleman. "They have brought matters to such a pass that there are no carts to be got. Nothing! . . . That's it again, do you hear?" he said, pointing in the direction from which the sounds of firing came.

"They have brought us all to ruin . . . The fools!" he declared again, and he went down the steps.

Alpatitch shook his head and went up. The waiting-room was full of merchants, women, and clerks, looking dumbly at one another. The door of the governor's room opened, all of them got up and stepped forward. A clerk ran out of the room, said something to a merchant, called a stout official with a cross on his neck to follow him, and vanished again, obviously trying to avoid all the looks and the questions addressed to him. Alpatitch moved forward, and the next time the same clerk came out, he put his hand into his buttoned coat, and addressed him, handing him the prince's letter.

"To his honour the Baron Ash from the general-in-chief Prince Bolkonsky," he boomed out with so much pomposity that the clerk turned to him and took the letter. A few minutes afterwards Alpatitch was shown into the presence of the governor, who said to him hurriedly, "Inform the prince and the princess that I knew nothing about it. I acted on the highest instructions—here. . . ."

He gave Alpatitch a document.

"Still, as the prince is not well my advice to him is to go to Moscow. I'm setting off myself immediately. Tell them . . . " But the governor did not finish; a dusty and perspiring officer ran into the room and began saying something in French. A look of horror came into the governor's face.

"You can go," he said, nodding to Alpatitch, and he put some questions to the officer. Eager, panic-stricken, helpless glances were turned upon Alpatitch when he came out of the governor's room. Alpatitch could not help listening now to firing, which seemed to come closer and to be getting hotter, as he hurried back to the inn. The document the governor had given to Alpatitch ran as follows:

"I guarantee that the town of Smolensk is not in the slightest danger, and it is improbable that it be threatened in any way. I myself from one side, and Prince Bagration from the other, will effect a junction before Smolensk on the 22nd instant, and both armies will proceed with their joint forces to defend their compatriots of the province under your government, till their efforts beat back the enemies of our country, or till their gallant ranks are cut down to the last warrior. You will see from this that you have a perfect right to reassure the inhabitants of Smolensk, as they are defended by two such valiant armies and can be confident of their victory.

"By order of Barclay de Tolly to the civil governor of Smolensk, Baron Ash. 1812."

Crowds of people were milling uneasily about the streets. Waggons, loaded up with household crockery, chairs, and cupboards, were moving along the streets. Carts were standing at the entrance of the house next to the inn, and women were wailing and exchanging good-byes. A dog was frisking about the horses, barking.

Alpatitch's step was more hurried than usual as he entered the yard, and went straight under the shed to his horses and cart. The coachman was asleep; he waked him up, told him to put the horses in, and went into the outer room of the inn. In the private room of the family, he heard the wailing of children, the heartrending sobs of a woman, and the furious, husky shouting of the inn-keeper. The cook came fluttering into the outer room like a frightened hen, just as Alpatitch walked in.

Alpatitch gathered up his purchases, handed them to the coachman, and settled his accounts with the inn-keeper.

It was now past noon, half the street lay in shadow, while half was in brilliant sunshine. Alpatitch went to the door. All of a sudden there came a strange sound of a faraway hiss and thump, followed by the boom of cannons, mingling into a dim roar that set the windows rattling.

Alpatitch went out into the street. Two men were running towards the bridge. From different sides came the hiss and thud of cannon balls and the bursting of grenades, as they fell in the town.

The sounds of the dropping grenades and cannon balls at first only excited the curiosity of the people. The inn-keeper's wife, who had till then been wailing in the shed, ceased, and with the baby in her arms went out to the gate, staring in silence at the people. The cook came out too. They were trying to get a glimpse of the cannon balls as they flew over their heads. Several persons came round the corner in eager conversation.

Others joined them. They stopped and described how a cannon ball had dropped on a house close by. Meanwhile another cannon ball, with a rapid, ominous hiss, and a grenade with a pleasant whistle flew over their heads.

Alpatitch got into his gig. The inn-keeper was standing at the gate.

"Will you never have done gaping!" he shouted to the cook, who in her red petticoat, with her sleeves tucked up and her bare elbows swinging, had stepped to the corner to listen to what was being said.

"A wonder it is!" she was saying, but hearing her master's voice, she came back, pulling down her tucked-up skirt.

Again something hissed, but very close this time, like a bird swooping down. There was a flash of fire in the middle of the street, the sound of a shot, and the street was filled with smoke.

At the same instant there rose a piteous wailing from the women. The baby set up a terrified howling, and the people crowded with pale faces round the cook. Above them all rose out of the crowd the moans and cries of the cook.

"O-o-oy, good kind souls, blessed friends! Don't let me die! Good kind souls! . . ."

Five minutes later no one was left in the street. The cook, with her leg broken by the bursting grenade, had been carried into the kitchen. Alpatitch, his coachman, the inn-keeper's wife and children and the porter were sitting in the cellar listening. The thunder of the cannon, the hiss of the balls, and the piteous moaning of the cook, which rose above all the noise, never ceased for an instant. The inn-keeper's wife alternately dandled and soothed her baby, and asked in a frightened whisper of every one who came into the cellar where was her husband. Someone told her that he had gone with the crowd to the cathedral, where they were raising on high the wonder-working, holy picture of Smolensk.

Towards dusk the cannonade began to subside. Alpatitch came out of the cellar and stood in the doorway.

The clear evening sky was all overcast with smoke. And a new crescent moon looked strange, shining high up in the sky, through that smoke. After the terrible thunder of the cannons had ceased, a hush seemed to hang over the town, broken only by footsteps, the sound of groans and distant shouts, and the crackle of fires. The cook's moans had stopped now. On two sides black clouds of smoke from fires rose up and drifted away. Russian soldiers in different uniforms walked and ran about the streets in different directions, not in ranks, but like ants out of a disturbed ant heap. Several of them ran into the inn yard before Alpatitch's eyes. He went out to the gate. A regiment, crowded and hurrying, blocked up the street.

"The town's surrendered. Get away, get away," said an officer noticing him. And turning immediately to the soldiers, he shouted, "I'll teach you to run through the yards!"

Alpatitch and the coachman with trembling hands pulled out the tangled reins and the traces of the horses under the shed. As he was driving out of the gate, he saw about a dozen soldiers in front of an open shop. They were filling their bags and knapsacks with flour and sunflower seeds. At that moment the shop-keeper returned. On seeing the soldiers, he was about to shout at them, but all at once he stopped short, and clutching at his hair broke into a sobbing laugh.

"Carry it all away! Don't leave it for the devils," he shouted, snatching up the sacks himself and pitching them into the street. Some of the soldiers ran away in fear, others went on filling up their bags. Seeing Alpatitch, the shop-keeper turned to him.

"It's all over with Russia!" he shouted. "It's all over! I'll set fire to it myself. It's over . . ."

An unbroken stream of soldiers was blocking up the whole street, so that Alpatitch could not pass and was obliged to wait. The inn-keeper's wife and children were sitting in a cart too, waiting till it was possible to start.

It was by now quite dark. There were stars in the sky, and from time to time the new moon shone through the veil of smoke. Alpatitch's gig and numberless other carriages moved slowly along in the rows of soldiers on the slope down to the Dnieper. In a lane not far from the cross-roads where the traffic had come to a full stop, there were shops and a house on fire. The fire was by now burning down. Talk and shouts could be heard above the crackling of the flames. Alpatitch, seeing that it would be some time before his gig could move forward, got out and went to look at the fire. He saw two soldiers with a man in a frieze coat dragging burning beams from the fire across the street to a house near by, while others carried armfuls of hay.

Alpatitch joined a great crowd of people standing before a high corn granary in full blaze. The walls were all in flames; the back wall had fallen in; the plank roof was breaking down, and the beams were glowing. The crowd was watching for the moment when the roof would fall in. Alpatitch too waited to see it.

"Alpatitch!" the old man suddenly heard a familiar voice calling to him.

"Mercy on us, your excellency," answered Alpatitch, instantly recognising the voice of his young master.

Prince André, wearing a cape, and mounted on a black horse, was in the crowd, and looking at Alpatitch.

"How did you come here?" he asked.

"Your . . . your excellency!" Alpatitch said, and he broke into sobs. . . . "Your, your . . . is it all over with us, really? Master . . ."

"How is it you are here?" repeated Prince André. The flames flared up at that instant, and Alpatitch saw in the bright light his young master's pale and worn face. Alpatitch told him how he had been sent to the town and had difficulty in getting away.

"What do you say, your excellency, is it all over with us?" he asked again.

Prince André, making no reply, took out his note-book, and raising his knee, scribbled in pencil on a leaf he had torn out. He wrote to his sister: "Smolensk has surrendered. Bleak Hills will be occupied by the enemy within a week. Set off at once for Moscow. Let me know when you start; send a messenger."

Handing Alpatitch the paper, he gave him further directions about sending off the old prince, the princess and his son with his tutor, and how and where to let him hear, as soon as they had gone.

There was a crash in the fire. The flames subsided for an instant; black clouds of smoke rolled under the roof. There was another fearful crash, and the falling of some enormous weight.

"Oh-oo!" the crowd yelled, as the ceiling of the granary fell in, and a smell of baked cakes rose from the burning wheat. The flames flared up again, and lighted up the delighted and careworn faces of the crowd around it.

The man in the frieze coat, waving his arms in the air, was shouting: "Good! Now she's started! Good! . . ."

"That's the owner himself," murmured voices.

From Smolensk the Russian army continued to retreat. The French followed them. On the 10th of August the regiment of which Prince André was in command was marching along the high-road past the avenue that led to Bleak Hills.

The heat and drought had lasted more than three weeks. Every day curly clouds passed over the sky, rarely covering the sun; but towards evening the sky cleared again and the sun set in a glowing, red mist. The wheat left in the fields was burnt up. The marshes were dry. The cattle lowed from hunger, finding nothing to graze on in the sun-baked meadows. The transports and artillery moved noiselessly, buried up to their axles, and the infantry sank to their ankles in the soft, stifling, burning dust. The sandy dust rose in a cloud over their heads, and got into the eyes and hair and lungs. There was no wind, and the men gasped for breath.

Although two days before Prince André had received the news that his father, his son and his sister had gone away to Moscow, he turned off from the main line of march towards his father's house, where he had been born and had spent his childhood. As he rode by the pond, where there always used to be dozens of peasant women gossiping, rinsing their linen, or beating it with washing bats, Prince André noticed that there was no one by the pond, and that the platform where they used to stand had been torn away, and was floating in the middle of the pond, half under water. Prince André rode up to the keeper's lodge. There was no one to be seen at the stone gates and the door was open. Cattle and horses were straying about the English park. Prince André rode up to the conservatory: the panes were smashed, and some of the trees in tubs were broken, others quite dried up. He called Taras, the gardener. No one answered. Going round the conservatory on the terrace, he saw that the paling-fence was all broken down, and branches of the plum-trees had been pulled off with the fruit. An old peasant, whom Prince André used to see in his childhood at the gate, was sitting on the green garden seat plaiting bast shoes.

He was deaf, and did not hear Prince André's approach. He was sitting on the seat on which the old prince liked to sit, and near him the bast was hanging on the branches of a broken and dried-up magnolia.

Prince André rode up to the house. Several lime-trees in the old garden had been cut down. A piebald mare and a colt were among the rose-trees just before the house. The shutters were all closed except on one window downstairs. A servant boy caught sight of Prince André and ran into the house.

Alpatitch had sent his family away, and was staying on alone at Bleak Hills. He was sitting indoors, reading the *Lives of the*

Saints. On hearing that Prince André had come, he ran out, buttoning himself up, and without uttering a word, burst into tears, kissing Prince André's knee.

Then he turned away in anger at his own weakness, and began giving his young master an account of what had happened. Everything valuable had been moved to Bogutcharovo. Corn to the amount of a hundred measures had been carried away, but the hay, and the wheat—an extraordinary crop that season, so Alpatitch said—had been cut green and carried off by the retreating Russian troops. The peasants were ruined: some of them, too, had gone to Bogutcharovo; a small number remained.

Prince André, not heeding his words, asked, "When did my father and sister go?" meaning when had they set off for Moscow. Alpatitch, assuming he was asking about the removal to Bogutcharovo, answered that they had set off on the 7th, and began going off again into details about the crops, asking for instructions.

"Is it your honour's orders that I let the oats go on getting a receipt from the officers?" asked Alpatitch. "We have still six hundred measures left."

"What am I to say to him?" Prince André wondered, looking at the old man's bald head shining in the sun.

"Yes, let it go," he said.

"If your excellency noticed any disorder in the garden," said Alpatitch, "it could not be prevented. Three regiments have been here and spent the night. The dragoons were the worst; I noted down the name and rank of the commanding officer to lodge a complaint."

"Well, and what are you going to do? Are you going to stay if the enemy occupies the place?" Prince André asked him.

Alpatitch turned his face towards Prince André and looked at him. Then all at once he lifted his hand upwards: "He is my protector, and His will be done!" he said.

A group of peasants and house-serfs were coming across the meadow, uncovering their heads as they drew near Prince André.

"Well, good-bye!" said Prince André, bending over to Alpatitch. "Go away yourself; take what you can; and tell the peasants to set off for the Ryazan estate or the property near Moscow."

Alpatitch hugged his leg and broke into sobs. Prince André gently moved him away, and spurring his horse galloped down the garden walk.

On the 8th of August a committee, consisting of General Field-Marshal Saltykov, Araktcheev and other high government officials, was held to consider the progress of the war.

This committee decided that the disasters were due to divided authority. And although the members of the committee were aware of the Tsar's dislike of Kutuzov, after a deliberation they advised the appointment of Kutuzov as commander-in-chief. And that same day Kutuzov was appointed commander-in-chief of the army, and intrusted with unlimited authority over the whole region occupied by the troops.

This appointment was hailed by the people. But in the salons of St. Petersburg and Moscow there was much criticism:

"Did any one hear of such a thing as appointing a man commander-in-chief who cannot sit a horse, who drops asleep at a council—a man, too, of the lowest morals! A pretty reputation he gained for himself in Bucharest! To say nothing of his qualities as a general, can we appoint, at such a moment, a man decrepit and blind—yes blind! A fine idea—a blind general! He sees nothing. Playing blind-man's buff—that's all he's fit for!"

"They say the Emperor was unwilling to give Kutuzov such authority. They say he blushed, saying to him, 'The sovereign and the country decree you this honour.' "

"I know for a fact that Kutuzov made it an express condition that the Grand Duke Konstantin, heir-apparent, should not be with the army. Kutuzov said to the Tsar: 'I can neither punish him if he does wrong, nor reward him if he does well.' Oh! he's a shrewd fellow, Prince Kutuzov."

"They say that Kutuzov even made it an express condition that the Emperor himself should not be with the army!"

Princess Mary was not in Moscow and out of danger as Prince André supposed.

After Alpatitch's return from Smolensk, the old prince seemed as though he had suddenly waked out of a sleep. He gave orders for the militiamen to assemble and to be armed. He wrote a letter to the local commander, in which he informed him of his intention to remain at Bleak Hills to the last and to defend himself, leaving it to his discretion to take steps or not for the defence of Bleak Hills, where he said one of the oldest Russian generals would be taken prisoner or die.

But though resolved himself to remain, the prince made arrangements for sending the princess with Dessalle and the little prince to Bogutcharovo, and from there on to Moscow. But Princess Mary could not bring herself to leave him alone, and for the first time in her life ventured not to obey him. She refused to go, and a fearful tempest of wrath burst upon her. Trying to find pretexts for reviling her, the old prince said she had done everything to worry him, that she had estranged him from his son, that she harboured the vilest suspicions of him, that she made it the object of her life to poison his existence. He drove her out of his study, telling her that he did not care if she did not go away. He told her that he did not want to hear of her existence, but gave her fair warning not to dare show herself before him. Princess Mary was relieved that he had not, as she had dreaded, ordered her to be forcibly removed from Bleak Hills, but had simply commanded her not to show herself. She knew that this meant that in the secret recesses of his heart he was glad she was staying at home.

The day after little Nicholas had left, the old prince dressed himself in the morning in full uniform, and prepared to make a call on the local commander. The carriage was standing ready. Princess Mary saw him in his uniform, with all his orders on his breast, walk out of the house and go down the garden to inspect the armed peasants and house-serfs. She sat at the window listening to his voice resounding from the garden. Suddenly several men came running up the avenue with panic-stricken faces.

Princess Mary ran out on to the steps, along the flower-bed path, and into the avenue. A great crowd of militiamen and servants were coming down it towards her, and in the middle of that crowd several men were carrying the old prince. Princess Mary ran towards him. On seeing her the old prince tried to move his lips, but all he could utter was a hoarse sound. It was impossible to understand what he meant. He was carried into his study, and laid on the couch, which had been such an object of dread to him of late.

The doctor, who was brought over the same night, bled him, and declared that the prince had had a stroke, paralysing his right side.

To remain at Bleak Hills was becoming more and more dangerous, and the next day they moved the prince to Bogutcharovo. The doctor travelled with him.

When they reached Bogutcharovo, they found Dessalle had already set off for Moscow with the little prince.

For three weeks the old prince lay unconscious. He lay like a deformed corpse. He muttered incessantly, twitching his eyebrows and lips, and it was impossible to tell whether he understood his surroundings or not. Only one thing could be said for certain: that was, that he was suffering, and had a craving to express something. But what that was no one could tell.

The doctor said that this uneasiness meant nothing; that it was due to physical causes. But Princess Mary believed that he wanted to tell her something.

"Wouldn't it be better if it were over, if all were over?" Princess Mary thought. Day and night, almost without sleep, she watched him, and, terrible to say, she watched him, not in the hope of finding symptoms of a change for the better, but often in the hope of seeing symptoms of the approaching end.

Strange as it was for the princess to admit it to herself, she had this feeling in her heart. And what was still more horrible to Princess Mary was the fact that ever since her father's illness all the forgotten hopes and desires slumbering within her awakened. Dreams of a life free from the terror of her father, even of the possibility of love and a happy married life, haunted her like temptations of the devil. In vain she tried to drive away these thoughts. She knew that the sole weapon against *him* was prayer, and she tried to pray. She gazed at the holy pictures, repeated the words of prayers, but still she could not pray. She felt herself carried off into a new world of real life free from bondage. She could not pray and could not weep.

To remain at Bogutcharovo was also becoming unsafe. Rumours came from all sides of the French being near, and in one village, fifteen miles from Bogutcharovo, a house had been sacked by French marauders. The doctor insisted on the necessity of moving the prince; the marshal of the province sent an official to Princess Mary to persuade her to get away as quickly as possible. The captain of the police visited Bogutcharovo to insist on the same thing, telling her that the French were only forty miles away; that French proclamations were circulating in the villages, and that if the princess did not move her father before the 15th, he could not answer for the consequences.

The princess made up her mind to leave on the 15th. The night of the 14th she spent as usual, without undressing, in the room next to the one where the old prince lay. Several times she waked up, hearing his groaning and muttering, the creak of the bedstead, and the steps of Tihon and the doctor moving him. Several times she listened at the door, and it seemed to her that he was muttering more loudly than usual and turning more restlessly. She went to the door, listening, tempted to go in, but she knew that her going in at night, at an unusual time, would irritate him. And again she began to dream of what would happen after his death, and how she would live her new life. But she drove away such thoughts with horror. Towards morning he was quieter, and she fell asleep.

She waked up late. She waked up, listened to what was passing through the door, and catching the sound of his muttering, she told herself with a sigh that there was no change.

"But what should there be? What did I hope for? I hope for his death," she cried, with inward loathing of herself.

The doctor came to her.

"He is a little better to-day," said the doctor. "I was looking for you. One can make out a little of what he says. His head is clearer. Come in. He is asking for you . . ."

Princess Mary's heart beat so violently at this news that she turned pale and leaned against the door to keep from falling. To see him, to talk to him, to be under his eyes now, when all her soul was filled with these fearful, sinful imaginings was full of an agonising terror for her.

"Let us go in," said the doctor.

Princess Mary went in to her father. He was lying raised high on his back; his little bony hands, covered with knotted purple veins, were laid on the quilt; his left eye was gazing straight before him, while the right eye was distorted, and his lips and eyebrows were motionless. He looked so thin, so small, and pitiable. His face looked withered. Princess Mary went up and kissed his hand. His left hand clasped her hand in a way that showed he had long been wanting her. His eyebrows and lips quivered.

She looked at him, trying to fathom what he wanted of her. When she changed her position so that his left eye could see her, he seemed satisfied, and for several seconds kept his eye fixed on her. Then his lips and tongue twitched; sounds came, and he tried to speak, looking with imploring timidity at her, evidently afraid she would not understand him.

"O . . . o . . . aye . . . aye . . . !" he repeated several times. It was impossible to interpret these sounds.

The doctor thought he had guessed it, and asked: "The princess is afraid?"

The old prince shook his head, and again repeated the same sounds.

Princess Mary pressed her head against his arm, trying to hide her tears.

He passed his hand over her hair. And again he tried to speak. "Darling!" . . . or "Dear one!" . . . Princess Mary could not distinguish the word; but from the expression of his eyes she had no doubt what was said was a word of caressing tenderness such as he had never used to her before.

"And I was wishing, wishing for his death!" thought Princess Mary.

Once more he spoke. This time more clearly. "Child, dear one! . . . Forgive . . . Forgive! . . ." And tears flowed from his eyes. "Call André," he said suddenly, and a look of childish misgiving came into his face. He seemed to be aware that his question had no meaning.

"I have had a letter from him," answered Princess Mary. "He is with the army, father, at Smolensk."

The old prince was silent for a long while, closing his eyes. Then, as though to answer his doubts, and to assert that now he understood it all and remembered, he nodded his head and opened his eyes.

He spoke softly and distinctly. "Russia is lost! They have lost her!"

And again he broke into sobs.

Then he said something, which, for a long while, no one could understand; and at last Tihon understood and interpreted.

Princess Mary looked for the drift of his words in the direction in which he had been speaking a minute before. She supposed he was speaking of Russia; then of Prince André, of herself, of his grandson, then of his own death. And this was just why she could not understand his words.

"Put on your white dress. I like it," he had said.

When she understood those words Princess Mary began to cry and the doctor led her out of the room on to the terrace. After Princess Mary had left the prince, he began talking again of his son, of the war, of the Tsar, twitched his eyebrows angrily, began to raise his hoarse voice, and was seized by a second and final stroke.

Princess Mary stayed on the terrace. She could grasp nothing, could think of nothing, and feel nothing but her passionate love for her father, of which it seemed to her that she had not been aware till that minute.

"Yes . . . I . . . I . . . I longed for his death! Yes, I wanted it soon to be over . . . I wanted to be at peace . . . And what will become of me? What use will peace be to me when he is gone?" Princess Mary mutttered aloud, walking back and forth.

Then coming back into her father's room she stood by his bed. He was still lying as before; but the stern look on his calm face struck Princess Mary.

"No, he is not dead, it cannot be!" she said to herself. She went up to him, and struggling with the terror that came upon her, she pressed her lips to his cheek. But she started back from him. All at once the tenderness she had been feeling for him vanished, and was followed by a feeling of horror for what lay before her. "No, no, he is no more! He is no more, and here in the place where he was, is something unfamiliar and sinister, some fearful, terrifying, and repulsive secret!" And hiding her face in her hands, Princess Mary sank to the floor leaning against his bed.

Towards night candles were lighted round the coffin, a pall was laid over it, juniper was strewn on the floor, a printed prayer was put under the dead withered head, and a deacon sat in the corner reading aloud the Psalter. Like horses crowding, snorting, and starting round a dead horse, numbers of familiar and unfamiliar figures crowded round the coffin—the marshal, and the village elder, and peasant women, and all with scared and fascinated eyes, crossed themselves, and bowed down and kissed the cold, stiff hand of the old prince.

Until Prince André's stay at Bogutcharovo, the estate had never had an owner in residence, and the Bogutcharovo peasants were of quite a different character from the peasants of Bleak Hills. They differed from them in speech, in dress, and in manners. They said they came from the steppes. The old prince praised them for their industry when they came to Bleak Hills for harvesting, or digging ponds and ditches; but he did not like them because of their savage manners.

Prince André's residence at Bogutcharovo, and his reforms—his hospitals and schools and the lowering of their rent—had not softened their manners, but, on the contrary, had intensified their traits of character, which the old prince called their savagery.

Obscure rumours were always current among them. At one time they believed that they were all to be carried off to be made Cossacks, then that they were to be converted to some new religion. At another time they believed they were to be freed. Now the rumours of the war, and Bonaparte and his invasion, were connected in their minds with vague ideas of Antichrist, of the end of the world, and perfect freedom.

Twenty years before, there had been a movement among the peasants of this district to emigrate to certain warm rivers. Hundreds of peasants, among them those of Bogutcharovo, had suddenly begun selling their cattle and moving away with their families towards the south-west. Like birds flying to unknown realms over the ocean, these men with their wives and children turned towards the south-west, where no one of them had ever been before. They set off in caravans, ran and drove and walked. Many were punished; some sent to Siberia; many died of cold and hunger on the road; many came back of their own accord. And the movement died down as it had begun. But the undercurrents still flowed among these people.

Alpatitch, who came to Bogutcharovo a little while before the old prince's death, noticed that there was some disturbance among the peasants. He noticed that, unlike the Bleak Hills peasants who had moved away, in the Bogutcharovo steppe country the peasants had entered into communication with the French, and were remaining in their homes. And there were some mysterious documents circulating among them, proclamations from the French army saying that no harm would be done to the peasants, and that everything taken from them would be paid for, if they would remain.

For nearly thirty years Bogutcharovo had been under the direction of a village elder called Dron.

The peasants were more afraid of him than of their master.

The old prince and the young one and the steward respected him, and called him in joke the minister. Dron had never once been drunk or ill since he had been appointed elder; he had never after sleepless nights or severe labour shown the slightest signs of fatigue; and though he could not read or write, he never forgot an account of the pounds of flour in the huge waggon-loads he sold, and of the money paid for them, nor missed a sheaf of wheat on an acre of the Bogutcharovo fields.

It was for this peasant Dron that Alpatitch sent, on coming from the plundered estate at Bleak Hills. He ordered him to get ready twelve horses for the princess's carriages, and eighteen waggons for the move which was to be made from Bogutcharovo. Though the peasants paid rent instead of working as serfs, Alpatitch expected to meet no difficulty on their part in carrying out this order, since there were two hundred and thirty efficient families in Bogutcharovo, and the peasants were well-to-do. But Dron, on receiving the order, dropped his eyes and made no reply. Alpatitch mentioned the names of peasants from whom he told him to take the waggons.

Dron replied that the horses belonging to those peasants were away on hire. Alpatitch mentioned the names of other peasants. They too, according to Dron, had no horses available: some were employed in government transport, others had gone lame, and others had died through the shortness of forage. In Dron's opinion, there was no hope of getting horses enough for the princess's carriages, not to speak of the transport of baggage.

Alpatitch looked intently at Dron and scowled. He saw at once that his answers were the expression of the general drift of opinion in the Bogutcharovo village. At the same time, he knew that Dron, who had saved money and was detested by the village, must be hesitating between two camps—the master's and the peasants'. And so frowning he came closer to him.

"Now, Dron," he said, "you listen to me! Don't you talk nonsense to me. His excellency, Prince André himself, gave me orders to move the folk away, and not leave them with the enemy, and the Tsar has issued a decree that it is to be so. Any one that stays is a traitor to the Tsar. Do you hear?"

"I hear," answered Dron, not raising his eyes.

Alpatitch was not satisfied with his reply.

"Dron, there'll be trouble!" said Alpatitch, shaking his head.

"It's for you to command!" said Dron dejectedly.

"Dron, drop it!" repeated Alpatitch, taking his hand out of the bosom of his coat, and pointing with a solemn gesture to the ground under Dron's feet. "I can see right through you; and more than that, I can see three yards into the earth under you," he said, knowing that his skill in bee-keeping, his knowledge of the right day to sow the oats, and his success in pleasing the old prince for twenty years had long ago gained him the reputation of a wizard, and that the power of seeing for three yards under a man is ascribed to wizards.

Dron was disconcerted; he looked furtively at Alpatitch, and dropped his eyes again.

"You drop this nonsense, and tell the folks to pack up to leave their homes and go to Moscow, and to get ready carts to-morrow morning for the princess's luggage. Do you hear?"

Dron would have said something, but Alpatitch interrupted him.

"What's this you've all got in your head? Eh? . . . What are you thinking about? Eh?"

"What am I to do with the people?" said Dron. "They're all in a ferment. I do tell them . . ."

"Then you listen to me. I'll go to the police-captain and you tell them so, and tell them to drop all this and get the carts ready."

Alpatitch did not insist further. He had experience in managing peasants, and knew that the chief means for securing obedience was not to show the slightest suspicion that they could do anything but obey. Having wrung from Dron a submissive "certainly," Alpatitch rested content with it, though he had more than doubts—he had a conviction—that the carts would not be provided without the intervention of the military authorities.

And as he feared when evening came, the carts had not been provided. There had been again a village meeting at the tavern, and it had been resolved to drive the horses out into the forest and not to provide the waggons. Without saying a word of all this to the princess, Alpatitch ordered his own baggage to be unloaded from the waggons that had come from Bleak Hills and the horses to be taken from them for the princess's carriage, while he rode off himself to the police authorities.

After her father's funeral Princess Mary locked herself in her room and would not let any one come near her. She said that she was never going away, and begged to be left in peace.

The sun was setting, and the slanting rays lighted up her room through the open window. She walked to the window, drawing a deep breath of the refreshing coolness of the clear, windy evening.

"Yes, now you can admire the sunset at your ease! He is not here, and there is no one to hinder you," she said to herself, and sinking into a chair, she let her head fall on the window-sill.

Some one spoke her name in a soft and tender voice from the garden and kissed her on the head. She looked up. It was Mademoiselle Bourienne in a black dress.

Princess Mary pictured quickly to herself Mademoiselle Bourienne's position, estranged from her of late, though dependent on her, and living among strangers. And she felt sorry for her. She looked at her and held out her hand to her. Mademoiselle Bourienne at once began kissing her hand with tears and talking of the princess's sorrow, making herself a partner in that sorrow. She said that her only consolation was that the princess permitted her to share it with her. She said that all their former misunderstandings must sink into nothing before their great sorrow: that she felt herself guiltless in regard to every one, and that *he* from above saw her love and gratitude.

"Your position is doubly dreadful, dear princess," said Mademoiselle Bourienne. " . . . Has Alpatitch spoken to you of moving? Do you know, my dear Mary, that we are in danger, that we are surrounded by the French; it is dangerous to move. If we move, we are almost certain to be taken prisoner, and God knows . . ."

Princess Mary looked at her with no notion of what she was saying.

"Oh, if any one knew how little anything matters to me now," she said. "Of course, I would not on any account move away from *him* . . . Alpatitch said something about going away. . . . You talk to him . . . I can't do anything, and I don't want . . ."

"I have been talking to him. He hopes that we may manage to get away to-morrow; but I think it would be better now to remain here," said Mademoiselle Bourienne. "Because you will agree, that to fall into the hands of soldiers or of rioting peasants would be awful."

Mademoiselle Bourienne took out of her pocket a document. It was the proclamation of General Rameau, announcing that protection would be given by the French commanders to all inhabitants who did not abandon their homes. She handed it to the princess.

"I think the best thing would be to appeal to this general," said Mademoiselle Bourienne. "I am convinced that all proper respect would be shown you."

Princess Mary read the document.

"Through whom did you get this?" she asked.

"They probably found out I was French from my name," said Mademoiselle Bourienne, flushing.

With the proclamation in her hand, Princess Mary got up from the window, and walked into Prince André's former study.

"Mademoiselle Bourienne can stay behind if she likes, but I . . . To set off at once! As quickly as possible!" said Princess Mary, appalled at the idea that she might be left in the power of the French.

"That Prince André should know that she was in the power of the French! That she, the daughter of Prince Nicholas Bolkonsky, should stoop to ask General Rameau to grant her his protection, and should take advantage of his good offices." The idea appalled her, made her shudder and turn crimson. She felt a rush of vindictive wrath and pride of which she had had no conception. All the bitterness, and still more the humiliation of her position rose vividly to her imagination. "They, the French, would take up their quarters in the house: M. le Général Rameau would occupy Prince André's study; would amuse himself by looking through and reading his letters and papers; Mademoiselle Bourienne would do the honours of Bogutcharovo; I should be given a room as a favour; the soldiers would break open my father's newly dug grave to take his crosses and decorations; they would tell me of their victories over the Russians, would affect hypocritical sympathy with my grief . . ." thought Princess Mary, thinking not the thoughts natural to her, but feeling it a duty to think as her father and brother would have done. To her personally it did not matter where she stayed and what happened to her, but, at the same time, she felt herself the representative of her dead father and Prince André. Unconsciously she thought their thoughts and felt their feelings. What they would have said, what they would have done now, she felt it incumbent upon her to do.

Flushed and excited she walked about the room, sending first for Alpatitch, then for Mihail Ivanitch, then for Tihon, then for Dron. Dunyasha, the old nurse, and the maids could not tell her how far Mademoiselle Bourienne's statements had been correct. Alpatitch was not in the house; he had gone to the police authorities. Mihail Ivanitch, the architect, came with sleepy eyes on being sent for, but could tell Princess Mary nothing. With the same smile of acquiescence with which he had been accustomed during the course of fifteen years to meet the old prince's remarks without committing himself, he now met the princess's questions, so that there was no getting any definite answer out of him. The old valet, Tihon, whose wan and sunken face wore the stamp of inconsolable grief, answered "Yes, princess," to all Princess Mary's questions, and could scarcely restrain his sobs as he looked at her.

Lastly, the village elder, Dron, came into the room, and bowing low to the princess, stood near the door.

"Dron," said Princess Mary, seeing in him a staunch friend,

the Dron who had every year brought back from the fair at Vyazma the same gingerbreads she connected with him, and had presented them to her with the same smile, "Dron now, after our misfortune," . . . she began, and paused, unable to go on.

"We are all in God's hands," he said, with a sigh.

They were silent.

"Dron, Alpatitch has gone off somewhere, I have no one to turn to. Is it true, as I'm told, that it is impossible for me to go away?"

"Why shouldn't you go away, your excellency? You can go," said Dron.

"I have been told there is danger from the enemy. I can do nothing, I know nothing about it, I have nobody. I want to set off without fail to-night or to-morrow morning early."

Dron did not speak. He looked up from under his brows at Princess Mary.

"There are no horses," he said. "I have told Alpatitch so already."

"How is that?" asked the princess.

"It's all the visitation of the Lord," said Dron. "Some horses have been carried off for the troops, and some are dead; it's a bad year, it is. If only we don't die of hunger ourselves, let alone feeding the horses! Here they've been three days without a bit of bread. There's nothing. They have been plundered to the last crust."

Princess Mary listened to what he said to her.

"The peasants have been plundered? They have no bread?" she asked.

"They are dying of hunger," said Dron. "No use talking of horses and carts."

"But why didn't you say so, Dron? Can't they be helped? I'll do everything I can . . ." It was strange to Princess Mary to think that at such a moment, when her heart was overflowing with such a sorrow, there could be rich people and poor, and that the rich could possibly not help the poor. She vaguely knew that there was a store of "seignorial corn," and that it was sometimes given to the peasants. She knew, too, that neither her brother nor her father would refuse the peasants in their need; she was only afraid of making some mistake in the wording of the order for this distribution.

"I suppose we have an extra store of wheat?" she asked.

"The wheat is all untouched," Dron declared with pride. "The prince gave me no orders about selling it."

"Give it to the peasants, give them all they need. I give you leave in my brother's name," said Princess Mary.

Dron made no answer.

"Distribute the corn among them, if it will be enough for

them. Distribute it all. And tell them, what's ours is theirs. We would grudge nothing for them. Tell them so."

Dron watched the princess intently all the while she was speaking. Suddenly he threw himself at her feet.

"Discharge me, ma'am, for God's sake, bid them take the keys from me," said he. "I have served twenty-three years, and done no wrong. Discharge me, for God's sake."

Princess Mary had no notion what he wanted of her and why he asked her to discharge him. She answered that she had never doubted his fidelity, and that she was ready to do everything for him and for the peasants.

An hour later Dunyasha came in to the princess with the news that all the peasants were assembled at the granary and desirous of speaking with their mistress.

In spite of Dunyasha's and the old nurse's attempts to dissuade her, Princess Mary went out on to the steps. Dron, Dunyasha, the old nurse, and Mihail Ivanitch followed her.

"They probably imagine I am offering them the grain to keep them here while I go away myself, leaving them at the mercy of the French," thought Princess Mary. "I will promise them food and lodgings on the Moscow estate. André would do more for them in my place," she thought, as she went out in the twilight towards the crowd.

The crowd stirred, and rapidly took off their hats. Princess Mary came closer to them. So many different eyes, old and young, were fixed upon her, there were so many different faces that Princess Mary did not see a single one of them, and feeling it necessary to address all at once, did not know how to set about it. But again the sense that she was the representative of her father and brother gave her strength, and she boldly began her speech.

"I am very glad you have come," she began, feeling the rapid and violent beating of her heart. "Dron has told me that the war has ruined you. That is our common trouble, and I will grudge nothing to aid you. I am going away myself because it is dangerous here . . . and the enemy is near . . . because . . . I give you everything, my friends, and I beg you to take everything, all our grain, that you may not suffer want. But if you have been told that I am giving you grain to keep you here, it is not true. On the contrary, I beg you to move away with all your belongings to our Moscow estate, and there I promise you that you shall not be in want. You shall be given houses and bread." The princess stopped. Nothing was to be heard from the crowd.

"I don't do this on my own account," the princess went on; "I do it in the name of my dead father, who was a good master to you, and for my brother and his son."

She paused again. No one broke the silence.

"We have trouble in common, and we will share it all equally. All that is mine is yours," she said, looking up at the faces before her. All the eyes were gazing at her with the same expression, the meaning of which she could not fathom. Whether it were curiosity, devotion, gratitude, or apprehension, and distrust, the expression on all the faces was alike.

"Very thankful for your kindness, only it's not for us to take the master's corn," said a voice from the back.

"But why not?" said the princess. No one answered, and Princess Mary, looking up at the crowd, noticed that now all the eyes dropped at once on meeting hers.

"Why don't you want to?" she asked again.

No one replied.

Princess Mary was oppressed by the silence; she tried to catch somebody's eye.

"Why don't you speak!" she said, addressing a very old man who was standing near her, his arms propped on his stick. "Tell me if you think something more is needed. I will do anything," she said. But as though angered he answered: "Why should we agree? We don't want your grain."

"Why should we give up everything? We're not willing . . . Not willing. It's not with our consent. We are sorry for you, but we are not willing. You go away by yourself, alone . . ." was protested from different parts of the crowd. And again all the faces in the crowd wore the same expression. And now it was unmistakably not an expression of curiosity and gratitude, but an expression of determination.

"But you misunderstand me," said Princess Mary. "Why don't you want to move away? I promise to settle you, to provide for you. And here the enemy will plunder you . . ." But her voice was drowned by the voices of the crowd.

"We're not willing, let him plunder us! We won't take your grain, we won't agree!"

Princess Mary tried again to catch some one's eye in the crowd, but no one was looking at her. Their eyes unmistakably avoided hers. She felt strange and awkward.

"To be sure, she would school us . . . a good dodge . . . follow her into slavery. Pull down your house and go into bondage. I dare say! I'll give you grain, says she!" voices were saying in the crowd.

Princess Mary moved out of the ring, and went to the house. Repeating her command to Dron that horses were to be ready next day for her to start, she went away to her own room.

On the 17th of August Nicholas Rostov and Ilyin rode out from Yankovo, fifteen miles from Bogutcharovo. They meant to try a new horse that Ilyin had bought, and to find out whether there was hay to be had in the village.

Bogutcharovo had been for the last three days between the two hostile armies, so that the Russian rearguard could reach the village as easily as the French vanguard; and therefore Rostov, like a careful officer, was anxious to get any provisions that might be left there.

Rostov and Ilyin were in the liveliest spirits. They were on their way to Bogutcharovo, which they knew to be an estate belonging to a prince, with a manor-house, where they hoped to find a large household, and, perhaps, pretty servant-girls. They raced their horses. Rostov had no notion that the village to which he was going was the property of the very Prince Bolkonsky who had been betrothed to his sister.

They galloped into the village street. Then they rode at a walking pace towards the granary, where there was a great crowd of peasants standing. Several of the peasants took off their caps, others stared at them without taking off their caps. Two old peasants, with wrinkled faces and scanty beards, came out of the tavern, reeling and singing a tuneless song.

A peasant came out of the crowd and went up to Rostov.

"Have you many troops here?" he asked.

"A great many," answered Rostov. "But why are you all gathered here?" he added. "Is it a holiday or what?"

"The old men are met about the village business," answered the peasant, moving away from him.

At that moment there came into sight two women and a man in a white hat running from the prince's house towards the officers.

"The princess sent me to ask of what regiment are you, and what is your name?"

"This is Count Rostov, the commander of the squadron, and I am your humble servant."

"I make bold to trouble your honour," Alpatitch said, putting one hand in his bosom, and speaking with a respectfulness in which there was a shade of contempt for the officer's youth. "My mistress, the daughter of general-in-chief Prince Nicholas Bolkonsky, who died on the 15th of this month, being in difficulties owning to the coarse ignorance of those people"—he pointed to the peasants—"begs you to come . . . Would you not be pleased," said Alpatitch, with a melancholy smile, "to move a little away, as it is not so convenient before . . ." Alpatitch indicated two peasants, who were hovering about him, like gadflies about a horse.

Rostov and he moved away. "What is the matter?" he inquired.

"I make bold to submit to your excellency that the rude

peasants here will not let their lady leave the estate, and threaten to take the horses out of her carriage."

Rostov got off his horse, and giving it to the orderly, walked with Alpatitch to the house, questioning him further.

The princess's offer of grain, and her interview with Dron and with the peasants, had, in fact, made the position so much worse that Dron had finally given up the keys of office, joined the peasants and refused to appear when Alpatitch sent for him. In the morning when the princess ordered the horses to be put in for her to set off, the peasants had come out in a great crowd to the granary, and had sent to say that they would not let the princess go out of the village; that there was an edict that people were not to leave their houses, and that they would unharness the horses. Alpatitch went out to lecture them; in reply they told him that the princess could not go, but that if she stayed they would serve her and obey her in everything as before.

Princess Mary was sitting helpless and distraught in the hall, when Nicholas Rostov was shown in to see her. She did not know who he was, or what brought him there, or what was happening to her. Seeing his Russian face, and recognising him at his first words and gait for a man of her own rank, she looked at him, with her deep, luminous gaze, and began speaking in a voice, broken and trembling with emotion.

When she had finished speaking, Rostov said: "I cannot express how glad I am, princess, that I happened to come this way, and am able to serve you." He rose. "I trust you will start at once, and I answer for it on my honour, no person shall dare to cause you annoyance, if you will only permit me to escort you," and making a deep bow, such as are made to ladies of the royal family, he turned to the door.

After Rostov and Ilyin had entered the village and Rostov had gone in to see the princess, a certain hesitation and division of opinion had become apparent in the crowd. Some of the peasants began to say that the officers might take it amiss that they had not let their young lady go. Dron was of that opinion; but as soon as he expressed it, others fell upon him.

"How many years have you been fattening on the village?" shouted one. "It's all one to you! You'll dig up your pot of money and make off with it. What is it to you if our homes are ruined or not?"

"We were told everything was to be in order and no one to leave their homes, and not a thing to be moved away," shouted another.

"It was your son's turn; but you spared your fat youngster," a little old man suddenly burst out, pouncing upon Dron, "and sent my Vanka to be shaved for a soldier."

As soon as Rostov, accompanied by Ilyin and Alpatitch, approached the crowd huddled closer together.

"Who is elder among you here?" shouted Rostov, walking quickly up to the crowd.

"The elder? What do you want him for? . . ." asked one. But he hardly had time to get the words out when his hat went flying off his head, and he was sent reeling from a violent blow.

"Caps off, traitors!" shouted Rostov's full-blooded voice. "Where is the elder?" he roared furiously.

"The elder, the elder's wanted. Dron, he calls you," voices were heard saying, hurriedly subservient, and caps were taken off.

"Talking? . . . Mutiny! . . . Scoundrels! Traitors!" Rostov shouted, without thinking, in a voice unlike his own, as he seized one of the peasants by the collar. "Bind him, bind him!" he shouted, though there was no one to bind him but Ilyin and Alpatitch.

Alpatitch turned to the peasants, calling upon two of them by name to bind the peasant. They obediently stepped out of the crowd and began undoing their belts.

"Where's the village elder?" shouted Rostov.

Dron with a pale and frowning face, stepped out of the crowd.

"Are you the elder? Bind him!" shouted Rostov, as though the order could meet with no sort of opposition. And in fact two peasants did begin binding Dron, who took off his sash, and gave it them as though to assist in the operation.

"And listen to me," Rostov turned to the peasants. "March straight to your homes this minute, and don't let me hear your voices again."

"We haven't done any harm. It was all foolishness. . . . I always said that it wasn't the right thing," said voices, blaming one another. And the crowd at once began to break up and to disperse about the village.

Within two hours the horses and carts required were standing in the courtyard of the Bogutcharovo house. The peasants were hurrying in and out and packing the carts. And Dron, who had at Princess Mary's desire, been released from the lumber-room, where they had shut him up, was standing in the yard, giving directions to the men.

Rostov, not wishing to force his acquaintance on the princess, did not go back to the house, but remained at the village waiting for her to drive out. When Princess Mary's carriage drove out from the house, Rostov mounted his horse and escorted her as far as the road occupied by the Russian troops, twelve miles from Bogutcharovo. There he parted from her, for the first time permitting himself to kiss her hand.

"How can you speak of it!" he said, blushing in response to Princess Mary's expression of gratitude to him for saving her. "If we only had to wage war with peasants, we would not have let the enemy advance so far," he said, trying with a sort of bashfulness to change the conversation. "I am only happy to have had the opportunity of making your acquaintance. Good-bye, princess. I trust you may find happiness and consolation, and I hope I may meet you again in happier circumstances."

But if the princess thanked him no more in words, she thanked him with the whole expression of her face, which was radiant with gratitude and warmth. To her mind it was an incontestable fact that had it not been for him, she must have fallen a victim to the rebellious peasants or the French; that *he,* to save her, had exposed himself to obvious and fearful danger.

When she had said good-bye to him and was left alone, Princess Mary suddenly felt tears in her eyes, and then the question occurred to her: "Was she in love with him?" On the rest of the way to Moscow, though the princess's position was by no means a joyful one, Dunyasha, who was in the carriage with her, noticed that her mistress's face wore a vaguely happy and pensive smile, as she looked out of the window.

"Well, what if I have fallen in love with him?" Though she was ashamed at acknowledging to herself that she had fallen in love with a man who would perhaps never care for her, she comforted herself with the reflection that no one would ever know it, and she was not to blame, if she loved in secret for the first and last time and for her whole life long.

"And to think that he should come to Bogutcharovo and at that very moment!" thought Princess Mary. "And that his sister should have refused André!" And in all that, Princess Mary saw the hand of Providence.

The impression made on Rostov by Princess Mary was a very agreeable one. When he thought of her, he felt pleased. And when his comrades, hearing of his adventure at Bogutcharovo, teased him on having gone to look for hay, and having picked up one of the greatest heiresses in Russia, it made him angry. He was angry just because the idea of marrying the gentle, and, to his mind, charming Princess Mary with her enormous fortune had more than once occurred to his mind. As far as he personally was concerned,

Nicholas could have asked nothing better than to have Princess Mary for his wife. To marry her would make the countess, his mother, happy, and would repair his father's broken fortunes. And it would even—Nicholas felt it—make the happiness of the princess herself.

But there was Sonya. And there was his promise.

On receiving the chief command of the army, Kutuzov remembered Prince André and sent for him.

Prince André reached headquarters on the very day and at the very hour when Kutuzov was making his first inspection of the troops. Prince André stopped in the village at the house of the priest, where the commander-in-chief's carriage was standing, and sat down on a bench at the gate to await his highness, as every one now called Kutuzov, for he had been honoured with the title of prince. From the plain beyond the village came the sounds of regimental music, and the roar of a vast multitude, shouting "Hurrah!" to the new commander-in-chief. At the gate stood two orderlies, a courier, and a butler, taking advantage of their master's absence to enjoy the fine weather. A swarthy little lieutenant-colonel of hussars, his face covered with bushy moustaches and whiskers, rode up to the gate, and glancing at Prince André asked whether his highness were putting up here and whether he would soon be back.

Prince André made room for him on the bench. The hussar sat down beside him.

"You, too, waiting for the commander-in-chief?" he began. "They say he is willing to see any one, thank God! It was a very different matter with the German sausage-makers! Now Russians may dare to speak again. And devil knows what they have been about. Nothing but retreating and retreating. Have you been in the field?" he asked.

"I have," said Prince André, "not only taking part in the retreat, but also losing everything I valued in the retreat—not to speak of my property and the home of my birth . . . my father, who died of grief. I am a Smolensk man."

"Ah! . . . Are you Prince Bolkonsky? Very glad to make your acquaintance. Lieutenant-colonel Denisov," said Denisov, pressing Prince André's hand and looking into his face with a kindly expression. "Yes, I had heard about it," he said sympathetically, and after a brief pause he added: "Yes, this warfare, it's all right, but not for those who have to pay the piper. So you are Prince André Bolkonsky?" He shook his head.

Prince André knew of Denisov from Natasha's stories of her first suitor. The recollection of them—both sweet and bitter—carried him back to the heart-sickness of which he had of late never thought, though it still lay buried within him. Of late so many different and grave matters, such as the abandonment of Smolensk, his visit to Bleak Hills, the recent news of his father's death—so many things had filled his heart that those memories had long been absent, and when they returned did not affect him nearly so violently. And for Denisov, the associations awakened by the name of Bolkonsky belonged to a far-away, romantic past, when, after supper and Natasha's singing, hardly knowing what he was doing, he had made an offer to the girl of fifteen. He smiled at the recollection of that time and his love for Natasha, and passed at once to what he was just now intensely and exclusively interested in. This was a plan of campaign he had formed while on duty at the outposts during the retreat. He had laid the plan before Barclay de Tolly, and now intended to lay it before Kutuzov. The plan was based on the fact that the French line was too extended. He began explaining his plan to Prince André.

"They are not able to defend all that line; it's impossible. I'll undertake to break through. Give me five hundred men and I will cut their communications! Guerilla warfare."

Suddenly they heard the shouts of the army, mingling with music and song. From the village came cheers and the tramp of horses' hoofs.

"Himself is coming," shouted the Cossack, who stood at the gate. He's coming!"

Prince André and Denisov moved up to the gate, where there stood a group of soldiers, a guard of honour, and they saw Kutuzov coming down the street mounted on a low bay horse. A suite of generals followed him. Barclay rode almost beside him.

Kutuzov impatiently kicked his horse, which ambled along slowly under his weight, and continually nodded his head and put his hand up to his white horse-guard's cap, with a red band and no peak. When he reached the guard of honour, saluting him, he looked at them for a minute in silence, with the intent, unflinching gaze of a man used to command; then he turned to the group of generals and officers standing round him. His face suddenly wore a subtle expression; he shrugged his shoulders with an air of perplexity. "And with fellows like that retreat and retreat!" he said. "Well, good-bye, generals," he added, and spurred his horse into the gateway by Prince André and Denisov.

"Hurrah! Hurrah! Hurrah!" rang out shouts behind him.

Since Prince André had seen him last Kutuzov had grown stouter. He seemed swimming in fat. But the familiar scar, and the white eye, and the expression of weariness in his face and figure were unchanged. He sat heavily swaying on his sturdy horse as he rode into the courtyard. His face expressed the relief of a man who looks forward to resting after a performance. He drew his left foot out of the stirrup, and with a lurch, frowning with the effort, brought it up to the saddle, leaned on his knee, and with a groan let himself drop into the arms of the Cossacks and adjutants, who stood ready to support him.

He pulled himself together, looked round with a half-shut eye, glanced at Prince André, and evidently not recognising him, moved with his shambling gait towards the steps.

Then again he looked round at Prince André. "Ah, how are you, how are you, my dear boy, come along . . ." he said wearily, and walked heavily up the steps that creaked under his weight. He unbuttoned his coat and sat down on a seat on the porch.

"Well, how's your father?"

"The news of his death reached me yesterday," said Prince André.

Kutuzov looked at him with his eye opened wide with dismay, then he took off his cap, and crossed himself. "The peace of heaven be with him! And may God's will be done with all of us!" He heaved a heavy sigh and paused. "I loved him deeply and respected him, and I feel for you with all my heart." He embraced Prince André, pressed him to his fat breast, and for some time did not let him go. When he released him, Prince André saw that Kutuzov's thick lips were quivering and there were tears in his eye. He sighed and pressed his hands on the seat to help himself in rising from it.

"Come in, come in, we'll have a chat," he said; but at that moment Denisov, who stood as little in dread of the authorities as he did of the enemy, walked boldly up, his spurs clanking on the steps. Kutuzov, his hands still pressed on the seat to help him up, looked at Denisov. Denisov, mentioning his name, announced that he had to communicate to his highness a matter of great importance for the welfare of Russia. Kutuzov bent his weary eyes on Denisov, and, lifting his hands with a gesture of annoyance, folded them across his stomach, and repeated, "For the welfare of Russia? Well, what is it? Speak." Denisov began boldly explaining his plan for cutting the enemy's line. Denisov's home was in that region now occupied by the French, and he knew the country well. His plan seemed unquestionably good. Kutuzov stared at his own feet, and occasionally looked round towards the yard of the next cottage, as though he were expecting something unpleasant to come from it. From the cottage there did in fact emerge, during Denisov's speech, a general with a portfolio under his arm.

"Eh?" Kutuzov inquired in the middle of Denisov's explanation. "Are you ready now?"

"Yes, your highness," said the general. Kutuzov shook his head with an air that seemed to say, "How is one man to get through it all?" and gave his attention again to Denisov.

"I give you my word of honour as a Russian officer," Denisov was saying, "that I will cut Napoleon's communications."

"Is Kirill Denisov, the ober-intendant, any relation of yours?" Kutuzov interposed.

"My uncle, your highness."

"Oh! We used to be friends," said Kutuzov. "Very good, very good, my dear boy; you stay here on the staff; we'll have a talk to-morrow." Nodding to Denisov, he turned away and put out his hand for the papers the general had brought him.

"Will your highness walk into the house?" said the general on duty in a discontented voice. "It's necessary to look through the plans and to sign some papers." An adjutant appeared at the door to announce that everything was in readiness within. But apparently Kutuzov preferred to be rid of business before going indoors. He paused . . .

"No; have a table placed here, my dear boy; I'll look through them here," he said. "Don't you go away," he added, addressing Prince André. Prince André remained.

Kutuzov heard the general's report, the subject of which was chiefly a criticism of the position of the troops, just as he had heard Denisov, and just as, seven years before, he had heard the discussions of the military council before Austerlitz. He was obviously hearing it simply because he had ears, and although one of them was stuffed up with cotton he could not help hearing. But it was obvious that nothing could surprise or interest him, that he knew beforehand all he would be told, and listened only because he had to listen to it, just as one has to listen to the litany being sung. All Denisov had said was practical and sensible. What the general was saying was even more practical and sensible, but apparently Kutuzov despised both knowledge and intellect, and knew of something else that would settle things—something different, quite apart from intellect and knowledge.

The only instruction of his own that Kutuzov inserted in the report related to acts of marauding by Russian troops. The general, at the end of the report, presented his highness a document for signature relating to a petition for damages from a landowner for the cutting of his oats by certain officers.

Kutuzov shook his head, as he listened.

"Into the stove . . . into the fire with it! And I tell you once for all, my dear fellow," he said, "all such things put into the fire. Let them cut the corn and burn the wood to their heart's content. It's not by my orders and it's not with my permission, but I can't pursue the matter. It can't be helped. You can't hew down trees without the chips flying." He glanced once more at the paper. "Oh, this German preciseness," he commented, shaking his head.

"Well, now, that's all," said Kutuzov, as he signed the last paper, and rising clumsily, he went to the door.

Half an hour later Kutuzov sent for Prince André. He was reclining in a low chair, still in the same unbuttoned military coat. He had a French novel in his hand, and at Prince André's entrance laid a paper-knife in it and put it aside.

"Well, sit down. Sit down here. Let us have a little talk," said Kutuzov. "It's sad; very sad. But remember, think of me as a father, another father, to you . . . !"

Prince André told Kutuzov all he knew about his father's end, and what he had seen at Bleak Hills.

"To think what we have been brought to!" Kutuzov cried suddenly, in a voice full of feeling, Prince André's story evidently bringing vividly before him the position of Russia.

"Wait a bit; wait a bit!" he added, with a vindictive look. And apparently unwilling to continue a conversation that stirred him too deeply, he said: "I sent for you to keep you with me."

"I thank your highness! But I am afraid I am no more good for staff work," said Prince André, with a smile, which Kutuzov noticed. He looked at him inquiringly. "And the great thing is," added Prince André, "I am used to my regiment. I like the officers; and I think the men have come to like me. I should be sorry to leave the regiment. If I decline the honour of being in attendance on you, believe me . . ."

Kutuzov's podgy face beamed with a shrewd, good-natured, and yet subtly ironical expression. He cut Prince André short.

"I'm sure you would have been of use to me. But you're right; you're right. It's not here that we need men. There are always a multitude of counsellors; but men are scarce. The regiments wouldn't be what they are if all the would-be counsellors would serve in them like you. I remember you at Austerlitz. I remember, I remember you with the flag!" said Kutuzov, and a flush of pleasure came into Prince André's face. Kutuzov held out his hand to him, and again Prince André saw tears in the old man's eye. Though Prince André knew Kutuzov's tears were apt to come easily, and that he was particularly affectionate and tender with him from the desire to show sympathy with his loss, yet he felt this reminder of Austerlitz agreeable and flattering.

"Go your own way, and God bless you in it. . . . I know your path is the path of honour!" He paused. "I missed you at Bucharest. I wanted some one to send . . ." And changing the subject, Kutuzov began talking of the Turkish war, and of the peace that had been concluded. "Yes, I have been roundly abused," he said, "both for the war and the peace . . . but it all happened in the nick of time. 'Everything comes in time for him who knows how to wait,'" he said, quoting the French proverb. "And there were as many counsellors there as here, . . ." he went on, returning to a subject which evidently occupied his mind. "Ugh, counsellors and counsellors!" he said. "If we had listened to all of them, we should be in Turkey now. We should not have made peace, and the war would never have been over. Always in haste, and more haste, worse speed. Kamensky would have come to grief there, if he hadn't died. He went storming fortresses with thirty thousand men. It's easy enough to take fortresses, but it's hard to finish off a campaign successfully. Storms and attacks are not what's wanted, but *time* and *patience*. Kamensky sent his soldiers to attack, but I trusted to them alone—*time* and *patience*—and I took more fortresses than Kamensky, and made the Turks eat horseflesh!" He shook his head. "And the French shall, too. Take my word for it," cried Kutuzov, growing warmer and slapping himself on the chest. "I'll make the French eat horseflesh!" And again his eye was dim with tears.

"We shall have to give battle, though, won't we?" said Prince André.

"We will, if every one wants to; there is no help for it. . . . But, mark my words! The strongest of all warriors are these two—*time* and *patience*."

As the French army drew nearer to Moscow its inhabitants grew more frivolous, as is always the case with people who see a great danger approaching. It was long since there had been so much gaiety in Moscow as that year.

Rastoptchin's posters were as much read and discussed. In the corner room of the club the members gathered together to read these posters; and some liked the way the simple character Karpushka was made to jeer at the French, saying that "they would be blown out with Russian cabbage, that Russian porridge would rip their guts open, and cabbage soup would finish them off; that they were all dwarfs, and a village girl could toss three of them on her pitchfork single-handed!"

Some people did not approve of this tone, and said it was vulgar and stupid. People said that Rastoptchin had sent all Frenchmen, and even foreigners, out of Moscow, and that there had been spies and agents of Napoleon among them. But they talked of this principally in order to repeat the witticisms uttered by Rastoptchin on the occasion. The foreigners had been put on a barque sailing to Nizhny, and Rastoptchin had said to them: "Keep yourselves to yourselves, get into the barque, and take care it does not become the barque of Charon to you." People talked too of all the government offices having been moved from Moscow. People said that Mamonov's regiment was costing him eight hundred thousand; that Pierre Bezuhov was spending even more on his; but that the noblest proof of Pierre's patriotism was that he was going to put on the uniform himself and ride at the head of his regiment, without any charge for seats to spectators.

"You have no mercy on any one," said Julie Drubetskoy, gathering up a pinch of scraped lint in her slender fingers covered with rings.

Julie was intending to leave Moscow next day, and was giving a farewell *soirée.*

"Bezuhov *est ridicule,* but he is so good-natured, so nice; how can you take pleasure in being so *caustique?*"

"Forfeit!" said a young man in a volunteer's uniform, whom Julie called *"mon chevalier,"* and was taking with her to Nizhny.

In Julie's circle, as in many circles in Moscow, it was a principle now to speak nothing but Russian, and those who made a mistake by speaking French had to pay a forfeit for the benefit of the committee of voluntary subscriptions.

"You have no mercy on any one," Julie continued. "And I'll pay for the pleasure of telling you the truth. I am ready to pay even more. I have neither the time nor the money to engage a teacher and learn Russian like Prince Galitzin. Ah, here is Pierre!" added Julie. *"Quand on* . . . No, no," she protested to the volunteer, "you're not going to catch me. When one speaks of the sun, one sees its rays. We were just talking of you," she said, smiling affably to Pierre, and adding, with the easy lying characteristic of society women, "We were saying your regiment was certain to be a finer one than Mamonov's."

"Oh, don't talk to me about my regiment," answered Pierre, kissing her hand, and sitting down beside her. "I am so sick of it!"

"You will take the command of it yourself, of course?" said Julie with a sly and sarcastic look towards the volunteer.

The latter was by no means so ready to be caustic in Pierre's presence. In spite of his absent-mindedness and good nature, Pierre's presence never failed to cut short any attempt at ridicule at his expense.

"No," answered Pierre, laughing and looking at his huge, bulky figure. "I should make too good a target for the French, and indeed I'm afraid I could hardly scramble on to a horse's back."

Among the people picked out as subjects for gossip, Julie's friends happened to hit on the Rostovs. "Their financial position is very serious, I am told," said Julie. "And the count is so unreasonable. Someone wanted to buy his house and his estate in the suburbs, and the matter is still dragging on. He asks too much."

"No, I fancy purchase will be concluded in a few days," said some one. "Though it's madness to buy anything in Moscow just now."

"Why?" said Julie. "Surely you don't suppose that Moscow is in any danger."

"Why are you leaving it then?"

"I? That's a strange question. I am going because . . . well, because everybody's going, and I am not a Jeanne d'Arc nor an Amazon."

"Oh, oh! Give me another strip of linen to scrape."

"He ought to be able to pay off all his debts, if he sets about it properly," the volunteer observed of Count Rostov.

"He's a good-hearted old fellow, but very foolish."

"And why are they staying on here so long? They were meaning to leave for the country long ago. Natasha is quite well again now, I suppose?" Julie asked Pierre, with a sly smile.

"They are waiting for their younger son," said Pierre. "He joined the army. But now they have transferred him to my regiment, and he is expected every day. The count wanted to get away long ago, but nothing would induce the countess to leave Moscow till Peter's return."

"I saw them the day before yesterday at a party. Natasha has quite recovered her looks and her spirits. She sang a song. How easily some people get over everything!"

"Get over what?" Pierre asked, looking displeased.

Julie smiled.

"Oh count, you know, such chivalrous knights as you are only to be found in novels."

"Knights! What do you mean?" Pierre asked blushing.

"Come now, my dear count. It's the talk of Moscow but I admire you just the same. Upon my word of honor," she said in French.

"Forfeit! forfeit!" cried the volunteer.

"Oh, very well. One cannot talk, what a bore it is!"

"What is the talk of all Moscow?" said Pierre angrily.

"Nonsense, count, you know!"

"I know nothing about it," said Pierre.

"I know what great friends you have always been with

Natasha, and so . . . But, I was always more friendly with Vera. That darling Vera."

"No," Pierre persisted in a tone of annoyance. "I have by no means taken upon myself the rôle of Countess Rostov's knight; indeed, it's almost a month since I have been near them. But I cannot understand the cruelty . . ."

"He who excuses himself, accuses himself," cried Julie in French, smiling, and waving the lint triumphantly. And so that she might have the last word, she promptly changed the subject. "By the way, I have heard poor Mary Bolkonsky arrived in Moscow yesterday. Have you heard she has lost her father?"

"Really? Where is she? I should like to see her," said Pierre.

"I spent the evening with her yesterday. She is going on to-day or to-morrow to their estate in the province with her little nephew."

"Well, how is she? Tell me," said Pierre.

"Oh, she is well, but very sad. But do you know who rescued her? It is quite a romance. Nicholas Rostov. She was surrounded; they tried to kill her and wounded her servants. He rushed in and saved her. . . ."

"Another romance," said the volunteer. "This general flight is evidently intended to marry off all the old maids."

"You know, I really do believe she's a little in love with the young man," she said in French.

"Forfeit! Forfeit! Forfeit!"

"But how is one to say that in Russian?"

When Pierre returned home, he was handed two new posters of Rastoptchin's that had just appeared.

The first declared that the rumour, that it was forbidden to leave Moscow, was false, and that, on the contrary, Count Rastoptchin was glad that ladies and merchants' wives were leaving the town. "There will be less panic and less false news," said the notice. "But I will stake my life on it that Bonaparte will never enter Moscow."

These words first showed Pierre clearly that the French certainly would enter Moscow. In the second poster it was announced that since many of the inhabitants of Moscow wanted to arm themselves, weapons were being provided in the arsenal; swords, pistols, and guns could be procured there at a low rate.

It was now evident to Pierre that the menacing storm cloud was coming closer.

"Shall I join the army or wait here?" Pierre thought, a question he had put to himself a hundred times already. He took up a pack of cards that lay on the table to deal them for a game of patience.

Just then he heard at the door of his study the voice of his cousin, the eldest princess, asking whether she might come in.

The eldest of his cousins, the one with the long waist and the stony face, was the only one still living in Pierre's house. The two younger sisters had both married.

"Excuse my coming to you, cousin," she said in a tone of reproach and excitement. "Some decision really must be made, you know. What is going to happen? Every one has left Moscow, and the people are becoming unruly. They won't obey any one now; even my maid has begun to be insolent. If it goes on like this, they will soon begin killing us. One can't walk about the streets. And the worst of it is, in another day or two the French will be here. Why are we waiting for them? One favour I beg of you, Pierre," said the princess, "give orders for me to be taken to Petersburg. Whatever I may be, I can't live under Bonaparte's rule. I'm not going to submit to Napoleon. Other people may do as they like. . . . If you won't do this for me . . ."

"But I will, I'll give orders for it at once. However, Count Rastoptchin says . . ."

"Rastoptchin," the princess began spitefully. "He's a hypocrite who has himself stirred the mob on to disorder. Didn't he write in his idiotic posters that they were to take anybody whoever it might be and drag them to the police. Honour and glory, says he, to the man who does so. And this is what he has brought us to. A friend of mine told me the mob almost killed her for speaking French."

Next day the princess set off in the evening, and Pierre's head-steward came to inform him that it was impossible to raise the money he required for the equipment of his regiment unless he sold one of his estates. Th head-steward impressed on Pierre generally that all this regimental craze would bring him to ruin. Pierre could hardly conceal a smile as he listened to the head-steward.

"Well, sell it then," he said. "I can't draw back now!"

The worse the position of affairs, and especially of his own affairs, the better pleased Pierre felt.

Scarcely any of Pierre's acquaintances were left in the town. Julie had gone, Princess Mary had gone. Of his more intimate acquaintances the Rostovs were the only people left; but Pierre did not go to see them.

To divert his mind that day, Pierre drove out to the village of Vorontsovo, to look at a great air balloon which was being constructed by Leppich to use against the enemy, and the test balloon which was to be sent up the following day.

On his way home Pierre drove through Bolotny Square, and seeing a crowd, stopped and got out of his carriage. The crowd was watching the flogging of a French cook, accused of being a spy. The flogging was just over, and the man who had administered it was untying from the whipping-post a stout, red-whiskered man in blue stockings and a green tunic, who was groaning piteously. Another victim, a thin, pale man, was standing by. Both, to judge by their faces, were Frenchmen.

Pierre pushed his way in among the crowd. "What is it? Who are they? What for?" he kept asking. But the crowd—clerks, artisans, shopkeepers, peasants, women in pelisses and jackets—was so intent on what was taking place that no one answered. The stout man got up, shrugged his shoulders frowning, and evidently trying to show fortitude, began putting on his tunic without looking about him. But all at once his lips quivered and to his own rage he began to cry. The crowd began talking loudly, to drown a feeling of pity in themselves.

"Some prince's cook. . . ."

"Eh, monsieur, Russian sauce is a bit strong for a French stomach . . . sets the teeth on edge," said a wrinkled clerk standing near Pierre, just when the Frenchman burst into tears. The clerk looked about him for signs of appreciation of his joke. Several laughed, but some were still gazing in dismay at the man who was undressing the second Frenchman and about to flog him.

Pierre choked, and turning quickly, went back to his carriage, muttering something to himself as he went. During the rest of the way he several times started, and cried out so loudly that the coachman at last asked him what he desired.

"Where are you driving?" Pierre shouted.

"You told me to drive to the governor's," answered the coachman.

"Fool! Idiot!" shouted Pierre, abusing his coachman, a thing he very rarely did. "I told you home. Blockhead! This very day I must set off," Pierre said to himself.

At the sight of the tortured Frenchman and the crowd, Pierre had decided that he could stay no longer in Moscow, and must that very day set off to join the army.

On reaching home Pierre told his head-coachman that he was going to drive that night to Mozhaisk to the army, and gave orders for his saddle horses to be sent on there.

The following morning when Pierre reached Mozhaisk, he found that troops were quartered in all the houses. And at the inn, where he was met by his coachman, there was not a room to spare. The whole place was full of officers.

Pierre pushed on as fast as possible. From Mozhaisk onwards troops were halting or marching everywhere. Cossacks, foot soldiers, horse soldiers, waggons, gun-carriages, and cannons were on all sides. And the further he got and the more deeply he plunged into this ocean of soldiers, the stronger became the thrill of uneasiness. It was a feeling akin to what he had felt at the Slobodsky Palace on the Tsar's visit, a sense of the urgent necessity of taking some step and making some sacrifice.

On the slope of a steep, and winding hill, leading out of the town, Pierre got out of the carriage, and walked by a cathedral, where a service was being held. A cavalry regiment followed him down the hill, the singers of the regiment in front. A train of carts came up the hill towards them, filled with wounded from a battle that had taken place the day before. The peasant drivers kept running from side to side, shouting and whipping the horses. The carts, in each of which three or four wounded soldiers were lying or sitting, jolted up and down on the rough road. The wounded men clung to the sides. Almost all of them stared with naïve and childlike curiosity at Pierre's white hat and green coat.

One cart full of wounded men came to a standstill close to Pierre. The driver, in bast shoes, ran panting up to his cart, pushed a stone under a hind wheel, and began setting straight the harness on his horse.

One of the soldiers sitting in the cart had been wounded in the cheek. His whole head was bandaged, and one cheek was swollen as large as a baby's head. All his mouth and nose were on one side. This soldier was looking at the cathedral and crossing himself. Another, a young fellow, a light-haired recruit, as white as though there were not a drop of blood in his thin face, gazed with a fixed, good-natured smile at Pierre. The third lay so that his face could not be seen.

"It's not soldiers only, but peasants, too, I have seen to-day! Peasants, too, they are hunting up," said a soldier standing by the cart, addressing himself to Pierre, with a melancholy smile. "They can't pick and choose now. . . . They want to mass all the people together—it's a matter of Moscow, you see. There is only one thing to do now." Pierre nodded his head.

The road was clear once more, and Pierre got back into his carriage. And after driving four miles he met an acquaintance, a doctor, one of the heads of the medical staff. He rode in a covered gig, with a young doctor sitting beside him.

"Count, your excellency, how do you come here?" asked the doctor.

"Oh, I wanted to have a look . . ."

Pierre got out of his carriage, and stopped to have a talk with the doctor, explaining to him his plan for taking part in the battle.

The doctor advised Pierre to go straight to Kutuzov.

"I would show you the way, but by God, you see," said

the doctor, "I'm racing to the commander of the corps. We're in such a fix, you see . . . you know, count, there's to be a battle to-morrow; with a hundred thousand troops. We must count on twenty thousand wounded at least; and we haven't the stretchers, nor beds, nor attendants, nor doctors for six thousand."

The strange idea that of those thousands of men, alive and well, young and old, who had been staring with such light-hearted amusement at his hat, twenty thousand were doomed to wounds and death disturbed Pierre. "They are going into battle, and . . ."

Pierre pushed on ahead to the little village of Gorky. And here for the first time he saw the peasants of the militia in white shirts, with crosses on their caps. With loud talk and laughter, eager and perspiring, they were working on the right of the road at a huge mound overgrown with grass.

Pierre got out of his carriage, and passing by the toiling peasants, clambered up a hill from which he could get a view of the field of battle.

It was eleven o'clock in the morning. And the huge panorama that stretched in an amphitheatre before him lay bathed in brilliant sunshine.

The Smolensk high-road ran winding through that amphitheatre, intersecting it towards the left at the top, and passing through a village with a white church, which lay some five hundred yards before and below the hill. This was Borodino. The road passed below the village, crossed a bridge, and ran winding uphill and downhill, mounting up and up to a hamlet, visible six miles away, where Napoleon now was. Behind this the road disappeared into a wood. In this wood of birch- and pine-trees, could be seen far away the shining cross and belfry of a monastery. Here and there in the blue distance, to right and to left of the wood and the road, could be seen smoking camp-fires and indistinct masses of troops. On the right, along the course of two rivers, the country was broken and hilly. Through the gaps between the hills could be seen other villages. On the left the ground was more level; there were fields of corn and a smoking village that had been set on fire.

"Are these our men there?" Pierre asked an officer standing nearby.

The officer, obviously pleased at an opportunity for conversation, went nearer to Pierre.

"Yes, and away further, those are the French," said the officer. "There they are, there you can see them."

"Where? Where?" asked Pierre.

"One can see them with the naked eye. Look!" the officer

pointed to smoke rising on the left beyond the river, and the same stern and grave expression came into his face that Pierre had noticed in many of the faces he had met.

"Ah, that's the French! And there? . . ." Pierre pointed to a knoll on the left about which troops could be seen.

"Those are our men."

"Oh! And there? . . ." Pierre pointed to another mound in the distance, with a big tree on it, near a village that could be seen in a gap between the hills, where there was a dark patch and the smoke of camp-fires.

"Ah! that's the French again!" said the officer. "Yesterday that was ours, but now it's theirs."

For a moment they were silent. "And who are you, not one of the doctors?"

"No, I am nothing in particular," answered Pierre. And he went downhill again, passing the peasant militiamen.

"Ah, the damned beasts!" said the officer hurrying by them with Pierre.

"Here they come! . . . They are bringing her, they are coming. . . . Here she is . . . They'll be here in a minute," cried voices suddenly, and officers, soldiers, and peasants ran forward along the road.

A church procession was coming up the hill from Borodino. In front of it a regiment of infantry marched smartly along the dusty road, with their shakoes off and their muskets lowered. Behind the infantry came the sounds of church singing.

Soldiers and peasants came running down bareheaded to meet it, overtaking Pierre.

"They are bringing the Holy Mother! Our defender . . . The Holy Mother of Smolensk . . ."

The militiamen who had been in the village and those who had been working at the battery, flinging down their spades, ran to meet the procession. The battalion marching along the dusty road was followed by priests in church robes, a little old man in a hood with attendant deacons and choristers. Behind them came soldiers and officers bearing a huge holy picture, with tarnished face in a setting of silver. This was the holy ikon that had been brought away from Smolensk when the French captured the city. It had accompanied the army ever since. Behind, before, and all around it, walked or ran crowds of soldiers with bared heads, bowing to the earth.

On the top of the hill the procession stopped; the men bearing the holy ikon were relieved by others; the deacons relighted their censers, and the service began. The burning rays of the sun beat down on the crowds; a faint, fresh breeze played with the hair of their bare heads, and fluttered the ribbons with which the holy picture was decked. The singing sounded subdued under the open sky. An immense crowd—officers, soldiers, and militiamen—stood round, all with bare heads.

As soon as the weary choristers (it was their twentieth service) began singing their chant, "O Mother of God, save Thy servants from calamity," and priest and deacon chimed in, "For to Thee we all fly as our invincible Bulwark and Protectress," there was a gleam on every face of that sense of the solemnity of the coming moment. And heads were bowed lower, while locks of hair fluttered in the breeze, and there was the sound of sighing and beating the breast as the soldiers crossed themselves.

The crowd suddenly parted and pressed back to make way for some one. It was Kutuzov, who had been making a round of inspection. He joined the service.

In a long military coat, with his enormously stout figure and bent back, with his white head uncovered, and his blind white eye, conspicuous in his puffy face, Kutuzov walked with his waddling, swaying gait into the ring and stood behind the priest. He crossed himself with an habitual gesture, bent down, with his hand touching the earth, and bowed his grey head. Kutuzov was followed by Bennigsen and his suite. In spite of the presence of the commander-in-chief, which drew the attention of all persons of higher rank, the militiamen and soldiers went on praying without looking at him.

When the service was over, Kutuzov went up to the holy picture, dropped heavily down on his knees, bowing to the earth, and for a long time he attempted to get up, and was unable from his weakness and heavy weight. His grey head twitched with the strain. At last he did get up, and putting out his lips in a naïve, childlike way kissed the holy picture, and again bowed down, with one hand touching the ground. The other generals followed his example. Then the officers, and after them the soldiers and militiamen ran up with excited faces, pushing each other, and shoving breathlessly forward.

Staggering from the crush of the crowd that carried him along with it, Pierre looked about him.

"Count! Pierre! How did you come here?" said a voice. Pierre looked round.

Boris Drubetskoy, brushing his knee with his hand—he had made it dusty in his devotions before the holy picture—came up to Pierre smiling. Boris was elegantly dressed. He wore a long military coat and had a riding-whip slung across his shoulder, as Kutuzov had.

Kutuzov had meanwhile reached the village, and sat down

in the shade of the nearest house on a bench. A large retinue of officers surrounded him.

The procession was moving on further, accompanied by the crowd. Pierre stood still about thirty yards from Kutuzov, talking to Boris.

He explained to him his desire to take part in the battle and to inspect the position.

"I tell you what you had better do," said Boris. "I will do the honours of the camp for you. You will see everything best of all from where Count Bennigsen is to be. I am in attendance on him. I will mention it to him. And if you want to go over the position, come along with us; we are just going to the left flank. And then when we come back, I beg you to stay the night with me, and we will make up a game of cards." He pointed to the third house in Gorky.

"But I should like to go through the whole position."

"Well, that you can do later, but the great thing is the left flank. . . . To tell you the truth, between ourselves, there's no making out how things stand with the left flank," said Boris confidentially, dropping his voice. "Count Bennigsen had proposed something quite different. He proposed to fortify that hill over there, not at all as it has . . . but . . ." Boris shrugged his shoulders. "His highness would not have it so, or he was talked out of it. You see . . ."

Although Kutuzov had cleared out the superfluous persons on his staff, Boris had succeeded in retaining a post at headquarters. Boris was in attendance on Count Bennigsen. Count Bennigsen, like every one on whom Boris had been in attendance, looked on young Prince Drubetskoy as an invaluable man. Among the chief officers of the army there were two clearly defined parties: Kutuzov's party and the party of Bennigsen, the chief of the staff. Boris belonged to the latter faction, and no one succeeded better than he did in paying the most servile adulation to Kutuzov, while managing to insinuate that the old fellow was not good for much, and that everything was really due to the initiative of Bennigsen. Now the decisive moment of battle had come, which must mean the downfall of Kutuzov and the transfer of the command to Bennigsen, or if Kutuzov should gain the battle, the credit of it must be skilfully put down to Bennigsen. In any case many promotions were bound to be made, and many new men were certain to be brought to the front after the battle. And Boris was consequently in a state of nervous exhilaration all that day.

Others of Pierre's acquaintances joined him; and he had not time to answer all the questions about Moscow that were showered upon him, nor to listen to all they had to tell him.

Kutuzov noticed Pierre and the group gathered about him.

"Call him to me," said Kutuzov.

Pierre went towards the bench. But a militiaman approached Kutuzov before him. It was Dolohov.

"How does that man come to be here?" asked Pierre.

"Oh, he's such a sly dog, he pokes himself in everywhere!" was the answer he received. "He has been degraded to the ranks, you know. Now he wants to pop up again. He has made plans of some sort and spies in the enemy's lines at night . . . But he's a plucky fellow . . ."

Pierre took off his hat and bowed respectfully to Kutuzov.

"I decided that if I were to lay the matter before your highness, you might dismiss me or say that you were aware of the facts and then I shouldn't lose anything," Dolohov was saying.

"To be sure."

"And if I were right, I should do a service for my country, for which I am ready to die."

"To be sure . . . to be sure . . ."

"And if your highness has need of a man who would not spare his skin, graciously remember me . . . perhaps I might be of use to your highness . . ."

"To be sure . . . to be sure . . ." repeated Kutuzov, looking with a laughing, half-closed eye at Pierre.

Meanwhile Boris, with his courtier-like tact, had moved close to the commander-in-chief with Pierre, and in the most natural manner, in a quiet voice, as though continuing his previous conversation, he said to Pierre: "The peasant militiamen have simply put on clean, white shirts to be ready to die. What heroism, count!"

Boris said this to Pierre with the evident intention of being overheard by his excellency. He knew Kutuzov's attention would be caught by those words, and his highness did in fact address him.

"What are you saying about the militia?" he said to Boris.

"They have put on white shirts, your highness, by way of preparing for to-morrow, to be ready for death."

"Ah! . . . A marvellous, unique people," said Kutuzov, and closing his eye he shook his head. "A unique people!" he repeated, with a sigh.

"Do you want a sniff of powder?" he said to Pierre. "Yes; a pleasant smell. I have the honour to be one of your wife's worshippers; is she quite well? My quarters are at your service." And Kutuzov began, as old people often do, gazing abstractedly about him, as though forgetting all he had to say or do.

When Pierre moved away from Kutuzov, Dolohov approached and took his hand.

"I am very glad to meet you here, count," he said, aloud, disregarding the presence of outsiders. "On the eve of a day which God knows who among us will be destined to survive I am glad to have the chance of telling you that I regret the misunderstandings there have been between us in the past; and I should be glad to think you had nothing against me. I beg you to forgive me."

Pierre looked with a smile at Dolohov, not knowing what to say to him. With tears starting into his eyes, Dolohov embraced and kissed Pierre.

Boris had said a few words to his general, and Count Bennigsen addressed Pierre, proposing that he should accompany them along the line.

"You will find it interesting," he said.

Half an hour later Kutuzov was on his way back to headquarters, while Bennigsen and his suite, with Pierre among them, were inspecting the position.

Prince André was on that bright August evening lying propped on his elbow in a broken-down barn at the further end of the encampment of his regiment. Through a gap in the broken wall he was looking at the line of thirty-year-old pollard birches in the hedge, at the field with sheaves of oats lying about it, and at the bushes where he saw the smoke of camp-fires, at which the soldiers were doing their cooking.

Cramped and useless and burdensome as his life seemed now to Prince André, he felt excited and irritable on the eve of battle, just as he had felt seven years earlier before Austerlitz.

He had received and given all orders for the next day's battle. He had nothing more to do. But thoughts—the simplest, most obvious, and therefore most awful—would not leave him in peace. He knew that the battle next day would be the most awful of all he had taken part in, and death, for the first time, presented itself to him, not in relation to his actual manner of life, or to the effect of it on others, but simply in relation to himself, and rose before him with a vividness that made it like reality. And from the height of this vision everything that had once occupied him seemed suddenly illumined by a cold, white light, without shade, without perspective or outline. His whole life seemed to him like a magic lantern, at which he had been looking by artificial light. Now he saw suddenly, in the clear light of day, those badly daubed pictures. The three chief sorrows of his life held his attention. His love for Natasha, his father's death, and the invasion of the French—now in possession of half of Russia.

"My father laid out Bleak Hills, and thought it was his place, his land, his air, his peasants. But Napoleon came along, and without even knowing of his existence, swept him away like a chip out of his path, and laid Bleak Hills in the dust, and all his life with it was brought to nought."

He closed his eyes. And then another image filled his mind. He vividly recalled one evening in Petersburg. Natasha with an eager, excited face had been telling him how in looking for mushrooms the previous summer she had lost her way in a great forest. She described incoherently the dark depths of the forest, and her feelings, and her talk with a bee-keeper she met, and every minute she broke off in her story, saying: "No, I can't, I'm not describing it properly; no, you won't understand me," although he tried to assure her that he understood and did really understand all she wanted to say. Natasha was dissatisfied with her own words; she felt that they did not convey the feeling she had known that day. "It was all so wonderful, that old man, and it was so dark in the forest . . . and such a kind look in his . . . no, I can't describe it," she had said, flushed and moved.

Prince André smiled now the same happy smile he had smiled then, gazing into her eyes. "I understood her," he thought. "And more than understood her: that spiritual force, that sincerity, that openness of soul, the very soul of her, which seemed bound up with her body, the very soul it was I loved in her . . . Loved so intensely, so passionately . . ." and all at once he thought how his love had ended. "*He* cared nothing for all that. *He* saw nothing of it, had no notion of it. He saw in her a pretty young girl . . . And I? . . . And *he* is still alive and happy." Prince André jumped up as though suddenly scalded, and went out of the barn and walked up and down.

He gazed at the row of birch trees with their motionless yellows and greens, and the white bark shining in the sun. "To die then, let them kill me to-morrow, let me be no more . . . Let it all go on, and let me be at an end." He vividly pictured his own absence from life. And those birch trees, with their light and shade, and the curling clouds and the smoke of the fires, everything around seemed suddenly transformed into something weird and menacing.

On the 25th of August, on the eve of the battle of Borodino, the prefect of the French Emperor's palace, M. de Beausset, and Colonel Fabvier arrived, the former from Paris, and the latter from Madrid, at Napoleon's headquarters.

After changing into a court uniform M. de Beausset ordered the package he had brought for the Emperor to be carried before him, and walked into the first compartment of Napoleon's tent, where he busied himself while conversing with the aides-de-camp in unpacking the box.

Fabvier stood talking with generals of his acquaintance in the entrance of the tent.

The Emperor Napoleon had not yet left his bedroom, he was finishing his toilet. With snorts and grunts of satisfaction, he was turning first his stout back and then his plump chest towards the flesh-brush with which a valet was rubbing him down. Another valet was sprinkling *eau de cologne* on the Emperor with an expression which seemed to say that he alone knew where and how much *eau de cologne* must be sprinkled. Napoleon's short hair was wet and matted on his brow. But his face, though puffy and yellow, expressed physical satisfaction.

"Go on, hard, go on . . ." he said, shrugging and clearing his throat, to the valet brushing him. An adjutant, who had come into the bedroom to report to the Emperor the number of prisoners taken in the last engagement, was standing at the door, after giving his message, awaiting permission to withdraw. Napoleon, frowning, glanced up from under his brows at the adjutant. "No prisoners," he repeated the adjutant's words. "They are working their own destruction. So much the worse for the Russian army," he said. "Harder, brush harder," he said, hunching his fat shoulders before the valet. "Good. Let Beausset come in and Fabvier too," he said to the adjutant, nodding.

"I obey, sire," and the adjutant disappeared.

The two valets rapidly dressed his majesty, and in the blue uniform of the guards he walked into the reception-room.

Beausset was setting up the present he had brought from the Empress on two chairs.

Napoleon at once noticed what he was doing and guessed he was not ready. He did not want to deprive him of the pleasure of preparing a surprise. He pretended not to see and beckoned Fabvier to him. Frowning sternly, he listened in silence to what Fabvier was saying of the gallantry and devotion of his army, fighting before Salamanca, at the other end of Europe. They had, he said, but one dream—to be worthy of their Emperor, and one fear—to displease him. The result of the battle however had been disastrous. Napoleon made ironical remarks during Fabvier's account of it, as though he had not expected it to be otherwise in his absence.

"I must make up for it at Moscow," said Napoleon. He then summoned Beausset, who had by this time finished unpacking the present and had thrown a cloth over it.

Beausset made a courtier's low bow and approached him, handing him a letter.

Napoleon addressed him gaily and pinched him by the

ear. To have one's ear pulled by the Emperor was regarded as the greatest honour and mark of favour at the French court.

"You have been quick, delighted to see you. Well, what is Paris saying?" he said.

"Sire, all Paris is regretting your absence," answered Beausset, as in duty bound. But though Napoleon knew Beausset was bound to say this or something like it, though at his lucid moments he knew it was all false, he was glad to hear this from him. He condescended to pinch his ear again.

"I am very sorry to have made you travel so far," he said.

"Sire, I expected to find you at least at the gates of Moscow," said Beausset.

Napoleon smiled, and lifting his head absently looked round to the right. An adjutant approached with a gold snuffbox and offered it. Napoleon took it.

"Yes, it's a happy chance for you," he said, putting the open snuffbox to his nose. "You are fond of travelling, and in three days you will see Moscow. You probably did not expect to see the Asiatic capital. You will have a delightful journey."

Beausset bowed with gratitude for this interest in his tastes for travel, of which he had till that moment been unaware.

"Ah! what's this?" said Napoleon, observing that all the courtiers were gazing at something concealed under a covering. Beausset with courtier-like agility retired two steps with a half turn, not showing his back, and at the same moment twitched off the covering, saying: "A present to your majesty from the Empress."

It was a portrait, painted in brilliant colours by Gérard, of the child of Napoleon and the daughter of the Austrian Emperor, the little boy whom every one called the King of Rome.

The very pretty, curly-headed child, with eyes like the Christ with the Sistine Madonna, had been portrayed playing cup and ball. The ball represented the globe and the cup in the other hand was a sceptre.

Though it was not altogether clear what the painter had intended to express by representing the King of Rome tossing the globe on a sceptre, the allegory apparently seemed to Napoleon, as it had to every one who had seen it in Paris, quite clear and extremely pleasing.

"The King of Rome!" he said, pointing with a graceful gesture to the portrait. "Admirable!" With the characteristic Italian facility for changing his expression at will, he went up to the portrait and assumed an air of pensive tenderness. He felt that what he might say or do at that moment would be historical. And it struck him that the best line he could take at that moment, at the height of his grandeur—so great that his child was playing cup and ball with the earth—would be to display, in contrast with that grandeur, the simplest, fatherly tenderness. His eyes were veiled by emotion; he moved up, looked round for a chair (a chair seemed to spring up under him), and sat down, facing the portrait. At a single gesture from him all withdrew on tip-toe, leaving the great man to himself and his feelings. After sitting there a little while and passing his fingers, he could not have said why, over the rough surface of the painting, he got up and again sent for Beausset and the officer on duty. He gave orders for the portrait to be carried out in front of his tent, so that the Old Guard, standing about his tent, might not be deprived of the happiness of seeing the King of Rome, the son and heir of their adored Emperor.

While he sat at breakfast with M. de Beausset—whom he had honoured by an invitation to join him—he heard, as he had expected, enthusiastic shouts from the soldiers and officers of the Old Guard, who had run up to see the portrait.

"Vive l'Empereur! Vive le roi de Rome! Vive l'Empereur!"

After breakfast, in Beausset's presence, Napoleon dictated his proclamation to the army.

"Short and vital!" Napoleon pronounced it, when he had read over the proclamation that he had dictated straight off without corrections. It was as follows: "Soldiers! This is the battle you have so greatly desired. Victory is in your hands. It is essential for us; it will give us everything we need: comfortable quarters and a speedy return to our own country. Behave as you behaved at Austerlitz, Friedland, Vitebsk, and Smolensk. May posterity recall with pride your achievement on this day! And may they say of each of you: he was at the great battle before Moscow!"

"Before Moscow," repeated Napoleon, and inviting M. de Beausset, so fond of travel, to accompany him on his ride, he went out of the tent to the saddled horses awaiting them outside.

"Your majesty is too kind," said Beausset, in response to the invitation to accompany the Emperor. He was very sleepy. He could not ride well, and was afraid of horses.

But Napoleon nodded to the traveller, and Beausset had to mount. When Napoleon came out of the tent the shouts of the Guards before his son's portrait were redoubled. Napoleon frowned.

"Take him away," he said, with a gracefully majestic gesture, pointing to the portrait. "It is too early yet for him to look upon the field of battle."

Beausset, dropping his eyelids, and bowing his head, heaved a deep sigh, to testify how well he was able to appreciate and comprehend the Emperor's words.

The whole of that day, the 25th of August, Napoleon spent, on horseback, inspecting the locality, criticising the plans submitted to him by his marshals, and giving commands in person to his generals.

On returning from a second careful inspection of the lines, Napoleon said.

"The pieces are on the board, the game will begin to-morrow."

He ordered some punch, and sending for Beausset began talking of Paris with him, discussing various changes he intended to make in the Empress's household, and surprising the prefect by his memory of the minutest details of court affairs.

He showed interest in trifles, jested at Beausset's love of travel, and chatted carelessly.

After emptying a second glass of punch, Napoleon went to rest. But he was so preoccupied with what lay before him that he could not sleep, and in spite of a cold, which got worse with the damp of evening, he got up at three o'clock, sneezing violently. He asked whether the Russians had not retreated. He was told that the enemy's fires were still in the same places. He nodded approval.

The adjutant on duty came into the tent.

"Well, Rapp, do you think we shall do good business to-day?" he asked him.

"Without doubt, sire!" answered Rapp.

Napoleon looked at him.

"Do you remember what you did me the honour to say at Smolensk?" said Rapp. "The wine is drawn, it must be drunk."

Napoleon frowned, and sat for a long while in silence, his head in his hand.

"This poor army, it has greatly diminished since Smolensk. Fortune is frank mistress, Rapp. I have always said so, and I begin to feel it; but the Guard, Rapp. The Guard is intact?" he said inquiringly.

"Yes, sire," replied Rapp.

Napoleon took a lozenge, put it in his mouth, and looked at his watch. He was not sleepy, and morning was still far off; and there were no instructions to be drawn up to get through the time, for all had been already given, and were even now being put into execution.

"Have the biscuits and the rice been distributed to the regiments of the Guard?" Napoleon asked severely.

"Yes, sire."

"The rice, too?"

Rapp answered that he had given the Emperor's orders

about the rice; but Napoleon shook his head with a dissatisfied air, as though he doubted whether his command had been carried out. A servant came in with punch. Napoleon ordered another glass for Rapp, and took a few sips from his own in silence. "I have neither taste nor smell," he said, sniffing at the glass. "I am sick of this cold."

Rapp was silent.

"To-morrow we shall have to do with Kutuzov. He is again in command," said Napoleon. "We shall see! Do you remember, he was in command at Braunau, and never once in three weeks mounted a horse to inspect his entrenchments. We shall see!"

He looked at his watch. It was still only four o'clock. He got up, walked up and down, put on a warm coat and hat and went out of the tent. The night was dark and damp; a slight drizzle was falling. Close by in the French Guard, the camp-fires burned dimly, and far away they were blazing brightly through the smoke along the Russian line. The air was still, and a faint stir and tramp could be heard from the French troops beginning to move into position.

Napoleon walked to and fro before the tent, looked at the fires, listened to the tramp, and passed by a tall guardsman in a fur cap, a sentinel at his tent, who drew himself up like a black post on seeing the Emperor. He stood still, facing him.

"Since what year have you served?" he asked, with that affectation of military bluntness and geniality with which he always addressed the soldiers. The soldier answered.

"Ah! one of the veterans! Have you all had rice in the regiment?"

"Yes, your majesty."

Napoleon nodded and walked away.

At half-past five it began to get light; the sky cleared, only a single storm cloud lay on the eastern horizon. The deserted camp-fires burned down in the pale light of morning.

A solitary, deep cannon shot boomed out on the right, hovered in the air, and died away in the stillness. Several minutes passed. A second, and a third shot was heard. A fourth and a fifth boomed out. Then more and more, their notes blending and overtaking one another.

The game had begun.

When Pierre woke that morning, the panes were rattling in the windows. The groom was at his side, shaking him. "Your excellency, your excellency, your excellency . . ." he kept saying persistently.

"Has it begun? Is it time?" said Pierre, waking up.

"Listen to the firing, your excellency," said the groom, an old soldier; "all the gentlemen are gone already. His highness set off long ago."

Pierre dressed quickly, and ran out on to the porch. The roar of the cannon could be heard more distinctly in the open air. An adjutant galloped down the street, followed by a Cossack.

"It's time, count, it's time!" cried the adjutant. Pierre gave orders that he should be followed with a horse, and walked along the street to the hill from which he had viewed the field of battle the day before. On this hill was a crowd of officers, and Pierre heard the French chatter of the staff, and saw Kutuzov's grey head sunk in his shoulders, and his white cap, with red braiding on it. Kutuzov was looking through a field-glass along the high-road before him.

Pierre glanced before him, and felt a thrill of delight at the beauty of the spectacle. It was the same scene that he had admired from that hill the day before. But now the whole panorama was filled with troops and the smoke of the guns, and in the pure morning air the slanting rays of the sun, behind Pierre on the left, shed on it a brilliant light full of gold and pink tones. The distant forests that bounded the scene lay in a crescent on the horizon, and through their midst behind Valuev ran the great Smolensk road, all covered with troops. In the foreground lay golden fields and woods glittering in the sun. Everywhere, to right, to left, and in front were soldiers.

About one of the rivers near Borodino, a mist still hung, melting, parting, shimmering with light in the bright sunshine, and giving fairy-like beauty to the shapes seen through it. The smoke of the guns mingled with this mist, and everywhere gleams of sunlight sparkled in it from the water, from the dew, from the bayonets of the soldiers crowding on the river banks. Through this mist could be seen a white church and here and there the roofs of Borodino.

Pierre longed to be there in the midst of the smoke, the glittering bayonets, the movement, and the noise. He looked round at Kutuzov and his suite to compare his own impression with that of others. All like him were looking before them at the field, and he believed, with the same feeling.

"Go, my dear fellow, go, and Christ be with you!" said Kutuzov, never taking his eyes off the field of battle, to a general standing beside him. The general, who received this order, ran by Pierre.

"To ride across! . . ." the general said coldly and severely, in answer to a question from one of the staff.

"And I too, I too," thought Pierre, and he went in the same direction.

The general mounted a horse. Pierre went up to the groom,

who was holding his horses. And mounting one of them he galloped after the general.

The general, after whom Pierre galloped, trotted downhill, turned off sharply to the left, and Pierre, losing sight of him, galloped into the middle of a battalion of infantry. He tried to get away from them, turning to left and to right; but there were soldiers everywhere, all with the same anxious faces.

Ahead of him he saw a bridge, and at the bridge stood soldiers firing. Pierre rode towards them. Though he did not know it, he rode into the very centre of the battle between the villages of Gorky and Borodino.

"What's that fellow doing in front of the line?" some one shouted at him.

"To the left," "To the right," men shouted to him. Pierre turned to the right, and unwittingly rode up to an adjutant, with whom he was acquainted. The adjutant glanced angrily at Pierre; and he, too, was about to shout at him, but recognising him, he nodded, and galloped on.

After passing in the smoke through the sixth corps behind the artillery, which had been moved forward and was keeping up a deafening cannonade, they rode into a small wood. There it was cool and still and full of the scents of autumn. Pierre and the adjutant got off their horses and walked on foot up the hill.

"Is the general here?" asked the adjutant.

"He was here just now; he went this way," some one answered, pointing to the right.

The adjutant looked round at Pierre, as though he did not know what to do with him.

"Don't trouble about me," said Pierre. "I'll go up on to the top; may I?"

"Yes, do; you can see everything from there, and it's not so dangerous, and I will come to get you."

Pierre went up to the battery, and the adjutant rode away. They did not see each other again, and only much later Pierre learned that the adjutant had lost an arm on that day.

The battery—afterwards known among the Russians as the battery mound, or Raevsky's battery, and among the French as "the great redoubt," "fatal redoubt," and "central redoubt" —was a spot at which tens of thousands of men were killed, and upon which the French looked as the key position.

But Pierre had no notion that this place, encircled by small trenches and protected by a few cannons, was the most important spot in the field. He sat down on the end of the earthwork surrounding the battery and gazed at what was passing around him with an unconscious smile of pleasure. At intervals he got up, and with the same smile on his face walked about the battery, trying not to get in the way of the soldiers, who were loading and discharging the cannons and were continually running by him with bags and ammunition. The cannons were firing, one after another, with deafening uproar, enveloping all the country round in clouds of smoke.

In contrast to the painful look of dread in the infantry soldiers who were guarding the battery, here in the battery itself, where a limited number of men were busily engaged in their work, and shut off from the rest of the trench, there was a general feeling of excitement, a sort of family feeling shared by all alike.

The soldiers cast sidelong glances of surprise and even alarm at Pierre as they ran by. The senior artillery officer, a tall, long-legged, pock-marked man, approached him, as though he wanted to examine the action of the cannon at the end, and stared inquisitively at him.

A boyish, round-faced, little officer, quite a child, evidently only just out of the cadets' school, and very conscientious in looking after the two cannons, addressed Pierre severely.

"Permit me to ask you to move out of the way, sir," he said. "You can't stay here."

The soldiers shook their heads as they looked at Pierre. But as the conviction gained ground among them that the man in the white hat was doing no harm, and either sat quietly on the slope of the earthwork, or, making way with a shy and courteous smile for the soldiers to pass, walked about the battery under fire as calmly as though he were strolling on a boulevard, their feeling of suspicious ill-will began to give way to a playful and kindly cordiality akin to the feeling soldiers always have for the dogs, cocks, goats, and other animals who share the fortunes of the regiment. The soldiers soon accepted Pierre in their own minds as one of their little circle, made him one of themselves, and gave him a name: "our gentleman" they called him, and laughed good-humouredly about him among themselves.

A cannon ball tore up the earth a couple of yards from Pierre. Brushing the earth off his clothes, he looked about him.

"And how is it you're not afraid, sir?" said a broad, red-faced soldier, showing his strong, white teeth in a grin.

"Why, are you afraid?" asked Pierre.

"To be sure!" answered the soldier. "Why, she has no mercy on you. She smashes into you, and your guts are sent flying. Nobody could help being afraid," he said laughing.

Several soldiers stood still near Pierre with amused and kindly faces. They seemed not to expect him to talk like any one else, and his doing so delighted them.

"It's our business—we're soldiers. But for a gentleman—it's surprising. It's queer in a gentleman!"

"To your places!" cried the little officer-boy to the soldiers, who had gathered round Pierre. It was evidently the first, or at most, the second time, this boy had been on duty as an officer, and so he behaved with the utmost formality both to the soldiers and his superior officer.

The roar of cannon and the rattle of musketry were growing louder all over the field, especially on the left, where Bagration's earthworks were, but from where Pierre was, hardly anything could be seen for the smoke. Moreover, watching the little group of men, shut off from all the world on the battery, engrossed all Pierre's attention. Sitting now on the slope of the earthwork, he watched the figures moving about him.

By ten o'clock some twenty men had been carried away from the battery; two cannons had been disabled, and more and more frequently shells fell on the battery, and cannon balls came with a hiss and whir, flying out of the distance. But the men on the battery did not seem to notice this: talk and jokes were to be heard on all sides.

Pierre noticed that after every ball that fell in their midst, after every loss, the general elation became more and more marked.

The closer the storm cloud swooped down upon them, the more bright and frequent were the gleams of latent fire that glowed like lightning flashes on those men's faces, called up, as it were, to meet and resist their danger.

Pierre did not look in front at the field of battle; he took no more interest in what was going on there. He was entirely engrossed in the contemplation of that growing fire, which he felt was burning in his own soul too.

At ten o'clock the infantry, who had been in advance of the battery, in the bushes and about the stream, retreated. From the battery they could see them running back past them, bearing their wounded on their guns. A general with a suite came on to the battery, and after talking to the colonel and looking angrily at Pierre, went away again, ordering the infantry standing behind the battery to lie down, so as to be less exposed to fire. After that a drum was heard in the ranks of the infantry, more to the right of the battery, and shouts gave the word of command, and they could see the ranks of infantry moving forward.

Pierre looked over the earthwork. One figure particularly caught his eye. It was the officer, walking backwards with a pale, boyish face. He held his sword downwards and kept looking uneasily round.

The rows of infantry soldiers vanished into the smoke, but

they could hear a prolonged shout from them and a rapid musketry fire. A few minutes later crowds of wounded men and a number of stretchers came back from that direction.

Shells fell more and more often in the battery. Several men lay on the ground, not picked up. The soldiers bustled more busily and briskly than ever about the cannons. No one took any notice of Pierre now. The senior officers strode rapidly from one cannon to another with a frowning face. The officer-boy, his cheeks crimson, gave the soldiers their orders more scrupulously than ever. The soldiers served out the charges, turned round, loaded, and did all their work with exaggerated smartness. They moved as though worked by springs.

The storm cloud was swooping closer; and more brightly than ever glowed in every face that fire which Pierre was watching. He was standing near the senior officer. The little officer-boy ran up, his hand to his shako, saluting his superior officer.

"I have the honour to inform you, colonel, only eight charges are left. Do you command to continue firing?" he asked.

"Grapeshot!" the senior officer shouted, looking away over the earthwork.

Suddenly something happened. The boy-officer groaned, and whirling round sat down on the ground, like a bird shot on the wing. All seemed strange, indistinct, and darkened before Pierre's eyes.

One after another the cannon balls came whistling, striking the breastwork, the soldiers, the cannons. Pierre, who had scarcely heard those sounds before, now could hear nothing else. On the right side of the battery, soldiers, with shouts of "hurrah," were running, not forward, it seemed to Pierre, but back.

A cannon ball struck the very edge of the earthwork, before which Pierre was sitting, and sent the earth flying. A dark, round mass flashed just before his eyes, and at the same instant flew with a thud into something. The militiamen, who had been coming into the battery, ran back.

"All with grapeshot!" shouted the officer.

The sergeant ran up to the officer, and in a frightened whisper said that there were no more charges.

The senior officer's face was red and perspiring. His piercing eyes glittered. "Run to the reserves, bring the ammunition-boxes!" he shouted angrily to the soldier.

"I'll go," said Pierre. The officer, making no reply, strode across to the other side.

"Cease firing . . . Wait!" he shouted.

The soldier who had been commanded to go for the ammunition ran off. Pierre ran after him, avoiding the spot where the boy-officer was sitting.

One cannon ball, a second and a third flew over him, hitting the ground in front, on each side, behind Pierre as he ran down. "Where am I going?" he suddenly wondered, just as he ran up to the green ammunition-boxes. He stopped short uncertain whether to go back or forward. Suddenly a fearful shock sent him flying backwards on to the ground. At the same instant a flash of flame dazed his eyes, and a roar, a hiss, and a crash set his ears ringing.

When he recovered his senses, Pierre found himself sitting on the ground leaning on his hands. The ammunition-box, near which he had been, was gone. There were a few charred green boards and rags lying scattered about on the scorched grass. A horse was galloping away with broken fragments of the shafts clattering after it; while another horse lay, like Pierre, on the ground groaning.

Pierre, beside himself with terror, jumped up and ran back to the battery as the one refuge from the horrors around him.

Just as he ran up, he noticed that there was no sound of firing from the battery, but that there were men there doing something or other. He had not time to make out what men they were. He caught sight of the senior officer lying with his back towards him on the earth wall, as though gazing intently at something below; and he noticed one soldier, who, tearing himself away from the men who were holding him, shouted "Mates!"

But before he had time to grasp that the colonel had been killed, that the soldier shouting "Mates!" was a prisoner, another soldier was stabbed in the back by a bayonet before his eyes.

Pierre dashed downhill, stumbling over the dead and wounded, who seemed to him to be clutching at his feet. But before he had reached the bottom he was met by dense crowds of Russian soldiers, who, stumbling against each other, were running towards the battery.

The French, who had captured the battery, now fled. Some Russian soldiers pursued them while others brought prisoners down from the battery, among them a wounded French general, surrounded by officers. Crowds of wounded, both French and Russians, walked, or crawled, or were borne on stretchers from the battery, their faces distorted by suffering.

Pierre went up into the battery, where he had spent over an hour; and found no one left of that little group that had accepted him as one of themselves. There were many dead there, whom he had not seen before. But several he recognised. The boy-officer was still sitting huddled up in a pool of blood at the edge of the earth wall. The red-faced soldier was still twitching convulsively; they did not carry him away.

Pierre ran down the slope.

"Oh, now they will stop it, now they will be horrified at what they have done!" thought Pierre, aimlessly following the crowds of stretchers moving off the battlefield.

But the sun still stood high behind the veil of smoke, and in front, and even more so to the left, there was still a turmoil seething in the smoke. And the roar of cannon and musketry, far from slackening, grew louder and more desperate, like a man putting all his force into one deafening outcry as a last despairing effort.

Napoleon, standing on a hill, was looking through a field-glass, and in the tiny circle of the glass saw smoke and men, sometimes his own, sometimes Russians. But where what he had seen was, he could not tell when he looked again with the naked eye.

From the battlefield adjutants were continually galloping up to Napoleon with reports from his marshals. But all the reports were deceptive; because in the heat of battle it was impossible to say what was happening at any given moment, and because many of the adjutants never reached the actual battlefield, but simply repeated what they heard from others, and also because, while the adjutant was galloping the two or three miles to Napoleon, circumstances had changed, and the news he brought had already become untrue.

In the middle of the day Murat sent his adjutant to Napoleon with a request for reinforcements.

Napoleon was sitting drinking punch, when Murat's adjutant galloped to him with the message that the Russians would be routed if his majesty would let them have another division.

"Reinforcements?" said Napoleon, with stern astonishment, staring, as though failing to comprehend his words. "Reinforcements!" thought Napoleon. "How can they want reinforcements when they have half the army already, concentrated against one weak, unsupported flank of the Russians?"

"Tell the King of Naples," said Napoleon sternly, "that I don't yet see clearly over my chess-board. You can go."

The adjutant, still holding his hand to his hat, galloped back to the slaughter.

Napoleon got up, and summoning Caulaincourt and Berthier, began talking with them of matters not connected with the battle.

In the middle of their conversation, Berthier's eye was caught by a general, who was galloping toward them, followed by his suite. It was Beliard. Dismounting from his horse, he walked rapidly up to the Emperor, and, in a loud voice, began boldly explaining the absolute necessity of reinforcements. He swore on his honour that the Russians would be annihilated if the Emperor would let them have another division.

Napoleon shrugged his shoulders, and began walking up and down.

"You are very hasty, Beliard," said Napoleon, going back again to him. "It is easy to make a mistake in the heat of battle. Go and look again and then come to me." Before Beliard was out of sight another messenger came galloping up from another part of the battlefield.

"Well, what is it now?" said Napoleon, in the tone of a man irritated by repeated interruptions.

"Sire, the prince . . ." began the adjutant.

"Asks for reinforcements?" said Napoleon, with an angry gesture. The adjutant bent his head affirmatively and was proceeding to give his message, but the Emperor turned and walked a couple of steps away, stopped, turned back, and beckoned to Berthier. "We must send the reserves," he said. "Whom shall we send there? What do you think?"

"Send Friant's division."

And a few minutes later Friant's division vanished like the rest into the smoke of the battlefield.

Adjutants still kept galloping up from every side, and all, as though in collusion, said the same thing. All asked for reinforcements; all told of the Russians standing firm and keeping up a hellish fire, under which the French troops were melting away.

Napoleon was experiencing the bitter feeling of a lucky gambler, who, after recklessly staking his money and always winning, suddenly finds, that the more he considers his course, the more certain he is of losing.

His soldiers were the same, his generals the same, there had been the same preparations, the same disposition, the same proclamation, *"short and vital."* He was himself the same,—he knew that; and the enemy was the same as at Austerlitz and Friedland. But the wave of his hand seemed robbed of its might by magic.

From all sides the same tidings kept pouring in of killed or wounded generals, of reinforcements needed, of the troops being in disorder, and the Russians impossible to move.

Napoleon after his long experience of war knew very well all that was meant by an unsuccessful attack after eight hours' straining every possible effort. He knew that this was almost equivalent to a defeat, and that the merest chance might now mean the overthrow of himself and his troops.

He sat in silence on a camp-stool, his elbows on his knees, and his head sunk in his hands. Berthier came up to him and suggested that they should inspect the lines.

"What? What do you say?" said Napoleon. "Yes, tell them to bring my horse." He mounted a horse and rode out.

In the slowly parting smoke, over the whole plain through which Napoleon rode, men and horses, singly and in heaps, were lying in pools of blood. Such a fearful spectacle, so great a mass of killed in so small a space, had never been seen by Napoleon nor any of his generals. The roar of the cannon that had not ceased for ten hours, exhausted the ear and gave a peculiar character to the scene.

It was not a battle. It was a prolonged massacre.

Napoleon pulled up his horse, and sank again into a brooding reverie.

One of his generals, riding up, ventured to suggest to him that the Old Guard should advance into action. Ney and Berthier, standing close by, exchanged glances and smiled contemptuously at the wild suggestion of this general.

"Eight hundred miles from France, I am not going to let my Guard be destroyed," he said. And turning his horse, he rode back.

Kutuzov, with his grey head hanging, and his heavy, corpulent frame sunk into a heap, was sitting on a bench covered with a rug, in the same place in which Pierre had seen him in the morning. He issued no orders, and simply gave or withheld his assent to what was proposed to him.

"Yes, yes, do so," he would say in reply to various suggestions. "Yes, yes, go across, my dear boy, and see," he would cry first to one and then to another of the adjutants near him; or, "No, better not. We'd better wait a bit," he would say. He listened to the reports brought him, and gave orders, when they were asked for. But as he heard the reports, he seemed to take little interest in the import of the words spoken; something else in the expression of his face, in the tone of the voice of the speaker, seemed to interest him more. From long years of military experience he had learned, and with the wisdom of old age he had recognised, that one man cannot guide hundreds of thousands of men struggling with death. He knew that the fate of battles is not decided by the orders given by the commander-in-chief, nor the place in which the troops are stationed, nor the number of cannons, nor of killed, but by that intangible force called the spirit of the army. And he followed that force and led it as far as it lay in his power.

At three o'clock the attacks of the French let up. On the faces of all who came from the battlefield, as well as of those standing round him, Kutuzov read of effort, strained to the utmost tension. His own physical force was failing him. Several times his head sank, as though he were falling, and he dropped asleep. Dinner was brought him.

The adjutant-general, Woltzogen, rode up to Kutuzov while he was at dinner. Woltzogen had come from Barclay de Tolly to report on the progress of the fight on the left flank. The sagacious Barclay de Tolly, seeing crowds of wounded men running back, and the ranks in disorder, and weighing all the circumstances of the case, made up his mind that the battle was lost, and sent his favourite adjutant to the commander-in-chief to tell him so.

Kutuzov was with difficulty chewing roast chicken, and his eye was screwed up as he glanced at Woltzogen.

With a half-contemptuous smile Woltzogen walked carelessly up to Kutuzov, scarcely touching the peak of his cap.

He behaved to his highness with a certain affected negligence, which aimed at showing that he, as a highly trained military man, left it to the Russians to make a prodigy of this useless old person, and was himself well aware what kind of a man he had to deal with. "The 'old gentleman' "—this was how Kutuzov was always spoken of in Woltzogen's German circle—"is making himself quite comfortable," he thought; and glancing at the dishes before Kutuzov, he began reporting to the old gentleman Barclay de Tolly's message and his own impressions and views. "Every point of our position is in the enemy's hands, and they cannot be driven back, because there are not the troops to do it; the men run away and there's no possibility of stopping them," he submitted.

Kutuzov, stopping short in his munching, stared at Woltzogen in amazement, as though not understanding what was said to him. Woltzogen, noticing the old gentleman's excitement, said with a smile:

"I did not consider I had a right to conceal from your highness what I saw. . . . The troops are completely routed. . . ."

"You saw? You saw? . . ." cried Kutuzov, getting up quickly. "How . . . how dare you! . . ." he cried, with a catch in his breath. "How dare you, sir, tell *me* that? You know nothing about it. Tell General Barclay from me that his information is incorrect, and that I, the commander-in-chief, know more of the course of the battle than he does."

Woltzogen wanted to protest, but Kutuzov interrupted him.

"The enemy has been repulsed on the left and defeated on the right flank. If you have seen amiss, sir, do not permit yourself to speak of what you do not understand. Kindly return to General Barclay and inform him of my unhesitating intention to attack the French to-morrow," Kutuzov said.

All were silent, and nothing was to be heard but the heavy breathing of the gasping, old general. "Repulsed at all points, for which I thank God and our brave men. The enemy is defeated, and to-morrow we will drive him out of the holy land of Russia!" said Kutuzov, crossing himself; and all at once he gave a sob from the rising tears.

Woltzogen, shrugging his shoulders, walked away in silence.

Prince André's regiment was in the reserves behind the lines, but in spite of this they were under hot artillery fire and lost over two hundred men.

At two o'clock they moved forward. But they were still behind the lines and could not discharge a single round of ammunition. In this position the regiment lost another third of its men. In front the cannons kept booming, and from the mysterious region of the smoke that hid all the country, there came flying swiftly hissing cannon balls and slowly whizzing grenades. Sometimes, as though to give them a breathing space, for a whole quarter of an hour all the cannon balls and grenades flew over them, but at other times, in the course of a single minute, several men would be killed. And they were busy the whole time dragging away the dead and carrying off the wounded.

At rare intervals there was the sound of talk in the ranks, but that sound was hushed every time the falling thud and the cry of "stretchers!" was heard. For the greater part of the time, by command of the officers, the men sat on the ground. One, taking off his shako, carefully loosened and then drew up the folds of it; another, crumbling the dry clay in his hands, rubbed up his bayonet with it; another shifted and fastened the buckle of his shoulder straps; while another carefully undid, and did up again, his leg bandages, and changed his boots. When men were killed or wounded, when the stretchers trailed by, when immense masses of the enemy came into view through the smoke, no one took any notice. Only those things that had nothing to do with the battle were what attracted their attention. Some batteries of artillery passed in front of their line. In one of the ammunition carriages a horse had put its legs through the traces.

"Hey! Look at the trace-horse! . . . Take her leg out! She'll fall! . . . Hey! they don't see! . . ." Shouts rose from the ranks all through the regiment.

Another time the attention of all was attracted by a little brown dog, with its tail in the air, who had come no one knew from where, and was running about fussily. All at once a cannon ball fell near it, and it squealed and dashed away with its tail between its legs! Roars and shrieks of laughter rang out from the whole regiment. But distractions of this kind did not last more than a minute. And the men who had been eight hours without food or occupation, with the terror of death never relaxing for an instant, grew pale and haggard.

Prince André, pale and haggard like every one else, walked

to and fro with his hands clasped behind his back, and his eyes fixed on the ground. There was no need for him to give orders, and nothing for him to do. Everything was done of itself. The killed were dragged behind the line; the wounded were removed, and the ranks closed up. He walked about dragging one leg after the other, making the grass rustle, and watching the dust, which covered his boots. Then he counted his steps, calculating how many would make a mile; or cut off the flowers of wormwood growing in the ruts, and crushing them in his hands, sniffed at the bitter-sweet, pungent odour. Of all the thoughts of the previous day not a trace remained. He thought of nothing at all. He listened wearily to the sounds that were ever the same, the whiz of the shells above the booming of the cannon, looked at the faces of the men of the first battalion, which he had gazed at to weariness already, and waited. "Here it comes . . . this one's for us again!" he thought, listening to the whiz of something flying out of the region of smoke. "One, another! More! Fallen" . . . He stopped short and looked towards the ranks. "No; it has flown over."

A whiz and a thud! Five yards from him the dry soil was thrown up, as a cannon ball sank into the earth. A chill ran down his back. He looked at the ranks. Probably a number had been struck: the men had gathered in a crowd in the second battalion.

"M. l'aide-de-camp," he shouted, "tell the men not to crowd together."

The adjutant, having obeyed this instruction, was approaching Prince André. From the other side the major in command of the battalion came riding up.

"Look out!" rang out a cry from a soldier, and like a bird, with swift, whirring wings alighting on the earth, a grenade dropped with a dull thud a couple of feet from Prince André, near the major's horse. The horse, with no question of whether it were right or wrong to show fear, snorted, reared, almost throwing the major, and galloped away.

"Lie down!" shouted the adjutant, throwing himself on the ground. Prince André hesitated. The shell was smoking and rotating like a top between him and the adjutant, near a bush of wormwood.

"Can this be death?" Prince André wondered, looking at the grass, at the wormwood and at the thread of smoke coiling from the rotating top. "I can't die, I don't want to die, I love this grass and earth and air . . ."

He thought this, and yet at the same time he did not forget that people were looking at him.

"For shame, M. l'aide-de-camp!" he said to the adjutant; "What sort of . . ." He did not finish. There was a tearing, crashing sound, like the smash of broken crockery, a puff of stifling fumes, and Prince André was sent spinning over, and flinging up one arm, fell on his face.

Several officers ran up to him. A great stain of blood was spreading over the grass from the right side of his stomach. He was breathing in hard, hoarse gasps.

"Pick him up!" shouted some one. The peasant stretcher-bearers lifted him by the shoulders and laid him on the stretcher.

"Oh, my God! My God! What is it? . . . The stomach! It's all over then! Ah, my God!" could be heard among the officers.

"It almost grazed my ear," the adjutant was saying.

The peasants, with the stretcher across their shoulders, hurried to the ambulance station.

Prince André was carried to the woods where there were vans and an ambulance station of three tents. In the woods stood the ambulance wagons and horses. The horses in nose-bags were munching oats, and sparrows flew up to them and picked up the grains they dropped. Some crows, scenting blood, flitted to and fro among the birches, cawing impatiently. For more than five acres round the tents there were sitting or lying men stained with blood.

From the tents came the sound of loud, angry wailing and piteous moans. At intervals a doctor's assistant ran out for water, or to point out those who were to be taken in next. The wounded, awaiting their turn, wept, shouted, swore, or begged for vodka. Several were raving in delirium.

Prince André, as a colonel, was carried through the crowd of wounded not yet treated, and brought close up to one of the tents, where his bearers halted awaiting instructions. He opened his eyes, and for a long while could not understand what was happening. The wormwood, the black, whirling ball, and his passionate rush of love for life came back to his mind.

"But isn't it all the same now?" he thought. "Why am I so sorry to part with life? There was something in this life that I didn't understand, and . . ."

There were three tables in the tent. Two were occupied, on the third they laid Prince André. For some time he was left alone. On the table nearest sat a Tatar, probably of a Cossack regiment, judging from the uniform that had been thrown down close by. Four soldiers were holding him. A doctor in spectacles was cutting something in his brown, muscular back.

"Ooh! Ooh! Ooh! . . ." the Tatar grunted, and all of a sudden, throwing up his broad, swarthy, sun-burned face, and showing his white teeth, he began shrieking. On the other table, a man lay with his head flung back. The colour and curliness of the hair and the shape seemed strangely familiar to Prince André. Several assistants were holding him, and weighing on his chest. One white, plump leg was incessantly moving with a rapid, spasmodic twitching. The man was sobbing and choking. Two doctors—one was pale and trembling—were doing something with the other red, gory leg. Having finished with the Tatar, over whom a cloak was thrown, the doctor in spectacles came up to Prince André, wiping his hands.

He glanced at his face, and hurriedly turned away. "Undress him! Why are you dawdling?" he shouted angrily to an assistant.

When the assistant had taken off his clothes, the doctor bent close down over the wound and felt it. The excruciating pain made Prince André lose consciousness. When he regained consciousness, the broken splinters of his thigh bone had been removed, the bits of ragged flesh had been cut off, and the wound bound up.

After the agony he had passed through, Prince André felt a blissful peace, such as he had not known for a long time. All the happiest moments of his life, especially his earliest childhood, when he had been undressed and put to bed, when his nurse had sung lullabies over him, when, burying his head in the pillows, he had felt happy in the mere consciousness of life, rose before his imagination as though it were the actual present.

The doctors were busily engaged with the wounded man, whose head had seemed somehow familiar to Prince André. They were lifting him up and trying to soothe him.

"Show it to me . . . Hoo! Hoo!" he could hear his suffering moans, broken by sobs. Hearing his moans, Prince André wanted to cry.

They showed the wounded man the leg that had been amputated, wearing a boot, and covered with dry gore. "O! Hooo!" he sobbed. The doctor who had been standing near him, screening his face, moved away.

"My God! How's this? Why is he here?" Prince André wondered.

It was Anatole Kuragin. It was Anatole they were holding up in their arms and offering a glass of water, the edge of which he could not catch with his trembling, swollen lips. "Yes, it is he; yes, that man is somehow closely and painfully bound up with me," thought Prince André, with no clear understanding yet of what was before him. "What is the connection between that man and my childhood, my life?" he asked himself, unable to find the clue. And all at once a new, unexpected memory from that childlike world of purity and love rose up before Prince André. He remembered Natasha, as he had seen her for the first time at the ball in 1810, with her slender neck and slender arms, and her frightened, happy face. And a love and tenderness awoke in his heart for her stronger and more loving than ever. He recalled now the bond that existed between him and this man, who was looking vaguely at him through the tears that filled his swollen eyes. Prince André remembered everything, and a passionate pity and love for that suffering man filled his heart.

Prince André could restrain himself no more and wept tears of love and tenderness over his fellow-men, over himself, and over their errors and his own. "Sympathy, love for our brothers, for those who love us. Love for those who hate us, love for our enemies. Yes, the love that God preached upon earth, that Mary sought to teach me, and I did not understand. That is why I am sorry to part with life. That is what was left me if I had lived. But now it is too late. I know that!"

1812

BOOK ELEVEN

Tens of thousands of men lay sacrificed on the battlefield of Borodino. At the ambulance stations the grass and earth were soaked with blood for two acres round. Crowds of men, wounded and unwounded, dragged themselves, on one side back to safety behind the Russian lines, on the other to safety behind the French lines. Others still held their ground, and went on firing.

Over all the plain, at first so bright and gay with its glittering bayonets and puffs of smoke in the morning sunshine, there now hung a dark cloud of damp mist and smoke, and a strange, sour smell of saltpetre and blood. Storm clouds had gathered, and a drizzling rain began to fall on the dead, on the wounded, on the panic-stricken, and exhausted, and hesitating soldiers. It seemed to say: "Enough, enough; cease. . . . Consider. What are you doing?"

But though towards the end of the battle the men felt all the horror of their actions, though they would have been glad to cease, some unfathomable, mysterious force still led them on, and the artillerymen—the third of them left—soaked with sweat, grimed with powder and blood, and panting with weariness, still brought the charges, loaded, aimed, and lighted the match. And the cannon balls flew as swiftly and cruelly from each side and crushed human flesh, and kept up the fearful work.

For the French, with the memory of fifteen years of victories, with confidence in Napoleon's all-vanquishing genius, with the consciousness of having taken a part of the battlefield, of having only lost a fourth of their men, and of having a body of twenty thousand—the Guards—intact—it was an easy matter to launch one more attack.

When the day was ending and the battle of Borodino was drawing to a close, Kutuzov truly believed that the Russian armies had won a great victory. He wrote to that effect to the Tsar. And he gave orders for his troops to be ready for a new attack on the following morning. But now with the French attacking once more and with the unbelievable reports of losses coming in from the battlefield—one half of the Russian army was wiped out—he was forced to abandon his plans for attack. Even to fight a defensive action was now out of the question. And so he ordered a retreat. For the next three days he drew his armies back closer and closer to Moscow.

The Russian army, retreating from Borodino, halted close to Fili, six miles outside of Moscow.

Kutuzov got out of his carriage and sat down on a bench by the side of the road. A great crowd of generals gathered about him. Count Rastoptchin, who had come out from Moscow, joined them. They talked among themselves. There was not a jest, not a laugh, not even a smile, to be seen among all these men. The commander-in-chief listened, and sometimes asked what had been said, but did not himself enter into conversation or express any opinion. For the most part, after listening to the talk of some group, he turned away with an air of disappointment, as though they were not speaking of anything he cared to hear about at all. Some were discussing the condition of the troops, plans proposed, and the situation of Moscow. Others argued that a blunder had been made earlier, that a battle ought to have been fought two days before. Count Rastoptchin was saying that he, with the Moscow city guard, was ready to die under the walls of the city, but that still he could not but complain of the uncertainty in which he had been left, and that had he known it earlier, things would have been different. . . .

Kutuzov's face grew more and more careworn and gloomy. He knew that Moscow could not possibly be defended, for his troops were not in condition. Besides he did not want to engage his forces in another battle with the French. He alone believed that the battle of Borodino had in truth been a defeat for the French; thousands of miles from France they had fought a costly battle, one that had drained their strength. Such a victory as theirs was really a defeat. And Kutuzov now looked upon Napoleon's Grand Armée as a wounded monster which would slowly bleed to death. He felt that with "time and patience" the monster would die. Let Napoleon's forces come further into Russia! Let him take Moscow itself! The loss of Moscow is not the loss of Russia!

Although Kutuzov was confident, still to give the command to abandon Moscow seemed a terrible thing. And unable to speak the words at this time, he rose from his bench and, mounting his horse, rode into Fili.

In the large best room of a peasant's cottage, at two o'clock, a council met. The men and women and children of the peasant's big family all crowded together in the room on the other side of the passage. Generals in uniform and with medals on their breast kept coming into the room one after another, and sat in a row on broad benches in the best corner under the holy images. Kutuzov was sitting apart from the rest in a dark corner behind the stove. He sat sunk all of a heap in a folding armchair, and was continually clearing his throat and straightening his collar, which, though it was unbuttoned, still seemed to gall his neck. The generals, as they came in one after another, walked up to the commander-in-chief: he shook hands with some, to others he merely nodded.

An adjutant wanted to draw back a curtain from the window facing Kutuzov, but he shook his hand angrily at him, and the adjutant saw that his highness did not care for them to see his face.

Round the peasant's table, on which lay maps, plans, pencils, and papers, there was such a crowd that the orderlies brought in another bench. In the foremost place, under the holy images, sat Barclay de Tolly, with his Order of St. George on his neck, with his pale, sickly face and high forehead that met his bald head. He had been in the throes of fever for the last two days, and was shivering and shaking. Beside him, resting his broad head on his hand, sat Count Osterman-Tolstoy, with his bold features and brilliant eyes, apparently plunged in his own thoughts.

They were all waiting for Bennigsen, who, on the pretext of a fresh inspection of the position, was engaged in finishing his luxurious dinner. They waited for him from four to six o'clock, and all that time did not enter on their deliberations, but talked of extraneous matters in subdued tones.

When Bennigsen had entered the hut, Kutuzov moved out of his corner and came up to the table, but sat there so that his face did not come within the light of the candles on it.

Bennigsen opened the council by the question: Whether to abandon the holy and ancient capital of Russia, or to defend it?

A prolonged silence followed. Every face was knitted, and in the stillness Kutuzov coughed and cleared his throat. All eyes turned on him. His face was working; he seemed to be going to cry. But he got control of himself.

"*The holy and ancient capital of Russia!*" he cried suddenly, in anger, repeating Bennigsen's words, and thereby underlining the false note in them. "Allow me to tell your excellency that that question has no meaning to a Russian." He lurched his unwieldy figure forward. "Such a question cannot be put; there is no sense in such a question. The question I have asked these gentlemen to meet to discuss is the question of the war. The question is: The safety of Russia lies in her army. Is it better to risk the loss of the army and of Moscow by giving battle, or to abandon Moscow without a battle? That is the question on which I desire to learn your opinion." He lurched back into his low chair again.

A debate began. Bennigsen did not yet consider that the game was lost. Overruled by the opinion of Barclay de Tolly and some of the others in admitting the impossibility of maintaining a defensive position at Fili, he proceeded to prove his Russian patriotism and devotion to Moscow by proposing to move the army during the night from the right to the left flank of the position, and to aim a blow at the French right flank next day. Opinions were divided, and arguments were advanced for and against this project. A number of generals sided with Bennigsen. Led by a feeling that a sacrifice was called for before abandoning the city, and by other personal considerations, these generals seemed unable to grasp that Moscow was already in effect abandoned. The other generals understood this, and leaving the question of Moscow on one side, talked of the direction the army ought to take in retreating.

Then quietly and gently Kutuzov began to speak. "I cannot approve of the count's plan, gentlemen," he said. "Movements of troops in close proximity to the enemy are always risky, and military history affords many examples of disasters arising from them. For instance . . ." Kutuzov seemed to ponder, seeking an example, and then looking with a frank, naïve expression at Bennigsen . . . "well, the battle of Friedland, which, as I have no doubt the count remembers, was not . . . completely successful owing to the change of the position of the troops in too close proximity to the enemy . . ."

A silence followed that seemed lengthy to all.

The debate was renewed; but pauses often interrupted it, and it was felt that there was nothing to talk about.

In one of these pauses Kutuzov heaved a heavy sigh, as though preparing to speak. All looked round at him.

"Well, gentlemen, I see that it is I who will have to pay for the broken pots," he said. And slowly rising from his seat, he walked up to the table. "Gentlemen, I have heard your opinions. Some of you will not agree with me. But I," he paused, "by the authority intrusted me by my Tsar and my country, give the order to retreat."

After dismissing the generals, Kutuzov sat a long while with his elbows on the table, pondering the terrible question: "When, when had it become inevitable that Moscow should be abandoned? When was the thing done that made it inevitable, and who is to blame for it?"

"This I did not expect!" he said to an adjutant, who came in to him late at night; "this I did not expect! This I never thought of!"

"You must rest, your highness."

"Yes; but they shall eat horse-flesh like the Turks!" Kutuzov cried, as he brought his podgy fist down on the table. "They, too, shall eat horse-flesh, if only . . . !"

While these things were going on at Borodino and Fili, while the people of Moscow began leaving the city which they sensed was going to be abandoned, life continued its usual pattern in fashionable Petersburg.

Helen had accompanied the court on its return from Vilna to Petersburg, and there found herself in a difficult position. In Petersburg Helen had enjoyed the special patronage of a great personage, who occupied one of the highest positions in the government. In Vilna she had formed a liaison with a young foreign prince.

When she returned to Petersburg the prince and the great dignitary were both in town; both claimed their rights, and Helen was confronted with a problem that had not previously arisen in her career—the preservation of the closest relations with both, without giving offence to either.

What might have seemed to any other woman a difficult or impossible task never cost a moment's thought to the Countess Bezuhov. Had she attempted concealment, had she allowed herself to get out of her awkward position by subterfuges, she would have spoilt her own case by acknowledging herself the guilty party. Helen at once assumed the correctness of her own position, of which she was convinced, and the guilty responsibility of every one else concerned.

The first time the young foreign prince ventured to reproach her, she lifted her beautiful head, and said firmly: "This is the egoism and the cruelty of men. I expected nothing lse. Woman sacrifices herself for you; she suffers, and this s her reward. What right have you to call me to account for ny friendships, my affections? He is a man who has been nore than a father to me!"

The prince wanted to say something. Helen interrupted him.

"I am not a person to be ungrateful. But in all that relates to ny private sentiments I will account only to God and to my onscience!"

"But listen to me, in God's name!" . . .

"Marry me, and I will be your slave!"

"But it is impossible."

"You do not deign to stoop to me, you . . ." Helen burst nto tears.

The prince attempted to console her. Helen, as though utterly distraught, declared through her tears that there was nothing to prevent her marrying; that there were precedents (Helen quoted the case of Napoleon and some other persons of exalted rank); that she had never been a real wife to her husband; that she had been dragged an unwilling victim into he marriage.

"But the law, religion . . ." murmured the prince, on the point of yielding.

"Religion, laws . . . What can they have been invented or, if they are unable to manage that?" said Helen.

The prince was astonished that so simple a reflection had never occurred to him, and applied to the council of the brotherhood of the Society of Jesus, with which he was in close relations.

A few days later, at one of the fêtes Helen used to give at her summer villa, a certain fascinating M. Jobert was presented to her; a man no longer young, with snow-white hair and brilliant black eyes, a Jesuit, who walked for a long while with Helen in the garden, conversing with her of the love of God, of Christ, of the heart of the Holy Mother, and of the consolations afforded in this life and the next by the one true Catholic faith. Helen was touched, and several times tears stood in her eyes. A dance, to which her partner fetched Helen away, cut short her conversation with the future "director of her conscience," but the next evening M. Jobert came alone to see Helen. And from that day he was a frequent visitor.

One day he took the countess into a Catholic church, where she fell on her knees before the altar, up to which she was conducted. The fascinating, middle-aged Frenchman laid his hands on her head, and as she herself afterwards described it, she felt something like a breath of fresh air, which seemed wafted into her soul. It was explained to her that this was the "grace of God."

Then an abbé was brought to her; he confessed her, and absolved her from her sins. Next day a box was brought containing the Sacred Host, and left for her to partake of at her house. Several days later Helen learned to her satisfaction that she had now been admitted into the true Catholic Church, and that in a few days the Pope himself would hear of her case, and send her a document of some sort from Rome.

All that was done with her and around her at this period, the attention paid her by so many clever men, and expressed in such agreeable and subtle forms, and her dovelike purity during her conversion (she wore nothing but white dresses and white ribbons all the time)—all afforded her gratification. But this gratification never led her for one instant to lose sight of her object. And, as always happens in contests of cunning, the stupid person gains more than the clever. Helen, fully grasping that the motive of all these words and all this manœuvring was by her conversion to Catholicism to get a round sum from her for the benefit of the Jesuit order (this was hinted at, indeed), held back the money, while insisting steadily on the various operations that would set her free from her marriage bonds. To her, the real object of every religion was to provide recognised forms of property for the satisfaction of human desires. And with this end in view, she insisted, in one of her conversations with her spiritual adviser, on demanding an answer to the question of how far her marriage was binding.

They were sitting in the drawing-room window. It was dusk. There was a scent of flowers from the window. Helen wore a white dress, transparent over the bosom and shoulders. The sleek, well-fed abbé, with his plump, clean-shaven chin, his amiable, strong mouth, and his white hands, clasped mildly on his knees, was sitting close by Helen. With a subtle smile on his lips, and a look of discreet admiration in his eyes, he gazed from time to time at her face, as he expounded his views on the subject. Helen, with a restless smile, stared at his curly hair and his smooth-shaven, blackish cheeks, and seemed every minute to be expecting the conversation to take a new turn.

But the abbé, though unmistakably aware of the beauty of his companion, was also interested in his own skilful handling of the question. The spiritual adviser adopted the following chain of reasoning: "In ignorance," said he, "of the significance of your promise, you took a vow of fidelity to a man who, on his side, was guilty of sacrilege in entering on the sacrament of matrimony with no faith in its religious significance. Your marriage had not the dual binding force it should have had. But in spite of that, your vow was binding upon you. You broke it. What did you commit? Venial sin or mortal sin? A venial sin, because you committed it with no intention of acting wrongly. If now, with the object of bearing children, you should enter into a new marriage, your sin might be forgiven. But the question again falls into two divisions. First . . ."

"But, I imagine," Helen, who was getting bored, said suddenly, with her fascinating smile, "that after being converted to the true religion, I cannot be bound by any obligations laid upon me by a false religion."

Her spiritual adviser was astounded at the simplicity of this solution, but could not abandon the edifice of subtle argument that had cost him mental effort.

"Let us understand each other," he said, with a smile; and began to find arguments to refute his spiritual daughter's contention.

Helen perceived that the matter was very simple and easy from the ecclesiastical point of view, but that her spiritual counsellors raised difficulties simply because they were apprehensive of the way in which it might be looked at by the temporal authorities.

And, consequently, Helen decided in her own mind that the way must be paved for society to look at the matter in the true light. She excited the jealousy of the old dignitary, and said the same thing to him as she had to her other suitor—that is, gave him to understand that the sole means of obtaining exclusive rights over her was to marry her. The elderly dignitary was, like the young foreign prince, for the first moment taken aback at this proposal of marriage from a wife whose husband was living. But Helen's unfaltering confidence in asserting that it was a matter as simple and natural as the marriage of an unmarried girl had its effect on him too. Had the slightest traces of hesitation, shame, or reserve been perceptible in Helen herself, her case would have been undoubtedly lost. But far from it; with perfect directness she told her intimate friends (and that term included all Petersburg) that both the prince and the dignitary had made her proposals of marriage, and that she loved both, and was afraid of grieving either.

The rumour was immediately all over Petersburg—not that Helen wanted a divorce from her husband (had such a rumour been discussed very many persons would have set themselves against any such illegal proceeding)—but that the unhappy, interesting Helen was in hesitation which of her two suitors to marry. The question was no longer whether a marriage was possible, but simply which would be the more suitable match for her, and how the court would look at the question. There were, indeed, certain strait-laced people who could not rise to the high level of the subject, and saw in the project a desecration of the sanctity of marriage. But such persons were few in number, and they held their tongues.

Marya Ahrosimov, "the terrible dragon," who had come that summer to Petersburg to see one of her sons, was the only person who ventured a contrary opinion. Meeting Helen at a ball, Marya Ahrosimov stopped her in the middle of the room, and in the midst of a general silence said to her, in her harsh voice: "So you are going to pass on from one husband to another, I hear! You think, I dare say, it's a new fashion you are setting. But you are not the first, madam. That's a very old idea. They do the same in all brothels." And with these words, Marya Ahrosimov tucked up her broad sleeves with her usual menacing action, and looking severely round her, walked across the ballroom.

Another person who ventured to question the legality of the proposed marriage was Helen's mother, Princess Kuragin. She had constantly suffered pangs of envy of her daughter, and now when the ground for such envy was the one nearest to her own heart, she could not reconcile herself to the idea of it.

She consulted a Russian priest to ascertain how far divorce and remarriage was possible for a woman in her husband's lifetime. The priest assured her that this was impossible; and to her delight referred her to the text in the Gospel in which re-marriage during the lifetime of the husband was directly forbidden.

Armed with these arguments, which seemed to her irrefutable, Princess Kuragin drove round to her daughter's early one morning in order to find her alone. Helen heard her mother's protests to the end, and smiled with bland sarcasm.

"You see it is plainly said: 'He who marryeth her that is divorced . . .' "

"Oh mother, don't talk nonsense. You don't understand. In my position I have duties . . ." Helen began.

"But, my dear . . ."

"Oh mother, how is it you don't understand that the Holy Father, who has the right of granting dispensations . . ."

At that moment the lady companion, who lived in Helen's house, came in to announce that his highness was in the drawing-room, and wished to see her.

"No, tell him I don't want to see him, that I am furious with him for not keeping his word."

"Countess, there is mercy for every sin," said a young man walking boldly into the room. He had fair hair and a long face and long nose.

The old princess rose respectfully and curtsied at his entrance. The young man took no notice of her. Princess Kuragin nodded to her daughter, and swam to the door.

"Yes, she is right," thought the old princess, all of whose convictions had been dissipated by the appearance of his highness on the scene. "She is right. But how was it that in my youth—gone now for ever—we knew nothing of this? And it is so simple," thought Princess Kuragin, as she settled herself in her carriage.

At the beginning of August Helen's affairs were settled, and she wrote to her husband a letter, in which she made known to him her intention of marrying N.N. She informed him also of her conversion to the one true faith, the Roman Catholic Church, and begged him to go through all the necessary formalities for obtaining a divorce, of which the bearer of the letter would give him further details. "On which I pray God to have you in His holy and powerful keeping. Your friend, Helen."

This letter was brought to Pierre's house at the time when he was on the field of Borodino.

The one thing Pierre desired, at the end of the battle of Borodino, was to get away from the terrible sensations in which he had passed that day, to get back into the ordinary conditions of life, and to go to sleep quietly indoors in his own bed. But the ordinary conditions of life were nowhere to be found. He followed the soldiers in retreat toward Mozhaisk.

Though bullets and cannon balls were not whistling here on the road along which he was going, still he saw on all sides the same sights as on the field of battle. There were everywhere the same suffering, exhausted, and sometimes strangely indifferent faces; everywhere the same blood and soldiers' overcoats, the same sound of firing at a distance.

After walking about three miles, Pierre sat down by the roadside.

Night was beginning to fall and the roar of cannon died down. Pierre gazed at the shadows passing by him in the dusk. He had no idea how long he was there, but in the middle of the night he got up and walked on.

Cocks were crowing when he reached Mozhaisk, and entered the yard of the inn where he had left his groom and carriage.

There was not a room at the inn: all were full. Pierre went out into the yard, and muffling his head up, lay down in his carriage.

He had hardly put his head on the cushion when he felt that he was dropping asleep. But all of a sudden he heard, almost with the distinctness of reality, the sound of the boom, boom, boom of the cannon, the groans and shrieks and dull thud of the falling shells, smelt the blood and powder; and the feeling of horror, of the dread of death came over him. He opened his eyes in a panic. All was quiet in the yard. The only sound came from a servant talking with the porter at the gate, and splashing through the mud. Over Pierre's head, under the dark, wooden eaves, he heard pigeons fluttering. The whole yard was pervaded by the strong smell of a tavern—full of peaceful suggestion and soothing relief to Pierre—the smell of hay, of dung, and of tar. Between two dark sheds he caught a glimpse of the pure, starlit sky.

"Thank God, that is all over!" thought Pierre, covering his head up again. "Oh, how awful terror is, and how shamefully I gave way to it! But they . . . *they* were firm and calm all the while up to the end . . ." he thought. *They*, in Pierre's mind, meant the soldiers, those who had been on the battery, and those who had prayed to the holy picture. *They*—those strange people, of whom he had known nothing before—*they* stood out clearly and sharply in his mind apart from all other people.

"To be a soldier, simply a soldier!" thought Pierre as he fell asleep. "To enter with one's whole nature into that common life, to be filled with what makes them what they are. But how is one to cast off all that is superfluous, devilish in one's self, all the burden of the outer man? At one time I might have been the same. I might have run away from my father as I wanted to. After the duel with Dolohov I might have been sent for a soldier."

A few hours later he was awakened by someone shouting.

"We want to harness the horses. It's time to harness the horses, your excellency! Your excellency," some voice was repeating. "We want to harness the horses. It's time . . ."

It was the groom waking Pierre. The sun was shining full in Pierre's face. He glanced at the dirty tavern yard. At the well in the middle of it soldiers were watering their thin horses and waggons were moving out of the gate.

The groom, the coachman, and the porter told Pierre that an officer had come with the news that the French were advancing on Mozhaisk and that the Russian troops were retreating.

Pierre got up, and ordering the carriage to be got out and to drive after him, crossed the town on foot.

The troops were marching out, leaving tens of thousands of wounded behind. The wounded could be seen at the windows of the houses, and were crowding the yards and streets. Screams, oaths, and blows could be heard in the streets about the carts which were to carry away the wounded.

Pierre put his carriage at the service of a wounded general of his acquaintance, and drove with him to Moscow. On the way he was told of the death of his brother-in-law, Anatole, and of the death of Prince André. Only half of this news was true. Prince André was still alive.

On the 30th Pierre reached Moscow. At the city gates he was met by an adjutant of Count Rastoptchin's.

"Why, we have been looking for you everywhere," said the adjutant. "The count urgently wants to see you. He begs you to come to him at once on very important business." Instead of going home, Pierre drove to the governor's.

The ante-room and waiting-room in Count Rastoptchin's house were full of officials, who had been summoned by him, or had come to him for instructions. He had already been informed that the defence of Moscow was out of the question, and the city would be surrendered. Though the news was being concealed from the citizens, the heads of various departments and officials of different kinds knew that Moscow would soon be in the hands of the enemy. And all of them, to escape personal responsibility, had come to the governor to inquire how to act in regard to the offices in their charge.

At the moment when Pierre went into the waiting-room, a courier from the army was just coming out from an interview with the count.

The courier waved his hand with a hopeless air at the questions with which he was besieged, and walked across the room.

While he waited, Pierre watched with weary eyes the various officials—young, old, military, and civilian, important and insignificant—who were gathered together in the room. All seemed dissatisfied and uneasy. Pierre went up to one group of functionaries, among whom he recognised an acquaintance. After greeting him, they went on with their conversation. They were discussing Rastoptchin's latest proclamation to the people which promised that Moscow would be defended.

"And oh, count," said one suddenly, addressing Pierre with a smile, "we have been hearing that you are in trouble. That the countess . . ."

"I have heard nothing about it," said Pierre indifferently. "What is it you have heard?"

"Oh, you know, stories are so often made up. I only repeat what I hear."

"What have you heard?"

"Oh, they say," said the man again with the same smile, "that the countess, your wife, is preparing to go abroad. It's most likely nonsense."

"It may be," said Pierre, looking absent-mindedly about him. "Who is that?" he asked, indicating a tall old man in a clean blue overcoat, with a big, snow-white beard and eyebrows and a ruddy face.

"That? Oh, he's a merchant; that is, he's the restaurant-keeper, Vereshtchagin. You have heard the story of the 'proclamation'?"

"Oh, so that's Vereshtchagin!" said Pierre, looking at the firm, calm face of the old merchant, and seeking in it some trace of treachery.

"That's not the man himself. That's the father of the fellow who wrote the 'proclamation'," said the man. "The young man himself is in custody, and I think it will go hard with him."

A little old gentleman with a star, and a German official with a cross on his neck, joined the group.

"It's a complicated story, you see," the man was relating. "The proclamation appeared two months ago. It was brought to the count. He ordered an investigation. The proclamation had passed through some sixty-three hands. We come to one and ask, From whom did you get it? From so and so. And the next refers us on to so and so; and in that way they traced it to Vereshtchagin . . . a half-educated merchant's son," said the man smiling. "He too was asked, From whom did you get it? And we knew very well from whom he had it really. He could have had it from no one but the director of the post-office. But it was clear there was an understanding between them. He says he got it from no one, but had composed it himself. And threaten him and question him as they would, he stuck to it, he had written it himself. So the matter was reported, and the count had him sent for. 'From whom did you get the proclamation?' 'I wrote it myself.' Well! you know the count," said the man, with a smile of pride and delight. "He was angry!"

"Oh! the count wanted him to say it was from Klutcharyov, director of the post-office. I understand," said Pierre.

"Oh no, not at all," said the man in dismay. "Klutcharyov had sins enough to answer for without that, and that's why he was banished. But any way, the count was very indignant. 'How could you write it?' says the count. He took up the *Hamburg Gazette* that was on the table. 'Here it is. You did not compose it, but translated it, and very badly too, because you don't even know French, you fool.' What do you think? 'No,' says he, 'I have never read any gazettes; I made it up.' 'But if so, you're a traitor, and I'll hand you over for judgment, and you will be hanged.' 'Tell us from whom you got it.' 'I have not seen any gazettes; I composed it.' So the matter rests. The count sent for the father; he sticks to the same story.

And they had him tried, and he was sentenced, I believe, to hard labour. Now the father has come to petition in his favour. But he is a worthless young scamp! You know the style of spoilt merchant's son, a regular dandy and lady-killer; has attended lectures of some sort, and so fancies that he's above everybody. A regular young scamp! His father has an eating-house here on the Kamenny bridge; and in the shop, you know, there is a great picture of God the Supporter of All, represented with a sceptre in one hand and the empire in the other. Well, he took that picture home for a few days, and what do you suppose he did! He got hold of some wretched painter . . ."

In the middle of this new story Pierre was summoned to the governor.

Rastoptchin, frowning, passed his hand across his forehead and eyes as Pierre entered.

"Ah! greetings to you, brave warrior," said Rastoptchin. "We have been hearing about your adventures! But that's not the point. Between ourselves, are you a mason?" said Count Rastoptchin in a severe tone, that suggested that it was a crime to be so, but that he intended to pardon it. Pierre did not speak. "My dear friend, I am well informed; but I know that there are masons and masons, and I hope you don't belong to those among them who, by way of regenerating the human race, are trying to ruin Russia."

"Yes, I am a mason," answered Pierre.

"Well then, look here. You are not unaware, I dare say, of the fact that Speransky and Magnitsky have been sent—to their proper place—and the same has been done with Klutcharyov and the others who, under the guise of building up the temple of Solomon, have been trying to destroy the temple of their fatherland. You may take it for granted there are good reasons for it, and that I could not have banished the director of the post-office here if he had not been a dangerous person. Now, it has reached my ears that you sent him your carriage to get out of the town, and that you have even taken charge of his papers. I like you, and wish you no harm, and as you are half my age, I advise you, as a father might, to break off all connection with people of that sort, and to get away from here yourself as quickly as you can."

"But what was Klutcharyov's crime?" asked Pierre.

"That's my business. And it's not yours to question me," cried Rastoptchin.

"If he is accused of having circulated Napoleon's proclamation, the charge has not been proved," said Pierre, not looking at Rastoptchin. "And Vereshtchagin . . ."

Rastoptchin suddenly broke in, scowling and shouting

louder than ever. "Vereshtchagin is a traitor and a deceiver, who will receive the punishment he deserves," he said, with the vindictiveness with which people speak at the recollection of an affront. "But I did not send for you to criticise my actions, but in order to give you advice. I tell you to break off all connection with Klutcharyov and his set, and to leave town." And, then becoming conscious that he was taking a heated tone with Pierre, who was as yet guilty of no offence, he added: "We are on the eve of a public disaster, and I haven't time to say civil things to every one who has business with me. Well, what are you going to do, you personally?"

"Oh, nothing," answered Pierre, with his eyes still downcast, and no change in the expression of his face.

The count frowned.

"Leave town as soon as possible, that's my advice. Good-bye. Oh, by the way," he called after him at the door, "is it true the countess has fallen into the clutches of the holy fathers of the Society of Jesus?"

Pierre made no answer. He walked out of Rastoptchin's room.

By the time he reached home it was getting dark. Eight people were waiting for him. A secretary of a committee, the colonel of his battalion of militia, his steward, his bailiff, and other persons with petitions. All of them had business matters with Pierre, which he had to settle. He had no understanding of their questions, nor interest in them, and answered them with the sole object of getting rid of them. At last he was left alone, and he broke open and read his wife's letter.

"*They*—the soldiers on the battery, Prince André killed . . . Osip. . . . Simplicity in submission to God's will. One has to suffer . . . The significance of the whole . . . One must harness all together . . . My wife is going to be married. . . . One must forget and understand . . ." And, without undressing, he threw himself on his bed and at once fell asleep.

When he woke up next morning his steward came in to announce that a police official was below, sent by Count Rastoptchin to find out whether Count Bezuhov had gone, or was going away.

A dozen different people were again waiting in the drawing-room to see Pierre on business. Pierre dressed quickly but instead of going down to see them, he ran down the back staircase and out by the back entry to the gates.

From that moment till the occupation of Moscow was over, no one of Pierre's household saw him again, nor could discover his whereabouts, in spite of every effort to track him down.

The Rostovs stayed in Moscow till the 1st of September, the day before the French entered the city.

After Peter had joined the army and gone away the countess fell into a panic of terror. The idea that both her sons were at the war, that they had both escaped from under her wing, that any day either of them—and possibly even both at once, like the three sons of a lady of her acquaintance—might be killed, struck her with cruel vividness. She tried to get Nicholas back, wanted to go herself after Peter, or to obtain some post for him in Petersburg; but all these seemed equally impossible. Peter could not be brought back except by the return of his regiment, or through being transferred to another regiment on active service. Nicholas was somewhere at the front, and nothing had been heard from him since the letter in which he had given a detailed account of his meeting with Princess Mary. The countess could not sleep at nights, and when she did sleep, she dreamed that her sons had been killed.

After talking the matter over, and many consultations with friends, the count at last hit on a means for soothing the countess. He got Peter transferred to Pierre's regiment which was being formed near Moscow. Though, even so, Peter remained in the army, by this exchange the countess had the consolation of seeing one son at least again under her wing. And she hoped to manage not to let her Peter escape her again, but to succeed in getting him always appointed to places where there would be no risk of his being in battle.

While Nicholas had been the only one in danger, the countess had fancied that she loved her elder son better than the other children. But now that her younger boy, always idle at his lessons, always in mischief, and teasing every one, her little Peter, with his snub-nose, his black eyes, his fresh colour, and the soft down just showing on his cheeks, had slipped away, now it seemed to the mother that she loved him more, far more, than all the rest. The nearer the time came for the return of her longed-for Peter to Moscow, the greater was the uneasiness of the countess. She positively thought she would never live to see such happiness.

Although by the 20th of August almost all the Rostovs' acquaintances had left Moscow, although everybody was trying to persuade the countess to get away as quickly as possible, she would not hear of leaving till her treasure, her idolised Peter, had come back. On the 28th of August Peter arrived. The morbidly passionate tenderness with which his mother received him was by no means gratifying to the sixteen-year-old officer. Though his mother concealed her intention of never letting him escape from under her wing again, Peter guessed her plan and he treated her rather coolly, avoided being with her, and during his stay in Moscow spent most of his time with Natasha.

The count, with his characteristic carelessness, had by the 28th made no preparations for leaving, and the waggons that were to come from their Moscow and Ryazan estate to remove their furniture and other possessions only arrived on the 30th.

From the 28th to the 31st, Moscow was all bustle and movement. Every day thousands of wounded men from the field of Borodino were brought in and carried across Moscow, and thousands of vehicles, full of residents and their belongings, drove out at the gates on the opposite side of the city. In spite of Rastoptchin's posters the strangest and most contradictory rumours were circulating about the town. Some said that every one was forbidden to leave the city; others asserted that all the holy pictures had been taken from the churches, and every one was to be driven out of Moscow by force. Some said there had been another battle after Borodino, in which the French had been utterly defeated; others declared that the whole Russian army had been annihilated. Some talked of the Moscow militia, which was to advance, preceded by priests, to Three Hills; others whispered that traitors had been caught, that the peasants were in revolt, and were plundering those who left the town. But all this was only talk.

During the three days preceding the occupation of Moscow, the whole Rostov family was busy. The count was continually driving about the town, picking up all the rumours that were in circulation, and while at home, gave superficial and hasty directions for the preparations for departure.

The countess superintended the sorting out of things to be packed; she was out of humour with every one, and was in continual pursuit of Peter, who was as continually escaping from her, and exciting her jealousy by spending all his time with Natasha. Sonya was the only person who really undertook the practical business of getting things packed. But Sonya had been particularly silent and melancholy of late. She had been present when Nicholas' letter mentioning Princess Mary had elicited the most delighted deductions from the countess, who saw in Nicholas' meeting with Princess Mary the direct intervention of Providence.

"I was never really happy," said the countess, "when Prince André was engaged to Natasha, but I have always longed for Nicholas to marry the princess, and I have always had a presentiment about it. And what a good thing it would be!"

Sonya felt that this was true; that the only possibility of retrieving the Rostovs' position was by Nicholas' marriage to an heiress, and that the princess would be an excellent match for him. But this reflection was very bitter for her. In spite, or perhaps in consequence, of her sadness, she undertook the difficult task of seeing after the sorting and packing of the household goods, and for whole days together she was busily employed. The count and countess referred to her when they had any orders to give. Peter and Natasha, on the contrary, did nothing to help their parents, but were in every one's way. All day long the house resounded with their flying footsteps and shouts and shrieks. They laughed and were gay, not in the least because there was reason for laughter. But they were gay and glad at heart, and so everything that happened was reason enough for gaiety and laughter in them. Peter was in high spirits because he had left home a boy, and come back (so every one told him) a fine young man, because he was at home, because he had come to Moscow where there would be fighting in a few days, and above all, because Natasha, whose lead he always followed, was in high spirits. Natasha was gay, because she had too long been sad, and now nothing reminded her of the cause of her sadness, and she was quite strong again. She was gay too, because she needed some one to adore her and Peter did adore her. They were both gay, because there was war at the very gates of Moscow, because there would be fighting. Because arms were being given out, and everybody was rushing about.

On Saturday, the 31st of August, the whole Rostov household seemed turned upside down. All the doors stood wide open, all the furniture had been moved about or carried out, looking-glasses and pictures had been taken down. The rooms were littered up with boxes, with hay and packing paper and cord. Peasants and house-serfs were tramping about the parquet floors carrying out the baggage. The courtyard was crowded with peasants' carts, some piled high with goods and corded up, others still standing empty.

The voices and steps of the numberless servants and of peasants, who had come with the carts, resounded through the courtyard and the house. The count had been out since early morning. The countess had a headache from the noise and bustle, and was lying down in the sitting-room with compresses steeped in vinegar on her head. Peter was not at home; he had gone off to see a friend with whom he was secretly planning to get transferred from the militia to a regiment at the front. Sonya was in the great hall, superintending the packing of the china and glass. Natasha was sitting on the floor in her dismantled room among heaps of dresses, ribbons, and scarfs. She sat gazing at the floor, holding in her hands an old ball-dress, the very dress, now out of fashion, in which she had been to her first Petersburg ball.

Natasha was ashamed of doing nothing when every one in the house was so busy, and several times that morning she had tried to set to work; but her soul was not in it. She stood over Sonya while she packed the china, and tried to help; but soon threw it up, and went to her room to pack her own things. At first she had found it amusing to give away her dresses and ribbons to the maids, but afterwards when it came to packing what was left, it seemed a wearisome task.

And when her maid undertook to do it all for her, Natasha sat down on the floor with the old ball-dress in her hands, and fell to dreaming on subjects far removed from what should have been occupying her mind. From the reverie she had fallen into, Natasha was aroused by the talk of the maids in the next room and their hurried footsteps from their room to the backstairs. Natasha got up and looked out of the window. A huge train of carts full of wounded men had stopped in the street.

The maids, the footmen, the housekeeper, the old nurse, the cooks, the coachmen, the grooms, and the scullion-boys were all at the gates, staring at the wounded men.

Natasha went out into the street.

The old housekeeper, Mavra Kuzminishna, had left the crowd standing at the gate, and gone up to a cart. She was talking to a pale young officer who was lying in this cart. Natasha took a few steps forward and stood still timidly, listening to what the housekeeper was saying.

"So you have no one in Moscow?" Mavra Kuzminishna was saying. "You'd be more comfortable in some apartment. . . . In our house even. The masters are all leaving."

"I don't know if it would be allowed," said the officer in a feeble voice. "There's our chief officer . . . ask him," and he pointed to a stout major who had turned back and was walking along the row of carts down the street.

Natasha glanced with frightened eyes into the face of the wounded officer, and at once went to meet the major.

"May the wounded men stay in our house?" she asked.

The major with a smile put his hand to his cap.

"What is your pleasure, ma'mselle?" he said smiling.

Natasha quietly repeated her question, and her face and her whole manner was so serious, that the major left off smiling, and after a moment's pondering—as though asking himself how far it were possible—he said, "Yes."

Natasha went to Mavra Kuminishna, who was still talking with sympathy to the young officer.

"They may; he said they might!" whispered Natasha.

The officer in the cart turned into the Rostovs' courtyard, and dozens of carts of wounded men then began at the invitation of the neighbours to drive up to the other houses of the street. Natasha was delighted at having to do with new people in conditions quite outside the ordinary routine of life. She joined Mavra Kuzminishna in trying to get as many as possible driven into their yard.

"We must ask your father though," said Mavra Kuzminishna.

"Nonsense, nonsense. What does it matter? For one day, we'll move into the drawing-room. We can give them all our half of the house."

"What an idea! What next? The lodge, may be, the men's room, and old nurse's room but . . ."

"Well, I will ask."

Natasha ran indoors, and straight to the sitting room.

"Are you asleep, mother?"

"Oh, what chance is there of sleep!" said the countess, who had just dropped into a doze.

"Mother, darling!" said Natasha, kneeling before her mother and leaning her face against her mother's. "I am sorry, forgive me, I'll never do it again, I waked you. Mavra Kuzminishna sent me; they have brought some wounded men in, officers, will you allow it? They have nowhere to go; I know you will allow it, . . ." she said rapidly, not taking breath.

"Officers? Who have been brought in? I don't understand," said the countess.

Natasha laughed. The countess too smiled faintly.

"I knew you would let me . . . So I will tell them so." And Natasha, kissing her mother, got up and went to the door.

In the hall she met her father, who had come home with bad news.

"We have lingered on too long!" said the count, with unconscious anger in his voice. "The club's shut up and the police are leaving."

"Father, you don't mind my having invited some of the wounded into the house?" said Natasha.

"Of course not," said the count absently. "But that's not to the point. I beg you now not to let yourself be taken up with any nonsense, but to help to pack and get off—to get off to-morrow . . ."

And the count gave his butler and servants the same orders.

Peter came back at dinner-time, and he too had news to tell them. He said that the mob was talking up arms in the Kremlin; that though Rastoptchin's placard said he would give the word two days later, it had really been arranged that all the people should go next day in arms to the Three Hills, and there a great battle was to be fought.

The countess looked in horror at her son's eager face as he

told them this. She knew that if she said a word to try and dissuade Peter from going to this battle, he would say something about the duty of a man, about honour, and the fatherland—something irrational, masculine, and perverse—which it would be useless to oppose. And, therefore, hoping to succeed in setting off before this battle, and in taking Peter with her, the countess called her husband aside, and with tears begged him to take her away as soon as could be, that night if possible. With the instinctive, feminine duplicity of love, she declared she should die of terror if they did not get away that very night. She was afraid now of everything.

Madame Schoss, the governess, who had gone out to visit her daughter, increased the countess's terrors by describing the scenes she had witnessed at a liquor dealer's in Myasnitsky Street. She entered that street on her way home, but could not pass through it owing to the drunken mob raging round the store. She had taken a cab and driven home by a roundabout route.

After dinner all the Rostovs set to work in earnest packing and preparing for their departure. The old count, suddenly rousing himself to the task, spent the rest of the day continually trotting from the courtyard into the house and back again, shouting confused instructions to the hurrying servants, and trying to spur them on to even greater haste. Peter looked after things in the yard. Sonya was quite bewildered by the count's contradictory orders, and did not know what to do. The servants raced about the rooms, shouting and quarrelling. Natasha, too, suddenly set to work with the ardour that was characteristic of her in all she did. At first her help was skeptically received. No one expected anything serious from her or would obey her instructions. But she insisted on being obeyed, got angry and almost cried, and did at last succeed in impressing them.

But with all their exertions, even late at night everything was not ready. The countess, completely exhausted, fell asleep, and the count put off their departure till morning and went to bed.

Sonya and Natasha slept in the sitting-room, without undressing.

That night another wounded officer was driven along their street, and Mavra Kuzminishna, who was standing at the gate, had him brought into the Rostovs' yard. The wounded officer must, she thought, be a man of importance. He was in a coach with the hood let down and a carriage apron completely covering it. An old man, a most respectable-looking valet, was sitting on the box with the driver. A doctor and two soldiers followed in another carriage.

"Come into our house, come in. The masters are going away, the whole house is empty," said the old woman, addressing the old servant.

"Well," answered the valet, sighing, "and indeed we have no hope of getting him home alive! We have a house of our own in Moscow, but it is a long way further, and there's no one living in it either."

"Pray come in, our masters have plenty of everything, and you are welcome," said Mavra Kuzminishna.

"I must ask the doctor." And the valet got down and went to the carriage behind.

"Very good," said the doctor.

The valet went up to the coach again, and told the coachman to turn into the yard.

Mavra Kuzminishna suggested the wounded man be carried into the house.

"The masters won't say anything . . ." she said.

But they had to avoid lifting him up the steps, and so they carried him instead into the lodge. The wounded officer was Prince André Bolkonsky.

Moscow's last day had come. It was a bright, clear autumn day. It was Sunday. The bells were ringing for service in all the churches, just as on all other Sundays. No one seemed yet able to grasp what was awaiting the city.

Early in the morning of this same day orderlies and servants were being continually sent into the Rostovs' courtyard by wounded officers, and wounded men were constantly dragging themselves there from the Rostovs' and neighbouring houses, to beseech the servants to try and get them a lift out of Moscow. The butler, to whom these requests were referred, resolutely refused, though he felt for the wounded men, and declared that he would never even dare to hint at such a thing to the count. Pitiable as the position of these wounded men was, it was obvious that if one gave up one cart to them, one might as well give all—and would then even have to put the carriages too at their service. Thirty waggons could not save all the wounded, and in the general catastrophe one must think of oneself and one's family first. So the butler reasoned on his master's behalf.

On waking up that morning the count slipped quietly out of his bedroom, so as not to wake his wife, and in his lilac silk dressing-gown he came out on to the steps. The loaded waggons were standing in the courtyard. The carriages were drawn up at the steps. The butler was standing in the entrance talking with an old orderly and a pale young officer with his arm in a sling. The butler, seeing his master, made a sign to them both to retire.

"Well, is everything ready, Vassilitch?" said the count, rubbing his bald head. And looking at the officer and the orderly, he nodded to them.

"Ready to put the horses in immediately, your excellency."

"Well, that's fine. The countess will soon be awake, and, please God, we set off! What can I do for you, sir?" he said, addressing the officer. "You are staying in my house?"

The officer came closer. His pale face suddenly flushed crimson.

"Count, do me a great favour, allow me . . . for God's sake . . . to get into one of your waggons. I have nothing here with me . . . I can go quite well with the luggage . . ."

Before the officer finished speaking, the orderly came up to make the same request for his master.

"Oh! Yes, yes, yes," said the count hurriedly. "I shall be very glad indeed. Vassilitch, you see to it; you have a waggon or two cleared, well . . . well . . . what's needed . . . ?" The count murmured some vague orders. But the look of gratitude on the officer's face instantly put the seal on the order. The count looked about him; everywhere—in the yard, at the gates, at the windows of the lodge—he saw wounded men and orderlies. They were all gazing at him and moving up towards the steps.

"Will you please walk into the gallery, your excellency. What are your orders about the pictures there?" said the butler. And the count went into the house with him, repeating his instructions that they were not to refuse the wounded men who begged to go with them.

"You can take something out of the loads, you know," he added, in a subdued voice, as though he were afraid of being overheard.

At nine o'clock the countess woke up, and her maid came in to report to her that Madame Schoss was very angry, and that the young ladies' summer dresses could not possibly be left behind. It appeared that Madame Schoss' trunk had been taken out of the waggon, and that all the waggons were being unloaded, and that the luggage was being taken out, as the waggons were to be given up to the wounded men, whom the count, with his usual readiness to be imposed upon, had consented to take away with them. The countess sent for her husband to come to her.

"What's this, my dear? I hear the luggage is being unloaded."

"I wanted to speak to you about it . . . Dear little countess . . . An officer came up to me—they are imploring us to let them have a few waggons for the wounded. It's a question of money loss to us, of course, but to be left behind . . .

think what it means to them! . . . Here they are in our very yard; we asked them in ourselves. There are officers. . . . You know, I really think, my dear . . . Well, let them take them. We are in no hurry."

The count spoke timidly, as he always did when the subject was in any way connected with money. The countess was used to that tone, which always ushered in some matter prejudicial to her children's interests, such as the building of a new gallery, or conservatory, or a new theatre in the house, or the training of an orchestra; and she made it a habit, and regarded it as a duty, to oppose everything that was communicated in that tone.

She assumed her air of tearful resignation, and said to her husband: "Listen, count, you have mismanaged things so, that we are getting nothing for the house, and now you want to throw away all our—all the *children's*—property. Why, you told me yourself that we have a hundred thousand roubles' worth of valuables in the house. I protest, and protest, my love. What would you have! It's for the Government to look after the wounded. They know that. Only think, the neighbours opposite cleared everything to the last stick out of their house the day before yesterday. That's how other people manage. It's only we who are such fools. If you have no consideration for me, do at least think of your children."

The count waved his hands in despair, and went out of the room without a word.

"Father! Why do you do that?" said Natasha, who had followed him into her mother's room.

"Nothing! It's no business of yours!" the count said angrily.

"But I heard," said Natasha. "Why won't mother . . . ?"

"It's no business of yours!" cried the count.

The countess came in with a look of weariness and annoyance on her face.

"I can't make out what the servants are about," said the countess, addressing her husband. "They told me just now nothing was ready. Some one really must go and look after them. It's at such times one misses Mitenka. There will be no end to it."

"Damnation! Damnation! Damnation!" cried the old count. "My head's going round." And he went out of the room.

The countess began to cry.

Natasha went out with her father, and as though unable to make up her mind on some difficult question, she followed him at first, then turned and ran downstairs.

Peter was standing at the entrance, giving out weapons to the servants, who were leaving Moscow. The loaded waggons were still standing in the yard. Two of them had been untied, and on to one of these the pale young wounded officer was clambering with the assistance of his orderly.

"Do you know what it was about?" Peter asked Natasha. Natasha knew that he meant, what their father and mother had been quarrelling about. She did not answer.

"It was because father wanted to give up all the waggons to the wounded," said Peter. "Vassilitch told me. And I think . . ."

"I think," Natasha suddenly screamed. "I think, that it's so vile, so loathsome . . . I don't know. Are we a lot of low Germans? . . ." Her throat was quivering with sobs, but afraid of being weak, or wasting the force of her anger, she turned and flew headlong up the stairs and burst like a tempest into the room where the countess was sitting.

The count was walking about the room.

"It's vile! It's loathsome!" she screamed. "Mother, it can't be true that it's your order."

The countess gazed at her in bewilderment. The count stood still in the window.

"Mother, it's impossible; look what's being done in the yard!" she cried. "They are being left . . ."

"What's the matter? Who are they? What do you want?"

"The wounded! It's impossible, mother, it's outrageous. . . . No, mother darling, it's all wrong. Forgive me, please, darling . . . Mother what is it to us what we take away. Look into the yard. . . . Mother! . . . It can't be done. . . ."

The count stood in the window, and listened to Natasha without turning his head. All at once he gave a sort of gulp, and put his face closer to the window.

The countess glanced at her daughter, saw her face full of shame for her, saw her emotion, felt why her husband would not look at her now, and looked about her with a distracted air.

"Oh, do as you please. Am I doing anything to hinder any one?" she said, not giving way all at once.

"Mother, darling, forgive me."

But the countess pushed away her daughter, and went up to the count.

"My dear, you order what is right. . . . I don't understand about it, you know," she said, dropping her eyes with a guilty air.

"The eggs . . . the eggs teaching the hen . . ." the count murmured through tears, and he embraced his wife, who was glad to hide her face on his breast.

"Father, Mother! may I give the order? May I? . . ." asked Natasha. "We'll take all that's quite necessary all the same," she added.

The count nodded. And Natasha flew across the hall into the vestibule, and down the steps into the yard.

The servants gathered round Natasha, and could hardly believe the strange order she gave them, till the count himself in his wife's name confirmed the order that all the waggons were to be placed at the disposal of the wounded, and the boxes were to be taken down to the storerooms.

Wounded soldiers came creeping out of their rooms, and crowded round the waggons with pale faces. The news spread to the neighbouring houses, and wounded men began to come into the yard from other houses too. Many of the wounded soldiers begged them not to take out the boxes, but only to let them sit on the top of them. But when once the work of unloading had begun there was no stopping it; it seemed of little consequence whether all were left or half. The cases of china, of bronzes, of pictures and looking-glasses, which had been so carefully packed during the previous night lay in the yard, and still they sought and found ways of taking out more and more, and leaving more and more room for the wounded.

By two o'clock the Rostovs' four carriages were packed and ready to start. The waggon-loads of wounded were filing one after another out of the yard.

The coach in which Prince André was being taken drove by the front door, and attracted the attention of Sonya, who was helping a maid to arrange the countess's seat comfortably in her huge, high carriage.

"Whose carriage is that?" asked Sonya, popping her head out of the carriage window.

"Why, haven't you heard, miss?" answered the maid. "The wounded prince; he stayed the night in the house, and is going on with us."

"Who is he? What's his name?"

"Our betrothed that was . . . Prince André Bolkonsky!" answered the maid, sighing. "They say he is dying."

Sonya jumped out of the carriage and ran in to the countess. The countess, dressed for the journey, in her hat and shawl, was walking wearily about the drawing-room, waiting for the rest of the household to come in and sit down with closed doors, for the usual silent prayer before setting out. Natasha was not in the room.

"Mother," said Sonya. "Prince André is here, wounded and dying. He is going with us."

The countess opened her eyes in dismay, and clutching Sonya's arm, looked about her.

"Natasha," she said.

Both to Sonya and the countess this news had for the first moment but one significance. They knew their Natasha, and alarm at the thought of the effect the news might have on her outweighed all sympathy for the man, though they both liked him.

"Natasha does not know yet, but he is going with us," said Sonya.

"You say he is dying?"

Sonya nodded.

The countess embraced Sonya and burst into tears. "The ways of the Lord are past our finding out!" she thought, feeling that in all that was passing now the Hand of the Almighty was beginning to be manifest.

"Well, mother, it's all ready. What is it? . . ." asked Natasha, running into the room.

"Nothing," said the countess. "If we're ready, then do let us start." And the countess tried to hide her feelings.

Natasha looked at her.

"What is it? What has happened?"

"Nothing . . . Oh, no . . ."

"Something . . . What is it?" asked Natasha.

At that moment the count, Peter, Madame Schoss, Mavra Kuzminishna, and Vassilitch came into the drawing-room. And closing the doors, they all sat down, and sat so in silence, without looking at each other for several seconds.

The count was the first to get up. With a loud sigh he crossed himself before the holy picture. All the others did the same. Then the count embraced Mavra Kuzminishna and Vassilitch, who were to remain in Moscow; and while they caught at his hand and kissed his shoulder, he patted them on the back with vaguely affectionate and reassuring phrases. The countess went off to the little chapel, and Sonya found her there on her knees before the holy pictures, that were still left here and there on the walls. All the holy pictures most precious through association with the traditions of the family were being taken with them.

On the porch and in the yard the servants who were going—all of whom had been armed with swords and daggers—with their trousers tucked in their boots, and their sashes or leather belts tightly braced, took leave of those who were being left behind.

The old coachman Efim, the only one whom the countess could trust to drive her, sat perched up on the box, and did not even look round at what was passing behind him. His thirty years' experience had taught him that it would be some time yet before they would say, "Now, in God's name, start!" and that when they had said it, they would stop him at least twice again to send back for things that had been forgotten; and after that he would have to pull up once more for the countess herself to put her head out of window and beg him to drive carefully downhill. He knew this, and therefore awaited what was to come with more patience than his horses, especially the left one, who was continually pawing the ground and champing at the bit. At last all were seated; the carriage steps were pulled up, and the door slammed, and the forgotten travelling-case had been sent for, and the countess had popped her head out and given the usual injunctions. Then Efim deliberately took his hat off and began crossing himself. The postillion and all the servants did the same.

"With God's blessing!" said Efim, putting his hat on. "Off!" The postillion started his horse. The right-shaft horse began to pull, the high springs creaked and the carriage swayed. The footman jumped up on the box. The carriage jolted as it drove out of the yard on to the uneven pavement; the other vehicles jolted in the same way as they followed in a procession up the street. All the occupants of the carriages, the coach and the covered gig, crossed themselves on seeing the church opposite. The servants, who were staying in Moscow, walked along on both sides of the carriages to see them off.

Natasha had rarely felt such a joyful sensation as she experienced at that moment sitting in the carriage by the countess and watching, as they slowly moved by her, the walls of forsaken Moscow. Now and then she put her head out of the carriage window and looked back, and then in front at the long train of waggons full of wounded soldiers preceding them. Foremost of them all she could see Prince André's closed carriage. She did not know who was in it, and every time she took stock of the procession of waggons she looked out for that coach. She knew it would be the foremost.

As they drove along several trains of vehicles, similar to the Rostovs', came driving out of side streets and joined the long file of moving carriages. By the time they reached the far side of Moscow the carriages and carts were two deep all along the road.

As they turned round Suharev Tower, Natasha, who was watching the crowd driving and walking by, uttered a cry of delight and surprise: "Good Heavens! Mother, Sonya, look; it's he!"

"Who? Who?"

"Look, look! Pierre," said Natasha, putting her head out of the carriage window and staring at a tall, stout man in a coachman's long coat, obviously a disguise. He was passing under the arch of the Suharev Tower beside a yellow-looking, beardless, little old man in a frieze cloak.

"Look! Pierre! In a coachman's coat," said Natasha. "Look! Look!"

"No, it's not Pierre. How can you be so absurd!"

"Mother," cried Natasha. "I am sure it is. Stop, stop," she

shouted to the coachman. But the coachman could not stop, because more carts and carriages were coming out of a side street, and people were shouting at the Rostovs to move on, and not to block the traffic.

"Pierre, come here! We recognised you!" Natasha cried, stretching out a hand to him. "How? Why are you dressed like this?"

Recognising Natasha Pierre ran toward the carriage. He took her outstretched hand, and awkwardly kissed it as he ran alongside their carriage.

"What has happened, count?" the countess asked him, in a surprised and commiserating tone.

"Eh? Why? Don't ask me," said Pierre, and he looked up at Natasha, the charm of whose radiant, joyous eyes he felt upon him.

"Are you staying in Moscow?"

"Yes, in Moscow. Good-bye. To-morrow . . . No! Good-bye; good-bye," he said. And he left the carriage and walked away to the pavement.

For a long while Natasha still looked out of the carriage window, smiling at him.

From the time of his disappearance, two days before, Pierre had been living in the home of his dead benefactor, Osip Alexyevitch. His widow and children had gone away to the country. But his old servant Gerasim, and his half-crazed and drunken brother, Makar, were still in the house.

The old servant welcomed Pierre. And when he learned that Pierre wanted to stay for some days in his old friend's home, he said: "Pray do, you are very welcome."

Pierre went into the house. A tall, bald old man in a dressing-gown, with a red nose and goloshes on his bare feet, was standing in the vestibule. Seeing Pierre, he muttered something angrily, and walked away into the corridor.

Pierre went into the gloomy study, which he had entered with such trepidation in the lifetime of his benefactor. Now covered with dust, and untouched since the death of Osip Alexyevitch, the room was gloomier than ever.

Gerasim opened one blind, and went out of the room on tiptoe. Pierre walked round the study, went up to the bookcase, where manuscripts were kept, and took one. He sat down to the dusty writing-table and laid the manuscript down before him, opened and closed it, and at last, pushing it away, sank into thought.

Several times Gerasim peeped cautiously into the study and saw that Pierre was sitting in the same attitude.

More than two hours passed by. Gerasim finally ventured to make a slight noise at the door to attract Pierre's attention.

"Listen," said Pierre, and hurriedly getting up and taking Gerasim by the button of his coat and looking down at him. "Listen! You know that to-morrow the French will enter the city and . . ."

"They have been saying so . . ." answered Gerasim.

"I beg you not to tell any one who I am. And do what I tell you . . ."

"Certainly, sir," said Gerasim. "Would your honour like something to eat?"

"No, but I want something else. I want a peasant dress and a pistol," said Pierre, suddenly flushing red.

"Certainly, sir," said Gerasim, after a moment's thought.

All the rest of that day Pierre spent alone in his benefactor's study, pacing restlessly from one corner to the other, as Gerasim could hear, and talking to himself; and he spent the night on a bed made up for him there.

Gerasim accepted Pierre's living in the house with the indifference of a servant, who had seen many queer things in his time, and he seemed, indeed, pleased at having some one to wait upon. Without even permitting himself to wonder with what object it was wanted, he obtained for Pierre that evening a coachman's coat and cap, and promised next day to procure the pistol.

Makar twice that evening approached the door, shuffling in his goloshes, and stood there, gazing at Pierre. But as soon as Pierre turned to him, he wrapped his dressing-gown round him with a shamefaced and angry look, and retreated.

Pierre put on the coachman's coat, carefully fumigated for him by Gerasim, and went out with the old servant to buy a pistol at the Suharev Tower. It was there he had met the Rostovs.

On the night of the 1st of September Kutuzov gave the Russian troops the command to fall back across Moscow to the Ryazan road. From two o'clock that night until late that morning, the Russian army retreated eastward across the city taking with them the last departing inhabitants.

Moscow was deserted. Although there were still people in the city—half of all the inhabitants remained—it seemed empty. There was scarcely a creature in the streets. The gates and the shops were all closed. Here and there near taverns could be heard shouts or drunken singing. No one was driving in the streets and there were no footsteps.

At ten o'clock in the morning of the 2nd of September the only troops left in the western suburbs were the regiments of the rearguard, and the crush was over. The army was already on the further side of Moscow, and out of the city altogether.

At the same time, at ten o'clock in the morning of the 2nd

of September, Napoleon was standing in the midst of his troops on Poklonny Hill, gazing at the spectacle that lay before him. Moscow lay stretching wide below with her river, her gardens, and her churches, and seemed to be living a life of her own, her cupolas twinkling like stars in the sunlight.

"This Asiatic city with its innumerable churches, Moscow the holy. Here it is at last, the famous city! It was high time," said Napoleon; and dismounting from his horse he bade them open the map of Moscow before him, and sent for his interpreter.

"A city occupied by the enemy is like a girl who has lost her honour," he thought. It was the phrase he had uttered when he took Smolensk. And with that point of view he gazed at the Oriental beauty who lay for the first time before his eyes. He felt it strange himself that the desire so long cherished, and thought so impossible, had at last come to pass. In the clear morning light he gazed at the city, and then at the map, looking up its details, and the certainty of possessing it awed him.

"But how could it be otherwise?" he thought. "Here is this capital, she lies at my feet awaiting her fate. Where is the Tsar Alexander now, and what is he thinking? A strange, beautiful, and grand city! And a strange and grand moment is this! In what light must I appear to them?" he mused, thinking of his soldiers. "Here is the city—the reward for all those of little faith," he thought, looking round at his suite and the approaching troops, forming into ranks.

"One word of mine, one wave of my arm, and the ancient capital of the Tsar is no more. But my clemency is ever prompt to stoop to the vanquished. I must be magnanimous and truly great. But no, it is not true that I am in Moscow," the idea suddenly struck him. "She lies at my feet, though, her golden domes and crosses flashing and twinkling in the sun. But I will spare her. On the ancient monuments of barbarism and despotism I will inscribe great words of justice and mercy . . . Alexander will feel that more bitterly than anything; I know him. From the heights of the Kremlin—yes, that's the Kremlin, yes—I will dictate to them the laws of justice, I will teach them the meaning of true civilisation, I will make the generations of boyards to enshrine their conqueror's name in love. I will tell the deputation that I have not sought, and do not seek, war; but I have been waging war only with the deceitful policy of their court; that I love and respect Alexander, and that in Moscow I will accept terms of peace worthy of myself and my peoples. I have no wish to take advantage of the fortune of war to humiliate their honoured Emperor. 'Boyards,' I will say to them, 'I do not seek war; I seek the peace and welfare of all my subjects.' But I know their presence will inspire me, and I shall speak to them as I always do, clearly, impressively, and greatly."

"Let the boyards be brought to me," he said, addressing his suite. A general, with a brilliant suite of adjutants, galloped off at once to fetch the boyards.

Two hours passed. His speech to the boyards had by now taken definite shape in his mind. It was full of dignity and of greatness, as Napoleon understood it. Napoleon was himself carried away by the magnanimity with which he intended to act in Moscow. In imagination he had already fixed the days for a "reunion in the Palace of the Tsars," at which the great Russian nobles were to mingle with French courtiers. In thought he had appointed a governor capable of winning the hearts of the people. Having heard that Moscow was full of religious institutions, he had mentally decided that his bounty was to be showered on these. He imagined that as in Africa he had had to sit in a mosque wearing a burnous, in Moscow he must be gracious and bountiful as the Tsars. . . . "But why is the deputation from the city so long in coming?" he wondered.

Meanwhile a whispered consultation was being held among his generals and marshals in the rear. The adjutants sent to bring the deputation had come back with the news that Moscow was empty, that every one had left or was leaving the city. The faces of all the suite were pale and perturbed. It was not that Moscow had been abandoned by its inhabitants that alarmed them. They were in alarm at the idea of making the fact known to the Emperor; they could not see how, without putting his majesty into a ridiculous position, to inform him that he had been waiting so long for the boyards in vain, that there was a drunken mob, but no one else in Moscow. Some of the suite maintained that come what may, they must anyway scrape up a deputation of some sort; others opposed this view, and asserted that the Emperor must be carefully and skilfully prepared, and then told the truth.

"We shall have to tell him all the same," said some gentleman of the suite. . . . "But, gentlemen . . ."

Meanwhile the Emperor, weary of waiting in vain, and with his actor's instinct feeling that the great moment, being too long deferred, was beginning to lose its grandeur, made a sign with his hand. A solitary cannon shot gave the signal, and the invading army marched into Moscow. More and more rapidly, vying with one another, the troops marched in, concealed in the clouds of dust they raised, and making the air ring with their deafening shouts.

Tempted on by the advance of the army, Napoleon too rode as far as the city wall, but there he halted again, and dismounting walked about for a long time, waiting for the deputation.

When, with due circumspectness, Napoleon was informed that Moscow was deserted, he looked wrathfully at his informant, and turning his back on him, went on pacing up and down in silence.

"My carriage," he said. He sat down in his carriage beside the adjutant on duty, and drove into the suburbs.

He did not drive right into the town, but put up for the night at an inn on the city's edge. The dramatic scene had not come off.

On the evening of the 1st of September, Count Rastoptchin had come away from an interview with Kutuzov, mortified and offended at not having been invited to the council of war, and at Kutuzov's having taken no notice of his offer to take part in the defence of the city. He was also astonished at the new view of things revealed to him in the camp, in which the tranquillity of the city and its patriotic fervour were treated as matters of quite secondary importance, if not altogether irrelevant and trivial. Mortified, offended, and astonished at all this, Count Rastoptchin had returned to Moscow. After supper, he lay down on a sofa without undressing, and at one o'clock was waked by a courier bringing him a letter from Kutuzov. The letter asked the count, since the troops were retreating to the Ryazan road behind Moscow, to send police officials to escort troops through the town. The letter told Rastoptchin nothing new. He had known that Moscow would be abandoned not merely since his interview the previous day with Kutuzov on the Poklonny Hill, but ever since the battle of Borodino; since when all the generals who had come to Moscow had with one voice declared that another battle was impossible, and with Rastoptchin's sanction government property had been removed every night, and half the inhabitants had left. But nevertheless the fact, communicated in the form of a simple note, with a command from Kutuzov, and received at night, breaking in on his first sleep, surprised and irritated the governor.

From the time when the enemy first entered Smolensk, Rastoptchin had in his own imagination been playing the part of leader of popular feeling—of the heart of Russia. He did not merely believe—as every governing official always does believe—that he was controlling the external acts of the inhabitants of Moscow, but imagined that he was shaping their mental attitude by means of his appeals and posters. The picturesque figure of leader of the popular feeling was so much to Rastoptchin's taste, and he so lived in it, that the necessity of abandoning it, the necessity of surrendering Moscow with no heroic effect of any kind, took him quite unawares; the very ground he was standing on seemed slipping from under his feet, and he was utterly at a loss what to do. Though he knew it was coming, he could not till the last minute fully believe in the abandonment of Moscow, and did nothing towards it. The inhabitants left the city against his wishes. If the courts were removed, it was only due to the insistence of the officials, to which Rastoptchin reluctantly gave way.

On being waked out of his sleep to read Kutuzov's cold note, Rastoptchin felt the more irritated the more he felt himself to blame. There was still left in Moscow all that was under his charge, all the government property which it was his duty to have removed to safety. There was now no possibility of getting it all away. "Who is responsible for it? Who has let it come to such a pass?" he wondered. "Of course, it's not my doing. I had everything in readiness; I held Moscow in my hand—like this! And see what they have brought things to! Traitors!" he thought, not exactly defining who were these traitors, but feeling a necessity to hate these vaguely imagined traitors, who were to blame for the false and ludicrous position in which he found himself.

All that night Rastoptchin was giving instructions, for which people were continually coming to him from every part of Moscow. His subordinates had never seen the count so gloomy and irascible.

To all inquiries he gave brief and curt replies, the drift of which was that his instructions were now not needed, that all his careful preparations had now been ruined by somebody, and that that somebody would have to take all responsibility for anything that might happen.

"Oh, tell that blockhead," he replied to the inquiry from the Estates Department, "to stay and keep guard over his deeds. Well, what nonsense are you asking about the fire brigade? There are horses, let them go off to Vladimir. Don't leave them for the French."

"Your excellency, the superintendent of the madhouse has come. What are your commands?"

"My commands? Let them all go free, that's all. . . . And let the madmen out into the city. When we have madmen in command of our armies, it seems it's God's will they should be free."

To the inquiry about the convicts in the prison, the count shouted angrily to the overseer:

"What, do you want me to give you two battalions for a convoy for them, when we haven't any battalions at all? Let them all go, and that settles it!"

"Your excellency, there are political prisoners—Myeshkov, Vereshtchagin . . ."

"Vereshtchagin! He is not yet hanged?" cried Rastoptchin. "Send him to me."

By nine o'clock in the morning, seeing the troops moving across Moscow, people stopped coming to Rastoptchin for instructions. All who could get away were going without asking leave; those who stayed decided for themselves what they had better do.

Count Rastoptchin ordered his horses to drive him to Sokolniky, his summer estate, and with a yellow and frowning face, sat in silence with folded arms in his study.

Rastoptchin felt helpless, weak, and useless and it drove him to frenzy. The head of the police, went in to see him at the same time as an adjutant, who came to announce that his horses were ready. Both were pale, and the head of the police, after reporting that he had discharged the commissions given to him, informed Count Rastoptchin that there was a great crowd of people in his courtyard waiting to see him.

"What is it they want?"

"Your excellency, they say they have come together to fight the French by your orders. They were shouting something about treachery. They say you promised that Moscow would not be surrendered, you promised to fight to the very end. . . . And now the army is retreating, the rich have fled, and they are being abandoned to die like dogs. It is an angry crowd. I had all I could do to get away from them."

Without replying, Count Rastoptchin got up and walked into his sumptuously furnished drawing-room. He went up to the balcony door, took hold of the door-handle, let go of it, and moved away to the window, from which the whole crowd could be better seen. A tall young fellow was standing in the front, waving his arms and saying something. A blood-bespattered blacksmith stood beside him. Through the closed windows could be heard the roar of voices.

"Is the carriage ready?" asked Rastoptchin, moving back from the window.

"Yes, your excellency," said the adjutant.

Rastoptchin went again to the balcony door.

"Your excellency . . . If I may venture to suggest, your excellency . . ."

"Kindly leave me; I know what to do without your assistance," cried Rastoptchin angrily. He stood at the door of the balcony looking at the crowd. "This is what they have done with Russia! This is what they have done with me!" thought Rastoptchin, feeling a rush of irrepressible rage against the undefined some one to whose fault what was happening could be set down. As is often the case with excitable persons, he was possessed by fury, while still seeking an object for it. "Here is the mob, the dregs of the people," he thought, looking at the crowd, "that they have stirred up by their folly. They want a victim," came into his mind, as he watched the waving arm of the tall fellow in front. And the thought struck him precisely because he too wanted a victim, an object for his wrath.

"Is the carriage ready?" he asked again.

"Yes, your excellency. What orders in regard to Vereshtchagin? He is waiting at the steps," answered the adjutant.

"Ah!" cried Rastoptchin.

And opening the door, he walked out on the balcony. The hum of talk instantly died down, caps and hats were lifted, and all eyes were raised upon the governor.

"Good-day, lads!" said the count, speaking loudly and quickly. "Thanks for coming. I'll come out to you in a moment, but we have first to deal with a criminal. We have to punish the wretch by whose doing Moscow is ruined. Wait for me!" And he went in again, slamming the door.

An approving murmur of satisfaction ran through the crowd.

A few minutes later an officer came hurriedly out of the main entrance, and gave some order, and the dragoons drew themselves up stiffly. The crowd moved greedily up from the balcony to the front steps. Coming out there, Rastoptchin looked about him hurriedly, as though seeking some one.

"Where is he?" he said, and at the moment he said it, he caught sight of a young man with a long, thin neck, and half of his head shaven and covered with short hair, coming round the corner of the house between two dragoons. This young man was dressed in a fox-lined blue cloth coat, that had once been foppish but was now shabby, and in filthy convict's trousers, stuffed into dirty battered boots. His uncertain steps were clogged by the heavy chains hanging about his thin, weak legs.

"Put him here!" said Rastoptchin, pointing to the bottom steps.

With a clank of chains the young man stepped with effort on to the steps. Putting his finger into the tight collar of his coat, he turned his long neck twice, and folded his thin, unworkmanlike hands before him with a resigned gesture.

For several seconds there was complete silence.

Rastoptchin scowled "Lads!" he said, with a metallic ring in his voice, "this man, Vereshtchagin, is the wretch by whose doing Moscow is lost."

The young man in the fox-lined coat stood bending a little forward. His wasted young face, with its look of hopelessness and the hideous disfigurement of the half-shaven head, was turned downwards. At the count's first words he slowly lifted his head and looked up. But Rastoptchin did not look at him. A blue vein behind the young man's ear stood out like a cord on his long, thin neck, and all at once his face flushed crimson.

All eyes were fixed upon him. He gazed at the crowd, and, as though made hopeful by the expression he read on the faces there, he smiled a timid, mournful smile, and dropping his head again, shifted his feet.

"He is a traitor to his Tsar and his country; he deserted to Bonaparte; he alone of all the Russians has disgraced the name of Russia, and through him Moscow is lost," cried Rastoptchin in a harsh, monotonous voice. But all at once he glanced down at Vereshtchagin, and as though that glance had driven him to frenzy, flinging up his arms, he almost yelled to the crowd: "You shall deal with him as you think fit! I hand him over to you!"

The people were silent, and only pressed closer and closer on one another. To bear each other's weight, to breathe in that tainted foulness, to be unable to stir, and to be expecting something vague, uncomprehended and awful, was becoming unbearable. The men in the front of the crowd, who saw and heard all that was passing before them, all stood with wide-open, horror-struck eyes and gaping mouths.

"Beat him! . . . Let the traitor perish and not shame the name of Russia!" screamed Rastoptchin. "Cut him down! I give the command!" Hearing not the words, but only the wrathful tones of Rastoptchin's voice, the mob moaned and heaved forward, but stopped again.

"Count!" . . . the timid voice of Vereshtchagin broke in upon the momentary stillness that followed. "Count, one God is above us . . ." said Vereshtchagin, lifting his head, and again the thick vein swelled on his thin neck and the colour swiftly came and faded again from his face. He did not finish what he was trying to say.

"Cut him down! I command it! . . ." cried Rastoptchin, suddenly turning as white as Vereshtchagin himself.

"Draw sabres!" shouted the officer to the dragoons, himself drawing his sabre.

Another still more violent wave passed over the crowd, and reaching the front rows, pushed them forward, and threw them staggering right up to the steps. The tall young man, with a stony expression and his lifted arm rigid in the air, stood close beside Vereshtchagin.

"Strike at him!" the officer said almost in a whisper to the dragoons. And one of the soldiers, his face suddenly convulsed by fury, struck Vereshtchagin on the head with the flat of his sword.

Vereshtchagin uttered a brief "Ah!" of surprise, looking

about him in alarm, as though he did not know what this was done to him for. A similar moan of surprise and horror ran through the crowd.

"O Lord!" some one was heard to utter mournfully. Then Vereshtchagin uttered a piteous cry of pain, and that cry was his undoing. The barrier of human feeling, that still held the mob back was snapped. The crime had been begun, its completion was inevitable. The piteous moan of reproach was drowned in the angry and menacing roar of the mob. The dragoon who had struck the victim would have repeated his blow. Vereshtchagin, with a scream of terror, putting his hands up before him, dashed into the crowd. The tall young man, against whom he stumbled, gripped Vereshtchagin's slender neck in his hands, and with a savage shriek fell with him under the feet of the trampling, roaring mob. Some beat and tore at Vereshtchagin, others at the tall young man. And the screams of those crushed in the crowd and of those who tried to rescue the tall young man only increased the frenzy of the mob. For a long while the dragoons were unable to get the bleeding, half-murdered young man away. And in spite of all the feverish haste with which the mob strove to make an end of what had once been begun, the men who beat and strangled Vereshtchagin and tore him to pieces could not kill him. The crowd pressed on them on all sides, heaved from side to side like one man with them in the middle, and would not let them kill him outright or let him go.

"Hit him with an axe . . . They have crushed him . . . Traitor, he sold Christ! . . . Living . . . Alive . . . Serve the thief right. With a bar! . . . Is he alive? . . ."

Only when the victim ceased to struggle, and his shrieks had passed into a long-drawn, rhythmic death-rattle, did the mob begin hurriedly to change places about the bleeding corpse on the ground. Every one went up to it, gazed at what had been done, and pressed back horror-stricken, surprised, and reproachful.

"And a young fellow too . . . Must have been a merchant's son . . . They say it's not the right man . . ." said the same people, looking at the dead body, with the blue face fouled with dust and blood, and the long, slender, broken neck.

A punctilious police official, feeling the presence of the body unseemly in the courtyard of his excellency, bade the dragoons drag the body away into the street. Two dragoons took hold of the mutilated legs, and dragged the body away. The dead, shaven head, stained with blood and grimed with dust, was trailed along the ground, rolling from side to side on the long neck. The crowd shrank away.

When Vereshtchagin fell, and the crowd with a savage yell closed in and heaved about him, Rastoptchin suddenly turned white, and instead of going to the back entrance, where horses were waiting for him, he walked rapidly along the corridor leading to the rooms of the lower story, looking at the floor and not knowing where or why he was going. His face was white, and he could not check the feverish twitching of his lower jaw.

"Your excellency, this way . . . where are you going? . . . This way," said a trembling, frightened voice behind him. Obediently turning, he went in the direction indicated. At the back entrance stood a carriage. The distant roar of the howling mob could be heard even there. Count Rastoptchin hurriedly got into the carriage, and bade them drive him to his house at Sokolniky beyond the town.

As he drove out into the street and lost the sound of the shouts of the mob, the count began to repent. He thought with dissatisfaction now of the excitement and terror he had betrayed before his subordinates. "The mob is terrible, it is hideous. They are like wolves that can only be appeased with flesh," he thought. "Count! There is one God over us!" Vereshtchagin's words suddenly recurred to him, and a disagreeable chill ran down his back. But that feeling was momentary, and Count Rastoptchin smiled contemptuously at himself. "I had other duties. The people had to be appeased. Many other victims have perished and are perishing for the public good," he thought. And he began to reflect on the social duties he had towards his family and towards the city intrusted to his care. "If I had been simply Rastoptchin, my course of action might have been quite different; but I was bound to preserve the dignity of the governor as the representative of authority intrusted with full powers by the Tsar."

Reaching his house in the country, the count completely regained his composure in arranging his domestic affairs.

Within half an hour the count was again driving with rapid horses across the Sokolniky plain, thinking no more now of the past, but absorbed in thought and plans for what was to come. He was approaching now the Yauzsky bridge where he had been told that Kutuzov was. In his own mind he was preparing the biting and angry speeches he would make, upbraiding Kutuzov for his deception. He would make that old court fox feel that the responsibility for all the disasters bound to follow the abandonment of Moscow, and the ruin of Russia, lay upon his old, doting head. Going over what he would say to Kutuzov, Rastoptchin angrily turned from side to side in his carriage, and looked about him.

The Sokolniky plain was deserted. Only at one end of it, by the almshouse and lunatic asylum, there were groups of people in white garments, wandering about, shouting and gesticulating.

One of them was running right across in front of Count Rastoptchin's carriage. And Count Rastoptchin himself and his coachman, and the dragoons, all gazed with a feeling of horror and curiosity at these released lunatics, and especially at the one who was running towards them.

Tottering on his long, thin legs in his fluttering dressing-gown, this madman ran, with his eyes fixed on Rastoptchin, shouting something to him in a husky voice, and making signs to him to stop. The gloomy and triumphant face of the madman was thin and yellow, with irregular tufts of beard growing on it. The black, agate-like pupils of his eyes moved restlessly, showing the saffron-yellow whites above. "Stay! Stop, I tell you!" he shouted shrilly, and again breathlessly fell to shouting something with emphatic gestures and intonations.

He reached the carriage and ran alongside it.

"Three times they slew me, three times I rose again from the dead. They stoned me, they crucified me . . . I shall rise again . . . I shall rise again . . . I shall rise again. My body they tore to pieces. The kingdom of heaven will be overthrown . . . Three times I will overthrow it, and three times I will set it up again," he screamed, his voice growing shriller and shriller. Count Rastoptchin suddenly turned white, as he had turned white when the crowd fell upon Vereshtchagin. He turned away. "G . . . go on, faster!" he cried in a trembling voice to his coachman.

The carriage dashed on. But for a long while yet Count Rastoptchin heard behind him the frantic, desperate scream getting further away, while before his eyes he saw nothing but the wondering, frightened, bleeding face of the traitor in the fur-lined coat. Fresh as that image was, Rastoptchin felt now that it was deeply for ever imprinted on his heart. He felt clearly now that the bloody print of that memory would never leave him, that the further he went the more cruelly, the more vindictively, would that fearful memory rankle in his heart to the end of his life. He seemed to be hearing now the sound of his own words: "Tear him to pieces, you shall answer for it to me!—Why did I say these words? I said it somehow without meaning to . . . I might not have said them," he thought, "and then nothing would have happened." He saw the terror-stricken, and then suddenly frenzied face of the dragoon who had struck the first blow, and the glance of silent, timid reproach cast on him by that lad in the fox-lined coat. "But I didn't do it on my own account. I was bound to act in that way. The people . . . The public good . . ."

The bridge over the Yauza was still crowded with troops. It was hot. Kutuzov, looking careworn and weary, was sitting on a bench near the bridge, playing with a whip on the sand, when Rastoptchin's carriage rattled noisily up to him. The count began addressing him in French, his eyes shifting uneasily, with a look between anger and terror in them. He told Kutuzov that he had come here, for since Moscow was no more, the army was all that was left. "It might have been very different if your highness had not told me you would not abandon Moscow without a battle; all this would not have been!"

Then, strange to tell! The governor of Moscow, the proud Count Rastoptchin, picking up a horse whip, went to the bridge, and fell to shouting and driving on the crowded carts.

At four o'clock in the afternoon, Murat's troops entered Moscow. In front rode a detachment of Würtemberg hussars, behind, with an immense suite, rode the King of Naples himself.

Just inside the city wall Murat halted to await information from the detachment in advance as to the condition in which the citadel of the city, *"le Kremlin,"* had been found.

A small group of inhabitants of Moscow had gathered about Murat. All stared with timid astonishment at the strange figure of the long-haired commander, decked in gold and feathers.

"Is this their Tsar himself?" voices were heard saying softly.

An interpreter approached the group of gazers.

"Caps . . . caps off," they muttered, turning to each other in the little crowd. The interpreter spoke to an old porter, and asked him if it were far to the Kremlin. The porter, listening with surprise to the unfamiliar Polish accent, and not recognising the interpreter's words for Russian, had no notion what was being said to him, and took refuge behind the others.

Murat approached the interpreter, and told him to ask where were the Russian troops. One of the Russians understood this question, and several voices began answering the interpreter simultaneously. A French officer rode up on Murat and reported that the gates into the Kremlin were blocked, and that probably there was an ambush there.

"Good," said Murat, and turning to one of the gentlemen of his suite, he commanded four light cannons to be moved forward, and the gates to be shelled.

The artillery came trotting out from the column following Murat, and advanced further into the city. When they reached the Kremlin square they halted and drew up. Several French officers superintended the placing of the cannon some distance apart, and looked at the Kremlin through a field-glass. A bell was ringing in the Kremlin for evening service, and that sound troubled the French. They thought it was a call to arms. Several infantry soldiers ran to the Kutafyev gateway. A barricade of beams and planks lay across the gateway. Two musket shots rang out from the gates, just as an officer with some men were running up to them. The general standing by the cannons shouted some words of command to the officer, and the officer and the soldiers ran back.

Three more shots were heard from the gate and the shout of several voices rose from behind the barricade. Instantaneously, as though at the word of command, the expression of good humour and serenity on the faces of the French general, officers, and men was replaced by a stubborn, concentrated expression of readiness for conflict and suffering. They felt it was a new battlefield, likely to be the scene of a bloody conflict. All were ready. The cannons were moved forward. An officer shouted "Fire!" The grapeshot fell rattling on the stone of the gateway, on the beams and screens of planks, and two clouds of smoke rolled over the square.

A flock of jackdaws rose above the walls and swept round in the air with loud caws, and the whir of thousands of wings. Together with this sound, there rose a solitary human cry at the gate, and the figure of a man bareheaded, in a long peasant's coat, came into sight through the smoke. Holding a gun up, he took aim at the French. "Fire!" repeated the artillery officer, and at the same instant one rifle shot and two cannon shots were heard. The gate was again hidden in smoke.

Nothing more stirred behind the barricade, and the French infantry soldiers with their officers passed in at the gate. In the gateway lay three men wounded and four dead. Two men in long peasant-coats had run away along the walls.

"Clear this away," said the officer, pointing to the beams and the corpses. And the French soldiers finished off the wounded, and flung the corpses over the fence below.

Murat was informed that the way had been cleared. The French entered the gates, and began pitching their camp on Senate-house Square. The soldiers threw chairs out of the windows of the Senate-house into the square, and began making fires.

Other detachments marched across the Kremlin and encamped in adjoining streets. Others pitched their camps in neighbouring districts. Not finding citizens to entertain them, the French everywhere bivouacked as in a camp pitched in a town, instead of quartering themselves on the houses.

Tattered, hungry, and exhausted, as they were, and dwindled to one-third their original numbers, still the French entered Moscow in good discipline. It was a harassed and exhausted, yet still active and menacing army. But it was an army only up to the moment when the soldiers of the army dispersed all over the city. As soon as the soldiers began to disperse about the wealthy, deserted houses, the army was lost for ever, and in its place was a multitude of men, neither citizens nor soldiers, but marauders.

Ten minutes after the French regiments had dispersed about the various quarters of Moscow, not a soldier nor an officer was left among them. At the windows of the houses men could be seen in military coats and Hessian boots, laughing and strolling through the rooms. In the cellars, in the storerooms other men were busily looking after the provisions; in the courtyards they were unlocking or breaking open the doors of sheds and stables; in the kitchens they were making up fires, and with bare arms mixing, kneading, and baking, and frightening, or trying to coax and amuse, women and children. Men there were in plenty everywhere, in all the shops and houses; but the French army was no more.

That day one order after another was issued by the French commanders forbidding the troops to disperse about the town, sternly forbidding violence to the inhabitants, and pillaging, and proclaiming that a general roll-call was to take place that evening. But in spite of all such measures the men, who had made up the Grande Armée, flowed about the wealthy, deserted city, so richly provided with luxuries and comforts.

Moscow was without its inhabitants, and the soldiers were sucked up in her, like water into sand, as they flowed away irresistibly in all directions from the Kremlin. Cavalry soldiers who had entered a merchant's house abandoned with all its belongings, and finding stabling for their horses and to spare, yet went on to take the house next door, which seemed to them better. Many took several houses, chalking their names on them, and quarrelled and even fought with other companies for their possession. Soldiers had no sooner succeeded in securing quarters than they ran along the street to look at the town, and on hearing that everything had been abandoned, hurried off where objects of value could be carried off for nothing. The officers followed to check the soldiers, and were involuntarily lured into doing the same. In Carriage Row shops had been abandoned stocked with carriages, and the generals flocked there to choose coaches for themselves. The few inhabitants who had stayed on invited the officers into their houses, hoping thereby to secure themselves against being robbed.

Wealth there was in abundance: there seemed no end to it. Everywhere all round the parts occupied by the French there were unexplored regions unoccupied beyond, in which the French fancied there were even more riches to be found. And Moscow absorbed them further and further into herself.

The absorption of the French into Moscow in a widening circle in all directions did not, till the evening of the 2nd of September, reach the quarter of the town in which Pierre was staying.

After the two last days spent in solitude Pierre was in a condition approaching madness. One haunting idea had complete possession of him. He could not have told how or when it had come to him, but that idea had now such complete possession of him that he remembered nothing in the past, and understood nothing in the present; and everything he saw and heard seemed passing in a dream.

When, in the deathlike stillness of Osip's study, he sat with his elbows on the dusty writing-table, there passed in calm and significant succession before his mental vision the impressions of the last few days, especially of the battle of Borodino, and of that overwhelming sense of his own pettiness and falsity in comparison with the truth and simplicity and force of that class of men, who were mentally referred to by him as "they." When Gerasim roused him from his reverie, the idea occurred to Pierre that he would take part in the defence of Moscow by the people, which was, he knew, expected. And with that object he had asked Gerasim to get him a peasant's coat and a pistol, and had told him that he intended to conceal his name, and to remain in Osip's house.

Next day with the simple aim of not sparing himself and not doing less than *they* would do, he had gone out to the Three Hills. But when he came back, convinced that Moscow would not be defended, he suddenly felt that he must remain in Moscow, concealing his name, must meet Napoleon, and kill him, so as either to perish or to put an end to the misery of all Europe, which was in Pierre's opinion entirely due to Napoleon alone.

Pierre's physical state, as is always the case, corresponded with his moral condition. The coarse fare to which he was unused, the vodka he drank during those days, the lack of wine and cigars, his dirty, unchanged linen, and two half-sleepless nights, spent on a short sofa without bedding, all reduced Pierre to a state of nervous irritability bordering on madness.

He brooded over his plan, going over all the details of it. In his dreams Pierre never clearly pictured the very act of striking the blow, nor the death of Napoleon, but with extraordinary vividness and mournful enjoyment dwelt on his own end and his heroic fortitude.

"Yes, one man for all, I must act or perish!" he thought. "Yes, I will approach . . . And then all at once . . . With a pistol or a dagger!" thought Pierre. "But that doesn't matter. It's not I but the Hand of Providence punishes you. . . . I shall say" (Pierre pondered over the words he would utter as he killed Napoleon). "Well, take me, execute me!" Pierre would murmur to himself, bowing his head.

While Pierre was standing in the middle of the room, musing

in this fashion, the door of the study opened, and Makar—always in the past so timid—appeared in the doorway, completely transformed.

His dressing-gown was hanging open. His face was red and distorted. He was unmistakably drunk. And with his thin, tottering legs walked into the middle of the room.

"They have grown fearful," he said, in a husky and confidential voice. "I will not surrender, I say . . . " He paused and suddenly catching sight of the pistol on the table, snatched it up and ran out.

Gerasim and the porter, who had followed Makar, stopped him in the vestibule, and tried to get the pistol away from him. Pierre coming out of the study looked at the half-insane old man. Makar, frowning with effort, succeeded in keeping the pistol, and was shouting in a husky voice, evidently imagining some heroic scene.

"To arms! Board them! You won't get it!" he was shouting.

"Give it to me. Give it to me. Do me the favour, sir, please be quiet. There now, if you please, sir, . . ." Gerasim was saying, cautiously trying to steer Makar by his elbow toward the door.

"Who are you? Bonaparte! . . ." yelled Makar.

"Come into your room and rest a little, sir. Let me have the pistol now."

"Away, base slave! Don't touch me! Do you see?" screamed Makar, brandishing the pistol. "Run them down!"

They seized Makar by the arms and dragged him towards the door.

The vestibule was filled with the sounds of scuffling and drunken, husky gasping.

Suddenly a new sound, a shrill, feminine shriek, was heard from the porch, and the cook ran into the vestibule.

"They! Merciful heavens! . . . My goodness, here they are! Four of them, horsemen!" she screamed.

Gerasim and the porter let Makar go, and in the hush that followed in the corridor they could distinctly hear several hands knocking at the front door.

There were two of them. One—an officer, a tall, handsome man of gallant bearing; the other, obviously a soldier or officer's servant. The officer walked first, limping and leaning on a stick. After advancing a few steps, the officer apparently making up his mind that these would be good quarters, stopped, turned round and shouted in a loud voice to the soldier standing in the doorway to tie up the horses. Having done this the officer turned and said gaily, smiling and looking about him, "*Bonjour* my friends!"

No one answered.

"Quartire, quartire, logement," said the officer, with a good-humoured smile. Then clapping the scared Gerasim on the shoulder he added, "Does no one speak French?"

The officer asked Gerasim to show him over the house.

"Master not here—no understand . . . Me you . . ." said Gerasim, trying to make his words more comprehensible by saying them in reverse.

The French officer, smiling, waved his hands in front of Gerasim's nose, to give him to understand that he too failed to understand him, and walked with a limp towards the door where Pierre was standing. Pierre was about to draw back, but at that very second he caught sight of Makar peeping out of the open kitchen door with a pistol in his hand. With a madman's cunning, Makar eyed the Frenchman, and lifting the pistol, took aim. "Run them down!" he yelled.

The French officer turned round at the scream, and at the same instant Pierre dashed at Makar. Just as Pierre snatched at the pistol and jerked it up a deafening shot rang out, wrapping every one in a cloud of smoke. The Frenchman turned pale and rushed back to the door.

Forgetting his intention of concealing his knowledge of French, Pierre pulled away the pistol, and throwing it on the ground, ran to the officer and addressed him in French. "You are not wounded?" he said.

"I think not," answered the officer, feeling himself. "But I have had a narrow escape this time," he added, pointing to the broken plaster in the wall. "Who is this man?" he asked, looking sternly at Pierre.

"Oh, I am really in despair at what has happened," said Pierre quickly, quite forgetting his part. "It is a madman, an unhappy creature, who did not know what he was doing."

The officer went up to Makar and took him by the collar.

Makar pouting out his lips, nodded, as he leaned against the wall, as though dropping asleep.

"Brigand, you shall pay for it," said the Frenchman, letting go of him. "We are clement after victory, but we do not pardon traitors," he added.

Pierre tried in French to persuade the officer not to be severe with this drunken imbecile. The Frenchman listened in silence, with a gloomy air, and then suddenly turned with a smile to Pierre. For several seconds he gazed at him mutely. His handsome face assumed an expression of melodramatic feeling, and he held out his hand.

"You have saved my life. You are French," he said. An heroic action, he felt, could only be performed by a Frenchman, and to save the life of him, M. Ramballe, captain of the 13th Light Brigade, was undoubtedly a most heroic action.

Pierre, however, thought it well to disillusion him.

"I am Russian," he said quickly.

"Tell that to others," said the Frenchman, smiling. "You shall tell me all about it directly," he said. "Charmed to meet a compatriot. Well, what are we to do with this man?" he added, applying to Pierre now as though to a comrade. To his last question Pierre explained once more who Makar was. He explained that just before his arrival the drunken imbecile had carried off a loaded pistol, which they had not succeeded in getting from him, and he begged him to let his action go unpunished. The Frenchman arched his chest, and made a majestic gesture with his hand.

"You have saved my life! You are a Frenchman. You ask me to pardon him. I grant you his pardon. Let this man be released." And taking Pierre's arm the French officer walked with him into the adjoining room.

The orderly, who had meanwhile been in the kitchen, came in to the officer.

"Captain, they have soup and a leg of mutton in the kitchen," he said. "Shall I bring it up?"

"Yes, and wine," said the captain.

As the French officer drew Pierre with him into the room, Pierre thought it his duty to assure the captain again that he was not a Frenchman. But the French officer would not hear of it. He was so polite, good-humoured, and genuinely grateful to him for saving his life that Pierre had not the heart to refuse, and sat down with him in the dining-room.

"Frenchman or Russian prince incognito," said the Frenchman, looking at Pierre's fine, though dirty linen, and the ring on his finger. "I owe my life to you, and I offer you my friendship. A Frenchman never forgets an insult or a service. I offer you my friendship. That's all I say."

In the tones of the voice, the expression of the face, and the gestures of the officer, there was so much naïve good nature and good breeding that Pierre unconsciously responded with a smile to his smile, as he took his outstretched hand.

"Captain Ramballe of the 13th Light Brigade," he introduced himself. "Will you tell me now to whom I have the honour of speaking so agreeably, instead of remaining in the ambulance with that madman's ball in my body?"

Pierre answered that he would not tell him his name, and was beginning with a blush, while trying to invent a name, to speak of the reasons for which he was unable to do so, but the Frenchman hurriedly interrupted him.

"Enough!" he said. "I understand your reasons; you are an officer . . . A staff officer, perhaps. You have borne arms against us. That's not my business. I owe you my life. That's enough for me. I am at your disposal. You are a nobleman?" he added, with an intonation of inquiry. Pierre bowed.

"Your baptismal name, if you please? I ask nothing more. M. Pierre, you say? Perfect! That's all I want to know."

When they had brought in the mutton, an omelette, a samovar, vodka, and wine, Ramballe begged Pierre to share his dinner; and at once with the greediness of a healthy, hungry man, set to work himself, munching vigorously with his strong teeth, and continually smacking his lips and exclaiming, "Excellent! Excellent!" Pierre was hungry, and pleased to share the meal. Morel, the orderly, brought in a pot of hot water, and put a bottle of red wine to warm in it. Ramballe then wrapped a napkin round the bottle, and poured out wine for himself and Pierre. The wine, and the satisfaction of his hunger, made the captain even more lively, and he chatted away without a pause all dinner-time.

"Yes, my dear M. Pierre, I owe you a fine votive candle for saving me from that maniac. I have bullets enough in my body, you know. Here is one from Wagram" (he pointed to his side), "and two from Smolensk" (he showed the scar on his cheek). "And this leg which won't walk, as you see. It was at the great battle of Borodino that I got that. My God it was wonderful! You ought to have seen that; it was a deluge of fire. You gave us a tough job; you can boast of that! And on my word, in spite of the cough I caught, I should be ready to begin again. I pity those who did not see it."

"I was there," said Pierre.

"Really!" pursued the Frenchman. "Well, so much the better. You are fine enemies, though. Oh, it was wonderful, M. Pierre. Your grenadiers were superb. I saw them six times in succession close ranks and march as though on parade. Fine fellows. Our king of Naples, who knows all about it, cried, Bravo! Ah, ah, soldiers like ourselves," he said after a moment's silence. "So much the better, so much the better, M. Pierre. Terrible in war . . . gallant, with the fair" (he winked with a smile)—"There you have the French, M. Pierre, eh?"

The captain was so naïvely gay and self-satisfied that Pierre almost winked in response. Probably the word "gallant" brought the captain to reflect on the state of things in Moscow.

"By the way, tell me, is it true that all the women have left Moscow? What a queer idea! What had they to fear?"

"Would not the French ladies quit Paris, if the Russians were to enter it?" said Pierre.

"Ha—ha—ha! . . ." The Frenchman gave vent to a gay chuckle, slapping Pierre on the shoulder. "That's a good one, that is," he went on. "Paris . . . But Paris . . ."

"Paris is the capital of the world," said Pierre, finishing the sentence for him.

The captain looked at Pierre. He had the habit of stopping short in the middle of conversation, and staring intently with his laughing eyes.

"Well, if you had not told me you are a Russian, I would have wagered you were a Parisian. You have that indescribable something . . ."

"I have been in Paris. I spent years there," said Pierre.

"One can see that! Paris! A man who does not know Paris is a savage . . . A Parisian can be told two leagues off. Paris—it is Talma, la Duschénois, Potier, the Sorbonne, the boulevards." Perceiving that the conclusion of his phrase was somewhat of an anticlimax, he added hurriedly, "There is only one Paris in the world. . . . You have been in Paris, and you remain Russian. Well, I don't think the less of you for that."

After the days he had spent alone with his gloomy thoughts, Pierre, under the influence of the wine he had drunk, could not help taking pleasure in being with this good-humoured and naïve person.

"To return to your ladies, they are said to be beautiful. What a silly idea to go and bury themselves in the steppes, when the French army is in Moscow. What a chance they have lost. Your peasants are different; but you civilised people ought to know better than that. We have taken Vienna, Berlin, Madrid, Naples, Rome, Warsaw—all the capitals in the world. We are feared, but we are loved. We are worth knowing. And then the Emperor . . ." he was beginning, but Pierre interrupted him.

"The Emperor," repeated Pierre, and his face suddenly wore an embarrassed look. "What of the Emperor?"

"The Emperor? He is generosity, mercy, justice, order, genius—that is the Emperor. It is I, Ramballe, who tell you that. I was his enemy eight years ago. My father was an exiled count. But he has conquered me, that man. He has taken hold of me. I could not resist the spectacle of the greatness and glory with which he was covering France. When I understood what he wanted, when I saw he was preparing a bed of laurels for us, I said to myself: 'That is a monarch.' And I gave myself up to him. Oh yes, he is the greatest man of the centuries, past and to come."

"And is he in Moscow?" Pierre asked, hesitating and looking guilty.

The Frenchman gazed at Pierre's guilty face, and grinned.

"No, he will make his entry to-morrow," he said, and went on.

Their conversation was interrupted by several voices shouting at the gates, and Morel coming in to tell the captain that some Würtemberg hussars had come and wanted to tie up their horses in the yard in which the captain's had been put up.

The captain went out to the entrance and gave some loud commands.

When he came back into the room, Pierre was sitting with his head in his hands. His face expressed suffering. He really was at that moment suffering. As soon as the captain had gone out, and Pierre had been left alone, he suddenly came to himself, and recognised the position he was in. It was not that Moscow had been taken, not that these lucky conquerors were making themselves at home there and patronising him, bitterly as Pierre felt it, that tortured him at that moment. He was tortured by the consciousness of his own weakness. The few glasses of wine he had drunk, the chat with this good-natured fellow, had dissipated that mood of concentrated gloom, which he had been living in for the last few days, and which was essential for carrying out his plan. The pistol and the dagger and the peasant's coat were ready, Napoleon was making his entry the next day. Pierre felt it absolutely necessary to kill him. But he felt now that he would not do it. He struggled against the consciousness of his own weakness, but he vaguely felt that he could not overcome it, that his past gloomy train of ideas, of vengeance, murder, and self-sacrifice, had been blown away like dust at contact with the first human being.

The captain came into the room, limping a little, and whistling some tune.

The Frenchman's chatter that had amused Pierre struck him now as revolting. And his whistling a tune, and his gait, and his gesture in twisting his moustaches, all seemed insulting to Pierre now.

"I'll go away at once, I won't say another word to him," thought Pierre. He thought this, yet went on sitting in the same place. Some strange feeling of weakness riveted him to his place.

The captain, on the contrary, seemed in exceedingly good spirits. He walked a couple of times up and down the room. His eyes sparkled and his moustaches slightly twitched as though he were smiling to himself at some amusing notion.

He sat down facing Pierre.

"Well, another bottle of this Moscow claret, eh? Morel, warm us another bottle!" the captain shouted gaily.

Morel brought another bottle of wine. The captain looked at Pierre and was obviously struck by his troubled face. With genuine regret and sympathy he bent over him.

"Eh, we are sad!" he said, touching Pierre on the hand. "Can I have hurt you? No, really, have you anything against me?" he questioned. "Perhaps it is owing to the situation of affairs?"

Pierre made no reply, but looked cordially into the Frenchman's eyes. This expression of sympathy was pleasant to him.

"My word of honour, to say nothing of what I owe you, I have a liking for you. Can I do anything for you? Dispose of me. It is for life and death. With my hand and my heart, I say so," he said, slapping himself on the chest.

"Thank you," said Pierre. The captain gazed at Pierre and his face suddenly brightened.

"Ah, in that case, I drink to our friendship," he cried gaily, pouring out two glasses of wine.

Pierre took the glass and emptied it. Ramballe emptied his and pressed Pierre's hand once more.

"Yes, my dear friend, such are the freaks of fortune," he began. "Who would have said I should be a soldier and captain of dragoons in the service of Bonaparte, as we used to call him. And yet here I am at Moscow with him. I must tell you, my dear fellow," he continued in the mournful and measured voice of a man who intends to tell a long story, "our name is one of the most ancient in France."

And with the easy and naïve unreserve of a Frenchman, the captain told Pierre the history of his forefathers, his childhood, boyhood, and manhood, and all his relations, his fortunes, and domestic affairs.

"But all that is only the setting of life; the real thing is love. Love! Eh, M. Pierre?" he said, warming up. "Another glass."

Pierre again emptied his glass, and filled himself a third.

"O women! Women!" and the captain, gazing with moist eyes at Pierre, began talking of love and his adventures. They were very numerous, as might readily be believed, judging from the officer's conceited, handsome face and the eager enthusiasm with which he talked of women. Although all Ramballe's accounts of his love affairs were characterised by that peculiar nastiness in which the French find the unique charm and poetry of love, the captain told his stories with such genuine conviction that he was the only man who had tasted and known all the sweets of love, and he described the women he had known in such an alluring fashion that Pierre listened to him with curiosity.

It was evident that *l'amour* the Frenchman was so fond of was neither that low and simple kind of love Pierre had at one time felt for his wife, nor the romantic love, exaggerated by himself, that he felt for Natasha. For both those kinds of love Ramballe had an equal contempt. *L'amour* for which the Frenchman had a weakness consisted principally in an unnatural relation to the woman, and in combinations of monstrous circumstances which lent the chief charm to the feeling.

Thus the captain related the touching history of his love for a fascinating marquise of five-and-thirty, and at the same time for a charming, innocent child of seventeen, the daughter of the fascinating marquise. The conflict of generosity between mother and daughter, ending in the mother sacrificing herself and offering her daughter in marriage to her lover, even now, though it was a memory in the remote past, moved the captain deeply. Then he related an episode in which the husband played the part of the lover, and he—the lover—the part of the husband, and several comic episodes among his reminiscences of Germany, where the husbands eat cabbage soup, and where the young girls are too flaxen-haired.

The last episode was one in Poland, still fresh in the captain's memory. The story was that he had saved the life of a Pole—the episode of saving life was continually cropping up in the captain's anecdotes—and that Pole had intrusted to his care his bewitching wife, a Parisian in heart, while he himself entered the French service. The captain had been happy, the bewitching Polish lady had wanted to elope with him; but moved by a magnanimous impulse, the captain had restored the wife to the husband with the words: "I saved your life, and I save your honour."

As men often do at a late hour at night, and under the influence of wine, Pierre listened to the captain's stories, and while he followed and understood all he told him, he was also following a train of personal reminiscences. As he listened to those love affairs, his own love for Natasha suddenly came into his mind, and going over all the pictures of that love in his imagination, he mentally compared them with Ramballe's stories. As he heard the account of the conflict between love and duty, Pierre saw before him every detail of the meeting with Natasha at the Suharev Tower. That meeting had not at the time made much impression on him; he had not once thought of it since. But now it seemed to him that there was something very significant and romantic in it.

"Pierre, come here, I recognise you"; he could hear her words now, could see her eyes, her smile, her travelling cap, and the curl peeping out below it . . . And he felt that there was something moving, touching in all that.

When he had finished his tale about the bewitching Polish lady, the captain turned to Pierre with the inquiry whether he had had any similar experience of self-sacrifice for love and envy of a lawful husband.

Pierre lifted his head and began to explain that he looked upon love somewhat differently. He said he had all his life long loved one woman, and still loved her, and that that woman could never be his.

"Well!" said the captain.

Then Pierre explained that he had loved this woman from his earliest youth, but had not dared to think of her because she was too young, and he had been an illegitimate son, with no name of his own. Then when he had received a name and wealth, he had not dared think of her because he loved her too much, because he set her too high above all the world, and so even more above himself. On reaching this point, Pierre asked the captain, did he understand.

The captain made a gesture expressing that whether he understood it or not, he begged him to proceed.

The wine he had drunk, or an impulse of frankness, or the thought that this man did not know and never would know, any of the persons concerned in his story, or all together loosened Pierre's tongue. With faltering lips he told all his story; his marriage and the story of Natasha's love for his dearest friend and her betrayal of him, and all his own simple relations with her. In response to questions from Ramballe, he told him, too, what he had at first concealed—his position in society—and even disclosed his name.

Late in the night they went out together into the street. The night was warm and clear. On the left there was the glow of a fire that had broken out in Moscow, in some distant district. On the right a young crescent moon stood high in the sky. At the gates of the yard stood Gerasim, the cook, and two Frenchmen. Pierre could hear their laughter and talk, incomprehensible to one another. They were looking at the glow of the fire burning in the city.

There was nothing alarming in a small remote fire in the immense city.

Gazing at the lofty, starlit sky, at the moon, and the glow of the fire, Pierre felt a thrill of joyous and tender emotion. "How fair it all is! What more does one want?" he thought. And all at once, when he recalled his plan, his head seemed going round; he felt so giddy that he leaned against the fence so as not to fall.

Without taking leave of his new friend, Pierre left the gate with unsteady steps, and going back to his room lay down on the sofa and at once fell asleep.

From different roads, and with different feelings, the inhabitants running and driving away from Moscow, and the retreating troops gazed at the glow of the first fire that broke out in the city on the 2nd of September.

The Rostovs stopped for that night at a village twenty miles from Moscow. They had started so late on the 1st of September, the road had been so blocked by waggons and troops, so many things had been forgotten, and servants sent back to get them, that they had decided to halt for the first night five miles from Moscow. On the second day they waked late, and there were again so many delays that they only travelled fifteen miles further. At ten o'clock the Rostov family, and the wounded soldiers travelling with them, had all found places for the night in the yards and huts of the village. The servants, the Rostovs' coachmen, and the orderlies of the wounded officers, after settling their masters for the night, ate, fed their horses, and came out on to the porch of a hut.

One of the servants noticed in the dark night sky another small glow of fire in distant Moscow.

"There's another fire," said the man. All of them looked towards the glow.

"It's a big fire," said one; "yes, it's in Moscow, my friends."

No one answered this remark. And for a good while all gazed in silence at the flames of this new fire glowing far away. An old man, the count's valet, Danilo, came up to the crowd and called Mishka.

"What are you gaping at? . . . The count may ask for you and nobody to be found; go and put the clothes together."

"Oh, I only ran out for some water," said Mishka.

"And what do you say, Danilo? That's a fire in Moscow, isn't it?" said one of the footmen.

Danilo made no reply, and for a long while all were silent again. The glow spread wider, and flickered further and further away.

"God have mercy! . . . A wind and the drought . . . The log houses!" said a voice again.

"Look how it's spreading. O Lord! why, one can see the jackdaws! Lord, have mercy on us poor sinners!"

"They'll put it out, never fear."

"Who's to put it out?" cried the voice of Danilo, silent till that moment. His voice was quiet and deliberate. "Moscow is on fire!" he said. "It's she, our mother, the white city . . ." his voice broke, and he suddenly burst into the sobs of old age. And it seemed as though all had been waiting for that to grasp the import of the glow they were watching. Sighs were heard and muttered prayers, and the sobs of the old valet.

The valet on going in informed the count that Moscow was on fire. The count put on his dressing-gown and went out to look. With him went Sonya, who had not yet undressed, and Madame Schoss. Natasha and the countess were left alone within. Peter was no longer with the family; he had gone on ahead with his regiment.

The countess wept on hearing that Moscow was in flames. Natasha, pale, with staring eyes, sat on the bench under the holy images, the spot where she had first thrown herself down on entering, and took no notice of her father's words.

"Oh! how awful!" cried Sonya, coming in chilled and frightened from the yard. "All Moscow is burning; there's an awful fire! Natasha, do look; you can see now from the window here," she said. But Natasha stared at her, as though she did not understand what was asked of her, and fixed her eyes again on the corner of the stove. Natasha had been in this condition ever since the morning, when Sonya, to the amazement and anger of the countess, had for some incomprehensible reason thought fit to tell Natasha of Prince André's wound, and his presence among their train. The countess had been angry with Sonya, as she was very rarely angry. Sonya had cried and begged forgiveness, and now she wanted to atone for her fault.

"Look, Natasha, how it's burning," said Sonya.

"What's burning?" asked Natasha. "Oh yes, Moscow."

And to get rid of Sonya, and not hurt her by a refusal, she moved her head towards the window, looking in such a way that it was evident she could see nothing, and sat down again in the same attitude as before.

"But you didn't see?"

"Yes, I really did see," she declared in a voice that implored to be left in peace.

The count came in again behind the partition wall and lay down. The countess went up to Natasha, put the back of her hand to her head, as she did when her daughter was ill, then touched her forehead with her lips, as though to find out whether she were feverish, and kissed her.

"You are chilled? You are shaking. You should lie down," she said.

"I'll lie down in a minute," said Natasha.

When Natasha had been told that morning that Prince André was seriously wounded, and was travelling with them, she had at the first moment asked a great many questions, how and why and where was he going; whether he were dangerously wounded, and whether she could see him. But after she had been told that she could not see him, that his wound was a serious one, but that his life was not in danger, though she plainly did not believe what was told her, she saw that she would get the same answer whatever she said, and gave up asking questions. All the way Natasha had sat motionless in the corner of the carriage with those wide eyes, the look in which the countess knew so well and dreaded so much. And she was sitting in just the same way now on the bench in the hut.

"Natasha, undress, darling, get into my bed."

For the countess only a bed had been made up on a bedstead. Madame Schoss and the two girls were to sleep on hay on the floor.

"No, mother, I'll lie here on the floor," said Natasha irritably. She went to the window and opened it. She put her head out into the damp night air, and the countess saw her slender neck shaking with sobs and heaving against the window frame. Natasha knew that Prince André was in the same block of huts that they were in, that he was in the next hut just across the porch, but . . .

"Go to bed, darling, go to bed, my pet," said the countess, lightly touching Natasha's shoulder. "Come, go to bed."

"Oh yes . . . I'll go to bed at once, at once," said Natasha, hurriedly undressing, and breaking the strings of her petticoats. Dropping off her dress, and putting on a dressing-jacket, she sat down on the bed made up on the floor, tucking her feet under her, and flinging her short, fine hair over her shoulder, began plaiting it. Then she sank softly down on the sheet laid on the hay nearest the door.

"Natasha, you lie in the middle," said Sonya.

"I'll stay here," said Natasha. "And do go to bed," she added in a tone of annoyance. And she buried her face in the pillow.

The countess, Madame Schoss, and Sonya hurriedly undressed and went to bed. The lamp before the holy images was the only light left in the room. But out of doors the fire in the distance lighted up the sky, and there were peasants shouting at the tavern across the street, and the moan of a wounded soldier could be heard.

For a long while Natasha listened to the sounds that reached her from within and without, and she did not stir. She heard at first her mother's prayers and sighs, the creaking of her bed under her, Madame Schoss's familiar, whistling snore, Sonya's soft breathing. Then the countess called to Natasha. Natasha did not answer.

"I think she's asleep," answered Sonya.

The countess, after a brief silence, spoke again, but this time no one answered her.

Soon after this Natasha caught the sound of her mother's even breathing. Natasha did not stir, though her little bare foot, poking out below the quilt, felt frozen against the uncovered floor.

A cricket chirped in a crack. A cock crowed far way, and another answered close by. The shouts died away in the tavern. Natasha sat up.

"Sonya! Are you asleep? Mother!" she whispered. No one answered. Slowly and cautiously Natasha got up, crossed herself, and stepped with her slender, supple, bare feet on to the dirty, cold floor. The boards creaked. She took hold of the cold door-handle.

It seemed to her that something with heavy, rhythmical strokes was banging on all the walls of the hut; it was the beating of her own heart, torn with dread, with love and terror.

She opened the door, stepped over the lintel, and on to the damp, cold earth of the passage outside. Her bare foot felt a man asleep; she stepped over him, and opened the door of the hut in which Prince André was lying.

In that hut it was dark. A tallow candle with a great, smouldering wick stood on a bench in the further corner, by a bed, on which something was lying.

An irresistible force drew her forward. She made one cautious step, another, and found herself in the middle of the small hut, cumbered up with baggage. On the bench, under the holy images, lay another man, and on the floor were two more figures, the doctor and the valet.

The smouldering candle flickered up, and she saw Prince André, lying with his arms stretched out on the quilt.

He was just the same as ever; but the flush on his face, his shining eyes, gazing at her, and especially the soft, childlike neck, showing above the lay-down collar of the nightshirt, gave him a peculiarly innocent, childlike look, such as she had never seen in him before. She ran up to him and dropped on her knees.

He smiled, and held out his hand to her.

He knew that it was the real, living Natasha, and did not wonder, but quietly rejoiced.

"Natasha! It is you. Natasha!" he whispered.

Natasha began kissing his hand, softly touching it with her lips.

"Forgive me!" she said in a whisper, lifting her head and glancing at him. "Forgive me!"

"I love you," said Prince André.

"Forgive . . ."

"Forgive what?" asked Prince André.

"Forgive me for what I di . . . id," Natasha murmured in a hardly audible, broken whisper, and again and again she softly put her lips to his hand.

"I love thee more, better than before," said Prince André, lifting her face with his hand so that he could look into her eyes that gazed at him with timid and joyful love.

At that moment there was a knock at the door. A maid had been sent by the countess in search of her daughter.

Like a sleep-walker awakened in the midst of her trance, Natasha walked out of the room, and getting back to her hut, sank sobbing on her bed.

From that day on, at all the halts and resting-places on the remainder of the Rostovs' journey, Natasha never left Prince André's side. And the doctor was forced to admit that he had not expected from a young girl so much fortitude, nor skill in nursing a wounded man.

Terrible as it was for the countess to think that Prince André might die on the road in her daughter's arms, she could not stop Natasha. Although with the renewal of affectionate relations between Prince André and Natasha the idea did occur that in case he recovered their old engagement would be renewed, no one—least of all Natasha and Prince André—spoke of this.

Pierre awoke late on the 3rd of September. His head ached, the clothes in which he had slept without undressing bound his body, and he had a vague sense in his heart of something shameful he had done the evening before. That something was his talk with Captain Ramballe.

It was eleven o'clock but it seemed a particularly dull day. Pierre stood up, rubbed his eyes, and seeing the pistol with its engraved stock—Gerasim had put it back on the writing-table—Pierre remembered where he was and what was in store for him that day.

"Am I not too late already?" Pierre wondered.

No, probably *he* would not make his entry into Moscow before twelve o'clock. Pierre did not allow himself to reflect on what lay before him, but hurried to act.

Fixing his clothes, Pierre took up the pistol and was about to set off. But then for the first time he wondered how he was to carry the weapon in the street. Even under his full coat it would be hard to conceal a big pistol. Moreover, the pistol was now unloaded, and Pierre could not succeed in reloading it in time. "The dagger will do as well," Pierre said to himself. And he hurriedly took the blunt, notched dagger in a green scabbard, which he had bought, together with the pistol, at the Suharev Tower, and hid it under his waistcoat.

Tying the sash round his peasant's coat, and pulling his cap forward, Pierre walked along the corridor, trying not to make any noise that might attract the captain, and slipped out into the street.

The fire, at which he had gazed so indifferently the evening before, had spread during the night. Moscow was on fire at several points. There were fires at the same time in Carriage Row, the Bazaar, and Povarsky, and the timber market and the barges in the river were also in a blaze.

Pierre's way lay across a side street, and from there across to the chapel of Nikola Yavlenny, where he had long before in his imagination fixed on the spot at which the deed ought to be done. Most of the houses had their gates and shutters closed. The streets and lanes were deserted; there was a smell of burning and smoke in the air. Now and then he met Russians with uneasy and timid faces, and Frenchmen with a look of the camp about them, walking in the middle of the street.

With haste and horror he bore within him his intention as something strange and fearful to him, fearing—from the experience of the previous night—to lose it. But Pierre was not destined to carry out his plan; he was detained on the way. Besides, Napoleon had four hours earlier crossed the city to the Kremlin; and he was by then sitting in the royal study in the Kremlin palace in the gloomiest temper, giving orders for immediately extinguishing the fires, preventing pillage, and reassuring the inhabitants. But Pierre knew nothing of that; entirely absorbed in what lay before him, he was suffering the anguish men suffer when they persist in undertaking a task impossible for them. He was tortured by the dread that he would be weak at the decisive moment, and so would lose his respect for himself.

As Pierre got nearer to the place he had chosen for the deed, the smoke grew thicker and thicker. Tongues of flame shot up here and there behind the house-tops. He met more people in the streets, and these people were in great excitement. As he walked along a path, across the large open space, Pierre suddenly heard close by him the sound of a woman, crying desperately. He stood still, as though awakened from a dream, and raised his head.

On the dried-up, dusty grass on one side of the path lay a heap of household goods: feather-beds, a samovar, holy images, and boxes. On the ground, near the boxes, sat a thin woman, no longer young, with long, projecting front teeth, dressed in a black cloak and cap. The woman was weeping violently, swaying to and fro, and muttering something. Two little girls, from ten to twelve years old, dressed in dirty, short frocks and cloaks, were gazing at their mother, with pale, frightened faces. A little boy of seven, in a coat and a huge cap, obviously not his own, was crying in an old nurse's arms. A bare-legged, dirty servant-girl was sitting on a chest; she had let down her blond hair, and was pulling out the singed hairs, sniffing at them. The husband, a short, stooping man, in a uniform, with little, wheel-shaped whiskers, and smooth locks of hair, peeping out from under his cap, was moving the chests from under one another and dragging garments of some sort from under them.

The woman almost flung herself at Pierre's feet as soon as she saw him.

"Merciful heavens, good Christian folk, save me, help me,

kind sir! . . . Somebody, help me," she cried. "My little girl! . . . My daughter! . . . My youngest girl left behind! . . . She's burnt! Oo . . . er! What a fate I have nursed thee for . . . Ooo!"

"Hush, Marya Nikolaevna," the husband said in a low voice to his wife, evidently only to justify himself before a stranger. "Sister must have taken her, nothing else can have happened to her!" he added.

"Monster!" the woman screeched furiously, her tears suddenly ceasing. "There is no heart in you, you have no feeling for your own child. Any other man would have rescued her from the fire. But he is a monster, not a man, not a father. You are a noble man," the woman turned to Pierre sobbing and talking quickly. "The row was on fire—they rushed in to tell us. The girl screamed: Fire! We rushed to get our things out. Just as we were, we escaped. . . . This is all we could snatch up . . . The blessed images, we look at the children, and the bed that was my dowry, and all the rest is lost. Katitchka's missing. Oooo! O Lord! . . ." And again she broke into sobs. "My darling baby! Burnt! Burnt!"

"But where, where was she left?" asked Pierre.

"Good, kind sir!" she screamed, clutching at his legs. "Benefactor, set my heart at rest anyway . . . Aniska, go, you slut, show the way," she bawled to the servant-girl, opening her mouth wide in her anger, and displaying her long teeth more than ever.

"Show me, I . . . I . . . I'll do something," Pierre gasped.

The dirty servant-girl came out from behind the box and walked on in front along the path with her coarse, bare feet.

Pierre followed the girl. The whole street was full of clouds of black smoke. Tongues of flame shot up here and there out of these clouds. A great crowd had gathered in front of the fire. In the middle of the street stood a French general, saying something to those about him. Pierre, accompanied by the servant-girl, was approaching the place where the French general stood; but the French soldiers stopped him.

"Can't pass," a voice shouted to him.

"This way, master," bawled the girl. "We'll cut across by the lane."

Pierre turned back, breaking into a run now and then to keep pace with her. The girl ran across the street, turned into a lane on the left, and passing three houses, turned in at a gate on the right.

"It's just here," she said, and running across a yard, she opened a little gate in a paling-fence, and stopping short, pointed out to Pierre a small wooden lodge, which was on fire.

As Pierre went in at the little gate, he felt a rush of heat, and stopped short. He could not go close to the lodge and drew back into the garden of a house which some French soldiers were looting.

Suddenly he heard a child wailing. Under a garden seat lay a girl of three years old, in a pink frock.

Pierre, breathless with joy, ran up to the child, and would have taken her in his arms. But seeing a stranger, the little girl—a scrofulous-looking, unattractive child, very like her mother—screamed and ran away. Pierre caught her, however, and lifted her up in his arms. She squealed in desperate fury, and tried to free herself with her little hands, and to bite him with her dirty, dribbling mouth. Pierre had a sense of horror and disgust. But he made an effort to overcome it, and not to drop the child, and ran back with it.

When Pierre, after running across courtyards and by-lanes, got back with his burden, he did not for the first moment recognise the place from which he had set out to look for the baby: it was so packed with people and goods, dragged out of the houses. Besides the Russian families with their belongings saved from the fire, there were a good many French soldiers.

Neither the official nor his wife were in the place where Pierre had left them. He walked about among the crowd, scanning the different faces he came across. He could not help noticing an Armenian family, consisting of a very old man, of a handsome Oriental cast of face, dressed in a new cloth-faced sheepskin and new boots; an old woman of a similar type; and a young woman. The young woman—a very young woman—struck Pierre as a perfect example of Oriental beauty, with her sharply marked, arched, black eyebrows, her extraordinarily soft, bright colour and beautiful, expressionless, oval face. In her rich satin mantle, she suggested a tender, tropical plant, thrown down in the snow. She was sitting on the baggage a little behind the old woman, and her big, black, long-shaped eyes, with their long lashes, were fixed immovably on the ground. Evidently she was aware of her beauty, and fearful because of it. Her face struck Pierre, and in his haste he looked round at her several times as he passed along by the fence. Reaching the fence, and still failing to find the people he was looking for, Pierre stood still and looked round.

Several Russians, both men and women, gathered about him.

"Have you lost some one, good sir? Are you a gentleman yourself, or what? Whose baby is it?" they asked him.

Pierre answered that the baby belonged to a woman in a black mantle, who had been sitting at this spot with her children. And he asked whether any one knew her, and where she had gone.

"Why, it must be the Anferovs," said an old deacon addressing a pock-marked peasant woman. "Lord, have mercy on us! Lord, have mercy on us!" he added, in his professional bass.

"The Anferovs," said the woman. "Why, the Anferovs have been gone since early this morning. It will either be Marya Nikolaevna's or Ivanova's."

"He says a woman, and Marya Nikolaevna's a lady," said a house-serf.

"You know her, then; a thin woman—long teeth," said Pierre.

"To be sure, Marya Nikolaevna. They moved off into the garden as soon as these wolves pounced down on us," said the woman, indicating the French soldiers.

"O Lord, have mercy on us!" the deacon added again.

"You go on yonder, they are there. It's she, for sure. She was quite beside herself with crying," said the woman again. "It's she. Here, this way."

But Pierre was not listening to the woman. He was looking at the Armenian family and two French soldiers, who had approached them. One of the soldiers, on going up to the Armenians, said something, and at once took hold of the old man's legs, and the old man began pulling off his boots. The other soldier stopped facing the beautiful Armenian girl, with his hands in his pockets, and stared at her without speaking or moving.

"Take it, take the child," said Pierre, handing the child to the peasant woman. "You give her to them, you take her," he almost shouted to the woman, setting the screaming child on the ground, and looking round again at the Frenchmen and the Armenian family. The old man was by now sitting barefoot. The French soldier had just taken the second boot from him, and was slapping the boots together. The old man was saying something with a sob. The second soldier moved up to the young woman, and taking his hands out of his pockets, caught hold of her neck.

The beautiful Armenian girl still sat in the same immobile pose, with her long lashes drooping, and seemed not to see and not to feel what the soldier was doing to her.

While Pierre ran the few steps that separated him from them, the French soldier tore the necklace from her neck. The young woman, clutching at her neck with both hands, screamed shrilly.

"Let that woman alone!" Pierre roared in a voice hoarse with rage, and seizing the soldier by the shoulders he shoved him away. The soldier fell down, got up, and ran away. His comrade, dropping the boots, pulled out his sword, and moved up to Pierre.

Pierre was in that frenzy in which he remembered nothing, and his strength was increased tenfold. He dashed at the Frenchman, and before he had time to draw his dagger, he knocked him down, and pounded him with his fists. Shouts of approval were heard from the crowd and at the same time a patrol of French came riding round the corner. They trotted up to Pierre, and surrounded him. Pierre had no recollection of what followed. He remembered that he beat somebody, and was beaten, and that in the end he found that his hands were tied, that a group of French soldiers were standing round him, ransacking his clothes.

"Lieutenant, he has a dagger," were the first words Pierre grasped the meaning of.

"Ah, a weapon," said the officer, and he turned to the soldier, who had been taken with Pierre. "Very good, very good; you can tell all your story at the court-martial," said the officer. And then he turned to Pierre: "Do you know French?"

Pierre looked about him with bloodshot eyes, and made no reply.

"Do you speak French?" the officer, keeping his distance, repeated the question. "Call the interpreter." From the ranks a little man came forward, in a Russian civilian dress. Pierre, from his dress and speech, at once recognised in him a French shopman from some Moscow store.

"He doesn't look like a common man," said the interpreter, looking at Pierre.

"Oh, oh, he looks very like an incendiary," said the officer. "Ask him who he is," he added.

"Who are you?" asked the interpreter in his Frenchified Russian. "You must answer the officer."

"I will not say who I am. I am your prisoner. Take me away." Pierre said suddenly in French.

"Ah! ah!" commented the officer, knitting his brows, "Well, march then!"

1812

BOOK TWELVE

On the 26th of August, the very day of the battle of Borodino, there was a *soirée* at Anna Pavlovna's, the chief attraction of which was to be the reading of the Metropolitan's letter, written on the occasion of his sending to the Tsar the holy picture of Saint Sergey. This letter was looked upon as a model of patriotic ecclesiastical eloquence. It was to be read by Prince Vassily himself, who was famed for his fine elocution.

This reading, as was always the case with Anna Pavlovna's entertainments, had a political significance. She was expecting at this *soirée* several important people who were to be made to feel ashamed of patronising the French theatre, and to be roused to patriotic fervour. A good many people had already arrived, but Anna Pavlovna did not yet see those persons whose presence in her drawing-room was necessary, and she was therefore starting general topics of conversation before proceeding to the reading.

The news of the day in Petersburg was the illness of Countess Bezuhov. The countess had been taken ill a few days before; she had missed several entertainments, of which she was usually the ornament, and it was said that she was seeing no one, and that instead of the celebrated Petersburg physicians, who usually attended her, she had put herself into the hands of some Italian doctor, who was treating her in some new and extraordinary way.

Everybody was well aware that the charming countess's illness was due to inconveniences arising from marrying two husbands at once, and that the Italian doctor's treatment consisted in the removal of such inconvenience. But in the presence of Anna Pavlovna no one ventured to think about this.

"They say the poor countess is very ill. The doctor says it is *angina pectoris.*"

"*Angina?* Oh, that's a terrible illness."

"They say the rivals are reconciled, thanks to the *angina* . . ." The word *angina* was repeated with great relish.

"I am told the old count is touching. He cried like a child when the doctor told him there was danger."

"Oh, it would be a terrible loss. She is a fascinating woman."

"You speak of the poor countess," said Anna Pavlovna, coming up. "I sent to inquire after her. I was told she was getting better. Oh, no doubt of it, she is the most charming woman in the world," said Anna Pavlovna, with a smile at her own enthusiasm. "We belong to different camps, but that does not prevent me from appreciating her as she deserves. She is very unhappy," added Anna Pavlovna.

Supposing that by these last words Anna Pavlovna had slightly lifted the veil of mystery that hung over the countess's illness, one unwary young man permitted himself to express surprise that no well-known doctor had been called in, and that the countess should be treated by a charlatan, who might make use of dangerous remedies.

"Your information may be better than mine," cried Anna Pavlovna, falling upon the inexperienced youth with sudden viciousness. "But I have it on good authority that this doctor is a very learned and skilful man. He is the private physician of the Queen of Spain."

An awkward silence followed and was broken by the arrival of those guests whom Anna Pavlovna was waiting to convert. Smiling, she summoned Prince Vassily to the table, and setting two candles and a manuscript before him, she begged him to begin. There was a general hush.

"Most high and gracious Emperor and Tsar!" Prince Vassily boomed out sternly, and he looked round at his audience as though to inquire whether any one had anything to say against that. But nobody said anything. "The chief capital city, Moscow, the New Jerusalem, receives *her* Messiah"—he threw a sudden emphasis on the *"her"*—"even as a mother in the embraces of her zealous sons, and through the gathering darkness, foreseeing the dazzling glory of thy dominion, sings aloud in triumph: 'Hosanna! Blessed be He that cometh!' "

Prince Vassily uttered these last words in a tearful voice.

Many of the guests were visibly cowed, as though wondering what they had done wrong. Anna Pavlovna murmured the words over beforehand, as old women whisper the prayer to come at communion: "Let the base and insolent Goliath . . ." she whispered.

Prince Vassily continued: "Let the base and insolent Goliath from the borders of France encompass the realm of Russia with the horrors of death; lowly faith, the sling of the Russian David, shall smite a swift blow at the head of his pride that thirsteth for blood. This holy image of the most venerable Saint Sergey, of old a zealous champion of our country's welfare, is borne to your imperial majesty. I grieve that my failing strength hinders me from the joy of your most gracious presence. Fervent prayers I am offering up to Heaven, and the Almighty will exalt the faithful and fulfil in His mercy the hopes of your majesty."

"What force! What style!" was murmured in applause of the reader and the author. Roused by this appeal, Anna Pavlovna's guests continued for a long while talking of the position of the country, and made various surmises as to the issue of the battle to be fought in a few days.

"You will see," said Anna Pavlovna, "that to-morrow on the Emperor's birthday we shall get news. I have a presentiment of something good."

Anna Pavlovna's presentiment was in fact fulfilled. Next day, during the special service at court in honour of the Tsar's birthday, Prince Volkonsky was called out of church and received a despatch from Kutuzov. This was the despatch Kutuzov had sent off on the day of the battle. Kutuzov wrote that the Russians had not retreated a single step, that the French had lost far more than the Russians, that he was writing off in haste from the field of battle before he had time to collect the latest intelligence. So it had been a victory, it appeared. And at once, without leaving church, the assembled court offered up thanks to the Creator for His help, and for the victory.

Anna Pavlovna's presentiment had been fulfilled, and the whole morning a mood of joyous festivity prevailed in the town. Every one accepted the victory as a conclusive one, and some people were already beginning to talk of Napoleon's having been taken prisoner, of his overthrow, and the selection of a new sovereign for France. The only note to darken the news was the fact that Bagration had lost his life.

Next day no news came from the army, and the public voice began to waver. The courtiers suffered agonies over the agonies of suspense which the Tsar was suffering.

"Think of the Emperor's position!" the courtiers said; and they no longer sang the praises of Kutuzov as two days before, but upbraided him as the cause of the Tsar's uneasiness that day. Prince Vassily no longer boasted of Kutuzov, but was mute when the commander-in-chief was the subject of conversation. Moreover, on the evening of that day everything seemed to conspire to throw the Petersburg world into agitation and uneasiness: a terrible piece of news came to add to their alarms. Countess Helen Bezuhov died.

At larger gatherings every one repeated the official story that Countess Bezuhov had died of a terrible attack of *angina pectoris*. But in intimate circles people told in detail how the Queen of Spain's own medical attendant had prescribed for Helen small doses of a certain drug; but that Helen, tortured by the old count's suspecting her, and by her husband's not having answered her letter, had suddenly taken an enormous dose of the drug prescribed, and had died in agonies before assistance could be given. The story ran that Prince Vassily and the old count had been going to start proceedings against the Italian; but the doctor had produced letters from the unhappy deceased of such a character that they had promptly dropped the matter.

Conversation centred round three melancholy facts—the Tsar's state of suspense, the loss of Bagration, and the death of Helen.

On the third day after Kutuzov's despatch, a country gentleman arrived in Petersburg from Moscow, and the news of the disaster at Borodino and of the surrender of Moscow to the French was all over the town. This was awful! Think of the position of the Emperor! Kutuzov was a traitor, and, during the "visits of condolence" paid to Prince Vassily on the occasion of his daughter's death, when he spoke of Kutuzov, whose praises he had once sung so loudly—it was pardonable in his grief to forget what he had said before—he said that nothing else was to be expected from a blind and dissolute old man.

"I only wonder how such a man could possibly be trusted with the fate of Russia."

Nine days after the abandonment of Moscow, a courier from Kutuzov reached Petersburg with the official news of the surrender of Moscow. This courier was a Frenchman, Michaud, who did not know Russian, yet was, "though a foreigner, Russian in heart and soul," as he used to say of himself.

The Tsar at once received the messenger in his study.

Michaud had such a melancholy face when he was shown into the Tsar's study that the Tsar asked him at once: "Do you bring me sad news, colonel?"

"Very sad, sire, the surrender of Moscow," answered Michaud, casting his eyes down with a sigh.

"Can they have surrendered my ancient capital without a battle?" the Tsar asked quickly, suddenly flushing.

Michaud respectfully gave the message he had been commanded to give from Kutuzov, that is, that there was no possibility of fighting before Moscow, and that seeing there was no chance but either to lose the army and Moscow or to lose Moscow alone, the commander-in-chief had been obliged to choose the latter.

The Tsar listened without a word, not looking at Michaud.

"Has the enemy entered the city?" he asked.

"Yes, sire, and by now the city is in ashes. I left it all in flames," said Michaud; but glancing at the Tsar, Michaud was horrified at what he had done. The Tsar was breathing hard and rapidly, his lower lip was twitching, and his fine blue eyes were for a moment wet with tears.

But that lasted only a moment. The Tsar suddenly frowned, as though vexed with himself for his own weakness; and raising his head, he addressed Michaud in a firm voice: "I see, colonel, from all that is happening to us that Providence requires great sacrifices of us. I am ready to submit to His will in everything.

A few days before the battle of Borodino, Nicholas Rostov was commissioned to go to Voronezh to purchase horses for his division.

Only one who has spent several months continuously in the atmosphere of an army in the field can imagine the delight Nicholas felt when he got out of the region overspread by the troops with their foraging parties, trains of provisions, and hospitals; when he saw no more soldiers, army waggons, and filthy traces of the camp, but villages of peasants and peasant women, gentlemen's country houses, fields with grazing oxen, and station-houses and sleepy overseers. He rejoiced as though he were seeing it all for the first time. What in particular remained for a long while a wonder and a joy to him was the sight of women, young and healthy, without dozens of officers hanging about every one of them.

In the happiest frame of mind, Nicholas reached the hotel at Voronezh at night, ordered everything of which he had so long been deprived in the army, and next day, after shaving with special care and putting on the full-dress uniform he had not worn for so long past, he drove off to present himself to the authorities.

The commander of the militia of the district was a civilian general, an old gentleman, who evidently found amusement in his military duties and rank. He gave Nicholas a brusque reception (supposing that this was the military manner), and cross-examining him with an important air, as though he had a right to do so, he expressed his approval and disapproval, as though called upon to give his verdict on the management of the war. Nicholas was in such high spirits that this only amused him.

From the commander of militia, he went to the governor's. The governor was a brisk little man, very affable and unpretentious. He mentioned to Nicholas the stud-farms, where he might obtain horses, recommended him to a horse-dealer in the town, and a gentleman living twenty miles from the town, who had the best horses. And promised him every assistance.

"You are Count Rostov's son? My wife was a great friend

of your mother's. We receive on Thursdays: to-day is Thursday, pray come in, quite without ceremony," said the governor, as he took leave of him.

Nicholas took a posting carriage, and making his quartermaster get in beside him, galloped straight off from the governor's to the gentleman with the stud of fine horses twenty miles away.

The country gentleman turned out to be an old cavalry officer, a bachelor, a great horse-fancier, a sportsman, and the owner of a smoking-room, of hundred-year-old herb-brandy, of some old Hungarian wine, and of superb horses.

Nicholas bought for six thousand roubles seventeen stallions, all perfect examples of their breeds. After dining and drinking a glass or so too much of the Hungarian wine, Nicholas galloped back over the most atrociously bad road in the happiest frame of mind, continually urging the driver on, so that he might be in time for the *soirée* at the governor's.

After dressing, scenting himself, and douching his head with cold water, Nicholas made his appearance at the governor's.

It was not a ball, and nothing had been said about dancing; but every one knew that Katerina Petrovna would play waltzes and écossaises on the clavichord, and that there would be dancing, and so every one had come dressed for a ball.

Provincial life in the year 1812 went on exactly the same as always, the only difference being that the provincial towns were livelier owing to the presence of many wealthy families from Moscow, that, as in everything going on at that time in Russia, there was perceptible in the gaiety a certain devil-may-care, desperate recklessness, and also that the small talk indispensable between people was now not about the weather and common acquaintances, but about Moscow and the army and Napoleon.

The gathering at the governor's consisted of the best society in Voronezh.

There were a great many ladies, among them several Moscow acquaintances of Nicholas'; but among the men there was no one who could be compared with the cavalier of St. George, the gallant hussar, and good-natured, well-bred, young Count Rostov.

As soon as Nicholas came in in his full-dress uniform, diffusing a fragrance of scent and wine, people clustered round him. All eyes were turned on him, and he felt at once that he had stepped into a position that just suited him in a provincial town—a position always agreeable, but now after months at the front, intoxicatingly delightful—that of a universal favourite. Not only at the posting-stations, at the taverns, and in the smoking-room of the horse-breeding gentleman, had he found servant-girls flattered by his attention, but here, at the governor's assembly, there were (so it seemed to Nicholas) an inexhaustible multitude of young married ladies and pretty girls, who were only waiting with impatience for him to notice them. The ladies and the young girls flirted with him, and the old people began even from this first evening bestirring themselves to try and get this gallant young rake of an hussar married and settled down. Among these was the governor's wife herself, who received Rostov as though he were a near kinsman.

Katerina Petrovna did in fact proceed to play waltzes and écossaises, and dancing began, in which Nicholas fascinated the company more than ever by his elegance. He surprised every one indeed by his peculiarly free and easy style in dancing. Nicholas was a little surprised himself at his own style of dancing at that *soirée*. He had never danced in that manner at Moscow, and would indeed have regarded such an extremely free and easy manner of dancing as not correct, as bad style; but here he felt it incumbent on him to astonish them all by something extraordinary, something that they would be sure to take for the usual thing in the capital, though new to them in the provinces.

All the evening Nicholas paid the most marked attention to a blue-eyed, plump, and pleasing little blonde, the wife of one of the provincial officials. With the naïve conviction of young men who are enjoying themselves, that other men's wives are created for their special benefit, Nicholas never left this lady's side, and treated her husband in a friendly way, almost as though there were a private understanding between them, as though they knew without speaking of it how well they, that is, how Nicholas and the wife, would get on. The husband did not, however, appear to share this conviction, and tried to take a gloomy tone with Rostov. But Nicholas' good-humoured naïveté was so limitless that at times the husband could not help being drawn into his gay humour. Towards the end of the evening, however, as the wife's face grew more flushed and animated, the husband's grew steadily more melancholy and stolid, as though they had a given allowance of liveliness between them, and as the wife's increased, the husband's dwindled.

With a smile that never left his lips, Nicholas sat bent a little forward on a low chair, and stooping close over his blonde beauty, he paid her compliments.

The good-natured governor's wife came up to them with a disapproving air.

"Anna Ignatyevna wants to see you, Nicholas," she said,

pronouncing the name in such a way that Rostov was at once aware that Anna Ignatyevna was a very great lady. "Come, Nicholas. You let me call you so, don't you?"

"Oh, yes, *ma tante*. Who is she?"

"Anna Ignatyevna Malvintsev. She has heard about you from her niece, how you rescued her . . . Do you guess? . . ."

"Oh, I rescued so many!" cried Nicholas.

"Her niece, Princess Bolkonsky. She is here in Voronezh with her aunt. Oho! how he blushes! Eh?"

"Not at all, nonsense, *ma tante*."

"Oh, very well, very well. Oh! oh! What a boy he is!"

The governor's wife led him up to a tall and very stout lady in a blue toque, who had just finished a game of cards with the people of greatest consequence in the town. This was Madame Malvintsev, Princess Mary's aunt on her mother's side, a wealthy, childless widow, who always lived in Voronezh. She was standing up, counting her losses, when Nicholas came up to her.

She dropped her eyelids with a severe and dignified air, glanced at him, and went on upbraiding the general who had been winning from her.

"Delighted, my dear boy," she said, holding out her hand to him. "Pray come and see me."

After saying a few words about Princess Mary and her late father, whom Madame Malvintsev had evidently disliked, and inquiring what Nicholas knew about Prince André, who was apparently also not in her good graces, the dignified old lady dismissed him, repeating her invitation to come and see her.

Nicholas promised to do so and blushed again as he took leave of Madame Malvintsev.

On leaving Madame Malvintsev, Rostov would have gone back to the dance, but the governor's wife laid her plump little hand on his sleeve, and saying that she wanted to have a few words with him, led him into a sitting-room.

"Do you know, my dear," said the governor's wife with a serious expression on her good-natured, little face, "this is really the match for you. If you like, I will try and arrange it."

"Whom do you mean, *ma tante?*" asked Nicholas.

"I will make a match for you with the princess. Katerina Petrovna talks of Lili, but I say, no—the princess. Do you wish it? I am sure your mother will be grateful. Really, she is such a splendid girl, charming! And she is by no means so very plain."

"Not at all so," said Nicholas, as though offended at the idea. "As for me, *ma tante,* as a soldier should, I don't force myself on any one, nor refuse anything that turns up," said Rostov, before he had time to consider what he was saying.

"So remember then. This is no jesting matter."

"How could it be!"

"Yes, yes," said the governor's wife, as though talking to herself. "And between ourselves my dear, you are too attentive to the other—the blonde. One feels sorry for the husband, really . . ."

"Oh no, we are quite friendly," said Nicholas in the simplicity of his heart: it had never occurred to him that such an agreeable pastime for him could be other than agreeable to any one else.

"What a stupid thing I said to the governor's wife though!" suddenly came into Nicholas' mind at supper. "She really will begin to arrange a match, and Sonya? . . ."

The governor's wife called on Madame Malvintsev the day after her *soirée* and talked over her plans with her, explaining that though under present circumstances a formal engagement was of course not to be thought of, yet they might bring the young people together. Having received the aunt's approval, they began to speak of Nicholas in Princess Mary's presence, singing his praises, and describing how he had blushed on hearing the princess's name. However Princess Mary's emotion was not one of joy, but of pain. Her inner harmony was destroyed, and desires, doubts, self-reproach, and hope sprang up again.

In the two days that followed before Nicholas called, Princess Mary was continually considering what her behaviour ought to be in regard to him. At one time, she made up her mind that she would not come down into the drawing-room when he came to see her aunt, that it was not suitable for her in her deep mourning to receive visitors. Then she thought this would be rude after what he had done for her. Then the idea struck her that her aunt and the governor's wife had views of some sort upon her and Rostov; their words and glances had seemed at times to confirm this suspicion. Then she told herself that it was only her own depravity that could make her think this of them: could they possibly fail to realise that in her position, still wearing the heaviest mourning, such match-making would be an insult both to her and to her father's memory? On the supposition that she would go down to see him, Princess Mary imagined the words he would say to her, and she would say to him. And at one moment, those words seemed to her undeservedly frigid, at the next, they struck her as carrying too much meaning. Above all she dreaded the embarrassment, which she felt would be sure to overcome her, and betray her, as soon as she saw him.

But when, on Sunday after morning prayers, the footman came into the drawing-room to announce that Count Rostov had called, the princess showed no sign of embarrassment, only a faint flush came into her cheeks, and her eyes shone with a new, radiant light.

When Rostov came into the room, the princess dropped her head for an instant, as though to give time for their visitor to greet her aunt; and then at the very moment when Nicholas turned to her, she raised her head and met his gaze. With a movement full of dignity and grace, she rose, held out her delicate, soft hand to him, and spoke in a voice in which for the first time there was the thrill of deep, womanly chest notes. Mademoiselle Bourienne, who was in the drawing-room, gazed at Princess Mary with bewildered surprise. The most accomplished coquette herself, she could not have manœuvred better on meeting a man whom she wanted to attract.

"Either black suits her wonderfully, or she really has grown better looking without my noticing it. And above all, such tact and grace!" thought Mademoiselle Bourienne.

Had Princess Mary been capable of reflection at that moment, she would have been even more astonished than Mademoiselle Bourienne at the change that had taken place in her. From the moment she set eyes on that sweet, loved face, some new force of life seemed to take possession of her, and to drive her to speak and act apart from her own will. From the time Nicholas entered the room, her face was transformed. For the first time all the pure, spiritual, inner travail in which she had lived till then came out in her face. All her inner searchings of spirit, her self-reproach, her sufferings, her striving for goodness, her resignation, her love, her self-sacrifice—all this was radiant now in those luminous eyes, in the delicate smile, in every feature of her face.

Nicholas saw all this as clearly as though he had known her whole life. He felt that he was in the presence of a creature utterly different from and better than all those he had met up to that moment, and, above all, far better than he was himself.

The conversation was of the simplest and most insignificant kind. They talked of the war, unconsciously, like every one else, exaggerating their sadness on that subject. They talked of their last meeting—and Nicholas then tried to change the subject; they talked of the kind-hearted governor's wife, of Nicholas' relations, and of Princess Mary's.

Princess Mary did not talk of her brother, but changed the conversation, as soon as her aunt mentioned Prince André. It was evident that of the troubles of Russia she could speak artificially, but her brother was a subject too near her heart, and she neither would nor could speak lightly of him. Nicholas noticed this, as indeed with a keenness of observation not usual with him, he noticed every shade of Princess Mary's character, and everything confirmed him in the conviction that she was an altogether rare and original being.

Princess Mary was not going into society at all on account of her mourning, and Nicholas did not think it proper to call on them again. But the governor's wife still persisted in her match-making, and repeating to Nicholas something flattering Princess Mary had said of him, and *vice versa,* kept urging that Nicholas should declare himself to Princess Mary. With this object, she arranged that the young people should meet at the reverend father's before Mass.

Though Rostov did tell the governor's wife that he would make no sort of declaration to Princess Mary, he promised to be there. He knew that to declare his feelings to Princess Mary after his promise to Sonya would be base.

After seeing Princess Mary, though his manner of life remained externally the same, all his former pleasures lost their charm for him, and he often thought of her. But he never thought of her, as he had thought of all the young girls he had met in society, nor as he had long, and sometimes with enthusiasm, thought of Sonya. Like almost every honest-hearted young man, he had thought of every young girl as of a possible future wife; the white morning wrapper, the wife behind the samovar, children, their attitude to one another. But when he thought of Princess Mary, he could never form any picture of his future married life with her. Even if he tried to do so, it all seemed incoherent and false. And it only filled him with dread.

The terrible news of the battle of Borodino, of the Russian losses in killed and wounded, and the even more terrible news of the loss of Moscow reached Voronezh in the middle of September. Princess Mary, learning of her brother's wound only from the newspapers, and having no definite information about him, was preparing to set off to try and reach him.

On hearing the news of the battle of Borodino and of the abandonment of Moscow, Nicholas felt, not despair, rage, revenge, nor any such feeling, but a sudden weariness and vexation with everything at Voronezh, and a sense of awkwardness and uneasy conscience. All the conversations he listened to seemed to him insincere. He did not know what to think of it all, and felt that only in the regiment would all become clear to him again. He hurried to conclude the purchase of horses, and was often without good cause ill-tempered with his servant and quartermaster.

Several days before his departure there was a service in the cathedral and Nicholas attended. He was a little behind the governor and when the service was ending, the governor's wife beckoned him to her.

"Did you see the princess?" she said, with a motion of her hand towards a lady in black standing behind the choir.

Nicholas recognised Princess Mary at once, not so much from the profile he saw under her hat as from the feeling of watchful solicitude, awe, and pity which came over him. Princess Mary, obviously buried in her own thoughts, was making the last signs of the cross before leaving the church.

Nicholas gazed in wonder at her face. It was the same face he had seen before; there was the same look of refined, inner, spiritual travail; but now there was an utterly different light in it. There was a touching expression of sadness, of prayer and of hope in it. With the same absence of hesitation as he had felt before in her presence, without waiting for the governor's wife to urge him, without asking himself whether it were right, whether it were proper for him to address her here in church, Nicholas went up to her, and said he had heard of her trouble and grieved with his whole heart to hear of it. As soon as she heard his voice, a vivid colour glowed in her face, lighting up at once her joy and her sorrow.

"One thing I wanted to tell you, princess," said Nicholas, "that is, that if Prince André were not alive, since he is a colonel, it would be announced immediately in the gazettes."

The princess looked at him.

"And I know from so many instances that a wound from a splinter" (the papers said it was from a grenade) "is either immediately fatal or else very slight," Nicholas went on. "We must hope for the best, and I am certain . . ."

Princess Mary interrupted him.

"Oh, it would be so aw . . ." she began. And choking up with tears she bent her head and, glancing gratefully at him, followed her aunt.

That evening Nicholas did not go out anywhere, but stayed at home to finish some accounts with the horse-traders. By the time he had finished his work it was rather late to go out anywhere, but still early to go to bed, and Nicholas spent a long while walking up and down the room, thinking over his life, a thing that he rarely did.

Princess Mary had made an agreeable impression on him at Bogutcharovo. The fact of his meeting her then in such striking circumstances, and of his mother having at one time pitched precisely on her as the wealthy heiress suitable for him, had led him to look at her with special attention. During his stay at Voronezh, that impression had become, not merely a pleasing, but a very strong one. Nicholas was impressed by the peculiar, moral beauty which he discerned in her at this time. But his meeting with Princess Mary that morning in church had, Nicholas felt, gone more deeply to his heart than he desired for his peace of mind. That pale, delicate, melancholy face, those luminous eyes, those soft, gracious gestures, and, above all, the deep and tender melancholy expressed in all her features, moved him with sympathy.

"She is a marvellous girl! An angel!" he said to himself. "Why am I not free? Why was I in such a hurry with Sonya?" And involuntarily he compared the two. He tried to picture what would have happened if he had been free, and in what way he would have made her an offer and she would have become his wife. No, he could not imagine that. A feeling of dread came over him and that picture would take no definite shape. With Sonya he had long ago made his picture of the future, and it was all so simple and clear, just because it was all made up and he knew all there was in Sonya. But with Princess Mary he could not picture his future life, because he did not understand her—he simply loved her.

There was something light-hearted, something of child's play in his dreams of Sonya. But to dream of Princess Mary was difficult and a little terrible.

"What do I want? Freedom, release from Sonya. Nothing but misery can come of my marrying her. Muddle, mother's grief . . . our position . . . a muddle, a fearful muddle! Besides, I don't even love her. No, I don't love her in the right way. . . ."

He had tears in his eyes and a lump in his throat when Lavrushka came in with papers.

"A courier has come," said Lavrushka in a sleepy voice, "from the governor. A letter for you."

Nicholas took the two letters. One was from his mother, the other from Sonya. He knew them from the handwriting, and broke open Sonya's letter first. He had hardly read a few lines when his face turned white and his eyes opened wide in dismay and joy.

The knot fastening his freedom, that had seemed so impossible to disentangle, had been undone by this unexpected letter from Sonya. She wrote that their late misfortunes, the loss of almost the whole of the Rostovs' property in Moscow, and the countess's frequently expressed desire that Nicholas should marry Princess Bolkonsky, and his silence and coldness of late, all taken together led her to decide to set him free from his promise, and to give him back complete liberty.

"It would be too painful to me to think that I could be a cause of sorrow and discord in the family which has overwhelmed me with benefits," she wrote. "And the one aim of my love is the happiness of those I love, and therefore I beseech you, Nicholas, to consider yourself free, and to know that in spite of everything, no one can love you more truly than your—SONYA."

His mother's letter described the last days in Moscow, the

departure, the fire and the loss of the whole of their property. The countess wrote too that Prince André had been among the train of wounded soldiers who had travelled with them. He was still in a very critical condition, but that the doctor said now that there was more hope. Sonya and Natasha were nursing him.

With this letter Nicholas went next day to call on Princess Mary. Neither Nicholas nor Princess Mary said a word as to all that was implied by the words: "Natasha is nursing him"; but thanks to this letter, Nicholas was brought suddenly into intimate relations, almost those of a kinsman, with the princess.

Sonya's letter to Nicholas was written at Troitsa. It had been prompted by the following. The idea of marrying Nicholas to a wealthy heiress had taken more and more possession of the old countess's mind. She knew that Sonya was the obstacle in the way of this. And Sonya's life had of late, and especially after the letter in which Nicholas described his meeting with Princess Mary at Bogutcharovo, become more and more difficult in the countess's house. The countess never let slip an opportunity for making some cruel or humiliating allusion to Sonya. And a few days before they set out from Moscow the countess, distressed and overwrought by all that was happening, sent for Sonya, and instead of insistence and upbraiding, besought her with tears and entreaties to repay all that had been done for her by sacrificing herself, and breaking off her engagement to Nicholas. "I shall have no peace of mind till you make me this promise," she said.

Sonya sobbed hysterically, answered through her tears that she would do anything, that she was ready for anything; but she did not give a direct promise, and in her heart she could not bring herself to what was demanded of her. She had to sacrifice herself for the happiness of the family that had brought her up and provided for her. To sacrifice herself for others was Sonya's habit. Her position in the house was such that only by way of sacrifice could she show her virtues, and she was accustomed to sacrificing herself and liked it. But in every self-sacrificing action in the past she had been happily conscious that by her very self-sacrifice she was heightening her value in the eyes of herself and others, and becoming more worthy of Nicholas, whom she loved beyond everything in life. But now her sacrifice would consist of the renunciation of what constituted for her the whole reward of sacrifice, and the whole meaning of life. And for the first time she felt bitterness against the people who had befriended her only to torment her. She felt envy of Natasha, who had never had any experience of the kind, who had never been required to make sacrifices, and made other people sacrifice themselves for her, and was yet loved by every one. And for the first time Sonya felt that there was beginning to grow up out of her quiet, pure love for Nicholas a passionate feeling, which stood above all principles, and virtue, and religion. And under the influence of that passion, Sonya, whose life of dependence had unconsciously trained her to reserve, gave the countess vague, indefinite answers, avoided talking with her, and resolved to wait until she saw Nicholas again, not to set him free, but, on the contrary, to bind him to her for ever.

The fuss and the horror of the Rostovs' last days in Moscow had smothered the gloomy thoughts that were weighing on Sonya. She was glad to find an escape from them in work. But when she heard of Prince André's presence in their house, in spite of all the genuine compassion she felt for him, and for Natasha, a joyful and superstitious feeling that it was God's will that she should not be parted from Nicholas took possession of her. She knew that brought together now, under such terrible circumstances, Natasha and Prince André would love one another again; and that then, owing to the relationship that would (in accordance with the laws of the Orthodox Church) exist between them, Nicholas could not be married to Princess Mary. In spite of all the awfulness of what was happening during the last day or two in Moscow and the first days of the journey, that feeling, that consciousness of the intervention of Providence in her personal affairs, was a source of joy to Sonya.

At the Troitsa monastery the Rostovs made the first long break in their journey. In the hostel of the monastery three big rooms were assigned to them, one of which was occupied by Prince André. He was a great deal better. Natasha was sitting with him. In the next room were the count and the countess reverently conversing with the superior, who was paying a visit to his old acquaintances and patrons. Sonya was sitting with them, tormented by curiosity as to what Prince André and Natasha were saying. She heard the sounds of their voices through the door.

The door of Prince André's room opened. Natasha came out with an excited face, and not noticing the monk, who rose to meet her, and pulled back his wide sleeve off his right hand, she went up to Sonya and took her by the arm.

"Natasha, what are you about! Come here," said the countess.

Natasha went up to receive the blessing, and the superior counselled her to turn for aid to God and to His saint.

Immediately after the superior had gone out, Natasha took her by the arm, and went with her into the empty third room.

"Sonya, yes, he will live," she said. "Sonya, how happy I am, and how wretched! Sonya, darling, everything is just as it used to be. He cannot die. . . . Because . . . Be . . . cause . . ." and Natasha burst into tears.

"Yes! I knew it would be! Thank God," said Sonya. "He will live."

Sonya was no less excited than Natasha, both by grief and fears, and by her own hopes, of which she had spoken to no one. Sobbing, she kissed and comforted Natasha. "If only he lives!" she thought.

A few minutes later, Prince André rang his bell, and Natasha went in to him; while Sonya, in a state of excitement and emotion such as she had rarely experienced, remained in the window, pondering over all the strangeness of what was happening.

That day there was an opportunity of sending letters to the army, and the countess wrote a letter to her son.

"Sonya," said the countess, raising her head, as her niece passed by her. "Sonya, won't you write to Nicholas?" said the countess, in a soft and trembling voice; and in the tired eyes, that looked at her over the spectacles, Sonya read all that the countess meant by those words. Those eyes expressed entreaty and dread of a refusal and shame at having to beg, and readiness for unforgiving hatred in case of refusal.

Sonya went up to the countess, and kneeling down, kissed her hand.

"I will write, mother," she said.

And she sat down, and several times interrupted by the tears that dimmed her velvety black eyes, she wrote to Nicholas.

In the guard-room to which Pierre had been taken, the officer and soldiers in charge treated him with respect. Their attitude to him betrayed doubt who he might be—perhaps a person of great importance.

But when on the morning of the next day the guard was relieved, they saw in him only number seventeen of the Russian prisoners who were to be detained for some reason by order of higher authorities. If there were anything peculiar about Pierre, in his coachman's coat, it lay only in his undaunted air of concentrated thought, and in his excellent French. In spite of that, Pierre was put that day with the other suspicious characters who had been arrested, since the room he had occupied was wanted for an officer.

All the Russians detained with Pierre were persons of the lowest class. And all of them, recognising Pierre as a gentleman, held aloof from him all the more for his speaking French. Pierre mournfully heard their jeers at his expense.

On the following evening, Pierre learned that all the prisoners were to be tried for arson. The day after, Pierre was taken with the rest to a house where were sitting a French general with white moustaches, two colonels, and other Frenchmen with scarfs on their shoulders. With that peculiar exactitude and definiteness, which is always employed in the examination of prisoners and is supposed to preclude all human weaknesses, they put questions to Pierre and the others, asking who he was, where he had been, with what object, and so on.

Pierre felt puzzled why all these questions were asked him. He had a feeling that the whole aim of the proceeding was to convict him. To the inquiry what he was doing when he was arrested, Pierre replied with a certain tragic dignity that he was carrying back to its parents a child he had "rescued from the flames." Why was he fighting with the soldiers? Pierre replied that he was defending a woman. . . . He was pulled up; this was irrelevant. With what object had he been in the courtyard of a burning house where he had been seen by several witnesses? He answered that he was going out to see what was going on in Moscow. He was pulled up again. He had not been asked, he was told, where he was going, but with what object he was near the fire. Who was he? The first question was repeated, to which he had said he did not want to answer. Again he replied that he could not answer that.

"Write that down, that's bad. Very bad," the general with the white whiskers and the red, flushed face said sternly.

After this Pierre was moved with thirteen of the others to a coach-house belonging to a merchant's house on the Crimean Ford. As he passed through the street, Pierre could hardly breathe for the smoke, which seemed hanging over the whole city. Fires could be seen in various directions. Pierre did not at that time grasp what was implied by the burning of Moscow, and he gazed with horror at the fires.

In the coach-house Pierre spent the next four days, and in the course of those four days he learned, from the conversation of the French soldiers, that all the prisoners were awaiting the decision of their fate by a marshal. What marshal, Pierre could not learn from the soldiers. For the soldiers, this marshal was evidently the highest and somewhat mysterious symbol of power.

On the 8th of September an officer came into the prisoners' coach-house. With an indolent and indifferent glance at all the prisoners, he gave the officer on guard orders to have them decently dressed before bringing them before the marshal. In an hour a company of soldiers arrived, and Pierre with the thirteen others was taken to the Virgin's Meadow. It was a fine day and the air was exceptionally clear. The smoke did not now hang low over the city but rose up in columns into the pure air. Flames were nowhere to be seen; but columns of smoke were rising up on all sides, and all Moscow, all that Pierre could see, was one great fire. On all sides he saw places laid waste, with stoves and pipes left standing in them, and now and then the charred walls of a stone house.

Here and there could be seen churches that had not been touched by the fire. The Kremlin uninjured, rose white in the distance, with towers and Ivan the Great. Close at hand, the cupola of the Monastery of the New Virgin shone brightly, and the bells for service rang out gaily from it. Those bells reminded Pierre that it was Sunday and the festival of the birth of the Virgin Mother. But there seemed to be no one to keep this holiday; on all sides they saw the ruin wrought by the fires, and the only Russians they met were a few tattered and frightened-looking people.

Pierre was led with the other prisoners to the right side of the Virgin's Meadow, not far from the monastery, and taken up to a big, white house with an immense garden. It was the house of Prince Shtcherbatov, and Pierre had often been inside it in former days to see its owner. Now, as he learnt from the talk of the soldiers, it was occupied by one of Napoleon's marshals, Davoust.

They were led up to the entrance, and taken into the house, one at a time. Pierre was the sixth to be led in. Through a glass-roofed gallery, a vestibule, and a hall, all familiar to Pierre, he was led to the long, low-pitched study, at the door of which stood an adjutant.

Davoust was sitting at a table at the end of the room, his spectacles on his nose, looking up something in a document that lay before him. Without raising his eyes, he asked: "Who are you?"

Pierre was silent. Davoust was not to Pierre simply a French general; to Pierre Davoust was a man notorious for his cruelty. Pierre felt that every second of delay might cost him his life. But he did not know what to say. To say the same as he had said at the first examination he did not dare; to disclose his name and his position would be both dangerous and shameful. But before he had time to come to any decision, Davoust raised his head, thrust his spectacles up on his forehead, and looked intently at Pierre.

"I know this man," he said, in a frigid, measured tone, obviously counting on frightening Pierre. The chill that had been running down Pierre's back seemed to clutch his head in a vice. "He's a Russian spy," said Davoust addressing a general in the room, whom Pierre had not noticed.

Pierre began speaking with sudden rapidity.

"Non, monseigneur," he said, suddenly recalling that Davoust was a duke, "you could not know me. I am a militia officer, and I have not quitted Moscow."

"Your name?" repeated Davoust.

"Bezuhov."

"What proof is there that you are not lying?"

"Monseigneur!" cried Pierre in a voice not of offence but of supplication.

Davoust looked intently at Pierre. "How can you prove to me the truth of what you say?" said Davoust coldly.

Pierre thought of Ramballe, and mentioned his name and regiment and the street and house where he could be found.

"You are not what you say," Davoust said again.

In a trembling, breaking voice, Pierre began to bring forward proofs of the truth of his testimony. But at that moment an adjutant came in and said something to Davoust.

Davoust beamed at the news brought him, and began buttoning up his uniform. Apparently he completely forgot about Pierre. When the adjutant reminded him of the prisoner, he nodded with a frown, and said to take him away. But where were they to take him—Pierre did not know: whether back to the shed or the place prepared for their execution which his companions had pointed out to him as they passed through the Virgin's Meadow.

From Prince Shtcherbatov's house the prisoners were taken straight down the Virgin's Meadow, to the left of the Convent of the Virgin, and toward a vegetable garden in which stood a post. Beyond the post a deep pit had been dug and the freshly turned earth had been heaped up around it. A large crowd stood in a semi-circle around the post and pit. The crowd consisted of a small number of Russians and a large number of Napoleon's soldiers off duty: Germans, Italians and Frenchmen in varied uniforms. To the right and to the left of the post stood ranks of French soldiers in dark-blue uniforms with red epaulettes, and wearing Hessians and shakos.

The "criminals" were lined up according to a certain order which was contained in a list (Pierre was sixth in line) and led to the post. Several drums suddenly rolled from both sides, and Pierre felt as though with this sound part of his soul was being torn away. He lost the capacity of thought and reflection. He was only able to see and hear. And he had only one desire, the desire to have done quickly that terrible thing that was about to be done.

A French official wearing a sash across his chest came up

to the right end of the row of prisoners and read the sentence in Russian and in French.

Then two pairs of French soldiers came over to the prisoners and, following the officer's order, took two convicts with shaven heads who were first on the line. The convicts, when they came to the post, both stopped, and while sacks were being brought they silently stared all around. One of them kept crossing himself, the other kept scratching his back and twisting his lips into a smile. The soldiers, with nervous hands, bandaged their eyes, put the sacks over their heads and tied them to the post.

A dozen sharpshooters with muskets marched out with firm, measured steps from behind the rows of soldiers and halted eight paces from the post. Pierre turned away so as not to see what was about to happen. Suddenly there was a crackling and a crashing that to Pierre seemed louder than the most terrifying thunderclap, and he turned to look. There was smoke, and the Frenchmen, their faces pale and their hands trembling, were doing something at the pit. The next two prisoners were now led up. And these two also looked around at everyone in exactly the same way, silently, with their eyes alone, begging for help and obviously neither comprehending nor believing what was about to happen.

Pierre tried not to look and again turned away; but again there was a horrible crash and with it smoke, somebody's blood and the pale, frightened faces of the French soldiers, once more busy at the post, fumbling with trembling hands. Pierre, breathing heavily, looked around as though to ask, "what does it all mean?" The same question was reflected in the eyes of everyone whose glance met Pierre's.

On the faces of all the Russians, on the faces of the French soldiers, and their officers, on all without exception, he read the same fear, horror and conflict that he felt in his own heart. "But who is doing this, really? They are all suffering as I am! Who is it? Who?"

"Sharpshooters of the 86th, forward!" somebody shouted. The fifth man, the one standing next to Pierre, was led forward—alone. Pierre did not understand that he was saved—that he and all the others had been brought here only to witness the execution. With growing horror, experiencing neither joy nor relief, he kept watching everything that happened around him. The fifth man was a young factory worker in a loose coat. As soon as they touched him he jumped back in terror and clutched at Pierre. Pierre shuddered and tore away from him. The factory worker was unable to walk. They dragged him off shouting and screaming. When they got him as far as the post he fell suddenly silent. He stood waiting for his eyes to be covered, waiting like the others, and like a wounded animal he kept looking around with burning eyes. He wrapped his loose coat around himself and scratched one bare foot with the other.

When they bandaged his eyes he adjusted the knot at the back of his head, which felt uncomfortable; then, when they stood him against the blood-spattered post, he pitched back, and, since he felt awkward in that position, shifted again, set his feet down evenly, and then leaned back quietly.

The word of command sounded, and after it the shots from eight muskets. But Pierre, however hard he tried afterwards to remember, heard not the slightest sound. He only saw how the factory worker suddenly sagged against the ropes, how blood appeared in two spots, and how the ropes slackened under the weight of the sagging body so that the factory worker, dropping his head unnaturally, sat down, one leg turning under. Pierre ran up to the post. No one stopped him. Around the factory worker some frightened, pale men were doing something. The lower jaw of one old, bewhiskered Frenchman was trembling as he untied the ropes. The body fell. The soldiers awkwardly and hurriedly dragged it beyond the post and began to push it down into the pit.

Pierre looked down into the pit and saw that the factory worker lay there with his knees up, close to his head, one shoulder higher than the other. And this shoulder was convulsively, rhythmically moving up and down. But already shovelfuls of dirt were falling on the whole body. One of the soldiers shouted at Pierre in an angry voice, telling him to get back. But Pierre failed to understand him and went on standing beside the post, and no one chased him away.

When the pit was finally filled, another command was heard. Pierre was led back to his place, and the French soldiers standing in formation made a half-turn and started to march slowly by the post. The twenty-four sharpshooters with unloaded muskets, who had stood in the center of the circle, now ran back to their places as their companies filed past.

Pierre stared with dazed eyes as these sharpshooters ran pair by pair from the circle. The crowd of Russians and Frenchmen now began to disperse. They all walked in silence, hanging their heads.

"That will teach them to set fires," said someone. Pierre looked around at the man who had spoken and saw that it was a French soldier who would have liked to find some sort of consolation for what had been done, but could not. Without finishing what he had started to say, he shrugged his shoulders and went on.

After the execution Pierre was separated from the other prisoners and left alone in a small, filthy church.

Towards evening a patrol sergeant, with two soldiers, came into the church and informed Pierre that he was pardoned, and was now going to the barracks of the prisoners of war. Pierre got up and went with the soldiers. He was taken to some sheds that had been rigged up in the upper part of the meadow out of charred boards, beams, and battens. Some twenty persons thronged round Pierre. He stared at them, with no idea of what these men were, why they were here, and what they wanted of him. He gazed at their faces and all seemed to him equally meaningless.

From the moment when Pierre saw that fearful murder committed by men who did not want to do it, it seemed as though the spring in his soul, by which everything was held together and given the semblance of life, had been wrenched out, and all seemed to have collapsed into a heap of meaningless refuse. It had annihilated in his soul all faith in the beneficent ordering of the universe, and in the soul of men, and in his own soul, and in God. This state of mind Pierre had experienced before, but never with such intensity as now. When such doubts had come upon him in the past they had arisen from his own fault. And at the very bottom of his heart Pierre had been aware then that salvation from that despair and from these doubts lay in his own hands. But now he felt that it was not his fault that the world was collapsing before his eyes, and that nothing was left but meaningless ruins. He felt that to get back to faith in life was not in his power.

Sitting in the straw against the wall, silent and motionless, Pierre opened, and then closed, his eyes. As soon as he shut his eyes he saw the face of the factory worker and the faces of the involuntary murderers. And he opened his eyes again and stared blankly about him in the darkness.

Close by him a little man was sitting bent up, of whose presence Pierre was first aware from the strong smell of sweat that rose at every movement he made. This man was unwinding his leg binders and although Pierre did not see his face, he was aware that he was continually glancing at him.

"You seen a lot of trouble, sir? Eh?" said the little man suddenly. And there was a tone of such friendliness and simplicity in the sing-song voice that Pierre wanted to answer, but his jaw quivered, and he felt tears rising.

At the same second, leaving no time for Pierre's embarrassment to appear, the little man said, in the same pleasant voice: "Ay, don't grieve," he said, in that tender, caressing sing-song in which old Russian peasant women talk. "Don't grieve, trouble lasts an hour, but life lasts for ever! Ay, ay, my dear. And we get on here fine, thank God. Nothing to vex us. They're men, too, and bad and good among them," he said; and, while still speaking, got with a supple movement on his knees to his feet, and clearing his throat walked away.

"Hey, the hussy, here she is!" Pierre heard at the end of the shed the same caressing voice. "Here she is, the hussy. She remembers me! There, there, lie down!" And the little man, pushing down a dog that was jumping up on him, came back to his place and sat down. In his hands he had something wrapped up in a cloth.

"Here, you taste this, sir," he said, returning to the respectful tone he had used at first, and untying and handing to Pierre several baked potatoes. "At dinner we had soup. But the potatoes are very good!"

Pierre had eaten nothing the whole day. He thanked the little man and began eating.

"Wait. You try them like this." He took out his clasp-knife and cut a potato in half and sprinkled it with salt from the cloth.

"The potatoes are good," he repeated. "You taste them like this."

It seemed to Pierre that he had never eaten anything so good.

"No, I am all right," said Pierre. "But why did they shoot those poor fellows? . . . The factory worker was not more than twenty."

"Tss . . . tss . . ." said the little man. "Sin, indeed . . . Sin . . . " he added quickly, just as though the words were already in his mouth and flew out of it by accident. He went on: "How was it, sir, you came to stay in Moscow like this?"

"I didn't think they would come so soon. I stayed by accident," said Pierre.

"But how did they take you? From your home?"

"No, I went out to see the fire, and they picked me up for arson."

"Where there's judgment, there there's falsehood," put in the little man.

"And have you been here long?" asked Pierre, as he munched the last potato.

"I? On Sunday they took me out of the hospital in Moscow."

"Who are you, a soldier?"

"We are soldiers of the Apsheron regiment. I was dying of fever. We were never told anything. There were twenty of us lying sick. And we had never a thought, never a guess of how it was."

"Well, and are you miserable here?" asked Pierre.

"Miserable, to be sure. My name's Platon, surname Karataev," he added, evidently to make it easier for Pierre to address him. "In the regiment they called me 'the little hawk.'

How can one help being sad? Moscow—she's the mother of cities. One must be sad to see it. Yes, the maggot gnaws the cabbage, but it dies before it's done; so the old folks used to say," he added quickly.

"What, what was that you said?" asked Pierre.

"I?" said Karataev. "I say it's not by our wit, but as God thinks fit," he said, supposing that he was repeating what he had said. And at once he went on: "Tell me, sir, and have you an estate from your fathers? And a house of your own? To be sure, your cup was overflowing! And a wife, too? And are your old parents living?" he asked. He was evidently disappointed that Pierre had no parents, especially that he did not have a mother.

"Wife for good counsel, mother-in-law for kind welcome, but none dear as your own mother!" said he. "And have you children?" he went on to ask. Pierre's answer seemed to disappoint him again, and he added: "Oh well, you are young. Please God, there will be. Only live in peace and happiness."

"But it makes no difference now," Pierre could not help saying.

"Ah, my dear man," answered Platon, "the beggar's bag and the prison walls none can be sure of escaping." He settled himself more comfortably, and cleared his throat, evidently preparing for a long story. "So it was like this, dear friend, when I used to be living at home," he began, "we have a rich heritage, a great deal of land, the peasants were well off, and our house—something to thank God for, indeed. Father used to go out to reap with six of us. We got along fine. Something like peasants we were. It came to pass . . ." and Platon Karataev told a long story of how he had gone into another man's land for wood, and had been caught by the keeper, how he had been flogged, tried, and sent for a soldier. "And do you know," said he, his voice changing from the smile on his face, "we thought it was a misfortune, while it was all for our happiness. My brother would have had to go if it hadn't been for my fault. And my younger brother had five little ones; while I, look, I left no one behind but my wife. I had a little girl, but God had taken her before I went for a soldier. I went home on leave, I must tell you. I find them all better off than ever. The yard full of beasts, the women folk at home, two brothers out earning wages. Only Mihailo, the youngest, at home. Father says all his children are alike; whichever finger's pricked, it hurts the same. And if they hadn't shaved Platon for a soldier, then Mihailo would have to go. He called us all together—would you believe it—made us stand before the holy picture. 'Mihailo,' says he, 'come here, bend down, and you, women, bow down; and you, grandchildren . . . Do you understand?' says he. Yes, so you see, my dear. Fate acts with reason. And we are always passing judgment; that's not right, and this doesn't suit us. Our happiness, is like water in a drag-net; you drag, and it is all puffed up, but pull it out and there's nothing. Yes, that's it." And Platon moved to a fresh seat in the straw.

After a short pause, Platon got up.

"Well, I dare say, you are sleepy?" he said, and he began crossing himself, murmuring: "Lord Jesus Christ, holy Saint Nikola, Frola and Lavra; Lord Jesus Christ, holy Saint Nikola, Frola and Lavra; Lord Jesus Christ—have mercy and save us!" he concluded, bowed down to the ground, got up, sighed, and sat down on his straw. "That's right. Let me lie down like a stone, O God, and rise up like new bread!" he murmured, and lay down, pulling his military coat over him.

"What prayer was that you recited?" asked Pierre.

"Eh?" said Platon. "Recited? I prayed to God. Don't you pray?"

"Yes, I do," said Pierre. "But what was it you said—Frola and Lavra?"

"Eh, to be sure," Platon answered quickly. "They're the horses' saints. One must think of the poor beasts, too," he said. "Why, the little hussy, she's curled up. You're warm, child of a bitch!" he said, feeling the dog at his feet; and, turning over again, he fell asleep at once.

In this shed, where Pierre spent four weeks, there were twenty-three soldiers, three officers, and two civilian officials, all prisoners.

They were all misty figures to Pierre afterwards, but Platon Karataev remained for ever in his mind the strongest and most precious memory, and the personification of everything Russian, kindly, and round. Platon's whole figure in his old military coat, girt round the waist with cord, in his forage-cap and bast shoes, was roundish. His head was perfectly round, his back, his chest, his shoulders, even his arms, which he always held as though he were about to embrace something, were round in their lines. His friendly smile and big, soft, brown eyes were also round.

Platon Karataev must have been over fifty to judge by his stories of the campaigns in which he had taken part. He did not himself know and could not determine how old he was. But his strong, dazzlingly white teeth showed in two unbroken semicircles whenever he laughed, as he often did, and all were good and sound. There was not a grey hair in his beard or on his head, and his whole frame had a look of suppleness and of unusual hardiness and endurance.

His face had an expression of innocence and youth in spite of the curving wrinkles on it; his voice had a pleasant sing-song note. But the great peculiarity of his talk was its spontaneity and readiness. He never thought of what he was saying, or of what he was going to say; and that gave a peculiar, irresistible persuasiveness to his rapid and genuine intonations.

His strength was such, during the first period of his imprisonment, that he seemed not to know what fatigue or sickness meant. Every evening as he lay down to sleep, he said: "Let me lie down, Lord, like a stone; let me rise up like new bread"; and every morning on getting up, he would shake his shoulder in the same way, saying: "Lie down and curl up, get up and shake yourself." And he had, in fact, only to lie down in order to sleep at once like a stone, and he had but to shake himself to be ready at once, on waking, without a second's delay, to set to work of some sort. He knew how to do everything, not particularly well, but not badly either. He baked, and cooked, and sewed, and planed, and cobbled boots. He was always busy, and only in the evenings allowed himself to indulge in conversation, which he loved. He sang songs, as the birds sing, obviously, because it was necessary to him to utter those sounds. And those sounds were always thin, tender, almost feminine, melancholy notes, and his face as he uttered them was very serious.

Being in prison, and having let his beard grow, he had apparently cast off all the soldier's ways that had been forced upon him and were not natural to him, and had unconsciously relapsed into his old peasant habits.

"A soldier discharged is the shirt outside the breeches again," he used to say. He did not care to talk of his life as a soldier, though he never complained, and often repeated that he had never once been beaten since he had been in the service. When he told stories, it was always by preference of his old and evidently precious memories of his life as a "Christian" or peasant. The proverbial sayings, of which his talk was full, were not the bold, and mostly indecent, sayings common among soldiers, but those peasant proverbs, which seem of so little meaning looked at separately, and gain all at once a significance of profound wisdom when uttered appropriately.

Often he would say something directly contrary to what he had said before, but both sayings were equally true. He liked talking, and talked well, adorning his speech with caressing epithets and proverbial sayings, which Pierre thought he often invented himself. But the great charm of his talk was that the simplest incidents, in his account of them, gained a character of seemliness and significance. He liked to listen to the fairy tales which one soldier used to tell—always the same ones over and over again. But most of all he liked to listen to stories of real life. He smiled as he listened to such stories, putting in words and asking questions, all aiming at bringing out clearly the moral beauty of the tale. Attachments, friendships, love, as Pierre understood them, Karataev had none; but he loved and lived on affectionate terms with every creature with whom he was thrown in life, and especially so with man—not with any particular man, but with the men who happened to be before his eyes. He loved his dog, loved his comrades, loved the French, loved Pierre, who was his neighbour. But Pierre felt that in spite of Karataev's affectionate tenderness to him, he would not suffer a moment's grief at parting from him. And Pierre began to have the same feeling towards Karataev.

To all the other soldiers Platon Karataev was the most ordinary soldier; they called him "little hawk," made good-humoured jokes at his expense, sent him to fetch things. But to Pierre, such as he appeared on that first night—an unfathomable, rounded-off, and everlasting personification of the spirit of simplicity and truth—so he remained to him for ever.

On hearing from Nicholas that her brother was at Yaroslavl with the Rostovs, Princess Mary, in spite of her aunt's efforts to dissuade her, prepared at once to go to him and to go not alone, but with her nephew.

Within a few days Princess Mary was ready for the journey. She rode in her immense travelling coach in which she had come to Voronezh, and had with her a covered trap and a waggon. She was accompanied by Mademoiselle Bourienne, little Nicholas, with his tutor, the old nurse, three maids, Tihon, a young valet, and a courier, whom her aunt was sending with her.

To travel by the usual route to Moscow was not to be thought of, and the roundabout route which Princess Mary was obliged to take was very long; from lack of posting horses difficult; and in the neighbourhood of Ryazan, where the French had begun to appear, dangerous.

After two long and hard weeks of travel, Princess Mary's party reached Yaroslavl, and her great coach, rumbling, jolting and swaying from side to side at last came to a standstill. It stopped in front of the house where the Rostovs were staying. The carriage-steps were let down with a crash.

The carriage-door was opened. On the left was water—a broad river; on the right, entrance steps. At the entrance were people, servants, and a rosy-faced girl with a thick coil of black hair, who smiled at her in an unpleasantly affected way. It was Sonya. The princess ran up the steps; the girl, smiling affectedly, said, "This way! This way!" and the princess found herself in the vestibule, facing an elderly woman of an Oriental type of face, who came to meet her. It was the countess. She embraced Princess Mary and kissed her.

"My child," she said, "I love you, and have known you a long while."

In spite of her emotion, Princess Mary knew it was the countess, and that she must say something to her. Not knowing how she did it, she uttered some polite French phrases in the tone in which she had been addressed, and asked, "How is he?"

"The doctor says there is no danger," said the countess. But as she said it she sighed.

"Where is he? Can I see him? Can I?" asked the princess.

"In a minute; in a minute, my dear. Is this his son?" the countess said, turning to little Nicholas, who came in with Dessalle. "We shall find room for every one; the house is large. Oh, what a charming boy!"

The countess led the princess into the drawing-room. Sonya began to talk with Mademoiselle Bourienne. The countess caressed the child. The old count came into the room to welcome the princess. He was extraordinarily changed since Princess Mary had seen him last. Then he had been a jaunty, gay, self-confident gentleman, now he seemed a pitiful, bewildered old creature. As he talked to the princess, he was continually looking about him, as though asking every one if he were doing the right thing. After the destruction of Moscow and the loss of his property, driven out of his accustomed rut, he had visibly lost the sense of his own importance, and felt that there was no place for him in life.

In spite of her one desire to see her brother without loss of time, and her vexation that at that moment, when all she wanted was to see him, they should entertain her conventionally with praises of her nephew, the princess observed all that was passing around her, and felt it inevitable for the time to fall in with the new order of things into which she had entered.

"This is my niece," said the countess, presenting Sonya. "You do not know her, princess?"

Princess Mary turned to Sonya, and trying to smother the feeling of hostility that rose up within her at the sight of this girl, she kissed her. But she felt painfully how out of keeping was the mood of every one around her with what was filling her own heart.

"Where is he?" she asked once more, addressing them all.

"He is downstairs. Natasha is with him," answered Sonya, flushing. "We have sent to ask. You are tired, I expect, princess?"

Tears of vexation came into Princess Mary's eyes. She turned away and was about to ask the countess again where she could see Prince André, when she heard at the door light, eager steps. She looked round and saw, almost running in, Natasha—that Natasha whom she had so disliked when they met long before in Moscow.

But Princess Mary had hardly glanced at Natasha's face before she understood that here was one who sincerely shared her grief, and was therefore her friend. And embracing her, burst into tears on her shoulder.

"Come, let us go to him, Mary," said Natasha at once, drawing her away into the next room.

Princess Mary lifted up her head, dried her eyes, and turned to Natasha. She felt that from her she would learn all, would understand all. "How . . ." she was beginning, but stopped short. She felt that no question nor answer could be put into words. Natasha's face and eyes would be sure to tell her all more clearly and more profoundly.

Natasha looked at her, but seemed to be in dread and in doubt whether to say or not to say all she knew. She seemed to feel that before those luminous eyes, piercing to the very bottom of her heart, it was impossible not to tell the whole truth. Natasha's lip suddenly twitched, and she broke into sobs, hiding her face in her hands.

Princess Mary then knew everything.

A few minutes later, Natasha told her that at first there had been danger from inflammation and the great pain, but that that had passed away at Troitsa, and the doctor had only been afraid of one thing—gangrene. But the risk of that, too, was almost over. When they reached Yaroslavl, the wound had began to suppurate, and the doctor had said that the suppuration might follow the regular course. Fever had set in. The doctor had said this fever was not so serious. "But two days ago," Natasha began, "all of a sudden a change came . . ." She struggled with her sobs. "O Mary, he is too good, he cannot, he cannot live, because . . ."

It happened in the evening. He was, as usual after dinner, slightly feverish, and his thoughts were particularly clear.

Natasha was in a low chair beside him, knitting a stocking, and sitting so as to screen the light of the candle from him. She had learned to knit since Prince André had once said to her that no one made such a good sick-nurse as an old nurse who knitted stockings, and that there was something soothing about knitting. Her slender fingers moved the needles rapidly with a slight click, and the dreamy profile of her drooping head could be clearly seen by him. She made a slight movement; the ball rolled off her knee. She started, glanced round at him, and, screening the light with her hand, bent over and picked up the ball.

He gazed at her without stirring. Then he began to think of the past. "Could it be, or could it not?" he wondered as he watched her and listened to the slight steel click of the needles. "Can fate have brought us together so strangely only for me to die? . . . Can the truth of life have been revealed to me only for me to have spent my life falsely? I love her more than anything in the world! But what am I to do if I love her?" Suddenly he unconsciously moaned from the habit he had fallen into in the course of his sufferings.

Hearing the sound, Natasha laid down her stocking, and went up to him.

"You must go to sleep."

"No. . . . I have been looking at you for a long while. No one but you gives me the same soft peace . . . The same light. I want to weep with gladness! Natasha, I love you too much! More than everything in the world!"

He was silent for a while.

"How good it would be!" And taking her hand, he kissed it.

His last hours passed in a simple and commonplace way. Princess Mary and Natasha, who never left his side, did not weep. The feelings of both of them were so strong that the external, horrible side of death did not affect them.

They saw Prince André slowly and quietly slipping further and further away from them, and both knew that this must be so, and that it was well. He received absolution and extreme unction; every one came to bid him good-bye. When his son was brought in to him, he pressed his lips to him and turned away, not because it was painful or sad to him, but simply because he supposed he had done all that was required of him. But he was told to give little Nicholas his blessing, he did what was required, and looked round as though to ask whether there was anything else he must do.

When the body, deserted by the spirit, passed through its last struggles, Princess Mary and Natasha were there.

"It is over!" said Princess Mary, after the body had lain for some moments motionless. Natasha went close, glanced at the dead eyes, closed them. She did not kiss them, but hung over what was the nearest memory of him. "Where has he gone? Where is he now? . . ."

When the body lay, dressed and washed, in the coffin on the table, every one came to take leave of him, and every one cried. Little Nicholas cried from the agonising bewilderment that was rending his heart. The countess and Sonya cried from pity for Natasha, and from grief that he was gone. The old count cried because he felt that he too must soon take the same terrible step.

Natasha and Princess Mary also wept now. But they did not weep for their personal sorrow; they wept from the emotion and awe that filled their souls before the simple and solemn mystery of death that had been accomplished before their eyes.

1812

BOOK THIRTEEN

NAPOLEON and his Grand Armée occupied Moscow through the whole of September and into the first week of October 1812. They pillaged and looted. And like a herd of cattle running wild and trampling under foot the fodder that might save them, they wasted the food and clothing and other provisions that they had found on entering the wealthy city. Disobeying all orders the soldiers and officers continued their vandalism, bringing their own ruin closer day by day.

Each week it grew colder. And each week Napoleon expected Russia to surrender. But Kutuzov and the Tsar held firm. Then suddenly seized with terror at the doom they saw hanging over them if they attempted to stay on through the winter, the Grand Armée led by Napoleon began to flee. They did not attempt to go north to conquer Petersburg. Neither did they go south to conquer the rich lands which lay open to them. They rushed back towards Europe over the road they had travelled before through Smolensk and Vilna, a road devastated and scorched.

Early in the morning of the 6th of October, Pierre came out of the shed, and stood in the doorway, playing with the long bandy-legged, purplish-grey dog, that jumped about him. This dog lived in their shed, sleeping with Karataev, though it sometimes went off on its own account into the town, and came back again. It had no master, and no name. Karataev called it "Grey-coat." The lack of a master, of a name, of any particular breed, and even of a definite colour, by no means troubled the purplish-grey dog. Its fluffy tail stood up firm and round like a plume; its bandy legs served it well. Everything was a source of satisfaction to it. At one moment, it was barking with joy, at another it would run about playing with a chip or a straw. Then it would bask in the sun with a dreamy and thoughtful air.

Pierre's clothing now consisted of a dirty, tattered shirt, a pair of soldier's trousers, tied with string round the ankles by Karataev's advice, for the sake of warmth, a full peasant's coat and a peasant's cap. Physically Pierre had changed greatly during this period. He no longer seemed stout, though he still had that look of solidity and strength that was characteristic of the Bezuhov family. His face was covered with a beard, his long, tangled hair, swarming with lice, formed a mat of curls on his head. His feet were bare.

Pierre looked over the meadow, across which waggons and men on horseback were moving that morning, then far away beyond the river, then at the dog, then at his bare feet, which he shifted with pleasure from one position to another, moving the dirty, big toes. And every time he looked at his bare feet, a smile of satisfaction flitted across his face. The sight of those bare feet reminded him of all he had passed through and learned during this time; and the thought of that was sweet to him.

Four weeks had passed since Pierre had been taken prisoner. Although the French had offered to transfer him from the common prisoners' shed to the officers', he had remained in the same shed as at first. And it was during this time that he attained that peace and content with himself, for which he had always striven in vain before. For long years of his life he had been seeking in various directions for that peace, that harmony with himself, which had struck him so much in the soldiers at Borodino. He had sought for it in philanthropy, in freemasonry, in the dissipations of society, in wine, in heroic feats of self-sacrifice, in his romantic love for Natasha; and all his efforts had failed him. And now without any thought of his own, he had gained that peace and that harmony with himself simply through the horror of death, through hardships, through what he had seen in Karataev. Those fearful moments that he had lived through during the execution had, as it were, washed for ever from his imagination and his memory the disturbing ideas and feelings that had once seemed to him so important. No thought came to him of Russia, of the war, of politics, or of Napoleon. It seemed obvious to him that all that did not concern him. His project of killing Napoleon struck him now as incomprehensible and positively ludicrous. His anger with his wife, and his dread of his name being disgraced by her, seemed to him trivial and amusing. And what did it matter to any one —least of all to him—whether they found out or not that their prisoner's name was Count Bezuhov?

It was warm out of doors in the sunshine, and that warmth

was particularly pleasant to Pierre as he stood there with the bracing freshness of the morning frost still in the air.

A French corporal, in a smoking-cap, with his coat comfortably unbuttoned, came round the corner of the shed, with a short pipe between his teeth, and with a friendly wink, approached Pierre.

"What sunshine. One would say it was spring." And the corporal leaned against the door, and offered Pierre his pipe, though he was always offering it, and Pierre always refused it.

"If one were marching in weather like this . . ." he began.

Pierre questioned him about what he had heard of the departure of the French, and the corporal told him that almost all the troops were setting out, and that instructions were expected that very day in regard to the prisoners. In the shed in which Pierre was, one of the Russian soldiers, Sokolov, was dangerously ill, and Pierre told the corporal that something ought to be done about this soldier. The corporal said that Pierre might set his mind at rest, that they had both travelling and stationary hospitals for such cases, that instructions would be given in regard to the sick, and that in fact every possible contingency was provided for by the General Staff.

"And then, M. Pierre, you have only to say a word to the captain, you know. Oh, he is a man who never forgets anything. Speak to the captain when he makes his round; he will do anything for you."

The captain of whom the corporal spoke used often to have long conversations with Pierre, and did him all kinds of favours.

"'You see,' he said to me the other day, 'M. Pierre is a man of education, who speaks French. He is a Russian lord who has had troubles, but he is a man. And he understands . . . If he wants anything, let him tell me, he shall not meet with a refusal. When one has studied, one likes education, you see, and well-bred people.' It's for your own sake I tell you that, M. Pierre."

Several of the prisoners heard Pierre talking to the corporal, and they came up immediately to ask what he had said. While Pierre was telling his companions what the corporal had said about setting off from Moscow, a thin, sallow, ragged French soldier came up to the door of the shed. With a shy and rapid gesture he put his fingers to his forehead by way of a salute, and addressing Pierre, asked him if the soldier, Platon, who was making a shirt for him, were in this shed.

The French soldiers had been provided with linen and leather a week before, and had asked the Russian prisoners to make them boots and shirts.

"It's ready, it's ready!" said Karataev, coming out with a

carefully folded shirt. On account of the heat and for greater convenience in working, Karataev was wearing nothing but a pair of drawers and a tattered shirt, as black as the earth. He had tied a wisp of bast round his hair, as workmen do, and his round face looked rounder and more pleasing than ever.

"Punctuality is brother to good business. I said Friday, and so I have done it," said Platon, smiling and displaying the shirt he had made.

The Frenchman looked about him uneasily, and as though overcoming some hesitation, rapidly slipped off his uniform and put on the shirt. Under his uniform he had no shirt, but a long, greasy, flowered silk waistcoat next his bare, yellow, thin body. The Frenchman was evidently afraid that the prisoners, who were looking at him, would laugh at him, and he made haste to put his head through the shirt. None of the prisoners said a word. "To be sure, it fits well," Platon observed, pulling the shirt down. The Frenchman, after putting his head and arms through, looked down at the shirt, and examined the stitching without lifting his eyes.

"Well, I'm not a tailor, you know, and I had no proper sewing materials, and there's a saying without the right tool you can't even kill a louse properly," said Karataev, still admiring his own handiwork.

"Very good, thanks. But you must have some stuff left . . ." said the Frenchman.

"It will be more comfortable as it wears to your body," said Karataev, still admiring his work. "There, you'll be nice and comfortable."

"Thanks, thanks, old fellow. But what is left . . . ?" repeated the Frenchman, giving Karataev a paper note. "Give me the pieces that are left over."

Pierre saw that Platon did not want to understand what the Frenchman said, and he looked on without interfering. Karataev thanked him for the rouble and went on admiring his own work. The Frenchman persisted in asking for what was left, and asked Pierre to translate what he said.

"What does he want with the pieces?" said Karataev. "They would have made me very good leg wrappers. Oh well, God bless the man."

And, looking suddenly crestfallen and melancholy, Karataev took a bundle of remnants out of his bosom and gave it to the Frenchman without looking at him. "Ach-ma!" he cried, and walked away. The Frenchman looked at the linen, he hesitated, glanced inquiringly at Pierre, and as though Pierre's eyes had told him something: "Here, Platon!" he cried in a shrill voice, suddenly blushing. "Keep them yourself," he said. And giving him the remnants, he turned and went out.

"There, look now," said Karataev, shaking his head. "They say they're not Christians, but they have souls too. It's true what the old folks used to say: a sweating hand is an open hand, but a dry hand is closefisted. His own back's bare, and yet he has given me this." Karataev paused for a while, smiling dreamily and gazing at the cuttings of linen. "First-rate leg binders they'll make me," he added, as he went back into the shed.

On the night of the 6th of October, the march of the retreating French army began: kitchens and shanties were broken up, waggons were packed, and troops and trains of baggage began moving.

At seven o'clock in the morning an escort of French soldiers in marching order, in shakos, with guns, knapsacks, and huge sacks, stood before the sheds and a running fire of eager French talk, interspersed with oaths, was kept up all along the line.

In the shed they were ready, dressed and belted and shod, only waiting for the word of command to come out. The sick soldier, Sokolov, pale and thin, with blue rings round his eyes, sat alone in his place, without boots or out-of-door clothes on. His eyes, that looked prominent from the thinness of his face, gazed at his companions, who took no notice of him, and he uttered low groans not so much from his sufferings as from the dread and grief of being left alone.

Pierre went up to the sick man, and squatted on his heels beside him.

"Come, Sokolov, they are not going away altogether, you know. They have a hospital here. You will be better off than us," said Pierre.

"O Lord! It will be the death of me! O Lord!" the soldier groaned.

"Well, I will ask them again in a minute," said Pierre, and getting up, he went to the door of the shed. While Pierre was going to the door, the same corporal, who had on the previous day offered Pierre a pipe, came in from outside, accompanied by two soldiers. Both the corporal and the soldiers were in marching order, with knapsacks on and shakos, with straps buttoned, that changed their familiar faces.

The corporal had come to the door so as to shut it in accordance with the orders given him. Before getting them out, he had to count over the prisoners.

"Corporal, what is to be done with the sick man?" Pierre was beginning, but at the very moment that he spoke the words he doubted whether it were the corporal he knew or some stranger—the corporal was so unlike himself at that moment. Moreover, at the moment Pierre was speaking, the roll of drums was suddenly heard on both sides. The corporal scowled at Pierre's words, and uttering a meaningless oath, he slammed the door. It was half-dark now in the shed; the drums beat a sharp tattoo on both sides.

"Here it is! . . . Here it is again!" Pierre said to himself, and an involuntary shudder ran down his back. In the changed face of the corporal, in the sound of his voice, in the stimulating and deafening din of the drums, Pierre recognised that mysterious, unsympathetic force which drove men, against their will, to do their fellow-creatures to death; that force, the effect of which he had seen at the execution. To be afraid, to try and avoid that force, to appeal with entreaties or with exhortations to the men who were serving as its instruments, was useless. That Pierre knew now. One could but wait and be patient. Pierre did not go near the sick man again, and did not look round at him. He stood at the door of the shed in silence.

When the doors of the shed were opened, and the prisoners, huddling against one another like a flock of sheep, crowded in the doorway, Pierre pushed in front of them, and went up to the very captain who was, so the corporal had declared, ready to do anything for him. The captain was in marching trim, and from his face, too, there looked out the same "it" Pierre had recognised in the corporal's words and in the roll of the drums.

"Step along! Step along!" the captain was saying, frowning sternly, and looking at the prisoners crowding by him.

Pierre knew his effort would be in vain, yet he went up to him.

"Well, what is it?" said the officer, scanning him coldly, as though he did not recognise him. Pierre spoke of the sick prisoner.

"He can walk, damn him!" said the captain.

"Step along! Step along!" he went on, without looking at Pierre.

"Well, no, he is in agony . . . !" Pierre was beginning.

"So what of it?" . . . shouted the captain.

"Dram-da-da-dam, dam-dam," rattled the drums, and Pierre knew that the mysterious force had already complete possession of those men, and that to say anything more now was useless.

The officers among the prisoners were separated from the soldiers and ordered to march in front.

The officers, among whom was Pierre, were thirty in number; the soldiers three hundred.

As the prisoners marched along through the streets they looked about in amazement at the charred remains of the city. And they talked about what was burnt, identifying this or that district as it came into view.

"Aie, aie, aie, what have they been doing?" the voices of the prisoners could be heard crying on one side and on another as they looked at the burnt districts. "Zamoskvoryetche, too, and Zubovo, and in the Kremlin. . . . Look, there's not half left. Why, didn't I tell you all Zamoskvoryetche was was gone, and so it is."

Passing through one of the few districts of Moscow that had not been burnt, by a church, the whole crowd of prisoners huddled suddenly on one side, with exclamations of horror.

"The wretches! The heathens! Yes; a dead man; a dead man it is . . . They have smeared it with something."

Pierre, too, drew near and he dimly discerned something leaning against the fence of the church enclosure. From the words of his companions, who saw better than he did, he learnt that it was the dead body of a man, propped up in a standing position, with his face smeared with soot.

"Move on, damn you! Go on, thirty thousand devils!" . . . They heard the escort swearing, and the French soldiers, with fresh vindictiveness, used the flat sides of their swords to drive on the prisoners, who had lingered to look at the dead man.

The prisoners marched alone with their escort, a train of carts and waggons, belonging to the soldiers of the escort, following behind them. But as they approached the main road leading westward out of Moscow, they found themselves in the middle of a huge train of artillery, moving with difficulty, and mixed up with private baggage-waggons.

The whole mass halted. The prisoners got a view of endless trains of baggage-waggons in front and behind and endless files of troops and waggons stretching away into the distance. The baggage-trains were so long that the last waggons had not yet got out of Moscow, while the vanguard of troops had already emerged.

The prisoners moved a few steps at a time and then halted, and again moved forward, and the crowd of vehicles and people grew greater and greater on all sides. After an hour, the prisoners were jammed in a close block. On all sides there was an unceasing sound, like the roar of the sea, of rumbling wheels, and tramping troops, and incessant shouts of anger and loud abuse.

Pierre stood squeezed against the wall of a charred house. Several of the Russian officers clambered up on to the wall so as to get a better view.

"The crowds! What crowds! . . . They have even loaded goods on the cannons! Look at the furs! . . ." they kept saying. "The vermin, they have been pillaging. . . . Look at what that one has got behind, on the cart. . . . Why, they are holy pictures, by God! . . . Those must be Germans. And a Russian peasant; by God! . . . Ah; the wretches! . . . See, how he's loaded; he can hardly move! Look at the carriages. They have taken them, too! . . . See, he has perched on the boxes. Heavens! . . . They have started fighting! . . . That's right; hit him in the face! We won't get by before evening like this. Look, look! . . . Why, that must surely be Napoleon himself. Do you see the horses! With the monograms and a crown! That's a portable house. He has dropped his sack, and doesn't see it. Fighting again. . . . A woman with a baby, and good-looking, too! Yes, that's the way they will let you pass. . . . Look; why, there's no end to it. Russian wenches! See how comfortable they are in the carriages!"

Again a wave of curiosity, as at the church, carried all the prisoners forward towards the road, and Pierre, thanks to his height, saw over the heads of the others. Three carriages were blocked between caissons, and in them a number of women with rouged faces, decked out in flaring colours, were sitting closely together, shouting something in shrill voices.

From the moment when Pierre had recognised the manifestation of that mysterious force, nothing seemed to him strange or terrible; not the corpse with its face blacked for a joke, nor these women hurrying away, nor the burnt ruins of Moscow. All that Pierre saw now made hardly any impression on him—as though his soul, in preparation for a hard struggle, refused to receive any impression that might weaken it.

The carriages of women drove by. They were followed again by carts, soldiers, waggons, soldiers, carriages, soldiers, caissons, and again soldiers, and at rare intervals more women.

It was almost evening when the officer in command of their escort rallied his men, and with shouts and oaths forced his way in among the baggage-trains; and the prisoners, surrounded on all sides, came out on the main road.

They marched very quickly now and only halted when the sun was setting. The baggage-carts were moved up close to one another, and the men began to prepare for the night. Every one seemed ill-humoured and dissatisfied. Angry shouts and fighting could be heard on all sides till late at night. A carriage, which had been following the escort, had driven into one of their carts and run a shaft into it. Several soldiers ran up to the cart from different sides; some hit the carriage horses on the head as they turned them round, others were fighting among themselves, and Pierre saw one German seriously wounded by a blow from the flat side of a sword on his head.

At this halting-place, the prisoners were even more roughly

treated by the French than at starting. In every one of the escort, from the officers to the lowest soldier, could be seen a sort of personal spite against every one of the prisoners, in surprising contrast with the friendly relations that had existed between them before. Pierre heard an officer reprimanding an under-officer for the escape of a prisoner, and threatening him with court-martial. On the under-officer's urging that the prisoner was ill and could not walk, the officer said that their orders were to shoot those who should lag behind.

The sun set. The immense, endless bivouac, which had been full of the sound of crackling fires and men talking, sank to rest. The red campfires burnt low and dim. High overhead in the lucid sky stood a full moon. Forests and fields, that before could not be seen beyond the camp, came into view now in the distance. And beyond those fields and forests could be seen the bright, shifting, alluring, boundless distance. Pierre glanced at the sky, at the far-away, twinkling stars. "And all that is mine, and all that is in me, and all that is I!" thought Pierre. "And all this they caught and shut up in a shed closed in with boards!" He smiled and went to lie down to sleep beside his companions.

Five days later a Russian messenger galloped through the night to Kutuzov's headquarters. It had been raining and the roads were slippery with mud, but changing horses twice he covered thirty miles in an hour and a half. It was past one o'clock when he reached the commander-in-chief's hut. Dismounting he rushed into the dark entry.

"The general on duty at once! Very important!" he cried to some one, who jumped up, wheezing in the darkness.

"His honour has been very unwell since the evening; he has not slept for three nights," an orderly's voice whispered, interposing. "You must wake the captain first."

"Very important!" said the messenger, feeling for the opened door and going in.

The orderly went in before him, and began waking some one up. "Your honour, your honour, a courier."

"What? What? From whom?" said a sleepy voice.

"From Dohturov and from Alexey Petrovitch. Napoleon is at Fominskoe," he said, not seeing the speaker in the darkness.

The man who had been waked yawned and stretched. "I don't want to wake him," he said, fumbling for something. "He's ill! Perhaps its only a rumour."

"Here is the report," said the messenger. "My instructions are to give it at once to the general on duty."

"Wait a minute, I'll strike a light. What do you do with

things, damn you!" said the sleepy voice addressing the orderly. The speaker was an adjutant. "I have found it, I have found it," he added.

The orderly struck a light, the adjutant felt for a candlestick.

By the light of the candle he had a glimpse of an officer asleep in the corner. The cockroaches that had been gnawing the candle ran away in all directions.

"Who sends the report?" asked the adjutant, taking the packet.

"The news is certain. Prisoners and Cossacks and spies, all tell the same story."

"Well there's no help for it, we must wake him," said the adjutant, getting up and going to the sleeping man who wore a nightcap and was covered up with a military cloak. "Wake up! Wanted at headquarters!" he said, knowing these words would be sure to wake him. And the head in the nightcap was in fact lifted at once.

"Well, what is it? From whom?" asked the officer blinking at the light. Hearing what the adjutant had to tell him, he broke open the packet and read it. He had hardly read it before he dropped his feet in worsted stockings on to the earth floor and began putting on his boots. Then he took off the nightcap, and combing his hair, put on a forage cap.

"Did you get here quickly? Let us go to his highness."

Like all old people, Kutuzov slept little at night. He often dropped into sudden naps during the daytime, but at night he lay on his bed without undressing, awake and thinking.

He was lying like that now on his bedstead. He was thinking with his one eye wide open, gazing into the darkness.

Since Bennigsen, who was in correspondence with the Tsar and had more weight than all the rest of the staff, had been avoiding him, Kutuzov was more at ease so far as not being compelled to lead his soldiers into useless offensive operations.

"They ought to understand that we can but lose by taking the offensive. *Time and patience,* these are my champions!" thought Kutuzov. He knew the apple must not be picked while it was green. It will fall of itself when ripe, but if you pick it green, you spoil the apple and the tree and set your teeth on edge. Like an experienced hunter, he knew the beast was wounded, wounded as only the whole force of Russia could wound it; but whether to death or not, was a question not yet solved. Now from reports brought by the irregulars, Kutuzov was almost sure that the wound was a deadly one. But more proof was wanted. He must wait.

"They want to run and look how they have wounded him. Wait a bit, you will see. Always manœuvres, attacks," he thought. "What for? Anything to distinguish themselves. As though there were any fun in fighting. They are like children from whom you can never get a sensible view of things because they all want to show how well they can fight. But that's not the point now. And what skilful manœuvres all these fellows propose! They think that when they have thought of two or three contingencies that they have thought of all of them. And there is no limit to them!"

The unanswered question, whether the wound dealt at Borodino were mortal or not, had been for a whole month hanging over Kutuzov's head. On one side, the French had taken possession of Moscow. On the other side, in all his being, Kutuzov felt that the terrible blow for which, together with all the Russians, he had strained all his strength must have been mortal. But in any case proofs were wanted, and he had been waiting for them now a month, and as time went on he grew more impatient. As he lay on his bed through sleepless nights, he did the very thing these younger generals did, the very thing he found fault with in them. He imagined all possible contingencies, but with this difference that he based no conclusion on the suppositions, and that he saw contingencies not as two or three, but as thousands. The more he pondered, the more of them he saw. He imagined all sorts of movements of Napoleon's army, acting as a whole or in part, on Petersburg, against him, to out-flank him. And also the possibility that Napoleon would fight against him with his own weapon, that he would stay on in Moscow waiting for him to move. But the one thing he could not foresee was what happened—the mad, convulsive stampede of Napoleon's army during the first eleven days of its march from Moscow—the stampede that made possible what Kutuzov did not yet dare to think about, the complete annihilation of the French.

The news brought by the irregulars of the miseries of Napoleon's army, rumours of preparations for leaving Moscow, all confirmed the supposition that the French army was beaten and preparing to take flight. But all this was merely supposition, that seemed of weight to the younger men, but not to Kutuzov. With his sixty years' experience he knew how much weight to attach to rumours; he knew how ready men are when they desire anything to manipulate all evidence so as to confirm what they desire; and he knew how readily in that case they let everything of an opposite significance pass unheeded. And the more Kutuzov desired this supposition to be correct, the less he permitted himself to believe it. This question absorbed all his spiritual energies. The destruction of the French, which he alone foresaw, was the one absorbing desire of his heart.

On the night of the 11th of October he lay thinking of that. There was a stir in the next room, and he heard steps.

"Hey, who is there? Come in, come in! Anything new?" he called.

While a footman lighted a candle, the officer told the drift of the news.

"Who brought it?" asked Kutuzov, with a face of frigid sternness.

"There can be no doubt of it, your highness."

"Call him, call him here!"

Kutuzov sat with one leg out of bed and his unwieldy, corpulent body propped on the other leg bent under him. He screwed up his one seeing eye to get a better view of the messenger, as though he hoped in his face to read what he cared to know.

"Tell me, tell me, my dear fellow," he said to the messenger in his low, aged voice, pulling the shirt together that had come open over his chest. "Come here, come closer. What news is this you have brought me? Eh? Napoleon has marched out of Moscow? Is it truly so? Eh?"

The messenger told him all and paused, awaiting instructions. The officer was beginning to speak, but Kutuzov checked him. He tried to say something, but all at once his face began to work, to pucker; waving his hand he turned the other way to the corner of the hut, which looked black with holy pictures. "Lord, my Creator! Thou hast heard our prayer . . ." he said in a trembling voice, clasping his hands. "Russia is saved. I thank Thee, O Lord." And he burst into tears.

From that time up to the end of the campaign, all Kutuzov's activity was limited to trying by the exercise of authority, by guile and by entreaties, to hold his army back from useless attacks, manœuvres, and skirmishes with the perishing enemy. A small force followed the French but Kutuzov lingered behind with the main army. But in spite of this the French fled in panic.

The men of what had been the Grand Armée fled with their leaders, not knowing whither they went. Napoleon and every soldier with him seemed filled with one desire: to make his own escape as quickly as possible.

Of the Russian generals no one but Kutuzov understood this. When the flight of the French army took its final direction along the Smolensk road, then what Kutuzov had foreseen began to come to pass. All the generals and officers of the Russian army were eager to distinguish themselves, to cut off the enemy's retreat, to overtake, to capture, to fall upon the French, and all clamoured for action.

Kutuzov alone used all his powers to resist this passion for attack. They laughed at him and slandered him. But he knew that there was no object in fighting and obstructing the road and losing his men, when the French army would, in its flight, melt away of itself without a battle. Drawing from the stores of his aged wisdom Kutuzov knew what they could not understand.

1812

BOOK FOURTEEN

KUTUZOV managed, for the most part, to keep the Russian army from engaging in a large and costly battle with the fleeing French. He did however allow guerrilla warfare. And as the French rushed towards Smolensk they were mercilessly attacked and destroyed piecemeal.

Some of the Russian guerrilla bands were detachments that followed all the usual make-up of an army, with infantry, artillery, staff-officers, and all the conveniences of life. Some consisted only of Cossacks, mounted men. Others were small bands of men, on foot and also mounted. Some were made up of peasants, or of landowners and their serfs. There was a deacon at the head of such a band, who took several hundred prisoners in a month. There was the village elder's wife, Vassilisa, who killed hundreds of the French.

On the 22nd of October, Denisov, who was a leader of a band of guerrillas, was engaged in a typical operation of this irregular warfare. From early morning he had been with his men moving about the woods that bordered the high road, watching a big convoy of cavalry baggage and Russian prisoners that had dropped behind the other French troops, and under strong escort—as he learned from his scouts and from prisoners—was making its way to Smolensk. But not only Denisov and Dolohov (who was also a leader of a small band acting in the same district) were aware of the presence of this convoy. Some generals in command of some larger detachments, with staff-officers also, knew of this convoy, and, as Denisov said, their mouths were watering for it. Two of these generals—one a Pole, the other a German—had almost at the same time sent Denisov an invitation to join their respective detachments in attacking the convoy.

"No, friend, I wasn't born yesterday!" said Denisov, on

reading these documents; and he wrote to the German that in spite of his ardent desire to serve under so brilliant and renowned a general, he must deprive himself of that happiness because he was already under the command of the Polish general. To the Pole he wrote the same thing, informing him that he was already serving under the command of the German.

Having disposed of that difficulty, Denisov, without communicating on the subject to the higher authorities, intended with Dolohov to attack and carry off this transport with his own small force.

The transport was, on the 22nd of October, going from the village of Mikulino to the village of Shamshevo. On the left side of the road between Mikulino and Shamshevo there were deep woods, which in places bordered on the road, and in places were a mile or more from the road. Denisov, with a small party of followers, had been the whole day riding about in these woods, sometimes plunging into their centre, and sometimes coming out at the edge, but never losing sight of the moving French. In the morning, not far from Mikulino, where the wood ran close to the road, the Cossacks of Denisov's party had pounced on two French waggonloads of saddles, stuck in the mud, and had carried them off. From that time right on to evening, they had been watching the movements of the French without attacking them. They wanted to avoid frightening them, and to let them go quietly on to Shamshevo, and then, joining Dolohov (who was to come that evening to a meeting-place in the wood, a mile from Shamshevo, to confer with them), from two sides to fall at dawn like an avalanche of snow on their heads, and to overcome and capture all of them at a blow.

Six Cossacks had been left behind, two miles from Mikulino, where the wood bordered the road. They were to bring word at once as soon as any fresh columns of French came into sight.

In front of Shamshevo, Dolohov was in the same way to watch the road to know at what distance there were other French troops. With the transport there were supposed to be fifteen hundred men. Denisov had two hundred men, and Dolohov might have as many more. But superiority in numbers was no obstacle to Denisov.

It was a warm, rainy, fall day. The sky and the horizon were all of the uniform tint of muddy water. Sometimes a mist seemed to be falling, and sometimes there was a sudden downpour of heavy, slanting rain.

Denisov, in a long cape and a high fur cap, both streaming with water, was riding a thin, pinched-looking, thoroughbred horse. With his head aslant, and his ears pricked up, like his horse, he was frowning at the driving rain, and anxiously looking before him. Beside Denisov, also wearing a long cape and a high cap, and mounted on a sleek, sturdy Don horse, rode a Cossack chief, Denisov's partner in his adventures.

A little ahead of them walked a peasant-guide, soaked through and through in his grey coat and white cap. A little behind, on a thin, delicate Kirghiz pony, with a flowing tail and mane, and a mouth flecked with blood, rode a young officer. Beside him rode a hussar, with a boy in a tattered French uniform and blue cap, perched upon his horse behind him. The boy held on to the hussar with hands red with cold, and kept moving his bare feet, trying to warm them. This was a French drummer, who had been captured in the morning during the attack on the waggons. All the French soldiers in charge of the waggons had been killed; only this boy had been captured alive. And he could tell them nothing certain about the troops of the column.

Along the narrow, muddy, cut-up forest-track there came hussars in knots of three and four at a time, and then Cossacks; some in capes, some in French cloaks; others with horse-cloths pulled over their heads. They sat huddled up, trying not to move, so as to keep warm the water that had already reached their skins, and not to let any fresh stream of cold rain trickle in anywhere under their seat, or at their knees or their necks. In the midst of the file of Cossacks two waggons, drawn by French horses, and Cossack saddle-horses hitched on in front, rumbled over stumps and branches, and splashed through the ruts full of water.

Denisov's horse, in avoiding a puddle in the track, knocked his knee against a tree.

"Ah, devil!" Denisov cried angrily. And he struck his horse three times with his whip, splashing himself and his comrades with mud. Denisov was out of humour, both from the rain and hunger; and, most of all, from having no news of Dolohov, and from no French prisoner having been caught to give him information.

"We will never have such another chance like this. To attack them alone would be risky, and to put it off for another day—some one else will carry the booty off from under our noses," thought Denisov.

Coming out into a clearing from which he could see some distance to the right, Denisov stopped.

"There's some one coming," he said.

The Cossack chief looked in the direction Denisov was pointing.

"There are two men coming," said the Cossack chief. The two figures, riding downhill, disappeared from sight, and came into view again a few minutes later. The first was an officer, soaked through, with his trousers tucked up above his knees;

he was lashing his horse into a weary gallop. Behind him a Cossack trotted along, standing up in his stirrups. The officer, a young boy, wth a broad face and keen, merry eyes, galloped up to Denisov, and handed him a sopping packet.

"From the general," he said. "I must apologise for its being wet . . ."

Denisov took the packet and broke it open.

"Why, they kept telling us it was dangerous," said the officer, turning to the Cossack chief while Denisov was reading the letter. "But Komarov"— and he indicated the Cossack—"and I were prepared. We both have two pistols. . . . But what's this?" he asked, seeing the French drummer-boy. "A prisoner? You have had a battle already? May I talk to him?"

"Rostov! Peter!" Denisov cried at that moment. "Why didn't you say who you were?" And Denisov, turning with a smile, held out his hand to Peter.

Peter had been all the way preparing himself to behave with Denisov as a grown-up person and an officer should, making no reference to their previous acquaintance. But as soon as Denisov smiled at him, Peter beamed, and forgetting all the formality he had been intending to preserve, he began telling him how he had ridden by the French, and how glad he was he had been given this commission, and how he had already been in a battle, and how a certain hussar had distinguished himself in it.

"Well, I am glad to see you," Denisov interrupted him, and his face looked anxious again.

Turning to the Cossack chief he said, "This is from the German again, you know. My friend Peter Rostov is in his suite." And Denisov told the Cossack chief that the letter, which had just been brought, repeated the German general's request that they should join him in attacking the transport. "If we don't catch them by to-morrow, he'll snatch them from under our noses," he concluded.

While Denisov was talking to the Cossack chief, Peter, disconcerted by Denisov's cold tone, and imagining that that tone might be due to the condition of his trousers, pulled them down under his cloak, trying to do so unobserved, and to maintain as martial an air as possible.

"Will your honour have any instructions to give me?" he said to Denisov, putting his hand to the peak of his cap, and going back to the comedy of adjutant and general, which he had prepared himself to perform, "or should I remain with your honour?"

"Instructions? . . ." said Denisov absently. "Well, can you stay till to-morrow?"

"As, please . . . May I stay with you?" cried Peter.

"Well, what were your instructions from your general—to go back at once?" asked Denisov.

Peter blushed. A few days before, he had disobeyed orders and rushed out under fire just for the thrill of it and his general had strictly forbidden him from taking part in any attack Denisov might be planning. "Oh, he gave me no instructions. I think I . . . ?" he said interrogatively.

"All right, then," said Denisov. And turning to his followers, he ordered a party of them to go to a hut in the wood, which they had fixed on as a meeting-place, and the officer on the Kirghiz horse to go and look for Dolohov, to find out where he was, and whether he were coming in the evening.

Denisov himself, with the Cossack chief and Peter, intended to ride to the edge of the wood near Shamshevo to have a look at the position of the French, where their attack next day was to take place.

"Come, my man," he said to a peasant guide, "take us to Shamshevo."

Denisov, Peter and the Cossack chief, accompanied by a few Cossacks and the hussar with the prisoner, turned to the left and crossed a ravine towards the edge of the wood.

The rain was over, but a mist was falling and drops of water dripped from the branches of the trees. The peasant, stepping lightly and noiselessly in his bast shoes over roots and wet leaves, led them out on to a road from where the French could be seen.

Just beyond the wood a field of grain ran downhill. On the right, across a steep ravine could be seen a little village and a manor-house with the roofs broken down. In that village and in the house and all over the high ground in the garden, by the wells and the pond, and all along the road uphill from the bridge to the village, not more than five hundred yards away, crowds of French soldiers could be seen in the shifting mist. They were shouting at the horses pulling the baggage uphill and calling to one another.

"Give me the prisoner here," said Denisov, in a low voice, never taking his eyes off the French.

A Cossack got off his horse, lifted the drummer-boy down, and came with him to Denisov. Denisov, pointing to the French, asked the boy what troops they were. The boy, looked in dismay at Denisov, and in spite of his unmistakable desire to tell all he knew, he was confused in his answers. Denisov, frowning, turned away from him, and addressing the Cossack chief, told him his own views on the matter.

"Whether Dolohov comes or not, we must take them. . . ." said Denisov.

"It is a good spot," said the Cossack chief.

"We will send the infantry down below, by the marshes," Denisov went on. "They will creep up to the garden; you dash down with the Cossacks from there"—Denisov pointed to the wood beyond the village—"and I from here with my hussars. And at a shot . . ."

It was getting dark when Denisov, with Peter and the Cossack chief, reached the hut in the wood which had been chosen as the meeting place. In the half-dark they could see saddled horses, Cossacks and hussars, rigging up shanties in the clearing, and building up a glowing fire in a hollow near, where the smoke would not be seen by the French. On the porch of the little hut there was a Cossack with his sleeves tucked up, cutting up a sheep. In the hut, three officers of Denisov's band were setting up a table made up of doors. Peter took off his wet clothes, gave them to be dried, and at once set to work to help the officers in fixing up a dining-table.

Within ten minutes the table was ready and covered with a cloth. On the table stood a bottle of vodka, a flask of rum, white bread and roast mutton and salt.

Sitting at the table with the officers and tearing the fat, savory mutton with his greasy fingers, Peter was in a state of childish rapture.

"So what do you think," he turned to Denisov, "is it all right if I remain with you a day or so?" And without waiting for an answer, he answered himself, "I have been ordered to find out, well then, I shall find out. . . Only you must let me go into the very. . . the main. . . I don't need any rewards. . . But I should like. . ."

"The very main. . ." repeated Denisov, smiling.

"But only, please, please give me a command where I'll really give the orders," Peter continued, "It would be easy for you. . . Oh, you need a knife?" he turned to an officer who was trying to tear off some mutton. And he gave him his pocket knife.

The officer praised the knife.

"Take it, please, keep it. I have many like it," Peter said, flushing. "Heavens! I clear forgot!" he suddenly cried. "I have some good raisins, you know, the kind without seeds. We have a new canteen-keeper, and he gets such wonderful things. I bought ten pounds. I like sweet things. Would you like some?" And Peter ran out to his Cossack and brought back some sacks with about five pounds of raisins. "Please take some."

"Do you need a coffee pot?" he turned to the Cossack chief. "I bought one from the canteen-keeper! He has wonderful things. And he's very honest. That's the main thing. I must send it to you without fail. Or maybe you're all out of flints, you've used yours up—that happens. I brought some with me, I have them right here," he pointed to the bags. "A hundred flints. I bought them very cheap. Please take whatever you need, take them all. . ." and suddenly afraid that he might have let his tongue run away with him, Peter stopped and turned red.

He began to wonder whether he had done anything else that was foolish. And as he went over the memories of the whole day he stopped at the memory of the French drummer-boy. "We are having a good time, but what about him? Where did they put him? Did they give him anything to eat? Have they been good to him?" he wondered.

But thinking he had said too much about the flints, he was afraid to speak now.

"Could I ask about him?" he wondered. "They'll say: he's a boy himself so he feels sorry for a boy. I'll show them to-morrow what a boy I am! Will I feel ashamed if I ask?" wondered Peter. "Oh, it doesn't matter!" And turning red again and watching the officers' faces for any possible signs of amusement, he said: "Would it be all right to call that boy who was taken prisoner, and give him something to eat. . . maybe. . ."

"Yes, poor little fellow," said Denisov, apparently finding nothing shameful in this. "Bring him in here. His name is Vincent Bosse. Bring him in here."

"I'll call him," said Peter.

"Yes, call him, call him. Poor little fellow," repeated Denisov.

Peter ran out into the yard.

"Bosse! Vincent!" he cried.

"Whom would you be wanting, sir?" said a voice out of the darkness. Peter answered that he was looking for the French boy whom they had captured that day.

"He was warming himself there by the fire. Hey Vincent! Vincent!" voices called in the darkness.

There were sounds of footsteps and the drummer-boy came splashing through the mud with his bare feet.

"Ah, it's you," said Peter. "Would you like to eat something? Don't be afraid, no one is going to hurt you," he added, gently and shyly touching his hand. "Come in, come in."

Denisov gave orders for the drummer-boy to be given some vodka and mutton, and to be put into a Russian coat, so that he should not be sent off with the other prisoners, but should stay with his band. Peter's attention was diverted from the boy by the sudden arrival of Dolohov. He had heard a great many stories of Dolohov's extraordinary daring and of his cruelty to the French. And therefore from the moment Dolohov entered the hut Peter could not take his eyes off him, and flinging up his head, he assumed a swaggering air, that he might not be unworthy of associating with such a hero.

Although in the old days he had worn a Persian dress in Moscow, Dolohov now looked like the most correct officer of the Guards. He was clean-shaven; he wore the wadded coat of the Guards with a St. George medal on a ribbon, and a plain forage cap, put on straight on his head. He took his wet cloak off in the corner and, without greeting any one, went straight up to Denisov and began at once asking questions. Denisov told him of the designs the larger detachment had upon the French convoy, of the message Peter had brought, and the answer he had given to both generals. Then he told him all he knew of the position of the French.

"That's so. But we must find out what troops they are, and what are their numbers," said Dolohov. "We must go and have a look at them. We can't rush into the thing without knowing for certain how many there are of them. I like to do things properly. Come, won't one of you come with me to pay them a call in their camp? I have an extra uniform with me."

"I, I . . . I'll come with you!" cried Peter.

"There's not the slightest need for you to go," said Denisov, addressing Dolohov. "And as for him I wouldn't let him go on any account."

"Why shouldn't I go? . . ." cried Peter.

"Why, because there's no reason to."

"Oh, well, excuse me . . . Because . . . Because . . . I'm going, and that's all. You will take me?" he cried, turning to Dolohov.

"Why not? . . ." Dolohov answered, absently.

Then turning to one of the Cossacks, he asked for his bag and opening it he gave Peter a French uniform.

To all Denisov's efforts to dissuade him from going, Peter replied that he too liked doing things properly and not in haphazard fashion, and that he never thought about danger to himself.

"For, you must admit, if we don't know exactly how many men there are there, it might cost the life of hundreds, and it is only we two, and so don't try to prevent me," he said. "It won't be any use . . ."

Peter and Dolohov, after dressing up in French uniforms and shakos, rode to the clearing from which Denisov had looked at the French camp, and coming out of the wood, descended into the hollow in the pitch darkness. When they had ridden downhill, Dolohov bade the Cossacks accompanying him to wait there, and set off at a smart trot along the road towards the bridge. Peter trotted along beside him.

"If we are caught, I won't be taken alive. I have a pistol," whispered Peter.

"Don't speak Russian," said Dolohov, in a rapid whisper, and at that moment they heard in the dark the challenge: "Who goes there?" and the click of a gun.

The blood rushed into Peter's face, and he clutched at his pistol.

"Uhlans of the Sixth Regiment," said Dolohov, neither hastening nor slackening his horse's pace.

The black figure of the French sentinel stood on the bridge.

"The password?"

Dolohov reined in his horse, and advanced at a walking pace.

"Tell me, is Colonel Gerard here?" he said.

"Password?" repeated the sentinel, making no reply and barring their way.

"When an officer makes his round, sentinels don't ask him for the password . . ." cried Dolohov, suddenly losing his temper and riding straight at the sentinel. "I ask you, is the colonel here?"

And not waiting for an answer from the sentinel, who moved aside, Dolohov rode at a walking pace uphill.

Noticing the black outline of a man crossing the road, Dolohov stopped the man, and asked where the colonel and officers were. The man, a French soldier with a sack over his shoulder, stopped, came close up to Dolohov's horse, stroking it with his hand, and told them in a simple and friendly way that the colonel and the officers were higher up the hill, on the right, in the courtyard of the farm, as he called the little manor-house.

After going further along the road, from both sides of which they heard French talk round the camp-fires, Dolohov turned into the yard of the manor-house. On reaching the gate, he dismounted and walked towards a big, blazing fire, round which several men were sitting. There was something boiling in a cauldron on one side, and a soldier in a peaked cap and blue coat, kneeling in the bright glow of the fire, was stirring it with his ramrod.

"Bonjour messieurs!" Dolohov called loudly and distinctly.

There was a stir among the officers in the shadow, and a tall officer with a long neck came round the fire and went up to Dolohov.

"Is that you, Clément?" said he. "Where the devil . . ." but realising his mistake, he did not finish, and with a slight frown greeted Dolohov as a stranger, and asked him what he could do for him. Dolohov told him that he and his comrade were trying to catch up with their regiment, and asked, addressing the company in general, whether the officers knew anything about the Sixth Regiment. No one could tell them anything about it. And Peter thought the officers began to look at him and Dolohov with unfriendly and suspicious eyes.

For several seconds no one spoke.

"If you're counting on some horsemeat you have come too late," said a voice from behind the fire, with a laugh.

Dolohov answered that they had had supper, and wanted to push on further that night.

He gave their horses to the soldier who was stirring the pot, and squatted down on his heels beside the officer with the long neck. The officer never took his eyes off Dolohov, and asked him again what regiment he belonged to.

Dolohov appeared not to hear the question. Making no answer, he lighted a short French pipe that he took from his pocket, and asked the officers whether the road ahead of them were clear of Cossacks.

"The Cossacks are everywhere," answered an officer from behind the fire.

Dolohov said that the Cossacks were only a danger for stragglers like himself and his comrade. "He supposed they would not dare to attack large detachments," he added inquiringly.

No one replied.

"Well, now he will come away," Peter was thinking every moment, as he stood by the fire listening to the talk.

But Dolohov took up the conversation that had dropped, and proceeded to ask them point-blank how many men there were in their battalion, how many battalions they had, and how many prisoners.

When he asked about the Russian prisoners, Dolohov added: "Nasty business dragging those corpses about. It would be better to shoot the vermin," and he broke into such a strange, loud laugh, that Peter thought the French must see through their disguise at once, and he involuntarily stepped back from the fire.

Dolohov's words and laughter brought no response, and a French officer whom they had not seen (he lay rolled up in a coat), sat up and whispered something to his companion. Dolohov stood up and called to the men, who held their horses.

"Will they give us our horses or not?" Peter wondered, unconsciously coming closer to Dolohov.

They did give them the horses. *"Bonsoir, messieurs,"* said Dolohov.

Peter tried to say *"Bonsoir,"* but he could not utter a sound. The officers were whispering together. Dolohov was a long while mounting his horse, who would not stand still; then he rode out of the gate at a walking pace. Peter rode beside him, not daring to look round, though he was longing to see whether the French were running after him or not.

When they came out to the road, Dolohov did not turn back towards the open country, but rode further along it into the village.

At one spot he stood still, listening. "Do you hear?" he said. Peter recognised the sound of voices speaking Russian, and saw round the camp-fire the dark outlines of Russian prisoners. When they reached the bridge again, Peter and Dolohov passed the sentinel, who, without uttering a word, paced gloomily up and down. They came out to the hollow where the Cossacks were waiting for them.

"Well now, good-bye. Tell Denisov, at sunrise, at the first shot," said Dolohov. And turning his horse's head he vanished into the darkness.

On reaching the hut in the wood, Peter found Denisov on the porch. He was waiting for Peter and was angry with himself for having let him go.

"Thank God!" he cried. "Well, thank God!" he repeated, hearing Peter's account. "And, damn you, you have prevented my sleeping!" he added. "Well, thank God. Now, go to bed. We can still get a nap before morning."

"Yes . . . no," said Peter. "I'm not sleepy yet. Besides, if I go to sleep, it will be all up with me. I can't sleep before a battle."

Peter sat for a long while in the hut, recalling the details of his adventure, and vividly imagining what was coming next day. Then seeing that Denisov had fallen asleep, he got up and went out.

It was still quite dark. The rain was over, but the trees were still dripping. Close by could be seen the black outlines of the Cossacks' shanties and the horses tied together. Behind the hut there was a dark blur where two waggons stood, and in the hollow there was a red glow from the dying fire. The Cossacks and the hussars were not all asleep; there mingled with the sound of the falling drops and the munching of the horses, the sound of low voices, that seemed to be whispering.

Peter went up to the waggons. Some one was snoring under the waggons, and saddled horses were standing round them munching oats. In the dark Peter recognised and approached his own mare, whom he called Karabach.

"Well, Karabach, to-morrow we shall do good service," he said, sniffing her nostrils and kissing her.

"Why, aren't you asleep, sir?" said a Cossack, sitting under the waggon.

"No; but . . . You know I have only just come back. We

have been calling on the French." And Peter gave the Cossack a detailed account, not only of his adventure, but also of his reasons for going, and why he thought it better to risk his life than to do things in a haphazard way.

"Well, get a little sleep," said the Cossack.

"No, I am used to it," answered Peter. "And how are the flints in your pistols—not worn out? I brought some with me. Don't you want any? Do take some."

The Cossack popped out from under the waggon to take a closer look at Peter.

"You see, I like to do everything carefully," said Peter. "Some men, you know, leave things to chance, and don't have things ready, and then they regret it. I don't like that."

"No, to be sure," said the Cossack.

"Oh, and another thing, please, sharpen my sabre for me; I have blunt . . ." (but Peter could not lie) . . . "It has never been sharpened. Will you do that?"

"Certainly I will."

The Cossack stood up and rummaged in the baggage for a whetstone. Peter clambered on to the waggon, and sat on the edge of it while the Cossacks sharpened his sabre.

"Are the other fellows asleep?" said Peter.

"Some are asleep, and some are awake, like us."

"And what about the boy?"

"He's lying in the hay. He's sleeping well after his fright. He was so pleased."

For a long while after that Peter sat quiet, listening to the low hum of talk and the muffled sounds of the camp and the grind of the whetstone on the sabre. He began to nod.

Suddenly he woke up. The Cossack was speaking to him.

"It's ready, your honour, you can cut the Frenchman in two now."

"Why, it's light already; it's really getting light," Peter cried. The horses were visible now, and through the leafless boughs there could be seen a watery light. Peter jumped down, took a rouble out of his pocket, and gave it to the Cossack. He brandished his sabre to try it, and thrust it into the scabbard. The Cossacks were untying the horses and fastening the saddlegirths.

"And here is the commander," said the Cossack.

Denisov came out of the hut, and calling to Peter, told him to get ready.

In the half-light of early dawn, the men picked out their horses, tightened saddlegirths, and formed into parties. Denisov stood by the hut, giving the last orders. The infantry of the detachment moved on along the road, hundreds of feet splashing through the mud. They quickly vanished among the trees in the mist. The Cossack chief gave some order to the Cossacks.

"Well, have you everything ready?" said Denisov. "Give us our horses."

They brought the horses up. Denisov was irritated because the saddlegirths were slack; he swore as he mounted his horse. Peter put his foot in the stirrup. The horse, as its habit was, made as though to nip at his leg; but Peter leaped into the saddle, unconscious of his own weight, and looking round at the hussars moving up from behind in the darkness.

"You will trust me with some commission? Please . . . For God's sake . . ." he said. Denisov seemed to have forgotten Peter. He looked round at him.

"One thing I beg of you," he said sternly, "to obey me and not go off on your own."

Denisov did not say another word to Peter; he rode on in silence. By the time they reached the edge of the wood, it was getting light. Denisov whispered something to the Cossack chief, and the Cossacks began riding by Peter and Denisov. When they had all passed on Denisov put his spurs to his horse, and rode downhill. Slipping and sinking back on their haunches, the horses slid down into the hollow with their riders. Peter kept beside Denisov. When he had reached the bottom, Denisov looked back and nodded to a Cossack.

"The signal," he said. The Cossack raised his arm, and a shot rang out. At the same moment they heard the tramp of horses galloping in front, shouts from different directions, and more shots.

The instant that he heard the first tramp of hoofs and shouts, Peter gave the rein to his horse, and lashing him on, galloped forward, heedless of Denisov, who shouted to him. He galloped to the bridge. The Cossacks were galloping along the road in front. At the bridge he ran against a Cossack who had lagged behind, and he galloped on. In front Peter saw men of some sort—the French he supposed—running across the road from right to left. One slipped in the mud under his horse's legs.

Cossacks were crowding about a hut, doing something. A fearful scream rose out of the middle of the crowd. Peter galloped to this crowd, and the first thing he saw was the white face and trembling lower-jaw of a Frenchman, who had clutched hold of a lance aimed at his breast.

"Hurrah!" shouted Peter and giving the rein to his excited horse, he galloped on down the village street.

He heard firing in front. Cossacks, hussars, and tattered Russian prisoners, running up from both sides of the road, were all shouting. A gallant-looking Frenchman, in a blue coat, with a red, frowning face, and no cap, was keeping back the hussars with a bayonet. By the time that Peter galloped up, the Frenchman had fallen. "Too late," flashed through Peter's brain, and he galloped to the spot where he heard the hottest fire. The shots came from the yard of the manor-house where he had been the night before with Dolohov. The French were ambushing there behind the fence in among the bushes of the overgrown garden, and firing at the Cossacks who were crowding round the gates. As he rode up to the gates, Peter caught a glimpse in the smoke of Dolohov's white face, as he shouted something to the men. "Go round. Wait for the infantry!" he was shouting, just as Peter rode up to him.

"Wait?" shouted Peter, and without pausing a moment, he galloped towards the spot where he heard the shots, and where the smoke was the thickest. There came a volley of shots with the sound of bullets whizzing by and thudding into something. The Cossacks and Dolohov galloped in at the gates after Peter. In the thick, hovering smoke the French flung down their arms and ran out of the bushes to meet the Cossacks, or fled downhill towards the pond. Peter was galloping on round the courtyard, but instead of holding the reins, he was flinging up both arms in a strange way, and slanting more and more to one side in the saddle. The horse stepped on to the ashes of the fire smouldering in the morning light, and stopped short. Peter fell heavily on the wet earth. The Cossacks saw his arms and legs twitching, though his head did not move. A bullet had passed through his brain.

After talking with the French senior officer, who came out of the house with a handkerchief on a sword to announce that they surrendered, Dolohov got off his horse and went up to Peter, who lay motionless with outstretched arms.

"Dead," he said frowning, and walked to the gate to Denisov, who was riding towards him.

"Killed?" cried Denisov, even from a distance recognising the familiar, unmistakably lifeless posture in which Peter's body was lying.

"Dead," Dolohov repeated, as though the utterance of those words afforded him satisfaction; and he walked towards the prisoners, whom the Cossacks were hurriedly surrounding. "No quarter!" he shouted to Denisov. Denisov made no reply. He went up to Peter, got off his horse, and with trembling hands turned over the blood-stained, mud-spattered face that was already turning white.

"I like sweet things. They are good raisins, take them all," came into his mind.

Among the Russian prisoners rescued by Denisov and Dolohov was Pierre.

The prisoners, of whom Pierre was one, were on the 22nd

of October not with the troops and transport, in whose company they had left Moscow, though no fresh instructions in regard to them had been given by the French authorities. Half of the transport with stores of biscuit, which had followed them during the early stages of the march, had been carried off by the Cossacks, the other half had got away in front. Of the cavalry soldiers on foot, who had marched in front of the prisoners, not one was left; they had all disappeared. The artillery, which the prisoners had seen in front during the early stages, was now replaced by an immense train of baggage belonging to some French marshal and convoyed by an escort of Westphalians. Behind the prisoners came a transport of cavalry supplies.

The French had at first marched in three columns, but after a hundred miles they had formed a single mass.

The road along which they marched was strewn on both sides with the carcases of dead horses. The tattered soldiers, stragglers from different French regiments, were continually changing, joining the column as it marched, and dropping behind it again. Several times there had been false alarms, and the soldiers of the convoy had raised their guns, and fired and fled, trampling one another underfoot. Then they had rallied again, and abused one another for their causeless panic.

These three bodies, travelling together—the cavalry transport, the convoy of prisoners, and the marshal's baggage transport—still made up a complete separate whole, though each of its three parts was rapidly dwindling away.

Of the cavalry transport, which had at first consisted of one hundred and twenty waggons, only sixty were left; the rest had been carried off or abandoned. Several waggonloads of the marshal's baggage, too, had been discarded or captured. Three waggons had been attacked and pillaged by stragglers from another French regiment. From the talk he overheard among the Germans, Pierre learned that a more careful watch was kept over the marshal's baggage-train than over the prisoners, and that one of their comrades, a German, had been shot by order of the marshal himself because a silver spoon belonging to him had been found in the soldier's possession.

The convoy of prisoners had dwindled even more than the other two convoys. Of the three hundred and thirty men who had started from Moscow there were now less than a hundred left. The prisoners were a burden even more irksome to the French soldiers than the cavalry stores and the marshal's baggage. The saddles and marshal's spoons they could understand might be of some use, but why cold and starving soldiers should stand as sentinels, keeping guard over Russians as cold and starving, who were continually dying and being left behind on the road, and whom they had orders to shoot—it was not only incomprehensible, but revolting. And the soldiers of the escort, apparently afraid in the miserable plight they were in themselves, to give way to the pity they felt for the prisoners, for fear of making their own lot harder, treated them with marked severity.

At one place the soldiers of the escort had gone off to plunder their own stores, leaving the prisoners locked in a stable, and several prisoners had burrowed under the wall and run away. But they were caught by the French and shot.

The arrangement, made at the start from Moscow, that the officers among the prisoners should march separately from the common soldiers, had long since been given up. All who could walk marched together; and at the third stage Pierre had rejoined Karataev and the bow-legged, purple-grey dog, who had chosen Karataev for her master.

On the third day after leaving Moscow, Karataev had a return of the fever, which had kept him in the Moscow hospital, and as Karataev's strength failed, Pierre held more aloof from him. Pierre could not have said why it was, but from the time Karataev fell sick, he had to make an effort to force himself to go near him. And when he did go near him and heard his moans, he moved away and tried not think about him.

He did not see and did not hear how the prisoners that lagged behind were shot, though more than a hundred of them had perished in that way. He did not think about Karataev, who was getting weaker every day, and would obviously soon fall a victim to the same fate. Still less did Pierre think about himself. The harder his lot became, the more terrible his future, the more independent of his present plight were the glad and soothing thoughts, memories, and images that occurred to him.

At midday on the 22nd, Pierre was walking along the muddy, slippery road uphill, looking at his feet and at the unevenness of the road. From time to time he glanced at the familiar crowd around him, and then again at his feet. Both that crowd and those feet were alike his and familiar to him. The purplish, bandy-legged, grey dog was running along at the side of the road, sometimes barking at the crows that perched on the carrion. All around lay the flesh of different animals—from men to horses—in different stages of decomposition, and because of the marching soldiers the wolves feared to come near it, so that the grey dog was able to feast to her heart's content.

Rain had been falling since early morning; and it seemed continually as though in another minute it would cease and the sky would clear, when, after a short break, the rain came on again more heavily.

Suddenly a voice shouted: "Take your places!"

There was a stir among the prisoners and the men of the convoy. On all sides shouted commands could be heard, and on the left, appeared a detachment of cavalry soldiers, well dressed and riding good horses. All faces wore that look of nervous strain which men take on at the approach of higher authorities. The prisoners huddled together, they were shoved off the road. The convoy soldiers formed into ranks.

"The Emperor! The Emperor! The Marshal! The Duke!" and no sooner had the well-fed cavalry soldiers trotted by than a coach drawn by grey horses rattled past. Pierre caught a glimpse of the calm, handsome, fat white face of a man in a three-cornered hat. It was one of the French marshals.

The general who was in charge of the convoy, his face red and frightened, galloped after the coach, whipping his horse. Several of the convoy officers gathered together; the soldiers crowded around them. They all had worried, tense expressions.

"What was it he said? What did he say?" Pierre heard.

It was then that Pierre caught sight of Karataev whom he had not yet seen that morning. Wrapped in his old coat, he was sitting and leaning against a birch tree.

Karataev looked at Pierre with his kind round eyes which were now filmed with tears, and, it seemed, he was appealing to him to come over, wanting to say something. But Pierre was too afraid for himself. He made believe he did not see that appealing look, and walked away hurriedly.

When the prisoners were again on the march, Pierre looked back. Karataev was still sitting by the roadside, under the birch tree, and two French soldiers were standing by him. Pierre did not look back again. He went on up the hill.

There was the sound of a shot. Pierre heard that shot clearly, but in the same instant as he heard it he remembered that he had not yet finished the calculations he had started before the marshal had ridden by, counting how many stages remained to Smolensk. And he began to count. Two French soldiers, one of whom was holding a smoking musket, ran by Pierre. They were both pale, and in their expression there was something reminiscent of what Pierre had seen in the faces of the soldiers at the execution in Moscow.

The purplish-grey dog began to howl behind at the spot where Pierre had last seen Karataev. "The silly fool, what is she howling about?" thought Pierre.

The prisoners, his companions, marching beside him, did not look back any more than he did, toward the spot where first the shot, then the dog's howling, had been heard. There was a grim look on all their faces.

The cavalry transport, and the prisoners, and the marshal's

baggage-train, halted at the village of Shamshevo. All crowded together round the camp fire. Pierre lay down with his back to the fire, and at once fell asleep.

The facts of real life mingled with his dreams.

Life is everything. All is changing and moving. The hardest and the most blessed thing is to love this life in one's sufferings, in undeserved suffering.

"Karataev!" flashed into Pierre's mind. And all at once there rose up, as vivid as though alive, the image, long forgotten, of the gentle old teacher, who had given Pierre geography lessons in Switzerland. "Wait a minute," the old man was saying. And he was showing Pierre a globe. This globe was a living, quivering ball, with no definite limits. Its whole surface consisted of drops, closely cohering together. And those drops were all in motion, and changing, several passing into one, and then one splitting up again into many. Every drop seemed striving to spread, to take up more space, but the others, pressing upon it, sometimes absorbed it, sometimes melted into it.

"This is life," the old teacher was saying.

"How simple it is and how clear," thought Pierre. "How was it I did not know that before? God is in the midst, and each drop strives to expand, to reflect Him on the largest scale possible. And it grows, and is absorbed and crowded out, and on the surface it disappears, goes back into the depths. That is how it is with him, with Karataev; he is absorbed and has disappeared."

"You understand, my child," said the teacher.

"You understand, damn you!" shouted a voice, and Pierre woke up.

He raised his head and sat up. A French soldier was squatting on his heels by the fire. He had just shoved away a Russian soldier, and was roasting a piece of horsemeat on the end of a ramrod. His brown face, with its sullen brows, could be clearly seen in the light of the glowing embers.

"It's just the same to him," he muttered, quickly addressing a soldier standing behind him. "Go!"

The Russian soldier, the one who had been pushed away, was sitting near the fire, patting something with his hand. Looking more closely, Pierre saw the purplish-grey dog. She was wagging her tail.

"Ah, she has come . . ." said Pierre. "And Plat . . ." he was beginning, but he did not go on. All at once, in close connection, there rose up the memory of the look Platon had fixed upon him, as he sat under the tree, the sound of the shot, of the dog's howl, the guilty faces of the soldiers, and the smoking gun. But at the same instant, at some mysterious summons, there rose up the memory of a summer evening he had spent with a beautiful Polish lady on the verandah of his house at Kiev. And making no effort to connect the impressions of the day and to deduce anything from them, Pierre closed his eyes, and the picture of the summer night in the country mingled with the thought of bathing and of that fluid, quivering globe, and he seemed to sink deep down so that the waters closed over his head.

Before sunrise he was wakened by loud and rapid shots and outcries. The French were flying by him.

"The Cossacks!" one of them shouted, and a minute later a crowd of Russians were surrounding Pierre. For a long while Pierre could not understand what had happened to him. He heard all about him his comrades' wails of joy.

The Russian prisoners cried, weeping, as they embraced the Cossacks and the hussars. The hussars and the Cossacks crowded round the prisoners, pressing on them clothes, and boots, and bread. Pierre sat sobbing in their midst, and could not utter one word; he hugged the first soldier who went up to him, and kissed him, weeping.

Dolohov was standing at the gates of a dilapidated house, letting the crowd of unarmed Frenchmen pass by him. The French, excited by all that had happened, were talking loudly among themselves; but as they passed before Dolohov, who stood switching his boots with his riding-whip, and watching them with his cold, glassy eyes, that boded nothing good, their talk died away. One of Dolohov's Cossacks stood on the other side, counting the prisoners, and marking off the hundreds with a chalk mark on the gate.

"How many?" Dolohov asked him.

"The second hundred," answered the Cossack.

"Step along. Step along," said Dolohov, who had picked up the expression from the French; and when he met the eyes of the passing prisoners, his eyes gleamed with a cruel light.

From the 28th of October, when the frosts began, the flight of the French assumed a more tragic aspect, from the men being frozen or roasted to death by the camp-fires, while the Emperor, and kings, and dukes, still drove on with their stolen booty in fur cloaks and closed carriages. But in its essentials, the process of the flight and disintegration of the French army went on unchanged.

Of the seventy-three thousands of the French army, counting the Guards, only thirty-six thousand were left, though only five thousand had been killed in battle.

Hardly a quarter of the men remained with the flags of their regiments; the rest wandered off in different directions, seeking food. All thought only of Smolensk, where they hoped to recover. Many threw away their cartridges and muskets.

But after struggling into Smolensk, the promised land of their dreams, the French killed one another fighting over food, sacked their own stores, and when everything had been pillaged, ran on further. All hastened on, not knowing whither or for what end they were going; least of all knew that great genius, Napoleon, since there was no one to give him orders. But still he and those about him clung to their old habits: wrote commands, letters, reports, orders of the day; called each other your majesty, *mon frère, Prince d'Eckmühl, roi de Naples,* and so on. But the orders and reports were all on paper: no attempt was made to carry them out, because they could not be carried out. And although they addressed each other as "majesty," "highness," and *"mon cousin,"* they all felt that they were pitiful and loathsome creatures. And in spite of their pretence of caring for the army, each was thinking only of himself, and how to make his escape as quickly as possible to safety.

Expecting the Russians in their rear and not in front, the French ran, straggling out, and getting separated as far as twenty-four hours' march from one another. In front of all fled the Emperor, then the kings, then the dukes.

The Russian army, supposing Napoleon would take the road to the right beyond the Dnieper—the only sensible course—turned also to the right, and came out on the high road at Krasnoe. And here the French came bearing straight down on the Russian vanguard. Seeing the enemy unexpectedly, the French were thrown into confusion, stopped short from the suddenness of the fright, but then ran on again, abandoning their own comrades in their rear. Then for three days, the separate parts of the French army passed, as it were, through the lines of the Russian army: first the viceroy's troops, then Davoust's, and then Ney's. They all abandoned one another, abandoned their heavy baggage, their artillery, and half their men, and fled, making semicircles to the right to get round the Russians by night.

Ney was the last, because in spite, or perhaps in consequence, of their miserable position, with a child's impulse to beat the floor that has bruised it, he lingered to demolish the walls of Smolensk, which had done nobody any harm. Ney, who was the last to pass with his corps of ten thousand, reached Napoleon at Orsha with only a thousand men, having abandoned all the rest, and all his cannons, and made his way by stealth at night, under cover of the woods, across the Dnieper.

From Orsha they fled on along the road to Vilna. At

Berezina again, they were thrown into confusion, many were drowned, many surrendered, but those that got across the river, fled on. Whoever could, ran away. And those who could not, surrendered or died.

Napoleon, their emperor, wrapped himself in a fur cloak, and getting into a sledge, galloped off alone, deserting his Grand Armée.

1812-1813

BOOK FIFTEEN

After Prince André's death, Natasha and Princess Mary both closed their eyes under the menacing cloud of death that hovered about them, and dared not look at life. They guarded their open wounds from every rough and painful touch. Everything—the carriage driving along the street, the summons to dinner, the maid asking which dress to get out; worse still—words of faint, feigned sympathy—set the wound smarting, seemed an insult to it, and jarred on that needful silence in which both were trying to listen to the stern, terrible litany that had not yet died away in their ears, and to gaze into the mysterious, endless vistas that seemed for a moment to have been unveiled before them.

Only alone together were they safe from such outrage and pain. They said little to one another. When they did speak, it was about the most trivial subjects. And both equally avoided all mention of anything connected with the future. To admit the possibility of a future seemed to them an insult to Prince André's memory. Still more did they avoid in their talk all that could be connected with him. It seemed to them that what they had felt and gone through could not be expressed in words.

But pure and perfect sorrow is as impossible as pure and perfect joy. From the isolation of her position, as the guardian and foster-mother of her nephew, and independent mistress of her own destinies, Princess Mary was the first to be called back to life from that world of mourning in which she lived for the first two weeks. She received letters from her relations which had to be answered; the room in which little Nicholas had been put was damp, and he had begun to cough. Alpatitch came to Yaroslavl with accounts. He had suggestions to make, and advised Princess Mary to move to Moscow to the house in Vozdvizhenka, which was uninjured, and only needed some trifling repairs. Life would not stand still, and she had to live. Painful as it was for Princess Mary to come out of that world of solitary contemplation, in which she had been living till then, and sorry, and, as it were, conscience-stricken, as she felt at leaving Natasha alone, the duties of daily life claimed her attention, and against her own will she had to give herself up to them. She went through the accounts with Alpatitch, consulted Dessalle about her little nephew, and began to make preparations for moving to Moscow.

Natasha was left alone, and from the time that Princess Mary began to busy herself with preparations for her journey, she held aloof from her too.

Princess Mary asked the countess to let Natasha come to stay with her in Moscow; and both count and countess eagerly agreed, for they saw their daughter's health failing every day, and they hoped that change of scene and the advice of Moscow doctors might do her good.

"I am not going anywhere," answered Natasha, when the suggestion was made to her. "All I ask is to be left alone," she said, and she ran out of the room, hardly able to restrain tears more of vexation and anger than of sorrow.

One day towards the end of December, Natasha, thin and pale in a black woollen gown, with her hair fastened up in a careless coil, sat perched up in the corner of the sofa in her room, her fingers nervously crumpling and smoothing out the ends of her sash. She was gazing into that world where she knew he was. But she could not see him, except as he had been here on earth. She was seeing him again as he had been years ago when she first knew him, as he had been during his illness, as he had been on that last night when he took her hand and . . .

Suddenly a loud rattle at the door handle broke with a painful shock on her. Her maid rushed into the room with frightened eyes.

"Come to your father, hurry," she said, with a strange excited expression. "A misfortune . . . Peter . . . A letter," she gasped out, sobbing.

As Natasha went into the drawing-room, her father came out of the countess's room. His face was wet with tears. Seeing Natasha, he waved his arms in despair, and went off into violent, miserable sobs, that convulsed his soft, round face.

"Peter . . . Peter . . . Go, go in, she's calling . . ." And sobbing like a child, he tottered with feeble legs to a chair, and almost dropped on to it, hiding his face in his hands.

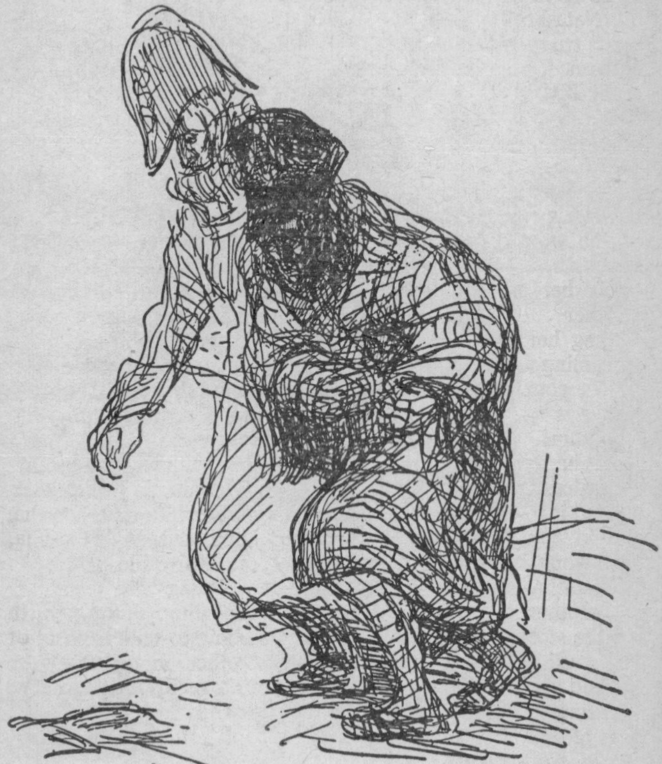

A fearful pain seemed to stab Natasha to the heart. She felt a poignant anguish; it seemed to her that something was being rent within her, and she was dying. But with the pain she felt an instant release from the seal that shut her out of life. At the sight of her father, she instantly forgot herself and her own sorrow.

She ran up to her father, but he feebly motioned her towards her mother's door. Princess Mary, with a white face, came out and took Natasha's hand, saying something to her. Natasha neither saw nor heard her. Struggling with herself, she ran in to her mother.

The countess was lying on a low chair. Sonya and some maid-servants were holding her by the arms.

"Natasha, Natasha! . . ." the countess was screaming. "It's not true, not true . . . it's false . . . Natasha!" she screamed, pushing the maids away. "All you go away, it's not true! Killed! . . . ha, ha, ha! . . . Not true! . . ."

Natasha knelt beside the low chair, bent over her mother, embraced her, with surprising strength lifted her up, turned her face to her, and pressed close to her.

"Mother! . . . Darling! . . . I'm here, dearest mother," she whispered to her, never ceasing for a second.

She would not let her mother go; she struggled tenderly with her, asked for pillows and water, unbuttoned and tore open her mother's dress. "Dearest . . . My darling . . . Mother . . . My precious," she whispered without pausing, kissing her head, her hands, her face, and feeling the tears streaming in irrepressible floods over her nose and cheeks.

The countess squeezed her daughter's hand, closed her eyes, and was quieter for a moment. All at once she sat up with unnatural swiftness, looked vacantly round, and seeing Natasha, began hugging her head to her with all her might. Natasha's face involuntarily worked with pain, as her mother turned it toward her, and gazed a long while into it. "Natasha, you love me," she said, in a soft, confiding whisper. "Natasha, you won't deceive me? You will tell me the whole truth?"

Natasha looked at her with eyes swimming with tears.

"Mother . . . Darling," she kept repeating, putting forth all the strength of her love to try somehow to take a little of the crushing load of sorrow off her mother on to herself.

And again in the helpless struggle with reality, the mother, refusing to believe that she could live while her adored boy, just blossoming into life, was dead, took refuge from reality in the world of delirium.

Natasha had no recollection of how she spent that day and that night, and the following day and the following night. She did not sleep, and did not leave her mother's side.

Natasha's love, patient and persistent, seemed to enfold the countess on all sides every second, offering no explanation, no consolation, simply beckoning her back to life.

On the third night the countess was quiet. She sat up in bed, and talking softly said: "Natasha, he is gone, he is no more." Then embracing her daughter, the countess for the first time began to weep.

Princess Mary put off her departure. Sonya and the count tried to take Natasha's place, but they could not. They saw that she was the only one who could keep the countess from the frenzy of despair. For three weeks Natasha never left her mother's side, slept on a lounge in her room, made her drink and eat, and without pause talked to her, talked because her tender, loving voice was the only thing that soothed the countess.

The wound in the mother's heart could never be healed. Peter's death had torn away half of her life. When the news of Peter's death reached her, she was a fresh-looking, vigorous woman of fifty; a month later she came out of her room an old woman, half dead and with no more interest in life. But the wound that half killed the countess, that fresh wound, brought Natasha back to life.

Natasha had believed that her life was over. But suddenly her love for her mother showed her that the essence of her life—love—was still alive within her. Love was awakened, and life waked with it.

The last days of Prince André had been a close bond between Natasha and Princess Mary. This fresh trouble brought them even closer together. Princess Mary put off her departure, and for the last three weeks she had been looking after Natasha, as though she were a sick child. Those weeks spent by Natasha in her mother's room had completely broken down her health.

Natasha had grown thin and pale, and was physically so weak that every one was continually talking about her health, and she was glad it was so. Yet sometimes she was suddenly seized, not simply by a dread of death, but by a dread of sickness, of ill-health, of losing her good looks; and sometimes she unconsciously examined her bare arms, marvelling at their thinness, or peeped in the looking-glass in the morning at her pinched face, and was touched by its piteous look. It seemed to her that this was as it should be, and yet she felt afraid and mournful at it.

Towards the end of January Princess Mary set off for Moscow, and the count insisted on Natasha going with her to consult the doctors.

On the 5th of November Kutuzov, who with his army was following the fleeing French, was riding along the main road about fifty miles west of Smolensk.

The day was clear, wintry. Kutuzov, with a large retinue of discontented, whispering generals behind him, was riding astride his fat little white horse. All along the road there were crowds of French prisoners huddling around fires to warm themselves. Seven thousand had been taken that day. Not far from Dobroe, the town where Kutuzov was to spend the night, a great crowd of prisoners, ragged, wrapped in whatever they had been able to scare up, hummed with loud talk as they stood in the roadway beside a long row of unharnessed French cannon. At the approach of the commander-in-chief the talk died away, and all eyes fastened on Kutuzov who, wearing a white cap with a red band and a cotton-quilted overcoat that hunched over his rounded shoulders, moved slowly along the road. One of the generals was reporting to Kutuzov where the guns and the prisoners had been captured.

Kutuzov seemed anxious about something and did not listen to the general's words. He screwed up his eye with displeasure and looked intently at the prisoners who presented a particularly pitiful appearance. The faces of the French soldiers were for the most part disfigured by frostbitten cheeks and noses, and almost all of them had red, swollen and pus-filled eyes.

One group of Frenchmen stood close to the road and two of the soldiers—the face of one of them was covered with sores—were tearing apart a piece of raw horse meat. There was something horrifying and bestial in the glance they cast on the approaching generals and in the manner in which the soldier with the sores turned away to continue with what he was doing.

Kutuzov looked long and searchingly at those two soldiers; then frowning, he shook his head thoughtfully. In another place he noticed a Russian soldier who, laughing and patting a Frenchman on the shoulder, was saying something kind to him. Again Kutuzov shook his head.

"What were you saying?" he suddenly asked the general who was now trying to draw the commander-in-chief's attention to the captured French flags which were set up in front of the Preobrazhensky regiment.

"Oh yes, the flags!" said Kutuzov, apparently shifting his attention with great effort away from the subject that was absorbing all his thoughts. He looked about absentmindedly. Thousands of eyes were fixed on him, waiting for what he would say.

In front of the Preobrazhensky regiment he came to a

standstill, sighed heavily, and closed his eye. Someone in the suite signaled to the soldiers holding the flags to come up and set up the flagstaffs around the commander-in-chief. Kutuzov remained silent a few moments. Then against his will, it seemed, yielding to the obligations of his position, he raised his head and began to speak. Crowds of officers surrounded him. He scanned them with an attentive eye, recognising some of them.

"I thank you all!" he said, addressing the soldiers, then again turning to the officers. In the stillness that now reigned around him his slowly-articulated words could be clearly heard. "I thank you all for your hard and faithful service. The victory is complete, and Russia will not forget you. Yours is eternal glory!" He grew silent, looking about.

"Lower, bow its head, bow it," he said to a soldier who was holding a French eagle and had accidentally lowered it before the standard of the Preobrazhensky regiment. "Lower, lower, like that! Hurrah, brothers!" he said, turning his head with a quick movement of the chin.

"Hurrah-r-rah-h!" roared thousands of voices.

While the soldiers were shouting, Kutuzov, bending in his saddle, bowed his head and his one eye shone with a gentle, and, it seemed, an ironical light.

"And now, brothers . . ." he said, when the shouts died away.

And suddenly his voice and the expression on his face changed: it was no longer the commander-in-chief talking, but an unassuming, aged man, who plainly wanted to say something important to his comrades.

"This is what I have to say, brothers. I know, it's hard for you, but what are we to do! Grin and bear it—it won't last much longer. First we will see our guests out, then we will rest. The Tsar won't forget your faithful services. It's hard for you, still, you are home; while they—you see for yourselves what they have come to—" he said, pointing to the prisoners. "They're worse than the lowest beggars. While they were strong we did not pity them, but now we can even afford them pity. They too are people. Isn't that so, brothers?"

He looked around. And in the intent, respectfully astonished glances directed at him he read sympathy for what he had said. His face grew suddenly brighter with the gentle smile of old age that brought wrinkles to the corners of his mouth and eyes. He was silent again, letting his head drop as if in doubt.

"But then, after all, who invited them to come here? It serves them right, the bastards!" he said suddenly, lifting his head. And raising his riding whip he rode off at a gallop, accompanied for the first time during the whole campaign by roars of hurrah and the laughter of the soldiers as they broke ranks.

The French army went on melting away. It fled like a wounded beast and could not be stopped.

Behind the French lay certain destruction; before them lay their only hope, Europe. And all were bent on this united flight.

The more precipitate the flight of the French, the more violent were the attacks made by the Russian generals on Kutuzov. They wanted to engage the French in battle, even though it was now more than obvious that Kutuzov had been right from the beginning. But so strong was the desire for battle among the higher army officials that a plan for catching Napoleon in a snare, before he left Russian soil, was drawn up in Petersburg and sent to Kutuzov with the Tsar's approval.

Assuming that the Petersburg plan would not please Kutuzov, the dissatisfaction with him, contempt of him, and jeering became more and more pronounced. This contempt and jeering was of course expressed in respectful form—in such a form that Kutuzov could not even ask what he was accused of. They did not talk to him seriously; they submitted their reports and asked for his decisions with an air of performing a melancholy ceremony, while they winked behind his back, and at every step tried to deceive him. It was accepted as a recognised thing by all those men that it was useless talking to the old man, simply because they could not understand him. They took it for granted that he could never comprehend the deep significance of their plans, that he would answer them with his phrases (they fancied they were only meaningless phrases) about the impossibility of going beyond the frontier and driving the enemy back to France. And everything he said—for instance, that they must wait for provisions, or that the men had no boots—all was so simple; while everything they proposed was so complicated and so clever, that it was obvious to them that he was stupid and in his dotage, while they were military officers of genius, without authority to take the lead.

Kutuzov saw all this, and simply sighed and shrugged his shoulders. Only once, he lost his temper and wrote to Bennigsen, who was in private correspondence with the Tsar: "I beg your Most High Excellency on the receipt of this letter to retire to Kaluga, on account of your attacks of ill-health, and there to await the further commands of His Majesty the Emperor."

But this dismissal of Bennigsen was followed by the arrival on the scene of the Grand Duke Konstantin, who had received a command at the beginning of the campaign and had been removed from the army by Kutuzov. Now the Grand Duke on rejoining the army informed Kutuzov of the Tsar's dissatisfaction at the poor successes of the Russian troops, and the slowness of their progress. The Tsar himself intended to be with the army in a few days.

The old man, as experienced in court methods as in warfare—who in the August of that year had been chosen commander-in-chief against the Tsar's will, who had dismissed the Grand Duke and heir-apparent from the army, and acting on his own authority, in opposition to the Tsar's will, had decreed the abandonment of Moscow—understood at once now that his day was over, that his part was played out, and that his supposed power was no more. And not only from the attitude of the court did he see this. On one side he saw the war—that war in which he had played his part—was over, and he felt that his work was done. On the other hand, at this very time, he began to be sensible of the physical weariness of his aged frame, and the necessity of rest.

On the 29th of November, Kutuzov reached Vilna—his dear Vilna, as he used to call it. Twice during his military career he had been governor of Vilna.

In that wealthy town, which had escaped injury, Kutuzov found old friends and old associations, as well as the comforts of which he had been so long deprived. And at once turning his back on all military and political cares, he plunged into the quiet routine of his accustomed life, so far as the passions raging all round him would permit. It was as though all that was being done, and had still to be done, in the world of history, was no concern of his now.

In opposition to the Tsar's wishes, Kutuzov kept the greater part of the troops in Vilna. He was said by all the persons about him to be getting much weaker, and breaking down physically during his stay in Vilna. He took no interest in the business of the army, left everything to his generals, and spent the time of waiting for the Tsar in social dissipation.

The Tsar, with his suite—Count Tolstoy, Prince Volkonsky, Araktcheev, and the rest—left Petersburg on the 7th of December, and reached Vilna on the 11th, and drove straight up to the castle in his travelling sledge. In spite of the intense cold there were some hundred generals and staff-officers in full parade uniform, and a guard of honour standing before the castle.

A courier, galloping up to the castle with steaming horses in advance of the Tsar, shouted: "He is coming!"

An adjutant rushed into the vestibule to inform Kutuzov, who was waiting in the porter's little room within.

A minute later the big, heavy figure of the old man in full

parade uniform, his breast covered with orders, and a scarf drawn tight about his bulky person, walked with a rolling gait on to the steps. He put his cocked hat on, with the flat side foremost, took his gloves in his hand, and going sideways with difficulty down the steps, took in his hand the report that had been prepared to give the Tsar.

All eyes were turned on the approaching sledge, in which the figures of the Tsar and Volkonsky could already be distinguished.

From the habit of fifty years, all this had a physically agitating effect on the old man. He felt himself over with nervous haste, set his hat straight, and pulling himself together and standing erect at the very moment when the Tsar stepping out of the sledge, turned his eyes upon him, he handed him the report, and began speaking in his measured, ingratiating voice.

The Tsar scanned Kutuzov from head to foot in a rapid glance, frowned for an instant; but at once overcoming his feelings, went up to him, and opening his arms, embraced the old general. Again, through old habitual association of ideas, arousing some deep feeling in his own heart, this embrace had its usual effect on Kutuzov. He gave a sob.

The Tsar greeted the officers and the guard of honour. And once more shaking hands with the old man, he went with him into the castle.

When he was alone with the commander-in-chief, the Tsar gave expression to his displeasure at the slowness of the pursuit of the enemy, and the blunders made, and to his views as to the coming campaign abroad. Kutuzov made no observation or explanation. The same expression of unreasoning submission with which seven years before he had listened to the Tsar's commands on the field of Austerlitz remained fixed now on his face.

When Kutuzov had left the room, and with downcast head walked across the reception-hall with his heavy, waddling step, a voice stopped him.

"Your highness," said some one.

He raised his head, and looked into the face of Count Tolstoy, who stood facing him with a small object on a silver dish. Kutuzov seemed for some time unable to grasp what was wanted of him.

All at once a faint smile gleamed on his pudgy face, and with a low, respectful bow, he picked up the object on the dish. It was the Order of St. George of the first rank.

The next day the commander-in-chief gave a dinner and a ball, which the Tsar honoured with his presence.

Kutuzov had received the Order of St. George of the first

rank; the Tsar has shown him the highest marks of respect, but every one was aware that the Tsar was displeased with the commander-in-chief. The proprieties were observed, and the Tsar set the first example in doing so. But every one felt that the old man was in fault, and had shown his incapacity. When, in accordance with the old custom of Catherine's time, Kutuzov gave orders for the captured standards to be lowered at the Tsar's feet on his entering the ball-room, the Tsar frowned with vexation, and muttered: "The old comedian."

The Tsar's displeasure was increased at Vilna by Kutuzov's obvious unwillingness or incapacity to see the importance of the approaching campaign.

When next morning the Tsar said to the officers gathered about him: "You have not only saved Russia, you have saved Europe," every one knew at once that the war was not over.

Kutuzov alone refused to see this, and frankly gave it as his opinion that no fresh war could improve the position of Russia, or add to her glory; that it could but weaken her position, and cast her down from that high pinnacle of glory at which in his view Russia was now standing. He tried to show the Tsar the impossibility of levying fresh troops, and talked of the hardships the people were suffering, the possibility of failure, and so on.

Such being his attitude on the subject, the commander-in-chief could naturally be looked upon only as a hindrance and a drag on the progress of the coming campaign.

To avoid friction with the old man, the obvious resource was—as with him at Austerlitz, and with Barclay de Tolly at the beginning of the war—to withdraw all real power from the commander-in-chief, without disturbing him by any open explanation on the matter, and to transfer it to the Tsar.

With this object, the staff was gradually transformed, and all the real power of Kutuzov's staff was removed and transferred to the Tsar.

Just as naturally, as simply, and as gradually as Kutuzov had come out of Turkey to take the command of the army just at the time when he was needed, did a new commander come now to replace him, when his part was played. Alexander was needed now just as Kutuzov was needed then for the deliverance and the glory of Russia.

Kutuzov did not see what was meant by Europe, the balance of power, and Napoleon. He could not understand all that.

After the enemy had been annihilated, Russia had been delivered and raised to the highest pinnacle of her glory, the representative of the Russian people, a Russian of the Russians, had no more left to do. Nothing was left for the representative of the national war but to die. And he did die.

As is generally the case, Pierre only felt the full strain of the physical hardships and privations he had suffered as a prisoner, when they were over. After he had been rescued, he went to Orel, and two days after getting there, as he was preparing to start for Kiev, he fell ill and spent three months in bed. He was suffering, so the doctors said, from a bilious fever.

Everything that had happened to Pierre from the time of his rescue up to his illness had left hardly any impression on his mind. He had only a memory of dark grey weather, sometimes rainy and sometimes sunshiny, of internal physical aches, of pain in his feet and his side. He remembered a general impression of the misery and suffering of men, remembered the worrying curiosity of officers and generals, who questioned him about his imprisonment, the trouble he had to get horses and a conveyance; and more than all he remembered his own dullness of thought and of feeling all that time.

On the day of his rescue he saw the dead body of Peter Rostov. The same day he learned that Prince André had lived for more than a month after the battle of Borodino, and had only a short time before died at Yaroslavl in the Rostovs' house. The same day Denisov, who had told Pierre this piece of news, happened to allude in conversation to the death of Helen, supposing Pierre to have been long aware of it. All this had at the time seemed to Pierre only strange. He felt that he could not take in the meaning of these facts. He was at the time simply in a hurry to get away from these places where men were slaughtering each other to some quiet refuge where he might rest and recover his faculties and think over all the new strange things he had learned.

But as soon as he reached Orel, he fell ill. On coming to himself after his illness, Pierre saw waiting on him two of his servants, who had come from Moscow, and the eldest of his cousins, who was staying at Pierre's estate in Elets, and hearing of his rescue and his illness had come to nurse him.

During his convalescence Pierre could only gradually recover from the impressions of the last few months, which had become habitual. Only by degrees could he become accustomed to the idea that there was no one to drive him on to-morrow, that no one would take his warm bed from him, and that he was quite sure of getting his dinner, and tea, and supper. But for a long while afterwards he was always in his dreams surrounded by his conditions as a prisoner.

And only in the same gradual way did Pierre grasp the meaning of the news he had heard since his escape: of the death of Prince André, of the death of his wife, and of the defeat of the French.

The joyful sense of freedom—that full, inalienable freedom

inherent in man, of which he had first had a consciousness a the first halting place outside Moscow—filled Pierre's sou during his convalescence. He was surprised that this inne freedom, independent as it was of all external circumstances was now as it were decked out in a luxury, a superfluity o external freedom. He was alone in a strange town withou acquaintances. No one made any demands on him; no on sent him anywhere. He had all he wanted; the thought of hi wife, that had in old days been a continual torture to him was no more.

What had worried him in old days, what he had always been seeking to solve, the question of the object of life, di not exist for him now. That seeking for an object in life wa over for him now. He felt that there was no such object, an could not be. And it was just the absence of an object tha gave him that complete and joyful sense of freedom that a this time made his happiness.

Just as it is difficult to explain why the ants hurry back tc a scattered ant-hill, some dragging away from it bits of refuse eggs, and corpses, while others run back again, and what is their object in crowding together, overtaking one another fighting with each other, so it would be hard to give the reasons that induced the Russians, after the departure of the French, to flock back to the place which had been known as Moscow. But just as looking at the ants hurrying about a ruined ant-heap, one can see by the tenacity, the energy, and the multitude of the busy insects that though all else is utterly destroyed, there is left something indestructible and immaterial that was the whole strength of the colony, so toc Moscow in the month of October, though without its governing authorities, without its churches, without its holy objects, without its wealth and its houses, was still the same Moscow as it had been in August. Everything was shattered except something immaterial, but mighty and indestructible.

Within a week there were fifteen thousand people in Moscow, within two weeks twenty-five thousand; and so it went on. The number went on mounting and mounting till by the autumn of 1813 it had reached a figure exceeding the population of the city before it was burnt.

The first Russians to enter Moscow were the Cossacks of Wintzengerode's detachment, the peasants from the nearest villages and the residents who had fled from Moscow and hidden themselves in the suburbs. On entering the ruined city, and finding it pillaged, the Russians fell to pillaging it too. They continued the work begun by the French. Trains of peasants' waggons drove into Moscow to carry away to the villages all that had been abandoned in the ruined Moscow houses and streets. The Cossacks carried off what they could to their tents; the householders collected all they could out of other houses, and removed it to their own under the pretence that it was their property.

The French had found Moscow deserted but with all the forms of an organically normal town life still existent, with various branches of trades and crafts, of luxury, and political government and religion. These forms were lifeless but they still existed. There were markets, shops, stores, grain-exchanges, and bazaars—most of them stocked with goods. There were factories and trading establishments. There were palaces and wealthy houses filled with articles of luxury. There were hospitals, prisons, courts, churches, and cathedrals. The longer the French remained, the more these forms of town life perished, and at the end all was lost in one indistinguishable, lifeless scene of pillage.

The longer the pillaging of the French lasted, the more complete was the destruction of the wealth of Moscow and of the forces of the pillagers. The longer the pillaging lasted that was carried on by the Russians on their first return to the capital, and the more there were taking part in it, the more rapidly was the wealth of Moscow and the normal life of the city re-established.

Apart from those who came for plunder, people of all sorts, drawn there, some by curiosity, some by the duties of office, some by self-interests—householders, priests, officials, high and low, traders, artisans, and peasants—flowed back to Moscow from all sides.

Within a week the peasants who had come with empty carts to carry off goods were detained by the authorities, and compelled to carry dead bodies out of the city. Other peasants, who had heard of this, drove into the town with wheat, and oats, and hay, knocking down each others' prices to a figure lower than it had been in former days. Gangs of carpenters, hoping for high wages, were arriving in Moscow every day; and on all sides there were new houses being built, or old half-burnt ones being repaired. Tradesmen carried on their business in booths. Cook-shops and taverns were opened in fire-blackened houses. The clergy held services in many churches that had escaped the fire. Church goods that had been plundered were restored as offerings. Government clerks set up their baize-covered tables and pigeon-holes of papers in little rooms. The higher authorities and the police organised a distribution of the goods left by the French. The owners of houses in which a great many of the goods plundered from other houses had been left complained of the injustice of all goods being taken to the Polygonal Palace. Others maintained that the French had collected all the things from different houses to one spot, and that it was therefore unfair to restore to the master of the house the things found in it. The police were abused and were bribed; estimates for government buildings that had been burnt were reckoned at ten times their value; and appeals for help were made. Count Rastoptchin wrote his posters again.

At the end of January Pierre arrived in Moscow and settled in the lodge of his mansion, as that had escaped the fire. He called on Count Rastoptchin and several acquaintances, and was intending in three days to set off for Petersburg.

Every one was triumphant at the victory; the ruined and reviving city was bubbling over with life. Every one was glad to see Pierre; everybody was eager to see him, and to ask him about all he had seen. Pierre had a particularly friendly feeling towards every one he met. But unconsciously he was a little on his guard with people to avoid fettering his freedom in any way. To all the questions put to him—important or trivial—whether they asked him where he meant to live, whether he were going to build, when he was starting for Petersburg, or whether he could take a parcel there for someone, he answered, "Yes, very possibly," "I dare say I may," and so on.

He heard that the Rostovs had not returned to Moscow but the thought of Natasha rarely came to his mind, and when it did occur to him it was as a pleasant memory of time long past. He felt himself set free, not only from the cares of daily life, but also from that feeling which, it seemed to him, he had voluntarily brought upon himself.

The third day after his arrival in Moscow he learnt from the Drubetskoys that Princess Mary was in Moscow and he went to call on her the same evening. The death, the sufferings, and the last days of Prince André had often filled Pierre's thoughts, and now recurred to him with fresh vividness.

Pierre drove up to the old prince's house. The house had remained entire. There were traces to be seen of the havoc wrought in it, but the character of the house was unchanged. The old footman met Pierre with a stern face, that seemed to wish to make the guest feel that the absence of the old prince made no difference in the severe routine of the household, and said that the princess had retired to her own apartments, and received on Sundays.

"Take my name to her, perhaps she will see me," said Pierre.

A few minutes later the footman returned accompanied by Dessalle. Dessalle brought a message from the princess that she would be very glad to see Pierre, and begged him, if he would excuse the lack of ceremony, to come upstairs to her apartment.

In a low-pitched room, lighted by a single candle, he found the princess, and some one with her in a black dress.

The princess rose to meet him, and held out her hand.

"Yes," she said, looking at his altered face, after he had kissed her hand. "So this is how we meet again. He often talked of you at the last," she said, turning her eyes from Pierre to her companion with a sort of bashfulness that struck him.

"I was so glad to hear of your safety. It was the only piece of good news we had had for a long time."

Again the princess glanced uneasily at her companion, and would have spoken.

But Pierre interrupted her. "Natasha! It is Natasha!" he cried.

And in that first minute Pierre betrayed to Natasha a secret that he had long had locked in his heart. He loved her.

1813-1820

EPILOGUE

NATASHA's marriage to Pierre, which took place in 1813, was the last happy event in the Rostov family. The old count died the same year; and as is always the case, with the death of the father the family was broken up.

The events of the previous year: the burning of Moscow and the flight from that city; the death of Prince André and Natasha's despair; the death of Peter and the grief of the countess fell like one blow after another on the old count's head. He seemed not to understand, and to feel himself incapable of understanding, the significance of all these events, and figuratively speaking, bowed his old head to the storm, as though expecting and seeking fresh blows to make an end of him. By turns he seemed scared and distraught, and then unnaturally lively and active.

Natasha's marriage for a time occupied him. He arranged dinners and suppers in honour of it, and obviously tried to be cheerful. But his cheerfulness was not infectious as in old days, but, on the contrary, aroused the pity of those who knew and liked him.

After Pierre and his wife had left, he collapsed and began

to complain of depression. A few days later he fell ill and took to his bed. In spite of the doctor's assurances, he knew from the first days of his illness that he would never get up again. For a whole two weeks the countess sat in a low chair by his bed. Every time she gave him his medicine, he silently kissed her hand, weeping. On the last day, sobbing, he begged forgiveness of his wife, and of his absent son, too, for squandering their property, the chief sin that lay on his conscience. And after receiving absolution and the last unction, he quietly died.

The next day the crowd of acquaintances that came to pay the last debt of respect to the deceased, filled the Rostovs' hired lodgings. All those acquaintances, who had so often dined and danced in his house, and had so often laughed at his expense, were saying now with the same inward feeling of contrition and self-reproach, as though seeking to justify themselves: "Yes, whatever he may have been, he was a splendid man. One doesn't meet such men nowadays . . . And who has not his weaknesses? . . ."

Nicholas was with the Russian army in Paris when the news of his father's death reached him. He at once applied for his discharge, and without waiting for it, obtained leave and went to Moscow. Within a month after the count's death the Rostovs' financial position had been made perfectly clear, astounding every one by the immense sum of various petty debts, the existence of which no one had suspected. The debts were more than double the assets of the estate.

Friends and relations advised Nicholas to refuse to accept his inheritance. But Nicholas looked on such a refusal as a slur on the honoured memory of his father; and so he would not hear of such a course, and accepted the inheritance with the obligation of paying the debts.

The creditors, who had so long been silent, held in check during the old count's lifetime by the vague but powerful influence of his easy good-nature, all beset Nicholas at once. There seemed, as so often happens, a sort of rivalry among them, which should get paid first; and the very people, such as Mitenka and others, who held promisory notes, not received in discharge of debts but as presents, were now the most insistent creditors. They would give Nicholas no peace. And those who had shown pity for the old man, were now ruthless in their persecution of the young heir, who was obviously guiltless as far as they were concerned, and had voluntarily undertaken to pay them.

Not one of the plans that Nicholas resorted to was successful: the estate was sold at auction at half its value, and half the debts remained still unpaid. Nicholas accepted a loan of thirty thousand roubles offered him by his brother-in-law

Pierre and paid that portion of the debts that he recognised as genuine obligations. And to avoid being thrown into prison for the remainder, as the creditors threatened, he once more entered the government service.

To return to the army, where at the next promotion he would have been colonel, was out of the question, because his mother now clung to him as her one hold on life. And so in spite of his not wanting to remain in Moscow, in the midst of a circle of acquaintances who had known him in former days, in spite of his distaste for the civil service, he accepted a civilian post in Moscow, and taking off his beloved uniform, established himself in a little lodging with his mother and Sonya.

Natasha and Pierre were living at this time in Petersburg, and had no very distinct idea of Nicholas' position. After having borrowed money from his brother-in-law, Nicholas did his utmost to conceal his poverty-stricken position from him. His situation was the more difficult because his mother would not submit to their poverty. The countess could not conceive of life being possible without the luxurious surroundings to which she had been accustomed from her childhood. And without any idea of its being difficult for her son, she was continually insisting on having a carriage, to send for a friend, or an expensive delicacy for herself, or wine, or money to buy a present, as a surprise for Natasha, for Sonya, or for Nicholas himself.

Sonya kept house, waited on her aunt, read aloud to her, and endured her caprices. Nicholas felt himself under a debt of gratitude to Sonya that he could never repay, for all she did for his mother; he admired her patience and devotion, but he tried to keep himself aloof from her.

In his heart he seemed to feel a sort of grudge against her for being too perfect, and for there being no fault to find with her. She had all the good qualities for which people are valued, but little of what would have made him love her. And he felt that the more he valued her the less he loved her. He had taken her at her word when she had written to him giving him his freedom, and now he behaved with her as though what had passed between them had been long, long ago forgotten, and could never under any circumstances be renewed.

At the beginning of the winter Princess Mary arrived in Moscow. From the gossip of the town she heard of the position of the Rostovs, and of how "the son was sacrificing himself for his mother." "It is just what I expected of him," Princess Mary said to herself, finding in it a delightful confirmation of her love for him. Remembering her intimate relations with the whole family, she thought it her duty to call on them.

Nicholas was the first to meet her, since it was impossible to reach the countess's room without passing through his room. Instead of the expression of delight Princess Mary had expected to see on his face at the first glance at her, he met her with a look of chilliness, stiffness, and pride that she had never seen before. Nicholas inquired after her health, conducted her to his mother, and, after staying five minutes, went out of the room.

"Why should she stroll in here? What does she want? I can't endure these ladies and all these civilities!" he said aloud before Sonya, obviously unable to restrain his irritation, after the princess's carriage had rolled away from the house.

Nicholas would have liked to say no more about Princess Mary. But after her visit the old countess talked about her several times every day.

She sang her praises. Insisted that her son should go and see her and expressed a wish to see more of her: "She is a very good and conscientious girl," she would say. "And you must go and call on her. Anyway, you will see some one; and it is boring for you, I expect, with us. Besides civility demands it, I should suppose . . . I have begged you to do so, and now I will meddle no further since . . ."

Next day, and the third, and the fourth, the same conversation was repeated again and again.

Finally to please his mother, Nicholas agreed to go.

Princess Mary was sitting in the schoolroom, supervising her nephew's lessons, when the servant announced that Nicholas Rostov was below. After the cold reception Nicholas had given her when she visited his mother Princess Mary was rather surprised and upset. She called Mademoiselle Bourienne, and with her went into the drawing-room.

At the first glance at Nicholas' face, she saw that he had come merely to perform the obligations of civility, and she determined to keep to the tone he adopted towards her.

They talked of the health of the countess, of common acquaintances, of the latest news of the war, and when the ten minutes required by propriety had elapsed, Nicholas got up to say good-bye.

With the aid of Mademoiselle Bourienne, Princess Mary had kept up the conversation very well. But at the very last moment, just when he was getting up, she was so weary of talking of what did not interest her, and she was so absorbed in wondering why to her alone so little joy had been given in life, that in a fit of abstraction, she sat motionless gazing straight before her with her luminous eyes.

Nicholas looked at her and felt suddenly sorry for her, and vaguely conscious that he might be the cause of the sadness. He longed to help her, to say something pleasant to her, but he could not think what to say.

"Good-bye, princess," he said. She started and flushed.

"Oh, I beg your pardon," she said. "You are going already, count. Well, good-bye! Oh, the cushion for the countess?"

"Wait a minute, I will get it," said Mademoiselle Bourienne, and she left the room.

They were both silent, glancing at each other now and then.

"Yes, princess," said Nicholas at last. "It seems not long ago, but how much has happened since the first time we met at Bogutcharovo. We all seemed in such trouble then, but I would give a great deal to have that time back . . . And there's no bringing it back."

Princess Mary looked intently at him with her luminous eyes, as he spoke.

"You have no need to regret the past, count," she said. She saw in him again now the man she had known and loved, and it was to that man only she was speaking now. "I thought you would . . ." she said. "I have been such intimate friends with you . . . and with your family, and I thought you would not feel my sympathy intrusive; but I made a mistake," she said. Her voice suddenly shook. "I don't know why," she went on, recovering herself. "You used to be different, and . . ."

"There are thousands of reasons *why*." He laid special stress on the word *why*. "I thank you, princess," he added softly. "It is sometimes hard . . ."

"Why, why?" she almost cried all at once, involuntarily moving nearer to him. "Why? Tell me. You must tell me." He was silent. "I do not understand your *why*," she went on. "But I am sad, I . . . I will admit that to you. You mean for some reason to deprive me of our old friendship. And it hurts me." There were tears in her eyes and in her voice. "I have had so little happiness in my life that every loss is hard for me . . . Excuse me, good-bye," she suddenly burst into tears, and was going out of the room.

"Princess! Stay, for God's sake," he cried, trying to stop her. "Princess!"

She looked round. For a few seconds they gazed silently at each other and the remote and impossible became all at once close at hand, possible and inevitable.

In the autumn of 1813, Nicholas married Princess Mary, and with his wife, and mother, and Sonya, went to live at Bleak Hills, which had been rebuilt.

Within four years he had paid off the remainder of his debts without selling his wife's estates, and coming into a small legacy on the death of a cousin, he also repaid the loan he had borrowed from Pierre.

In another three years, by 1820, Nicholas had so well managed his affairs that he was able to buy a small estate adjoining Bleak Hills, and was opening negotiations for the re-purchase of his ancestral estate of Otradnoe, which was his cherished dream.

Though he took up the management of the land at first from necessity, he soon acquired such a passion for agriculture, that it became his favourite and almost his exclusive interest.

Countess Mary was jealous of this passion of her husband's for agriculture, and regretted she could not share it. Her sole interest lay in her home and their three children. She was unable to understand the joys and disappointments he met with in that world apart that was so alien to her. She could not understand why he used to be so happy when after getting up at dawn and spending the whole morning in the fields or the threshing-floor he came back to tea with her from the sowing, the mowing, or the harvest. She could not understand why he was so delighted when he told her with enthusiasm of the well-to-do, thrifty peasant, who had been up all night with his family, carting his sheaves, and had all harvested when no one else had begun carrying. She could not understand why, stepping out of the window on to the balcony, he smiled when a warm, fine rain began to fall on his young oats that were suffering from the drought, or why, when a menacing cloud blew over in mowing or harvest time, he would come in from the barn red, sunburnt, and perspiring, with the smell of wormwood in his hair, and rubbing his hands would say: "Come, another day of this and my lot, and the peasants' too, will all be in the barn."

Still less could she understand how it was that with his good heart and everlasting readiness to anticipate her wishes, he would be thrown almost into despair when she brought him petitions from peasants or their wives who had appealed to her to be let off tasks, why it was that he, her good-natured Nicholas, obstinately refused her, angrily begging her not to meddle in his business. She felt that he had a world apart, that was intensely dear to him, governed by laws of its own which she did not understand.

Sometimes trying to understand him she would talk to him of the good work he was doing in striving for the good of his serfs; but at this he was angry and answered: "Not in the least. It never even entered my head; and for their good I would not lift my little finger. That's all romantic nonsense and old wives' cackle—all that doing good to one's neighbour. I don't want our children to be beggars; I want to build up our fortunes in my lifetime; that is all. And to do that one must have discipline, one must have strictness . . . So there!" he would declare, clenching his fist. "And justice too—of course," he would add, "because if the peasant is naked and hungry, and has but one poor horse, he can do no good for himself or me."

During the fall and early winter of 1820, Natasha, with her three little daughters and infant son, was staying at Bleak Hills. Pierre was in Petersburg, where he had gone on private business of his own, as he said, for three weeks. He had already been away for six, and was expected home every minute. There was also staying with the Rostovs Nicholas' old friend, Denisov, now a retired general on half-pay.

Natasha had grown stouter, so that it was hard to recognise in the robust-looking young mother the slim, mobile Natasha of old days. Her features had become more defined, and wore an expression of calm softness and serenity. Her face had no longer that ever-glowing fire of eagerness that had once constituted her chief charm. Only on rare occasions now the old fire glowed in her again. That happened only when Pierre returned after a trip, when a sick child recovered, or on the rare occasions when something happened to attract her to her singing, which she had entirely laid aside since her marriage. And at those rare moments, when the old fire glowed again, she was more attractive, with her handsome, fully-developed figure, than she had ever been in the past.

Since her marriage Natasha and her husband had lived in Moscow, in Petersburg, on their estate near Moscow, and at her mother's; that is to say, at Bleak Hills with Nicholas and Mary.

The young Countess Bezuhov was little seen in society. Every one who had known Natasha before her marriage marvelled at the change that had taken place in her, as though it were something extraordinary. Only the old countess, with her mother's insight, had seen that what was at the root of all Natasha's wild outbursts of feeling was simply the need of children and a husband of her own, as she often used to declare, more in earnest than in joke.

Natasha did not follow the golden rule that recommends that a girl on marrying should not neglect herself, should not give up her accomplishments, should think even more of her appearance than when a young girl, and should try to fascinate her husband as she had fascinated him before he was her husband. She felt that the tie that bound her to her husband did not rest on those romantic feelings which had attracted him to her, but rested on something else undefined, but as strong as the tie that bound her soul to her body.

To curl her hair, put on a crinoline, and sing songs to attract her husband would have seemed to her as strange as to deck herself up so as to please herself. Natasha neglected herself to such a degree that her dresses, her untidy hair, and her jealousy—she was jealous of Sonya, the governess, of every woman, pretty and ugly—were a continual subject of jests among her friends.

The subject in which Natasha was completely absorbed was her family, that is, her husband, on whom she kept a hold so that he should belong entirely to her, to his home and her children, whom she had to carry, to bear, to nurse and to bring up.

The general opinion was that Pierre was tied to his wife's apron strings, and it really was so. From the earliest days of their marriage Natasha had made plain her claims. Pierre had been greatly surprised at his wife's view—to him a completely novel idea—that every minute of his life belonged to her and their home. He was surprised at his wife's demands, but he was flattered by them, and he submitted. He did not dare to be attentive, or even to speak with a smile, to any other woman; did not dare go to dine at the club, without good reason, simply for entertainment; did not dare spent money on idle whims, and did not dare to be away from home for any long time, except on business. To make up for all this Pierre had complete power in his own house. He had only to show the slightest preference, for what he desired to be at once carried out. He had but to express a wish and Natasha jumped up at once and ran for what he wanted.

The whole household was ruled by the wishes of Pierre, which Natasha tried to guess. Their manner of life and place of residence, their acquaintances and ties, Natasha's pursuits, and the bringing up of the children—all followed, not only Pierre's expressed wishes, but even the deductions Natasha strove to draw from the ideas he explained in conversation with her. And she guessed very correctly what was the essential point of Pierre's wishes, and having once guessed it she was steadfast in adhering to it: even when Pierre himself would have veered round she opposed him with his own weapons.

After seven years of married life, Pierre had a firm and joyful consciousness that he was not a bad fellow, and he felt this because he saw himself reflected in his wife. In himself he felt all the good and bad mingled together, and obscuring one another. But in his wife he saw reflected only what was really good; everything not quite good was left out.

And this result was not reached by the way of logical thought, but by way of a mysterious, direct reflection of himself.

Two months previously, Pierre was already settled at the Rostovs' when he received a letter from a certain Prince Fyodor, urging him to come to Petersburg for the discussion of various important questions that were agitating the Petersburg members of a society, of which Pierre had been one of the chief founders.

Natasha read this letter, as she did all her husband's letters, and bitterly as she always felt his absence, she urged him herself to go to Petersburg. All she asked was that he would fix an absolutely certain date for his return. To everything pertaining to Pierre's intellectual pursuits she ascribed immense consequence, though she had no understanding of them, and she was always in dread of being a hindrance.

Ever since the day fixed for his return, two weeks before, Natasha had been in a continual state of alarm, depression, and irritability, especially when her mother, her brother, Sonya, or Countess Mary tried to console her by excusing Pierre, and inventing good reasons for his delay in returning.

"It's all nonsense," Natasha would say. "His projects never lead to anything, and all those foolish societies," she would declare of the very matters in the immense importance of which she firmly believed. And she would march off to the nursery to nurse her only boy, the baby Peter.

No one could give her such soothing consolation as that little three months' old creature, when it lay at her breast, and she felt the movement of its lips and the snuffling of its nose.

Natasha was nursing the baby when Pierre's carriage drove noisily up to the entrance, and the nurse, knowing how to please her mistress, came to the door with a beaming face.

"He has come, ma'am," whispered the nurse.

The blood rushed to Natasha's face, and her feet involuntarily moved, but to jump up and run was out of the question. The baby opened its little eyes, glanced, as though to say, "You are here," and gave another lazy smack with its lips.

Cautiously withdrawing her breast, Natasha dandled him, handed him to the nurse, and went softly and quickly towards the door.

Then she ran to the vestibule. Pierre was there in a fur coat, fumbling with his scarf.

She hugged him, squeezing her head to his breast, and then drawing back, glanced at the frosty, red, and happy face of Pierre. "Yes, here he is happy, satisfied . . ."

And all at once she remembered all the tortures of suspense she had passed through during the last two weeks. She frowned, and a torrent of reproaches and angry words broke upon Pierre.

"Yes, you are all right, you have been happy, you have been enjoying yourself . . . But what about me! You might at least think of your children. I am nursing, my milk went wrong . . . Peter nearly died of it. And you have been enjoying yourself. Yes, enjoying yourself . . ."

Pierre knew he was not to blame, because he could not have come sooner. He knew this outburst on her part was unseemly, and would be all over in two minutes. Above all, he knew that he was himself happy and joyful. He would have liked to smile, but dared not even think of that. He made a piteous, dismayed face, and bowed before the storm.

"I could not, upon my word . . ."

"Aren't you ashamed? If you could see what I am like without you, how wretched I am . . . But come along, come along," she said, not letting go of his hand. And they went off to their rooms.

When Nicholas and Mary came to look for Pierre, they found him in the nursery, with his baby son awake in his arms. There was a smile on the baby's broad face and open, toothless mouth. The storm had long blown over, and a bright, sunny radiance of joy flowed all over Natasha's face, as she gazed tenderly at her husband and son.

Pierre, not letting go of his son, stooped down, kissed them, and answered their questions. But it was obvious that in spite of the many interesting things they had to discuss, the baby, with the wobbling head in the little cap, was absorbing Pierre's whole attention.

"Oh, Pierre is a wonderful nurse," said Natasha. "He says his hand is just made for a baby's bottom. Just look."

"Oh yes, but not for this," Pierre cried laughing, and hurriedly snatching up the baby, he handed him back to his nurse.

As in every real family, there were several quite separate worlds living together at Bleak Hills, and while each of these preserved its own individuality, they mixed into one harmonious whole. Every event that occurred in the house was alike important and joyful or distressing to all those circles. But each circle had its own private grounds for rejoicing or mourning at every event quite apart from the rest.

So Pierre's arrival was a joyful and important event, reflected as such in all the circles of the household.

The children and their governesses were delighted at Pierre's return, because no one drew them into the general social life of the house as Pierre did. He it was who could play on the avichord that écossaise (his one piece) to which, as he said, ıe could dance all possible dances; and he was quite sure, o, to have brought all of them presents.

Young Nicholas Bolkonsky, who was now a thin, delicate, telligent boy of fifteen, with curly light hair and beautiful 'es, was delighted because Uncle Pierre, as he called him, as the object of his passionate love and adoration. Countess Iary, who had brought him up, had done her utmost to make oung Nicholas love her husband, as she loved him; and the oy did like his uncle, but Pierre he adored. He did not want be an hussar or a Cavalier of St. George like his Uncle Iicholas; he wanted to be learned, clever, and kind like Pierre. Ie never missed a word that Pierre uttered, and afterwards lone or with Dessalle recalled every phrase, and wondered at s exact significance. Pierre's past life, his unhappiness before 812, his adventures in Moscow, and captivity with the 'rench, Platon Karataev, his love for Natasha, whom the boy oved too with quite a special feeling, and, above all, his riendship with his father, whom young Nicholas did not remember, all made Pierre a hero and a saint in his eyes.

The grown-up members of the household were glad to see friend who always made daily life run more smoothly and asily.

The old ladies were pleased both at the presents Pierre rought them, and still more at Natasha's being herself again.

Pierre felt the various views those different sets of people took of him, and tried to satisfy the expectations of all of them.

Though he was the most absent-minded and forgetful of men, by the help of a list Natasha had made for him, he had bought everything, not forgetting a single commission from his mother-in-law or brother-in-law, nor the presents of a dress for Madame Byelov, the old Countess Rostov's companion, and toys for the children.

The countess was by now over sixty. Her hair was completely grey, and she wore a cap that surrounded her whole face with a frill. Her face was wrinkled, her upper lip had sunk, and her eyes were dim.

After the deaths of her son and her husband that had followed so quickly on one another, she had felt herself a creature forgotten in this world, with no object and no interest in life. She ate and drank, slept and lay awake, but she did not live. Life gave her no impressions. She wanted nothing from life but peace, and that peace she could find only in death. But until death came to her she had to go on living—that is, using her vital forces. No external aim could be seen in her existence; all that could be seen was the need to exercise her various capacities. She had to eat, to sleep, to think, to talk, to weep, to work, to get angry, and so on, simply because she had a stomach, a brain, muscles, nerves, and spleen. All this sh did, but not at the promptings of any external motive. Sh only talked because she needed to exercise her lungs and he tongue. She cried like a child, because she needed the physica relief of tears. What for people in their full vigour is a motiv with her was obviously a pretext.

Thus in the morning, especially if she had eaten anythin too rich the night before, she sought an occasion for ange and pitched on the first excuse—the deafness of Madam Byelov.

From the other end of the room she would begin to sa something to her in a low voice.

"I think it is warmer to-day, my dear," she would say in whisper. And when Madame Byelov replied: "To be sure they have come," she would mutter angrily: "Mercy on us how deaf and stupid she is!"

Another excuse was her snuff, which she fancied either too dry, or too moist, or badly pounded. After these outbursts o irritability, a bilious hue came into her face. And her maid knew by infallible tokens when Madame Byelov would be deaf again, and when her snuff would again be damp, and her face would again be yellow. Just as she had to exercise her spleen, she had sometimes to exercise her remaining facul ties; and for thought the pretext was a game of patience. When she wanted to cry, the subject of her tears was the late count When she needed excitement, the subject was Nicholas and anxiety about his health. When she wanted to say something spiteful, the pretext was the Countess Mary. When she re quired exercise for her organs of speech—this was usually about seven o'clock, after she had had her after-dinner rest in a darkened room—then the pretext was found in repetition of anecdotes, always the same, and always to the same listeners.

The old countess's condition was understood by all the household, though no one ever spoke of it, and every possible effort was made by every one to satisfy her. Only rarely a mournful half-smile passed between Nicholas, Pierre, Natasha, and Countess Mary that betrayed their understanding of her condition.

But those glances said something else besides. They said that she had done her work in life already, that she was not all here in what was seen in her now, that they would all be the same, and that they were glad to give way to her, to restrain themselves for the sake of this poor creature, once so dear, once as full of life as they.

When Pierre and Natasha came into the drawing-room, the old countess happened to be in her customary condition of needing the mental exercise of a game of patience, and therefore, although from habit she uttered the words, she always repeated on the return of Pierre or her son after absence: "It was high time, high time, my dear boy; we have been expecting you a long while. Well, thank God, you are here." And on the presents being given her, pronounced another stock phrase: "It's not the gift that is precious, my dear. . . . Thank you for thinking of an old woman like me. . . ." It was evident that Pierre's entrance at that moment was unwelcome, because it interrupted her in dealing her cards. She finished her game of patience, and only then really looked at her presents. The presents for her consisted of a card-case of fine workmanship, a bright blue Sèvres cup with a lid and a picture of shepherdesses on it, and a gold snuff-box with the count's portrait on it, which Pierre had had done by a miniature-painter in Petersburg. The countess had long wished to have this; but just now she had no inclination to weep, and so she looked unconcernedly at the portrait, and took more notice of the card-case.

"Thank you, my dear, you are a comfort to me," she said, as she always did. "But best of all, you have brought yourself back. It has been beyond everything; you must really scold your wife. She is like one possessed without you. She sees nothing, thinks of nothing," she said as usual. "Look, Madame Byelov," she added, "at the card-case my son has brought us."

Madame Byelov admired the present, and was enchanted with the dress material.

Pierre, Natasha, Nicholas, Countess Mary, and Denisov had a great deal they wanted to talk about, which was not talked of before the old countess; not because anything was concealed from her, but simply because she had dropped so out of things, that if they had begun to talk freely before her they would have had to answer so many questions put by her at random, and to repeat so many things that had been repeated to her so many times already; to tell her that this person was dead and that person was married, which she could never remember. Yet they sat as usual at tea in the drawing-room, and Pierre answered the countess's quite superfluous questions, which were of no interest even to her, and told her that Prince Vassily was looking older, and that Countess So-and-so sent her kind regards and remembrances.

Such conversation, was kept up all tea-time. All the grown-up members of the family were gathered about the round tea-table with the samovar, at which Sonya presided. The children with their tutors and governesses had already had tea, and their voices could be heard in the next room. At tea every one sat in his own place. Nicholas sat by the stove at a little table apart, where his tea was handed him. An old terrier bitch, with a perfectly grey face, lay on a chair beside him. Denisov, with streaks of grey in his curly hair, wearing his general's coat unbuttoned, sat beside Countess Mary. Pierre was sitting between his wife and the old countess. He was telling what he knew might interest the old lady and be intelligible to her. He talked of external social events and of the persons who had once made up the circle of the old countess's contemporaries, and had once been a real living circle of people, but were now for the most part scattered about the world, and, like her, living out their remnant of life, gleaning up the stray ears of what they had sown in life.

By Pierre's eagerness, Natasha saw that his visit had been an interesting one, that he was longing to tell them about it, but dared not speak freely before the countess. Denisov, not being a member of the family, did not understand Pierre's caution, and, moreover, being dissatisfied with the course of events, took a very great interest in all that was going on in Petersburg.

"Well, what is all this idiocy, Gossner and Madame Tatarinov," Denisov asked, "is that still going on?"

"Going on?" said Pierre. "Worse than ever. The Bible Society is now the whole government."

"What is that?" asked the old countess, who, having drunk her tea, was obviously seeking a pretext for ill-humour after taking food. "What are you saying about the government? I don't understand that."

"Why, you know, mother," said Nicholas, who knew how to translate things into his mother's language. "Prince Alexander Nikolaevitch Golitsin had founded a society, so he has great influence they say."

"Araktcheev and Golitsin," said Pierre incautiously, "are practically the government now. And what a government! They see conspiracy in everything, they are afraid of everything."

"What, Prince Alexander found fault with! He is a most admirable man. I used to meet him in old days," said the countess in an offended tone. And still more offended by the general silence, she went on, "Nowadays people find fault with every one. A Gospel Society, what harm is there in that?" and she got up, and with a severe face sailed out to her table in the adjoining sitting-room.

In the midst of the silence that followed, they heard the sound of children's voices and laughter from the next room.

"Finished, finished!" the gleeful shriek of little Natasha was heard above all the rest. Pierre exchanged glances with Countess Mary and Nicholas, and he smiled happily.

"Delightful music!" he said.

"Anna Makarovna has finished her stockings," said Countess Mary.

"Oh, I'm going to have a look at them," said Pierre, jumping up.

"I know, I know," Nicholas chimed in. "I mustn't come—the stockings are a surprise for me."

Pierre went in to the children, and the shrieks and laughter were louder than ever. "Now, Anna Makarovna," cried Pierre's voice, "here in the middle of the room and at the word of command—one, two, and when I say three, you stand here. You in my arms. Now, one, two . . ." there was complete silence. "Three!" and an enthusiastic roar of children's voices rose in the room. "Two, two!" cried the children.

They meant the two stockings, which, by a secret only known to her, Anna Makarovna used to knit on her needles at once. She always made a solemn ceremony of pulling one stocking out of the other in the presence of the children when the pair was finished.

Soon after this the children came in to say good-night. The children kissed every one, the tutors and governesses said good-night and went away. Dessalle alone remained with his pupil. The tutor whispered to his young charge to come downstairs.

"No, M. Dessalle, I will ask my aunt if I may stay," young Nicholas answered, also in a whisper. "Aunt Mary, will you let me stay?" he asked, going up to his aunt. His face was full of entreaty, excitement, and enthusiasm. Countess Mary looked at him and turned to Pierre.

"When you are here, there is no tearing him away . . ." she said.

"I will bring him directly, M. Dessalle. Good-night," said Pierre, giving his hand to the Swiss tutor, and he turned smiling to young Nicholas. "We have not seen each other at all yet. Mary, how like he is growing . . ."

"Like my father?" said the boy, flushing crimson and looking up at Pierre.

Pierre nodded to him, and went on with the conversation that had been interrupted by the children. Countess Mary had some canvas embroidery in her hands; Natasha sat with her eyes fixed on her husband. Nicholas and Denisov got up, asked for pipes, smoked, and took cups of tea from Sonya, still sitting with weary pertinacity at the samovar, and asked questions of Pierre. The curly-headed, delicate boy, with his shining eyes, sat unnoticed by any one in a corner.

The conversation turned on the scandals of the day in the higher government circles. Denisov, who was dissatisfied with the government on account of his own disappointments in the service, heard with pleasure of all the follies, as he considered them, that were going on now in Petersburg, and made his comments on Pierre's words in harsh and in cutting phrases.

"In old days you had to be a German to be anybody, nowadays you have to dance with the Tatarinov woman and Madame Krüdner, to read . . . Eckartshausen, and the rest of that crew. Ugh! I would let good old Bonaparte loose again! He would knock all the nonsense out of them."

Though Nicholas did not have Denisov's disposition to find everything wrong, he too thought it dignified and becoming to criticise the government, and he believed that the fact, that a certain person had been appointed minister of such a department, and the Tsar had said this, and the minister had said that, were all matters of the greatest importance. And he thought it necessary to take an interest in the subject and to question Pierre about it. So the questions put by Nicholas and Denisov kept the conversation on the usual lines of gossip about the higher government circles.

But Natasha, who knew every thought and expression in her husband, saw that Pierre wanted to lead the conversation into another channel, and to open his heart on his own idea, the idea about which he had gone to Petersburg to consult his new friend Prince Fyodor. She saw too that he could not lead up to this, and she came to the rescue with a question: How had he settled things with Prince Fyodor?

"All the same thing over and over again," said Pierre, looking about him. "Every one sees that things are all going so wrong that they can't be endured, and that it's the duty of all honest men to oppose it to the utmost of their power."

"Why, what can honest men do?" said Nicholas, frowning slightly. "What can be done?"

"Why, this . . ."

"Let us go into the study," said Nicholas.

Natasha, who had a long while been expecting to be called to her baby, heard the nurse calling her, and went off to the nursery. Countess Mary went with her. The men went to the study, and young Nicholas stole in, unnoticed by his uncle, and sat down at the writing-table, in the dark by the window.

"Well, what are you going to do?" said Denisov.

"Everlastingly these fantastic schemes," said Nicholas.

"Well," Pierre began, not sitting down, but pacing the room, and coming to an occasional standstill, lisping rapidly as he talked. "This is the position of things in Petersburg: the Tsar lets everything go. He is entirely wrapped up in mysticism. All he asks for is peace; and he can only get peace through these men of no faith and no conscience, who are stifling and destroying everything, Magnitsky and Araktcheev, and . . . You will admit that if you did not look after your property yourself, and only asked for peace and quiet, the crueller your bailiff were, the more easily you would attain your object," he said, turning to Nicholas.

"Well, but what is the drift of all this?" said Nicholas.

"Why, everything is going to ruin. Bribery in the law-courts, in the army nothing but coercion and drill: exile—people are being tortured, and enlightenment is suppressed. Everything youthful and honourable—they are crushing! Everybody sees that it can't go on like this. The strain is too great, and the string must snap," said Pierre. "I told them one thing in Petersburg."

"Told whom?" asked Denisov.

"Oh, you know whom," said Pierre, with a meaning look from under his brows, "Prince Fyodor and all of them. Zeal in educational and philanthropic work is all very good of course. Their object is excellent and all the rest of it; but in present circumstances what is wanted is something else."

At that moment Nicholas noticed his nephew. His face fell; he went up to him.

"Why are you here?"

"Oh, let him be," said Pierre, taking hold of Nicholas' arm; and he went on. "That's not enough, I told them; something else is wanted now. While you stand waiting for the string to snap every moment; while every one is expecting the inevitable revolution, as many people as possible should join hands to withstand the general catastrophe. All the youth and energy is being drawn away and dissipated. One lured by women, another by honours, a third by display or money—they are all going over to the wrong side. As for independent, honest men, like you and me—there are none of them left. I say: enlarge the scope of the society: let the motto be not loyalty only, but independence and action."

Nicholas, leaving his nephew, had angrily moved out a chair, and sat down in it. As he listened to Pierre, he coughed in a dissatisfied way, and frowned more and more.

"But action with what object?" he cried. "And what attitude do you take to the government?"

"Why, the attitude of supporters! The society will perhaps not even be a secret one, if the government will allow it. So far from being hostile to the government, we are the real conservatives. It is a society of *gentlemen*, in the full significance of the word. It is simply to prevent corrupt government officials from coming to massacre my children and yours, to prevent Araktcheev from transporting me to a military settlement, that we are joining hands, with the sole object of the common welfare and security."

"Yes; but it's a secret society, and consequently a hostile and mischievous society, which can only lead to evil."

"Why so? Did the *Tugend-bund* which saved Europe lead to evil? A *Tugend-bund* it is, an alliance of virtue; it is love and mutual help; it is what Christ preached on the cross . . ."

Natasha, coming into the room in the middle of the conversation, looked happily at her husband. She was not rejoicing in what he was saying. It did not interest her indeed, because it seemed to her that it was all so excessively simple, and that she had known it long ago. She thought this, because she knew all that it sprang from—all Pierre's soul. She was happy to see his eager face.

Pierre was watched with even more rapturous gladness by the young boy Nicholas, who had been forgotten by all of them. Every word Pierre uttered set his heart in a glow, and his fingers moving nervously. He unconsciously picked up and broke to pieces the sticks of sealing-wax and pens on his uncle's table.

"It's not at all what you imagine, but just such a society as the German *Tugend-bund* is what I propose."

"Well, that's all very well for the sausage-eaters—a *Tugend-bund*—but I don't understand it, and I can't even pronounce it," Denisov's loud, positive voice broke in. "Everything's rotten and corrupt; I agree there; only your *Tugend-bund* I don't understand, but if one is dissatisfied . . ."

Pierre smiled, Natasha laughed; but Nicholas knitted his brows more than ever, and began arguing with Pierre that no revolution was to be expected, and that the danger he talked of had no existence but in his imagination. Pierre maintained his view, and as his intellectual faculties were keener and more resourceful, Nicholas was soon at a loss for an answer. This angered him still more, as in his heart he felt convinced, not by reasoning, but by something stronger than reasoning, of the truth of his own view.

"Well, let me tell you," he said, getting up and nervously setting his pipe down in the corner, and then flinging it away; "I can't prove it to you. You say everything is all rotten, and there will be a revolution; I don't see it; but you say our oath of allegiance is a conditional thing, and as to that, let me tell you, you are my greatest friend, you know that, but if you start a secret society, you begin working against the government—whatever it may be, I know it's my duty to obey it. And if Araktcheev bids me march against you with a squadron and cut you down, I won't hesitate for a second. And then you may think what you like about it."

An awkward silence followed these words. Natasha was the first to break it by defending her husband and attacking her brother. Her defence was weak and clumsy. But it attained her object. The conversation was taken up again, and no longer in the unpleasantly hostile tone in which Nicholas' last words had been spoken.

When they all got up to go in to supper, young Nicholas went up to Pierre with a pale face and shining eyes.

"Uncle Pierre . . . you . . . no . . . If father had been alive . . . He would have been on your side?" he asked.

Pierre saw in a flash all the original, complicated and violent thought and feeling that must have been going on in this boy during the conversation. And recalling all he had been saying, he felt annoyed that the boy should have heard him. He had to answer him, however.

"I believe he would," he said reluctantly, and he went out of the study.

The boy looked down, and then for the first time seemed to become aware of the havoc he had been making on the writing-table. He flushed and went up to his uncle Nicholas.

"Uncle, forgive me; I did it—not on purpose," he said, pointing to the fragments of sealing-wax and pens.

Nicholas bounded up angrily. "All right, all right," he said, throwing the bits of pens and sealing-wax under the table. And with evident effort mastering his fury, he turned away from him.

"You ought not to have been here at all," he said.

At supper no more was said of politics and societies, but the conversation turned on the subject most agreeable to Nicholas—reminiscences of 1812. Denisov started the talk, and Pierre was particularly cordial and amusing. And the party broke up on the friendliest terms.

Nicholas, after undressing in his study, and giving instructions to his steward, who was awaiting him, went in his dressing-gown to his bedroom, and found his wife Mary at her writing-table.

"I have behaved badly. You were not in the study. Pierre and I were arguing, and I lost my temper," he said. "I couldn't help it. He is such a child. I don't know what would become of him if Natasha didn't keep him at her apron-strings. Can you imagine what he went to Petersburg about? . . . They have made a . . ."

"Yes, I know," said Countess Mary. "Natasha told me."

"Oh, well, you know, then," Nicholas went on, getting angry at the mere recollection of the discussion. "He wants to persuade me that it's the duty of every honest man to work against the government when one's sworn allegiance and duty. . . . I am sorry you were not there. As it was, they all fell upon me, Denisov, and Natasha, too. . . . Natasha is too amusing when it comes to discussion—she hasn't an idea to call her own—she simply repeats his words."

"Yes, I have noticed that," said Countess Mary.

"When I told him that duty and sworn allegiance come before everything, he began arguing God knows what. It was a pity you were not there. What would you have said?"

"To my thinking, you were quite right. I told Natasha so. Pierre says that every one is suffering, and being ill-treated and corrupted, and that it's our duty to help our neighbours. Of course, he is right," said Countess Mary. "But he forgets that we have other nearer duties, which God Himself has marked out for us, and that we may run risks for ourselves, but not for our children."

"Yes, yes, that's just what I told him," cried Nicholas, who actually believed he had said just that. "And they had all their say out about loving one's neighbour, and Christianity, and all the rest of it, before young Nicholas, who had slipped in there, and was pulling all my things to pieces."

"Ah, do you know, Nicholas, I am so often worried about young Nicholas," said Countess Mary. "He is such an exceptional boy. And I am afraid I neglect him for my own. All of us have our children; we all have our own ties; while he has nobody. He is always alone with his thoughts."

"Well, I don't think you have anything to reproach yourself with on his account. Everything the fondest mother could do for her son you have done, and are doing, for him."

"Still I am not the same as a mother," said Countess Mary. "I feel that it's not the same, and it worries me. He's a wonderful boy; but I am awfully afraid for him."

"Yes, Pierre always was, and always will be, a dreamer," he went on, returning to the discussion in the study, which had worked on his feelings. "Why, what concern is all that of mine—Araktcheev's misdoings, and all the rest of it—what concern was it of mine, when at the time of our marriage I had so many debts that they were going to put me in prison, and a mother who couldn't see it or understand it. And then you, and the children, and my work. It's not for my own pleasure I am from morning to night looking after the men, or in the counting-house. No, I know I must work to comfort my mother, repay you, and not leave my children in poverty, as I was left myself."

Countess Mary wanted to tell him that man does not live by bread alone; that he attached too much importance to this *work*. But she knew that she must not say this, and that it would be useless. She only took his hand and kissed it.

Natasha, as soon as she was alone with her husband, had

begun talking too, as only husband and wife can talk, that is, understanding and communicating their thoughts to each other, with extraordinary clearness and rapidity.

From the moment they were alone together and Natasha, with wide open, happy eyes, crept softly up to him and suddenly, seizing his head, pressed it to her bosom, saying, "Now you're all mine, mine! You shan't escape!" that conversation began that contravened every rule of logic, especially because they talked of several different subjects at once. This discussion of all sorts of things at once, far from hindering clearness of comprehension, was the surest token that they understood one another fully.

Natasha talked to Pierre of the daily round of existence at her brother's. She said that she was fonder of Mary than ever. Pierre told her how intolerable he had found the evening parties and dinners with ladies in Petersburg.

"I have lost the art of talking to ladies," he said. "It was horribly tiresome. Especially as I was so busy."

Natasha looked intently at him, and went on. "Mary, now she is wonderful!" she said. "The insight she has into children. She seems to see straight into their souls. Yesterday, for instance, her baby Nicholas was naughty . . ."

"And isn't he like his father?" Pierre put in.

Natasha knew why he made this remark about baby Nicholas' likeness to his father. He disliked the thought of his dispute with his brother-in-law, and was longing to hear what she thought about it.

"It's a weakness of Nicholas', that if anything is not generally accepted, he will never agree with it."

"No, the real thing is that to Nicholas," said Pierre, "thoughts and ideas are an amusement, almost a pastime. Here he's forming a library and has made it a rule not to buy a new book till he has read through the last he has bought –Sismondi and Rousseau and Montesquieu," Pierre added with a smile. "You know how I . . ."

"You say ideas to him are not serious . . ."

"Yes, and to me nothing else is serious. All the while I was in Petersburg, I seemed to be seeing every one in a dream. When I am absorbed by an idea, nothing else is serious. . . . Nicholas says we ought not to think. But I can't help it. To say nothing of the fact, I can say so to you, that in Petersburg I felt that the whole thing would go to pieces without me, every one pulled his own way. But I succeeded in bringing them all together; and then my idea is so clear and simple. I don't say we ought to work against so-and-so. We may be mistaken. But I say: let those join hands who care for the good cause, and let our one standard be energy and honesty."

"Do you know what I am thinking about?" she said. "About Platon Karataev. What would he have said? Would he have approved of you now?"

Pierre was not in the least surprised at this question. He understood the connection of his wife's ideas.

"Platon Karataev?" he said, and he pondered, evidently trying sincerely to picture what Karataev's judgment would have been on the subject. "He would not have understood, and yet, perhaps, he would."

"I like you awfully!" said Natasha all at once. "Awfully! Awfully!"

"No, he wouldn't have approved," said Pierre. "What he would have approved of is our home life. He liked to see happiness, peace in everything, and I could have shown him all of us with pride. You talk about separation. But you would not believe what a special feeling I have for you after separation . . ."

"And, besides . . ." Natasha was beginning.

"No, not so. I never leave off loving you. And one couldn't love more; but it's something special. . . ." He did not finish, because their eyes meeting said the rest.

They were both silent for some seconds. Then all at once, at the same moment, they turned to each other and began talking. Pierre was beginning with self-satisfaction and enthusiasm, Natasha with a soft, happy smile. Interrupting each other, both stopped, waiting for the other to go on.

"No, what is it? Tell me, tell me."

"No, you tell me, it wasn't anything, only nonsense," said Natasha.

Pierre said what he had been going to say. It was the sequel to his complacent reflections on his success in Petersburg. It seemed to him at that moment that he was destined to give a new direction to the progress of the whole of Russian society and of the whole world.

"I only meant to say that all ideas that have immense results are always simple. All my idea really is that if vicious people are united and form a power, honest men must do the same. It's so simple, you see."

Meanwhile, below in young Nicholas Bolkonsky's bedroom a lamp was burning as usual. The boy was afraid of the dark and could not be cured of this weakness. Dessalle was asleep with his head high on his four pillows, and his Roman nose gave forth rhythmic sounds of snoring. Young Nicholas had just waked up in a cold sweat, and was sitting up in bed, gazing with wide-open eyes straight before him. He had been waked by a fearful dream. In his dream his Uncle Pierre and he in helmets, such as appeared in the illustrations in his

Plutarch, were marching at the head of an immense army. This army was made up of slanting, white threads that filled the air like those spider-webs that float in autumn and that Dessalle used to call the threads of the Virgin. Ahead of them was glory, which was something like those threads too, only somewhat more opaque. They—he and Pierre—were flying lightly and happily nearer and nearer to their goal. All at once the threads that moved them seemed to grow weak and tangled; and it was all difficult. And Uncle Nicholas stood before them in a stern and menacing attitude.

"Have you done this?" he said, pointing to broken pens and sticks of sealing-wax. "I did love you, but Araktcheev has bidden me, and I will kill the first that moves forward."

Young Nicholas looked round for Pierre; but Pierre was not there. Instead of Pierre, there was his father—Prince André—and his father had no shape or form, but he was there. And seeing him, young Nicholas felt the weakness of love; he felt powerless, limp, and relaxed. His father caressed him and pitied him, but his Uncle Nicholas was moving down upon them, coming closer and closer. A great horror came over young Nicholas and he woke up.

"My father!" he thought. Although there were two very good portraits of Prince André in the house, young Nicholas never thought of his father in human form. "My father has been with me, and has caressed me. He approved of me; he approved of Uncle Pierre. Whatever he might tell me, I would do it. I know they want me to study. And I am going to study. But some day I will have finished, and then I will act. One thing only I pray God for, that the same sort of thing may happen with me as with Plutarch's men, and I will act in the same way. I will do more. Every one shall know of me, shall love me, and admire me." And all at once young Nicholas felt his breast heaving with sobs, and he burst into tears.

"Are you ill?" he heard Dessalle's voice.

"No," he answered, and he lay back on his pillow. "How good and kind he is; I love him!" He thought of Dessalle. "But Uncle Pierre! Oh, what a wonderful man! And my father? Father! Father! Yes, I will do something that even *he* would be proud of . . ."

JOHN GROTH

the distinguished illustrator of this Bantam edition of WAR AND PEACE, is one of the most widely known graphic artists in America. In addition to his notable illustrations for books and magazines his work is exhibited in the Library of Congress, the National Gallery at Washington, and New York's Museum of Modern Art, as well as in many private collections. Mr. Groth has been honored, also, for his brilliant visual reporting in World War II, in Korea and Indo-China.